When Mary Norton created the Borrowers she invented a world of adventure that has enchanted adults and children alike ever since.

Mary Norton was born in 1903 and brought up in a house in Bedfordshire, which was to become the setting for *The Borrowers*. First published in 1952, *The Borrowers* was an immediate success, winning the Library Association's Carnegie Medal. Four more adventures followed: *The Borrowers Afield* (1955), *The Borrowers Afloat* (1959), *The Borrowers Aloft* (1961) and *The Borrowers Avenged* (1982). Also included in this omnibus edition is *Poor Stainless*, the last story about the Borrowers that Mary Norton wrote. Mary Norton died in 1992.

The Complete Borrowers

MARY NORTON

PUFFIN

PUFFIN BOOKS

Published by the Penguin Group
Penguin Books Ltd, 80 Strand, London WC2R ORL, England
Penguin Group (USA) Inc., 375 Hudson Street, New York, New York 10014, USA
Penguin Group (Canada), 90 Eglinton Avenue East, Suite 700, Toronto, Ontario, Canada M4P 2Y3
(a division of Pearson Penguin Canada Inc.)
Penguin Ireland, 25 St Stephen's Green, Dublin 2, Ireland (a division of Penguin Books Ltd)
Penguin Group (Australia), 250 Camberwell Road, Camberwell, Victoria 3124, Australia
(a division of Pearson Australia Group Pty Ltd)
Penguin Books India Pvt Ltd, 11 Community Centre, Panchsheel Park, New Delhi – 110 017, India
Penguin Group (NZ), 67 Apollo Drive, Rosedale, North Shore 0632, New Zealand
(a division of Pearson New Zealand Ltd)
Penguin Books (South Africa) (Pty) Ltd, 24 Sturdee Avenue, Rosebank, Johannesburg 2196, South Africa

Penguin Books Ltd, Registered Offices: 80 Strand, London WC2R ORL, England

puffinbooks.com

The Borrowers first published by J. M. Dent & Sons Ltd 1952
Published in Puffin Books 1958
Copyright © Mary Norton, 1952
Illustrations copyright © J. M. Dent & Sons Ltd, 1952

The Borrowers Afield first published by J. M. Dent & Sons Ltd 1955
Published in Puffin Books 1960
Copyright © Mary Norton, 1955
Illustrations copyright © J. M. Dent & Sons Ltd, 1955

The Borrowers Afloat first published by J. M. Dent & Sons Ltd 1959
Published in Puffin Books 1970
Copyright © Mary Norton, 1959
Illustrations copyright © J. M. Dent & Sons, Ltd, 1959

The Borrowers Aloft first published by J. M. Dent & Sons Ltd 1961
Published in Puffin Books 1970
Copyright © Mary Norton, 1961
Illustrations copyright © J. M. Dent & Sons Ltd, 1961

The Borrowers Avenged first published by Kestrel Books 1982
Copyright © Mary Norton, 1982
Illustrations copyright © Pauline Baynes, 1982

Poor Stainless first published 1966
Revised version published 1971
Poor Stainless first appeared in *The Eleanor Farjeon Book* in 1966.
The beginning and end of the story have since been revised.
Revised version copyright © Mary Norton, 1971

Published together as *The Complete Borrowers* 1982
Revised edition published 1994, 2007

011

Set in VIP Baskerville
Made and printed in England by Clays Ltd, St Ives plc

British Library Cataloguing in Publication Data
A CIP catalogue record for this book is available from the British Library

ISBN: 978-0-141-32270-4

CONTENTS

CONTENTS

INTRODUCTION

To John Cromwell, Esq.

Dear John,

It is early morning in this small whitewashed room, and I am sitting up in bed trying to answer this question of yours about what kind of events or circumstances led me first to think about the Borrowers.

Looking back, the idea seems to be part of an early fantasy in the life of a very short-sighted child, before it was known that she needed glasses. Detailed panorama of lake and mountain, the just-glimpsed boat on a vague horizon, the scattered constellations of a winter sky, the daylight owl – carven and motionless against the matching tree trunk – the sight of romping hares in a distant field, the swift recognition of a rare bird on the wing, were not for her (although the pointing fingers and shouted 'look-looks' in no way passed her by: on tiptoed feet and with screwed-up searching eyes she would join in an excitement which for her held the added element of mystery).

On the other hand, for her brothers country walks with her must have been something of a trial: she was an inveterate lingerer, a gazer into banks and hedgerows, a rapt investigator of shallow pools, a lier-down by stream-like teeming ditches. Such walks were punctuated by loud, long-suffering cries: 'Oh, come *on* . . . for goodness' sake . . . we'll never get there. . . . What on earth are you staring at *now*?'

It might only be a small toad, with striped eyes, trying to hoist himself up – on his bulging washerwoman's arms – from the dank depths of the ditch on to a piece of floating bark; or wood violets quivering on their massed roots from the passage of some sly, desperate creature pushing its way to safety. What would it be like, this child would wonder, lying prone upon the moss, to live among such creatures – human oneself to all intents and purposes, but as small and vulnerable as they? What would one live on? Where make one's home? Which would be one's enemies and which one's friends?

She would think of these things, as she scuffed her shoes along the sandy lane on her way to join her brothers. All three would climb the gate, jumping clear of the pocked mud and the cow pats, and stroll along the path between the coarse grass and the thistles. On this particular walk they would carry bathing suits in rolled towels because, beyond the wood ahead, lay a rocky cove with a deserted patch of beach.

'Look, there's a buzzard! There! On that post!' But it wasn't a buzzard to her: there was a post (or something like a post) slightly thickened at the top. 'There she goes! What a beauty!' The thickened end of the post had broken off and she saw for a second a swift, dim shadow of flight, and the post seemed a great deal shorter.

Buzzards, yes, they would be the enemies of her little people. Hawks too – and owls. She thought back to the gate which so easily the three human children had climbed. How would her small people manipulate it? They would go underneath of course – there was plenty of room – but, suddenly, she saw through their eyes the great lava-like (sometimes almost steaming) lakes of cattle dung, the pock-like craters in the mud – chasms to them, whether wet or dry. It would take them, she thought, almost half an hour of teetering on ridges, helping one another, calling out warnings, holding one another's hands before, exhausted, they reached the dry grass beyond. And then, she thought, how wickedly sharp, how dizzily high and rustling those thistle plants would seem! And suppose one of these creatures (Were they a little family? She thought perhaps they might be) called out as her brother had just done, 'Look, there's a buzzard!' What a different intonation in the voice and a different implication in the fact. How still they would lie – under perhaps a dock leaf! How deathly still, except for their beating hearts!

Then for this child, as for all children, there were the ill days – mumps, chicken-pox, measles, flu, tonsillitis. Bored with jigsaw puzzles, coloured chalks, familiar story-books (and with hours to go before the welcome rattle of a supper tray), she would bring her small people indoors – and set them mountain climbing among the bedroom furniture. She would invent for them commando-like assault courses: from window seat to bedside table without touching the floor; from curtain-rod to picture rail; from corner cupboard, via the chimney-piece to coal-scuttle. To help them achieve such feats she would allow them any material assistance they could lay their hands on: work baskets were for rifling – threads and wools for climbing ropes, needles and pins for alpenstocks. She would allow them the run of any half-opened drawer or gaping toy cupboard; then, having exhausted all the horizontal climbs, she would decide to start them from the floor and send them upwards towards the ceiling. This, she found, was the hardest task of all: chair and table legs were polished and slippery and the walls (except for a large picture called 'Bubbles' and one called 'Cherry Ripe') terrifyingly stark. At this point she would encourage them to build teetering pagodas of strong-smelling throat lozenges on down-turned medicine glasses which would serve them as stairways to greater heights. Long curtains helped with this too, of course, and trailing bedclothes where they touched the carpet. Wicker-work waste-paper baskets also had their uses. After a while she began to realize that there was no place in the room they could not reach at last – given time, privacy and patience.

What did they live on? she began to wonder. The answer was easy: they live on human left-overs as mice do, and birds in winter. They would be as shy as mice or birds, and as fearful of the dangers surrounding them, but more discerning in their tastes and more adventurously ambitious.

In the dull, safe routine of those nursery years, it was exciting to imagine there were others in the house, unguessed at by the adult human beings, who were living so close but so dangerously.

It was the maturing demands of boarding-school which swept them away at last. The Powers That Were discovered that she could not see the blackboard. There were eye tests; and eventually the much stamped, oblong box arrived by morning post, fiercely bound by sticky tape; and (after some nail-breaking and sharp work with a penknife) there at last, in cotton wool, lay a round-rimmed pair of spectacles.

Magic. The girls on the far side of the long classroom had faces suddenly; the trees outside the window had separate leaves; there was a crack in the ceiling like the coast of Brittany; the heel of Miss Hollingworth's stocking, as she turned towards the blackboard, had been darned in a lighter wool; and, not only that, she was losing a hairpin.

They were off-and-on sort of spectacles, easily mislaid, because while more distant objects stood out with eye-smiting clarity, close things became more blurred. It had to be 'glasses off' to read a book, write a letter, examine an ant nest, search for wild strawberries or four-leaved clovers – or even to pick up a pin; 'glasses on' to follow the hockey ball, see the unrolled map on the wall, watch the weekly lantern lecture or the fourth-form Latin play ('Where did you last have them? Try to think! Very tiresome! Take an order mark!').

In the midst of such diversions there was little time for the Borrowers who, denied even humble attention, slid quietly back to the past.

Anyway, ghosts had become the craze by then – ghosts and ghost stories (as small girls, wide-eyed, huddled in groups around the bubbling radiators of the 'gym'); heavy objects heard after dark, dragging across the boot-room floor; skeletal shadows in the ill-lit corridors joining up the houses; a silent figure who, in moonlit white, would be seen to cross a dormitory. We knew in our hearts that the heavy objects dragged across the cloakroom floor were the sacks of muddy hockey boots collected by the boot-boy; that the skeletal shadows were a trick of the corridor lights where preceding and receding outlines momentarily met and blended; we knew too that our cubicled dormitories were *peopled* by white-robed figures – most of whom were snoring gently and safely tucked in bed; and that one or two of these, in the silent hours, would make slippered expeditions to the bathroom.

But we loved to frighten ourselves. Life perhaps in those days seemed a little too secure – in spite of the 1914–18 war and the mud and blood across the Channel which engaged our elder brothers, but which to us, at our convent school, seemed wearily familiar yet somehow not quite real. As we told our stories, grouped around the radiators, we knitted balaclava helmets and long, long khaki scarves.

It was only just before the 1940 war, when a change was creeping over the world as we had known it, that one thought again about the Borrowers. There were human men and women who were being forced to live (by stark and tragic necessity) the kind of lives a child had once envisaged for a race of mythical creatures. One could not help but realize (without any thought of conscious symbolism) that the world at any time could produce its Mrs Drivers who in their turn would summon their Rich Williams. And there we would be. Apart from this thought, these are meant to be very practical books. Pod's balloon does work. I wonder if anyone has tried it?

With love, dear John. I hope this answers your question.

Yours,

Mary

Positano, June, 1966

THE
BORROWERS

WITH ILLUSTRATIONS BY
Diana Stanley

For
SHARON RHODES

CHAPTER ONE

IT was Mrs May who first told me about them. No, not me. How could it have been me – a wild, untidy, self-willed little girl who stared with angry eyes and was said to crunch her teeth? Kate, she should have been called. Yes, that was it – Kate. Not that the name matters much either way: she barely comes into the story.

Mrs May lived in two rooms in Kate's parents' house in London; she was, I think, some kind of relation. Her bedroom was on the first floor, and her sitting-room was a room which, as part of the house, was called 'the breakfast-room'. Now breakfast-rooms are all right in the morning when the sun streams in on the toast and marmalade, but by afternoon they seem to vanish a little and to fill with a strange silvery light, their own twilight; there is a kind of sadness in them then, but as a child it was a sadness Kate liked. She would creep in to Mrs May just before tea-time and Mrs May would teach her to crochet.

9

Mrs May was old, her joints were stiff, and she was – not strict exactly, but she had that inner certainty which does instead. Kate was never 'wild' with Mrs May, nor untidy, nor self-willed; and Mrs May taught her many things besides crochet: how to wind wool into an egg-shaped ball; how to run-and-fell and plan a darn; how to tidy a drawer and to lay, like a blessing, above the contents, a sheet of rustling tissue against the dust.

'Why so quiet, child?' asked Mrs May one day, when Kate was sitting hunched and idle upon the hassock. 'What's the matter with you? Have you lost your tongue?'

'No,' said Kate, pulling at her shoe button, 'I've lost the crochet hook . . .' (they were making a bed-quilt – in woollen squares: there were thirty still to do), 'I know where I put it,' she went on hastily; 'I put it on the bottom shelf of the book-case just beside my bed.'

'On the bottom shelf?' repeated Mrs May, her own needle flicking steadily in the firelight. 'Near the floor?'

'Yes,' said Kate, 'but I looked on the floor. Under the rug. Everywhere. The wool was still there though. Just where I'd left it.'

'Oh dear,' exclaimed Mrs May lightly, 'don't say they're in this house too!'

'That what are?' asked Kate.

'The Borrowers,' said Mrs May, and in the half light she seemed to smile.

Kate stared a little fearfully. 'Are there such things?' she asked after a moment.

'As what?'

Kate blinked her eyelids. 'As people, other people, living in a house who . . . borrow things?'

Mrs May laid down her work. 'What do you think?' she asked.

'I don't know,' said Kate, looking away and pulling hard at her shoe button. 'There can't be. And yet' – she raised her head – 'and yet sometimes I think there must be.'

'Why do you think there must be?' asked Mrs May.

'Because of all the things that disappear. Safety-pins, for instance. Factories go on making safety-pins, and every day people go on buying safety-pins and yet, somehow, there never is a safety-pin just when you want one. Where are they all? Now, at this minute? Where do they go to? Take needles,' she went on. 'All the needles my mother ever bought – there must be hundreds – can't just be lying about this house.'

'Not lying about the house, no,' agreed Mrs May.

'And all the other things we keep on buying. Again and again and again. Like pencils and match-boxes and sealing-wax and hair-slides and drawing-pins and thimbles –'

'And hat-pins,' put in Mrs May, 'and blotting-paper.'

'Yes, blotting-paper,' agreed Kate, 'but not hat-pins.'

'That's where you're wrong,' said Mrs May, and she picked up her work again. 'There was a reason for hat-pins.'

Kate stared. 'A reason?' she repeated. 'I mean – what kind of a reason?'

'Well, there were two reasons really. A hat-pin is a very useful weapon and' – Mrs May laughed suddenly – 'but it all sounds such nonsense and' – she hesitated – 'it was so very long ago!'

'But tell me,' said Kate, 'tell me how you *know* about the hat-pin. Did you ever see one?'

Mrs May threw her a startled glance. 'Well, yes –' she began.

'Not a hat-pin,' exclaimed Kate impatiently, 'a – whatever-you-called-them – a Borrower?'

Mrs May drew a sharp breath. 'No,' she said quickly, 'I never saw one.'

'But someone else saw one,' cried Kate, 'and you know about it. I can see you do!'

'Hush,' said Mrs May, 'no need to shout!' She gazed downwards at the upturned face and then she smiled and her eyes slid away into distance. 'I had a brother –' she began uncertainly.

Kate knelt upon the hassock. 'And he saw them!'

'I don't know,' said Mrs May, shaking her head, 'I just don't know!' She smoothed out her work upon her knee. 'He was such a tease. He told us so many things – my sister and me – impossible things. He was killed,' she added gently, 'many years ago now on the North-West Frontier. He became colonel of his regiment. He died what they call "a hero's death" . . .'

'Was he your only brother?'

'Yes, and he was our little brother. I think that was why' – she thought for a moment, still smiling to herself – 'yes, why he told us such impossible stories, such strange imaginings. He was jealous, I think, because we were older – and because we could read better. He wanted to impress us; he wanted, perhaps, to shock us. And yet' – she looked into the fire – 'there was something about him – perhaps because we were brought up in India among mystery and magic and legend – something that made us think that he saw things that other people

could not see; sometimes we'd know he was teasing, but at other times
– well, we were not so sure . . .' She leaned forward and, in her tidy
way, brushed a fan of loose ashes under the grate, then, brush in hand,
she stared again at the fire. 'He wasn't a very strong little boy: the first
time he came home from India he got rheumatic fever. He missed a
whole term at school and was sent away to the country to get over it. To
the house of a great-aunt. Later I went there myself. It was a strange
old house . . .' She hung up the brush on its brass hook and, dusting her
hands on her handkerchief, she picked up her work. 'Better light the
lamp,' she said.

'Not yet,' begged Kate, leaning forward. 'Please go on. Please tell
me –'

'But I've told you.'

'No you haven't. This old house – wasn't that where he saw – he
saw . . .?'

Mrs May laughed. 'Where he saw the Borrowers? Yes, that's what he
told us . . . what he'd have us believe. And, what's more, it seems that
he didn't just see them but that he got to know them very well; that he
became part of their lives, as it were; in fact, you might almost say that
he became a borrower himself . . .'

'Oh, *do* tell me. Please. Try to remember. Right from the very
beginning!'

'But I do remember,' said Mrs May. 'Oddly enough I remember it
better than many real things which have happened. Perhaps it was a
real thing. I just don't know. You see, on the way back to India my
brother and I had to share a cabin – my sister used to sleep with our
governess – and, on those very hot nights, often we couldn't sleep; and
my brother would talk for hours and hours, going over old ground,
repeating conversations, telling me details again and again – wondering
how they were and what they were doing and –'

'They? Who were they – exactly?'

'Homily, Pod, and little Arrietty.'

'Pod?'

'Yes, even their names were never quite right. They imagined they
had their own names – quite different from human names – but with
half an ear you could tell they were borrowed. Even Uncle Hendreary's
and Eggletina's. Everything they had was borrowed; they had nothing
of their own at all. Nothing. In spite of this, my brother said, they were
touchy and conceited, and thought they owned the world.'

'How do you mean?'

'They thought human beings were just invented to do the dirty work – great slaves put there for them to use. At least, that's what they told each other. But my brother said that, underneath, he thought they were frightened. It was because they were frightened, he thought, that they had grown so small. Each generation had become smaller and smaller, and more and more hidden. In the olden days, it seems, and in some parts of England, our ancestors talked quite openly about the "little people".'

'Yes,' said Kate, 'I know.'

'Nowadays, I suppose,' Mrs May went on slowly, 'if they exist at all, you would only find them in houses which are old and quiet and deep in the country – and where the human beings live to a routine. Routine is their safeguard: it is important for them to know which rooms are to be used and when. They do not stay long where there are careless people, unruly children, or certain household pets.

'This particular old house, of course, was ideal – although as far as some of them were concerned, a trifle cold and empty. Great Aunt Sophy was bed-ridden, through a hunting accident some twenty years before, and as for other human beings there was only Mrs Driver the cook, Crampfurl the gardener, and, at rare intervals, an odd housemaid or such. My brother, too, when he went there after rheumatic fever, had to spend long hours in bed, and for those first weeks it seems the Borrowers did not know of his existence.

'He slept in the old night-nursery, beyond the schoolroom. The schoolroom, at that time, was sheeted and shrouded and filled with junk – odd trunks, a broken sewing-machine, a desk, a dressmaker's dummy, a table, some chairs, and a disused pianola – as the children who had used it, Great Aunt Sophy's children, had long since grown up, married, died, or gone away. The night-nursery opened out of the schoolroom and, from his bed, my brother could see the oil-painting of the battle of Waterloo which hung above the schoolroom fireplace and, on the wall, a corner cupboard with glass doors in which was set out, on hooks and shelves, a doll's tea-service – very delicate and old. At night, if the schoolroom door was open, he had a view down the lighted passage which led to the staircase, and it would comfort him to see, each evening at dusk, Mrs Driver appear at the head of the stairs and cross the passage carrying a tray for Aunt Sophy with Bath Oliver biscuits and the tall, cut-glass decanter of Fine Old Pale Madeira. On her way out Mrs Driver would pause and lower the gas jet in the passage to a dim, blue flame, and then he would watch her as she stumped away downstairs, sinking slowly out of sight between the banisters.

'Under this passage, in the hall below, there was a clock, and through the night he would hear it strike the hours. It was a grandfather clock and very old. Mr Frith of Leighton Buzzard came each month to wind it, as his father had come before him and his great-uncle before that. For eighty years, they said (and to Mr Frith's certain knowledge), it had not stopped and, as far as anyone could tell, for as many years before that. The great thing was – that it must never be moved. It stood against the wainscot, and the stone flags around it had been washed so often that a little platform, my brother said, rose up inside.

'And, under this clock, below the wainscot, there was a hole . . .'

CHAPTER TWO

IT was Pod's hole – the keep of his fortress; the entrance to his home. Not that his home was anywhere near the clock: far from it – as you might say. There were yards of dark and dusty passage-way, with wooden doors between the joists and metal gates against the mice. Pod used all kinds of things for these gates – a flat leaf of a folding cheese-grater, the hinged lid of a small cash-box, squares of pierced zinc from an old meat-safe, a wire fly-swotter . . . 'Not that I'm afraid of mice,' Homily would say, 'but I can't abide the smell.' In vain Arrietty had begged for a little mouse of her own, a little blind mouse to bring up by hand – 'like Eggletina had had'. But Homily would bang with the pan lids and exclaim: 'And look what happened to Eggletina!' 'What,' Arrietty would ask, 'what did happen to Eggletina?' But no one would ever say.

It was only Pod who knew the way through the intersecting passages to the hole under the clock. And only Pod could open the gates. There were complicated clasps made of hair-slides and safety-pins of which Pod alone knew the secret. His wife and child led more sheltered lives in homelike apartments under the kitchen, far removed from the risks and dangers of the dreaded house above. But there was a grating in the brick wall of the house, just below the floor level of the kitchen above, through which Arrietty could see the garden – a piece of gravelled path and a bank where crocus bloomed in spring; where blossom drifted from an unseen tree; and where later an azalea bush would flower; and where birds came – and pecked and flirted and sometimes fought. 'The hours you waste on them birds,' Homily would say, 'and when there's a little job to be done you can never find the time. I was brought up in a house,' Homily went on, 'where there wasn't no grating, and we were all the happier for it. Now go off and get me the potato.'

That was the day when Arrietty, rolling the potato before her from the storehouse down the dusty lane under the floorboards, kicked it ill-temperedly so that it rolled rather fast into their kitchen, where Homily was stooping over the stove.

'There you go again,' exclaimed Homily, turning angrily; 'nearly pushed me into the soup. And when I say "potato" I don't mean the whole potato. Take the scissor, can't you, and cut off a slice.'

'Didn't know how much you wanted,' Arrietty had mumbled, as Homily, snorting and sniffing, unhooked the blade and handle of half a pair of manicure scissors from a nail on the wall, and began to cut through the peel.

'You've ruined this potato,' she grumbled. 'You can't roll it back now in all that dust, not once it's been cut open.'

'Oh, what does it matter?' said Arrietty. 'There are plenty more.'

'That's a nice way to talk. Plenty more. Do you realize,' Homily went on gravely, laying down the half nail scissor, 'that your poor father risks his life every time he borrows a potato?'

'I meant,' said Arrietty, 'that there are plenty more in the store-room.'

'Well, out of my way now,' said Homily, bustling around again, 'whatever you meant – and let me get the supper.'

Arrietty had wandered through the open door into the sitting-room – the fire had been lighted and the room looked bright and cosy. Homily was proud of her sitting-room: the walls had been papered with scraps of old letters out of waste-paper baskets, and Homily had arranged the handwriting sideways in vertical stripes which ran from floor to ceiling. On the walls, repeated in various colours, hung several portraits of Queen Victoria as a girl; these were postage stamps, borrowed by Pod some years ago from the stamp-box on the desk in the morning-room. There was a lacquer trinket-box, padded inside and with the lid open, which they used as a settle; and that useful stand-by – a chest of drawers made of match-boxes. There was a round table with a red velvet cloth, which Pod had made from the wooden bottom of a pill-box supported on the carved pedestal of a knight from the chess-set. (This had caused a great deal of trouble upstairs when Aunt Sophy's eldest son, on a flying mid-week visit, had invited the vicar for 'a game after dinner'. Rosa Pickhatchet, who was housemaid at the time, gave in her notice. Not long after she had left other things were found to be missing and, from that time onwards, Mrs Driver ruled supreme.) The knight itself – its bust, so to speak – was standing on a column in the corner, where it looked very fine, and lent that air to the room which only statuary can give.

Beside the fire, in a tilted wooden book-case, stood Arrietty's library. This was a set of those miniature volumes which the Victorians loved to print, but which to Arrietty seem-ed the size of very large church Bibles. There was Bryce's *Tom Thumb Gazetteer of the World*, including the last census; Bryce's *Tom Thumb Dictionary*, with short explana-tions of scientific, philosophical, lit-erary, and technical terms; Bryce's *Tom Thumb Edition of the Comedies of William Shakespeare*, including a fore-word on the author; another book, whose pages were all blank, called *Memoranda*; and, last but not least, Arrietty's favourite Bryce's *Tom Thumb Diary and Proverb Book* with a saying for each day of the year and, as a preface, the life story of a little man called General Tom Thumb, who married a girl called Mercy Lavinia Bump. There was an engraving of their carriage and pair, with little horses – the size of mice. Arrietty was not a stupid girl. She knew that horses could not be as small as mice, but she did not realize that Tom Thumb, nearly two feet high, would seem a giant to a Borrower.

Arrietty had learned to read from these books, and to write by leaning sideways and copying out the writings on the walls. In spite of this, she did not always keep her diary, although on most days she would take the book out for the sake of the saying which sometimes would comfort her. Today it said: 'You may go farther and fare worse' and, underneath: 'Order of the Garter, instituted 1348.' She carried the book to the fire and sat down with her feet on the hob.

'What are you doing, Arrietty?' called Homily from the kitchen.

'Writing my diary.'

'Oh,' exclaimed Homily shortly.

'What did you want?' asked Arrietty. She felt quite safe; Homily liked her to write; Homily encouraged any form of culture. Homily herself, poor ignorant creature, could not even say the alphabet. 'Nothing. Nothing,' said Homily crossly, banging away with the pan lids; 'it'll do later.'

Arrietty took out her pencil. It was a small white pencil, with a piece of silk cord attached, which had come off a dance programme, but, even so, in Arrietty's hand, it looked like a rolling-pin.

'Arrietty!' called Homily again from the kitchen.

'Yes?'

'Put a little something on the fire, will you?'

Arrietty braced her muscles and heaved the book off her knees, and stood it upright on the floor. They kept the fuel, assorted slack and crumbled candle-grease, in a pewter mustard-pot, and shovelled it out with the spoon. Arrietty trickled only a few grains, tilting the mustard spoon, not to spoil the blaze. Then she stood there basking in the warmth. It was a charming fireplace, made by Arrietty's grandfather, with a cog-wheel from the stables, part of an old cider-press. The spokes of the cog-wheel stood out in starry rays, and the fire itself nestled in the centre. Above there was a chimney-piece made from a small brass funnel, inverted. This, at one time, belonged to an oil-lamp which matched it, and which stood, in the old days, on the hall table upstairs. An arrangement of pipes, from the spout of the funnel, carried the fumes into the kitchen flues above. The fire was laid with match-sticks and fed with assorted slack and, as it burned up, the iron would become hot, and Homily would simmer soup on the spokes, in a silver thimble, and Arrietty would broil nuts. How cosy those winter evenings could be. Arrietty, her great book on her knees, sometimes reading aloud; Pod at his last (he was a shoemaker, and made button-boots out of kid-gloves – now, alas, only for his family); and Homily, quiet at last, with her knitting.

Homily knitted their jerseys and stockings on black-headed pins, and, sometimes, on darning needles. A great reel of silk or cotton would stand, table high, beside her chair, and sometimes, if she pulled too sharply, the reel would tip up and roll away out of the open door into the dusty passage beyond, and Arrietty would be sent after it, to rewind it carefully as she rolled it back.

The floor of the sitting-room was carpeted with deep red blotting-paper, which was warm and cosy, and soaked up the spills. Homily would renew it at intervals when it became available upstairs, but since Aunt Sophy had taken to her bed, Mrs Driver seldom thought of blotting-paper unless, suddenly, there were guests. Homily liked things which saved washing because drying was difficult under the floor; water they had in plenty, hot and cold, thanks to Pod's father who had tapped the pipes from the kitchen boiler. They bathed in a small tureen, which once had held *pâté de foie gras*. When you had wiped out your bath you were supposed to put the lid back, to stop people putting things in it. The soap, too, a great cake of it, hung on a nail in the scullery, and they

scraped pieces off. Homily liked coal tar, but Pod and Arrietty preferred sandalwood.

'What are you doing now, Arrietty?' called Homily from the kitchen.

'Still writing my diary.'

Once again Arrietty took hold of the book and heaved it back on to her knees. She licked the lead of her great pencil, and stared a moment, deep in thought. She allowed herself (when she did remember to write) one little line on each page because she would never – of this she was sure – have another diary, and if she could get twenty lines on each page the diary would last her twenty years. She had kept it for nearly two years already, and today, March 22, she read last year's entry: 'Mother cross.' She thought a while longer then, at last, she put ditto marks under 'mother', and 'worried' under 'cross'.

'What did you say you were doing, Arrietty?' called Homily from the kitchen.

Arrietty closed the book. 'Nothing,' she said.

'Then chop me up this onion, there's a good girl. Your father's late tonight . . .'

CHAPTER THREE

Sighing, Arrietty put away her diary and went into the kitchen. She took the onion ring from Homily and slung it lightly round her shoulders, while she foraged for a piece of razor blade. 'Really, Arrietty,' exclaimed Homily, 'not on your clean jersey! Do you want to smell like a bit-bucket? Here, take the scissor –'

Arrietty stepped through the onion ring as though it were a child's hoop, and began to chop it into segments.

'Your father's late,' muttered Homily again, 'and it's my fault, as you might say. Oh dear, oh dear, I wish I hadn't –'

'Hadn't what?' asked Arrietty, her eyes watering. She sniffed loudly and longed to rub her nose on her sleeve.

Homily pushed back a thin lock of hair with a worried hand. She stared at Arrietty absently. 'It's that tea-cup you broke,' she said.

'But that was days ago –' began Arrietty, blinking her eyelids, and she sniffed again.

'I know. I know. It's not you. It's me. It's not the breaking that matters, it's what I said to your father.'

'What did you say to him?'

'Well, I just said – there's the rest of the service, I said – up there, where it always was, in the corner cupboard in the schoolroom.'

'I don't see anything bad in that,' said Arrietty, as, one by one, she dropped the pieces of onion into the soup.

'But it's a high cupboard,' exclaimed Homily. 'You have to get up by the curtain. And your father at his age –' She sat down suddenly on a metal-topped champagne cork. 'Oh, Arrietty, I wish I'd never mentioned it!'

'Don't worry,' said Arrietty, 'papa knows what he can do.' She pulled a rubber scent-bottle cork out of the hole in the hot-water pipe and let a trickle of scalding drops fall into the tin lid of an aspirin bottle. She added cold and began to wash her hands.

'Maybe,' said Homily. 'But I went on about it so. What's a tea-cup! Your Uncle Hendreary never drank a thing that wasn't out of a common acorn cup, and he's lived to a ripe old age and had the strength

21

to emigrate. My mother's family never had nothing but a little bone thimble which they shared around. But it's once you've *had* a tea-cup, if you see what I mean . . .'

'Yes,' said Arrietty, drying her hands on a roller towel made out of surgical bandage.

'It's that curtain,' cried Homily. 'He can't climb a curtain at his age – not by the bobbles!'

'With his pin he could,' said Arrietty.

'His pin! I led him into that one too! Take a hat-pin, I told him, and tie a bit of name-tape to the head, and pull yourself upstairs. It was to borrow the emerald watch from Her bedroom for me to time the cooking.' Homily's voice began to tremble. 'Your mother's a wicked woman, Arrietty. Wicked and selfish, that's what she is!'

'You know what?' exclaimed Arrietty suddenly.

Homily brushed away a tear. 'No,' she said wanly, 'what?'

'I could climb a curtain.'

Homily rose up. 'Arrietty, you dare stand there in cold blood and say a thing like that!'

'But I could! I could! I could borrow! I know I could!'

'Oh!' gasped Homily. 'Oh, you wicked heathen girl! How could you speak so!' and she crumpled up again on the cork stool. 'So it's come to this!' she said.

'Now, mother, please,' begged Arrietty, 'now, don't take on!'

'But don't you see, Arrietty . . .' gasped Homily; she stared down at the table at loss for words and then, at last, she raised a haggard face. 'My poor child,' she said, 'don't speak like that of borrowing. You don't know – and, thank goodness, you never will know' – she dropped her voice to a fearful whisper – 'what it's like upstairs . . .'

Arrietty was silent. 'What is it like?' she asked after a moment.

Homily wiped her face on her apron and smoothed back her hair. 'Your Uncle Hendreary,' she began, 'Eggletina's father –' and then she paused. 'Listen!' she said. 'What's that?'

Echoing on the wood was a faint vibration – the sound of a distant click. 'Your father!' exclaimed Homily. 'Oh, look at me! Where's the comb?'

They had a comb: a little, silver, eighteenth-century eyebrow comb from the cabinet in the drawing-room upstairs. Homily ran it through her hair and rinsed her poor red eyes and, when Pod came in, she was smiling and smoothing down her apron.

CHAPTER FOUR

POD came in slowly, his sack on his back; he leaned his hat-pin, with its dangling name-tape, against the wall and, on the middle of the kitchen table, he placed a doll's tea-cup; it seemed the size of a mixing-bowl.

'Why, Pod –' began Homily.

'Got the saucer too,' he said. He swung down the sack and untied the neck. 'Here you are,' he said, drawing out the saucer. 'Matches it.'

He had a round, currant-bunny sort of face; tonight it looked flabby.

'Oh, Pod,' said Homily, 'you do look queer. Are you all right?'

Pod sat down. 'I'm fair enough,' he said.

'You went up the curtain,' said Homily. 'Oh, Pod, you shouldn't have. It's shaken you –'

Pod made a strange face, his eyes swivelled round towards Arrietty. Homily stared at him, her mouth open, and then she turned. 'Come along, Arrietty,' she said briskly, 'you pop off to bed, now, like a good girl, and I'll bring you some supper.'

'Oh,' said Arrietty, 'can't I see the rest of the borrowings?'

'Your father's got nothing now. Only food. Off you pop to bed. You've seen the cup and saucer.'

Arrietty went into the sitting-room to put away her diary, and took some time fixing her candle on the upturned drawing-pin which served as a holder.

'Whatever are you doing?' grumbled Homily. 'Give it here. There, that's the way. Now off to bed and fold your clothes, mind.'

'Good night, papa,' said Arrietty, kissing his flat white cheek.

'Careful of the light,' he said mechanically, and watched her with his round eyes until she had closed the door.

'Now, Pod,' said Homily, when they were alone, 'tell me. What's the matter?'

Pod looked at her blankly. 'I been "seen",' he said.

Homily put out a groping hand for the edge of the table; she grasped it and lowered herself slowly on to the stool. 'Oh, Pod,' she said.

There was silence between them. Pod stared at Homily and Homily

23

stared at the table. After a while she raised her white face. 'Badly?' she asked.

Pod moved restlessly. 'I don't know about badly. I been "seen". Ain't that bad enough?'

'No one,' said Homily slowly, 'hasn't never been "seen" since Uncle Hendreary and he was the first they say for forty-five years.' A thought struck her and she gripped the table. 'It's no good, Pod, I won't emigrate!'

'No one's asked you to,' said Pod.

'To go and live like Hendreary and Lupy in a badger's set! The other side of the world, that's where they say it is – all among the earthworms.'

'It's two fields away, above the spinney,' said Pod.

'Nuts, that's what they eat. And berries. I wouldn't wonder if they don't eat mice –'

'You've eaten mice yourself,' Pod reminded her.

'All draughts and fresh air and the children growing up wild. Think of Arrietty!' said Homily. 'Think of the way she's been brought up. An only child. She'd catch her death. It's different for Hendreary.'

'Why?' asked Pod. 'He's got five.'

'That's why,' explained Homily. 'When you've got five, they're brought up rough. But never mind that now. . . Who saw you?'

'A boy,' said Pod.

'A what?' exclaimed Homily, staring.

'A boy.' Pod sketched out a rough shape in the air with his hands. 'You know a boy.'

'But there isn't – I mean, what sort of a boy?'

'I don't know what you mean "what sort of a boy". A boy in a nightshirt. A boy. You know what a boy is, don't you?'

'Yes,' said Homily, 'I know what a boy is. But there hasn't been a boy, not in this house, these twenty years.'

'Well,' said Pod, 'there's one here now.'

Homily stared at him in silence, and Pod met her eyes. 'Where did he see you?' asked Homily at last.

'In the schoolroom.'

'Oh,' said Homily, 'when
you was getting the cup?'

'Yes,' said Pod.

'Haven't you got eyes?'
asked Homily. 'Couldn't you
have looked first?'

'There's never nobody in the
schoolroom. And what's more,'
he went on, 'there wasn't
today.'

'Then where was he?'

'In bed. In the night-nursery
or whatever it's called. That's
where he was. Sitting up in
bed. With the doors open.'

'Well, you could have looked
in the nursery.'

'How could I – half-way up
the curtain!'

'Is that where you was?'

'Yes.'

'With the cup?'

'Yes. I couldn't get up or
down.'

'Oh, Pod,' wailed Homily, 'I should never have let you go. Not at
your age!'

'Now, look here,' said Pod, 'don't mistake me. I got up all right. Got
up like a bird, as you might say, bobbles or no bobbles. But' – he leaned
towards her – 'afterwards – with the cup in me hand, if you see what I
mean . . .' He picked it up off the table. 'You see, it's heavy like. You
can hold it by the handle, like this . . . but it drops or droops, as you
might say. You should take a cup like this in your two hands. A bit of
cheese off a shelf, or an apple – well, I drop that . . . give it a push and
it falls and I climbs down in me own time and picks it up. But with a
cup – you see what I mean? And coming down, you got to watch your
feet. And, as I say, some of the bobbles was missing. You didn't know
what you could hold on to, not safely . . .'

'Oh, Pod,' said Homily, her eyes full of tears, 'what did you do?'

'Well,' said Pod, sitting back again, 'he took the cup.'

'What do you mean?' exclaimed Homily, aghast.

Pod avoided her eyes. 'Well, he'd been sitting up in bed there watching me. I'd been on that curtain a good ten minutes, because the hall clock had just struck the quarter –'

'But how do you mean – "he took the cup"?'

'Well, he'd got out of bed and there he was standing, looking up. "I'll take the cup," he said.'

'Oh!' gasped Homily, her eyes staring, 'and you give it to him?'

'He took it,' said Pod, 'ever so gentle. And then, when I was down, he give it me.' Homily put her face in her hands. 'Now don't take on,' said Pod uneasily.

'He might have caught you,' shuddered Homily in a stifled voice.

'Yes,' said Pod, 'but he just give me the cup. "Here you are," he said.'

Homily raised her face. 'What are we going to do?' she asked.

Pod sighed. 'Well, there isn't nothing we can do. Except –'

'Oh, no,' exclaimed Homily, 'not that. Not emigrate. Not that, Pod, now I've got the house so nice and a clock and all.'

'We could take the clock,' said Pod.

'And Arrietty? What about her? She's not like those cousins. She can *read*, Pod, and sew a treat –'

'He don't know where we live,' said Pod.

'But they look,' exclaimed Homily. 'Remember Hendreary! They got

the cat and –'

'Now, now,' said Pod, 'don't bring up the past.'

'But you've got to think of it! They got the cat and –'

'Yes,' said Pod, 'but Eggletina was different.'

'How different? She was Arrietty's age.'

'Well, they hadn't told her, you see. That's where they went wrong. They tried to make her believe that there wasn't nothing but was under the floor. They never told her about Mrs Driver or Crampfurl. Least of all about cats.'

'There wasn't any cat,' Homily pointed out, 'not till Hendreary was "seen".'

'Well, there was, then,' said Pod. 'You got to tell them, that's what I say, or they try to find out for themselves.'

'Pod,' said Homily solemnly, 'we haven't told Arrietty.'

'Oh, she knows,' said Pod; he moved uncomfortably. 'She's got her grating.'

'She doesn't know about Eggletina. She doesn't know about being "seen".'

'Well,' said Pod, 'we'll tell her. We always said we would. There's no hurry.'

Homily stood up. 'Pod,' she said, 'we're going to tell her tonight.'

CHAPTER FIVE

ARRIETTY had not been asleep. She had been lying under her knotted coverlet staring up at the ceiling. It was an interesting ceiling. Pod had built Arrietty's bedroom out of two cigar-boxes, and on the ceiling lovely painted ladies dressed in swirls of chiffon blew long trumpets against a background of blue sky; below there were feathery palm-trees and small white houses set about a square. It was a glamorous scene, above all by candlelight, but tonight Arrietty had stared without seeing. The wood of a cigar-box is thin and Arrietty, lying straight and still under the quilt, had heard the rise and fall of worried voices. She had heard her own name; she had heard Homily exclaim: 'Nuts and berries, that's what they eat!' and she had heard, after a while, the heart-felt cry of 'What shall we do?'

So when Homily appeared beside her bed, she wrapped herself obediently in her quilt and, padding in her bare feet along the dusty passage, she joined her parents in the warmth of the kitchen. Crouched on her little stool she sat clasping her knees, shivering a little, and looking from one face to another.

Homily came beside her and, kneeling on the floor, she placed an arm round Arrietty's skinny shoulders. 'Arrietty,' she said gravely, 'you know about upstairs?'

'What about it?' asked Arrietty.

'You know about the two giants?'

'Yes,' said Arrietty, 'Great Aunt Sophy and Mrs Driver.'

'That's right,' said Homily, 'and Crampfurl in the garden.' She laid a roughened hand on Arrietty's clasped ones. 'You know about Uncle Hendreary?'

Arrietty thought awhile. 'He went abroad?' she said.

'Emigrated,' corrected Homily, 'to the other side of the world. With Aunt Lupy and all the children. To a badger's set – a hole in a bank under a hawthorn hedge. Now why do you think he did this?'

'Oh,' said Arrietty, her face alight, 'to be out of doors . . . to lie in the sun . . . to run in the grass . . . to swing on twigs like the birds do . . . to suck honey . . .'

28

'Nonsense, Arrietty,' exclaimed Homily sharply, 'that's a nasty habit! And your Uncle Hendreary's a rheumatic sort of man. He emigrated,' she went on, stressing the word, 'because he was "seen".'

'Oh,' said Arrietty.

'He was "seen" on 23rd of April, 1892, by Rosa Pickhatchet, on the drawing-room mantelpiece. Of all places . . .' she added suddenly in a wondering aside.

'Oh,' said Arrietty.

'I have never heard nor no one has never seen fit to tell why he went on the drawing-room mantelpiece in the first place. There's nothing on it, your father assures me, which cannot be seen from the floor or by standing sideways on the handle of the bureau and steadying yourself on the key. That's what your father does if he ever goes into the drawing-room –'

'They said it was a liver pill,' put in Pod.

'How do you mean?' asked Homily, startled.

'A liver pill for Lupy.' Pod spoke wearily. 'Someone started a rumour,' he went on, 'that there were liver pills on the drawing-room mantelpiece . . .'

'Oh,' said Homily and looked thoughtful, 'I never heard that. All the same,' she exclaimed, 'it was stupid and foolhardy. There's no way down except by the bell-pull. She dusted him, they say, with a feather duster, and he stood so still, alongside a cupid, that she might never have noticed him if he hadn't sneezed. She was new, you see, and didn't know the ornaments. We heard her screeching right here under the kitchen. And they could never get her to clean anything much after that that wasn't chairs or tables – least of all the tiger-skin rug.'

'I don't hardly never bother with the drawing-room,' said Pod. 'Everything's got its place like and they see what goes. There might be a little something left on a table or down the side of a chair, but not without there's been company, and there never is no company – not for the last ten or twelve year. Sitting here in this chair, I can tell you by heart every blessed thing that's in that drawing-room, working round from the cabinet by the window to the –'   'There's a mint of things in that cabinet,' interrupted Homily, 'solid silver some of them. A solid silver violin, they got there, strings and all – just right for our Arrietty.'

'What's the good,' asked Pod, 'of things behind glass?'

'Couldn't you break it?' suggested Arrietty. 'Just a corner, just a little tap, just a . . .' Her voice faltered as she saw the shocked amazement on her father's face.

'Listen here, Arrietty,' began Homily angrily, and then she controlled
herself and patted Arrietty's clasped hands. 'She don't know much
about borrowing,' she explained to Pod. 'You can't blame her.' She
turned again to Arrietty. 'Borrowing's a skilled job, an art like. Of all
the families who've been in this house, there's only us left, and do you
know for why? Because your father, Arrietty, is the best Borrower that's
been known in these parts since – well, before your grandad's time.
Even your Aunt Lupy admitted that much. When he was younger I've
seen your father walk the length of a laid dinner-table, after the gong
was rung, taking a nut or sweet from every dish, and down by a fold in
the tablecloth as the first people came in at the door. He'd do it just for
fun, wouldn't you, Pod?'

Pod smiled wanly. 'There weren't no sense in it,' he said.

'Maybe,' said Homily, 'but you did it! Who else would dare?'

'I were younger then,' said Pod. He sighed and turned to Arrietty.
'You don't break things, lass. That's not the way to do it. That's not
borrowing . . .'

'We were rich then,' said Homily. 'Oh, we did have some lovely
things! You were only a tot, Arrietty, and wouldn't remember. We
had a whole suite of walnut furniture out of the doll's house and a
set of wineglasses in green glass, and a musical snuff-box, and the
cousins would come and we'd have parties. Do you remember, Pod?
Not only the cousins. The Harpsichords came. Everybody came –
except those Overmantels from the morning-room. And we'd dance
and dance and the young people would sit out by the grating. Three
tunes that snuff-box played – *Clementine*, *God Save the Queen*, and the
Post-Chaise Gallop. We were the envy of everybody – even the Overmantels . . .'

'Who were the Overmantels?' asked Arrietty.

'Oh, you must've heard me talk of the Overmantels,' exclaimed Homily, 'that stuck-up lot who lived in the wall high up – among the lath and plaster behind the mantelpiece in the morning-room. And a queer lot they were. The men smoked all the time because the tobacco jars were kept there; and they'd climb about and in and out the carvings of the overmantel, sliding down pillars and showing off. The women were a conceited lot too, always admiring themselves in all those bits of overmantel looking-glass. They never asked anyone up there and I, for one, never wanted to go. I've no head for heights, and your father never liked the men. He's always lived steady, your father has, and not only the tobacco jars, but the whisky decanters too, were kept in the morning-room and they say those Overmantel men would suck up the dregs in the glasses through those quill pipe-cleaners they keep there on the mantelpiece. I don't know whether it's true but they do say that those Overmantel men used to have a party every Tuesday after the bailiff had been to talk business in the morning-room. Laid out, they'd be, dead drunk – or so the story goes – on the green plush tablecloth, all among the tin boxes and the account books –'

'Now, Homily,' protested Pod, who did not like gossip, 'I never see'd 'em.'

'But you wouldn't put it past them, Pod. You said yourself when I married you not to call on the Overmantels.'

'They lived so high,' said Pod, 'that's all.'

'Well, they were a lazy lot – that much you can't deny. They never had no kind of home life. Kept themselves warm in winter by the heat of the morning-room fire and ate nothing but breakfast food; breakfast, of course, was the only meal served in the morning-room.'

'What happened to them?' asked Arrietty.

'Well, when the Master died and She took to her bed, there was no more use for the morning-room. So the Overmantels had to go. What else could they do? No food, no fire. It's a bitter cold room in winter.'

'And the Harpsichords?' asked Arrietty.

Homily looked thoughtful. 'Well, they were different. I'm not saying they weren't stuck up too, because they were. Your Aunt Lupy, who married your Uncle Hendreary, was a Harpsichord by marriage and we all know the airs she gave herself.'

'Now, Homily –' began Pod.

'Well, she'd no right to. She was only a Rain-Pipe from the stables before she married Harpsichord.'

'Didn't she marry Uncle Hendreary?' asked Arrietty.

'Yes, later. She was a widow with two children and he was a widower with three. It's no good looking at me like that, Pod. You can't deny she took it out of poor Hendreary: she thought it was a comedown to marry a Clock.'

'Why?' asked Arrietty.

'Because we Clocks live under the kitchen, that's why. Because we don't talk fancy grammar and eat anchovy toast. But to live under the kitchen doesn't say we aren't educated. The Clocks are just as old a family as the Harpsichords. You remember that, Arrietty, and don't let anyone tell you different. Your grandfather could count and write down the numbers up to – what was it, Pod?'

'Fifty-seven,' said Pod.

'There,' said Homily, 'fifty-seven! And your father can count, as you know, Arrietty; he can count and write down the numbers, on and on, as far as it goes. How far does it go, Pod?'

'Close on a thousand,' said Pod.

'There!' exclaimed Homily, 'and he

knows the alphabet because he taught you, Arrietty, didn't he? And he would have been able to read – wouldn't you, Pod? – if he hadn't had to start borrowing so young. Your Uncle Hendreary and your father had to go out borrowing at thirteen – your age, Arrietty, think of it!'

'But I should like –' began Arrietty.

'So he didn't have your advantages,' went on Homily breathlessly, 'and just because the Harpsichords lived in the drawing-room – they moved in there, in 1837, to a hole in the wainscot just behind where the harpsichord used to stand, if ever there was one, which I doubt – and were really a family called Linen-Press or some such name and changed it to Harpsichord –'

'What did they live on,' asked Arrietty, 'in the drawing-room?'

'Afternoon tea,' said Homily, 'nothing but afternoon tea. No wonder the children grew up peaky. Of course, in the old days it was better – muffins and crumpets and such, and good rich cake and jams and jellies. And there was one old Harpsichord who could remember sillabub of an evening. But they had to do their borrowing in such a rush, poor things. On wet days, when the human beings sat all afternoon in the drawing-room, the tea would be brought in and taken away again without a chance of the Harpsichords getting near it – and on fine days it might be taken out into the garden. Lupy has told me that, sometimes, there were days and days when they lived on crumbs and on water out of the flower-vases. So you can't be too hard on them; their only comfort, poor things, was to show off a bit and talk like ladies and gentlemen. Did you ever hear your Aunt Lupy talk?'

'Yes. No. I can't remember.'

'Oh, you should have heard her say "Parquet" – that's the stuff the drawing-room floor's made of – "Parkay . . . Parr-r-kay", she'd say. Oh, it was lovely. Come to think of it, your Aunt Lupy was the most stuck up of them all . . .'

'Arrietty's shivering,' said Pod. 'We didn't get the little maid up to talk about Aunt Lupy.'

'Nor we did,' cried Homily, suddenly contrite, 'you should've stopped me, Pod. There, my lamb, tuck this quilt right round you and I'll get you a nice drop of piping hot soup!'

'And yet,' said Pod as Homily, fussing at the stove, ladled soup into the tea-cup, 'we did in a way.'

'Did what?' asked Homily.

'Get her up to talk about Aunt Lupy. Aunt Lupy, Uncle Hendreary, and' – he paused – 'Eggletina.'

'Let her drink up her soup first,' said Homily.

'There's no call for her to stop drinking,' said Pod.

CHAPTER SIX

'YOUR mother and I got you up,' said Pod, 'to tell you about upstairs.'

Arrietty, holding the great cup in both hands, looked at him over the edge.

Pod coughed. 'You said a while back that the sky was dark brown with cracks in it. Well, it isn't.' He looked at her almost accusingly. 'It's blue.'

'I know,' said Arrietty.

'You know!' exclaimed Pod.

'Yes, of course I know. I've got the grating.'

'Can you see the sky through the grating?'

'Go on,' interrupted Homily, 'tell her about the gates.'

'Well,' said Pod ponderously, 'if you go outside this room, what do you see?'

'A dark passage,' said Arrietty.

'And what else?'

'Other rooms.'

'And if you go farther?'

'More passages.'

'And, if you go walking on and on, in all the passages under the floor, however they twist and turn, what do you find?'

'Gates,' said Arrietty.

'Strong gates,' said Pod, 'gates you can't open. What are they there for?'

'Against the mice?' said Arrietty.

'Yes,' agreed Pod uncertainly, as though he gave her half a mark, 'but mice never hurt no one. What else?'

'Rats?' suggested Arrietty.

'We don't have rats,' said Pod. 'What about cats?'

'Cats?' echoed Arrietty, surprised.

'Or to keep you in?' suggested Pod.

'To keep me in?' repeated Arrietty, dismayed.

'Upstairs is a dangerous place,' said Pod. 'And you, Arrietty, you're all we've got, see? It isn't like Hendreary – he still has two of his own

35

and three of hers. Once,' said Pod, 'Hendreary had three – three of his
own.'

'Your father's thinking of Eggletina,' said Homily.

'Yes,' said Pod, 'Eggletina. They never told her about upstairs. And
they hadn't got no grating. They told her the sky was nailed up, like,
with cracks in it –'

'A foolish way to bring up a child,' murmured Homily. She sniffed
slightly and touched Arrietty's hair.

'But Eggletina was no fool,' said Pod; 'she didn't believe them. So
one day,' he went on, 'she went upstairs to see for herself.'

'How did she get out?' asked Arrietty, interested.

'Well, we didn't have so many gates then. Just the one under the
clock. Hendreary must have left it unlocked or something. Anyway,
Eggletina went out . . .'

'In a blue dress,' said Homily, 'and a pair of button-boots your father made her, yellow kid with jet beads for buttons. Lovely they were.'

'Well,' said Pod, 'any other time it might have been all right. She'd have gone out, had a look around, had a bit of a fright, maybe, and come back – none the worse and no one the wiser . . .'

'But things had been happening,' said Homily.

'Yes,' said Pod, 'she didn't know, as they never told her, that her father had been "seen" and that upstairs they had got in the cat and –'

'They waited a week,' said Homily, 'and they waited a month and they hoped for a year but no one ever saw Eggletina no more.'

'And that,' said Pod after a pause and eyeing Arrietty, 'is what happened to Eggletina.'

There was silence except for Pod's breathing and the faint bubble of the soup.

'It just broke up your Uncle Hendreary,' said Homily at last. 'He never went upstairs again – in case, he said, he found the button-boots. Their only future was to emigrate.'

Arrietty was silent a moment, then she raised her head. 'Why did you tell me?' she asked. 'Now? Tonight?'

Homily got up. She moved restlessly towards the stove. 'We don't never talk of it,' she said, 'at least, not much, but tonight, we felt –' She turned suddenly. 'Well, we'll just say it straight out: your father's been "seen", Arrietty!'

'Oh,' said Arrietty, 'who by?'

'Well, by a – something you've never heard of. But that's not the point: the point is –'

'You think they'll get a cat?'

'They may,' said Homily.

Arrietty set down the soup for a moment; she stared into the cup as it stood beside her almost knee high on the floor; there was a dreamy, secret something about her lowered face. 'Couldn't we emigrate?' she ventured at last, very softly.

Homily gasped and clasped her hands and swung away towards the wall. 'You don't know what you're talking about,' she cried, addressing a frying-pan which hung there. 'Worms and weasels and cold and damp and –'

'But supposing,' said Arrietty, 'that I went out, like Eggletina did, and the cat ate me. Then you and papa would emigrate. Wouldn't you?' she asked, and her voice faltered. 'Wouldn't you?'

Homily swung round again, this time towards Arrietty; her face looked very angry. 'I shall smack you, Arrietty Clock, if you don't behave yourself this minute!'

Arrietty's eyes filled with tears. 'I was only thinking,' she said, 'that I'd like to be there – to emigrate too. Uneaten,' she added softly and the tears fell.

'Now,' said Pod, 'this is enough! You get off to bed, Arrietty, uneaten and unbeaten both – and we'll talk about it in the morning.'

'It's not that I'm afraid,' cried Arrietty angrily; 'I like cats. I bet the cat didn't eat Eggletina. I bet she just ran away because she hated being cooped up . . . day after day . . . week after week . . . year after year. . . . Like I do!' she added on a sob.

'Cooped up!' repeated Homily, astounded.

Arrietty put her face into her hands. 'Gates . . .' she gasped, 'gates, gates, gates . . .'

Pod and Homily stared at each other across Arrietty's bowed shoulders. 'You didn't ought to have brought it up,' he said unhappily, 'not so late at night . . .'

Arrietty raised her tear-streaked face. 'Late or early, what's the difference?' she cried. 'Oh, I know papa is a wonderful Borrower. I know we've managed to stay when all the others have gone. But what has it done for us, in the end? I don't think it's so clever to live on alone, for ever and ever, in a great, big, half-empty house; under the floor, with no one to talk to, no one to play with, nothing to see but dust and passages, no light but candlelight and firelight and what comes through the cracks. Eggletina had brothers and Eggletina had half-brothers; Eggletina had a tame mouse; Eggletina had yellow boots with jet buttons, and Eggletina did get out – just once!'

'Shush,' said Pod gently, 'not so loud.' Above their heads the floor creaked and heavy footfalls heaved deliberately to and fro. They heard Mrs Driver's grumbling voice and the clatter of the fire-irons. 'Drat this stove,' they heard her say, 'wind's in the east again.' They then heard her raise her voice and call, 'Crampfurl!'

Pod sat staring glumly at the floor; Arrietty shivered a little and hugged herself more tightly into the knitted quilt and Homily drew a long, slow breath. Suddenly she raised her head.

'The child is right,' she announced firmly.

Arrietty's eyes grew big. 'Oh, no –' she began. It shocked her to be right. Parents were right, not children. Children could say anything, Arrietty knew, and enjoy saying it – knowing always they were safe and wrong.

'You see, Pod,' went on Homily, 'it was different for you and me. There was other families, other children . . . the Sinks in the scullery, you remember? And those people who lived behind the knife machine – I forget their names now. And the Broom-Cupboard boys. And there was that underground passage from the stables – you know, that the Rain-Pipes used. We had more, as you might say, freedom.'

'Ah, yes,' said Pod, 'in a way. But where does freedom take you?' He looked up uncertainly. 'Where are they all now?'

'Some of them may have bettered themselves, I shouldn't wonder,' said Homily sharply. 'Times have changed in the whole house. Pickings aren't what they were. There were those that went, you remember, when they dug a trench for the gas-pipe. Over the fields, and through the wood, and all. A kind of tunnel it gave them, all the way to Leighton Buzzard.'

'And what did they find there?' said Pod unkindly. 'A mountain of coke!'

Homily turned away. 'Arrietty,' she said, in the same firm voice, 'supposing one day – we'd pick a special day when there was no one about, and providing they don't get a cat which I have my reasons for thinking they won't – supposing, one day, your father took you out borrowing, you'd be a good girl, wouldn't you? You'd do just what he said, quickly and quietly, and no arguing?'

Arrietty turned quite pink; she clasped her hands together. 'Oh –' she began in an ecstatic voice, but Pod cut in quickly:

'Now, Homily, we got to think. You can't just say things like that without thinking it out proper. I been "seen" remember. This is no kind of time for taking a child upstairs.'

'There won't be no cat,' said Homily; 'there wasn't no screeching. It's not like that time with Rosa Pickhatchet.'

'All the same,' said Pod uncertainly, 'the risk's there. I never heard of no *girl* going borrowing before.'

'The way I look at it,' said Homily, 'and it's only now it's come to me: if you had a son, you'd take him borrowing, now, wouldn't you? Well, you haven't got no son – only Arrietty. Suppose anything happened to you or me, where would Arrietty be – if she hadn't learned to borrow?'

Pod stared down at his knees. 'Yes,' he said after a moment, 'I see what you mean.'

'And it'll give her a bit of interest like and stop her hankering.'

'Hankering for what?'

'For blue sky and grass and suchlike.' Arrietty caught her breath and

Homily turned on her swiftly: 'It's no good, Arrietty, I'm not going to emigrate – not for you nor anyone else!'

'Ah,' said Pod and began to laugh, 'so that's it!'

'Shush!' said Homily, annoyed, and glanced quickly at the ceiling. 'Not so loud! Now kiss your father, Arrietty,' she went on briskly, 'and pop off back to bed.'

As Arrietty snuggled down under the bed-clothes she felt, creeping up from her toes, a glow of happiness like a glow of warmth. She heard their voices rising and falling in the next room: Homily went on and on, measured and confident – there was, Arrietty felt, a kind of conviction behind it; it was the winning voice. Once she heard Pod get up and the scrape of a chair. 'I don't like it!' she heard him say. And she heard Homily whisper 'Hush!' and there were tremulous footfalls on the floor above and the sudden clash of pans.

Arrietty, half dozing, gazed up at her painted ceiling. 'FLOR DE HAVANA' proclaimed the banners proudly. 'Garantizados . . . Superiores . . . Non Plus Ultra . . . Esquisitos . . .' and the lovely gauzy ladies blew their trumpets, silently, triumphantly, on soundless notes of glee . . .

CHAPTER SEVEN

For the next three weeks Arrietty was especially 'good': she helped her mother tidy the store-rooms; she swept and watered the passages and trod them down: she sorted and graded the beads (which they used as buttons) into the screwtops of aspirin bottles; she cut old kid gloves into squares for Pod's shoemaking; she filed fish-bone needles to a bee-sting sharpness; she hung up the washing to dry by the grating so that it blew in the soft air; and at last the day came – that dreadful, wonderful, never-to-be-forgotten day – when Homily, scrubbing the kitchen table, straightened her back and called 'Pod!'

He came in from his workroom, last in hand.

'Look at this brush!' cried Homily. It was a fibre brush with a plaited, fibre back.

'Aye,' said Pod, 'worn down.'

'Gets me knuckles now,' said Homily, 'every time I scrub.'

Pod looked worried. Since he had been 'seen', they had stuck to kitchen borrowing, and bare essentials of fuel and food. There was an old mouse-hole under the kitchen stove upstairs which, at night when the fire was out or very low, Pod could use as a chute to save carrying. Since the window-curtain incident they had pushed a match-box chest of drawers below the mouse-hole, and had stood a wooden stool on the chest of drawers; and Pod, with much help and shoving from Homily, had learned to squeeze up the chute instead of down. In this way he need not venture into the great hall and passages; he could just nip out, from under the vast black stove in the kitchen for a clove or a carrot or a tasty piece of ham. But it was not a satisfactory arrangement: even when the fire was out, often there were hot ash and cinders under the stove and once, as he emerged, a great brush came at him wielded by Mrs Driver; and he slithered back, on top of Homily, singed, shaken, and coughing dust. Another time, for some reason, the fire had been in full blaze and Pod had arrived suddenly beneath a glowing inferno, dropping white-hot coals. But usually, at night, the fire was out, and Pod could pick his way through the cinders into the kitchen proper.

'Mrs Driver's out,' Homily went on. 'It's her day off. And She' – they always spoke of Aunt Sophy as 'She' – 'is safe enough in bed.'

'It's not them that worries me,' said Pod.

'Why,' exclaimed Homily sharply, 'the boy's not still here?'

'I don't know,' said Pod; 'there's always a risk,' he added.

'And there always will be,' retorted Homily, 'like when you was in the coal-cellar and the coal-cart came.'

'But the other two,' said Pod, 'Mrs Driver and Her, I always know where they are, like.'

'As for that,' exclaimed Homily, 'a boy's even better. You can hear a boy a mile off. Well,' she went on after a moment, 'please yourself. But it's not like you to talk of risks . . .'

Pod sighed. 'All right,' he said and turned away to fetch his borrowing-bag.

'Take the child,' called Homily after him.

Pod turned. 'Now, Homily,' he began in an alarmed voice.

'Why not?' asked Homily sharply, 'it's just the day. You aren't going no farther than the front door. If you're nervous you can leave her by the clock, ready to nip underneath and down the hole. Let her just *see* at any rate. Arrietty!'

As Arrietty came running in Pod tried again. 'Now listen, Homily –' he protested.

Homily ignored him. 'Arrietty,' she said brightly, 'would you like to go along with your father and borrow me some brush fibre from the door-mat in the hall?'

Arrietty gave a little skip. 'Oh,' she cried, 'could I?'

'Well, take your apron off,' said

Homily, 'and change your boots. You want light shoes for borrowing – better wear the red kid.' And then as Arrietty spun away Homily turned to Pod: 'She'll be all right,' she said; 'you'll see.'

As she followed her father down the passage Arrietty's heart began to beat faster. Now the moment had come at last she found it almost too much to bear. She felt light and trembly, and hollow with excitement.

They had three borrowing-bags between the two of them ('In case,' Pod had explained, 'we pick up something. A bad Borrower loses many a chance for lack of an extra bag'), and Pod laid these down to open the first gate, which was latched by a safety-pin. It was a big pin, too strongly sprung for little hands to open, and Arrietty watched her father swing his whole weight on the bar and his feet kick loose off the ground. Hanging from his hands, he shifted his weight along the pin towards the curved sheath, and, as he moved, the pin sprang open and he, in the same instant, jumped free. 'You couldn't do that,' he remarked, dusting his hands; 'too light. Nor could your mother. Come along now. Quietly . . .'

There were other gates; all of which Pod left open ('Never shut a gate on the way out,' he explained in a whisper, 'you might need to get back quick') and, after a while, Arrietty saw a faint light at the end of the passage. She pulled her father's sleeve. 'Is that it?' she whispered.

Pod stood still. 'Quietly, now,' he warned her. 'Yes, that's it: the hole under the clock!' As he said these words, Arrietty felt breathless, but outwardly she made no sign. 'There are three steps up to it,' Pod went on, 'steep like, so mind how you go. When you're under the clock you just stay there; don't let your mind wander and keep your eyes on me: if all's clear, I'll give you the sign.'

The steps were high and a little uneven but Arrietty took them more lightly than Pod. As she scrambled past the jagged edges of the hole she had a sudden blinding glimpse of molten gold: it was spring sunshine on the pale stones of the hall floor. Standing upright, she could no longer see this; she could only see the cave-like shadows in the great case above her and the dim outline of the hanging weights. The hollow darkness around her vibrated with sound; it was a safe sound – solid and regular; and, far above her head, she saw the movement of the pendulum; it gleamed a little in the half light, remote and cautious in its rhythmic swing. Arrietty felt warm tears behind her eyelids and a sudden swelling pride: so this, at last, was The Clock! Their clock . . . after which her family was named! For two hundred years it had stood there, deep-voiced and patient, guarding their threshold, and measuring their time.

But Pod, she saw, stood crouched beneath the carved archway against the light: 'Keep your eyes on me,' he had said, so Arrietty crouched too. She saw the gleaming golden stone floor of the hall stretching away into distance; she saw the edges of rugs, like richly coloured islands in a molten sea, and she saw, in a glory of sunlight – like a dreamed-of gateway to fairyland – the open front door. Beyond she saw grass and, against the clear, bright sky, a waving frond of green. Pod's eyes slewed round. 'Wait,' he breathed, 'and watch.' And then in a flash he was gone. Arrietty saw him scurry across the sunlit floor. Swiftly he ran – as a mouse runs or a blown dry leaf – and suddenly she saw him as 'small'. But she told herself, 'He isn't small. He's half a head taller than mother . . .' She watched him run round a chestnut-coloured island of door-mat into the shadows beside the door. There, it seemed, he became invisible.

Arrietty watched and waited. All was still except for a sudden whirr within the clock. A grinding whirr it was, up high in the hollow darkness above her head, then the sliding grate of slipped metal before the clock sang out its chime. Three notes were struck, deliberate and mellow: 'Take it or leave it,' they seemed to say, 'but that's the time –'

A sudden movement near the shadowed lintel of the front door and there was Pod again, bag in hand, beside the mat; it rose knee deep before him like a field of chestnut corn. Arrietty saw him glance towards the clock and then she saw him raise his hand.

Oh, the warmth of the stone flags as she ran across them . . . the gladdening sunlight on her face and hands . . . the awful space above and around her! Pod caught her and held her at last, and patted her shoulder. 'There, there . . .' he said, 'get your breath – good girl!'

Panting a little, Arrietty gazed about her. She saw great chair legs rearing up into sunlight; she saw the shadowed undersides of their seats spread above her like canopies; she saw the nails and the strapping and odd tags of silk and string; she saw the terraced cliffs of the stairs, mounting up into the distance, up and up . . . she saw carved table legs and a cavern under the chest. And all the time, in the stillness, the clock spoke – measuring out the seconds, spreading its layers of calm.

And then, turning, Arrietty looked at the garden. She saw a gravelled path, full of coloured stones – the size of walnuts they were, with, here and there, a blade of grass between them, transparent green against the light of the sun. Beyond the path she saw a grassy bank rising steeply to a tangled hedge; and beyond the hedge she saw fruit trees, bright with blossom.

'Here's a bag,' said Pod in a hoarse whisper; 'better get down to work.'

Obediently Arrietty started pulling fibre; stiff it was and full of dust. Pod worked swiftly and methodically, making small bundles, each of which he put immediately in the bag. 'If you have to run suddenly,' he explained, 'you don't want to leave nothing behind.'

'It hurts your hands,' said Arrietty, 'doesn't it?' and suddenly she sneezed.

'Not my hands it doesn't,' said Pod, 'they're hardened like,' and Arrietty sneezed again.

'Dusty, isn't it?' she said.

Pod straightened his back. 'No good pulling where it's knotted right in,' he said, watching her. 'No wonder it hurts your hands. See here,' he exclaimed after a moment, 'you leave it! It's your first time up like. You sit on the step there and take a peek out of doors.'

'Oh, no –' Arrietty began ('If I don't help,' she thought, 'he won't want me again') but Pod insisted.

'I'm better on me own,' he said. 'I can choose me bits, if you see what I mean, seeing as it's me who's got to make the brush.'

CHAPTER EIGHT

THE step was warm but very steep. 'If I got down on to the path,' Arrietty thought, 'I might not get up again,' so for some moments she sat quietly. After a while she noticed the shoe-scraper.

'Arrietty,' called Pod softly, 'where have you got to?'

'I just climbed down the shoe-scraper,' she called back.

He came along and looked down at her from the top of the step. 'That's all right,' he said after a moment's stare, 'but never climb down anything that isn't fixed like. Supposing one of them came along and moved the shoe-scraper – where would you be then? How would you get up again?'

'It's heavy to move,' said Arrietty.

'Maybe,' said Pod, 'but it's movable. See what I mean? There's rules, my lass, and you got to learn.'

'This path,' Arrietty said, 'goes round the house. And the bank does too.'

'Well,' said Pod, 'what of it?'

Arrietty rubbed one red kid shoe on a rounded stone. 'It's my grating,' she explained. 'I was thinking that my grating must be just round the corner. My grating looks out on to this bank.'

'Your grating!' exclaimed Pod. 'Since when has it been your grating?'

'I was thinking,' Arrietty went on. 'Suppose I just went round the corner and called through the grating to mother?'

'No,' said Pod, 'we're not going to have none of that. Not going round corners.'

'Then,' went on Arrietty, 'she'd see I was all right like.'

46

'Well,' said Pod, and then he half smiled, 'go quickly then and call. I'll watch for you here. Not loud mind!'

Arrietty ran. The stones in the path were firmly bedded and her light, soft shoes hardly seemed to touch them. How glorious it was to run – you could never run under the floor: you walked, you stooped, you crawled – but you never ran. Arrietty nearly ran past the grating. She saw it just in time after she turned the corner. Yes, there it was quite close to the ground, embedded deeply in the old wall of the house; there was moss below it in a spreading, greenish stain.

Arrietty ran up to it. 'Mother!' she called, her nose against the iron grille. 'Mother!' She waited quietly and, after a moment, she called again.

At the third call Homily came. Her hair was coming down and she carried, as though it were heavy, the screw lid of a pickle jar, filled with soapy water. 'Oh,' she said in an annoyed voice, 'you didn't half give me a turn! What do you think you're up to? Where's your father?'

Arrietty jerked her head sideways. 'Just there – by the front door!' She was so full of happiness that, out of Homily's sight, her toes danced on the green moss. Here she was on the other side of the grating – here she was at last, on the outside – looking in!

'Yes,' said Homily, 'they open that door like that – the first day of spring. Well,' she went on briskly, 'you run back to your father. And tell him, if the morning-room door happens to be open that I wouldn't say no to a bit of red blotting-paper. Mind out of my way now – while I throw the water!'

'That's what grows the moss,' thought Arrietty as she sped back to her father, 'all the water we empty through the grating . . .'

Pod looked relieved when he saw her but frowned at the message. 'How's she expect me to climb that desk without me pin? Blotting-paper's a curtain-and-chair job and she should know it. Come on now! Up with you!'

'Let me stay down,' pleaded Arrietty, 'just a bit longer. Just till you finish. They're all out. Except Her. Mother said so.'

'She'd say anything,' grumbled Pod, 'when she wants something quick. How does she know She won't take it into her head to get out of that bed of Hers and come downstairs with a stick? How does she know Mrs Driver ain't stayed at home today – with a headache? How does she know that boy ain't still here?'

'What boy?' asked Arrietty.

Pod looked embarrassed. 'What boy?' he repeated vaguely and then went on: 'Or maybe Crampfurl –'

'Crampfurl isn't a boy,' said Arrietty.

'No, he isn't,' said Pod, 'not in a manner of speaking. No,' he went
on as though thinking this out, 'no, you wouldn't call Crampfurl a boy.
Not, as you might say, a boy – exactly. Well,' he said, beginning to
move away, 'stay down a bit if you like. But stay close!'

Arrietty watched him move away from the step and then she looked
about her. Oh, glory! Oh, joy! Oh, freedom! The sunlight, the grasses,
the soft, moving air and half-way up the bank, where it curved round
the corner, a flowering cherry-tree! Below it on the path lay a stain of
pinkish petals and at the tree's foot, pale as butter, a nest of primroses.

Arrietty threw a cautious glance towards the front door-step and
then, light and dancey, in her soft red shoes, she ran towards the petals.
They were curved like shells and rocked as she touched them. She
gathered several up and laid them one inside the other . . . up and
up . . . like a card castle. And then she spilled them. Pod came again to
the top of the step and looked along the path. 'Don't you go far,' he said
after a moment. Seeing his lips move, she smiled back at him: she was
too far already to hear the words.

A greenish beetle, shining in the sunlight, came towards her across
the stones. She laid her fingers lightly on its shell and it stood still,
waiting and watchful, and when she moved her hand the beetle went
swiftly on. An ant came hurrying in a busy zig-zag. She danced in front
of it to tease it and put out her foot. It stared at her, nonplussed, waving
its antennae; then pettishly, as though put out, it swerved away. Two
birds came down, quarrelling shrilly, into the grass below the tree. One
flew away but Arrietty could see the other among the moving grass
stems above her on the slope. Cautiously she moved towards the bank
and climbed a little nervously in amongst the green blades. As she
parted them gently with her bare hands, drops of water plopped on her
skirt and she felt the red shoes become damp. But on she went, pulling
herself up now and again by rooty stems into this jungle of moss and
wood-violet and creeping leaves of clover. The sharp-seeming grass
blades, waist high, were tender to the touch and sprang back lightly
behind her as she passed. When at last she reached the foot of the tree,
the bird took fright and flew away and she sat down suddenly on a
gnarled leaf of primrose. The air was filled with scent. 'But nothing will
play with you,' she thought and saw the cracks and furrows of the
primrose leaves held crystal beads of dew. If she pressed the leaf these
rolled like marbles. The bank was warm, almost too warm here within
the shelter of the tall grass, and the sandy earth smelled dry. Standing

up, she picked a primrose. The pink stalk felt tender and living in her hands and was covered with silvery hairs, and when she held the flower, like a parasol, between her eyes and the sky, she saw the sun's pale light through the veined petals. On a piece of bark she found a wood-louse and she struck it lightly with her swaying flower. It curled immediately and became a ball, bumping softly away downhill in amongst the grass roots. But she knew about wood-lice. There were plenty of them at home under the floor. Homily always scolded her if she played with them because, she said, they smelled of old knives. She lay back among the stalks of the primroses and they made a coolness between her and the sun, and then, sighing, she turned her head and looked sideways up the bank among the grass stems. Startled, she caught her breath. Something had moved above her on the bank. Something had glittered. Arrietty stared.

CHAPTER NINE

It was an eye. Or it looked like an eye. Clear and bright like the colour of the sky. An eye like her own but enormous. A glaring eye. Breathless with fear, she sat up. And the eye blinked. A great fringe of lashes came curving down and flew up again out of sight. Cautiously, Arrietty moved her legs: she would slide noiselessly in among the grass stems and slither away down the bank.

'Don't move!' said a voice, and the voice, like the eye, was enormous but, somehow, hushed – and hoarse like a surge of wind through the grating on a stormy night in March.

Arrietty froze. 'So this is it,' she thought, 'the worst and most terrible thing of all: I have been "seen"! Whatever happened to Eggletina will now, almost certainly, happen to me!'

There was a pause and Arrietty, her heart pounding in her ears, heard the breath again drawn swiftly into the vast lungs. 'Or,' said the voice, whispering still, 'I shall hit you with my ash stick.'

Suddenly Arrietty became calm. 'Why?' she asked. How strange her own voice sounded! Crystal thin and harebell clear, it tinkled on the air.

'In case,' came the surprised whisper at last, 'you ran towards me, quickly, through the grass . . . in case,' it went on, trembling a little, 'you scrabbled at me with your nasty little hands.'

Arrietty stared at the eye; she held herself quite still. 'Why?' she asked again, and again the word tinkled – icy cold it sounded this time, and needle sharp.

'Things do,' said the voice. 'I've seen them. In India.'

Arrietty thought of her Gazetteer of the World. 'You're not in India now,' she pointed out.

'Did you come out of the house?'

'Yes,' said Arrietty.

'From whereabouts in the house?'

Arrietty stared at the eye. 'I'm not going to tell you,' she said at last bravely.

'Then I'll hit you with my ash stick!'

'All right,' said Arrietty, 'hit me!'

'I'll pick you up and break you in half!'

Arrietty stood up. 'All right,' she said and took two paces forward.

There was a sharp gasp and an earthquake in the grass: he spun away from her and sat up, a great mountain in a green jersey. He had fair, straight hair and golden eyelashes. 'Stay where you are!' he cried.

Arrietty stared up at him. So this was 'the boy'! Breathless, she felt, and light with fear. 'I guessed you were about nine,' she gasped after a moment.

He flushed. 'Well, you're wrong, I'm ten.' He looked down at her, breathing deeply. 'How old are you?'

'Fourteen,' said Arrietty. 'Next June,' she added, watching him.

There was silence while Arrietty waited, trembling a little. 'Can you read?' the boy said at last.

'Of course,' said Arrietty. 'Can't you?'

'No,' he stammered. 'I mean – yes. I mean I've just come from India.'

'What's that got to do with it?' asked Arrietty.

'Well, if you're born in India, you're bilingual. And if you're bilingual, you can't read. Not so well.'

Arrietty stared up at him: what a monster, she thought, dark against the sky.

'Do you grow out of it?' she asked.

He moved a little and she felt the cold flick of his shadow.

'Oh yes,' he said, 'it wears off. My sisters were bilingual; now they aren't a bit. They could read any of those books upstairs in the schoolroom.'

'So could I,' said Arrietty quickly, 'if someone could hold them, and turn the pages. I'm not a bit bilingual. I can read anything.'

'Could you read out loud?'

'Of course,' said Arrietty.

'Would you wait here while I run upstairs and get a book now?'

'Well,' said Arrietty; she was longing to show off; then a startled look came into her eyes. 'Oh –' she faltered.

'What's the matter?' The boy was standing up now. He towered above her.

'How many doors are there to this house?' She squinted up at him against the bright sunlight. He dropped on one knee.

'Doors?' he said. 'Outside doors?'

'Yes.'

'Well, there's the front door, the back door, the gun room door, the kitchen door, the scullery door . . . and the french windows in the drawing-room.'

'Well, you see,' said Arrietty, 'my father's in the hall, by the front door, working. He . . . he wouldn't want to be disturbed.'

'Working?' said the boy. 'What at?'

'Getting material,' said Arrietty, 'for a scrubbing-brush.'

'Then I'll go in the side door'; he began to move away but turned suddenly and came back to her. He stood a moment, as though embarrassed, and then he said: 'Can you fly?'

'No,' said Arrietty, surprised; 'can you?'

His face became even redder. 'Of course not,' he said angrily; 'I'm not a fairy!'

'Well, nor am I,' said Arrietty, 'nor is anybody. I don't believe in them.'

He looked at her strangely. 'You don't believe in them?'

'No,' said Arrietty; 'do you?'

'Of course not!'

Really, she thought, he is a very angry kind of boy. 'My mother believes in them,' she said, trying to appease him. 'She thinks she saw one once. It was when she was a girl and lived with her parents behind the sand pile in the potting-shed.'

He squatted down on his heels and she felt his breath on her face. 'What was it like?' he asked.

'About the size of a glow-worm with wings like a butterfly. And it had a tiny little face, she said, all alight and moving like sparks and tiny moving hands. Its face was changing all the time, she said, smiling and sort of shimmering. It seemed to be talking, she said, very quickly – but you couldn't hear a word.'

'Oh,' said the boy, interested. After a moment he asked: 'Where did it go?'

'It just went,' said Arrietty. 'When my mother saw it, it seemed to be caught in a cobweb. It was dark at the time. About five o'clock on a winter's evening. After tea.'

'Oh,' he said again and picked up two petals of cherry-blossom which he folded together like a sandwich and ate slowly. 'Supposing,' he said, staring past her at the wall of the house, 'you saw a little man, about as tall as a pencil, with a blue patch in his trousers, half-way up a window curtain, carrying a doll's tea-cup – would you say it was a fairy?'

'No,' said Arrietty, 'I'd say it was my father.'

'Oh,' said the boy, thinking this out, 'does your father have a blue patch on his trousers?'

'Not on his best trousers. He does on his borrowing ones.'

'Oh,' said the boy again. He seemed to find it a safe sound, as lawyers do. 'Are there many people like you?'

'No,' said Arrietty. 'None. We're all different.'

'I mean as small as you?'

Arrietty laughed. 'Oh, don't be silly!' she said. 'Surely you don't think there are many people in the world your size?'

'There are more my size than yours,' he retorted.

'Honestly –' began Arrietty helplessly and laughed again. 'Do you really think – I mean, whatever sort of a world would it be? Those great chairs . . . I've seen them. Fancy if you had to make chairs that size for everyone? And the stuff for their clothes . . . miles and miles of it . . . tents of it . . . and the sewing! And their great houses, reaching up so you can hardly see the ceilings . . . their great beds . . . the *food* they eat . . . great, smoking mountains of it, huge bogs of stew and soup and stuff.'

'Don't you eat soup?' asked the boy.

'Of course we do,' laughed Arrietty. 'My father had an uncle who had a little boat which he rowed round in the stock-pot picking up flotsam and jetsam. He did bottom-fishing too for bits of marrow until the cook got suspicious through finding bent pins in the soup. Once he was nearly shipwrecked on a chunk of submerged shin-bone. He lost his oars and the boat sprang a leak but he flung a line over the pot handle and pulled himself alongside the rim. But all that stock – fathoms of it! And the size of the stock-pot! I mean, there wouldn't be enough stuff in the world to go round after a bit! That's why my father says it's a good thing they're dying out . . . just a few, my father says, that's all we need – to keep us. Otherwise he says, the whole thing gets' – Arrietty hesitated trying to remember the word – 'exaggerated, he says –'

'What do you mean,' asked the boy, ' "to keep us"?'

CHAPTER TEN

So Arrietty told him about borrowing – how difficult it was and how dangerous. She told him about the store-rooms under the floor; about Pod's early exploits, the skill he had shown and the courage; she described those far-off days, before her birth, when Pod and Homily had been rich; she described the musical snuff-box, of gold filigree, and the little bird which flew out of it made of kingfisher feathers, how it flapped its wings and sang its song; she described the doll's wardrobe and the tiny green glasses; the little silver teapot out of the drawing-room case; the satin bedcovers and embroidered sheets . . . 'those we have still,' she told him, 'they're Her handkerchiefs . . .' 'She', the boy realized gradually, was his Great Aunt Sophy upstairs; he heard how Pod would borrow from her bedroom, picking his way – in the firelight – among the trinkets on her dressing-table, even climbing her bed-curtains and walking on her quilt. And of how she would watch him and sometimes talk to him because, Arrietty explained, every day at six o'clock they brought her a decanter of Fine Old Pale Madeira, and how before midnight she would drink the lot. Nobody blamed her, not even Homily, because, as Homily would say, 'She' had so few pleasures, poor soul, but, Arrietty explained, after the first three glasses Great Aunt Sophy never believed in anything she saw. 'She thinks my father comes out of the decanter,' said Arrietty, 'and one day when I'm older he's going to take me there and she'll think I come out of the decanter too. It'll please her, my father thinks, as she's used to him now. Once he took my mother, and Aunt Sophy perked up like anything and kept asking why my mother didn't come any more and saying they'd watered the Madeira because once, she says, she saw a little man *and* a little woman and now she only sees a little man . . .'

'I wish she thought I came out of the decanter,' said the boy. 'She gives me dictation and teaches me to write. I only see her in the mornings when she's cross. She sends for me and looks behind my ears and asks Mrs D. if I've learned my words.'

'What does Mrs D. look like?' asked Arrietty. (How delicious it was to say 'Mrs D.' like that . . . how careless and daring!)

'She's fat and has a moustache and gives me my bath and hurts my bruise and my sore elbow and says she'll take a slipper to me one of these days . . .' The boy pulled up a tuft of grass and stared at it angrily and Arrietty saw his lip tremble. 'My mother's very nice,' he said. 'She lives in India. Why did you lose all your worldly riches?'

'Well,' said Arrietty, 'the kitchen boiler burst and hot water came pouring through the floor into our house and everything was washed away and piled up in front of the grating. My father worked night and day. First hot, then cold. Trying to salvage things. And there's a dreadful draught in March through that grating. He got ill, you see, and couldn't go borrowing. So my Uncle Hendreary had to do it and one or two others and my mother gave them things bit by bit, for all their trouble. But the kingfisher bird was spoilt by the water; all its feathers fell off and a great twirly spring came jumping out of its side. My father used the spring to keep the door shut against draughts from the grating and my mother put the feathers in a little moleskin hat.

After a while I got born and my father went borrowing again. But he gets tired now and doesn't like curtains, not when any of the bobbles are off . . .'

'I helped him a bit,' said the boy, 'with the tea-cup. He was shivering all over. I suppose he was frightened.'

'My father frightened!' exclaimed Arrietty angrily. 'Frightened of you!' she added.

'Perhaps he doesn't like heights,' said the boy.

'He loves heights,' said Arrietty. 'The thing he doesn't like is curtains. I've told you. Curtains make him tired.'

The boy sat thoughtfully on his haunches, chewing a blade of grass. 'Borrowing,' he said after a while. 'Is that what you call it?'

'What else could you call it?' asked Arrietty.

'I'd call it stealing.'

Arrietty laughed. She really laughed. 'But we *are* Borrowers,' she explained, 'like you're a – a Human Bean or whatever it's called. We're part of the house. You might as well say that the fire-grate steals the coal from the coal-scuttle.'

'Then what is stealing?'

Arrietty looked grave. 'Supposing my Uncle Hendreary borrowed an emerald watch from Her dressing-table and my father took it and hung it up on our wall. That's stealing.'

'An emerald watch!' exclaimed the boy.

'Well, I just said that because we have one on the wall at home, but my father borrowed it himself. It needn't be a watch. It could be anything. A lump of sugar, even. But Borrowers don't steal.'

'Except from human beans,' said the boy.

Arrietty burst out laughing; she laughed so much that she had to hide her face in the primrose. 'Oh dear,' she gasped with tears in her eyes, 'you are funny!' She stared upwards at his puzzled face. 'Human beans are *for* Borrowers – like bread's for butter!'

The boy was silent awhile. A sigh of wind rustled the cherry-tree and shivered among the blossom.

'Well, I don't believe it,' he said at last, watching the falling petals. 'I don't believe that's what we're for at all and I don't believe we're dying out!'

'Oh, goodness!' exclaimed Arrietty impatiently, staring up at his chin. 'Just use your common sense: you're the only real human bean I ever saw (although I do just know of three more – Crampfurl, Her, and Mrs Driver). But I know lots and lots of Borrowers: the Overmantels and the Harpsichords and the Rain-Barrels and the Linen-Presses and the Boot-Racks and the Hon. John Studdingtons and –'

He looked down. 'John Studdington? But he was our grand-uncle –'

'Well, this family lived behind a picture,' went on Arrietty, hardly listening, 'and there were the Stove-Pipes and the Bell-Pulls and the –'

'Yes,' he interrupted, 'but did you see them?'

'I saw the Harpsichords. And my mother was a Bell-Pull. The others were before I was born . . .'

He leaned closer. 'Then where are they now? Tell me that.'

'My Uncle Hendreary has a house in the country,' said Arrietty coldly, edging away from his great lowering face; it was misted over, she noticed, with hairs of palest gold. 'And five children, Harpsichords and Clocks.'

'But where are the others?'

'Oh,' said Arrietty, 'they're somewhere.' But where? she wondered. And she shivered slightly in the boy's cold shadow which lay about her, slantwise, on the grass.

He drew back again, his fair head blocking out a great piece of sky. 'Well,' he said deliberately after a moment, and his eyes were cold, 'I've only seen two Borrowers but I've seen hundreds and hundreds and hundreds and hundreds and hundreds –'

'Oh no –' whispered Arrietty.

'Of human beans.' And he sat back.

Arrietty stood very still. She did not look at him. After a while she said: 'I don't believe you.'

'All right,' he said, 'then I'll tell you –'

'I still won't believe you,' murmured Arrietty.

'Listen!' he said. And he told her about railway stations and football matches and racecourses and royal processions and Albert Hall concerts. He told her about India and China and North America and the British Commonwealth. He told her about the July sales. 'Not hundreds,' he said, 'but thousands and millions and billions and trillions of great, big, enormous people. Now do you believe me?'

Arrietty stared up at him with frightened eyes: it gave her a crick in the neck. 'I don't know,' she whispered.

'As for you,' he went on, leaning closer again, 'I don't believe that there are any more Borrowers anywhere in the world. I believe you're the last three,' he said.

Arrietty dropped her face into the primrose. 'We're not. There's Aunt Lupy and Uncle Hendreary and all the cousins.'

'I bet they're dead,' said the boy. 'And what's more,' he went on, 'no one will ever believe I've seen *you*. And you'll be the very last because you're the youngest. One day,' he told her, smiling triumphantly, 'you'll be the only Borrower left in the world!'

He sat still, waiting, but she did not look up. 'Now you're crying,' he remarked after a moment.

'They're not dead,' said Arrietty in a muffled voice: she was feeling in her little pocket for a handkerchief. 'They live in a badger's set two fields away, beyond the spinney. We don't see them because it's too far. There are weasels and things and cows and foxes . . . and crows . . .'

'Which spinney?' he asked.

'I don't KNOW!' Arrietty almost shouted. 'It's along by the gas-pipe – a field called Parkin's Beck.' She blew her nose. 'I'm going home,' she said.

'Don't go,' he said, 'not yet.'

'Yes, I'm going,' said Arrietty.

His face turned pink. 'Let me just get the book,' he pleaded.

'I'm not going to read to you now,' said Arrietty.

'Why not?'

She looked at him with angry eyes. 'Because –'

'Listen,' he said, 'I'll go to that field. I'll go and find Uncle Hendreary. And the cousins. And Aunt What-ever-she-is. And, if they're alive, I'll tell you. What about that? You could write them a letter and I'd put it down the hole –'

Arrietty gazed up at him: 'Would you?' she breathed.

'Yes, I would. Really I would. Now can I go and get the book? I'll go in by the side door.'

'All right,' said Arrietty absently. Her eyes were shining. 'When can I give you the letter?'

'Any time,' he said, standing above her. 'Where in the house do you live?'

'Well –' began Arrietty and stopped. Why once again did she feel this chill? Could it only be his shadow . . . towering above her, blotting out the sun? 'I'll put it somewhere,' she said hurriedly, 'I'll put it under the hall mat.'

'Which one? The one by the front door?'

'Yes, that one.'

He was gone. And she stood there alone in the sunshine, shoulder deep in grass. What had happened seemed too big for thought; she felt unable to believe it really had happened: not only had she been 'seen' but she had been talked to; not only had she been talked to but she had –

'Arrietty!' said a voice.

She stood up, startled, and spun round: there was Pod, moon-faced, on the path looking up at her. 'Come on down!' he whispered.

She stared at him for a moment as though she did not recognize him; how round his face was, how kind, how familiar!

'Come on!' he said again, more urgently; and obediently because he sounded worried, she slithered quickly towards him off the bank, balancing her primrose. 'Put that thing down,' he said sharply, when she stood at last beside him on the path. 'You can't lug great flowers about – you got to carry a bag. What you want to go up there for?' he grumbled as they moved off across the stones. 'I might never have seen you. Hurry up now. Your mother'll have tea waiting!'

CHAPTER ELEVEN

HOMILY was there, at the last gate, to meet them. She had tidied her hair and smelled of coal-tar soap. She looked younger and somehow excited. 'Well –!' she kept saying. 'Well!' taking the bag from Arrietty and helping Pod to fasten the gate. 'Well, was it nice? Were you a good girl? Was the cherry tree out? Did the clock strike?' She seemed, in the dim light, to be trying to read the expression on Arrietty's face. 'Come along now. Tea's all ready. Give me your hand . . .'

Tea was indeed ready, laid on the round table in the sitting-room with a bright fire burning in the cog-wheel. How familiar the room seemed, and homely, but, suddenly, somehow strange; the fire-light flickering on the wall-paper – the line which read: '. . . it would be so charming if –' If what? Arrietty always wondered. If our house were less dark, she thought, that would be charming. She looked at the home-made dips set in upturned drawing-pins which Homily had placed as candle-holders among the tea things; the old teapot, a hollow oak-apple, with its quill spout and wired-on handle – burnished it was now and hard with age; there were two roast sliced chestnuts which they would eat like toast with butter and a cold boiled chestnut which Pod would cut like bread; there was a plate of hot dried currants, well plumped before the fire; there were cinnamon breadcrumbs, crispy golden, and lightly dredged with sugar, and in front of each place, oh, delight of delights, a single potted shrimp. Homily had put out the silver plates – the florin ones for herself and Arrietty and the half-crown one for Pod.

'Come along, Arrietty, if you've washed your hands,' exclaimed Homily, taking up the teapot, 'don't dream!'

Arrietty drew up a cotton-reel and sat down slowly. She watched her mother pulling on the spout of the teapot; this was always an interesting moment. The thicker end of the quill being inside the teapot, a slight pull just before pouring would draw it tightly into the hole and thus prevent a leak. If, as sometimes happened, a trace of dampness appeared about the join, it only meant a rather harder pull and a sudden gentle twist.

'Well?' said Homily, gingerly pouring. 'Tell us what you saw!'

'She didn't see so much,' said Pod, cutting himself a slice of boiled chestnut to eat with his shrimp.

'Didn't she see the overmantel?'

'No,' said Pod, 'we never went in the morning-room.'

'What about my blotting-paper?'

'I never got it,' said Pod.

'Now that's a nice thing –' began Homily.

'Maybe,' said Pod, munching steadily, 'but I had me feeling. I had it bad.'

'What's that?' asked Arrietty. 'His feeling?'

'Up the back of his head and in his fingers,' said Homily. 'It's a feeling your father gets when' – she dropped her voice – 'there's someone about.'

'Oh,' said Arrietty and seemed to shrink.

'That's why I brought her along home,' said Pod.

'And was there anyone?' asked Homily anxiously.

Pod took a mouthful of shrimp. 'Must have been,' he said, 'but I didn't see nothing.'

Homily leaned across the table. 'Did you have any feeling, Arrietty?'

Arrietty started. 'Oh,' she said, 'do we all have it?'

'Well, not in the same place,' said Homily. 'Mine starts at the back of me ankles and then me knees go. My mother – hers used to start just under her chin and run right round her neck –'

'And tied in a bow at the back,' said Pod, munching.

'No, Pod,' protested Homily, 'it's a fact. No need to be sarcastic. All the Bell-Pulls were like that. Like a collar, she said it was –'

'Pity it didn't choke her,' said Pod.

'Now, Pod, be fair; she had her points.'

'Points!' said Pod. 'She was all points!'

Arrietty moistened her lips; she glanced nervously from Pod to Homily. 'I didn't feel anything,' she said.

'Well,' said Homily, 'perhaps it was a false alarm.'

'Oh no,' began Arrietty, 'it wasn't –' and, as Homily glanced at her sharply, she faltered: 'I mean if papa felt something – I mean – Perhaps,' she went on, 'I don't have it.'

'Well,' said Homily, 'you're young. It'll come, all in good time. You go and stand in our kitchen, just under the chute, when Mrs Driver's raking out the stove upstairs. Stand right up on a stool or something – so's you're fairly near the ceiling. It'll come – with practice.'

After tea, when Pod had gone to his last and Homily was washing up, Arrietty rushed to her diary: 'I'll just open it,' she thought, trembling with haste, 'anywhere.' It fell open at July 9 and 10: 'Talk of Camps but Stay at Home. Old Cameronian Colours in Glasgow Cathedral, 1885' – that's what it said for the 9th. And on the 10th the page was headed: 'Make Hay while the Sun Shines. Snowdon Peak sold for £5,750, 1889.' Arrietty tore out this last page. Turning it over she read on the reverse side: 'July 11: Make Not a Toil of your Pleasure. Niagara passed by C. D. Graham in a cask, 1886.' No, she thought, I'll choose the 10th, 'Make Hay while the Sun Shines' and crossing out her last entry ('Mother out of sorts'), she wrote below it:

Dear Uncle Hendreary,

I hope you are quite well and the cousins are well and Aunt Lupy. We are very well and I am learning to borrow.

Your loving neice,
Arrietty Clock.

Write a letter on the back, please.

XXOXOXX

'What are you doing, Arrietty?' called Homily from the kitchen.

'Writing in my diary.'

'Oh,' said Homily shortly.

'Anything you want?' asked Arrietty.

'It'll do later,' said Homily.

Arrietty folded the letter and placed it carefully between the pages of Bryce's *Tom Thumb Gazetteer of the World* and, in the diary, she wrote: 'Went borrowing. Wrote to H. Talked to B.' After that Arrietty sat for a long time staring into the fire, and thinking and thinking and thinking . . .

> **10th July.**
> Make hay while the sun shines.
> Snowdon Peak sold for £5750, 1889.
>
> ~~Mother out of sorts~~
> Dear Uncle Hendreary,
>   I hope you are ~~go~~ quite
> well and the cousins are
> well and Aunt Lupy.
> We are very well and I
> am learning to borrow,
>   your loving neice
>   Arrietty Clock
> Write a letter on the back
> please × × o × o × ×

CHAPTER TWELVE

BUT it was one thing to write a letter and quite another to find some means of getting it under the mat. Pod, for several days, could not be persuaded to go borrowing: he was well away on his yearly turn-out of the store-rooms, mending partitions, and putting up new shelves. Arrietty usually enjoyed this spring sorting, when half-forgotten treasures came to light and new uses were discovered for old borrowings. She used to love turning over the scraps of silk or lace; the odd kid gloves; the pencil stubs; the rusty razor blades; the hairpins and the needles; the dried figs, the hazel-nuts, the powdery bits of chocolate, and the scarlet stubs of sealing-wax. Pod, one year, had made her a hairbrush from a toothbrush, and Homily had made her a small pair of Turkish bloomers from two glove fingers for 'knocking about in the mornings'. There were reels and reels of coloured silks and cottons and small variegated balls of odd wool, pen-nibs which Homily used as flour scoops, and bottle-tops galore.

But this year Arrietty banged about impatiently and stole away whenever she dared, to stare through the grating, hoping to see the boy. She now kept the letter always with her, stuffed inside her jersey, and the edges became rubbed. Once he did run past the grating and she saw his woollen stockings; he was making a chugging noise in his throat like some kind of engine, and as he turned the corner he let out a piercing 'Ooooo – oo' (it was a train whistle, he told her afterwards) so he did not hear her call. One evening, after dark, she crept away and tried to open the first gate, but swing and tug as she might she could not budge the pin.

Homily, every time she swept the sitting-room, would grumble about the carpet. 'It may be a curtain-and-chair job,' she would say to Pod, 'but it wouldn't take you not a quarter of an hour, with your pin and name-tape, to fetch me a bit of blotting-paper from the desk in the morning-room . . . anyone would think, looking at this floor, that we lived in a toad-hole. No one could call me house-proud,' said Homily. 'You couldn't be, not with my kind of family, but I do like,' she said, 'to keep "nice things nice".' And at last, on the fourth day, Pod gave in. He laid down his hammer (a small electric-bell clapper) and said to Arrietty: 'Come along . . .'

Arrietty was glad to see the morning-room; the door luckily had been left ajar and it was fascinating to stand at last in the thick pile of the carpet gazing upwards at the shelves and pillars and towering gables of the famous overmantel. So that's where they had lived, she thought, those pleasure-loving creatures, remote and gay and self-sufficient. She imagined the Overmantel women – a little 'tweedy', Homily had described them, with wasp waists and piled Edwardian hair – swinging carelessly outwards on the pilasters, lissom and laughing; gazing at themselves in the inset looking-glass which reflected back the tobacco jars, the cut-glass decanters, the book-shelves, and the plush-covered table. She imagined the Overmantel men – fair, they were said to be, with long moustaches and nervous, slender hands – smoking and drinking and telling their witty tales. So they had never asked Homily up there! Poor Homily with her bony nose and never tidy hair . . . They would have looked at her strangely, Arrietty thought, with their long, half-laughing eyes, and smile a little and, humming, turn away. And they had lived only on breakfast food – on toast and egg and tiny snips of mushroom; sausage they'd have had and crispy bacon and little sips of tea and coffee. Where were they now? Arrietty wondered. Where could such creatures go?

Pod had flung his pin so it stuck into the seat of the chair and was up the leg in a trice, leaning outwards on his tape; then, pulling out the pin, he flung it like a javelin, above his head, into a fold of curtain. This is the moment, Arrietty thought, and felt for her precious letter. She slipped into the hall. It was darker, this time, with the front door closed, and she ran across it with a beating heart. The mat was heavy, but she lifted up the corner and slid the letter under by pushing with her foot. 'There!' she said, and looked about her ... shadows, shadows, and the ticking clock. She looked across the great plain of floor to where, in the distance, the stairs mounted. 'Another world above', she thought, 'world on world ...' and shivered slightly.

'Arrietty,' called Pod softly from the morning-room, and she ran back in time to see him swing clear of the chair seat and pull himself upwards on the name-tape, level with the desk. Lightly he came down feet apart and she saw him, for safety's sake, twist the name-tape lightly round his wrist. 'I wanted you to see that,' he said, a little breathless. The blotting-paper, when he pushed it, floated down quite softly, riding lightly on the air, and lay at last some feet beyond the desk, pink and fresh, on the carpet's dingy pile.

'You start rolling,' whispered Pod. 'I'll be down,' and Arrietty went on her knees and began to roll the blotting-paper until it grew too stiff for her to hold. Pod soon finished it off and lashed it with his name-

tape, through which he ran his hat-pin, and together they carried the long cylinder, as two house-painters would carry a ladder, under the clock and down the hole.

Homily hardly thanked them when,

panting a little, they dropped the bundle in the passage outside the sitting-room door. She looked alarmed. 'Oh, there you are,' she said. 'Thank goodness! That boy's about again. I've just heard Mrs Driver talking to Crampfurl.'

'Oh!' cried Arrietty. 'What did she say?' and Homily glanced sharply at her and saw that she looked pale. Arrietty realized she should have said: 'What boy?' It was too late now.

'Nothing real bad,' Homily went on, as though to reassure her. 'It's just a boy they have upstairs. It's nothing at all, but I heard Mrs Driver say that she'd take a slipper to him, see if she wouldn't, if he had the mats up once again in the hall.'

'The mats up in the hall!' echoed Arrietty.

'Yes. Three days running, she said to Crampfurl, he'd had the mats up in the hall. She could tell, she said, by the dust and the way he'd put them back. It was the hall part that worried me, seeing as you and your father – What's the matter, Arrietty? There's no call for that sort of face! Come on now, help me move the furniture and we'll get down the carpet.'

'Oh dear, oh dear,' thought Arrietty miserably, as she helped her mother empty the match-box chest of drawers. 'Three days running he's looked and nothing there. He'll give up hope now . . . he'll never look again.'

That evening she stood for hours on a stool under the chute in their kitchen, pretending she was practising to get 'a feeling' when really she was listening to Mrs Driver's conversations with Crampfurl. All she learned was that Mrs Driver's feet were killing her, and that it was a pity that she hadn't given in her notice last May, and would Crampfurl have another drop, considering there was more in the cellar than anyone would drink in Her lifetime, and if they thought she was going to clean the first-floor windows single-handed they had better think again. But on the third night, just as Arrietty had climbed down off the stool before she overbalanced with weariness, she heard Crampfurl say: 'If you ask me, I'd say he had a ferret.' And quickly Arrietty climbed back again, holding her breath.

'A ferret!' she heard Mrs Driver exclaim shrilly. 'Whatever next? Where would he keep it?'

'That I wouldn't like to say,' said Crampfurl in his rumbling earthy voice; 'all I know is he was up beyond Parkin's Beck, going round all the banks and calling-like down all the rabbit-holes.'

'Well, I never,' said Mrs Driver. 'Where's your glass?'

'Just a drop,' said Crampfurl. 'That's enough. Goes to your liver, this sweet stuff – not like beer, it isn't. Yes,' he went on, 'when he saw me coming with a gun he pretended to be cutting a stick like from the hedge. But I'd see'd him all right and heard him. Calling away, his nose down a rabbit-hole. It's my belief he's got a ferret.' There was a gulp, as though Crampfurl was drinking. 'Yes,' he said at last, and Arrietty heard him set down the glass, 'a ferret called Uncle something.'

Arrietty made a sharp movement, balanced for one moment with arms waving, and fell off the stool. There was a clatter as the stool slid sideways, banged against a chest of drawers and rolled over.

'What was that?' asked Crampfurl.

There was silence upstairs and Arrietty held her breath.

'I didn't hear nothing,' said Mrs Driver.

'Yes,' said Crampfurl, 'it was under the floor like, there by the stove.'

'That's nothing,' said Mrs Driver. 'It's the coals falling. Often sounds like that. Scares you sometimes when you're sitting here alone ... Here, pass your glass, there's only a drop left – might as well finish the bottle ...'

They're drinking Fine Old Madeira, thought Arrietty, and very carefully she set the stool upright and stood quietly beside it, looking up. She could see light through the crack, occasionally flicked with shadow as one person or another moved a hand or arm.

'Yes,' went on Crampfurl, returning to his story, 'and when I come up with m'gun he says, all innocent like – to put me off, I shouldn't wonder: "Any old badgers' sets round here?" '

'Artful,' said Mrs Driver; 'the things they think of ... badgers' sets ...' and she gave her creaking laugh.

'As a matter of fact,' said Crampfurl, 'there did used to be one, but when I showed him where it was like he didn't take no notice of it. Just stood there, waiting for me to go.' Crampfurl laughed. 'Two can play at that game, I thought, so I just sits m'self down. And there we were the two of us.'

'And what happened?'

'Well, he had to go off in the end. Leaving his ferret. I waited a bit, but it never came out. I poked around a bit and whistled. Pity I never heard properly what he called it. Uncle something it sounded like –'

Arrietty heard the sudden scrape of a chair. 'Well,' said Crampfurl, 'I'd better get on now and shut up the chickens –'

The scullery door banged and there was a sudden clatter overhead as Mrs Driver began to rake the stove. Arrietty replaced the stool and stole softly into the sitting-room, where she found her mother alone.

Homily was ironing, bending and banging and pushing the hair back out of her eyes. All round the room underclothes hung airing on safety-pins which Homily used like coat-hangers.

'What happened?' asked Homily. 'Did you fall over?'

'Yes,' said Arrietty, moving quietly into her place beside the fire.

'How's the feeling coming?'

'Oh, I don't know,' said Arrietty. She clasped her knees and laid her chin on them.

'Where's your knitting?' asked Homily. 'I don't know what's come over you lately. Always idle. You don't feel seedy, do you?'

'Oh,' exclaimed Arrietty, 'let me be!' And Homily for once was silent. 'It's the spring,' she told herself. 'Used to take me like that sometimes at her age.'

'I must see that boy,' Arrietty was thinking – staring blindly into the fire. 'I must hear what happened. I must hear if they're all right. I don't want us to die out. I don't want to be the last Borrower. I don't want' – and here Arrietty dropped her face on to her knees – 'to live for ever and ever like this . . . in the dark . . . under the floor . . .'

'No good getting supper,' said Homily, breaking the silence; 'your father's gone borrowing. To Her room. And you know what that means!'

Arrietty raised her head. 'No,' she said, hardly listening; 'what does it mean?'

'That he won't be back,' said Homily sharply, 'for a good hour and a half. He likes it up there, gossiping with Her and poking about on the dressing-table. And it's safe enough once that boy's in bed. Not that there's anything we want special,' she went on. 'It's just these new shelves he's made. They look kind of bare, he says, and he might, he says, just pick up a little something . . .'

Arrietty suddenly was sitting bolt upright: a thought had struck her, leaving her breathless and a little shaky at the knees. 'A good hour and a half,' her mother had said and the gates would be open!

'Where are you going?' asked Homily as Arrietty moved towards the door.

'Just along to the store-rooms,' said Arrietty, shading with one hand her candle-dip from the draught. 'I won't be long.'

'Now don't you untidy anything!' Homily called out after her. 'And be careful of that light!'

As Arrietty went down the passage she thought: 'It is true. I am going to the store-rooms – to find another hat-pin. And if I do find a hat-pin (and a piece of string – there won't be any name-tape) I still "won't be long" because I'll have to get back before papa. And I'm doing it for their sakes,' she told herself doggedly, 'and one day they'll thank me.' All the same she felt a little guilty. 'Artful' – that's what Mrs Driver would say she was.

There was a hat-pin – one with a bar for a top – and she tied on a piece of string, very firmly, twisting it back and forth like a figure of eight and, as a crowning inspiration, she sealed it with sealing-wax.

The gates were open and she left the candle in the middle of the passage where it could come to no harm, just below the hole by the clock.

The great hall when she had climbed out into it was dim with shadows. A single gas jet, turned low, made a pool of light beside the locked front door and another faintly flickered on the landing half-way up the stairs. The ceiling sprang away into height and darkness and all around was space. The night-nursery, she knew, was at the end of the upstairs passage and the boy would be in bed – her mother had just said so.

Arrietty had watched her father use his pin on the chair and single stairs, in comparison, were easier. There was a kind of rhythm to it after a while: a throw, a pull, a scramble, and an upward swing. The stair rods glinted coldly, but the pile of the carpet seemed soft and warm and delicious to fall back on. On the half-landing she paused to get her breath. She did not mind the semi-darkness; she lived in darkness; she was at home in it and, at a time like this, it made her feel safe.

On the upper landing she saw an open door and a great square of golden light which like a barrier lay across the passage. 'I've got to pass through that,' Arrietty told herself, trying to be brave. Inside the lighted room a voice was talking, droning on. '. . . And this mare,' the voice said, 'was a five-year-old which really belonged to my brother in Ireland, not my elder brother but my younger brother, the one who owned Stale Mate and Oh My Darling. He had entered her for several point-to-points . . . but when I say "several" I mean three or at least two . . . Have you ever seen an Irish point-to-point?'

'No,' said another voice, rather absent-mindedly. 'That's my father,' Arrietty realized with a start, 'my father talking to Great Aunt Sophy or rather Great Aunt Sophy talking to my father.' She gripped her pin with its loops of string, and ran into the light and through it to the passage beyond. As she passed the open door she had a glimpse of firelight and lamplight and gleaming furniture and dark-red silk brocade.

Beyond the square of light the passage was dark again and she could see, at the far end, a half-open door. 'That's the day-nursery,' she thought, 'and beyond that is the night-nursery.'

'There are certain differences,' Aunt Sophy's voice went on, 'which would strike you at once. For instance . . .' Arrietty liked the voice. It was comforting and steady, like the sound of the clock in the hall, and as she moved off the carpet on to the strip of polished floor beside the skirting-board, she was interested to hear there were walls in Ireland instead of hedges. Here by the skirting she could run and she loved running. Carpets were heavy going – thick and clinging, they held you up. The boards were smooth and smelled of beeswax. She liked the smell.

The schoolroom, when she reached it, was shrouded in dust sheets and full of junk. Here, too, a gas jet burned, turned low to a bluish flame. The floor was oilcloth, rather worn, and the rugs were shabby. Under the table was a great cavern of darkness. She moved into it, feeling about, and bumped into a dusty hassock higher than her head. Coming out again, into the half light, she looked up and saw the corner cupboard with the doll's tea-service, the painting above the fire-place, and the plush curtain where her father had been 'seen'. Chair legs were everywhere and chair seats obscured her view. She found her way among them to the door of the night-nursery, and there she saw, suddenly, on a shadowed plateau in the far corner, the boy in bed. She saw his great face, turned towards her on the edge of the pillow; she saw the gaslight reflected in his open eyes; she saw his hand gripping the bed-clothes, holding them tightly pressed against his mouth.

She stopped moving and stood still. After a while, when she saw his fingers relax, she said softly: 'Don't be frightened . . . It's me, Arrietty.'

He let the bed-clothes slide away from his mouth and said: 'Arri-*what*-y?' He seemed annoyed.

'Etty,' she repeated gently. 'Did you take the letter?'

He stared at her for a moment without speaking, then he said, 'Why did you come creeping, creeping, into my room?'

'I didn't come creeping, creeping,' said Arrietty. 'I even ran. Didn't you see?'

He was silent, staring at her with his great, wide-open eyes.

'When I brought the book,' he said at last, 'you'd gone.'

'I had to go. Tea was ready. My father fetched me.'

He understood this. 'Oh,' he said matter of factly, and did not reproach her.

'Did you take the letter?' she asked again.

'Yes,' he said, 'I had to go back twice. I shoved it down the badger's hole . . .' Suddenly he threw back the bed-clothes and stood up in bed, enormous in his pale flannel night-shirt. It was Arrietty's turn to be afraid. She half turned, her eyes on his face, and began backing slowly towards the door. But he did not look at her; he was feeling behind a picture on the wall. 'Here it is,' he said, sitting down again, and the bed creaked loudly.

'But I don't want it back!' exclaimed Arrietty, coming forward again. 'You should have left it there! Why did you bring it back?'

He turned it over in his fingers. 'He's written on it,' he said.

'Oh, please,' cried Arrietty excitedly, 'show me!'

She ran right up to the bed and tugged at the trailing sheet. 'Then they are alive! Did you see him?'

'No,' he said, 'the letter was there, just down the hole where I'd put it.' He leaned towards her. 'But he's written on it. Look!'

She made a quick dart and almost snatched the letter out of his great fingers, but was careful to keep out of range of his grasp. She ran with it to the door of the schoolroom where the light, though dim, was a little brighter. 'It's very faint,' she said, holding it close to her eyes. 'What's he written it with? I wonder. It's all in capitals –' She turned suddenly. 'Are you sure you didn't write it?' she asked.

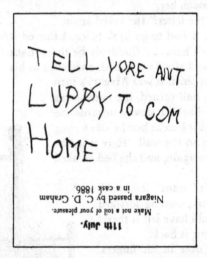

'Of course not,' he began. 'I write small –' But she had seen by his face that he spoke the truth and began to spell out the letters. 'T – e – double l,' she said. 'Tell y – o – r – e.' She looked up. 'Yore?' she said.

'Yes,' said the boy, 'your.'

'Tell your a – n – t, ant?' said Arrietty. 'Ant? My ant?' The boy was silent, waiting. 'Ant L – u – Oh, Aunt Lupy!' she exclaimed. 'He says – listen, this is what he says: "Tell your Aunt Lupy to come home"!'

There was silence. 'Then tell her,' said the boy after a moment.

'But she isn't here!' exclaimed Arrietty. 'She's never been here! I don't even remember what she looked like!'

'Look,' said the boy, staring through the door, 'someone's coming!'

Arrietty whipped round. There was no time to hide: it was Pod, borrowing-bag in one hand and pin in the other. He stood in the doorway of the schoolroom. Quite still he stood, outlined against the light in the passage, his little shadow falling dimly in front of him. He had seen her.

'I heard your voice,' he said, and there was a dreadful quietness about the way he spoke, 'just as I was coming out of Her room.' Arrietty stared back at him, stuffing the letter up her jersey. Could he see beyond her into the shadowed room? Could he see the tousled shape in bed?

'Come on home,' said Pod, and turned away.

CHAPTER FOURTEEN

Pod did not speak until they reached the sitting-room. Nor did he look at her. She had had to scramble after him as best she might. He had ignored her efforts to help him shut the gates, but once, when she tripped, he had waited until she had got up again, watching her, it seemed, almost without interest while she brushed the dust off her knees.

Supper was laid and the ironing put away and Homily came running in from the kitchen, surprised to see them together.

Pod threw down his borrowing-bag. He stared at his wife.

'What's the matter?' faltered Homily, looking from one to the other.

'She was in the night-nursery,' said Pod quietly, 'talking to that boy!'

Homily moved forward, her hands clasped tremblingly against her apron, her startled eyes flicking swiftly to and fro. 'Oh, no –' she breathed.

Pod sat down. He ran a tired hand over his eyes and forehead; his face looked heavy like a piece of dough. 'Now what?' he said.

Homily stood quite still; bowed she stood over her clasped hands and stared at Arrietty. 'Oh, you never –' she whispered.

'They are frightened,' Arrietty realized; 'they are not angry at all – they are very, very frightened.' She moved forward. 'It's all right –' she began.

Homily sat down suddenly on the cotton-reel; she had begun to tremble. 'Oh,' she said, 'whatever shall we do?' She began to rock herself, very slightly, to and fro.

'Oh, mother, don't!' pleaded Arrietty. 'It isn't so bad as that. It really isn't.' She felt up the front of her jersey; at first she could not find the letter – it had slid round her side to the back – but at last she drew it out, very crumpled. 'Look,' she said, 'here's a letter from Uncle Hendreary. I wrote to him and the boy took the letter –'

'You wrote to him!' cried Homily on a kind of suppressed shriek. 'Oh,' she moaned, and closed her eyes, 'whatever next! Whatever shall we do?' and she fanned herself limply with her bony hand.

'Get your mother a drink of water, Arrietty,' said Pod sharply.

Arrietty brought it in a sawn-off hazel shell – it had been sawn off at the pointed end and was shaped like a brandy glass.

'But whatever made you do such a thing, Arrietty?' said Homily more calmly, setting the empty cup down on the table. 'Whatever came over you?'

So Arrietty told them about being 'seen' – that morning under the cherry-tree. And how she had kept it from them not to worry them.

And what the boy said about 'dying out'. And how – more than important – how imperative it had seemed to make sure the Hendrearys were alive. 'Do understand,' pleaded Arrietty, 'please understand! I'm trying to save the race!'

'The expressions she uses!' said Homily to Pod under her breath, not without pride.

But Pod was not listening. 'Save the race!' he repeated grimly. 'It's people like you, my girl, who do things sudden-like with no respect for tradition, who'll finish us Borrowers once for all. Don't you see what you've done?'

Arrietty met his accusing eyes. 'Yes,' she said falteringly, 'I've – I've got in touch with the only other ones still alive. So that,' she went on bravely, 'from now on we can all stick together . . .'

'All stick together!' Pod repeated angrily. 'Do you think Hendreary's lot would ever come to live back here? Can you see your mother emigrating to a badger's set, two fields away, out in the open and no hot water laid on?'

'Never!' cried Homily in a full, rich voice which made them both turn and look at her.

'Or do you see your mother walking across two fields and a garden,' went on Pod, 'two fields full of crows and cows and horses and what-not, to take a cup of tea with your Aunt Lupy whom she never liked much anyway? But wait,' he said as Arrietty tried to speak, 'that's not the point – as far as all that goes we're just where we was – the point,' he went on, leaning forward and speaking with great solemnity, 'is this: that boy knows now where we live!'

'Oh no,' said Arrietty, 'I never told him that. I –'

'You told him,' interrupted Pod, 'about the kitchen pipe bursting; you told him how all our stuff got washed away to the grating.' He sat back again glaring at her. 'He's only got to think,' he pointed out. Arrietty was silent and Pod went on: 'That's a thing that has never happened before, never, in the whole long history of the Borrowers. Borrowers have been "seen" – yes; Borrowers have been caught – maybe: but no human bean has ever known where any Borrower lived. We're in very grave danger, Arrietty, and you've put us there. And that's a fact.'

'Oh, Pod,' whimpered Homily, 'don't frighten the child.'

'Nay, Homily,' said Pod more gently, 'my poor old girl! I don't want to frighten no one, but this is serious. Suppose I said to you pack up tonight, all our bits and pieces, where would you go?'

'Not to Hendreary's,' cried Homily, 'not there, Pod! I couldn't never share a kitchen with Lupy –'

'No,' agreed Pod, 'not to Hendreary's. And don't you see for why? The boy knows about that too!'

'Oh!' cried Homily in real dismay.

'Yes,' said Pod, 'a couple of smart terriers or a well-trained ferret, and that'd be the end of that lot.'

'Oh, Pod . . .' said Homily and began again to tremble. The thought of living in a badger's set had been bad enough, but the thought of not having even that to go to seemed almost worse. 'And I dare say I could have got it nice in the end,' she said, 'providing we lived quite separate –'

'Well, it's no good thinking of it now,' said Pod. He turned to Arrietty: 'What does your Uncle Hendreary say in his letter?'

'Yes,' exclaimed Homily, 'where's this letter?'

'It doesn't say much,' said Arrietty, passing over the paper; 'it just says "Tell your Aunt Lupy to come home".'

'What?' exclaimed Homily sharply, looking at the letter upside-down. 'Come home? What can he mean?'

'He means,' said Pod, 'that Lupy must have set off to come here and that she never arrived.'

'Set off to come here?' repeated Homily. 'But when?'

'How should I know?' said Pod.

'It doesn't say when,' said Arrietty.

'But,' exclaimed Homily, 'it might have been weeks ago!'

'It might,' said Pod. 'Long enough anyway for him to want her back.'

'Oh,' cried Homily, 'all those poor little children!'

'They're growing up now,' said Pod.

'But something must have happened to her!' exclaimed Homily.

'Yes,' said Pod. He turned to Arrietty. 'See what I mean, Arrietty, about those fields?'

'Oh, Pod,' said Homily, her eyes full of tears. 'I don't suppose none of us'll ever see poor Lupy again!'

'Well, we wouldn't have anyway,' said Pod.

'Pod,' said Homily soberly, 'I'm frightened. Everything seems to be happening at once. What are we going to do?'

'Well,' said Pod, 'there's nothing we can do tonight. That's certain. But have a bit of supper and a good night's rest.' He rose to his feet.

'Oh, Arrietty,' wailed Homily suddenly, 'you naughty, wicked girl! How could you go and start all this? How could you go and talk to a human bean? If only –'

'I was "seen",' cried Arrietty. 'I couldn't help being "seen". Papa was "seen". I don't think it's all as awful as you're trying to make out. I don't think human beans are all that bad –'

'They're bad and they're good,' said Pod; 'they're honest and they're artful – it's just as it takes them at the moment. And animals, if they could talk, would say the same. Steer clear of them – that's what I've always been told. No matter what they promise you. No good never really came to no one from any human bean.'

CHAPTER FIFTEEN

THAT night, while Arrietty lay straight and still under her cigar-box ceiling, Homily and Pod talked for hours. They talked in the sitting-room, they talked in the kitchen, and later, much later, she heard them talk in their bedroom. She heard drawers shutting and opening, doors creaking, and boxes being pulled out from under beds. 'What are they doing?' she wondered. 'What will happen next?' Very still she lay in her soft little bed with her familiar belongings about her: her postage stamp view of Rio harbour; her silver pig off a charm bracelet; her turquoise ring which sometimes, for fun, she would wear as a crown, and, dearest of all, her floating ladies with the golden trumpets, tooting above their peaceful town. She did not want to lose these, she realized suddenly, lying there straight and still in bed, but to have all the other things as well, adventure and safety mixed – that's what she wanted. And that (the restless bangings and whisperings told her) is just what you couldn't do.

As it happened, Homily was only fidgeting: opening drawers and shutting them, unable to be still. And she ended up, when Pod was already in bed, by deciding to curl her hair. 'Now, Homily,' Pod protested wearily, lying there in his night-shirt, 'there's really no call for that. Who's going to see you?'

'That's just it,' exclaimed Homily, searching in a drawer for her curl-rags; 'in times like these one never knows. I'm not going to be caught out,' she said irritably, turning the drawer upside-down and picking over the spilled contents, 'with me hair like this!'

She came to bed at last, looking spiky, like a washed-out golliwog, and Pod with a sigh turned over at last and closed his eyes.

Homily lay for a long time staring at the oil-lamp; it was the silver cap of a scent-bottle with a tiny, floating wick. She felt unwilling, for some reason, to blow it out. There were movements upstairs in the kitchen above and it was late for movements – the household should be asleep – and the lumpy curlers pressed uncomfortably against her neck. She gazed – just as Arrietty had done – about the familiar room (too full, she realized, with little bags and boxes and make-shift cupboards) and thought: 'What now? Perhaps nothing will happen after all; the child perhaps is right, and we are making a good deal of fuss about nothing very much; this boy, when all's said and done, is only a guest; perhaps,' thought Homily, 'he'll go away again quite soon, and that,' she told herself drowsily, 'will be that.'

Later (as she realized afterwards) she must have dozed off because it seemed she was crossing Parkin's Beck; it was night and the wind was blowing and the field seemed very steep; she was scrambling up it, along the ridge by the gas-pipe, sliding and falling in the wet grass. The trees, it seemed to Homily, were threshing and clashing, their branches waving and sawing against the sky. Then (as she told them many weeks later) there was a sound of splintering wood . . .

And Homily woke up. She saw the room again and the oil-lamp flickering, but something, she knew at once, was different: there was a strange draught and her mouth felt dry and full of grit. Then she looked up at the ceiling: 'Pod!' she shrieked, clutching his shoulder.

Pod rolled over and sat up. They both stared at the ceiling: the whole surface was on a steep slant and one side of it had come right away from the wall – this was what had caused the draught – and down into the room, to within an inch of the foot of the bed, protruded a curious object: a huge bar of grey steel with a flattened, shining edge.

'It's a screwdriver,' said Pod.

They stared at it, fascinated, unable to move, and for a moment all was still. Then slowly the huge object swayed upwards until the sharp edge lay against their ceiling and Homily heard a scrape on the floor above and a sudden human gasp. 'Oh, my knees,' cried Homily, 'oh, my feeling –' as, with a splintering wrench, their whole roof flew off and fell down with a clatter, somewhere out of sight.

Homily screamed then. But this time it was a real scream, loud and shrill and hearty; she seemed almost to settle down in her scream, while her eyes stared up, half interested, into empty lighted space. There was another ceiling, she realized, away up above them – higher, it seemed, than the sky; a ham hung from it and two strings of onions. Arrietty appeared in the doorway, scared and trembling, clutching her nightgown. And Pod slapped Homily's back. 'Have done,' he said, 'that's enough,' and Homily, suddenly, was quiet.

A great face appeared then between them and that distant height. It wavered above them, smiling and terrible: there was silence and Homily sat bolt upright, her mouth open. 'Is that your mother?' asked a surprised voice after a moment, and Arrietty from the doorway whispered: 'Yes.'

It was the boy.

Pod got out of bed and stood beside it, shivering in his night-shirt. 'Come on,' he said to Homily, 'you can't stay there!'

But Homily could. She had her old night-dress on with the patch in the back and nothing was going to move her. A slow anger was rising up in Homily: she had been caught in her hair-curlers; Pod had raised his hand to her; and she remembered that, in the general turmoil and for once in her life, she had left the supper washing-up for morning, and there it would be, on the kitchen table, for all the world to see!

She glared at the boy – he was only a child after all. 'Put it back!' she said, 'put it back at once!' Her eyes flashed and her curlers seemed to quiver.

He knelt down then, but Homily did not flinch as the great face came slowly closer. She saw his under lip, pink and full – like an enormous exaggeration of Arrietty's – and she saw it wobble slightly. 'But I've got something for you,' he said.

Homily's expression did not change, and Arrietty called out from her place in the doorway: 'What have you got?'

The boy reached behind him and very gingerly, careful to keep it upright, he held a wooden object above their heads. 'It's this,' he said, and carefully, his tongue out and breathing heavily, he lowered the object slowly into their hole: it was a doll's dresser, complete with plates. It had two drawers in it and a cupboard below; he adjusted its position at the foot of Homily's bed. Arrietty ran round to see better.

'Oh,' she cried ecstatically. 'Mother, look!'

Homily threw the dresser a glance – it was dark oak and the plates were hand-painted – and then she looked quickly away again. 'Yes,' she said coldly, 'it's very nice.'

There was a short silence which no one knew how to break.

'The cupboard really opens,' said the boy at last, and the great hand came down all amongst them, smelling of bath soap. Arrietty flattened herself against the wall and Pod exclaimed, nervous: 'Now then!'

'Yes,' agreed Homily after a moment, 'I see it does.'

Pod drew a long breath – a sigh of relief as the hand went back.

'There, Homily,' he said placatingly, 'you've always wanted something like that!'

'Yes,' said Homily – she still sat bolt upright, her hands clasped in her lap. 'Thank you very much. And now,' she went on coldly, 'will you please put back the roof?'

'Wait a minute,' pleaded the boy. Again he reached behind him;

again the hand came down; and there, beside the dresser, where there was barely room for it, was a very small doll's chair; it was a Victorian chair, upholstered in red velvet. 'Oh!' Arrietty exclaimed again and Pod said shyly: 'Just about fit me, that would.'

'Try it,' begged the boy, and Pod threw him a nervous glance. 'Go on!' said Arrietty, and Pod sat down – in his night-shirt, his bare feet showing. 'That's nice,' he said after a moment.

'It would go by the fire in the sitting-room,' cried Arrietty; 'it would look lovely on red blotting-paper!'

'Let's try it,' said the boy, and the hand came down again. Pod sprang up just in time to steady the dresser as the red velvet chair was whisked away above his head and placed presumably in the next room but one. Arrietty ran out of the door and along the passage to see. 'Oh,' she called out to her parents, 'come and see. It's lovely!'

But Pod and Homily did not move. The boy was leaning over them, breathing hard, and they could see the middle buttons of his night-shirt. He seemed to be examining the farther room.

'What do you keep in that mustard-pot?' he asked.

'Coal,' said Arrietty's voice. 'And I helped to borrow this new carpet. Here's the watch I told you about, and the pictures . . .'

'I could get you some better stamps than those,' the boy said. 'I've got some jubilee ones with the Taj Mahal.'

'Look,' cried Arrietty's voice again, and Pod took Homily's hand, 'these are my books –'

Homily clutched Pod as the great hand came down once more in the direction of Arrietty. 'Quiet,' he whispered; 'sit still . . .' The boy, it seemed, was touching the books.

'What are they called?' he asked, and Arrietty reeled off the names.

'Pod,' whispered Homily, 'I'm going to scream –'

'No,' whispered Pod. 'You mustn't. Not again.'

'I feel it coming on,' said Homily.

Pod looked worried. 'Hold your breath,' he said, 'and count ten.'

The boy was saying to Arrietty: 'Why couldn't you read me those?'

'Well, I could,' said Arrietty, 'but I'd rather read something new.'

'But you never come,' complained the boy.

'I know,' said Arrietty, 'but I will.'

'Pod,' whispered Homily, 'did you hear that? Did you hear what she said?'

'Yes, yes,' Pod whispered; 'keep quiet –'

'Do you want to see the store-rooms?' Arrietty suggested next and Homily clapped a hand to her mouth as though to stifle a cry.

Pod looked up at the boy. 'Hey,' he called, trying to attract his attention. The boy looked down. 'Put the roof back now,' Pod begged him, trying to sound matter of fact and reasonable; 'we're getting cold.'

'All right,' agreed the boy, but he seemed to hesitate: he reached across them for the piece of board which formed their roof. 'Shall I nail you down?' he asked, and they saw him pick up the hammer; it swayed above them, very dangerous-looking.

'Of course nail us down,' said Pod irritably.

'I mean,' said the boy, 'I've got some more things upstairs –'

Pod looked uncertain and Homily nudged him. 'Ask him,' she whispered, 'what kind of things?'

'What kind of things?' asked Pod.

'Things from an old doll's house there is on the top shelf of the cupboard by the fire-place in the schoolroom.'

'I've never seen no doll's house,' said Pod.

'Well, it's in the cupboard,' said the boy, 'right up by the ceiling; you can't see it – you've got to climb on the lower shelves to get to it.'

'What sort of things are there in the doll's house?' asked Arrietty from the sitting-room.

'Oh, everything,' the boy told her; 'carpets and rugs and beds with mattresses, and there's a bird in a cage – not a real one, of course – and cooking pans and tables, and five gilt chairs and a pot with a palm in it – a dish of plaster tarts and an imitation leg of mutton –'

Homily leaned across to Pod. 'Tell him to nail us down lightly,' she whispered. Pod stared at her and she nodded vigorously, clasping her hands.

Pod turned to the boy. 'All right,' he said, 'you nail us down. But lightly, if you see what I mean. Just a tap or two here and there . . .'

CHAPTER SIXTEEN

THEN began a curious phase in their lives: borrowings beyond all dreams of borrowing – a golden age. Every night the floor was opened and treasures would appear: a real carpet for the sitting-room, a tiny coal-scuttle, a stiff little sofa with damask cushions, a double bed with a round bolster, a single ditto with a striped mattress, framed pictures instead of stamps, a kitchen stove which didn't work, but which looked 'lovely' in the kitchen; there were oval tables and square tables and a little desk with one drawer; there were two maple wardrobes (one with a looking-glass) and a bureau with curved legs. Homily grew not only accustomed to the roof coming off but even went so far as to suggest to Pod that he put the board on hinges. 'It's just the hammering, I don't care for,' she explained; 'it brings down the dirt.'

When the boy brought them a grand piano Homily begged Pod to build a drawing-room. 'Next to the sitting-room,' she said, 'and we could move the store-rooms farther down. Then we could have those gilt chairs he talks about and the palm in a pot . . .' Pod, however, was a little tired of furniture removing; he was looking forward to the quiet evenings when he could doze at last beside the fire in his new velvet chair. No sooner had he put a chest of drawers in one place when Homily, coming in and out of the door – 'to get the effect' – made him 'try' it somewhere else. And every evening, at about his usual bedtime, the roof would fly up and more stuff would arrive. But Homily was tireless; bright-eyed and pink-cheeked, after a long day's pushing and pulling, she still would leave nothing until morning. 'Let's just *try* it,' she would beg, lifting up one end of a large doll's sideboard, so that Pod would have to lift the other; 'it won't take a minute!' But as Pod well knew, in actual fact it would be several hours before, dishevelled and aching, they finally dropped into bed. Even then Homily would sometimes hop out 'to have one last look'.

In the meantime, in payment for these riches, Arrietty would read to the boy – every afternoon in the long grass beyond the cherry-tree. He would lie on his back and she would stand beside his shoulder and tell him when to turn the page. They were happy days to look back on afterwards, with the blue sky beyond the cherry boughs, the grasses softly stirring, and the boy's great ear listening beside her. She grew to know that ear quite well, with its curves and shadows and sunlit pinks and golds. Sometimes, as she grew bolder, she would lean against his shoulder. He was very still while she read to him and always grateful. What worlds they would explore together – strange worlds to Arrietty. She learned a lot and some of the things she learned were hard to accept. She was made to realize once and for all that this earth on which they lived turning about in space did not revolve, as she had believed, for the sake of little people, 'Nor for big people either,' she reminded the boy when she saw his secret smile.

In the cool of the evening Pod would come for her – a rather weary Pod, dishevelled and dusty – to take her back for tea. And at home there would be an excited Homily and fresh delights to discover. 'Shut your eyes!' Homily would cry. 'Now open them!' and Arrietty, in a dream of joy, would see her home transformed. All kinds of surprises there were – even, one day, lace curtains at the grating, looped up with pink string.

Their only sadness was that there was no one there to see: no visitors, no casual drop-  pers-in, no admiring cries and envious glances! What would Homily have not given for an Overmantel or a Harpsi- chord? Even a Rain-Barrel would have been better than no one at all. 'You write to your Uncle Hendreary,' Homily suggested, 'and tell *him*. A nice long letter, mind, and don't leave anything out!' Arrietty began the letter on the back of one of the discarded pieces of blotting-paper, but it became as she wrote it just a dull list, far too long, like a sale catalogue or the inventory of a house to let; she would have to keep jumping up to count spoons or to look up words in the dictionary, and after a while she laid it aside: there was so much else to do, so many new books to read, and so much, now, that she could talk of with the boy.

'He's been ill,' she told her mother and father; 'he's been here for the quiet and the country air. But soon he'll go back to India. Did you know,' she asked the amazed Homily, 'that the Arctic night lasts six months, and that the distance between the two poles is less than that between the two extremities of a diameter drawn through the equator?'

Yes, they were happy days and all would have been well, as Pod said afterwards, if they had stuck to borrowing from the doll's house. No one in the human household seemed to remember it was there and, consequently, nothing was missed. The drawing-room, however, could not help but be a temptation: it was so seldom used nowadays; there were so many knick-knack tables which had been out of Pod's reach, and the boy, of course, could turn the key in the glass doors of the cabinet.

The silver violin he brought them first and then the silver harp; it stood no higher than Pod's shoulder and Pod restrung it with horse-hair from the sofa in the morning-room. 'A musical conversazione, that's what we could have!' cried the exulting Homily as Arrietty struck a tiny, tuneless note on a horse-hair string. 'If only,' she went on fervently, clasping her hands, 'your father would start on the drawing-room!' (She curled her hair nearly every evening nowadays and, since the house was more or less straight, she would occasionally change for dinner into a satin dress; it hung like a sack, but Homily called it 'Grecian'.) 'We could use your painted ceiling,' she explained to Arrietty, 'and there are quite enough of those toy builders' bricks to make a parquet floor.' ('Parkay,' she would say, 'Par-r-r-kay . . .', just like a Harpsichord.)

Even Great Aunt Sophy, right away upstairs in the littered grandeur of her bedroom, seemed distantly affected by a spirit of endeavour which seemed to flow, in gleeful whorls and eddies, about the staid old house. Several times lately Pod, when he went to her room, had found her out of bed. He went there nowadays not to borrow, but to rest: the room, one might almost say, had become his club; a place to which he could go 'to get away from things'. Pod was a little irked by his riches; he had never visualized, not in his wildest dreams, borrowing such as this. Homily, he felt, should call a halt; surely, now, their home was grand enough; these jewelled snuff-boxes and diamond-encrusted miniatures, these filigree vanity-cases and Dresden figurines – all, as he knew, from the drawing-room cabinet – were not really necessary: what was the good of a shepherdess nearly as tall as Arrietty or an outsize candle-snuffer? Sitting just inside the fender, where he could warm his hands at the fire, he watched Aunt Sophy hobble slowly round the room on her two sticks. 'She'll be downstairs soon, I shouldn't wonder,' he thought glumly, hardly listening to her oft-told tale about a royal luncheon aboard a Russian yacht, 'then she'll miss these things . . .'

It was not Aunt Sophy, however, who missed them first. It was Mrs Driver. Mrs Driver had never forgotten the trouble over Rosa Pick-hatchet. It had not been, at the time, easy to pin-point the guilt. Even Crampfurl had felt under suspicion. 'From now on,' Mrs Driver had said, 'I'll manage on me own. No more strange maids in *this* house!' A drop of Madeira here, a pair of old stockings there, a handkerchief or so, an odd vest, or an occasional pair of gloves – these, Mrs Driver felt, were different; these were within her rights. But trinkets out of the drawing-room cabinet – that, she told herself grimly, staring at the depleted shelves, was a different story altogether!

Standing there, on that fateful day, in the spring sunshine, feather duster in hand, her little black eyes had become slits of anger and cunning. She felt tricked. It was, she calculated, as though someone, suspecting her dishonesty, were trying to catch her out. But who could it be? Crampfurl? That boy? The man who came to wind the clocks? These things had disappeared gradually, one by one: it was someone, of that she felt sure, who knew the house – and someone who wished her ill. Could it, she wondered suddenly, be the mistress herself? The old girl had been out of bed lately and walking about her room. Might she not have come downstairs in the night, poking about with her stick, snooping and spying (Mrs Driver remembered suddenly the empty Madeira bottle and the two glasses which, so often, were left on the kitchen table). Ah, thought Mrs Driver, was not this just the sort of thing she might do – the sort of thing she would cackle over, back upstairs again among her pillows, watching and waiting for Mrs Driver to report the loss? 'Everything all right downstairs, Driver?' – that's what she'd always say and she would look at Mrs Driver sideways out of those mocking old eyes of hers. 'I wouldn't put it past her!' Mrs Driver exclaimed aloud, gripping her feather duster as though it were a club. 'And a nice merry-andrew she'd look if I caught her at it – creeping about the downstairs rooms in the middle of the night. All right, my lady,' muttered Mrs Driver grimly, 'pry and potter all you want – two can play at that game!'

CHAPTER SEVENTEEN

MRS DRIVER was short with Crampfurl that evening; she would not sit down and drink with him as usual, but stumped about the kitchen, looking at him sideways every now and again out of the corners of her eyes. He looked uneasy – as indeed he was: there was a kind of menace in her silence, a hidden something which no one could ignore. Even Aunt Sophy had felt it when Mrs Driver brought up her wine; she heard it in the clink of the decanter against the glass as Mrs Driver set down the tray and in the rattle of the wooden rings as Mrs Driver drew the curtains; it was in the tremble of the floor-boards as Mrs Driver crossed the room and in the click of the latch as Mrs Driver closed the door. 'What's the matter with her now?' Aunt Sophy wondered vaguely as delicately, ungreedily, she poured the first glass.

The boy had felt it too. From the way Mrs Driver had stared at him as he sat hunched in the bath; from the way she soaped the loofah and the way she said: 'And now!' She had scrubbed him slowly, with a careful, angry steadiness, and all through the bathing time she did not say a word. When he was in bed she had gone through all his things, peering into cupboards and opening his drawers. She had pulled his suit-case out from under the wardrobe and found his dear dead mole and his hoard of sugar-lumps and her best potato knife. But even then she had not spoken. She had thrown the mole into the waste-paper basket and had made sharp noises with her tongue; she pocketed the potato knife and all the sugar-lumps. She had stared at him a moment before she turned the gas low – a strange stare it had been, more puzzled than accusing.

Mrs Driver slept above the scullery. She had her own back-stairs. That night she did not undress. She set the alarm clock for midnight and put it, where the tick would not disturb her, outside her door; she unbuttoned her tight shoes and crawled, grunting a little, under the eiderdown. She had 'barely closed her eyes' (as she told Crampfurl afterwards) when the clock shrilled off – chattering and rattling on its four thin legs on the bare boards of the passage-way. Mrs Driver tumbled herself out of bed and fumbled her way to the door. 'Shush,' she said to the clock as she felt for the catch. 'Shush!' and clasped it to her bosom. She stood there, in her stockinged feet, at the head of the scullery stairs: something, it seemed, had flickered below -- a hint of light. Mrs Driver peered down the dark curve of the narrow stairway. Yes, there it was again – a moth-wing flutter! Candlelight – that's what it was! A moving candle – beyond the stairs, beyond the scullery, somewhere within the kitchen.

Clock in hand, Mrs Driver creaked down the stairs in her stockinged feet, panting a little in her eagerness. There seemed a sigh in the darkness, an echo of movement. And it seemed to Mrs Driver, standing there on the cold stone flags of the scullery, that this sound that was barely a sound could only mean one thing; the soft swing-to of the green baize door – that door which led out of the kitchen into the main hall beyond. Hurriedly Mrs Driver felt her way into the kitchen and fumbled for matches along the ledge above the stove; she knocked off a pepper-pot and a paper bag of cloves, and glancing quickly downwards saw a filament of light; she saw it in the second before she struck a match – a glow-worm thread, it looked like, on the floor beside her feet; it ran in an oblong shape, outlining a rough square. Mrs Driver gasped and lit the gas and the room leapt up around her: she glanced quickly at the baize door; there seemed to her startled eye a quiver of movement in it, as though it had just swung to; she ran to it and pushed it open, but the passage beyond was still and dark – no flicker of shadow nor sound of distant footfall. She let the door fall to again and watched it as it swung back, slowly, regretfully, held by its heavy spring. Yes, that was the sound she had heard from the scullery – that sighing whisper – like an indrawn breath.

Cautiously, clutching back her skirts, Mrs Driver moved towards the stove. An object lay there, something pinkish, on the floor beside the jutting board. Ah, she realized, that board – that was where the light had come from! Mrs Driver hesitated and glanced about the kitchen: everything else looked normal and just as she had left it – the plates on the dresser, the saucepans on the wall, and the row of tea-towels hanging symmetrically on their string above the stove. The pinkish object, she saw now, was a heart-shaped cachou-box – one that she knew well -- from the glassed-in tray-table beside the fire-place in the drawing-room. She picked it up; it was enamel and gold and set with tiny brilliants. 'Well, I'm –' she began, and stooping swiftly with a sudden angry movement, she wrenched back the piece of floor.

And then she shrieked, loud and long. She saw movement: a running, a scrambling, a fluttering! She heard a squeaking, a jabbering, and a gasping. Little people, they looked like, with hands and feet . . . and mouths opening. That's what they looked like . . . but they couldn't *be* that, of course! Running here, there, and everywhere. 'Oh! oh! oh!' she shrieked and felt behind her for a chair. She clambered on to it and it wobbled beneath her and she climbed, still shrieking, from the chair to the table.

And there she stood, marooned, crying and gasping, and calling out for help, until, after hours it seemed, there was a rattling at the scullery door. Crampfurl it was, roused at last by the light and the noise. 'What is it?' he called. 'Let me in!' But Mrs Driver would not leave the table. 'A nest! A nest!' she shouted. 'Alive and squeaking!'

Crampfurl threw his weight against the door and burst open the lock. He staggered, slightly dazed, into the kitchen, his corduroy trousers pulled on over his nightshirt. 'Where?' he cried, his eyes wide beneath his tousled hair. 'What sort of a nest?'

Mrs Driver, sobbing still with fright, pointed at the floor. Crampfurl walked over in his slow, deliberate way and stared down. He saw a hole in the floor, lined and cluttered with small objects – children's toys, they looked like, bits of rubbish – that was all. 'It's nothing,' he said after a moment; 'it's that boy, that's what it is.' He stirred the contents with his foot and all the partitions fell down. 'There ain't nothing alive in there.'

'But I saw them, I tell you,' gasped Mrs Driver, 'little people – like with hands – or mice dressed up . . .'

Crampfurl stared into the hole. 'Mice dressed up?' he repeated uncertainly.

'Hundreds of them,' went on Mrs Driver, 'running and squeaking. I saw them, I tell you!'

'Well, there ain't nothing there now,' said Crampfurl and he gave a final stir round with his boot.

'Then they've run away,' she cried, 'under the floor . . . up inside the walls . . . the place is alive with them.'

'Well,' said Crampfurl stolidly, 'maybe. But if you ask me, I think it's that boy – where he hides things.' His eye brightened and he went down on one knee. 'Where he's got the ferret, I shouldn't wonder.'

'Listen,' cried Mrs Driver, and there was a despairing note in her voice, 'you've got to listen. This wasn't no boy and it wasn't no ferret.' She reached for the back of the chair and lowered herself clumsily on to the floor; she came beside him to the edge of the hole. 'They had hands and faces, I tell you. Look,' she said, pointing, 'see that? It's a bed. And now I come to think of it one of 'em was in it.'

'Now you come to think of it,' said Crampfurl.

'Yes,' went on Mrs Driver firmly, 'and there's something else I come to think of. Remember that girl, Rosa Pickhatchet?'

'The one that was simple?'

'Well, simple or not, she saw one – on the drawing-room mantelpiece, with a beard.'

'One what?' asked Crampfurl.

Mrs Driver glared at him. 'What I've been telling you about – one of these – these –'

'Mice dressed up?' said Crampfurl.

'Not mice!' Mrs Driver almost shouted. 'Mice don't have beards.'

'But you said –' began Crampfurl.

'Yes, I know I said it. Not that these had beards. But what would you call them? What could they be but mice?'

'Not so loud!' whispered Crampfurl. 'You'll wake the house up.'

'They can't hear,' said Mrs Driver, 'not through the baize door.' She went to the stove and picked up the fire-tongs. 'And what if they do? We ain't done nothing. Move over,' she went on, 'and let me get at the hole.'

One by one Mrs Driver picked things out – with many shocked gasps, cries of amazement, and did-you-evers. She made two piles on the floor – one of valuables and one of what she called 'rubbish'. Curious objects dangled from the tongs: 'Would you believe it – her best lace

handkerchiefs! Look, here's another . . . and another! And my big
mattress needle – I knew I had one – my silver thimble, if you please,
and one of hers! And look, oh my, at the wools . . . the cottons! No
wonder you can never find a reel of white cotton if you want one.
Potatoes . . . nuts . . . look at this, a pot of caviare . . . CAVIARE! No, it's
too much, it really is. Doll's chairs . . . tables . . . and look at all this
blotting-paper – so that's where it goes! Oh, my goodness gracious!' she
cried suddenly, her eyes staring. 'What's this?' Mrs Driver laid down
the tongs and leaned over the hole – tentatively and fearfully as though
afraid of being stung. 'It's a watch – an emerald watch – her watch!
And she's never missed it!' Her voice rose. 'And it's going! Look, you
can see by the kitchen clock! Twenty-five past twelve!' Mrs Driver sat
down suddenly on a hard chair; her eyes were staring and her face
looked white and flabby, as though deflated. 'You know what this
means?' she said to Crampfurl.

'No?' he said.

'The police,' said Mrs Driver, 'that's what this means – a case for the
police.'

CHAPTER EIGHTEEN

THE boy lay, trembling a little, beneath the bed-clothes. The screwdriver was under his mattress. He had heard the alarm clock; he had heard Mrs Driver exclaim on the stairs and he had run. The candle on the table beside his bed still smelt a little and the wax must still be warm. He lay there waiting, but they did not come upstairs. After hours, it seemed, he heard the hall clock strike one. All seemed quiet below, and at last he slipped out of bed and crept along the passage to the head of the stairway. There he sat for a while, shivering a little, and gazing downwards into the darkened hall. There was no sound but the steady tick of the clock and occasionally that shuffle or whisper which might be wind, but which, as he knew, was the sound of the house itself – the sigh of the tired floors and the ache of knotted wood. So quiet it was that at last he found courage to move and to tiptoe down the staircase and along the kitchen passage. He listened awhile outside the baize door, and at length, very gently, he pushed it open. The kitchen was silent and filled with greyish darkness. He felt, as Mrs Driver had done, along the shelf for the matches and he struck a light. He saw the gaping hole in the floor and the objects piled beside it and, in the same flash, he saw a candle on the shelf. He lit it clumsily, with trembling hands. Yes, there they lay – the contents of the little home – higgledy-piggledy on the boards and the tongs lay beside them. Mrs Driver had carried away all she considered valuable and had left the 'rubbish'. And rubbish it looked thrown down like this – balls of wool, old potatoes, odd pieces of doll's furniture, match-boxes, cotton-reels, crumpled squares of blotting-paper . . .

He knelt down. The 'house' itself was a shambles – partitions fallen, earth floors revealed (where Pod had dug down to give greater height to the rooms), match-sticks, an old cog-wheel, onion-skins, scattered bottle-tops . . . The boy stared, blinking his eyelids and tilting the candle so that the grease ran hot on his hand. Then he got up from his knees and, crossing the kitchen on tiptoe, he closed the scullery door. He came back to the hole and, leaning down, he called softly: 'Arrietty . . . Arrietty!' After a while he called again. Something else fell hot on his hand: it was a tear from his eye. Angrily he brushed it away, and, leaning farther into the hole, he called once more. 'Pod,' he whispered. 'Homily!'

They appeared so quietly that at first, in the wavering light of the candle, he did not see them. Silent they stood, looking up at him with scared white faces from what had been the passage outside the store-rooms.

'Where have you been?' asked the boy.

Pod cleared his throat. 'Up at the end of the passage. Under the clock.'

'I've got to get you out,' said the boy.

'Where to?' asked Pod.

'I don't know. What about the attic?'

'That ain't no good,' said Pod. 'I heard them talking. They're going to get the police and a cat and the sanitary inspector and the rat-catcher from the town hall at Leighton Buzzard.'

They were all silent. Little eyes stared at big eyes. 'There won't be nowhere in the house that's safe,' Pod said at last. And no one moved.

'What about the doll's house on the top shelf in the schoolroom?' suggested the boy. 'Even a cat can't get there.'

Homily gave a little moan of assent. 'Yes,' she said, 'the doll's house . . .'

'No,' said Pod in the same expressionless voice, 'you can't live on a shelf. Maybe the cat can't get up, but no more can't you get down. You're stuck. You got to have water.'

'I'd bring you water,' said the boy; he touched the pile of 'rubbish'. 'And there are beds and things here.'

'No,' said Pod, 'a shelf ain't no good. Besides, you'll be going soon, or so they say.'

'Oh, Pod,' pleaded Homily in a husky whisper, 'there's stairs in the doll's house, and two bedrooms, and a dining-room, and a kitchen. And a bathroom!' she said.

'But it's up by the ceiling,' Pod explained wearily. 'You got to eat, haven't you,' he asked, 'and drink?'

'Yes, Pod, I know. But –'

'There ain't no buts,' said Pod. He drew a long breath. 'We got to emigrate,' he said.

'Oh,' moaned Homily softly and Arrietty began to cry.

'Now don't take on,' said Pod in a tired voice.

Arrietty had covered her face with her hands and her tears ran through her fingers; the boy, watching, saw them glisten in the candlelight. 'I'm not taking on,' she gasped. 'I'm so happy . . . happy.'

'You mean,' said the boy to Pod, but with one eye on Arrietty, 'you'll go to the badger's set?' He too felt a mounting excitement.

'Where else?' asked Pod.

'Oh, my goodness gracious!' moaned Homily, and sat down on the broken match-box chest of drawers.

'But you've got to go somewhere tonight,' said the boy. 'You've got to go somewhere before tomorrow morning.'

'Oh, my goodness gracious!' moaned Homily again.

'He's right at that,' said Pod. 'Can't cross them fields in the dark. Bad enough getting across them in daylight.'

'I know,' cried Arrietty. Her wet face glistened in the candlelight; it was alight and tremulous and she raised her arms a little as though about to fly, and she swayed as she balanced on her toe-tips. 'Let's go to the doll's house just for tonight and tomorrow' – she closed her eyes against the brightness of the vision – 'tomorrow the boy will take us – take us –' and she could not say to where.

'Take us?' cried Homily in a strange hollow voice. 'How?'

'In his pockets,' chanted Arrietty; 'won't you?' Again she swayed, with lighted upturned face.

'Yes,' he said, 'and bring the luggage up afterwards – in a fish basket.

'Oh, my goodness!' moaned Homily.

'I'll pick all the furniture out of this pile here. Or most of it. They'll hardly notice. And anything else you want.'

'Tea,' murmured Homily. 'Enough for our life-times.'

'All right,' said the boy. 'I'll get a pound of tea. And coffee too if you like. And cooking pots. And matches. You'll be all right,' he said.

'But what do they eat?' wailed Homily. 'Caterpillars?'

'Now, Homily,' said Pod, 'don't be foolish. Lupy was always a good manager.'

'But Lupy isn't there,' said Homily. 'Berries. Do they eat berries? How do they cook? Out of doors?'

'Now, Homily,' said Pod, 'we'll see all that when we get there.'

'I couldn't light a fire of sticks,' said Homily, 'not in the wind. What if it rains?' she asked. 'How do they cook in the rain?'

'Now, Homily –' began Pod – he was beginning to lose patience – but Homily rushed on.

'Could you get us a couple of tins of sardines to take?' she asked the boy. 'And some salt? And some candles? And matches? And could you bring us the carpets from the doll's house?'

'Yes,' said the boy, 'I could. Of course I could. Anything you want.'

'All right,' said Homily. She still looked wild, partly because some of her hair had rolled out of the curlers, but she seemed appeased. 'How are you going to get us upstairs? Up to the schoolroom?'

The boy looked down at his pocketless night-shirt. 'I'll carry you,' he said.

'How?' asked Homily. 'In your hands?'

'Yes,' said the boy.

'I'd rather die,' said Homily. 'I'd rather stay right here and be eaten by the rat-catcher from the town hall at Leighton Buzzard.'

The boy looked round the kitchen; he seemed bewildered. 'Shall I carry you in the peg-bag?' he asked at last, seeing it hanging in its usual place on the handle of the scullery door.

'All right,' said Homily. 'Take out the pegs first.'

But she walked into it bravely enough when he laid it out on the floor. It was soft and floppy and made of woven raffia. When he picked it up Homily shrieked and clung to Pod and Arrietty. 'Oh,' she gasped as the bag swayed a little, 'oh, I can't! Stop it! Put me out! Oh! Oh!' And, clutching and slipping, they fell into a tangle at the bottom.

'Be quiet, Homily, can't you!' exclaimed Pod angrily, and held her tightly by the ankle. It was not easy to control her as he was lying on his back with his face pushed forward on his chest and one leg, held upright by the side of the bag, somewhere above his head. Arrietty climbed up, away from them, clinging to the knots of raffia, and looked out over the edge.

'Oh, I can't! I can't!' cried Homily. 'Stop it, Pod. I'm dying. Tell him to put us down.'

'Put us down,' said Pod in his patient way, 'just for a moment. That's right. On the floor,' and, as once again the bag was placed beside the hole, they all ran out.

'Look here,' said the boy unhappily to Homily, 'you've got to try.'

'She'll try all right,' said Pod. 'Give her a breather, and take it slower, if you see what I mean.'

'All right,' agreed the boy, 'but there isn't much time. Come on,' he said nervously, 'hop in.'

'Listen!' cried Pod sharply, and froze.

The boy, looking down, saw their three upturned faces catching the light – like pebbles they looked, still and stony, against the darkness within the hole. And then in a flash they were gone – the boards were empty and the hole was bare. He leaned into it. 'Pod!' he called in a frantic whisper. 'Homily! Come back!' And then he too became frozen, stooped and rigid above the hole. The scullery door creaked open behind him.

It was Mrs Driver. She stood there silent, this time in her night-dress. Turning, the boy stared up at her. 'Hallo,' he said, uncertainly, after a moment.

She did not smile, but something lightened in her eyes – a malicious gleam, a look of triumph. She carried a candle which shone upwards on her face, streaking it strangely with light and shadow. 'What are you doing down here?' she asked.

He stared at her, but he did not speak.

'Answer me,' she said. 'And what are you doing with the peg-bag?'

Still he stared at her, almost stupidly. 'The peg-bag?' he repeated and looked down as though surprised to see it in his hand. 'Nothing,' he said.

'Was it you who put the watch in the hole?'

'No,' he said, staring up at her again, 'it was there already.'

'Ah,' she said and smiled, 'so you knew it was there?'

'No,' he said; 'I mean yes.'

'Do you know what you are?' asked Mrs Driver, watching him closely. 'You are a sneaking, thieving, noxious little dribbet of no-good!'

His face quivered. 'Why?' he said.

'You know why. You're a wicked, black-hearted, fribbling little pickpocket. That's what you are. And, so are they. They're nasty, crafty, scampy, scurvy, squeaking little –'

'No they're not,' he put in quickly.

'And you're in league with them!' She came across to him and, taking him by the upper arm, she jerked him to his feet. 'You know what they do with thieves?' she asked.

'No,' he said.

'They lock them up. That's what they do with thieves. And that's what's going to happen to you!'

'I'm not a thief,' cried the boy, his lips trembling. 'I'm a Borrower.'

'A what?' She swung him round by tightening the grip on his arm.

'A Borrower,' he repeated; there were tears on his eyelids; he hoped they would not fall.

'So that's what you call it!' she exclaimed (as he himself had done – so long ago, it seemed now – that day with Arrietty).

'That's their name,' he said. 'The kind of people they are – they're Borrowers.'

'Borrowers, eh?' repeated Mrs Driver wonderingly. She laughed. 'Well, they've done all the borrowing they're ever going to do in this house!' She began to drag him towards the door.

The tears spilled over his eyelids and ran down his cheeks. 'Don't hurt them,' he begged. 'I'll move them. I promise. I know how.'

Mrs Driver laughed again and pushed him roughly through the green baize door. 'They'll be moved all right,' she said. 'Don't worry. The rat-catcher will know how. Crampfurl's old cat will know how. So will the sanitary inspector. And the fire brigade, if need be. The police'll know how, I shouldn't wonder. No need to worry about moving them. Once you've found the nest,' she went on, dropping her voice to a vicious whisper as they passed Aunt Sophy's door; 'the rest is easy!'

She pushed him into the schoolroom and locked the door and he heard the boards of the passage creak beneath her tread as, satisfied, she moved away. He crept into bed then, because he was cold, and cried his heart out under the blankets.

CHAPTER NINETEEN

'AND that,' said Mrs May, laying down her crochet hook, 'is really the end.'

Kate stared at her. 'Oh, it can't be,' she gasped, 'oh, please . . . *please* . . .'

'The last square,' said Mrs May, smoothing it out on her knee, 'the hundred and fiftieth. Now we can sew them together –'

'Oh,' said Kate, breathing again, 'the quilt! I thought you meant the story.'

'It's the end of the story too,' said Mrs May absently, 'in a way,' and she began to sort out the squares.

'But,' stammered Kate, 'you can't – I mean –' and she looked, quite suddenly, everything they had said she was – wild, self-willed, and all the rest of it. 'It's not fair,' she cried, 'it's cheating. It's –' Tears sprang to her eyes; she threw her work down on the table and darning needle after it, and she kicked the bag of wools which lay beside her on the carpet.

'Why, Kate, why?' Mrs May looked genuinely surprised.

'Something more must have happened,' cried Kate angrily. 'What about the rat-catcher? And the policeman? And the –'

'But something more did happen,' said Mrs May, 'a lot more happened. I'm going to tell you.'

'Then why did you say it was the end?'

'Because,' said Mrs May (she still looked surprised), 'he never saw them again.'

'Then how can there be more?'

'Because,' said Mrs May, 'there is more.'

Kate glared at her. 'All right,' she said, 'go on.'

Mrs May looked back at her. 'Kate,' she said after a moment, 'stories never really end. They can go on and on and on. It's just that sometimes, at a certain point, one stops telling them.'

'But not at this kind of point,' said Kate.

'Well, thread your needle,' said Mrs May, 'with grey wool, this time. And we'll sew these squares together. I'll start at the top and you can start at the bottom. First a grey square, then an emerald, then a pink, and so on –'

'Then you didn't really mean it,' said Kate irritably, trying to push the folded wool through the narrow eye of the needle, 'when you said he never saw them again?'

'But I did mean it,' said Mrs May. 'I'm telling you just what happened. He had to leave suddenly – at the end of the week – because there was a boat for India and a family who could take him. And for the three days before he left they kept him locked up in those two rooms.'

'For three days!' exclaimed Kate.

'Yes. Mrs Driver, it seemed, told Aunt Sophy that he had a cold. She wasn't unkind to him, but she was determined, you see, to keep him out of the way until she'd got rid of the Borrowers.'

'And did she?' asked Kate. 'I mean – did they all come? The policeman? And the rat-catcher? And the –'

'The sanitary inspector didn't come. At least, not while my brother was there. And they didn't have the rat-catcher from the town hall, but they had the local man. The policeman came –' Mrs May laughed. 'During those three days Mrs Driver used to give my brother a running commentary on what was going on below. She loved to grumble, and my brother, rendered harmless and shut away upstairs, became a kind of neutral. She used to carry his meals up, and, on that first morning, she brought all the doll's furniture up on the breakfast tray and made my brother climb the shelves and put it back in the doll's house. It was then she told him about the policeman. Furious he said she was. He felt almost sorry for her.'

'Why?' asked Kate.

'Because the policeman turned out to be Nellie Runacre's son Ernie, a boy Mrs Driver had chased many a time for stealing russet apples from the tree by the gate – "A nasty, thieving, good-for-nothing dribbet of no-good," she told my brother. "Sitting down there he is now, in the kitchen, large as life with his note-book out, laughing fit to bust . . . twenty-one, he says he is now, and as cheeky as you make 'em . . ." '

'And was he,' asked Kate, round-eyed, 'a dribbet of no-good?'

'Of course not. Any more than my brother was. Ernie Runacre was a fine, upstanding young man and a credit to the police force. And he did not actually laugh at Mrs Driver when she told him her story, but he gave her what Crampfurl spoke of afterwards as "an old-fashioned look" when she described Homily in bed – "Take more water with it," it seemed to say.'

'More water with what?' asked Kate.

'The Fine Old Pale Madeira, I suppose,' said Mrs May. 'And Great Aunt Sophy had the same suspicion: she was furious when she heard that Mrs Driver had seen several little people when she herself on a full decanter had only risen to one or, at most, two. Crampfurl had to bring all the Madeira up from the cellar and stack the cases against the wall in a corner of Aunt Sophy's bedroom where, as she said, she could keep an eye on it.'

'Did they get a cat?' asked Kate.

'Yes, they did. But that wasn't much of a success either. It was Crampfurl's cat, a large yellow tom with white streaks in it. According to Mrs Driver, it had only two ideas in its head – to get out of the house or into the larder. "Talk of borrowers," Mrs Driver would say as she slammed down the fish-pie for my brother's luncheon, "that cat's a borrower, if ever there was one; borrowed the fish, that cat did, and a good half-bowl of egg sauce!" But the cat wasn't there long. The first thing the rat-catcher's terriers did was to chase it out of the house. There was a dreadful set-to, my brother said. They chased it everywhere – upstairs and downstairs, in and out all the rooms, barking their heads off. The last glimpse my brother had of the cat was streaking away through the spinney and across the fields with the terriers after it.'

'Did they catch it?'

'No,' Mrs May laughed. 'It was still there when I went, a year later. A little morose, but as fit as a fiddle.'

'Tell about when *you* went.'

'Oh, I wasn't there long,' said Mrs May rather hastily, 'and after that the house was sold. My brother never went back.'

Kate stared at her suspiciously, pressing her needle against the centre of her lower lip. 'So they never caught the little people?' she said at last.

Mrs May's eyes flicked away. 'No, they never actually caught them, but' – she hesitated – 'as far as my poor brother was concerned, what they did do seemed even worse.'

'What did they do?'

Mrs May laid down her work and stared for a moment, thoughtfully, at her idle hands. 'I hated the rat-catcher,' she said suddenly.

'Why, did you know him?'

'Everybody knew him. He had a wall eye and his name was Rich William. He was also the pig-killer, and, well – he did other things as well – he had a gun, a hatchet, a spade, a pick-axe, and a contraption with bellows for smoking things out. I don't know what the smoke was exactly – poison fumes of some kind which he made himself from herbs and chemicals. I only remember the smell of it; it clung round the barns or wherever he'd been. You can imagine what my brother felt on that third day, the day he was leaving, when suddenly he smelled that smell . . .

'He was all dressed and ready to go. The bags were packed and down in the hall. Mrs Driver came and unlocked the door and took him down the passage to Aunt Sophy. He stood there, stiff and pale, in gloves and overcoat beside the curtained bed. "Seasick already?" Aunt Sophy mocked him, peering down at him over the edge of the great mattress.

' "No," he said, "it's that smell."

'Aunt Sophy lifted her nose. She sniffed. "What smell is it, Driver?"

' "It's the rat-catcher, my lady," explained Mrs Driver, reddening, "down in the kitchen."

' "What!" exclaimed Aunt Sophy, "are you smoking them out?" and she began to laugh. "Oh dear . . . oh dear!" she gasped, "but if you don't like them, Driver, the remedy's simple."

' "What is that, my lady?" asked Mrs Driver uncomfortably, and even her chins were red.

'Helpless with laughter Aunt Sophy waved a ringed hand: "Keep the bottle corked," she managed at last and motioned them weakly away. They heard her laughing still as they went on down the stairs.

' "She don't believe in them," muttered Mrs Driver, and she tightened her grip on my brother's arm. "More fool her! She'll change her tune, like enough, when I take them up afterwards, laid out in sizes, on a clean piece of newspaper . . ." and she dragged him unceremoniously across the hall.

'The clock had been moved, exposing the wainscot, and, as my brother saw at once, the hole had been blocked and sealed. The front door was open as usual and the sunshine streamed in. The bags stood there beside the fibre mat, cooking a little in the golden warmth. The fruit trees beyond the bank had shed their petals and were lit with tender green, transparent in the sunlight. "Plenty of time," said Mrs Driver, glancing up at the clock, "the cab's not due till three-thirty –"

' "The clock's stopped," said my brother.

'Mrs Driver turned. She was wearing her hat and her best black coat, ready to take him to the station. She looked strange and tight and chapel-going – not a bit like "Driver". "So it has," she said; her jaw dropped and her cheeks became heavy and pendulous. "It's moving it," she decided after a moment. "It'll be all right," she went on, "once we get it back. Mr Frith comes on Monday," and she dragged again at his arm above the elbow.

‘ "Where are we going?" he asked, holding back.

‘ "Along to the kitchen. We've got a good ten minutes. Don't you want to see them caught?"

‘ "No," he said, "no!" and pulled away from her.

‘Mrs Driver stared at him, smiling a little. "I do," she said; "I'd like to see 'em close. He puffs this stuff in and they come running out. At least, that's how it works with rats. But first, he says, you have to block up all the exits . . ." and her eyes followed my brother's to the hole below the wainscot.

‘ "How did they find it?" he asked then (puttied it looked, and with a square of brown paper pasted on crooked).

‘ "Rich William found it. That's his job."

‘ "They could unstick that," said the boy after a moment.

‘Mrs Driver laughed – quite amiably for once. "Oh no they couldn't. Not now, they couldn't! Cemented, firm, that is. A great block of it, right inside, with a sheet of iron across from the front of that old stove in the outhouse. He and Crampfurl had to have the morning-room floor up to get at it. All Tuesday they was working, up till tea-time. We aren't going to have no more capers of that kind. Not under the clock. Once you get that clock back, it can't be moved again in a hurry. Not if you want it to keep time, it can't. See where it's stood – where the floor's washed away like?" It was then my brother saw, for the first and last time, that raised platform of unscrubbed stone. "Come on now," said Mrs Driver and took him by the arm. "We'll hear the cab from the kitchen."

‘But the kitchen, as she dragged him past the baize door, seemed a babel of sound. No approaching cab could be heard here. "Steady, steady, steady, steady, steady . . ." Crampfurl was saying, on one loud note, as he held back the rat-catcher's terriers which shrilled and panted on the leash. The policeman was there, Nellie Runacre's son Ernie. He had come out of interest and stood back from the others a little in view of his calling, with a cup of tea in his hand and his helmet pushed off his forehead. But his face was pink with boyish excitement and he stirred the teaspoon round and round. "Seeing's believing!" he said cheerfully to Mrs Driver when he saw her come in at the door. A boy from the village was there with a ferret. It kept sort of pouring out of his pocket, my brother said, and the boy kept pushing it back. Rich

William himself was crouched on the floor by the hole. He had lighted something beneath a piece of sacking and the stench of its smouldering eddied about the room. He was working the bellows now, with infinite care, stooping over them – rapt and tense.

'My brother stood there as though in a dream ("Perhaps it was a dream," he said to me later – much later, after we were all grown up). He gazed round the kitchen. He saw the sunlit fruit trees through the window and a bough of the cherry-tree which stood upon the bank; he saw the empty teacups on the table, with spoons stuck in them and one without a saucer; he saw, propped against the wall close beside the baize door, the rat-catcher's belongings – a frayed coat, patched with leather; a bundle of rabbit snares; two sacks, a spade, a gun, and a pick-axe . . .

' "Stand by now," Rich William was saying; there was a rising note of excitement in his voice, but he did not turn his head. "Stand by. Ready now to slip the dogs."

'Mrs Driver let go my brother's arm and moved towards the hole. "Keep back," said the rat-catcher, without turning. "Give us room –" and Mrs Driver backed nervously towards the table. She put a chair beside it and half raised one knee, but lowered it again when she caught Ernie Runacre's mocking glance. "All right, ma," he said, cocking one eyebrow, "we'll give you a leg up when the time comes," and Mrs Driver threw him a furious look; she snatched up the three cups from the table and stumped away with them, angrily, in the direction of the scullery. ". . . seemingless smutch of something-or-other . . ." my brother heard her mutter as she brushed past him. And at those words, suddenly, my brother came to life . . .

'He threw a quick glance about the kitchen: the men were absorbed; all eyes were on the rat-catcher – except those of the village boy who was getting out his ferret. Stealthily my brother drew off his gloves and began to move backwards . . . slowly . . . slowly . . . towards the green baize door; as he moved, gently stuffing his gloves into his pocket, he kept his eyes on the group around the hole. He paused a moment beside the rat-catcher's tools, and stretched out a wary, groping hand; his fingers closed at last on a wooden handle – smooth it was and worn with wear; he glanced down quickly to make sure – yes, it was, as he hoped, the pick-axe. He leaned back a little and pushed – almost imperceptibly – against the door with his shoulders: it opened sweetly, in its silent way. Not one of the men had looked up. "Steady now," the rat-catcher was saying, stooping closely over the bellows, "it takes a moment like to go right through . . . . there ain't much ventilation, not under a floor . . . ."

'My brother slid through the barely opened door and it sighed to behind him, closing out the noise. He took a few steps on tiptoe down the dark kitchen passage and then he ran.

'There was the hall again, steeped in sunshine, with his bags beside the door. He bumped against the clock and it struck a note, a trembling note – urgent and deep. He raised the pick-axe to the height of his shoulder and aimed a sideways blow at the hole below the wainscot. The paper tore, a few crumbs of plaster fell out, and the pick-axe rebounded sharply, jarring his hands. There was indeed iron behind the cement – something immovable. Again he struck. And again and again. The wainscot above the hole became split and scratched, and the paper hung down in strips, but still the pick-axe bounced. It was no good; his hands, wet with sweat, were sliding and slipping on the wood. He paused for breath and, looking out, he saw the cab. He saw it on the road, beyond the hedge on the far side of the orchard; soon it would reach the russet apple-tree beside the gate; soon it would turn into the drive. He glanced up at the clock. It was ticking steadily – the result, perhaps, of his knock. The sound gave him comfort and steadied his thumping heart; time, that's what he needed, a little more time. "It takes a moment like," the rat-catcher had said, "to go right through . . . there ain't much ventilation, not under a floor . . . ."

' "Ventilation" – that was the word, the saving word. Pick-axe in hand my brother ran out of the door. He stumbled once on the gravel path and nearly fell; the pick-axe handle came up and struck him a sharp blow on the temple. Already, when he reached it, a thin filament of smoke was eddying out of the grating and he thought, as he ran towards it, that there was a flicker of movement against the darkness between the bars. And that was where they would be, of course, to get the air. But he did not stop to make sure. Already he heard behind him the crunch of wheels on the gravel and the sound of the horse's hoofs. He was not, as I have told you, a very strong little boy, and he was only nine (not ten, as he had boasted to Arrietty) but, with two great blows on the brickwork, he dislodged one end of the grating. It fell down sideways, slightly on a slant, hanging – it seemed – by one nail. Then he clambered up the bank and threw the pick-axe with all his might into the long grass beyond the cherry-tree. He remembered thinking as he stumbled back, sweaty and breathless, towards the cab, how that too – the loss of the pick-axe – would cause its own kind of trouble later.'

CHAPTER TWENTY

'But,' exclaimed Kate, 'didn't he see them come out?'

'No. Mrs Driver came along then, in a flurry of annoyance, because they were late for the train. She bustled him into the cab because she wanted to get back again, she said, as fast as she could to be "in at the death". Mrs Driver was like that.'

Kate was silent a moment, looking down. 'So that *is* the end,' she said at last.

'Yes,' said Mrs May, 'in a way: or the beginning . . .'

'But' – Kate raised a worried face – 'perhaps they didn't escape through the grating? Perhaps they were caught after all?'

'Oh, they escaped all right,' said Mrs May lightly.

'But how do you know?'

'I just know,' said Mrs May.

'But how did they get across those fields? With the cows and things? And the crows?'

'They walked, of course. The Hendrearys did it. People can do anything when they have a mind to.'

'But poor Homily! She'd be so upset.'

'Yes, she was upset,' said Mrs May.

'And how would they know the way?'

'By the gas-pipe,' said Mrs May. 'There's a kind of ridge all along, through the spinney and across the fields. You see, when men dig a trench and put a pipe in it all the earth they've dug out doesn't quite fit when they've put it back. The ground looks different.'

'But poor Homily – she didn't have her tea or her furniture or her carpets or anything. Do you suppose they took anything?'

'Oh, people always grab something,' said Mrs May shortly, 'the oddest things sometimes – if you've read about shipwrecks.' She spoke hurriedly, as though she were tired of the subject. 'Do be careful, child – not grey next to pink. You'll have to unpick it.'

'But,' went on Kate in a despairing voice as she picked up the scissors, 'Homily would hate to arrive there all poor and destitute in front of Lupy.'

'Destitute,' said Mrs May patiently, 'and Lupy wasn't there, remember. Lupy never came back. And Homily would be in her element. Can't you see her? "Oh, these poor silly men . . ." she would cry and would tie on her apron at once.'

'Were they all boys?'

'Yes, Harpsichords and Clocks. And they'd spoil Arrietty dreadfully.'

'What did they eat? Did they eat caterpillars, do you think?'

'Oh, goodness, child, of course they didn't. They would have a wonderful life. Badgers' sets are almost like villages – full of passages and chambers and storehouses. They could gather hazel-nuts and beech-nuts and chestnuts; they could gather corn – which they could store and grind into flour, just as humans do – it was all there for them: they didn't even have to plant it. They had honey. They could make elderflower tea and lime tea. They had hips and haws and blackberries and sloes and wild strawberries. The boys could fish in the stream and a minnow to them would be as big as a mackerel is to you. They had birds' eggs – any amount of them – for custards and cakes and omelettes. You see, they would know where to look for things. And they had greens and salads, of course. Think of a salad made of those tender shoots of young hawthorn – bread and cheese we used to call it – with sorrel and dandelion and a sprinkling of thyme and wild garlic. Homily was a good cook remember. It wasn't for nothing that the Clocks had lived under the kitchen.'

'But the danger,' cried Kate; 'the weasels and the crows and the stoats and all those things?'

'Yes,' agreed Mrs May, 'of course there was danger. There's danger

everywhere, but no more for them than for many of us. At least, they didn't have *wars*. And what about the early settlers in America? And those people who farm in the middle of the big game country in Africa and on the edge of the jungles in India? They get to know the habits of the animals. Even rabbits know when a fox isn't hunting; they will run quite near when he's full fed and lazing in the sun. These were boys, remember; they would learn to hunt for the pot and how to protect themselves. I don't suppose it's very likely that Arrietty and Homily would wander far afield.'

'Arrietty would,' said Kate.

'Yes,' agreed Mrs May, laughing, 'I suppose Arrietty might.'

'So they'd have meat?' said Kate.

'Yes, sometimes. But Borrowers are Borrowers; not killers. I think,' said Mrs May, 'that if a stoat, say, killed a partridge they might borrow a leg!'

'And if a fox caught a rabbit they'd use the fur?'

'Yes, for rugs and things.'

'Supposing,' said Kate excitedly, 'when they had a little roast, they skinned haws and baked them, would they taste like browned potatoes?'

'Perhaps,' said Mrs May.

'But they couldn't cook in the badger's set. I suppose they cooked out of doors. How would they keep warm then in winter?'

'Do you know what I think?' said Mrs May; she laid down her work and leaned forward a little. 'I think that they didn't live in the badger's set at all. I think they used it, with all its passages and store-rooms, as a great honeycomb of an entrance hall. None but they would know the secret way through the tunnels which led at last to their home. Borrowers love passages and they love gates; and they love to live a long way from their own front doors.'

'Where *would* they live then?'

'I was wondering,' said Mrs May, 'about the gas-pipe –'

'Oh yes,' cried Kate, 'I see what you mean!'

'The soil's all soft and sandy up there. I think they'd go right through the badger's set and dig out a circular chamber, level with the gas-pipe. And off this chamber, all around it, there'd be little rooms, like cabins. And I think,' said Mrs May, 'that they'd bore three little pin-holes in the gas-pipe. One would be so tiny that you could hardly see it and that one would be always alight. The other two would have stoppers in them which, when they wanted to light the gas, they would pull out. They would light the bigger ones from the small burner. That's where they'd cook and that would give them light.'

'But would they be so clever?'

'But they are clever,' Mrs May assured her, 'very clever. Much too clever to live near a gas-pipe and not use it. They're Borrowers remember.'

'But they'd want a little air-hole?'

'Oh,' said Mrs May quickly, 'they did have one.'

'How do you know?' asked Kate.

'Because once when I was up there I smelled hotpot.'

'Oh,' cried Kate excitedly; she twisted round and knelt up on the hassock, 'so you did go up there? So that's how you know! You saw them too!'

'No, no,' said Mrs May, drawing back a little in her chair, 'I never saw them. Never.'

'But you went up there? You know something! I can see you know!'

'Yes, I went up there.' Mrs May stared back into Kate's eager face; hesitant, she seemed, almost a little guilty. 'Well,' she conceded at last, 'I'll tell you. For what it's worth. When I went to stay in that house it was just before Aunt Sophy went into the nursing home. I knew the place was going to be sold, so I' – again Mrs May hesitated, almost shyly – 'well, I took all the furniture out of the doll's house and put it in a pillow-case and took it up there. I bought things too out of my pocket money – tea and coffee beans and salt and pepper and cloves and a great packet of lump sugar. And I took a whole lot of little pieces of silk which were over from making a patchwork quilt. And I took them some fish-bones for needles. I took the tiny thimble I had got in a Christmas pudding and a whole collection of scraps and cracker things I'd had in a chocolate box –'

'But you never saw them!'

'No. I never saw them. I sat for hours against the bank below the hawthorn hedge. It was a lovely bank, twined with twisted hawthorn roots and riddled with sandy holes and there were wood-violets and primroses and early campion. From the top of the bank you could see for miles across the fields: you could see the woods and the valleys and the twisting lanes; you could see the chimneys of the house.'

'Perhaps it was the wrong place.'

'I don't think so. Sitting there in the grass, half dreaming and watching beetles and ants, I found an oak-apple; it was smooth and polished and dry and there was a hole bored in one side of it and a slice off the top –'

'The teapot!' exclaimed Kate.

'I think so. I looked everywhere, but I couldn't find the quill spout. I called then, down all the holes – as my brother had done. But no one answered. Next day, when I went up there, the pillow-case had gone.'

'And everything in it?'

'Yes, everything. I searched the ground for yards around, in case there might be a scrap of silk or a coffee bean. But there was nothing. Of course, somebody passing might just have picked it up and carried it away. That was the day,' said Mrs May, smiling, 'that I smelled hot-pot.'

'And which was the day,' asked Kate, 'that you found Arrietty's diary?'

Mrs May laid down her work. 'Kate,' she began in a startled voice, and then, uncertainly, she smiled, 'what makes you say that?' Her cheeks had become quite pink.

'I guessed,' said Kate. 'I knew there was something – something you wouldn't tell me. Like – like reading somebody else's diary.'

'It wasn't the diary,' said Mrs May hastily, but her cheeks had become even pinker. 'It was the book called *Memoranda*, the book with blank pages. That's where she'd written it. And it wasn't on that day I found it, but three weeks later – the day before I left.'

Kate sat silent, staring at Mrs May. After a while she drew a long breath. 'Then that proves it,' she said finally, 'underground chamber and all.'

'Not quite,' said Mrs May.

'Why not?' asked Kate.

'Arrietty used to make her "e's" like little half-moons with a stroke in the middle –'

'Well?' said Kate.

Mrs May laughed and took up her work again. 'My brother did, too,' she said.

THE
BORROWERS
AFIELD

WITH ILLUSTRATIONS BY
Diana Stanley

For
CHARLOTTE AND VICTORIA

CHAPTER ONE

'WHAT HAS BEEN, MAY BE'
First recorded eclipse of the moon, 721 B.C.
[*Extract from Arrietty's Diary and Proverb Book, 19th March*]

IT was Kate who, long after she was grown up, completed the story of the borrowers. She wrote it all out, many years later, for her four children, and compiled it as you compile a case-history or a biographical novel from all kinds of evidence – things she remembered, things she had been told, and one or two things – we had better confess it – at which she just guessed. The most remarkable piece of evidence was a miniature Victorian notebook with gilt-edged pages, discovered by Kate in a gamekeeper's cottage on the Studdington estate near Leighton Buzzard, Bedfordshire.

Old Tom Goodenough, the gamekeeper, had never wanted the story put in writing, but as he had been dead now for so many years and as Kate's children were so very much alive, she thought perhaps that wherever he might be (and with a name like Goodenough it was bound to be heaven) he would have overcome this kind of prejudice and would by now perhaps forgive her and understand. Anyway, Kate, after some thought, decided to take the risk.

When Kate had been a child herself and was living with her parents in London, an old lady shared their home (she was, I think, some kind of relation): her name was Mrs May. And it was Mrs May on those long winter evenings beside the fire when she was teaching Kate to crochet, who had first told Kate about the borrowers.

At the time, Kate never doubted their existence – a race of tiny creatures, as like to humans as makes no matter, who live their secret lives under the floors and behind the wainscots of certain quiet old houses. It was only later that she began to wonder (and how wrong she was you will very soon be told. There were stranger happenings to come – developments more unlooked for and extraordinary than any Mrs May had dreamed of).

The original story had smacked a little of hearsay: Mrs May admitted – in fact, had been at some pains to convince Kate – that she, Mrs May, had never actually seen a borrower herself; any knowledge of such beings she had gained at second hand from her younger brother, who she admitted was a little boy with not only vivid imagination but well known to be a tease. So there you were, Kate decided – thinking it over afterwards – you could take it or leave it.

And, truth to tell, in the year or so which followed Kate tended rather to leave it: the story of the borrowers became pushed away in the back of her mind with other childish fantasies. During this year she changed her school, made new friends, acquired a dog, took up skating, and learned to ride a bicycle. And there was no thought of 'borrowers' in Kate's mind (nor did she notice the undercurrent of excitement in Mrs May's usually calm voice) when, one morning at breakfast in early spring, Mrs May passed a letter across the table, saying: 'This will interest you, Kate, I think.'

It didn't interest Kate a bit (she was about eleven years old at the time): she read it through twice in a bewildered kind of way but could make neither head nor tail of it. It was a lawyer's letter from a firm called Jobson, Thring, Beguid & Beguid; not only was it full of long words like 'beneficiary' and 'disentailment' but even the medium-sized words were arranged in such a manner that, to Kate, they made no sense at all (what, for instance, could 'vacant possession' mean? However much you thought about it, it could only describe a state of affairs which was manifestly quite impossible). Names there were in plenty – Studdington, Goodenough, Amberforce, Pocklinton – and quite a family of people who spelled their name 'deceased' with a small 'd'.

'Thank you very much,' Kate had said politely, passing it back.

'I thought, perhaps,' said Mrs May (and her cheeks, Kate noticed, looked slightly flushed as though with shyness), 'you might like to go down with me.'

'Go down where?' asked Kate, in her vaguest manner.

'My dear Kate,' exclaimed Mrs May, 'what was the point of showing you the letter? To Leighton Buzzard, of course.'

Leighton Buzzard? Years afterwards, when Kate described this scene to her children, she would tell them how, at these words, her heart began to bump long before her mind took in their meaning: Leighton Buzzard . . . she knew the name, of course: the name of an English country town . . . somewhere in Bedfordshire, wasn't it?

'Where Great-aunt Sophy's house was,' said Mrs May, prompting her. 'Where my brother used to say he saw the borrowers.' And before Kate could get back her breath she went on, in a matter-of-fact voice: 'I have been left a little cottage, part of the Studdington estate, and,' her colour deepened as though what she was about to say now might sound slightly incredible, 'three hundred and fifty-five pounds. Enough,' she added, in happy wonderment, 'to do it up.'

Kate was silent. She stared at Mrs May, her clasped hands pressed against her middle as though to still the beat of her heart.

'Could we see the house?' she said at last, a kind of croak in her voice.

'Of course, that's why we're going.'

'I mean the big house, Aunt Sophy's house?'

'Oh, that house? Firbank Hall, it was called.' Mrs May seemed a little taken aback. 'I don't know. We could ask, perhaps; it depends of course on whoever is living there now.'

'I mean,' Kate went on, with controlled eagerness, 'even if we couldn't get inside, you could show me the grating, and Arrietty's bank; and even if they opened the front door only ever so little, you could show me where the clock was. You could kind of point with your finger, quickly . . .' and, as Mrs May still seemed to hesitate, Kate added suddenly on a note of anguish: 'You did believe in them, didn't you? Or was it' – her voice faltered – 'only a story?'

'And what if it were only a story,' said Mrs May quickly, 'so long as it was a good story? Keep your sense of wonder, child, and don't be so literal. And anything we haven't experienced for ourselves sounds like a story. All we can ever do about such things is' – she hesitated, smiling at Kate's expression – 'keep an open mind and try to sift the evidence.'

Sift the evidence? There was, Kate realized, calming down a little, a fair amount of that: even before Mrs May had spoken of such creatures, Kate had suspected their existence. How else to explain the steady, but inexplicable, disappearance of certain small objects about the house?

Not only safety-pins, needles, pencils, blotting-paper, match-boxes, and those sort of things, but, even in Kate's short life, she had noticed that if you did not open a drawer for any length of time you never found it quite as you left it: something was always missing – your best handkerchief, your only bodkin, your carnelian heart, your lucky sixpence . . . 'But I *know* I put it in this drawer' – how often had she said these words herself, and how often had she heard them said? As for attics – 'I am absolutely certain,' Kate's mother had wailed only last week, on her knees before an open trunk searching vainly for a pair of shoe buckles, 'that I put them in this box with the ostrich-fan. They were wrapped in a piece of black wadding and I slipped them here, just below the handle . . .' And the same thing with writing-desks, sewing-baskets, button-boxes: there was never as much tea next day as you had seen in the caddy the evening before. Nor rice for that matter, nor lump sugar. Yes, Kate decided, evidence there was in plenty, if only one knew how to sift it.

'I suppose,' she remarked thoughtfully, as she began to fold up her napkin, 'some houses are more apt to have them than others.'

'Some houses,' said Mrs May, 'do not have them at all. And according to my brother,' she went on, 'it's the tidier houses, oddly enough, which attract them most. Borrowers, he used to say, are nervous people; they must know where things are kept and what each human being is likely to be doing at any hour of the day. In untidy, noisy, badly run houses, oddly enough, you can leave your belongings about with impunity – as far as borrowers are concerned, I mean.' And she gave a short laugh.

'Could borrowers live out of doors?' asked Kate suddenly.

'Not easily, no,' said Mrs May. 'They need human beings; they live by the same things human beings live by.'

'I was thinking,' went on Kate, 'about Pod and Homily, and little Arrietty. I mean – when they were smoked out from under the floor, how do you think they managed?'

'I often wonder,' said Mrs May.

'Do you think,' asked Kate, 'that Arrietty did become the last living borrower? Like your brother said she would?'

'Yes, he said that, didn't he – the last of her race? I sincerely hope not. It was unkind of him,' Mrs May added reflectively.

'I wonder, though, how they got across those fields? Do you think they ever did find the badgers' set?'

'We can't tell. I told you about the pillow-case incident – when I took all the doll's house furniture up there in a pillow-case?'

'And you smelled something cooking? But that doesn't say our family ever got there – Pod and Homily and Arrietty. The cousins lived in the badgers' set too, didn't they – the Hendrearys? It might have been their cooking.'

'It might, of course,' said Mrs May.

Kate was silent for a while, lost in reflection; suddenly her whole face lit up and she swivelled round in her chair.

'If we do go,' she cried (and there was an awed look in her eyes as though vouchsafed by some glorious vision), 'where shall we stay? In an *inn*?'

CHAPTER TWO

'WITHOUT PAINS, NO GAINS'
British Residency at Manipur attacked 1891
[*Extract from Arrietty's Diary and Proverb Book, 24th March*]

BUT nothing turns out in fact as you have pictured it; the 'inn' was a case in point – and so, alas, was Great-aunt Sophy's house. Neither of these, to Kate, were at all as they should be:

An inn, of course, was a place you came to at night, not at three o'clock in the afternoon, preferably a rainy night – wind, too, if it could be managed; and it should, of course, be situated on a moor ('bleak', Kate knew, was the adjective here). And there should be scullions; mine host should be gravy-stained and broad in the beam with a tousled apron pulled across his stomach; and there should be a tall, dark stranger – the one who speaks to nobody – warming thin hands before the fire. And the fire should *be* a fire – crackling and blazing, laid with an impossible size log and roaring its great heart out up the chimney. And there should be some sort of cauldron, Kate felt, somewhere about – and a couple of mastiffs, perhaps, thrown in for good measure.

But, here, were none of these things: there was a quiet-voiced young woman in a white blouse who signed them in at the desk; there was a waitress called Maureen (blonde) and one called Margaret (mousy, with pebble glasses) and an elderly waiter, the back part of whose hair did not at all match the front; the fire was not made out of logs but of bored-looking coals tirelessly licked by an abject electric flicker; and (worst of all) standing in front of it, instead of a tall dark stranger, was Mr Beguid, the lawyer (pronounced 'Begood') – plump, pink, but curiously cool-looking, with his silvery hair and steel-grey eye.

But outside Kate saw the bright spring sunshine and she liked her bedroom with its view over the marketplace, its tall mahogany wardrobe, and its constant H. and C. And she knew that tomorrow they would see the house – this legendary, mysterious house which now so surprisingly had become real, built no longer of airy fantasy but, she gathered, of solid bricks and mortar, standing firmly in its own grounds not two miles along the road. Close enough, Kate realized, if only Mrs May would not talk so much with Mr Beguid, for them to have walked there after tea.

But when, next morning, they did walk there (Mrs May in her long, slightly deer-stalker-looking coat and with her rubber-tipped walking-stick made of cherry wood), Kate was disappointed; the house looked nothing at all like she had imagined it: a barrack of red brick, it appeared to her, with rows of shining windows staring blankly through her, as though they were blind.

'They've taken the creeper down,' said Mrs May (she too sounded a little surprised), but after a moment, as they stood there at the head of the drive, she rallied slightly and added on a brisker note: 'And quite right too – there's nothing like creeper for damaging brickwork,' and, as they began to walk on down the driveway, she went on to explain to Kate that this house had always been considered a particularly pure example of early Georgian architecture.

'Was it really *here*?' Kate kept asking in an incredulous voice as though Mrs May might have forgotten.

'Of course, my dear, don't be so silly. This is where the apple-tree was, the russet apple by the gate . . . and the third window on the left, the one with bars across, used to be my bedroom the last few times I slept here. The night-nursery, of course, looks out over the back. And there's the kitchen garden. We used to jump off that wall, my brother and I, and on to the compost heap. Ten feet high, it's supposed to be – I remember one day Crampfurl scolding us and measuring it with his besom.'

(Crampfurl? So there had been such a person . . .)

The front door stood open (as it must have stood, Kate realized suddenly, years ago on that never-to-be-forgotten day for Arrietty when she first saw the 'great outdoors'), and the early spring sunshine poured across the newly whitened step into the high dark hall beyond; it made a curtain of light through which it was hard to see. Beside the step, Kate noticed, was an iron shoe-scraper. Was this the one down which Arrietty had climbed? Her heart began to beat a little faster. 'Where's the grating?' she whispered, as Mrs May pulled the bell (they heard it jangle far off in the dim distance, miles away it seemed).

'The grating?' said Mrs May, stepping backwards on the gravel path and looking along the house front. 'There,' she said, with a slight nod – keeping her voice low. 'It's been repaired,' she whispered, 'but it's the same one.'

Kate wandered towards it: yes, there it was, the actual grating through which they had escaped – Pod, Homily, and little Arrietty; there was the greenish stain and a few bricks which looked newer than the others. It stood higher than she had imagined; they must have had a bit of a jump to get down. Going up to it, she stooped, trying to see inside; dank darkness, that was all. So this had been their home . . .

'Kate!' called Mrs May softly, from beside the door-step (as Pod must have called that day to Arrietty when she ran off down the path), and Kate, turning, saw suddenly a sight she recognized, something which at last was like she had imagined it – the primrose bank. Tender, blue-green blades among the faded winter grasses – sown, spattered, almost drenched they seemed – with palest gold. And the azalea bush, Kate saw, had become a tree.

After a moment Mrs May called again and Kate came back to the front door. 'We'd better ring again,' she said, and once more they heard the ghostly jangle. 'It rings near the kitchen,' explained Mrs May, in a whisper, 'just beyond the green baize door.'

('The Green Baize Door' . . . she seemed, Kate thought, to speak these words in capitals.)

At last they saw a figure through the sunbeams; it was a slatternly girl in a wet, sack-cloth apron, her bare feet in run-down sandals.

'Yes?' she said, staring at them and frowning against the sun.

Mrs May stiffened. 'I wonder,' she said, 'if I could see the owner of the house?'

'You mean Mr Dawsett-Poole?' said the girl, 'or the headmaster?' She raised her forearm, shading her eyes, a wet floor-cloth, dripping slightly, clasped in her grimy hand.

'Oh!' exclaimed Mrs May. 'Is it a school?' Kate caught her breath – that, then, explained the barracky appearance.

'Well, it always has been, hasn't it?' said the girl.

'No,' replied Mrs May, 'not always. When I was a child I used to stay here. Perhaps, then, I might speak to whoever is in charge?'

'There's only my mum,' said the girl; 'she's the caretaker. They're all away over Easter – the masters and that.'

'Well, in that case,' began Mrs May uncertainly, 'I mustn't trouble you –' and was preparing to turn away when Kate, standing her ground, addressed the girl: 'Can't we just see inside the hall?'

'Help yourself,' said the girl, looking mildly surprised, and she re-treated slightly into the shadows as though to make way. 'It's okay by me.'

They stepped through the veil of sunlight into a dimmer coolness. Kate looked about her: it was wide and high and panelled and there were the stairs 'going up and up, world upon world', as Arrietty had described them – all the same, it was nothing like she had imagined it. The floor was covered with burnished, dark green linoleum; there was a sourish smell of soapy water and the clean smell of wax.

'There's a beautiful stone floor under this,' said Mrs May, tapping the linoleum with her rubber-tipped walking-stick.

The girl stared at them curiously for a moment and then, as though bored, she turned away and disappeared into the shadowy passage beyond the staircase, scuffling a little in her downtrodden shoes.

Kate, about to comment, felt a touch on her arm. 'Listen,' hissed Mrs May sharply; and Kate, holding her breath to complete the silence, heard a curious sound, a cross between a sigh and a moan. Mrs May nodded. 'That's it,' she whispered, 'the sound of the green baize door.'

'And where was the clock?' asked Kate.

Mrs May indicated a piece of wall, now studded with a row of coat pegs. 'There; Pod's hole must have been just behind where that radiator is now. A radiator, they'd have liked that . . .' She pointed to a door across the hall, now labelled, in neat white lettering, 'Headmaster's Study'. 'And that was the morning-room,' she said.

'Where the Overmantels lived? And Pod got the blotting-paper?' Kate stared a moment and then, before Mrs May could stop her, ran across and tried the handle.

'No, Kate, you mustn't. Come back.'

'It's locked,' said Kate, turning back. 'Could we just peep upstairs?' she went on. 'I'd love to see the night-nursery. I could go terribly quietly . . .'

'No, Kate, come along: we must go now. We've no business to be here at all,' and Mrs May walked firmly towards the door.

'Couldn't I just peep in the kitchen window?' begged Kate at last, when they stood once again in the sunshine.

'No, Kate,' said Mrs May.

'Just to see where they lived? Where that hole was under the stove which Pod used as a chute – *please*.'

'Quickly, then,' said Mrs May; she threw a nervous glance in each direction as Kate sped off down the path.

This too was a disappointment. Kate knew where the kitchen was because of the grating, and making blinkers of her cupped hands against the reflected sunshine, she pushed her face up close against the glass. Dimly the room came into view, but it was nothing like a kitchen: shelves of bottles, gleaming retorts, heavy bench-like tables, rows of Bunsen burners: the kitchen was now a lab.

And that was that. On the way home Kate picked a very small bunch of dog-violets; there was veal and ham pie for luncheon, with salad, with the choice of plums and junket or baked jam roll; and, after luncheon, Mr Beguid arrived with car and chauffeur to take them to see the cottage.

At first Kate did not want to go: she had a secret plan of walking up to the field called Parkin's Beck and mooching about by herself, looking for badgers' sets, but when Mrs May explained to her that the field was just behind the cottage, and by the time Mr Beguid had stared long enough and pointedly enough out of the window with a bored, dry, if-this-were-my-child kind of expression on his face, Kate decided to go in the car after all, just to spite him. And it was a good thing (as she so often told her own children years afterwards) that she did: otherwise, she might never have talked to – or (which was more important) made friends with – Thomas Goodenough.

CHAPTER THREE

'AND about vacant possession,' Mrs May asked in the car, 'he really is going, this old man? I've forgotten his name –'

'Old Tom Goodenough? Yes, he's going all right; we've got him an almshouse. Not,' Mr Beguid added, with a short laugh, 'that he deserves it.'

'Why not?' asked Kate in her blunt way.

Mr Beguid glanced at her – a little put out, he seemed, as though the dog had spoken. 'Because,' he said, ignoring Kate and addressing Mrs May, 'he's a tiresome old humbug, that's why.' He laughed again, his complacent, short laugh. 'And the biggest liar in five counties, as they put it down in the village.'

The stone cottage stood in a field; it stood high, its back to the woods; it had a derelict look, Kate thought, as they toiled up the slope towards

it, but the thatch seemed good. Beside the front door stood a water-butt leaking a little at the seams and green with moss; there was slime on the brick path and a thin trickle of moisture which lost itself among the dock and thistles. Against the far end was a wooden out-house on the walls of which Kate saw the skins of several small mammals nailed up to dry in the sun.

'I didn't realize it was quite so remote,' panted Mrs May, as Mr Beguid knocked sharply on the blistered paint of the front door. She waved her rubber-tipped stick towards the sunken lane below the sloping field of meadow grass. 'We'll have to make some kind of path up to here.'

Kate heard a shuffling movement within and Mr Beguid, rapping again, called out impatiently: 'Come on, old Tom. Open up.'

There were footsteps and, as the door creaked open, Kate saw an old man – tall, thin, but curiously heavy about the shoulders. He carried his head sunk a little on to his chest, and inclined sideways; and when he smiled (as he did at once) this gave him a sly look: he had bright, dark, strangely luminous eyes which he fixed immediately on Kate.

'Well, Tom,' said Mr Beguid briskly, 'how are you keeping? Better, I hope. Here is Mrs May, the lady who owns your cottage. May we come in?'

'There's naught to hide,' said the old man, backing slightly to let them pass, but smiling only at Kate, it was, Kate thought, as though he could not see Mr Beguid.

They filed past him into the principal room; it was barish but neat enough, except for a pile of wood shavings on the stone floor and a stack of something Kate took to be kindling beside the window embrasure. A small fire smouldered in a blackened grate which seemed to be half oven.

'You've tidied up a bit, I see,' said Mr Beguid, looking about him. 'Not that it matters much. But,' he added, speaking aside to Mrs May, and barely lowering his voice, 'before the builders come in, if I were you I'd get the whole place washed through and thoroughly fumigated.'

'I think it looks lovely,' cried Kate warmly, shocked by this want of manners, and Mrs May hastened to agree with her, addressing a friendly look towards the old man.

But old Tom gave no sign of having noticed: quietly he stood, looking down at Kate, smiling his secret smile.

'The stairs are through here,' said Mr Beguid, leading the way to a farther door; 'and here,' they heard him say, 'is the scullery.' Mrs May, about to follow, hesitated on the threshold. 'Don't you want to come, Kate, and see round the cottage?'

Kate stood stolidly where she was; she threw a quick glance at the old man, and back again to Mrs May. 'No thanks,' she said shortly. And as Mrs May, a little surprised, followed Mr Beguid into the scullery, Kate moved towards the pile of peeled sticks. There was a short silence. 'What are you making?' Kate asked at last, a little shyly. The old man came back from his dream. 'Them?' he said in his soft voice. 'Them's sprays – for thatching.' He picked up a knife, tested the blade on his horny thumb, and pulling up a lowish stool, he sat down. 'Come you here,' he said, 'by me, and I'll show 'ee.'

Kate drew up a chair beside him and watched him in silence as he cut several small lengths of the hazel sapling which at first she had taken for kindling. After a moment he said softly without looking up: 'You don't want to take no notice of him.'

'Mr Beguid?' said Kate. 'I don't. Be good! It's a silly kind of name.

Compared to yours, I mean,' she added warmly; 'whatever you did wouldn't matter really with a name like Good Enough.'

The old man turned his head in a warning gesture towards the scullery; he listened a moment and then he said: 'They're going upstairs,' and Kate, listening too, heard clumping footsteps on wooden treads. 'You know how long I bin in this cottage?' the old man asked, his head still cocked as though listening while the footsteps crossed and recrossed what must have been his bedroom. 'Nigh on eighty years,' he added after a moment. He took up a peeled sapling, grasping it firmly at either end.

'And now you've got to go?' said Kate, watching his hands as he took a firmer grip on the wood.

The old man laughed as though she had made a joke: he laughed quite silently, Kate noticed, shaking his head. 'So they make out,' he said in an amused voice, and with a twist of his two wrists he wrung the tough sapling as you wring out a wet cloth, and in the same movement doubled it back on itself. 'But I bain't going,' he added, and he threw the bent stick on the pile.

'But they wouldn't want to turn you out,' said Kate, 'not if you don't want to go. At least,' she added cautiously, 'I don't think Mrs May would.'

'Her-r-r?' he said, rolling the 'r's' and looking up at the ceiling; 'she's hand and glove with him.'

'She used to come and stay here,' Kate told him, 'when she was a child, did you know? Down at the big house. Firbank, isn't it?'

'Ay,' he said.

'Did you know her?' asked Kate curiously. 'She was called Miss Ada.'

'I knew Miss Ada all right,' said the old man, 'and her aunty. *And* her brother.' He laughed again. 'I knew the whole lot of 'em, come to that.'

As he spoke, Kate had a strange feeling; it was as though she had heard these words before, spoken by just such an old man as this and, she seemed to remember, it was in some such similar place – the sunlit window of a darkish cottage on a bright but cold spring day. She looked round wonderingly at the whitewashed walls – flaking a little they were, in a pattern she seemed to recognize; even the hollows and cracks of the worn brick floor also seemed curiously familiar – strange, because (of this she was certain) she had never been here before. She looked back at the old man, getting up courage to go a step farther. 'Did you know Crampfurl?' she asked after a moment, and before he spoke she knew what would be his answer.

'I knew Crampfurl all right,' said the old man. and he laughed again, nodding his head, enjoying some secret joke.

'And Mrs Driver, the cook?'

Here the joke became almost too much for old Tom. 'Av,' he said, wheezing with silent laughter, 'Mrs Driver!' and he wiped the corner of his eye with his sleeve.

'Did you know Rosa Pickhatchet?' went on Kate, 'that housemaid, the one who screamed?'

'Nay,' said old Tom, nodding and laughing. 'But I heard tell of her – screamed the house down, so they say.'

'But do you know why?' cried Kate excitedly.

He shook his head. 'No reason at all, as I can see.'

'But didn't they tell you that she saw a little man, on the drawing-room mantel-shelf, about the size of the china cupid; that she thought he was an ornament and tried to dust him with a feather duster – and suddenly he sneezed? Anyone would scream,' Kate concluded breathlessly.

'For why?' said old Tom, deftly sliding the bark from the wood as though it were a glove finger. 'They don't hurt you, borrowers don't. And they don't make no mess neither. Not like field-mice. Beats me, always has, the fuss folk'll make about a borrower, screeching and screaming and all that caper.' He ran an appreciative finger along the peeled surface. 'Smoking 'em out and them kind of games. No need for it, not with borrowers. They go quiet enough, give 'em time, once they know they've been seen. Now take field-mice –' The old man broke off to twist his stick, catching his breath with the effort.

'Don't let's,' cried Kate, 'please! I mean, tell me some more about borrowers.'

'There's naught to tell,' said the old man, tossing his stick on the pile and selecting a fresh one. 'Borrowers is as like to humans as makes no matter, and what's to tell about humans? Now you take field-mice – once one of them critturs finds a way indoors, you're done and strung up as you might say: you can't leave the place not for a couple of hours but you don't get the whole lot right down on you like a flock of starlings. Mess! And it ain't a question of getting 'em out: they've come and they've gone, if you see what I mean. Plague o' locusts ain't in it. Yes,' he went on, 'no doubt about it – in a house like this, you're apt to get more trouble from field-mice than ever you get from any borrower; in a house like this,' he repeated, 'set away like at the edge of the woods, borrowers can be company like as not.' He glanced up at the ceiling, which creaked slightly as footsteps passed and repassed in the room above. 'What you reckon they're up to?' he said.

'Measuring,' Kate said. 'Mrs May brought a yard-stick. They'll be down soon,' she went on hurriedly, 'and I want to ask you something – something important. If they send me for a walk tomorrow – by myself, I mean, while they talk business, could I come up and be with you?'

'I don't see no reason why not,' said the old man, at work on his next stick. 'If you brings along a sharp knife, I'll learn you to make sprays.'

'You know,' said Kate impressively, with a glance at the ceiling, dropping her voice. 'Her brother, Mrs May's brother – or Miss Ada's or whatever you like to call her – he *saw* those borrowers down at the big house!' She paused for effect, watching his face.

'What of it?' said the old man impassively. 'You only got to keep your eyes skinned. I seen stranger things in my time than them sort of critturs – take badgers – now you come up here tomorrow and I'll tell you summat about badgers you wouldn't credit, but that I seen it with my own two eyes –'

'But have you ever seen a *borrower?*' cried Kate impatiently. 'Did you ever see any of these ones down at the big house?'

'Them as they had in the stables?'

'No, the ones who lived under the kitchen?'

'Oh, them,' he said, 'smoked out, they were. But it ain't true –' he began, raising his face suddenly, and Kate saw that it was a sad face when it was not smiling.

'What isn't true?'

'What they say: that I set the ferret on 'em. I wouldn't. Not once I knew they were borrowers.'

'Oh!' exclaimed Kate, kneeling up on her chair with excitement, 'you were the boy with the ferret?'

Old Tom looked back at her – his sideways look. 'I were a boy,' he admitted guardedly, 'and I did have a ferret.'

'But they did escape, didn't they?' Kate persisted anxiously. 'Mrs May says they escaped by the grating.'

'That's right,' said old Tom, 'made off across the gravel and up the bank.'

'But you don't know for certain,' said Kate; 'you didn't see them go. Or *could* you see them from the window?'

'I know for certain all right,' said old Tom. 'True enough I saw 'em from the window, but that ain't how –' he hesitated, looking at Kate; amused he seemed but still wary.

'Please tell me. Please –' begged Kate.

The old man glanced upwards at the ceiling. 'You know what he is?' he said, inclining his head.

'Mr Beguid? A lawyer.'

The old man nodded. 'That's right. And you don't want nothing put down in writing.'

'I don't understand,' said Kate.

The old man sighed and took up his whittling knife. 'What I tells *you*, you tells *her*, and *he* puts it all down in writing.'

'Mrs May wouldn't tell,' said Kate, 'she's –'

'She's hand in glove with him, that's what I maintain. And it's no good telling me no different. Seemingly, now, you can't die no more where you reckons to die. And you know for why?' he said, glaring at Kate. 'Because of what's put down in writing.' And with a curiously vicious twist he doubled back his stick. Kate stared at him nonplussed. 'If I promised not to tell?' she said at last, in a timid voice.

'Promises!' exclaimed the old man; staring at Kate, he jerked a thumb towards the ceiling. 'Her-r-r great-uncle, old Sir Montague that was, *promised* me this cottage – "It's for your lifetime, Tom," he says. Promises!' he repeated angrily, and he almost spat the word. 'Promises is pie-crust.'

Kate's eyes filled with tears. 'All right,' she snapped, 'I don't care – then don't tell me!'

Tom's expression changed too, almost as violently. 'Now don't 'ee cry, little maid,' he begged, surprised and distressed.

But Kate, to her shame, could not stop; the tears ran down her cheeks and she felt the familiar hot feeling at the tip of her nose as though it were swelling. 'I was only wondering,' she gasped, fumbling for a handkerchief, 'if they were all right – and how they managed – and whether they found the badgers' set –'

'They found the badgers' set all right,' said old Tom. 'Now, don't 'ee cry, my maiden, not no more.'

'I'll stop in a minute,' Kate assured him in a stifled voice, blowing her nose.

'Now look 'ee here,' the old man went on – very upset he sounded, 'you dry your eyes and stop your weeping and old Tom'll show you summat.' Awkwardly he got up off his stool and hovered over her, drooping his shoulders like some great protective bird. 'Something you'd like. How's that, eh?'

'It's all right,' Kate said, giving a final scrub. She stuffed away her handkerchief and smiled up at him. 'I've stopped.'

Old Tom put his hand in his pocket and then, throwing a cautious glance towards the ceiling, he seemed to change his mind: for a moment it had sounded as though the footsteps had been moving towards the stairs. 'It's all right,' whispered Kate, after listening, as he searched again and drew out a battered tin box, the kind in which pipe-smokers keep tobacco, and with his knotted fingers fumbled awkwardly with the lid; at last it was open and, breathing heavily, he turned it over

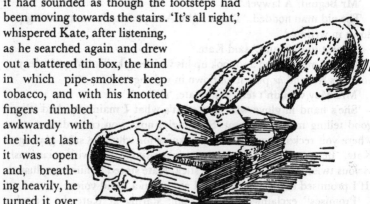

and slid some object out. 'Here . . .' he said, and there on his calloused palm Kate saw the tiny book.

'Oh . . .' she breathed, staring incredulously.

'Take it up,' said old Tom, 'it won't bite you.' And, as gingerly Kate put out her hand, he added smiling: ''Tis Arrietty's diary.'

But Kate knew this, even before she saw the faded gilt lettering – 'Diary and Proverb Book', and in spite of the fact that it was weather-stained and time-worn, that when she opened it the bulk of its pages slipped out from between the covers, and the ink or pencil or sap – or whatever Arrietty had used to write with – had faded to various shades of brown and sepia and a curious sickly yellow. It had opened at August the 31st, and the proverb, Kate saw, was 'Earth is the Best Shelter', and below this the bald statement, 'Disastrous Earthquake at Charleston, U.S., 1866', and on the page itself, in Arrietty's scratchy hand-writing, were three entries for the three successive years:

'Spiders in store-room.'

'Mrs D. dropped pan. Soup-leak in ceiling.'

'Talked to Spiller.'

Who was Spiller? Kate wondered. August 31st? That was after they left the big house: Spiller, she realized, must be part of the new life, the life out of doors. At random she turned back a few pages:

'Mother bilious.'

'Threaded green beads.'

'Climbed hedge. Eggs bad.'

Climbed hedge? Arrietty must have gone birds'-nesting – and the eggs would be bad in (Kate glanced at the date) . . . yes, it was still August, and the motto for that day was 'Grasp all, lose all'.

'Where did you get this book?' Kate asked aloud in a stunned voice.

'I found it,' said old Tom.

'But where?' cried Kate.

'Here,' said old Tom, and Kate saw his eyes stray in the direction of the fire-place.

'In this house,' she exclaimed in an unbelieving voice and, staring up at his mysterious old face, Mr Beguid's unkind words came back to her suddenly, 'the biggest liar in five counties'. But here, in her hand, was the actual book; she stared down at it trying to sort out her thoughts.

'You want I should show you summat else?' he asked her, suddenly and a little pathetically, as though aware of her secret doubts. 'Come you here,' and getting up slowly from his chair, Kate followed like a sleep-walker as he went towards the fire-place.

The old man stooped down, and panting a little with the effort, he dragged and tugged at the heavy wood-box: as he shifted it aside a board fell forward with a slight clatter and the old man, alarmed, glanced up at the ceiling; but Kate, leaning forward, saw the board had covered a sizeable rat-hole gouged out of the skirting and Gothic in shape, like an opened church door.

'See?' said old Tom, after listening a moment – a little breathless from tugging, 'goes right through to the scullery: they'd got fire this side and water t'other. Years, they lived there.'

Kate knelt down, staring into the hole. 'Here? In your house?' Her voice became more and more scared and unbelieving. 'You mean . . . Pod? And Homily? . . . And little Arrietty?'

'Them, too,' said old Tom, 'in the end, as it were.'

'But didn't they live out of doors? That's what Arrietty was longing to do –'

'They lived out of doors all right.' He gave a short laugh. 'If you call it living. Or come to that, if you can call it outdoors! But you take a look at this,' he went on softly, with a note in his voice of thinly disguised pride, 'goes right up inside the wall, stairs they got and all betwixt the lath and the plaster. Proper tenement, they got here – six floors – and water on every floor. See that?' he asked, laying his hand on a rusty pipe; 'comes down from the cistern in the roof, that does, and goes on through to the scullery. Tapped it, they did, in six different places – and never a drop or a leak!'

He was silent a moment, lost in thought, before he propped back the board again and shoved the wood-box back into place. 'Years they lived here,' he said affectionately, and he sighed a little as he straightened up, dusting his hands together.

'But *who* lived here?' Kate whispered hurriedly (the footsteps above had crossed the landing and were now heard approaching the head of the stairs). 'You don't mean my ones? You said they found the badgers' set?'

'They found the badgers' set all right,' said old Tom, and gave his short laugh.

'But how do you know? Who told you?' Twittering with anxiety she followed behind him as he limped towards his stool.

Old Tom sat down, selected a stick, and with maddening deliberation tested the edge of his knife. 'She told me,' he said at last, and he cut the stick in three lengths.

'You mean you talked to Arrietty!'

He made a warning sign at her raised voice, lifting his eyebrows and jerking his head: the footsteps, Kate heard, were clumping now down the wooden treads of the stairs. 'You don't talk to that one,' he whispered, 'not while she's got a tongue to wag.'

Kate went on staring; if he had hit her on the head with a log from the log-box, she could not have appeared more stunned. 'Then she must have told you everything!' she gasped.

'Hush!' said the old man, his eye on the door.

Mrs May and Mr Beguid, it seemed, had reached the bottom of the stairs, and from the sound of their voices had turned again into the scullery for a last look round. 'Two fitted basins, at least,' Mrs May was heard saying, in a matter-of-fact tone.

'Pretty nigh on everything, I reckon,' whispered old Tom. 'She'd creep out most evenings, pretty regular.' He smiled as he spoke, glancing towards the hearth. And Kate, watching his face, suddenly saw the picture: the firelit cottage, the lonely boy at his whittling, and almost invisible in the shadows this tiny creature, seated maybe on a match-box; the fluty, monotonous voice going on and on and on ... after a while, Kate thought, he would hardly hear it: it would merge and become part of the room's living stillness, like the simmer of the kettle or the ticking of the clock. Night after night; week after week; month after month; year, perhaps, after year ... yes, indeed, Kate realized (staring at old Tom in the same stunned way even though, at this minute, Mrs May and Mr Beguid came back to the room talking so loudly about washbasins), Arrietty must have told Tom everything!

CHAPTER FOUR

'NO TALE LOSES IN THE TELLING'
Longfellow, American poet, died 1882;
also Walt Whitman, 1891
[*Extract from Arrietty's Diary and Proverb Book, 26th March*]

AND all that was needed now, she thought (as she lay that night in bed, listening to the constant gurgle in the pipes of the constant H. and C.), was for old Tom to tell *her* everything in fullest detail – as Arrietty must have told it to him. And, having gone so far, he might do this, she felt – in spite of his fear of things put down in writing. And she wouldn't tell either, she resolved staunchly – at any rate, not during his lifetime (although why he should mind so much she couldn't understand, seeing that he was known already as 'the biggest liar in five counties'). But what seemed still more hopeful was that, having shown her the little book, he had not asked for it back: she had it now in bed with her stuffed beneath her pillow and this, at any rate, was full of 'things in writing'. Not that she could understand them quite: the entries were too short, little headings, they seemed like, jotted down by Arrietty to remind herself of dates. But some of them sounded extraordinarily weird and mysterious . . . yes, she decided – suddenly inspired – that was the way to work it: she would ask old Tom to explain the headings – 'What could Arrietty have meant,' she would ask, 'by "Black men. Mother saved"?'

And this, more or less, was what did happen. While Mrs May talked business each day with Messrs Jobson, Thring, Beguid & Beguid, or argued with builders and plumbers and plumbers' mates, Kate would wander off alone across the fields and find her own way to the cottage, seeking out old Tom.

On some days (as Kate, in later years, would explain to her children) he would seem a bit 'cagey' and uninterested, but on other days a particular heading in the diary would seem to inspire him and his imagination would take wings and sail away on such swirls and eddies of miraculous memory that Kate, spellbound, could hardly believe that he had not at some time (in some other life, perhaps) been a borrower himself. And Mrs May, Kate remembered, had once said just this of her younger brother: this brother who, although three years his junior, had been known to old Tom (old Tom himself had admitted this much).

Had they been friends? Great friends, perhaps? They certainly seemed birds of a feather – one famous for telling tall stories because 'he was such a tease'; the other more simply described as 'the biggest liar in five counties'. And it was this thought which, long after she was grown up, decided Kate to tell the world what was said to have happened to Pod and Homily and little Arrietty after that dreadful day when, smoked out of their house under the kitchen, they sought for refuge in the wild outdoors.

Here is her story – all 'put down in writing'. We can sift the evidence ourselves.

CHAPTER FIVE

'STEP BY STEP CLIMBS THE HILL'

Victoria Tubular Bridge, Montreal, opened 1866

[Extract from Arrietty's Diary and Proverb Book, 25th August]

WELL, at first, it seems they just ran, but they ran in the right direction – up the azalea bank, where (so many months ago now) Arrietty had first met the boy, and through the long grass at the top; how they got through that, Homily used to say afterwards, she never knew – nothing but stalks, close set. And insects: Homily had never dreamed there could be so many different kinds of insect – slow ones, hanging on things; fast, scuttling ones, and ones (these were the worst) which stared at you and did not move at once and then backed slowly, still staring; it was as though, Homily said, they had made up their mind to bite you and then (still malicious) changed it out of caution. 'Wicked,' she said, 'that's what they were; oh, wicked, wicked, wicked . . .'

As they shoved their way through the long grass, they were choked with pollen loosened in clouds from above; there were sharp-edged leaves, deceptively sappy and swaying, which cut their hands, gliding across the skin like the softly drawn bow of a violin but leaving blood behind; there were straw-dry, knotted stems, which caught them round the shins and ankles and which made them stumble and trip forward; often they would land on that cushiony plant with silvery, hairlike spines – spines which pricked and stung. Long grass . . . long grass . . . for ever afterwards it was Homily's nightmare.

Then, to get to the orchard, came a scramble through the privet hedge: dead leaves, below the blackened boughs of privet . . . dead leaves and rotting, desiccated berries which rose waist high as they swam their way through them, and, below the leaves, a rustling dampness. And here again were insects: things which turned over on their backs or hopped suddenly, or slyly slid away.

Across the orchard – easier going this, because the hens had fed there, achieving their usual 'blasted heath' effect – a flattened surface of lava-coloured earth; and the visibility was excellent. But, if they could see, they could also be seen: the fruit trees were widely spaced, giving little cover; anyone glancing from a first-floor window in the house might well exclaim curiously: 'What's that, do you think, moving across the orchard? There by the second tree on the right – like leaves

blowing. But there isn't a wind. More like something being drawn along
on a thread – too steady to be birds . . .' This was the thought in Pod's
mind as he urged Homily onwards. 'Oh, I can't,' she would cry. 'I
must sit down! Just a moment, Pod – please!'

But he was adamant. 'You can sit down,' he'd say, gripping her
below the elbow, and spinning her forward across the rubble, 'once we
get to the wood. You take her other arm, Arrietty, but keep her moving!'

Once within the wood, they sank down on the side of the well-worn
path, too exhausted to seek further cover. 'Oh dear . . . oh dear . . . oh
dear . . .' Homily kept saying (mechanically, because she always said
it), but behind her bright dark eyes in her smudged face they could see
her brain was busy: and she was not hysterical, they could see that too:
they could see, in other words, that Homily was 'trying'. 'There's no
call for all this running,' she announced after a moment, when she
could get her breath, 'nobody didn't see us go: for all they know we're
still there, trapped-like – under the floor.'

'I wouldn't be so sure,' said Arrietty, 'there was a face at the kitchen
window. I saw it as we were going up the bank. A boy it looked like,
with a cat or something.'

'If anyone'd seen us,' remarked Homily, 'they'd have been after us,
that's what I say.'

'That's a fact,' said Pod.

'Well, which way do we go from here?' asked Homily, gazing about
among the tree-trunks. There was a long scratch across her cheek and
her hair hung down in wisps.

'Well, we'd better be getting these loads sorted out first,' said Pod. 'Let's see what we've brought. What have you got in that borrowing-bag, Arrietty?'

Arrietty opened the bag she had packed so hurriedly two days before against just this emergency; she laid out the contents on the hardened mud of the path and they looked an odd collection. There were three tin lids of varying sizes of pill bottles which fitted neatly one inside the other; a sizeable piece of candle and seven wax-vestas; a change of underclothes and an extra jersey knitted by Homily on blunted darning-needles from a much washed, unravelled sock, and last, but most treasured, her pencil from a dance programme and her Diary and Proverb Book.

'Now why did you want to cart that along?' grumbled Pod, glancing sideways at this massive tome as he laid out his own belongings. For the same reason, Arrietty thought to herself as she glanced at Pod's unpacking, that you brought along your shoemaker's needle, your hammer made from an electric bell-clapper, and a stout ball of twine: each to his hobby and the tools of the craft he loves (and hers she knew to be literature).

Besides his shoemaking equipment, Pod had brought the half nail-scissor, a thin sliver of razor-blade, ditto of child's fret-saw, an aspirin bottle with screw lid filled with water, a small twist of fuse wire, and two steel hat-pins, the shorter of which he gave to Homily. 'It'll help you up the hill,' he told her; 'we may have a bit of a climb.'

Homily had brought her knitting-needles, the rest of the unravelled sock, three pieces of lump sugar, the finger of a lady's kid glove filled with salt and pepper mixed, tied up at the neck with cotton, some broken pieces of digestive biscuit, a small tin box made for phonograph needles which now contained dry tea, a chip of soap, and her hair curlers.

Pod gazed glumly at the curious collection. 'Like as not we brought the wrong things,' he said, 'but it can't be helped now. Better pack 'em up again,' he went on, suiting the action to the word, 'and let's get going. Good idea of yours, Arrietty, the way you fitted together them tin lids. Not sure, though, we couldn't have done with a couple more –'

'We've only got to get to the badgers' set,' Arrietty excused herself. 'I mean Aunt Lupy will have most things, won't she – like cooking utensils and such?'

'I never knew anyone as couldn't do with extra,' remarked Homily, stuffing in the remains of the sock and lashing up the neck of her bag with a length of blue embroidery silk, 'especially when they live in a badgers' set. And who's to say your Aunt Lupy's there at all?' She went on, 'I thought she got lost or something, crossing them fields out walking.'

'Well, she may be found again by now,' said Pod. 'Over a year ago, wasn't it, when she set out walking?'

'And anyway,' Arrietty pointed out, 'she wouldn't go walking with the cooking-pots.'

'I never could see,' said Homily, standing up and trying out the weight of her bag, 'nor never will, no matter what nobody tells me, what your Uncle Hendreary saw fit to marry in a stuck-up thing like that Lupy.'

'That's enough,' said Pod, 'we don't want none of that now.'

He stood up and slung his borrowing-bag on his steel hat-pin, swinging it over his shoulder. 'Now,' he asked, looking them up and down, 'sure you're both all right?'

'Not that, when put to it,' went on Homily, 'that she isn't good-hearted. It's the kind of way she does it.'

'What about your boots?' asked Pod. 'They quite comfortable?'

'Yes,' said Homily, 'for the moment,' she added.

'What about you, Arrietty?'

'I'm all right,' said Arrietty.

'Because,' said Pod, 'it's going to be a long pull. We're going to take it steady. No need to rush. But we don't want no stopping. Nor no grumbling. Understand?'

'Yes,' said Arrietty.

'And keep your eyes skinned,' Pod went on, as they all moved off along the path. 'If you see anything, do as I do – and sharp, mind. We don't want no running every which way. We don't want no screaming.'

'I know,' said Arrietty irritably, adjusting her pack. She moved ahead as though trying to get out of earshot.

'You *think* you know,' called Pod after her. 'But you don't know nothing really; you don't know nothing about cover; nor does your mother: cover's a trained job, an art-like –'

'I know,' repeated Arrietty; 'you told me.' She glanced sideways into the shadowy depths of the brambles beside the path; she saw a great spider, hanging in space, his web was invisible: he seemed to be staring at her – she saw his eyes. Defiantly, Arrietty stared back.

'You can't tell no one in five minutes,' persisted Pod, 'things you got to learn from experience. What I told you, my girl, that day I took you out borrowing, wasn't even the ABC. I tried my best, because your mother asked me. And see where it's got us!'

'Now, Pod,' panted Homily (they were walking too fast for her), 'no need to bring up the past.'

'That's what I mean,' said Pod, 'the past *is* experience: that's all you got to learn from. You see, when it comes to borrowing –'

'But you had a lifetime of it, Pod: you was in training – Arrietty'd only been out that once –'

'That's what I *mean*,' cried Pod, and, in stubborn desperation, he stopped in his tracks for Homily to catch up, 'about cover, if only she'd known the ABC –'

'Look out!' sang Arrietty shrilly, now some way ahead.

There was a rushing clatter and a dropped shadow and a hoarse, harsh cry: and, suddenly, there was Pod – alone on the path – face to face with a large, black crow.

The bird stared, wickedly, but a little distrustfully, his cramped toes turned in slightly, his great beak just open. Frozen to stillness Pod stared back – something growing in the path, that's what he looked like – a rather peculiar kind of chunky toadstool. The great bird, very curious, turned his head sideways and tried Pod with his other eye. Pod, motionless, stared back. The crow made a murmur in its throat – a tiny bleat – and, puzzled, it moved forward. Pod let it come, a couple of sideways steps, and then – out of a still face – he spoke: 'Get back to where you was,' he said evenly, almost conversationally, and the bird seemed to hesitate. 'We don't want no nonsense from you,' Pod went on steadily; 'pigeon-toed, that's what you are! Crows is pigeon-toed, first time it struck me. Staring away like that, with one eye, and your head turned sideways . . . think it pretty, no doubt' – Pod spoke quite pleasantly – 'but it ain't, not with *that* kind of beak . . .'

The bird became still, its expression no longer curious: there was stark amazement in every line of its rigid body and, in its eye, a kind of ghastly disbelief. 'Go on! Get off with you!' shouted Pod suddenly, moving towards it. 'Shoo . . .!' And, with a distraught glance and panic-stricken croak, the great bird flapped away. Pod wiped his brow with his sleeve as Homily, white faced and still trembling, crawled out from under a foxglove leaf. 'Oh, Pod,' she gasped, 'you were brave – you were wonderful!'

'It's nothing,' said Pod, 'it's a question of keeping your nerve.'

'But the size of it!' said Homily. 'You'd never think seeing them flying they was that size!'

'Size is nothing,' said Pod, 'it's the talk that gets them.' He watched Arrietty climb out from a hollow stump and begin to brush herself down. When she looked up he looked away. 'Well,' he said, after a moment, 'we'd better keep moving.'

Arrietty smiled; she hesitated a moment then ran across to him.

'What's that for?' asked Pod weakly, as she flung her arms round his neck. 'Oh,' cried Arrietty, hugging him, 'you deserve a medal – the way you faced up to it, I mean.'

'No, lass,' said Pod, 'you don't mean that: the way I was caught out, that's what you mean – caught out, good and proper, talking of cover.' He patted her hand. 'And, what's more, you're right: we'll face up to that one, too. You and your mother was trigger quick and I'm proud of you.' He let go her hand and swung his pack up on to his shoulders. 'But another time, remember,' he added, turning suddenly, 'not stumps. Hollow they may be but not always empty, see what I mean, and you're out of the frying-pan into the fire . . .'

On and on they went, following the path which the workmen had made when they dug out the trench for the gas-pipe. It led them through two fields of pasture land, on a gradually rising slope alongside; they could walk with perfect ease under the lowest rungs of any five-barred gate, picking a careful way across the clusters of sun-dried cattle tracks; these were crater-like but crumbling, and Homily, staggering a little beneath her load, slipped once and grazed her knee.

On the third field the gas-pipe branched away obliquely to the left, and Pod, looking ahead to where against the skyline he could just make out a stile, decided that they could safely now forsake the gas-pipe and stick to the path beside the hedge. 'Won't be so long now,' he explained comfortingly when Homily begged to rest, 'but we got to keep going. See that stile? That's what we're aiming for and we got to make it afore sunset.'

So on they plodded and, to Homily, this last lap seemed the worst: her tired legs moved mechanically like scissors; stooping under her load, she was amazed each time she saw a foot come forward – it no longer seemed to be her foot; she wondered how it got there.

Arrietty wished they could not see the stile: their tiny steps seemed to bring it no nearer; it worked better she found to keep her eyes on the ground and then every now and again if she looked up she could see they had made progress.

But at last they reached the crest of the hill; towards the right, on the

far side of the cornfield beyond the hazel hedge, lay the woods, and
ahead of them, after a slight dip, rose a vast sloping field, crossed with
shadow from where the sun was setting behind the trees.

On the edge of this field they stood and stared, awed by its vastness,
its tilted angle against the rosy sky; on this endless sea of lengthening
shadows and dreaming grassland floated an island of trees dimmed
already by its long-thrown trail of dusk.

'This is it,' said Pod, after a long moment, 'Parkin's Beck.' They
stood, all three of them, underneath the stile, loath to lose its shelter.

'Parkin's what?' asked Homily uneasily.

'Parkin's Beck. You know – the name of the field. This is where they
live, the Hendrearies.'

'You mean,' said Homily, after a pause, 'where the badgers' set is?'

'That's right,' said Pod, staring ahead.

Homily's tired face looked yellow in the golden light; her jaw hung
loose. 'But where?' she asked.

Pod waved his arm. 'Somewhere; it's in this field anyway.'

'In this field . . .' repeated Homily dully, her eyes fixed on the dim boundaries, the distant group of shadowy trees.

'Well, we got to look,' explained Pod uneasily. 'You didn't think we'd go straight to it, did you?'

'I thought you knew where it was,' said Homily. Her voice sounded husky. Arrietty, between them, stood strangely silent.

'Well, I've brought you this far. Haven't I?' said Pod. 'If the worst comes to the worst, we can camp for the night, and look round in the morning.'

'Where's the stream?' asked Arrietty. 'There's supposed to be a stream.'

'Well, there is,' said Pod, 'it flows down there, along that distant hedge, and then comes in like – do you see? – across that far corner. That thicker green there – can't you see? – them's rushes.'

Arrietty screwed up her eyes. 'Yes,' she said uncertainly, and added: 'I'm thirsty.'

'And so am I,' said Homily; she sat down suddenly as though deflated. 'All the way up that hill, step after step, hour after hour, I bin saying to meself "Never mind, the first thing we'll do as soon as we get to that badgers' set is sit down and have a nice cup o' tea" – it kept me going.'

'Well, we will have one,' said Pod. 'Arrietty's got the candle.'

'And I'll tell you another thing,' went on Homily, staring ahead, 'I couldn't walk across that there field, not if you offered me a monkey in a cage: we'll have to go round by the edges.'

'Well, that's just what we're going to do,' said Pod, 'you don't find no badgers' sets in the middle of a field. We'll work round, systematic-like, bit by bit, starting out in the morning. But we got to sleep rough tonight, that's one thing certain. No good poking about tonight: it'll be dark soon; the sun's near off that hill already.'

'And there are clouds coming up,' said Arrietty, gazing at the sunset, 'and moving fast.'

'Rain?' cried Homily, in a stricken voice.

'Well, we'll move fast,' said Pod, slinging his pack up. 'Here, give me yours, Homily, you'll travel lighter . . .'

'Which way are we going?' asked Arrietty.

'We'll keep along by this lower hedge,' said Pod, setting off. 'And make towards the water. If we can't make it before the rain comes, we'll just take any shelter.'

'What sort of shelter?' asked Homily, stumbling after him through the tussocky grass. 'Look out, Pod, them's nettles!'

'I can see them,' said Pod (they were walking in a shallow ditch). 'A hole or something,' he went on. 'There's a hole there, for instance. See? Under that root.'

Homily peered at it as she came abreast. 'Oh, I couldn't go in there,' she said, 'there might be something in it.'

'Or we could go right into the hedge,' Pod called back.

'There's not much shelter in the hedge,' said Arrietty. She walked alone, on the higher ground where the grass was shorter. 'I can see

from here: it's all stems and branches.' She shivered a little in a light wind which set the leaves of the hedge plants suddenly a-tremble, clashing the drying teazles as they swung and locked together. 'It's clouding right over,' she called.

'Yes, it'll be dark soon,' said Pod, 'you'd better come down here with us; you don't want to get lost.'

'I won't get lost; I can see better from here. Look!' she called out suddenly, 'there's an old boot. Wouldn't that do?'

'An old what?' asked Homily incredulously.

'Might do,' said Pod, looking about him. 'Where is it?'

'To your left. There. In the long grass . . .'

'An old boot!' cried Homily, as she saw him set down the borrowing-bags. 'What's the matter with you, Pod – have you gone out of your mind?' Even as she spoke, it began to rain, great summer drops which bounced among the grasses.

'Take the borrowing-bags and get under that dock-leaf – both of you – while I look.'

'An old boot . . .' repeated Homily incredulously, as she and Arrietty crouched under the dock-leaf; she had to raise her voice – the rain, on

the swaying leaf, seemed to clatter rather than patter. 'Hark at it!' complained Homily. 'Come in closer, Arrietty, you'll catch your death. Oh, my goodness me – it's running down my back!'

'Look – he's calling to us,' said Arrietty, 'come on!'

Homily bent her neck and peered out from under the swaying leaf: there stood Pod, some yards away, barely visible among the steaming grasses, dimmed by the curtain of rain. 'A tropical scene,' Arrietty thought, remembering her *Gazetteer of the World.* She thought of man against the elements, jungle swamps, steaming forests, and Mr Living-stone she presumed . . . 'What's he want?' she heard her mother complaining. 'We can't go out in this – look at it!'

'It's coming in under-foot now,' Arrietty told her, 'can't you see? This is a ditch. Come on, we must run for it; he wants us.'

They ran, half-crouching, stunned by the pounding water. Pod pulled them up into the longer grass, snatching their borrowing-bags, gasping instructions, as they slid and slithered after him through – what Arrietty thought of as 'the bush'.

'Here it is,' said Pod. 'Get in here.'

The boot lay on its side; they had to crouch to enter. 'Oh, my goodness,' Homily kept saying. 'Oh, my goodness me . . .' and would glance fearfully about the darkness inside. 'I wonder whoever wore it.'

'Go on,' said Pod, 'get farther down; it's all right.'

'No, no,' said Homily, 'I'm not going in no farther: there might be something in the toe.'

'It's all right,' said Pod, 'I've looked: there's nothing but a hole in the toe.' He stacked the borrowing-bags against the inner side. 'Something to lean against,' he said.

'I wish I knew who'd wore this boot,' Homily went on, peering about uncomfortably, wiping her wet face on her wetter apron.

'What good would that do you?' Pod said, untying the strings of the largest bag.

'Whether he was clean or dirty or what,' said Homily, 'and what he died of. Suppose he died of something infectious?'

'Why suppose he died?' said Pod. 'Why shouldn't he be hale and hearty, and just had a nice wash and be sitting down to a good tea this very minute.'

'Tea?' said Homily, her face brightening. 'Where's the candle, Pod?'

'It's here,' said Pod. 'Give me a wax-vesta, Arrietty, and a medium-sized aspirin lid. We got to go careful with the tea, you know; we got to go careful with everything.'

Homily put out a finger and touched the worn leather. 'I'll give this boot a good clean out in the morning,' she said.

'It's not bad,' said Pod, taking out the half nail-scissor. 'If you ask me, we been lucky to find a boot like this. There ain't nothing to worry about: it's disinfected, all right – what with the sun and the wind and the rain, year after year of it.' He stuck the blade of the nail-scissor through an eyelet hole and lashed it firm with a bit of old bootlace.

'What are you doing that for, Papa?' asked Arrietty.

'To stand the lid on, of course,' said Pod, 'a kind of bracket over the candle; we haven't got no tripod. Now you go and fill it with water, there's a good girl – there's plenty outside . . .'

There was plenty outside: it was coming down in torrents; but the mouth of the boot faced out of the wind and there was a little dry patch before it. Arrietty filled the tin lid quite easily by tipping a large pointed fox-glove leaf towards it so the rain ran off and down the point. All about her was the steady sound of rain, and the lighted candle within the boot made the dusk seem darker: there was a smell of wildness, of space, of leaves and grasses and, as she turned away with the filled tin-lid, another smell – winy, fragrant, spicy. Arrietty took note of it to remember it for morning – it was the smell of wild strawberries.

After they had drunk their hot tea and eaten a good half of sweet, crumbly digestive biscuit, they took off their wet outer clothes and hung them out along the handle of the nail-scissor above the candle. With the old woollen sock about their three shoulders, they talked a little. '. . . Funny,' Arrietty remarked, 'to be wrapped in a sock and inside a boot.' But Pod, watching the candle flame, was worried about wastage and, when the clothes had steamed a little, he doused the flame. Tired out, they lay down at last among the borrowing-bags, cuddled together for warmth. The last sound Arrietty heard as she fell asleep was the steady drumming of the rain on the hollow leather of the boot.

CHAPTER SIX

'SUCH IS THE TREE, SUCH IS THE FRUIT'
End of great railway strike at Peoria, Ill., 1891
[*Extract from Arrietty's Diary and Proverb Book, 26th August*]

ARRIETTY was the first to wake. 'Where am I!' she wondered. She felt warm – too warm, lying there between her mother and father – and when slightly she turned her head she saw three little golden suns, floating in the darkness; it was a second or two before she realized what they were, and with this knowledge memory flooded back – all that happened yesterday: the escape, the frenzied scramble across the orchard, the weary climb, the rain – the little golden suns, she realized, were the lace-holes of the boot!

Stealthily Arrietty sat up; a balmy freshness stole in upon her and, framed in the neck of the boot, she saw the bright day: grasses, softly stirring, tenderly sunlit: some were broken, where yesterday they had pushed through them dragging the borrowing-bags; there was a yellow buttercup, sticky and gleaming, it looked – like wet paint; on a tawny stalk of sorrel she saw an aphis – of a green so delicate that, against the sunlight, it looked transparent. 'Ants milk them,' Arrietty remembered, 'perhaps we could.'

She slid out from between her sleeping parents and, just as she was, with bare feet and in her vest and petticoat, she ventured out of doors.

It was a glorious day, sunlit and rain-washed – the earth breathing out its scents. 'This,' Arrietty thought, 'is what I have longed for; what I have imagined; what I knew existed – what I knew we'd have!'

She pushed through the grasses and soft drops fell on her benignly, warmed by the sun. Downhill a little way she went, towards the hedge, out of the jungle of higher grass, into the shallow ditch where, last night, the rain and darkness had combined to scare her.

There was warm mud here, between the shorter grass blades, fast-drying now in the sun; a bank rose between her and the hedge: a glorious bank, it was, filled with roots; with grasses; with tiny ferns; with small sandy holes; with violet leaves and with pale scarlet pimpernel and, here and there, a globe of deeper crimson – wild strawberries!

She climbed the bank – leisurely and happily, feeling the warm sun through her vest, her bare feet picking their way more delicately than clumsy human feet. She gathered three strawberries, heavy with juice, and ate them luxuriously, lying full-length on a sandy terrace before a mouse-hole. From this bank she could see across the field, but today it looked different – as large as ever; as oddly tilted; but alight and alive with the early sunshine: now all the shadows ran a different way, dewy – they seemed – on the gleaming golden grass. She saw in the distance the lonely group of trees: they still seemed to float on a grassy ocean. She thought of her mother's fear of open spaces. 'But I could cross this field,' she thought, 'I could go anywhere . . .' Was this, perhaps, what Eggletina had thought? Eggletina – Uncle Hendreary's child – who, they said, had been eaten by the cat. Did enterprise, Arrietty wondered, always meet with disaster? Was it really better, as her parents had always taught her, to live in secret darkness underneath the floor?

The ants were out, she saw, and busy about their business – flurried, eager, weaving their anxious routes among the grass stems; every now and again, Arrietty noticed, waving its antennae, an ant would run up a grass stem and look around. A great contentment filled Arrietty: yes – here they were, for better or worse – there could be no going back!

Refreshed by the strawberries, she went on up the bank and into the shade of the hedge: here was sun-flecked greenness and a hollowness above her. Up and up as far as she could see there were layers and storeys of green chambers, crossed and recrossed with springing branches: cathedral-like, the hedge seemed from the inside.

Arrietty put her foot on a lower branch and swung herself up into the green shadows: quite easy, it was, with branches to her hand on all sides – easier than climbing a ladder; a ladder as high as this would mean a feat of endurance, and a ladder at best was a dull thing, whereas

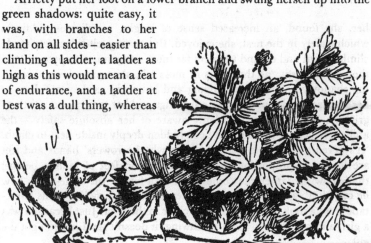

here was variety, a changing of direction, exploration of heights unknown. Some twigs were dry and rigid, shedding curls of dusty bark; others were lissom and alive with sap: on these she would swing a little (as so often she had dreamed of swinging in that other lifetime under the floor!). 'I will come here when it is windy,' she told herself, 'when the whole hedge is alive and swaying in the wind . . .'

Up and up she went. She found an old bird's-nest, the moss inside was straw-dry. She climbed into it and lay for a while and, leaning over the edge, dropped crumbled pieces of dried moss through the tangled branches below her; to watch them plummet between the boughs gave

her, she found, an increased sense of height, a delicious giddiness which, safely in the nest, she enjoyed. But having felt this safety made climbing out and on and up seem far more dangerous. 'Suppose I fell,' thought Arrietty, 'as those bits of moss fell, skimming down through the shadowy hollows and banging and bouncing as they go?' But, as her hands closed round the friendly twigs and her toes spread a little to grip the bark, she was suddenly aware of her absolute safety – the ability (which for so long had been hidden deeply inside her) to climb. 'It's heredity,' she told herself, 'that's why borrowers' hands and feet are longer in proportion than the hands and feet of human beings; that's how my father can come down by a fold in the table-cloth; how he can climb a curtain by the bobbles; how he can swing on his name-tape from a desk to a chair, from a chair to the floor. Just because I was a girl, and not allowed to go borrowing, it doesn't say I haven't got the gift . . .'

Suddenly, raising her head, she saw the blue sky above her, through
the tracery of leaves – leaves which trembled and whispered as, in her
haste, she swayed their stems. Placing her foot in a fork and swinging
up, she caught her petticoat on a wild rose thorn and heard it rip. She
picked the thorn out of the stuff and held it in her hand (it was the size
to her of a rhinoceros-horn to a human being): it was light in proportion
to its bulk, but very sharp and vicious looking. 'We could use this for
something,' Arrietty thought. 'I must think . . . some kind of

weapon . . .' One more pull and her head and shoulders were outside
the hedge; the sun fell hot on her hair, and dazzled by the brightness
she screwed her eyes up as she gazed about her.

Hills and dales, valleys, fields and woods – dreaming in the sunshine;
she saw there were cows in the next field but one. Approaching the
wood, from a field on the lower side, she saw a man with a gun – very
far away, he looked, very harmless. She saw the roof of Aunt Sophy's
house and the kitchen chimney smoking. On the turn of a distant road,
as it wound between the hedges, she saw a milk-cart: the sunlight
flashed on the metal churn and she heard the faint fairy-like tinkle of
the harness brasses. What a world – mile upon mile, thing after thing,

layer upon layer of unimagined richness – and she might never have seen it! She might have lived and died as so many of her relations had done, in dusty twilight – hidden behind a wainscot.

Coming down, she felt a rhythm: a daring swing, a letting go, and a light drop into thickly clustered leaves which her instinct told her would act as a safety net – a cage of lissom twigs, which sprang to hand and foot – lightly to be caught, lightly to be let go. Such leaves clustered more thickly towards the outside of the hedge, not in the bare hollows within, and her passage amongst them was almost like surf-riding – a controlled and bouncing slither. The last bough dropped her lightly on the slope of a grassy bank, springing back into place above her head, as lightly she let it go, with a graceful elastic shiver.

Arrietty examined her hands: one was slightly grazed. 'But they'll harden up,' she told herself. Her hair stood on end and was filled with bark dust and there in her white embroidered petticoat she saw a great tear.

Hurriedly she picked three more strawberries as a peace-offering and, wrapping them in a violet leaf so as not to stain her vest, she scrambled down the bank, across the ditch, and into the clump of long grass.

Homily, at the entrance to the boot, looked worried as usual.

'Oh, Arrietty, wherever have you been? Breakfast's been ready this last twenty minutes. Your father's out of his mind.'

'Why?' asked Arrietty, surprised.

'With worrying about you – with looking for you.'

'I was quite near,' Arrietty said. 'I was only in the hedge. You could have called me.'

Homily put her finger on her lip and glanced in a fearful way from one side to another: 'You can't *call*,' she said, dropping her voice to an angry whisper. 'We're not to make any noise at all, your father says. No calling or shouting – nothing to draw attention. Danger, that's what he said there is – danger on all sides . . .'

'I don't mean you have to whisper,' Pod said, appearing suddenly from behind the boot, carrying the half nail-scissor (he had been cutting a small trail through the thickest grass). 'But don't you go off, Arrietty, never again, without you say just where you're going, and what for, and for how long. Understand?'

'No,' said Arrietty, uncertainly, 'I don't quite. I mean I don't always know what I'm going *for*.' (For what, for instance, had she climbed to the top of the hedge?) 'Where is all this danger? I didn't see any. Excepting three cows two fields away.'

Pod looked thoughtfully to where a sparrow-hawk hung motionless in the clear sky.

'It's everywhere,' he said, after a moment. 'Before and Behind, Above and Below.'

CHAPTER SEVEN

'PUFF AGAINST THE WIND'
Oxford and Harvard Boat Race, 1869
[*Extract from Arrietty's Diary and Proverb Book, 27th August*]

WHILE Homily and Arrietty were finishing breakfast, Pod got busy: he walked thoughtfully around the boot, surveying it from different angles; he would touch the leather with a practised hand, peer at it closely, and then stand back, half-closing his eyes; he removed the borrowing-bags, one by one, carefully stacking them on the grass outside, and then he crawled inside; they could hear him grunting and panting a little as he knelt, and stopped and measured – he was, they gathered, making a carefully calculated examination of seams, joins, floor space, and quality of stitching.

After a while he joined them as they sat there on the grass. 'Going to be a hot day,' he said thoughtfully, as he sat down, 'a real scorcher.' He removed his neck-tie and heaved a sigh.

'What was you looking at, Pod?' asked Homily, after a moment.

'You saw,' said Pod, 'that boot.' He was silent a moment, and then, 'That's no tramp's boot,' he said, 'nor that boot weren't made for no working man neither: that boot,' went on Pod, staring at Homily, 'is a gentleman's boot.'

'Oh,' breathed Homily in a relieved voice, half-closing her eyes and fanning her face with a limp hand, 'thank goodness for that!'

'Why, Mother,' asked Arrietty, irritated, 'what's wrong with a working man's boot? Papa's a working man, isn't he?'

Homily smiled and shook her head in a pitying way. 'It's a question,' she said, 'of quality.'

'Your mother's right there,' said Pod. 'Hand-sewn that boot is, and as fine a bit of leather as ever I've laid me hand on.' He leaned towards Arrietty. 'And you see, lass, a gentleman's boot is well cared for, well greased and dubbined – years and years of it. If it hadn't been, don't you see, it would never have stood up – as this boot has stood up – to wind and rain and sun and frost. They pays dear for their boots, gentlemen do, but they sees they gets good value.'

'That's right,' agreed Homily, nodding her head and looking at Arrietty.

'Now, that hole in the toe,' Pod went on, 'I can patch that up with a bit of leather from the tongue. I can patch that up good and proper.'

'It's not worth the time nor the thread,' exclaimed Homily. 'I mean to say, just for a couple o' nights or a day or two: it's not as though we were going to *live* in a boot,' she pointed out, with an amused laugh.

Pod was silent a moment and then he said slowly: 'I bin thinking.'

'I mean to say,' Homily went on, 'we do know we got relations in this field and — though I wouldn't call a badgers' set a proper home, mind – at least it's somewhere.'

Pod raised solemn eyes. 'Maybe,' he said, in the same grave voice, 'but all the same, I bin thinking. I bin thinking,' he went on; 'relations or no relations, they're still borrowers, ain't they? And among human beings, for instance, who ever sees a borrower?' He gazed round challengingly.

'Well, that boy did,' began Arrietty, 'and –'

'Ah,' said Pod, 'because you, Arrietty, who wasn't no borrower – who hadn't even learned to borrow – went up and talked to him: sought him out, shameless – knowing no better. And I told you just what would happen; hunted out, I said we'd be, by cats and rat-catchers – by policemen and all. Now was I right or wasn't I?'

'Yes, you were right,' said Arrietty, 'but –'

'There ain't no buts,' said Pod. 'I was right. And if I was right then, I'm right now. See? I bin thinking and what I bin thinking is right – and, this time, there ain't going to be no nonsense from you. Nor from your mother, neither.'

'There won't be no nonsense from me, Pod,' said Homily in a pious voice.

'Now,' said Pod, 'this is how it strikes me: human beings stand high and move fast; when you stand higher you can see farther – do you get me? What I mean to say is – if, with them advantages, a human being can't never find a borrower ... even goes as far as to say they don't believe borrowers *exist*, why should we borrowers – who stand lower and move slower, compared to them like – hope to do much better? Living in a house, say, with several families – well, of course, we know each other ... stands to reason: we been brought up together. But come afield, to a strange place like this and – this is how it seems to me – borrowers is hid from borrowers.'

'Oh my –' said Homily unhappily.

'We don't move "slow" exactly,' said Arrietty.

'Compared to them, I said. Our legs move *fast* enough – but theirs is longer: look at the ground they cover!' He turned to Homily. 'Now don't upset yourself. I don't say we won't find the Hendrearies – maybe we will . . . quite soon. Or anyway before the winter –'

'The winter . . .' breathed Homily in a stricken voice.

'But we got to plan,' went on Pod, 'and act, as though there weren't no badgers' set. Do you see what I mean?'

'Yes, Pod,' said Homily huskily.

'I bin thinking it out,' he repeated. 'Here we are, the three of us, with what we got in the bags, two hat-pins, and an old boot: we got to face up to it and, what's more,' he added solemnly, 'we got to live different.'

'How different?' asked Homily.

'Cold food, for instance. No more hot tea. No coffee. We got to keep the candle and the matches in hand for winter. We got to look about us and see what there is.'

'Not caterpillars, Pod,' pleaded Homily, 'you promised! I couldn't never eat a caterpillar.'

'Nor you shall,' said Pod, 'not if I can help it. There's other things, this time o' year, plenty. Now, I want you to get up, the two of you, and see how this boot drags.'

'How do you mean?' asked Homily, mystified, but obediently they both stood up.

'See these laces?' said Pod, 'good and strong – been oiled, that's why . . . or tarred. Now, you each take a lace over your shoulder and pull. Turn your back to the boot – that's right – and just walk forward.'

Homily and Arrietty leaned on the traces and the boot came on with a bump and a slither so fast across the slippery grass that they stumbled and fell – they had not expected it would be so light.

'Steady on!' cried Pod, running up beside them. 'Take it steady, can't you? Up you get – that's the way . . . steady, steady . . . that's fine. You see,' he said, when they paused for breath, having dragged the boot to

the edge of the long grass, 'how it goes – like a bird!' Homily and Arrietty rubbed their shoulders and said nothing; they even smiled slightly, a pale reflection of Pod's pride and delight. 'Now sit down, both of you. You was fine. Now, you'll see, this is going to be good.'

He stood beaming down at them as, meekly, they sat on the grass. 'It's like this,' he explained. 'I talked just now of danger – to you, Arrietty – and that's because, though brave we must be (and there's none braver than your mother when she's put to it), we can't never be foolhardy: we got to make our plans and we got to keep our heads; we can't afford to waste no energy – climbing hedges just for fun, and suchlike – and we can't afford to take no risks. We got to make our plan and we got to stick to it. Understand?'

'Yes,' said Arrietty, and Homily nodded her head.

'Your father's right,' she said.

'You got to have a main object,' went on Pod, 'and ours is there, ready-made – we got to find the badgers' set. Now how are we going to set about it? It's a big field – take us the best part of a day to get along one side of it, let alone have time to look down holes; and we'd be wore out, that's what we'd be. Say I went off looking by myself – well, your mother would never know a moment's peace all day long, till she had me safe back again: there's nothing bad enough for what she'd be imagining. *And* going on at you, Arrietty. Now, that's all wear and tear, and we can't afford too much of it. Folk get silly when they're fussed, if you see what I mean, and that's when accidents happen.

'Now, my idea,' Pod went on, 'is this: we'll work our way all round this field, like I said last night, by the edges –'

'Hedges,' corrected Arrietty, under her breath, without thinking.

'I heard what you said, Arrietty,' remarked Pod quietly (he seldom grudged her superior education); 'there's hedges and edges, and I meant edges.'

'Sorry,' murmured Arrietty, blushing.

'As I was saying,' Pod went on, 'we'll work our way round, systematic-like, exploring the banks and' – he looked at Arrietty pointedly – 'hedges – and camping as we go: a day here, a day or two there, just as we feel; or depending on the holes and burrows; there'll be great bits of bank where there couldn't be no badgers' set – we can skip those, as you might say. Now you see, Homily, we couldn't do this if we had a settled home.'

'You mean,' asked Homily sharply, 'that we've got to drag the boot?'

'Well,' said Pod, 'was it heavy?'

'With all our gear in it, it would be.'

'Not over grass,' said Pod.

'And uphill!' exclaimed Homily.

'*Level* here at the bottom of the field,' corrected Pod patiently, 'as far as them rushes; then uphill at the top of the field, alongside the stream; then across – *level* again; then the last lap of all, which brings us back to the stile again, and it's downhill all the way!'

'Um-m-m,' said Homily, unconvinced.

'Well,' said Pod, 'out with it – speak your mind: I'm open to suggestions.'

'Oh, Mother –' began Arrietty in a pleading voice, and then became silent.

'Has Arrietty and me got to drag all the time?' asked Homily.

'Now, don't be foolish,' said Pod, 'we take it in turns, of course.'

'Oh well,' sighed Homily, 'what can't be cured, needs must.'

'That's my brave old girl,' said Pod. 'Now about provender – *food*,' he explained, as Homily looked up bewildered, 'we better become vegetarian, pure and simple, one and all, and make no bones about it.'

'There won't be no bones to make,' remarked Homily grimly, 'not if we become vegetarian.'

'The nuts is coming on,' said Pod; 'nearly ripe they'll be down in that sheltered corner – milky like. Plenty of fruit – blackberries, them wild strawberries. Plenty of salad, dandelion, say, and sorrel. There's gleanings still in that cornfield t'other side of the stile. We'll manage – the thing is you got to get used to it: no hankering for boiled ham, chicken rissoles, and that kind of fodder. Now, Arrietty,' he went on, 'as you're so set on hedge-climbing, you and your mother had better go off and gather us some nuts, how's that, eh? And I'll get down to a bit of cobbling.' He glanced at the boot.

'Where do you find the nuts?' asked Arrietty.

'There, about half-way along' – Pod pointed to a thickening of pale green in the hedge – 'before you get to the water. You climb up, Arrietty, and throw 'em down, and your mother can gather 'em up. I'll come down and join you later: we got to dig a pit.'

'A pit? Whatever for?' asked Arrietty.

'We can't carry that weight of nuts around,' explained Pod, 'not in a boot this size. Wherever we find provender, we got to make a cache like, and mark it down for winter.'

'Winter . . .' moaned Homily softly.

Nevertheless, as Arrietty helped her mother over the rough places in

the ditch, which – because it was
shallow, well drained, and fairly sheltered – could be used as a highway,
she felt closer to Homily than she had felt
for years: more like a sister, as she put it.
'Oh, look,' cried Homily, when they saw
a scarlet pimpernel; she stooped and
picked it by its hair-pin stalk. 'In't it
lovely?' she said in a tender voice; touching the fragile petals with a work-worn
finger, she tucked it into the opening of
her blouse. Arrietty found a pale-blue
counterpart in the delicate bird's-eye, and
put it in her hair; and suddenly the day
began to seem like a holiday. 'Flowers
made for borrowers,' she thought.

At last they reached the nutty part of
the hedge. 'Oh, Arrietty,' exclaimed
Homily, gazing up at the spreading
branches with mingled pride and fear,
'you can't never go up there.'

But Arrietty could and would: she was
delighted to show off her climbing. In a
workmanlike manner she stripped off her
jersey, hung it on a grey-green spike of
thistle, rubbed her palms together (in
front of Homily she did not like to spit on
them), and clambered up the bank.

Homily watched below, her two hands
clasped and pressed against her heart,
how the outer leaves shivered and shook
as Arrietty, invisible, climbed up inside.
'Are you all right?' she kept calling. 'Oh,
Arrietty, do be careful. Suppose you fell
and broke your leg?' And then after a
while the nuts began to come down, and
poor Homily, under fire, ran this way and
that, in her panting efforts to retrieve
them.

Not that they came down fast enough

to be really dangerous. Nut-gathering was not quite so easy as Arrietty had imagined: for one thing, it was still a little early in the season and the nuts were not quite ripe; each was still encased in what to Arrietty looked something like a tough, green fox-glove bell, and was fixed firmly to the tree. It was quite an effort, until she learned the trick of a sharp twist, for Arrietty to detach the clusters. And what was more, even to reach them was not easy: it meant climbing or swinging or edging her body along a perilously swaying branch tip (later Pod made her, with a piece of lead, some twine, and a supple dock root, a kind of swinging cosh with which she could strike them down); but she persevered, and soon there was a sizeable pile in the ditch, neatly stacked up by the perspiring Homily.

'That'll do now,' Homily called out breathlessly after a while. 'No more or your poor pa will never get through with the digging,' and Arrietty, hot and dishevelled, with scratched face and smarting hands, thankfully climbed down. She flung herself full length in the speckled shade of a clump of cow-parsley and complained of feeling thirsty.

'Well, there's water farther along, so your pa says. Do you think you could walk it?'

Of course Arrietty could walk it. Tired she might be, but determined to foster this new-found spirit of adventure in her mother. She caught up her jersey and they set off along the ditch.

The sun was higher now and the ground was hotter. They came to a place where some beetles were eating a long-dead mole. 'Don't look,' said Homily, quickening her step and averting her eyes, as though it were a street accident.

But Arrietty, more practical for once, said: 'But when they've finished, perhaps we ought to have the skin. It might come in useful,' she pointed out, 'for winter.'

'Winter . . .' breathed Homily. 'You say it to torment me,' she added in a sudden spurt of temper.

The stream when they reached it seemed less a stream than a small clear pond, disturbed as they approached by several plops and spreading silvery circles as frogs, alarmed, dived in. It meandered out of a tangled wood beyond the hedge and, crossing the corner of the field, had spread into a small marsh of cresses, mud, and deep-sunk cattle-tracks. On the farther side of the stream the field was bounded, not by a junction of hedges but by several mildewed posts hung with rusty wire slung across the water; beyond this frail barrier the shadowed tree trunks of the wood seemed to crowd and glower as though they longed to rush forward across the strip of water into the sunlit field. Arrietty saw a powdery haze of wild forget-me-not, with here and there a solitary bulrush; the dry-edged cattle-tracks were water-filled chasms criss-crossed with dikes and there was a delicious smell of fragrant slime, lightly spiced with spearmint. A sinuous feathered current of clear ripples broke the still, sky-reflecting surface of the miniature lake. It was very beautiful, Arrietty thought, and strangely exciting; she had never seen so much water before.

'Watercress!' announced Homily in a flat voice. 'We'll take a bit o' that for tea . . .'

They picked their way along the raised ridges of the cow craters whose dark pits of stagnant water reflected the cloudless sky. Arrietty, stooping over them, saw her own clear image sharply focused against the dreaming blue, but oddly tilted and somehow upside-down.

'Careful you don't fall in, Arrietty,' warned Homily, 'you only got one change, remember. You know,' she went on in an interested voice, pointing at a bulrush, 'I could have used one of those back home, under the kitchen. Just the thing for cleaning out the flues. Wonder your father never thought of it. And don't drink yet,' advised Homily, 'wait till we get where the water's running. Same with watercress, you don't want to pick it where the water's stagnant. You never know what you might get.'

At last they found a place from where it would be possible to drink: a solid piece of bark, embedded firmly in the mud yet stretching out into the stream forming a kind of landing stage or rough jetty. It was grey and knobbly and looked like a basking crocodile. Arrietty stretched her length on the cork-like surface and cupping her hands took long draughts of the cool water. Homily, after some hesitation and arrange-ments of skirts, did the same. 'Pity,' she remarked, 'we don't have a jug nor a pail, nor some kind of bottle. We could do with some water in the boot.'

Arrietty did not reply; she was gazing happily down past the drifting surface into the depths below.

'Can vegetarians eat fish?' she asked, after a while.

'I don't rightly know,' said Homily; 'we'll have to ask your father.' Then the cook in Homily reasserted itself. 'Are there any?' she asked, a trifle hungrily.

'Plenty,' Arrietty murmured dreamily, gazing down into the shifting depths: the stream, she thought, seemed to be gently breathing. 'About as long as my forearm. And some invisible things,' she added, 'like shrimps –'

'How do you mean – *invisible?*' asked Homily.

'Well,' explained Arrietty in the same absent voice, 'I mean you can see through them. And some black things,' she went on, 'like blobs of expanding velvet –'

'Leeches, I shouldn't wonder,' remarked Homily with a slight shudder, and added dubiously after a moment's thought: 'Might be all right stewed.'

'Do you think papa could make a fishing-net?' asked Arrietty.

'Your father can make anything,' asserted Homily loyally. 'No matter what – you've only got to name it.'

Arrietty lay quiet for a while, dozing she seemed on this sun-soaked piece of bark, and when at last she spoke Homily gave a startled jump – she, too, lulled for once into quietness, had begun to float away. 'Never do,' she thought, 'to drop off to sleep on a log like this: you might turn over.' And she roused herself by an inward shake and rapidly blinked her eyes.

'What did you say, Arrietty?' she asked.

'I said,' Arrietty went on after a moment in a lilting lazy voice (she spoke as though she too had been dreaming), 'couldn't we bring the boot down here? Right beside the water?'

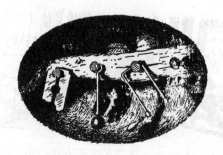

CHAPTER EIGHT

'EVERYMAN'S HOUSE IS HIS CASTLE'
Great Fire of London began 1666
[*Extract from Arrietty's Diary and Proverb Book, 2nd September*]

AND that is just what they did do. Pod, consulted, had looked over the site, weighed the pros and cons, and rather ponderously, as though it was his own idea, decided they should move camp. They would choose a site farther along the hedge as near as was safe to the brook. 'Homily can do her washing. You got to have water,' he announced, but rather defensively as though he had only just thought of it. 'And I *might* make a fish-net, at that.'

The boot, though fully loaded, ran quite easily along the shallow ditch with all three of them in harness. The site Pod had chosen was a platform or alcove halfway up the steepish bank below the hedge.

'You want to keep fairly high,' he explained (as, to make it lighter for hauling, they unpacked the boot in the ditch), 'with rain like we had the other night and the brook so near. You got to remember,' he went on, selecting a sharp tool, 'that flood we had back home when the kitchen boiler burst.'

'What do you mean,' sniffed Homily, 'got to remember? Scalding hot, that one was, too.' She straightened her back and gazed up the slope at the site.

It was well chosen: a kind of castle, Arrietty had called it, in which they would live in the dungeons, but in their case the dungeon was more like an alcove, open to the sun and air. A large oak-tree, at one time part of the hedge, had been sawn off at the base; solid and circular, it stood above the bank where the hedge thinned, like the keep of a fortress, its roots flung out below as flying buttresses. Some of these were not quite dead and had shot forth here and there a series of suckers like miniature oak-trees. One of these saplings overhung their cave, shading its lip with sun-flecked shadow.

The underside of a large root formed the roof of their alcove and other smaller roots supported the walls and floor. These last, Pod pointed out, would come in handy as beams and shelves.

He was busy now (while the boot still lay in the ditch) extracting some nails from the heel.

169

'It seems a shame,' remarked Homily as she and Arrietty sorted out belongings for earlier transportation. 'You'll loosen the whole heel.'

'What good's the heel to us?' asked Pod, perspiring with effort; 'we ain't going to wear the boot. And I need the nails,' he added firmly.

The flat top of the tree-trunk, they decided, would come in useful as a look-out, a bleaching-ground for washing, and a place for drying herbs and fruit. Or for grinding corn. Pod was urged to chip out foot-holes in the bark for easier climbing. (This he did later, and for years after these foot-holes were considered by naturalists to be the work of the greater spotted woodpecker.)

'We got to dig a cache for these nuts,' remarked Pod, straightening his aching back, 'but better we get all ship-shape here first and snug for the night, as you might say. Then after the digging we can come home straight to bed.'

Seven nails, Pod decided, were enough for the moment (it was tough work extracting them). The idea had come to him when he had been mending the hole in the toe. Heretofore he had only worked on the softest of glove leathers and his little cobbler's needle was too frail to pierce the tough hide of the boot. Using the electric bell-clapper as a hammer, he had pierced (with the help of a nail) a series of matching holes – in the boot itself and the tongue which was meant to patch it; then all he had to do was to thread in some twine.

By the same token, he had made a few eyelet holes round the ankle of the boot so they could, if necessary, lash it up at night – as campers would close a tent flap.

It did not take them long to drag the empty boot up the slope, but wedging it firmly in the right position under the main root of the alcove was a tricky business and took a good deal of manoeuvring. At last it was done – and they left panting but relieved.

The boot lay on its side, sole against the rear wall and ankle facing outwards, so that if disturbed at night they could spot the intruder approaching, and when they woke in the morning they would get the early sun.

Pod drove a series of nails along one shelf-like root on the right wall of the alcove (the left wall was almost completely taken up by the boot), on which he hung his tools: the half nail-scissor, the fret-saw, the bell-clapper, and the piece of razor-blade.

Above this shelf was a sandy recess which Homily could use as a larder; it went in quite deep.

When Pod had placed the larger hat-pin in a place of strategic importance near the mouth of the alcove (the smaller one they were to keep in the boot in case, Pod said, 'of these alarms at night') they felt they had met the major demands of the moment and, though tired, they felt a pleasant sense of achievement and of effort well spent.

'Oh, my back,' exclaimed Homily, her hands in the small of it. 'Let's just sit down, Pod, for a moment and rest quietly and look at the view.' And it was worth looking at in the afternoon sunlight: they could see right away across the field. A pheasant flew out of the far group of trees and whirred away to the left.

'We can't sit for long,' said Pod, after a moment; 'we got to dig that cache.'

Wearily, they collected the half nail-scissor and a borrowing-bag for anything they might see on the way, and the three of them climbed down the bank.

'Never mind,' Pod comforted Homily as they made their way along the ditch, 'we can go straight to bed after. And you haven't got no cooking,' he reminded her.

Homily was not comforted. As well as tired she realized suddenly she was feeling very hungry, but not – she reflected glumly – somehow, for nuts.

When they reached the place and Pod had removed the first sods in order to reach the soil (great shrubs these were to him, like uprooting clumps of pampas), Homily revived a little – determined to play her part: courageous helpmate, it was today. She had never dug before but the prospect faintly excited her. Strange things are possible in this odd world and she might (one never knew) discover a new talent.

They had to take it in turns with the half nail-scissor. ('Never mind,' Pod told them. 'I'll set to work tomorrow and rig us up a couple of spades.')

Homily screamed when she saw her first worm: it was as long as she was – even longer, she realized as the last bit wriggled free. 'Pick it up,' shouted Pod; 'it won't hurt you. You got to learn.' And before Arrietty (who was not too keen on worms herself) could volunteer to help, she saw her mother, with set face and tensed muscles, lay hold of the writhing creature and drop it some inches beyond the hole, where gratefully it writhed away among the grasses. 'It was heavy,' Homily remarked – her only comment – as she went back to her digging; but Arrietty thought she looked a trifle pale. After her third worm, Homily became slightly truculent – she handled it with the professional casualness of an experienced snake charmer – almost bored, she seemed. Arrietty was much impressed. It was a different story, however, when her mother dug up a centipede – then Homily not only screamed but ran, clutching her skirts, half-way up the bank, where she stood on a flat stone, almost gibbering. She only consented to rejoin them when Pod, tickling the squirming creature with the tip of the nail-scissor, sent it scuttling angrily into the 'bush'.

They carried a few nuts home for supper: these, and several wild strawberries, a leaf or two of watercress, washed down with cold water, made an adequate though dismal repast. There seemed to be something lacking; a bit of digestive biscuit would have been nice, or a good cup of hot tea. But the last piece of biscuit, Homily decided, must be kept

for breakfast, and the tea (Pod had ordained) only for celebrations and emergencies.

But they slept well all the same; and felt safe, tucked away under their protecting root, with the boot laced up in front. It was a little airless, perhaps, but they were far less cramped for space because so many of their belongings could be stacked outside now in the sandy, root-filled annexe.

CHAPTER NINE

'AS YE SOW, SO SHALL YE REAP'
Oliver Cromwell, Protector of England, died 1658
[*Extract from Arrietty's Diary and Proverb Book, 3rd September*]

'Now, today,' said Pod, at breakfast next morning, 'we'd better go gleaning. There's a harvested cornfield yonder. Nuts and fruit is all right,' he went on, 'but for winter we're going to need bread.'

'Winter?' moaned Homily. 'Aren't we supposed to be looking for the badgers' set? And,' she went on, 'who's going to grind the corn?'

'You and Arrietty, couldn't you?' said Pod, 'between two stones.'

'You'll be asking us to make fire with two sticks next,' grumbled Homily, 'and how do you think I make bread without an oven? And what about yeast? Now, if you ask me,' she went on, 'we don't want to go gleaning and trying to make bread and all that nonsense: what we want to do is to put a couple of nuts in our pockets, pick what fruit we see on the way, and have a real good look for the Hendrearies.'

'As you say,' agreed Pod, after a moment, and heaved a sigh.

They tidied away breakfast, put the more precious of their belongings inside the boot and carefully laced it up, and struck out uphill, beyond the water, along the hedge which lay at right angles to the bank in which they had passed the night.

It was a weary trapes. Their only adventure was at midday, when they rested after a frugal luncheon of rain-sodden, overripe blackberries. Homily, lying back against the bank, her drowsy eyes fixed on the space between a stone and a log, saw the ground begin to move; it streamed past the gap, in a limited but constant flow.

'Oh, my goodness, Pod,' she breathed, after watching a moment to make sure it was not an optical illusion, 'do you see what I see? There, by that log . . .' Pod, following the direction of her eyes, did not speak straight away, and when he did it was hardly above a whisper.

'Yes,' he said, seeming to hesitate, 'it's a snake.'

'Oh, my goodness . . .' breathed Homily again in a trembling voice, and Arrietty's heart began to beat wildly.

'Don't move,' whispered Pod, his eyes on the steady ripple: there seemed to be no end – the snake went on and on and on (unless it was, as Arrietty thought afterwards, that Time itself, in a moment of danger,

has often been said to slow down), but just when they felt they could bear the sight not a moment longer, they saw the flick of a tail.

They all breathed again. 'What was it, Pod?' asked Homily weakly. 'An adder?'

'A grass snake, I think,' said Pod.

'Oh,' exclaimed Arrietty, with a relieved little laugh, 'they're harmless.'

Pod looked at her gravely; his currant-bunnish face seemed more doughy than usual. 'To humans,' he said slowly. 'And what's more,' he added, 'you can't talk to snakes.'

'Pity,' remarked Homily, 'that we did not bring one of the hat-pins.'

'What good would that have done?' asked Pod.

By about tea-time (rose-hips, this time: they were sick of sodden blackberries) they found, to their surprise, that they were more than half-way along the third side of the field. There had been more walking than searching; none of the ground they had covered so far could have housed the Hendrearies, let alone a badger colony; the bank, as they made their way uphill beside the hedge, had become lower in proportion until, here where they sat drearily munching rose-hips, there was no bank at all.

'It's almost as far now,' said Pod, 'to go back the same way as we came as to keep on round. What do you say, Homily?'

'We better keep on round, then,' said Homily hoarsely, a hairy seed of a rose-hip being stuck in her throat. She began to cough. 'I thought you said you cleaned them?' she complained to Arrietty, when she could get back her breath.

'I must have missed one,' said Arrietty. 'Sorry,' and she passed her mother a new half-hip, freshly scoured; she had rather enjoyed opening the pale scarlet globes and scooping out the golden nest of close-packed seeds, and she liked the flavour of the hips themselves – they tasted, she thought, of apple-skins honeyed over with a dash of rose petal.

'Well, then,' said Pod, standing up, 'we better start moving.'

The sun was setting when they reached the fourth and last side of the field, where the hedge threw out a ragged carpet of shadow. Through a gap in the dark branches they could see a blaze of golden light on a sea of harvested stubble.

'As we're here,' suggested Pod, standing still and staring through the gap, 'and it's pretty well downhill most the way back now, what's the harm in an ear or two of corn?'

'None,' said Homily wearily, 'if it would walk out and follow us.'

'Corn ain't heavy,' said Pod; 'wouldn't take us no time to pick up a few ears . . .'

Homily sighed. It was she who had suggested this trip, after all. In for a penny, she decided wanly, in for a pound.

'Have it your own way,' she said resignedly.

So they clambered through the hedge and into the cornfield.

And into a strange world (as it seemed to Arrietty), not like the Earth at all: the golden stubble, lit by the evening sun, stood up in rows like a blasted colourless forest; each separate bole threw its own long shadow and all the shadows, combed by the sun in one direction, lay parallel – a bizarre criss-cross of black and gold which flicked and fleckered with every footstep. Between the boles, on the dry straw-strewn earth, grew scarlet pimpernel in plenty, with here and there a ripened ear of wheat.

'Take a bit of stalk, too,' Pod advised them. 'Makes it easier to carry.'

The light was so strange in this broken, beetle-haunted forest that, every now and again, Arrietty seemed to lose sight of her parents but, turning panic-stricken, would find them again quite close, zebra-striped with sun and shadow.

At last they could carry no more and Pod had mercy; they forgathered on their own side of the hedge, each with two bunches of wheat ears, carried head downwards by a short length of stalk. Arrietty was reminded of Crampfurl, back home in the big house, going past the gratings with onions for the kitchen; they had been strung on strings and looked much like these corn grains and in something the same proportion.

'Can you manage all that?' asked Pod anxiously of Homily as she started off ahead down the hill.

'I'd sooner carry it than grind it,' retorted Homily tartly, without looking back.

'There wouldn't be no badgers' sets along this side,' panted Pod (he was carrying the heaviest load), coming abreast of Arrietty. 'Not with all the ploughing, sowing, dogs, men, horses, harrows, and what-not as there must have been –'

'Where could one be, then?' asked Arrietty, setting down her corn for a moment to rest her hands. 'We've been all round.'

'There's only one place to look now,' said Pod; 'them trees in the middle,' and standing still in the deep shadow, he gazed across the stretch of pasture land. The field looked in this light much as it had on that first day (could that only be the day before yesterday?). But from this angle they could not see the trail of dusky shadow thrown by the island of trees.

'Open ground,' said Pod, staring; 'your mother would never make it.'

'I could,' said Arrietty. 'I'd like to go . . .'

Pod was silent. 'I got to think,' he said, after a moment. 'Come on, lass. Take up your corn, else we won't get back before dark.'

They didn't. Or, rather, it was deep dusk along the ditch of their home stretch and almost dark when they came abreast of their cave. But even in the half-light there seemed something suddenly home-like and welcoming about the sight of their laced-up boot.

Homily sank down at the foot of the bank, between her bunches of corn. 'Just a breather,' she explained weakly, 'before that next pull up.'

'Take your time,' said Pod. 'I'll go ahead and undo the laces.' Panting a little, dragging his ears of corn, he started up the bank. Arrietty followed.

'Pod,' called Homily from the darkness below, without turning, 'you know what?'

'What?' asked Pod.

'It's been a long day,' said Homily; 'suppose, tonight, we made a nice cup of tea?'

'Please yourself,' said Pod, unlacing the neck of the boot and feeling cautiously inside. He raised his voice, shouting down at her: 'What you have now, you can't have later. Bring the half-scissor, Arrietty, will you? It's on a nail in the store-room.' After a moment he added impatiently: 'Hurry up. No need to take all day, it's just there to your hand.'

'It isn't,' came Arrietty's voice, after a moment.

'What do you mean – it isn't?'

'It isn't here. Everything else is, though.'

'Isn't there!' exclaimed Pod unbelievingly. 'Wait a minute, let *me* look.' Their voices sounded muffled to Homily, listening below; she wondered what the fuss was about.

'Something or someone's been mucking about in here,' she heard Pod say, after what seemed a distressed pause; and picking up her ears of wheat Homily scrambled up the bank: heavy going, she found it, in the half-light.

'Get a match, will you,' Pod was saying in a worried voice, 'and light the candle,' and Arrietty foraged in the boot to find the wax-vestas.

As the wick guttered, wavered, then rose to a steady flame, the little hollow, half-way up the bank, became illumined like a scene on a stage; strange shadows were cast on the sandy walls of the annexe. Pod and Homily and little Arrietty appeared as they passed back and forth curiously unreal, like characters in a play. There were the borrowing-bags, stacked neatly together as Pod had left them, their mouths tied up with twine; there hung the tools from their beam-like root, and, leaning beside them – as Pod had left it this morning – the purple thistle-head with which he had swept the floor. He stood there now, white-faced in the candlelight, his hand on a bare nail. 'It was here,' he was saying, tapping the nail; 'that's where I left it.'

'Oh, goodness!' exclaimed Homily, setting down her wheat ears. 'Let's just look again.' She pulled aside the borrowing-bags and felt behind them. 'And you, Arrietty,' she ordered, 'could you get round to the back of the boot?'

But it was not there, nor, they discovered suddenly, was the larger hat-pin. 'Anything but them two things,' Pod kept on saying in a worried voice as Homily, for the third or fourth time, went through the contents of the boot. 'The smaller hat-pin's here all right,' she kept repeating, 'we still got one. You see no animal could unlace a boot –'

'But what kind of animal,' asked Pod wearily, 'would take a half nail-scissor?'

'A magpie might,' suggested Arrietty, 'if it looked kind of shiny.'

'Maybe,' said Pod. 'But what about the hat-pin? I don't see a magpie carrying the two. No,' he went on thoughtfully, 'it doesn't look to me like no magpie, nor like any other race of bird. Nor no animal neither, if it comes to that. Nor I wouldn't say it was any kind of human being. A human being, like as not, finding a hole like this smashes the whole place up. Kind of kick with their feet, human beings do out walking 'fore they touch a thing with their hands. Looks to me,' said Pod, 'like something more in the style of a borrower.'

'Oh,' cried Arrietty joyfully, 'then we've found them!'

'Found what?' asked Pod.

'The cousins . . . the Hendrearies . . .'

Pod was silent a moment. 'Maybe,' he said uneasily again.

'Maybe!' mimicked Homily, irritated. 'Who else could it be? They live in this field, don't they? Arrietty, put some water on to boil, there's a good girl; we don't want to waste the candle.'

'Now see here –' began Pod.

'But we can't fix the tin-lid,' interrupted Arrietty, 'without the ring part of the nail-scissor.'

'Oh, goodness me,' complained Homily, 'use your head and think of something! Suppose we'd never had a nail-scissor! Tie a piece of twine round an aspirin lid and hang it over the flame from a nail or a bit of root or something. What were you saying, Pod?'

'I said we got to go careful on the tea, that's all. We was only going to make tea to celebrate like, or in what you might call a case of grave emergency.'

'Well, we are, aren't we?'

'Are what?' asked Pod.

'Celebrating. Looks like we've found what we come for.'

Pod glanced uneasily towards Arrietty who, in the farther corner of the annexe, was busily knotting twine round a ridged edge of a screw-on lid. 'You don't want to go so fast, Homily,' he warned her, lowering his voice, 'nor you don't want to jump to no conclusions. Say it was one of the Hendrearies. All right then, why didn't they leave a word or sign or stay a while and wait for us? Hendreary knows our gear all right – that Proverb book of Arrietty's, say, many's the time he's seen it back home under the kitchen.'

'I don't see what you're getting at,' said Homily in a puzzled voice, watching Arrietty anxiously as gingerly she suspended the water-filled aspirin lid from a root above the candle. 'Careful,' she called out, 'you don't want to burn the twine.'

'What I'm getting at is this,' explained Pod. 'Say you look at the nail-scissor as a blade, a sword, as you might say, and the hat-pin as a spear, say, or a dagger. Well, whoever took them things has armed himself, see what I mean? And left us weaponless.'

'We got the other hat-pin,' said Homily in a troubled voice.

'Maybe,' said Pod, 'but he doesn't know that. See what I mean?'

'Yes,' whispered Homily, subdued.

'Make tea, if you like,' Pod went on, 'but I wouldn't call it a celebration. Not yet, at any rate.'

Homily glanced unhappily towards the candle: above the aspirin lid (she noticed longingly) already there rose a welcome haze of steam. 'Well,' she began, and hesitated, then suddenly she seemed to brighten, 'it comes to the same thing.'

'How do you mean?' asked Pod.

'About the tea,' explained Homily, perking up. 'Going by what you said, stealing our weapons and such – this looks to be something you might call serious. Depends how it strikes you. I mean,' she went on hurriedly, 'there's some I know as might even name it a state of grave emergency.'

'There's some as might,' agreed Pod wanly. Then, suddenly, he sprang aside beating the air with his hands. Arrietty screamed and Homily, for a second, thought they had both gone mad. Then she saw.

A great moth had lumbered into the alcove, attracted by the candle; it was fawn-coloured and (to Homily) hideous, drunk, and blinded with light. 'Save the tea!' she cried, panic-stricken, and seizing the purple thistlehead, beat wildly about the air. Shadows danced every way and, in their shouting and scolding, they hardly noticed a sudden, silent thickening of night swerve in on the dusk; but they felt the wind of its passing, watched the candle gutter, and saw the moth was gone.

'What was that?' asked Arrietty at last, after an awed silence.

'It was an owl,' said Pod. He looked thoughtful.

'It ate the moth?'

'As it would eat you,' said Pod, 'if you went mucking about after dusk. We're living and learning,' he said. 'No more candles after dark. Up with the sun and down with the sun: that's us, from now on.'

'The water's boiling, Pod,' said Homily.

'Put the tea in,' said Pod, 'and douse the light: we can drink all right

in the dark,' and turning away he propped the broom handle back
against the wall and, while Homily was making the tea, he tidied up the
annexe, stacking the ears of wheat alongside the boot, straightening the
borrowing-bags, and generally seeing all was ship-shape for the night.
When he had finished he crossed to the recessed shelf and ran a loving
hand along his neatly hanging row of tools. Just before they doused the
light, he stood for a long time, deep in thought – a quiet hand on a
grimly empty nail.

CHAPTER TEN

'LIKE TURNS TO LIKE'
Republic declared in France, 1870
[*Extract from Arrietty's Diary and Proverb Book, 4th September*]

THEY slept well and woke next morning bright and early. The sun poured slantwise into the alcove and, when Pod had unlaced it, into the neck of the boot. For breakfast Arrietty gathered six wild strawberries and Homily broke up some wheat grains with Pod's small bell-clapper which, sprinkled with water, they ate as cereal. 'And, if you're still hungry, Arrietty,' remarked Homily, 'you can get yourself a nut.' Arrietty was and did.

The programme for the day was arranged as follows: Pod, in view of last night's happening, was to make a solitary expedition across the field to the island of trees in the centre in one last bid to find the badgers' set. Homily, because of her fear of open spaces, would have to stay behind, and Arrietty, Pod said, must keep her company. 'There's plenty of jobs about the house,' he told them. 'To start with you can weather-proof one of the borrowing-bags, rub it all over hard with a bit of candle, and it'll do for carting water. Then you can take the fret-saw and saw off a few hazel-nuts for drinking out of, and while you're about it you can gather a few extra nuts and store them in the annexe, seeing as we don't have a spade. There's a nice bit o' horse-hair I saw, in the hedge going towards the stile, caught on a bramble bush; you can fetch a bit o' that along, if you feel like it, and I'll see about making a fish-net. And a bit more corn-crushing wouldn't come amiss . . .'

'Oh, come on, Pod,' protested Homily. 'Oblige you we'd like to, but we're not black slaves . . .'

'Well,' said Pod, gazing thoughtfully across the ocean of tussocky grass, 'it'll take me pretty near all day – getting there, searching around, and getting back: I don't want you fretting . . .'

'I knew it would end like this,' said Homily later, in a depressed voice, as she and Arrietty were waxing the borrowing-bag. 'What did I tell you always, back home, when you wanted to emigrate? Didn't I tell you just how it would be – draughts, moths, worms, snakes, and what not? And you saw how it was when it rained? What's it going to be like in winter? You tell me that. No one can say I'm not trying,' she went on, 'and no one won't hear a word of grumble pass my lips, but

you mark my words, Arrietty; we won't none of us see another spring.'
And a round tear fell on the waxed cloth and rolled away like a marble.

'What with the rat-catcher,' Arrietty pointed out, 'we wouldn't have
if we'd stayed back home.

'And I wouldn't be surprised,' Homily persisted, 'if that boy wasn't
right. Remember what he said about the end of the race? Our time is
come, I shouldn't wonder. If you ask me, we're dying out.'

But she cheered up a bit when they took the bag down to the
water to fill it up and a sliver of soap to wash with: the drowsy heat
and the gentle stir of ripples past their landing-stage of bark seemed
always to calm her and she even encouraged Arrietty to have a bath
and let her splash about a little in the shallows. For a being so light
the water was incredibly buoyant and it would not be very long,
Arrietty felt, before she would learn to swim. Where she had used
the soap the water went cloudy and softly translucent, the shifting
colour of moonstones.

After her bath Arrietty felt refreshed and left Homily in the annexe
to 'get the tea' and went on up the hedge to collect the horse-hair (not
that there was anything to 'get', Homily thought irritably, setting out
a few hips and haws, some watercress, and, with the bell-clapper, she
cracked a couple of nuts).

The horse-hair, caught on a bramble, was half-way up the hedge, but
Arrietty, refreshed by her dip, was glad of a chance to climb. On the
way down, seeking a foothold, she let out a tiny scream; her toes had
touched, not the cool bark, but something soft and warm. She hung
there, grasping the horse-hair and staring through the leaves: all was
still – nothing but tangled branches, flecked with sunlight. After a
second or two, in which she did not dare to move, a flicker of movement
caught her eye, as though the tip of a branch had moved. Staring she
saw, like a bunch of budding twigs the shape of a brownish hand. It
could not be a hand, of course, she told herself, but that's what it looked
like, with tiny, calloused fingers no larger than her own. Picking up
courage, she touched it with her foot and the hand grasped her toes.
Screaming and struggling, she lost her balance and came tumbling
through the few remaining branches on to the dead leaves below. With
her had fallen a small laughing creature no taller than herself. 'That
frightened you,' it said.

Arrietty stared, breathing quickly. He had a brown face, black
eyes, tousled dark hair, and was dressed in what she guessed to be
shabby moleskin, worn smooth side out. He seemed so soiled and

earth-darkened that he matched not only the dead leaves into which they had fallen but the blackened branches as well. 'Who are you?' she asked.

'Spiller,' he said cheerfully, lying back on his elbows.

'You're filthy,' remarked Arrietty disgustedly after a moment; she still felt breathless and very angry.

'Maybe,' he said.

'Where do you live?'

His dark eyes became sly and amused. 'Here and there,' he said, watching her closely.

'How old are you?'

'I don't know,' he said.

'Are you a boy or a grown-up?'

'I don't know,' he said.

'Don't you ever wash?'

'No,' he said.

'Well,' said Arrietty, after an awkward silence, twisting the coarse strands of greyish horse-hair about her wrist, 'I'd better be going –'

'To that hole in the bank?' he asked – the hint of a jeer in his voice.

Arrietty looked startled. 'Do you know it?' When he smiled, she noticed, his lips turned steeply upwards at the corners making his mouth a 'V': it was the most teasing kind of smile she had ever seen.

'Haven't you ever seen a moth before?' he asked.

'You were watching last night?' exclaimed Arrietty.

'Were it private?' he asked.

'In a way; it's our home.'

But he looked bored suddenly, turning his bright gaze away as though searching the more distant grasses. Arrietty opened her mouth to speak but he silenced her with a peremptory gesture, his eyes on the field below. Very curious, she watched him rise cautiously to his feet and then, in a single movement, spring to a branch above his head, reach for something out of sight, and drop again to the ground. The object, she saw, was a taut, dark bow strung with gut and almost as tall as he was; in the other hand he held an arrow.

Staring into the long grass he laid the arrow to the bow, the gut twanged, and the arrow was gone. There was a faint squeak.

'You've killed it,' cried Arrietty, distressed.

'I meant to,' he replied, and sprang down the bank into the field. He made his way to the tussock of grass and returned after a moment with a dead field-mouse swinging from his hand. 'You got to eat,' he explained.

Arrietty felt deeply shocked, she did not know quite why – at home, under the kitchen, they had always eaten meat; but borrowed meat from the kitchen upstairs; she had seen it raw but she had never seen it killed.

'We're vegetarians,' she said primly. He took no notice: this was just a word to Spiller, one of the noises which people made with their mouths. 'Do you want some meat?' he asked casually. 'You can have a leg.'

'I wouldn't touch it,' cried Arrietty indignantly. She rose to her feet, brushing down her skirt. 'Poor thing,' she said, referring to the field-mouse, 'and I think you're horrid,' she said, referring to him.

'Who isn't?' remarked Spiller, and reached above his head for his quiver.

'Let me look,' begged Arrietty, turning back, suddenly curious.

He passed it to her. It was made, she saw, of a glove finger – the thickish leather of a country glove; the arrows were dry pine-needles, weighted, and tipped with blackthorn.

'How do you stick the thorns to the shaft?' she asked.

'Wild-plum-gum,' sang out Spiller, all in one word.

'Wild-plum-gum?' repeated Arrietty. 'Are they poisoned?' she asked.

'No,' said Spiller, 'fair's fair. Hit or miss. They got to eat – I got to eat. And I kill 'em quicker than an owl does. Nor I don't eat so many,' It was quite a long speech for Spiller. He slung his quiver over his shoulder and turned away. 'I'm going,' he said.

Arrietty scrambled quickly down the bank. 'So am I,' she told him.

They walked along in the dry ditch together. Spiller, she noticed, as she walked glanced sharply about him: the bright black eyes were never still. Sometimes, at a slight rustle in grass or hedge, he would become motionless: there would be no tensing of muscles – he would just cease to move; on such occasions, Arrietty realized, he exactly matched his background. Once he dived into a clump of dead bracken and came out again with a struggling insect.

'Here you are,' he said, and Arrietty, staring, saw some kind of angry beetle.

'What is it?' she asked.

'A cricket. They're nice. Take it.'

'To eat?' asked Arrietty, aghast.

'Eat? No. You take it home and keep it. Sings a treat,' he added.

Arrietty hesitated. 'You carry it,' she said, without committing herself.

When they came abreast of the alcove, Arrietty looked up and saw that Homily, tired of waiting, had dozed off: she was sitting on the sunlit sand and had slumped against the boot.

'Mother,' she called softly from below, and Homily woke at once. 'Here's Spiller . . .' Arrietty went on, a trifle uncertainly.

'Here's what?' asked Homily, without interest. 'Did you get the horse-hair?'

Arrietty, glancing sideways at Spiller, saw that he was in one of his stillnesses and had become invisible. 'It's my mother,' she whispered. 'Speak to her. Go on.'

Homily, hearing a whisper, peered down, screwing her eyelids against the setting sun.

'What shall I say?' asked Spiller. Then, clearing his voice, he made an effort. 'I got a cricket,' he said. Homily screamed. It took her a moment to add the dun-coloured patches together into the shapes of face, eyes, and hands; it was to Homily as though the grass had spoken.

'Whatever is it?' she gasped. 'Oh, my goodness gracious, whatever have you got there?'

'It's a cricket,' said Spiller again, but it was not to this insect Homily referred.

'It's Spiller,' Arrietty repeated more loudly, and in an aside she whispered to Spiller: 'Drop that dead thing and come on up . . .'

Spiller not only dropped the field-mouse but a fleeting echo of some dim, half-forgotten code must have flicked his memory, and he laid aside his bow as well. Unarmed, he climbed the bank.

Homily stared at Spiller rather rudely when he stepped on to the sandy platform before the boot. She moved right forward, keeping him at bay. 'Good afternoon,' she said coldly; it was as though she spoke from the threshold.

Spiller dropped the cricket and propelled it towards her with his toe. 'Here you are,' he said. Homily screamed again, very loudly and angrily, as the cricket scuttled knee high past her skirts and made for the darker shadow behind the boot. 'It's a present, Mother,' Arrietty explained indignantly. 'It's a cricket: it sings –'

But Homily would not listen. 'How dare you! How dare you! How dare you! You naughty, dirty, unwashed boy.' She was nearly in tears. 'How could you? You go straight out of my house this minute. Lucky,' she went on, 'that my husband's not at home, nor my brother Hendreary neither –'

'Uncle Hendreary –' began Arrietty, surprised, and, if looks could kill, Arrietty would have died.

'Take your beetle,' Homily went on to Spiller, 'and go! And never let me

see you here again!' As Spiller hesitated, she added in a fury: 'Do you hear what I say?'

Spiller threw a swift look towards the rear of the boot and a somewhat pathetic one towards Arrietty. 'You better keep it,' he muttered gruffly, and dived off down the bank.

'Oh, Mother!' exclaimed Arrietty reproachfully. She stared at the 'tea' her mother had set out, and even the fact that her mother had filled the half-hips with clover honey milked from the blooms failed to comfort her. 'Poor Spiller! you were rude –'

'Well, who is he? What does he want here? Where did you find him? Forcing his way on respectable people and flinging beetles about! Wouldn't be surprised if we all woke up one day with our throats cut. Did you see the dirt? Ingrained! I wouldn't be surprised if he hadn't left a flea,' and she seized the thistlebroom and briskly swept the spot where the miserable Spiller had placed his unwelcome feet. 'I never had such an experience as this. Never. Not in all my born days. Now, that's the type,' she concluded fiercely, 'who would steal a hat-pin!'

Secretly Arrietty thought so too but she did not say so, using her tongue instead to lick a little of the honey out of the split rose-hip. She also thought, as she savoured the sun-warmed honey, that Spiller, the huntsman, would make better use of the hat-pin than either her mother or father could. She wondered why he wanted the half nail-scissor. 'Have you had your tea?' she asked Homily after a moment.

'I've eaten a couple of wheat grains,' admitted Homily in a martyred voice. 'Now I must air the bedding.'

Arrietty smiled, gazing out across the sunlit field: the bedding was one piece of sock – poor Homily with practically no housework had little now on which to vent her energy. Well, now she'd had Spiller and it had done her good – her eyes looked brighter and her cheeks pinker. Idly, Arrietty watched a small bird picking its way amongst the grasses – no, it was too steady for a bird. 'Here comes Papa,' she said after a moment.

They ran down to meet him. 'Well?' cried Homily eagerly, but as they drew closer, she saw by his face that the news he brought was bad. 'You didn't find it?' she asked in a disappointed voice.

'I found it all right,' said Pod.

'What's the matter then? Why do you look so down? You mean – they weren't there? You mean – they've left?'

'They've left, all right. Or been eaten.' Pod stared unhappily.

'What can you mean, Pod?' stammered Homily.

'It's full o' foxes,' he told them ponderously, his eyes still round with shock. 'Smells awful . . .' he added after a moment.

CHAPTER ELEVEN

'MISFORTUNES MAKE US WISE'
Louis XIV of France born 1638
[Extract from Arrietty's Diary and Proverb Book, 5th September]

HOMILY carried on a bit that evening. It was understandable – what were they faced with now? This kind of Robinson Crusoe existence for the rest of their lives? Raw food in the summer was bad enough but in the stark cold of winter, Homily protested, it could not sustain life. Not that they had the faintest chance of surviving the winter, anyway, without some form of heat. A bit of wax candle would not last for ever. Nor would their few wax-vestas. And supposing they made a fire of sticks, it would have to be colossal – an absolute conflagration it would appear to a borrower – to keep alight at all. And the smoke of this, she pointed out, would be seen for miles. No, she concluded gloomily, they were in for it now and no two ways about it, as Pod and Arrietty would see for themselves, poor things, when the first frosts came.

It was the sight of Spiller, perhaps, which had shaken Homily, confirming her worst premonitions – uncouth, unwashed, dishonest, and ill-bred, that's what she summed him up to be, everything she most detested and feared. And this was the level (as she had often warned them back home) to which borrowers must sink if ever, for their sins, they took to the great outdoors.

To make matters worse, they were awakened that night by a strange sound – a prolonged and maniac bellow, it sounded to Arrietty, as she lay there trembling, breath held and heart aching. 'What was it?' she whispered to Pod, when at last she dare speak.

The boot creaked as Pod sat up in bed. 'It's a donkey,' he said, 'but close.' After a moment he added: 'Funny – I ain't ever seen a donkey hereabouts.'

'Nor I,' whispered Arrietty. But she felt somehow relieved and was just preparing to settle down again when another sound, closer, caught her ear. 'Listen!' she said sharply, sitting up.

'You don't want to lie awake listening,' Pod grumbled, turning over and pulling after him an unfair share of the sock. 'Not at night, you don't.'

'It's in the annexe,' whispered Arrietty.

The boot creaked again as Pod sat up. 'Keep quiet, Pod, do,' grumbled Homily, who had managed to doze off.

'Quiet yourself,' said Pod, trying to concentrate. It was a small whirring sound he heard, very regular. 'You're right,' he breathed to Arrietty, 'it's in the annexe.' He threw off the sock, which Homily clutched at angrily, pulling it back about her shoulders. 'I'm going out,' he said.

'No, Pod, you don't!' implored Homily huskily. 'We're all right here, laced up. Stay quiet –'

'No, Homily, I got to see.' He felt his way along the ankle of the boot. 'Stay quiet, the two of you, I won't be long.'

'Oh dear,' exclaimed Homily in a scared voice. 'Then take the hat-pin,' she implored nervously as she saw him begin to unthread the laces. Arrietty, watching, saw the boot fall open and her father's head and shoulders appear suddenly against the night sky; there was a scrabbling, a rustling, and a skittering – and Pod's voice shouting – 'Dang you . . . dang you . . . dang you!' Then there was silence.

Arrietty crept along the ankle of the boot and put her head out into the air; the alcove was filled with bright moonlight, and every object could be plainly seen. Arrietty stepped out and looked about her. A silvery Pod stood on the lip of the alcove, staring down at the moon-drenched field.

'What was it?' called Homily from the depths of the boot.

'Danged field-mice,' called Pod, 'been at the corn.'

And Arrietty saw in that pale, friendly light that the sandy floor of the annexe was strewn with empty husks.

'Well, that's that,' said Pod, turning back and kicking the scattered husks. 'Better get the thistle,' he added, 'and sweep up the mess.'

Arrietty did so, almost dancing. Enchanted, she felt, by this friendly radiance which lent an unfamiliar magic to even the most matter-of-fact objects – such as Pod's bell-clapper hanging from its nail and the whitened stitching on the boot. When she had made three neat piles of husks she joined Pod at the lip of the alcove and they sat silent for a while on the still warm sand, listening to the night.

An owl called from the spinney beside the brook – a fluting, musical note which was answered, at great distance by a note as haunting in a slightly higher key, weaving a shuttle of sound back and forth across the sleeping pasture, linking the sea of moonlight and the velvet shadowed woods.

'Whatever the danger,' Arrietty thought, sitting there at peace beside her father, 'whatever the difficulty, I am still glad we came!'

'What we need in this place,' said Pod at last, breaking the long silence, 'is some kind of tin.'

'Tin?' repeated Arrietty vaguely, not sure she had understood.

'Or a couple of tins. A cocoa tin would do. Or one of them they use for baccy.' He was silent awhile, and then he added: 'That pit we dug weren't deep enough; bet them danged field-mice have been at the nuts.'

'Couldn't you learn to shoot a bow and arrow?' asked Arrietty after a moment.

'Whatever for?' asked Pod.

Arrietty hesitated, then, all in a breath, she told him about Spiller: the well-sprung bow, the thorn-tipped, deadly arrows. And she described how Spiller had been watching them from the darkness when they played out their scene with the moth on the stage of the lighted alcove.

'I don't like that,' said Pod after a moment's thought, 'not neighbours watching I don't like. Can't have that, you know. Not by night nor by day neither, it ain't healthy, if you get my meaning.'

Arrietty did get his meaning. 'What we want here is some kind of shutter or door. A piece of chicken wire might do. Or that cheese-grater, perhaps – the one we had at home. It would have to be something that lets the light in, I mean,' she went on. 'We can't go back to living in the dark.'

'I got an idea,' said Pod suddenly. He stood up and, turning about, craned his neck upwards to the overhang above. The slender sapling, silvery with moonlight, leaned above their bank. Pod stared a moment at the leaves against the sky as though calculating distances; then, looking down he kicked about the sand with his feet.

'What is it?' whispered Arrietty, thinking he had lost something.

'Ah,' said Pod, in a pleased voice, and went down on his knees, 'this 'ould do.' And he shovelled about with his hands, uncovering, after a moment, a snaking loop of tough root – seemingly endless. 'Yes,' he repeated, 'this'll do fine.'

'What for?' asked Arrietty, wildly curious.

'Get me the twine,' said Pod. 'There on that shelf, where the tools are . . .'

Arrietty, standing on tiptoe, reached her hand into the sandy recess and found the ball of twine.

'Give it here,' said Pod, 'and get me the bell-clapper.'

Arrietty watched her father tie a length of twine on to the bell-clapper and, balancing a little perilously on the very edge of their terrace, take careful aim and, with a violent effort, fling the clapper up into the branches above; it caught hold, like an anchor, among a network of twigs.

'Now, come on,' said Pod to Arrietty, breathing steadily, 'take hold and pull. Gently does it . . . steady now. Gently . . . gently . . .' and leaning together their full weight on the twine, hand over hand they drew down the stooping branch. The alcove became dark suddenly with broken shadow, cut and trembling with filtered moonlight.

'Hold on,' panted Pod, guiding the twine to the loop of root, 'while I make her fast.' He gave a grunt. 'There,' he said, and stood up, rubbing the strain out of his hands (he was flecked all over, Arrietty noticed, with trembling blobs of silver), 'get me the half-scissor. Dang it, I forgot – the fret-saw will do.'

It was hard to lay hands on the fret-saw in this sudden darkness, but at last she found it and Pod cut his halyard. 'There,' he said again in a satisfied voice. 'She's fast – and we're covered. How's that for an idea? You can let her up or down, depending on what goes on, wind, weather, and all the rest of it . . .'

He removed the bell-clapper and made the twine fast to the main branch. 'Won't keep the field-mice out, nor them kind of cattle – but,' he gave a satisfied laugh, 'there won't be no more watching.'

'It's wonderful,' said Arrietty, her face among the leaves, 'and we can still see out.'

'That's the idea,' said Pod. 'Come on now: time we got back to bed!'

As they felt their way towards the mouth of the boot, Pod tripped against a pile of wheat-husks and stumbled, coughing, into their dusty scatter. As he stood up and brushed himself down, he remarked thoughtfully: 'Spiller – you said his name was?' He was silent a moment and then added thoughtfully: 'There's a lot worse food, when you come to think of it, than a piping-hot, savoury stew made of corn-fed field-mouse.'

CHAPTER TWELVE

'OUT OF SIGHT, OUT OF MIND'
H.M.S. *Captain* lost, 1870
[Extract from Arrietty's Diary and Proverb Book, 7th September]

HOMILY was in a worried mood next morning. 'What's all this?' she grumbled when, a little tousled, she crept out of the boot and saw that the alcove was filled with a greenish, underwater light.

'Oh, Mother,' exclaimed Arrietty reproachfully, 'it's lovely!' A faint breeze stirred the clustered leaves which, parting and closing, let pass bright spears and arrows of dancing light. A delightful blend of mystery and gaiety (or so it seemed to Arrietty). 'Don't you see,' she went on as its inventor preserved a hurt silence, 'Papa made it: it's quick cover – lets in the light but keeps out the rain; and we can see out but they can't see in.'

'Who's they?' asked Homily.

'Anything . . . anybody passing. Spiller,' she added on a gleam of inspiration.

Homily relented. 'H'mm,' she vouchsafed in a non-committal tone, but she examined the uncovered root in the floor, noted the running clove-hitch, and ran a thoughtful finger down the taut twine.

'The thing to remember,' Pod explained earnestly, aware of her tardy approval, 'is – when you let her go – keep hold of the halyard: you don't want this here halyard ever to leave the root. See what I mean?'

Homily saw. 'But you don't want to waste the sunshine,' she pointed out, 'not while it's summer, you don't. Soon it will be –' She shuddered slightly and tightened her lips, unable to say the word.

'Well, winter ain't here yet,' exclaimed Pod lightly. 'Sufficient unto the day, as they say.' He was busy with the halyard. 'Here you are – up she goes!' and, as the twine ran squeaking under the root, the leaves flew up out of sight and the alcove leapt into sudden sunlight.

'See what I mean?' said Pod again in a satisfied voice.

During breakfast the donkey brayed again, loud and long, and was answered almost at once by the neigh of a horse.

'I don't like it,' said Homily suddenly, setting down her half hazel-shell of honey and water. Even as she spoke a dog yelped – too close for comfort. Homily started – and over went the honey and water, a dark

195

stain on the sandy floor. 'Me nerves is all to pieces,' Homily wailed, clapping her hands to her temples and looking from side to side with wild eyes.

'It's nothing, Mother,' Arrietty explained, irritated. 'There's a lane just below the spinney: I saw it from the top of the hedge. It's people passing, that's all; they're bound to pass sometimes –'

'That's right,' agreed Pod, 'you don't want to worry. You eat up your grain –'

Homily stared distastefully at the bitten-into grain of corn, dry and hard as a breakfast roll three days after a picnic. 'Me teeth ain't up to it,' she said unhappily.

'According to Arrietty,' explained Pod, holding up the spread fingers of his left hand and knocking each back in turn, 'between us and that lane we got five barriers: the stream down at the corner – one; them posts with rusty wire across the stream – two; a fair-sized wood – three; another hedge – four; and a bit o' rough grazing ground – five.' He turned to Arrietty. 'Ain't that right, lass? You been up the hedge?'

Arrietty agreed. 'But that bit of grazing ground belongs to the lane – a kind of grass verge.'

'There you are then,' exclaimed Pod triumphantly, slapping Homily on the back. 'Common land! And someone's tethered a donkey there. What's wrong with that? Donkeys don't eat you – no more don't horses.'

'A dog might,' said Homily. 'I heard a dog.'

'And what of it?' exclaimed Pod. 'It wasn't the first time and it won't be the last. When I was a lad, down at the big house, the place was awash with setters, as you might say. Dogs is all right: you can talk to dogs.'

Homily was silent a moment, rolling the wheat grain backwards and forwards on the flat piece of slate which they used as a table.

'It's no good,' she said at last.

'What's no good?' asked Pod, dismayed.

'Going on like this,' said Homily. 'We got to do something before winter.'

'Well, we are doing something, aren't we?' said Pod. He nodded towards Arrietty. 'Like it says in her book – Rome weren't built in a day.'

'Find some kind of human habitation,' went on Homily, 'that's what we've got to do – where there's fires and pickings and proper sort of cover.' She hesitated. 'Or,' she went on in a set, determined voice, 'we got to go back home.'

There was a stunned silence. 'We got to do what?' asked Pod weakly, when he could find his voice; and Arrietty, deeply upset, breathed: 'Oh, Mother –'

'You heard me, Pod,' said Homily; 'all these hips and haws and watercress and dogs barking and foxes in the badgers' set and creeping in the night and stealing and rain coming up and nothing to cook on. You see what I mean? Back home, in the big house, it wouldn't take us no time to put a few partitions up and get kind of straight again under the kitchen. We did it once, that time the boiler burst: we can do it again.'

Pod stared across at her and when he spoke he spoke with the utmost gravity. 'You don't know what you're saying, Homily. It's not just that they'll be waiting for us; that they've got the cat, set traps, laid down poison, and all that caper: it's just that you don't *go back*, Homily, not once you've come out, you don't. And we ain't *got* a home. That's all over and done with. Like it or not, we got to go on now. See what I mean?' When Homily did not reply, he turned his grave face to Arrietty.

'I'm not saying we're not up against it; we are – right up against it. More than I like to let on. And if we don't stick together, we're finished – see? And it will be the end – like you once said, Arrietty – the end of our race! Never let me hear another word from either of you, you or your mother, about –' with great solemnity he slightly raised his voice, stressing each word, 'going back anywhere – let alone under the floor!'

They were very impressed; they both stared back at him, unable, for the moment, to speak.

'Understand?' asked Pod sternly.

'Yes, Papa,' whispered Arrietty; and Homily swallowed, nodding her head.

'That's right,' Pod told them more gently. 'Like it says in your book, Arrietty, "A Word is enough to the Wise".'

'Now get me the horse-hair,' he went on more jovially. 'It's a nice day. And while you two clear breakfast, I'll start on the fish-net. How's that?' Homily nodded again. She did not even ask him (as on any other occasion she would immediately have) how, when they had caught the fish, he proposed that they should cook it. 'There's a nice lot of dry bark about. Do fine,' said Pod, 'for floats.'

But Pod, though good at knots, had quite a bit of trouble with the horse-hair: the long tail-strands were springy and would slide from the eye of the needle. When the chores were done, however, and Arrietty sent off to the brook with two borrowing-bags – the waxed one for water and the other for bark, Homily came to Pod's rescue and, working together, they evolved a close mesh on the spider-web principle, based on Homily's knowledge of tatting.

'What about this Spiller?' Pod asked uneasily after a while, as he sat beside Homily, watching her fingers.

Homily snorted, busy with her knots. 'Don't talk to me of that one,' she said after a moment.

'Is he a borrower, or what?' asked Pod.

'I don't know what he is,' cried Homily, 'and what's more, I don't care neither. Threw a beetle at me, that's all I know. And stole the pin and our nail-scissor.'

'You know that for sure?' asked Pod, on a rising note.

'Sure as I'm sitting here,' said Homily. 'You ain't seen him.'

Pod was silent a moment. 'I'd like to meet him,' he said after a while, staring out across the sunlit field.

The net grew apace and the time went by almost without their noticing. Once when, each taking an end, they held the work for inspection, a grasshopper sprang from the bank below, bullet-like, into the meshes; and it was only after – with infinite care for the net – they had freed the struggling creature that Homily thought of luncheon.

'Goodness,' she cried, staring across the field, 'look at them shadows! Must be after two. What can have happened to Arrietty?'

'Playing down there with the water, I shouldn't wonder,' said Pod.

'Didn't you tell her "there and back and no dawdling"?'

'She knows not to dawdle,' said Pod.

'That's where you're wrong, Pod, with Arrietty. With Arrietty you got to say it every time!'

'She's going on for fourteen now,' said Pod.

'No matter,' Homily told him, rising to her feet, 'she's young for her age. You always got to tell her, else she'll make excuses.'

Homily folded up the net, brushed herself down, and bustled across the annexe to the shelf above the tool rack.

'You hungry, Pod?' (It was a rhetorical question: they were always hungry, all of them, every hour of the day. Even after meals they were hungry.)

'What is there?' he asked.

'There's a bunch of haws, a couple of nuts, and a mildewed blackberry.'

Pod sighed. 'All right,' he said.

'But which?' asked Homily.

'The nut's more filling,' said Pod.

'But what can I do, Pod?' cried Homily unhappily.

'Any suggestion? Do you want to go and pick us a couple of wild strawberries?'

'That's an idea,' said Pod, and he moved towards the bank.

'But you got to look careful,' Homily told him, 'they've got a bit scarce now. Something's been at them. Birds maybe. Or,' she added bitterly, 'more likely that Spiller.'

'Listen!' cried Pod, raising a warning hand. He stood quite still at the edge of their cave, staring away to his left.

'What was it?' whispered Homily, after a moment.

'Voices,' said Pod.

'What kind of voices?'

'Human,' said Pod.

'Oh, my –' whispered Homily tearfully.

'Quiet,' said Pod.

They stood quite still, ears attuned. There was a faint hum of insects from the grasses below and the buzzing of a fly which had blundered into the alcove; it flew jerkily about between them and settled greedily at last on the sandy floor where at breakfast Homily had spilled the honey. Then suddenly, uncomfortably close, they heard a different sound, a sound which drove the colour from their cheeks and which filled their hearts with dread – and it was, on the face of it, a cheerful sort of sound: the sound of a human laugh.

Neither moved; frozen they stood – pale and tense with listening. There was a pause and, nearer now, a man's voice cursed – one short, sharp word and, immediately after, they heard the yelp of a dog.

Pod stooped; swiftly, with a jerk of the wrist, he released the halyard and, hand over steady hand, he pulled on the swaying tree: this time he used extra strength, drawing the branches lower and closer until he had stuffed the mouth of their cave with a close-knit network of twigs.

'There,' he gasped, breathing hard, 'take some getting through, that will.'

Homily, bewildered by the dappled half-light, could not make out his expression, but somehow she sensed his calm. 'Will it look all right from outside?' she asked evenly, matching her tone to his.

'Should do,' said Pod. He went up to the leaves and peered out between them, and with steady hands and sure grip tried the set of the branches. 'Now,' he said, stepping back and drawing a deep breath, 'hand me that other hat-pin.'

Then it was that a further strange thing happened. Pod put out his hand – and there at once was the hat-pin, but it had been put in his grasp too quietly and too immediately to have been put there by Homily: a shadowy third shared their dim-lit cavern, a dun-coloured creature of invisible stillness. And the hat-pin was the hat-pin they had lost.

'Spiller!' gasped Homily hoarsely.

CHAPTER THIRTEEN

'MEAT IS MUCH, BUT MANNERS ARE MORE'
New Style introduced into Britain, 1752
[*Extract from Arrietty's Diary and Proverb Book, 11th September*]

HE must have slid in with the lowering of the leaves – a shadow among shadows. Now she could see the blob of face, the tangled thatch of hair, and that he carried two borrowing-bags, one empty and one full. And the bags, Homily realized with a sinking heart, were the bags which that morning she had handed to Arrietty.

'What have you done with her?' Homily cried, distraught. 'What have you done with Arrietty?'

Spiller jerked his head towards the back of the alcove. 'Coming up over yon field,' he said, and his face remained quite expressionless. 'I floated her off down the current,' he added carelessly. Homily turned wild eyes towards the back of the alcove as though she might see through the sandy walls and into the field beyond: it was the field through which they had trapsed on the day of their escape.

'You what?' exclaimed Pod.

'Floated her off down the river,' said Spiller, 'in half of a soap-box,' he explained irritably, as though Pod were being dense.

Pod opened his mouth to reply, then, staring, remained silent: there was a sound of running footsteps in the ditch below; as they came abreast of the alcove and thundered past outside, the whole of the bank seemed to tremble and the bell-clapper fell off its nail – they heard the steady rasp of men's harsh breathing and the panting of a dog.

'It's all right,' said Spiller, after a tense pause, 'they cut off left, and across. Gipsies,' he added tersely, 'out rabbiting.'

'Gipsies?' echoed Pod dully, and he wiped his brow with his sleeve.

'That's right,' said Spiller, 'down there by the lane; coupla caravans.'

'Gipsies . . .' breathed Homily in a blank kind of wonderment, and for a moment she was silent – her breath held and her mouth open, listening.

'It's all right,' said Spiller, listening too, 'they gone across now, alongside the cornfield.'

'And what's this now about Arrietty?' stammered Pod.

'I told you,' said Spiller.

'Something about a soap-dish?'

'Is she all right?' implored Homily, interrupting. 'Is she safe? Tell us that –'

'She's safe,' said Spiller, 'I told you. Box, not dish,' he corrected and glanced interestedly about the alcove. 'I slept in that boot once,' he announced conversationally, nodding his head towards it.

Homily repressed a shudder. 'Never mind that now,' she said, hurriedly dismissing the subject, 'you go on and tell us about Arrietty. This soap-dish, or box, or whatever it was. Tell us just what happened.'

It was difficult to piece the story together from Spiller's terse sentences, but at last some coherence emerged. Spiller, it seemed, owned a boat – the bottom half of an aluminium soap-case, slightly dented; in this, standing up, he would propel himself about the stream. Spiller had a summer camp (or hunting lodge) in the sloping field behind – an old blackened tea kettle it was – wedged sideways in the silt of the stream (he had several of these bases it appeared, of which, at some time, the boot had been one) – and he would borrow from the caravans, transporting the loot by water; this boat gave him a speedy getaway, and one which left no scent. Coming up against the current was slower, Spiller explained, and for this he was grateful for the hat-pin, which not only served as a sharp and pliable punt-pole, but as a harpoon as well. He became so lyrical about the hat-pin that Pod and Homily began to feel quite pleased with themselves, as though, out of the kindness of their hearts, they had achieved some benevolent gesture. Pod longed to ask to what use Spiller had put the half nail-scissor but could not bring himself to do so, fearing to strike a discordant note in so bland a state of innocent joy.

On this particular afternoon, it seemed, Spiller had been transporting two lumps of sugar, a twist of tea, three leaden hair-curlers, and one of those plain gold earrings for pierced ears known as sleepers across the wider part of the brook where, pond-like, it spread into their field, when (he told them) he had seen Arrietty at the water's edge, barefoot in the warm mud, playing some kind of game. She had a quill-like leaf of bulrush in her hand and seemed to be stalking frogs: she would steal up behind her prey, where innocently it sat basking in the sun, and – when

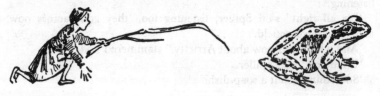

she was close enough – she would tap the dozing creature smartly in the small of its back with her swaying length of wand; there would then be a croak, a plop, a splash – and it was one up to Arrietty. Sometimes she was seen approaching – then, of course, it was one up to the frog. She challenged Spiller to a match, completely unaware (he said) that she had another interested spectator – the gipsies' dog, a kind of mongrel greyhound, which stared with avid eyes from the woodland edge of the pond. Nor (he added) had she heard the crackling in the underbrush which meant that its masters were close behind.

Spiller, it seemed, had just had time to leap ashore, push Arrietty into the shallow soap-box and, with a few hurried directions about the whereabouts of the kettle, shove her off down-stream.

'But will she ever find it?' gasped Homily. 'The kettle, I mean?'

'Couldn't miss it,' said Spiller, and went on to explain that the current fetched up close against the spout, in a feathery pile-up of broken ripples – and there the soap-box always stuck. 'All she got to do,' he pointed out, 'is make fast, tip the stuff out, and walk back up.'

'Along the ridge of the gas-pipe?' asked Pod. Spiller threw him a startled glance, shrewd but somehow closed. 'She could do,' he said shortly.

'Half a soap-box . . .' murmured Homily wonderingly, trying to picture it, '. . . hope she'll be all right.'

'She'll be all right,' said Spiller, 'and there b'aint no scent on the water.'

'Why didn't you get in too,' asked Pod, 'and go along with her like?'

Spiller looked faintly uncomfortable. He rubbed his dark hand on the back of his moleskin trousers; he frowned slightly, glancing at the ceiling. 'There b'aint room for two,' he said at last, 'not with cargo.'

'You could have tipped the cargo out,' said Pod.

Spiller frowned more deeply, as though the subject bored him. 'Maybe,' he said.

'I mean,' Pod pointed out, 'there you were, weren't you, out in the open, left without cover. What's a bit of cargo compared to that?'

'Yes,' said Spiller, and added uncomfortably, referring to his boat: 'She's shallow – you ain't seen her: there b'aint room for two.'

'Oh, Pod –' cried Homily, suddenly emotional.

'Now what?' asked Pod.

'This boy,' went on Homily in ringing tones, 'this – well, anyway, there he stands!' and she threw out an arm towards Spiller.

Pod glanced at Spiller. Yes, indeed, there he stood, very embarrassed and indescribably grubby.

'He saved her life,' went on Homily, throaty with gratitude, 'at the expense of his own!'

'Not expense,' Pod pointed out after a moment, staring thoughtfully at Spiller. 'I mean he's here, isn't he?' And added reasonably in surprised afterthought: 'And she's not!'

'She will be,' said Homily, suddenly confident, 'you'll see; everything's all right. And he's welcome to the hat-pin. This boy's a hero.' Suddenly herself again, she began to bustle about. 'Now you sit here, Spiller,' she urged him hospitably, 'and rest yourself. It's a long pull up from the water. What'll you take? Could you do with a nice half a rose-hip filled with something or other? We haven't much,' she explained with a nervous laugh, 'we're newcomers, you see . . .'

Spiller put a grubby hand into a deep pocket. 'I got this,' he said, and threw down a sizeable piece of something heavy which bounced juicily as it hit the slate table. Homily moved forward; curiously, she stooped. 'What is it?' she asked in an awed voice. But even as she spoke she knew: a faint gamy odour rose to her nostrils – gamy, but deliciously savoury, and for one fleeting, glorious second she felt almost faint with greed: it was a roast haunch of –

'Meat,' said Spiller.

'What kind of meat?' asked Pod. He too looked rather glassy-eyed – an exclusive diet of hips and haws might be non-acid-forming but it certainly left corners.

'Don't tell me,' Homily protested, clapping her hands to her ears. And, as they turned towards her surprised, she looked apologetic but added eagerly: 'Let's just eat it, shall we?'

They fell to, slicing it up with the sliver of razorblade. Spiller looked on surprised: surfeited with regular protein, he was not feeling particularly hungry. 'Lay a little by for Arrietty,' Homily kept saying, and every now and again she remembered her manners and would press Spiller to eat.

Pod, very curious, kept throwing out feelers. 'Too big for field-mouse,' he would say, chewing thoughtfully, 'yet too small for rabbit. You couldn't eat stoat . . . might be a bird, of course.'

And Homily, in a pained voice, would cry: 'Please, Pod . . .' and would turn coyly to Spiller. 'All *I* want to know is how Spiller cooks it. It's delicious and hung just right.'

But Spiller would not be drawn. 'It's easy,' he admitted once (to

Homily's bewilderment: how could it be 'easy' out here in a grateless wilderness devoid of coke or coal? And, natural gratitude apart, she made more and more fuss of Spiller: she had liked him, she was convinced now, from the first.)

Arrietty returned in the middle of this feast. She staggered a little when she had pushed her way through the tight-packed screen of leaves, swayed on her two feet, and sat down rather suddenly in the middle of the floor.

Homily was all concern. 'What have they done to you, Arrietty? What's the matter? Are you sick?'

Arrietty shook her head. 'Seasick,' she said weakly, 'my head's all awhirl.' She glanced reproachfully across at Spiller. 'You spun me out

in the current,' she told him accusingly. 'The thing went round and round and round and round and round and round and –'

'Now, that's enough, Arrietty,' interrupted Homily, 'or you'll have us all whirling. Spiller was very kind. You should be grateful. He gave his life for yours –'

'He didn't give his life,' explained Pod again, slightly irritated.

But Homily took no notice. 'And then came on up here with the borrowing-bags to say you were all right. You should thank him.'

'Thank you, Spiller,' said Arrietty, politely but wanly, looking up from her place on the floor.

'Now, get up,' said Homily, 'that's a good girl. And come to the table. Not had a bite since breakfast – that's all that's the matter with you. We've saved you a nice piece of meat –'

'A nice piece of what?' asked Arrietty in a dazed voice, not believing her ears.

'Meat,' said Homily firmly, without looking at her.

Arrietty jumped up and came across to the table; she stared blankly down at the neat brown slices. 'But I thought we were vegetarians . . .' After a moment she raised her eyes to Spiller: there was a question in them. 'Is it –?' she began unhappily.

Spiller shook his head quickly; it was a firm negative and settled her misgivings. 'We never ask,' put in Homily sharply, tightening her lips and creating a precedent; 'let's just call it a bit of what the gipsies caught and leave it at that.'

'Not leave it . . .' murmured Arrietty dreamily. Quite recovered she seemed suddenly; and arranging her skirts she joined them at the low table round which they sat picnic-wise on the floor. Tentatively she took up a slice in two fingers, took a cautious bite, then closed her eyes and almost shuddered, so welcome and downright was the flavour. '*Did* the gipsies catch it?' she asked incredulously.

'No,' said Pod, 'Spiller did.'

'I thought so,' Arrietty said. 'Thank you, Spiller,' she added. And this time her voice sounded heartfelt – alive and ringing with proper gratitude.

CHAPTER FOURTEEN

'LOOK HIGH, AND FALL LOW'
First Balloon Ascent in England, 1784
[Extract from Arrietty's Diary and Proverb Book, 15th September]

MEALS became different after that – different and better – and this had something to do, Arrietty decided, with their stolen half nail-scissor. Stolen? An unpleasant-sounding word, seldom applied to a borrower. 'But what else can you call it?' Homily wailed as she sat one morning on the edge of the alcove while Pod sewed a patch on her shoe, 'or expect even? Of a poor, homeless, ignorant boy dragged up, as they say, in the gutter –'

'Ditch, you mean,' put in Arrietty drowsily, who was lying below on the bank.

'I mean gutter –' repeated Homily, but she looked a little startled: she had not known Arrietty was near, 'it's a manner of speaking. No,' she went on primly, adjusting the hem of her skirt to hide her stockinged foot (there was a slight hole, she had noticed, in the toe), 'you can't blame the lad. I mean, with that sort of background, what could he learn about ethics?'

'About whatticks?' asked Pod. Homily, poor ignorant soul, occasionally hit on a word which surprised him and, what surprised him still more, sometimes she hit on its meaning.

'Ethics,' repeated Homily coolly and with perfect confidence. 'You know what ethics are, don't you?'

'No, I don't,' Pod admitted simply, sewing away on his patch; 'sounds to me like something you pick up in the long grass.'

'Them's ticks,' said Homily.

'Or,' Pod went on, smoothing the neat join with a licked thumb, 'that thing that horses get from drinking too quick.'

'It's funny . . .' mused Arrietty, 'that you can't have just one.'

'One what?' asked Homily sharply.

'One ethic,' said Arrietty.

'That's where you're wrong,' snapped Homily. 'As a matter of fact there is only one. And Spiller's never learned it. One day,' she went on, 'I'm going to have a nice, quiet, friendly talk with that poor lad.'

'What about?' asked Arrietty.

Homily ignored the question: she had composed her face to a certain kind of expression and was not going to change it. ' "Spiller," I'll say, "you never had a mother –" ' '

'How do you know he never had a mother?' asked Pod. 'He must have had,' he added reasonably, after a moment's reflection.

'Yes,' put in Arrietty, 'he did have a mother. That's how he knows his name.'

'How?' asked Homily, suddenly curious.

'Because his mother told him, of course! Spiller's his surname. His first name's Dreadful.'

There was a pause.

'What is it?' asked Homily then, in an awed voice.

'Dreadful!'

'Never mind,' snapped Homily, 'tell us: we're not children.'

'That's his name: Dreadful Spiller. He remembers his mother saying it one day, at table. "A Dreadful Spiller, that's what you are," she said, "aren't you?" It's about all he does remember about his mother.'

'All right,' said Homily, after a moment, composing her features back to gentle tolerance, 'then I'll say to him' (she smiled her sad smile), ' "Dreadful," I'll say, "dear boy, my poor orphan lad –" ' '

'How do you know he's orphaned?' interrupted Pod. 'Have you ever asked him if he's orphaned?'

'You can't ask Spiller things,' put in Arrietty quickly. 'Sometimes he tells you, but you can't ask him. Remember when you tried to find out how he did the cooking? He didn't come back for two days.'

'That's right,' agreed Pod glumly, 'couple o'days without meat. We don't want that again in a hurry. Look here, Homily,' he went on, turning suddenly towards her, 'better leave Spiller alone.'

'It's for his own good,' protested Homily angrily, 'and it's *telling*, not *asking*! I was only going to say –' (again she smiled her smile) ' "Spiller, my poor lad," or "Dreadful" or whatever his name is –'

'You can't call him Dreadful, Mother,' put in Arrietty, 'not unless he asks you –'

'Well, "Spiller" then!' Homily threw up her eyes. 'But I got to tell him.'

'Tell him what?' asked Pod, irritated.

'This *ethic*!' Homily almost shouted, 'this what we all been brought up on! That you don't never borrow from a borrower!'

Impatiently Pod snapped off his thread. 'He knows that,' he said. He handed the shoe to Homily. 'Here you, put it on.'

'Then what about the hat-pin?' persisted Homily.

'He give it back,' Pod said.

'He didn't give back the nail-scissor!'

'He skins the game with it,' said Arrietty quickly. 'And we get the meat.'

'Skins the game?' pondered Homily. 'Well, I never.'

'That's right,' agreed Pod, 'and cuts it up. See what I mean, Homily?' He rose to his feet. 'Better leave well alone.'

Homily was struggling absent-mindedly with the laces of her shoe. 'Wonder how he does cook?' she mused aloud after a moment.

'Wonder away,' said Pod. He crossed to the shelf to replace his tools. 'No harm in that, so long as you don't ask.'

'Poor orphaned lad . . .' said Homily again. She spoke quite lightly but her eye was thoughtful.

CHAPTER FIFTEEN

'NO JOY WITHOUT ALLOY'
Columbus discovered New World, 1492
[*Extract from Arrietty's Diary and Proverb Book, 25th September*]

THE next six weeks (according to Tom Goodenough) were the happiest
Arrietty ever spent out of doors. Not that they could be called halcyon
exactly: they ran, of course, the usual gamut of English summer weather
– days when the fields were drowned in opal mist and spiders' webs
hung jewelled in the hedges; days of breathless heat and stifling
closeness; thundery days with once a searing strike of lightning across
the woods when Homily, terrified, had buried the razor-blade saying
that 'steel attracts'; and one whole week of dismal, steady rain with
scarcely a let-up, when the ditch below their bank became a roaring
cataract on which Spiller, guiding his tin soap-case with uncanny speed
and skill, intrepidly shot the rapids; during this week Homily and
Arrietty were kept house-bound in case, Pod told them, they should slip
on the mud and fall in: it would be no joke, he explained, to be swept
along down the ditch to the swollen stream at the corner and on and on
through the lower fields until they met the river and eventually, he
concluded, be carried out to sea.

'Why not say "across to America" and have done with it?' Homily
had remarked tartly, remembering Arrietty's *Gazetteer of the World*. But
she got ahead with her winter knitting, saw the men had hot drinks,
and dried out poor
Spiller's clothes over the
candle while he huddled
naked, but clean for
once, in the boot. The
rain never actually beat
into the alcove but there
was an unpleasant damp-
ness all over everything,
white mildew on the
leather of the boot, and,
once, a sudden crop of
yellow toadstools where
none had been before.

Another morning, when Homily crept forth shivering to get breakfast, a silvery track of slime wound ribbon-like across the floor and, putting her hand on the tool shelf for the matches, she gave a startled scream – stuffed, the shelf was, and flowing over with a heaving mass of slug. A slug that size cannot be easily tackled by a borrower, but luckily this one shrunk up and feigned dead: once they had prized it out of its closely-fitting retreat, they could bowl it over across the sandy floor and roll it away down to the bank.

After this, towards the end of September, there did come some halcyon days – about ten of them: sun and butterflies and drowsy heat; and a second burst of wild flowers. There was no end to Arrietty's amusements out of doors. She would climb down the bank, across the ditch, and into the long grass, and stretched between the stems would lie there watching. Once she became used to the habits of the insects she no longer feared them: her world, she realized, was not their world and for them hers had little interest; except, perhaps, for that bug-like horror (an ethic to Pod) which, crawling sluggishly across bare skin, would bury its head and cling.

Grasshoppers would alight like prehistoric birds on the grasses above her head; strange, armour-plated creatures, but utterly harmless to such as she. The grass stems would sway wildly beneath their sudden weight, and Arrietty, lying watchful below, would note the machine-like slicing of the mandibles as the grasshopper munched its fill.

Bees, to Arrietty, were as big as birds are to humans; and if honey-bees were pigeon-sized, a bumble-bee in weight and girth could be compared to a turkey. These too she found, if unprovoked, were harmless. A quivering bumble-bee, feeding greedily on clover, became strangely still all at once when, with gentle fingers, she stroked his fur. Benignity met with benignity: and anger, she found, was only roused through fear. Once she was nearly stung when, to tease it, she imprisoned a bee in that bloom called wild snapdragon by closing the lip with her hands. The trapped bee buzzed like a dynamo and stung, not Arrietty this time, but the enclosing calyx of the flower.

A good deal of time she would spend by the water – paddling, watching, learning to float. The frogs fought shy of her: At Arrietty's approach, they would plop away with bored bleats of distaste, their bulging eyes resigned but nervous; 'look where it comes again . . .'[1] they seemed to croak.

After bathing, before putting on her clothes, sometimes she would dress up: a skirt of violet leaves, stalks uppermost, secured about the waist with a twist of faded columbine, and, aping the fairies, a foxglove bell for a hat. This, Arrietty thought as she stared at her bright reflection in the stagnant water of a hoof crater, might look all right on gnomes, elves, brownies, pixies, and what not, but she had to admit that it looked pretty silly on a common or garden borrower: for one thing, if the lip fitted the circumference of her head, the whole thing stood up too high like some kind of pinkish sausage or a very drawn-out chef's cap. Yet if, on the other hand, the lip of the bell flowed out generously in a gentle, more hat-like curve, the whole contraption slid down past her face to rest on her shoulders in a Klu-Klux-Klan effect.

And to get hold of these bells at all was not easy: foxglove plants were high. Fairies, Arrietty supposed, just flew up to them with raised chins and neatly pointed toes, trailing a wisp of gauze. Fairies did everything so gracefully: Arrietty, poor girl, had to hook down the plant with a forked stick and sit on it as heavily as she could while she plucked any bells within reach. Sometimes the plant would escape her and fly up again. But usually, by shifting her weight along the stalk, she would manage to get five or six bells – sufficient anyway to try some out for size.

1. Tom Thumb edition of Shakespeare's Tragedies, with foreword on the Author.

Spiller, gliding by in his cleverly loaded boat, would stare with some surprise: he was not altogether approving of Arrietty's games; having spent all his life out of doors, fending for himself against nature, he had no picture of what such freedom could mean to one who had spent her childhood under a kitchen floor; frogs were just meat to Spiller; grass was 'cover'; and insects a nuisance, especially gnats; water was there to drink, not to splash in; and streams were highways which held fish. Spiller, poor harried creature, had never had time to play.

But he was a fearless borrower; that even Pod conceded; as skilful in his own way as ever Pod had been. The two gentlemen would have long discussions of an evening after supper, on the finer points of a multiplex art. Pod belonged to a more moderate school: the daily sortie and modest loot – a little here, a little there – nothing to rouse suspicion. Spiller preferred a make-hay-while-the-sun-shines technique: a swift whip-round of whatever he could lay hands on and a quick getaway. This difference in approach was understandable, Arrietty thought, as listening she helped her mother with the dishes: Pod was a house-borrower, long established in traditional routine; whereas Spiller dealt exclusively with gipsies – here today and gone tomorrow – and must match his quickness with theirs.

Sometimes a whole week would elapse without their seeing Spiller, but he would leave them well stocked with cooked food: a haunch of this or that, or a little stew flavoured with wild garlic which Homily would heat over the candle. Flour, sugar, tea, butter – even bread – they had now in plenty. Spiller,

in his nonchalant way, would sooner or later provide almost anything they asked for – a piece of plum-coloured velvet out of which Homily made a new skirt for Arrietty, two whole candles to augment their stub, four empty cotton-reels on which they raised their table, and, to Homily's joy, six mussel shells for plates.

Once he brought them a small glass medicine bottle, circular in shape. As he uncorked it, Spiller said: 'Know what this is?'

Homily, wry-faced, sniffed at the amber liquid. 'Some kind of hair-wash?' she asked, grimacing.

'Elder-flower wine,' Spiller told her, watching her expression. 'Good, that is.'

Homily, about to taste, suddenly changed her mind. 'When wine is in,' she told Spiller – quoting from Arrietty's *Diary and Proverb Book*, 'wit is out. Besides, I was brought up teetotal.'

'He makes it in a watering-can,' explained Spiller, 'and pours it out of the spout.'

'Who does?' asked Homily.

'Mild Eye,' said Spiller.

There was a short silence, tense with curiosity. 'And who might Mild Eye be?' asked Homily as last. Airily pinning up her back hair, she moved slightly away from Spiller and began softly to hum below her breath.

'He that had the boot,' said Spiller carelessly.

'Oh?' remarked Homily. She took up the thistlehead and began to sweep the floor – without seeming to be rude she managed to convey a gentle dismissal of the now-I-must-get-on-with-the-housework kind – 'What boot?'

'This boot,' said Spiller, and kicked the toe.

Homily stopped sweeping; she stared at Spiller. 'But this was a gentleman's boot,' she pointed out evenly.

' "Was" is right,' said Spiller.

Homily was silent a moment. 'I don't understand you,' she said at last.

'Afore Mild Eye pinched 'em,' explained Spiller.

Homily laughed. 'Mild Eye . . . Mild Eye . . . who is this Mild Eye?' she asked airily, determined not to be rattled.

'I told you,' said Spiller, 'the gipsy as took up the boots.'

'Boots?' repeated Homily, raising her eyebrows and stressing the plural.

'They was a pair. Mild Eye picked 'em up outside the scullery door . . .' Spiller jerked his head, 'that big house down yonder. Went there selling clothes-pegs and there they was, set out on the cobbles, pairs of 'em – all shapes and sizes, shined up nice, set out in the sunshine . . . brushed and all.'

'Oh,' said Homily thoughtfully – this sounded a good 'borrow', 'and he took the lot?'

Spiller laughed. 'Not Mild Eye. Took up the pair and closed up the gap.'

'I see,' said Homily. After a moment she asked: 'And who borrowed this one? You?'

'In a manner of speaking,' said Spiller, and added, as though in part explanation: 'He's got this piebald cat.'

'What's the cat got to do with it?' asked Homily.

'A great tom comes yowling round the place one night and Mild Eye ups and heaves a boot at it – this boot.' Again Spiller kicked at the leather. 'Good and watertight this boot was afore a weasel bit into the toe. So I gets hold of her, drags her through the hedge by the laces, heaves her into the water, jumps aboard, sails downstream to the corner, brings her aground on the mud and dries her out after, up in the long grass.'

'Where we found it?' asked Homily.

'That's right,' said Spiller. He laughed. 'You should have heard old Mild Eye in the morning. Knew just where he'd heaved the boot, cussin' and swearin'. Couldn't make it out.' Spiller laughed again. 'Never passes that way,' he went on, 'but he has another look.'

Homily turned pale. 'Another look?' she repeated nervously.

Spiller shrugged. 'What's the difference? Wouldn't think to look this side of the water. Knows where he heaved the boot, Mild Eye does: that's what he can't fathom.'

'Oh, my,' faltered Homily unhappily.

'You've no call to worry,' said Spiller. 'Anything you'm wanting?'

'A bit of something woollen, I wouldn't mind,' said Homily; 'we was cold last night in the boot.'

'Like a bit of sheep's fleece?' asked Spiller. 'There's plenty down to the lane along them brambles.'

'Anything,' agreed Homily, 'providing it's warm. And providing –' she added, suddenly struck by a horrid thought, 'it ain't a sock.' Her eyes widened. 'I don't want no sock belonging to Mild Eye.'

Spiller dined with them that night (cold boiled minnow with sorrel salad). He had brought them a splendid wad of cleanish fleece and a strip of red rag off the end of a blanket. Pod, less teetotal than Homily, poured him out a half hazel-shell of elderberry wine. But Spiller would not touch it. 'I've things to do,' he told them soberly, and they guessed he was off on a trip.

'Be away long?' asked Pod casually as, just to sample it, he took a sip of wine.

'A week,' said Spiller, 'ten days, maybe . . .'

'Well,' said Pod, 'take care of yourself.' He took another sip of wine. 'It's nice,' he told Homily, proffering the hazel-shell, 'you try it.'

Homily shook her head and tightened her lips. 'We'll miss you, Spiller,' she said, batting her eyelids and ignoring Pod, 'and that's a fact –'

'Why have you got to go?' asked Arrietty suddenly.

Spiller, about to push his way through the screen of leaves, turned back to look at her.

Arrietty coloured. 'I've asked him a question,' she realized unhappily, 'now he'll disappear for weeks.' But this time Spiller seemed merely hesitant.

'Me winter clothes,' he said at last.

'Oh!' exclaimed Arrietty, raising her head – delighted. 'New?'

Spiller nodded.

'Fur?' asked Homily.

Spiller nodded again.

'Rabbit?' asked Arrietty.

'Mole,' said Spiller.

There was a sudden feeling of gaiety in the candlelit alcove: a pleasant sense of something to look forward to. All three of them smiled at Spiller and Pod raised his 'glass'. 'To Spiller's new clothes,' he said, and Spiller, suddenly embarrassed, dived quickly through the branches. But before the living curtain had stopped quivering they saw his face again; amused and shy, it poked back at them framed in leaves. 'A lady makes them,' he announced self-consciously, and quickly disappeared.

CHAPTER SIXTEEN

'EVERY TIDE HAS ITS EBB'
Burning of the Tower of London, 1841
[*Extract from Arrietty's Diary and Proverb Book, 30th October*]

NEXT morning early Pod, on the edge of the alcove, summoned Arrietty from the boot. 'Come on out,' he called, 'and see this.'

Arrietty, shivering, pulled on a few clothes, and wrapping the piece of red blanket around her shoulders she crept out beside him. The sun was up and the landscape shimmered, dusted over with what, to Arrietty, looked like powdered sugar.

'This is it,' said Pod, after a moment, 'the first frost.'

Arrietty pushed her numbed fingers under her arm-pits, hugging the blanket closer. 'Yes,' she said soberly, and they stared in silence.

After a bit Pod cleared his throat. 'There's no call to wake your mother,' he said huskily; 'like as not, with this sun, it'll be clear in less than an hour.' He became silent again, thinking deeply. 'Thought you'd like to see it,' he said at last.

'Yes,' said Arrietty again, and added politely: 'It's pretty.'

'What we better do,' said Pod, 'is get the breakfast quietly and leave your mother sleeping. She's all right,' he went on, 'deep in that fleece.'

'I'm perished,' grumbled Homily at breakfast, her hands wrapped round a half hazel-shell filled with piping hot tea (there was less need, now they had Spiller, to economize on candles). 'It strikes right through to the marrow. You know what?' she went on.

'No,' said Pod (it was the only reply). 'What?'

'Say we went down to the caravan site and had a look round? There won't be no gipsies: when Spiller goes, it means they've moved off. Might find something,' she added, 'and in this kind of weather there ain't no sense in sitting around. What about it, Pod? We could wrap up warm.'

Arrietty was silent, watching their faces: she had learned not to urge.

Pod hesitated. Would it be poaching, he wondered – was this Spiller's preserve? 'All right,' he agreed uncertainly, after a moment.

It was not a simple expedition. Spiller having hidden his boat, they had to ferry themselves across the water on a flat piece of bark, and it was rough going when, once in the wood, they tried to follow the stream

by land: both banks were thickly grown with brambles, ghastly forests of living barbed wire which tore at their hair and clothes; by the time they had scrambled through the hedge on to the stretch of grass beside the lane, they were all three dishevelled and bleeding.

Arrietty looked about her at the camping site and was depressed by what she saw: this wood through which they had scrambled now shut off the last pale gleams of sun; the shadowed grass was bruised and yellow; here and there were odd bones, drifting feathers, bits of rag, and every now and again a stained newspaper flapped in the hedge.

'Oh dear,' muttered Homily, glancing from side to side, 'somehow, now, I don't seem to fancy that bit o' red blanket.'

'Well,' said Pod, after a pause, 'come on. We may as well take a look round . . .' And he led the way down the bank.

They poked about rather distastefully and Homily thought of fleas. Pod found an old iron saucepan without a bottom: he felt it might do for something but could not think for what; he walked around it speculatingly and, once or twice, he tapped it sharply with the head of his hat-pin, which made a dull clang. Anyway, he decided at last as he moved away, it was no good to him here and was far too heavy to shift.

Arrietty found a disused cooking-stove: it was flung into the bank below the hedge – so sunk it was in the grasses and so thickly engrained with rust that it must have been there for years. 'You know,' she remarked to her mother, after studying it in silence, 'you could live in a stove like this.'

Homily stared. 'In that?' she exclaimed disgustedly. The stove lay tilted, partially sunk in earth; as stoves went it was a very small one,

with a barred grate and a miniature oven of the kind which are built into caravans. Beside it, Arrietty noticed, lay a small pile of fragile bones.

'Not sure she isn't right,' agreed Pod, tapping the bars of the grate, 'you could have a fire in here, say, and live in the oven like.'

'Live!' exclaimed Homily. 'Be roasted alive, you mean.'

'No,' exclaimed Pod, 'needn't be a big fire. Just enough to warm the place through like. And there you'd be' – he looked at the brass latch on the door of the oven – 'safe as houses. Iron, that is,' he rapped the stove with his hat-pin; 'nothing couldn't gnaw through that.'

'Field-mice could slip through them bars,' said Homily.

'Maybe,' said Pod, 'but I wasn't thinking so much about field-mice as about' – he paused uneasily – 'stoats and foxes and them kind of cattle.'

'Oh, Pod,' exclaimed Homily, clapping her hands flat to her cheeks and making her eyes tragic, 'the things you do bring up! Why do you do it?' she implored him tearfully. 'Why? You know what it does to me!'

'Well, there are such things,' Pod pointed out stolidly. 'In this life,' he went on, 'you got to see what *is*, as you might say, and then face up to what you wish there wasn't.'

'But foxes, Pod,' protested Homily.

'Yes,' agreed Pod, 'but there they are; you can't deny 'em. See what I mean?'

'I see all right,' said Homily, eyeing the stove more kindly, 'but say you lit it, the gipsies would see the smoke.'

'And not only the gipsies,' admitted Pod, glancing aside at the lane, 'anyone passing would see it. No,' he sighed, as he turned to go, 'this stove ain't feasible. Pity – because of the iron.'

The only really comforting find of the day was a piping-hot blackened potato: Arrietty found it on the site of the gipsies' fire. The embers were still warm, and, when stirred with a stick, a line of scarlet sparks ran snakewise through the ash. The potato steamed when they broke it open, and comforted they ate their fill, sitting as close as they dared to the perilous warmth.

'Wish we could take a bit of this ash home,' Homily remarked. 'This is how Spiller cooks, I shouldn't wonder – borrows a bit of the gipsies' fire. What do you think, Pod?'

Pod blew on his crumb of hot potato. 'No,' he said, taking a bite and speaking with his mouth full, 'Spiller cooks regular-like whether the gipsies are here or not. Spiller's got his own method. Wish I knew what it was.'

Homily leaned forward, stirring the embers

with a charred stick. 'Say we kept this fire alight,' she suggested, 'and brought the boot down here?'

Pod glanced about uneasily. 'Too public,' he said.

'Say we put it in the hedge,' went on Homily, 'alongside that stove? What about that? Say we put it *in* the stove?' she added suddenly, inspired but fearful.

Pod turned slowly and looked at her. 'Homily –' he began and paused, as though stumped for words. After a moment he laid a hand on his wife's arm and looked with some pride towards his daughter. 'Your mother's a wonderful woman,' he said in a moved voice. 'And never you forget it, Arrietty.'

Then it was 'all hands to the plough': they gathered sticks like maniacs, and wet leaves to keep up the smoulder. Backwards and forwards they ran, up into the hedges, along the banks, into the spinney . . . they tugged and wrenched and tripped and stumbled . . . and soon a white column of smoke spiralled up into the leaden sky.

'Oh my,' panted Homily, distressed, 'folks'll see this for miles!'

'No matter,' gasped Pod, as he pushed on a lichen-covered branch, 'they'll think it's the gipsies. Pile on some more of them leaves, Arrietty, we got to keep this going till morning.'

A sudden puff of wind blew the smoke into Homily's eyes and the tears ran down her cheeks. 'Oh my,' she exclaimed – again distressed. 'This is what we'll be doing all winter, day in, day out, till we're wore to the bone and run out of fuel. It ain't no good, Pod. See what I mean?'

And she sat down suddenly on a blackened tin-lid and wept in earnest. 'You can't spend the rest of your life,' she whimpered, 'tending an open fire.'

Pod and Arrietty had nothing to say: they knew suddenly that Homily was right: borrowers were too little and weak to create a full-sized blaze. The light was fading and the wind sharpening, a leaden wind which presaged snow.

'Better we start for home,' said Pod, at last. 'We tried anyway. Come on, now,' he urged Homily, 'dry your eyes: we'll think of something else . . .'

But they didn't think of anything else. And the weather became colder. There was no sign of Spiller and, after ten days, they ran out of meat and started (their sole source of warmth) on the last bit of candle.

'I don't know,' Homily would moan unhappily, as at night they crept under the fleece, 'what we're going to do, I'm sure. We won't see Spiller again, that's one thing certain. Dare say he's met with an accident.'

Then came the snow. Homily, tucked up in the boot, would not get up to see it. To her it presaged the end. 'I'll die here,' she announced, 'tucked up comfortable. You and father,' she told Arrietty, 'can die as you like.'

It was no good Arrietty assuring her that the field looked very pretty, that the cold seemed less severe, and that she had made a sledge of the blackened tin-lid which Pod had retrieved from the ashes: she had made her grave and was determined to lie in it.

In spite of this, and rather heartlessly, Arrietty still enjoyed her toboggan runs down the bank with a wide sweep into the ditch at the bottom. And Pod, brave soul, still went out to forage – though there was little left to eat in the hedgerows and for this little, a few remaining berries, they had to compete with the birds. Though appreciably thinner, none of them felt ill and Arrietty's snow-tanned cheeks glowed with healthy colour.

But five days later it was a different story: intense cold and a second fall of snow – snow which piled up in air-filled drifts, too light and feathery to support a matchstick, let alone a borrower. They became house-bound and, for most of the time, joined Homily in the boot. The fleece was warm but, lying there in semi-darkness, the time passed slowly and the days were very boring. Homily would revive occasionally and tell them stories of her childhood: she could be as long-winded as she liked with this audience which could not get away.

They came to the end of the food. 'There's nothing left,' announced Pod, one evening, 'but one lump of sugar and a quarter inch of candle.'

'I couldn't never eat that,' complained Homily, '– not paraffin wax.'

'No one's asking you to,' said Pod. 'And we've still that drop of elderberry wine.'

Homily sat up in bed. 'Ah!' she said, 'put the sugar in the wine and heat it up over the quarter inch of candle.'

'But, Homily,' protested Pod, surprised, 'I thought you was teetotal.'

'Grog's different,' explained Homily. 'Call me when it's ready,' and she lay down again, piously closing her eyes.

'She will have her way,' muttered Pod, aside to Arrietty. He eyed the bottle dubiously. 'There's more here than I thought there was. I hope she'll be all right . . .'

It was quite a party: so long it had been since they had lit the candle; and it was pleasant to gather round it and feel its warmth.

When at last, warmed and befuddled, they snuggled down in the fleece, a curious contentment filled Arrietty – a calmness akin to hope. Pod, she noticed, drowsed with wine, had forgotten to lace up the boot . . . well, perhaps it didn't matter – if it was their last night on earth.

CHAPTER SEVENTEEN

'WHAT HEAVEN WILL, NO FROST CAN KILL'
Great Earthquake at Lisbon, 50,000 killed, 1755
[*Extract from Arrietty's Diary and Proverb Book, 1st November*]

IT was not their last night on earth: it seldom is, somehow; it was, however, their last night *in* earth.

Arrietty was the first to wake. She woke tired, as though she had slept badly, but it was only later (as she told Tom) that she remembered her dream of the earthquake. She not only woke tired but she woke cramped, and in a most uncomfortable position. There seemed more light than was usual, and then she remembered the unlaced opening. But why, she wondered, as she roused a little, did the daylight seem to come in from above, as from a half-concealed skylight? And suddenly she understood – the boot, which lay always on its side, for some extraordinary reason was standing upright. Her first thought (and it made her heart beat faster) was that her dream of an earthquake had been fact. She glanced at Pod and Homily: from what she could see of them, so enmeshed they were in fleece, they appeared to be sleeping soundly, but not, she thought, quite in the same positions as when they had gone to bed. Something had happened – she was sure of it – unless she was still dreaming.

Stealthily Arrietty sat up; although the boot was open, the air felt surprisingly warm – almost stuffy; it smelt of wood smoke and onions and of something else – a smell she could not define – could it be the scent of a human being?

Arrietty crept along the sole of the boot until she stood under the opening. Staring up she saw, instead of the sandy roof of the annexe, a curious network of wire springs and some kind of striped ceiling. They must be under some bed, she realized (she had seen this view of beds back home); but what bed? And where?

Trembling a little, but too curious not to be brave, she put her foot as high as she could into an eyelet hole and pulled herself erect on a loop of shoe-lace; another step up, a harder pull – and she found she could see out: the first thing she saw, standing close beside her – so close that she could see into it – was a second boot exactly like their own.

That was about all she could see from her present position: the bed

224

was low, stretching up she could almost touch the springs with her hands. But she could hear things – the liquid purr of a simmering kettle, the crackle of a fire, and a deeper, more rhythmic, sound – the sound of a human snore.

Arrietty hesitated: she was in half a mind to wake her parents, but, on second thoughts, she decided against it. First to find out a bit more. She unloosed a couple of lace-holes and eased out through the gap and, via the boot's instep, she walked out to the toe. Now she could really see.

As she had guessed, they were in a caravan. The boots stood under a collapsible bed which ran along one side of its length; and facing her on the opposite side, parallel to this bed, she saw a miniature coal range very like the one in the hedge, and a light-grained overmantel. The shelves of the overmantel, she saw, were set with pieces of looking-glass and adorned with painted vases, old coronation mugs, and trails of paper flowers. Below and on each side were set-in drawers and cupboards. A kettle simmered gently on the flat of the stove and a fire glowed redly through the bars.

At right angles, across the rear end of the caravan, she saw a second bunk, built in more permanently above a locker, and the locker, she noted, thinking of cover, was not set in flush with the door: there was space below into which, if crouching, a borrower might creep. In the bunk above the locker she saw a heaving mountain of patchwork which she knew must contain, by the sound of the snoring, a human being asleep. Beside the head of the bunk stood a watering-can, a tin mug balanced on the spout. Elder-flower wine, she thought – that last night had been their undoing.

To her left, also at right angles, was the door of the caravan, the top half open to the winter sunshine; it faced, she knew, towards the shafts. A crack of sunlight ran down the latch side of this door – a crack through which, if she dared approach it, she might perhaps see out.

She hesitated. It was only a step to the crack – a yard and a half at most: the human mountain was still heaving, filling the air with sound. Lightly, Arrietty slid from the toe of the boot to the worn piece of carpet and, soundless in her stockinged feet, she tiptoed to the door. For a moment the sunlight striking brightly through the crack almost seemed to blind her, then she made out a stretch of dirty grass, sodden with melting snow, a fire smoking sulkily between two stones, and beyond that, some way distant below the hedge, she saw a familiar object – the remains of a disused stove. Her spirits rose: so they were still at the same old caravan site – they had not, as she had feared at first, been travelling in the night.

As, her nose in the crack, she stood there staring, a sudden silence behind her caused her to turn; and, having turned, she froze: the human being was sitting up in bed. He was a huge man, fully dressed, dark-skinned, and with a mass of curling hair; his eyes were screwed up, his fists stretched, and his mouth wide open in a long-drawn groaning yawn.

Panic-stricken, she thought about cover. She glanced at the bed to her right – the bed under which she had awakened. Three strides would do it; but better to be still, that's what Pod would say: the shadowed part of the door against which she stood would seem still darker because of that opened half above, filled so brightly with winter sunshine. All Arrietty did was to move aside from the crack of light against whose brightness she might be outlined.

The human being stopped yawning and swung his legs down from the bunk and sat there a moment, pensively, admiring his stockinged feet. One of his eyes, Arrietty noticed, was dark and twinkling, the other paler, hazel-yellow, with a strangely drooping lid. This must be Mild Eye – this great, fat, terrifying man, who sat so quietly smiling at his feet.

As Arrietty watched, the strange eyes lifted a little and the smile broadened: Mild Eye, Arrietty saw, was looking at the boots.

She caught her breath as she saw him lean forward and (a stretch of the long arm was enough) snatch them up from below the other bed. He examined them lovingly, holding them together as a pair, and then, as though struck by some discrepancy in the weight, he set one down on the floor. He shook the other gently, turning its opening towards his palm and, as nothing fell out, he put his hand inside.

The shout he gave, Arrietty thought afterwards, must have been heard for miles. He dropped the boot, which fell on its side, and Arrietty, in an anguish of terror, saw Homily and Pod run out and disappear between his legs (but not, she realized, before he had glimpsed them) into the shallow space between his bunk and the floor.

There was a horrified pause.

Arrietty was scared enough, but Mild Eye seemed even more so: his strange eyes bulged in a face which had turned the colour of putty. Two tiny words hung in the silence, a thread-thin echo, incredible to Mild Eye: someone . . . something . . . somewhere . . . on a note of anguish, had stammered out 'Oh dear!'

And that was controlled enough, Arrietty thought, for what Homily must be feeling: to be woken from a deep sleep and shaken out of the boot; to have seen those two strange eyes staring down at her; to have heard that thunderous shout. The space between the locker and the floor, Arrietty calculated, could not be more than a couple of inches; it would be impossible to stand up in there and, although safe enough for the moment, there they would have to stay: there seemed no possible way out.

For herself – glued motionless against the shadows – she was less afraid: true enough she stood face to face with Mild Eye; but he would not see her, of this she felt quite sure, providing she did not move: he seemed too shaken by those half-glimpsed creatures which so inexplicably had appeared between his feet.

Stupefied, he stared for a moment longer; then awkwardly he got down on all fours and peered under the locker; as though disappointed, he got up again, found a box of matches, struck a light, and once again explored the shadows as far as the light would carry. Arrietty took advantage of his turned back to take her three strides and slip back under the bed. There was a cardboard box under here, which she could use as cover, some ends of rope, a bundle of rabbit snares, and a slimy saucer which once had contained milk.

She made her way between these objects until she reached the far end – the junction of the bed with the locker below the bunk. Peering out through the tangle of rabbit snares she saw that Mild Eye – despairing of matchlight – had armed himself with a hefty knobkerrie stick which he was now running back and forth in a business-like manner along the space between the bunk and the floor. Arrietty, her hands pressed tight against her heart, once thought she heard a strangled squeak and a muttered: 'Oh, my gracious –!'

At that moment the door of the caravan opened, there was a draught of cold air, and a wild-eyed woman looked in. Wrapped in a heavy shawl against the cold, she was carrying a basket of clothes-pegs. Arrietty, crouching among the rabbit snares, saw the wild eyes open still more wildly, and a flood of questions in some foreign tongue was aimed at Mild Eye's behind. Arrietty saw the woman's breath smoke in the clear sunshine and could hear her ear-rings jangle.

Mild Eye, a little shamefaced, rose to his feet; he looked very big to Arrietty and, though she could no longer see his face, his hanging hands looked helpless. He replied to the woman in the same language: he said quite a lot; sometimes his voice rose on a curious squeak of dismayed excitement.

He picked up the boot, showed it to the woman, said a lot about it, and – somewhat nervously, Arrietty noticed – he put his hand inside; he pulled out the wad of fleece, the unravelled sock, and – with some surprise because it had once been his – the strip of coloured blanket. As he showed these to the woman, who continued to jeer, his voice became almost tearful. The woman laughed then – a thin, high peal of raucous laughter. Completely heartless, Arrietty thought, completely unkind. She wanted almost for Mild Eye's sake to run out and show this doubting creature that there were such things as borrowers ('it's so awful and sad,' she once admitted to Tom Goodenough, 'to belong to a race that no sane person believes in'). But tempting as this thought was she thought better of it, and instead she edged herself out from the end of the bed into the darker space below the bunk.

And only just in time: there was a faint thud on the carpet, and there, not a foot from where she had stood, she saw the four paws of a cat – three black and one white; saw him stretch, roll over, and rub his whiskered face on the sun-warmed carpet: he was black, she saw, with a white belly. He or she? Arrietty did not know: a fine beast anyway, sleek and heavy as cats are who hunt for themselves out of doors.

Sidling crab-wise into the shadows, her eyes on the basking cat, she felt her hand taken suddenly, held, and squeezed tight. 'Oh, thank goodness . . .' Homily breathed in her ear, 'thank heaven you're safe.'

Arrietty put a finger to her lips. 'Hush,' she whispered, barely above her breath, staring towards the cat.

'It can't get under here,' whispered Homily. Her face, Arrietty saw, looked pallid in the half-light, grey and streaked with dust. 'We're in a caravan,' she went on, determined to tell the news.

'I know,' said Arrietty, and pleaded: 'Mother, we'd better be quiet.'

Homily was silent a moment, then she said: 'He caught your father's back with that stick. The soft part,' she added reassuringly.

'Hush,' whispered Arrietty again. She could not see much from where she was, but Mild Eye, she gathered, was struggling into a coat; after a moment he stooped, and his hand came near when he felt under the settee for the bundle of rabbit snares; the woman was still out of doors busy about the fire.

After a while, her eyes growing used to the dimness she saw her father sitting some way back, leaning against the wall. She crawled across to him, and Homily followed.

'Well, here we are,' said Pod, barely moving his lips, 'and not dead yet,' he added, with a glance at Homily.

CHAPTER EIGHTEEN

'HIDDEN TROUBLES DISQUIET MOST'
Gun Powder Plot, 1605
[Extract from Arrietty's Diary and Proverb Book, 5th November]

THEY crouched there listening, holding their breaths as Mild Eye unlatched the door, re-latched it, and clumped off down the steps.

There was a pause.

'We're alone now,' remarked Homily at last in her ordinary speaking voice, 'I mean, we could get out, I shouldn't wonder, if it weren't for that cat.'

'Hush –' whispered Pod. He had heard the woman shoot some mocking question at Mild Eye and, at Mild Eye's mumbled reply, the woman had laughed her laugh. Arrietty, too, was listening.

'*He* knows we're here,' she whispered, 'but *she* won't believe him . . .'

'And that cat'll know we're here, too, soon enough,' replied Pod.

Arrietty shivered. The cat, she realized, must have been asleep on the bed, while she, Arrietty, had been standing unprotected beside the door.

Pod was silent a while, thinking deeply. 'Yes,' he said at last, 'it's a rum go: he must have come round at dusk last night, seeing after his snares . . . and there he finds his lost boot in our hollow.'

'We should have pulled down the screen,' whispered Arrietty.

'We should that,' agreed Pod.

'We didn't even lace up the boot,' went on Arrietty.

'Yes,' said Pod, and sighed. 'A bottle at night and you're out like a light. That how it goes?' he asked.

'More or less,' agreed Arrietty in a whisper.

They sat waist-high in dusty trails of fluff. 'Disgusting,' remarked Homily, suppressing a sneeze. 'If I'd built this caravan,' she grumbled, 'I'd have set the bunk in flush with the floor.'

'Then thank goodness you didn't build it,' remarked Pod, as a whiskered shadow appeared between them and the light: the cat had seen them at last.

'Don't panic,' he went on calmly, as Homily gave a gasp, 'this bunk's too low, we're all right here.'

'Oh my goodness,' whispered Homily, as she saw a luminous eye. Pod squeezed her hand to silence her.

The cat, having sniffed his way along the length of the opening, lay down suddenly on its side and ogled them through the gap; quite friendly, it looked, and a little coy, as though coaxing them out to play.

'They don't *know*,' whispered Homily then, referring to cats in general.

'You keep still,' whispered Pod.

For a long time nothing much happened: the shaft of sunshine moved slowly across the worn carpet, and the cat, motionless, seemed to doze.

'Well,' whispered Homily, after a while, 'in a way, it's kind of nice to be indoors.'

Once the woman came in and fumbled in the dresser for a wooden spoon and took away the kettle; they heard her swearing as she tended

the outdoor fire, and once a gust of acrid smoke blew in through the doorway, making Arrietty cough. The cat woke up at that and cocked an eye at them.

Towards midday, they smelt a savoury smell – the gamy smell of stew: it would drift towards them as the wind veered and then, tormentingly, would drift away.

Arrietty felt her mouth water.

'*Oh*, I'm hungry . . .' she sighed.

'I'm thirsty,' said Homily.

'I'm both,' said Pod. 'Now be quiet, the two of you,' he told them, 'shut your eyes and think of something else.'

'Whenever I shut my eyes,' protested Homily, 'I see a nice hot thimbleful of tea, or I think of that teapot we had back home: that oak-apple teapot, with a quill spout.'

'Well, think of it,' said Pod; 'no harm in that, if it does you good . . .'

The man came back at last. He unlatched the door and threw a couple of snared rabbits down on the carpet. He and the woman ate their meal on the steps of the caravan using the floor as a table.

At this point the smell of food became unbearable; it drew the three borrowers out of the shadows to the very edge of their shelter: the tin plates, filled with savoury stew, were at eye level; they had a splendid view of the floury potatoes and the richly running gravy. 'Oh my . . .' muttered Homily unhappily, 'pheasant – and what a way to cook it.'

Once Mild Eye threw a morsel on the carpet. Enviously they watched the cat pounce and leisurely fall to, crunching up the bones like the hunter it was. 'Oh my . . .' muttered Homily again, 'those teeth!'

At length Mild Eye pushed aside his plate. The cat stared with interest at the pile of chewed bones to which here and there clung slivers of tender meat. Homily stared too: the plate was almost in range. 'Dare you, Pod?' she whispered.

'No,' said Pod – so loudly and firmly that the cat turned round and looked at him; gaze met gaze with curious mutual defiance; the cat's tail began slowly to swish from side to side.

'Come on,' gasped Pod, as the cat crouched, and all three dodged back into the shadows in the split half-second before the pounce.

Mild Eye turned quickly. Staring, he called to the woman, pointing towards the bunk, and both man and woman stooped their heads to floor-level, gazing across the carpet . . . and gazing, it seemed to Arrietty, crouched with her parents against the back wall of the caravan, right into their faces. It seemed impossible that they could not be seen: but – 'It's all right,' Pod told them, speaking with still lips in the lightest of whispers, 'don't panic – just you keep still.'

There was silence: even the woman now seemed uneasy – the cat, padding and peering, back and forth along the length of the locker, had aroused her curiosity. 'Don't you move,' breathed Pod again.

A sudden shadow fell across the patch of sunlight on the carpet: a third figure, Arrietty noted with surprise, loomed up behind the crouching gipsies in the doorway; someone less tall than Mild Eye. Arrietty, rigid between her parents, saw three buttons of a stained corduroy waistcoat and, as its wearer stopped, she saw a young face, and a tow-coloured head of hair. 'What's up?' asked a voice which had a crack in it.

Arrietty saw Mild Eye's expression change: it became all at once sulky and suspicious. He turned slowly and faced the speaker, but before he did so he slid his right hand inconspicuously across the floor of the caravan, pushing the two dead rabbits out of sight.

'What's up, Mild Eye?' asked the boy again. 'Looks like you'm seeing ghosties.'

Mild Eye shrugged his great shoulders. 'Maybe I am,' he said.

The boy stooped again, staring along the floor, and Arrietty could see that, under one arm, he carried a gun. 'Wouldn't be a ferret by any chance?' he asked slily.

The woman laughed then. 'A ferret!' she exclaimed, and laughed again. 'You're the one for ferrets . . .' Pulling her shawl more tightly about her she moved away towards the fire. 'You think the cat act *kind* like that for a ferret?'

The boy stared curiously past the cat across the floor, screwing his eyelids to see beyond the pacing cat and into the shadows. 'The cat bain't acting so kind,' he remarked thoughtfully towards the fire.

'A couple of midgets he's got in there,' the woman told him, '– dressed up to kill – or so he says,' and she went off again into screams of jeering laughter.

The boy did not laugh; his expression did not change: calmly he stared at the crack below the bunk. 'Dressed up to kill . . .' he repeated and, after a moment, he added: 'Only two?'

'How many do you want?' asked the woman. 'Half a dozen? A couple's enough, ain't it?'

'What do you reckon to do with them?' asked the boy.

'Do with them?' repeated the woman, staring stupidly.

'I mean, when you catch them?'

The woman gave him a curious look, as though doubting his reason. 'But there ain't nothing there,' she told him.

'But you just said –'

The woman laughed, half angry, half bewildered. 'Mild Eye sees 'em – not me. Or so he makes out. There ain't nothing there, I tell you –'

'I seen 'em all right,' said Mild Eye. He stretched his first finger and thumb. 'This high, I'd say – a bit of a woman, it looked like, and a bit of a man.'

'Mind if I look?' asked the boy, his foot on the steps. He laid down his gun, and Arrietty, watching, saw him put his hand in his pocket; there was a stealthiness about his movement which drove the blood from her heart. 'Oh,' she gasped, and grabbed her father's sleeve.

'What is it?' breathed Pod, leaning towards her.

'His pocket –' stammered Arrietty. 'Something alive in his pocket!'

'A ferret,' cried Homily, forgetting to whisper. 'We're finished.'

'Hush –' implored Pod. The boy had heard something; he had seated himself on the top step and was now leaning forward gazing towards them across the strip of faded carpet. At Homily's exclamation, Pod had seen his eyes widen, his face become alert.

'What's the good of whispering?' complained Homily, lowering her voice all the same. 'We're for it now. Wouldn't matter if we sang –'

'Hush –' said Pod again.

'How would you think to get 'em out?' the boy was asking, his eyes on the gap; his right hand, Arrietty saw, still feeling in his pocket.

'Easy,' explained Mild Eye; 'empty the locker and take up them boards underneath.'

'You see?' whispered Homily, almost in triumph, 'it doesn't matter what we do now!'

Pod gave up. 'Then sing,' he suggested wearily.

'Nailed down, them boards are, aren't they?' asked the boy.

'No,' said Mild Eye. 'I've had 'em out after rats; they comes out in a piece.'

The boy, his head lowered, was staring into the gap. Arrietty, from where she crouched, was looking straight into his eyes: they were thoughtful eyes, bland and blue.

'Say you catch them,' the boy went on, 'what then?'

'What then?' repeated Mild Eye, puzzled.

'What do you want to do with 'em?'

'Do with 'em? Cage 'em up. What else?'

'Cage 'em up in what?'

'In that.' Mild Eye touched the bird cage, which swung slightly. 'What else?'

('And feed us on groundsel, I shouldn't wonder,' muttered Homily below her breath.)

'You want to keep 'em?' asked the boy, his eyes on the shadowed gap.

'Keep 'em, naow! Sell 'em!' exclaimed Mild Eye. 'Fetch a pretty penny, that lot would – cage and all complete.'

'Oh, my goodness,' whimpered Homily.

'Quiet,' breathed Pod, 'better the cage than the ferret.'

'No,' thought Arrietty, 'better the ferret.'

'What would you feed 'em on?' the boy was asking; he seemed to be playing for time.

Mild Eye laughed indulgently. 'Anything. Bits o' left-overs . . .'

('You hear that?' whispered Homily, very angry.

'Well, to-day it was pheasant,' Pod reminded her; but he was glad she was angry: anger made her brave.)

Mild Eye had climbed right in now – blotting out the sunshine. 'Move over,' he said to the boy, 'we got to get at the locker.'

The boy shifted, a token shift. 'What about the cat?' he said.

'That's right,' agreed Mild Eye, 'better have the cat out. Come on, Tiger –'

But the cat, it seemed, was as stubborn as the boy and shared his interest in borrowers; evading Mild Eye's hand, it sprang away to the bed, and (Arrietty gathered from a slight thump immediately above their heads) from the end of the bed to the locker. Mild Eye came after it: they could see his great feet close against the gap – their own dear boot was there just beside them, with the patch which Pod had sewn! It seemed incredible to see it worn, and by such a hostile foot.

'Better cart it out to the missus,' suggested the boy, as Mild Eye grabbed the cat; 'if it bain't held on to it'll only jump back in.'

'Don't you dare,' moaned Homily, just below her breath.

Pod looked amazed. 'Who are you talking to?' he asked in a whisper.

'Him – Mild Eye; the minute he leaves this caravan that boy'll be after us with the ferret.'

'Now, see here –' began Pod.

'You mark my words,' went on Homily in a panic-stricken whisper. 'I know who he is now. It's all come back to me: young Tom Goodenough. I heard speak of that one many a time back home under the kitchen. And I wouldn't be surprised if it wasn't him we saw at the window – that day we made off, remember? Proper devil he's reckoned to be with that ferret –'

'Quiet, Homily!' implored Pod.

'Why? For heaven's sake – they know we're here: quiet or noisy – what's the difference to a ferret?'

Mild Eye swore suddenly as though the cat had scratched him. 'Cart him right out,' said the boy again, 'and see she holds him.'

'Don't fret,' said Mild Eye, 'we can shut the door.'

'That bain't no good,' said the boy; 'we can't shut the top half; we got to have light.'

On the threshold Mild Eye hesitated. 'Don't you touch nothin',' he said, and stood there a moment, waiting, before he clumped off down the steps. On the bottom rung he seemed to slip: the borrowers could

hear him swearing. 'This blamed boot,' they heard him say, and
something about the heel.

'You all right?' called out the boy carelessly. The answer was an
oath.

'Block your ears,' whispered Homily to Arrietty. 'Oh, my goodness
me, did you hear what he said?'

'Yes,' began Arrietty obligingly, 'he said –'

'Oh, you wicked, heathen girl,' cried Homily angrily, 'shame on
yourself for listening!'

'Quiet, Homily,' begged Pod again.

'But you know what happened, Pod?' whispered Homily excitedly.
'The heel came off the boot! What did I tell you, up in the ditch, when
you would take out them nails!' For one brief moment she forgot her
fears and gave a tiny giggle.

'Look,' breathed Arrietty suddenly, and reached for her mother's
hand. They looked.

The boy, leaning towards them on one elbow, his steady gaze fixed
on the slit of darkness between the locker and floor, was feeling stealthily
in the right-hand pocket of his coat – it was the deep, pouched pocket
common to gamekeepers.

'Oh, my . . .' muttered Homily, as Pod took her hand.

'Shut your eyes,' said Pod. 'No use running and you won't know
nothing: a ferret strikes quick.'

There was a pause, tense and solemn, while three small hearts beat
quickly. Homily broke it.

'I've tried to be a good wife to you, Pod,' she announced tearfully,
one eye screwed obediently shut, the other cautiously open.

'You've been first-rate,' said Pod, his eyes on the boy. Against the
light it was hard to see, but something moved in his hand: a creature he
had taken from his pocket.

'A bit sharp sometimes,' went on Homily.

'It doesn't matter now,' said Pod.

'I'm sorry, Pod,' said Homily.

'I forgive you,' said Pod absently. A deeper shadow now had fallen
across the carpet: Mild Eye had come back up the steps. Pod saw the
woman had sneaked up behind him, clasping the cat in her shawl.

The boy did not start or turn. 'Make for my pocket . . .' he said
steadily, his eyes on the gap.

'What's that?' asked Mild Eye, surprised.

'Make for my pocket,' repeated the boy, 'do you hear what I say?' And suddenly he loosed on the carpet the thing he had held in his hand.

'Oh, my goodness –' cried Homily, clutching on to Pod.

'Whatever is it?' she went on, after a moment, both eyes suddenly open. Some kind of living creature it was, but certainly not a ferret . . . too slow . . . too angular . . . too upright . . . too –

Arrietty let out a glad cry: 'It's Spiller!'

'What?' exclaimed Homily, almost crossly – tricked, she felt, when she thought of those grave 'last words'.

'It's Spiller,' Arrietty sang out again, 'Spiller . . . Spiller . . . Spiller!'

'Looking quite ridiculous,' remarked Homily; and indeed he did look rather odd and sausage-like, stuffed out in his stiff new clothes; he would render them down gradually to a wearable suppleness.

'What are you waiting for?' asked Spiller. 'You heard what he said. Come on now. Get moving, can't you?'

'That boy?' exclaimed Homily, 'was he speaking to us?'

'Who else?' snapped Spiller. 'He don't want Mild Eye in his pocket. Come on –'

'His pocket!' exclaimed Homily in a frantic whisper. She turned to Pod. 'Now let's get this right: young Tom Goodenough wants me' – she touched her own chest – 'to run out there, right in the open, get meself over his trouser-leg, across his middle, up to his hip, and potter down all meek and mild into his pocket?'

'Not you only,' explained Pod, 'all of us.'

'He's crazy,' announced Homily firmly, tightening her lips.

'Now, see here, Homily –' began Pod.

'I'd sooner perish,' Homily asserted.

'That's just what you will do,' said Pod.

'Remember that peg-bag?' she reminded him. 'I couldn't face it, Pod. And where's he going to take us? Tell me that?'

'How should I know?' exclaimed Pod. 'Now, come on, Homily, you do what he says, there's me brave old girl . . . take her by the wrist, Spiller, she's got to come . . . ready, Arrietty? Now for it –' and suddenly there they were, the whole group of them – out in the open.

CHAPTER NINETEEN

'FORTUNE FAVOURS THE BRAVE'
Sherman's March to the Coast began, 1864
[Extract from Arrietty's Diary and Proverb Book, 13th November]

THE woman screeched when she saw them: she dropped the cat, and ran for her life, making hell for leather towards the main road. Mild Eye, too, was taken aback: he sat down on the bed with his feet in the air as though a contaminated flood were swirling across the carpet: the cat, unnerved by the general uproar, made a frantic leap for the overmantel, bringing down two mugs, a framed photograph, and a spray of paper rosebuds.

Pod and Arrietty made their own slithering way across the folds of trouser-leg to the rising slope of hip; but poor Spiller, pulling and pushing a protesting Homily, was picked up and dropped in. For one awful moment, attached by the wrist to Spiller, Homily dangled in air, before the boy's quick fingers gathered her up and tidied her neatly away. Only just in time – for Mild Eye, recovering, had made a sudden

238

grab, missing her by inches ('Torn us apart, he would have,' she said later, 'like a couple of bananas!'). Deep in the pocket, she heard his angry shout of 'Four of 'em you got there. Come on: fair's fair – hand over them first two!'

They did not know what happened next: all was darkness and jumble. Some sort of struggle was going on – there was the sound of heavy breathing, muttered swear words, and the pocket swayed and bounced. Then, by the bumping, they knew the boy was running and Mild Eye, shouting behind him, was cursing his heelless boot. They heard these shouts grow fainter, and the crackle of breaking branches as the boy crashed through a hedge.

There was no conversation in the pocket: all four of them felt too dazed. At last Pod, wedged, upside-down in a corner, freed his mouth from fluff. 'You all right, Homily?' he gasped. Homily, tightly interwoven with Spiller and Arrietty, could not quite tell. Pod heard a slight squeak. 'Me leg's gone numb,' said Homily unhappily.

'Not broken, is it?' asked Pod anxiously.

'Can't feel nothing in it,' said Homily.

'Can you move it?' asked Pod.

There was a sharp exclamation from Spiller as Homily said 'No.'

'If it's the leg you're pinching,' remarked Spiller, 'stands to reason you can't move it.'

'How do you know?' asked Homily.

'Because it's mine,' he said.

The boy's steps became slower: he seemed to be going uphill; after a while he sat down. The great hand came down amongst them. Homily began to whimper, but the fingers slid past her; they were feeling for Spiller. The coat was pulled round and the pocket flap held open, so the boy could peer at them. 'You all right, Spiller?' he asked.

Spiller grunted.

'Which is Homily?' asked the boy.

'The noisy one,' said Spiller. 'I told you.'

'You all right, Homily?' asked the boy.

Homily, terrified, was silent.

The great fingers came down again, sliding their way into the pocket.

Spiller, standing now with legs apart and back supported against the upright seam, called out tersely: 'Leave 'em be.'

The fingers stopped moving. 'I wanted to see if they were all right,' said the boy.

'They're all right,' said Spiller.

'I'd like to have 'em out,' the boy went on. 'I'd like to have a look at 'em.' He peered downwards at the open pocket. 'You're not dead, are you?' he inquired anxiously. 'You bain't none of you dead?'

'How could we say, if we was?' muttered Homily irritably.

'You leave 'em be,' said Spiller again; 'it's warm in here: you don't want to bring 'em out sudden into the cold. You'll see 'em often enough,' he consoled the boy, 'once you get back home.'

The fingers withdrew and they were in the dark again; there was a rocking and the boy stood up. Pod, Homily, and Arrietty slid the length of the bottom seam of the pocket, fetching up against the opposite corner; it was full of dried breadcrumbs; jagged and hard as concrete. 'Ouch!' cried Homily, unhappily. Spiller, Arrietty noticed, though he swayed on his feet, managed to keep upright. Spiller, she guessed, had travelled by pocket before: the boy was walking again now, and the coat swayed with a more predictable rhythm. 'After a while,' Arrietty thought, 'I'll have a go at standing myself.'

Pod experimentally broke off a jagged piece of breadcrumb which, after patient sucking, slowly began to dissolve. 'I'll try a bit of that,' said Homily, holding out her hand; she had revived a little and was feeling peckish.

'Where's he taking us?' she asked Spiller after a while.

'Round the wood and over the hill.'

'Where he lives with his grandpa?'

'That's right,' admitted Spiller.

'I ain't ever heard tell much about gamekeepers,' said Homily, 'nor what they'd be apt to do with – a borrower, say. Nor what sort of boy this is neither. I mean,' she went on in a worried voice, 'my mother-in-law had an uncle once who was kept in a tin box with four holes in the lid and fed twice a day by an eye-dropper . . .'

'He ain't that sort of boy,' said Spiller.

'Whatever's an eye-dropper?' asked Pod. He took it to be some strange sort of craft or profession.

'Then there was Lupy's cousin, Oggin, you remember,' went on Homily. 'They made a regular kind of world for him in the bottom of an old tin bath in the outhouse; grass, pond, and all. And they gave him a cart to ride in and a lizard for company. But the sides of the bath were good and slippery: they knew he couldn't get out . . .'

'Lupy?' repeated Spiller wonderingly. 'Wouldn't be two called that?'

'This one married my brother Hendreary,' said Homily. 'Why,' she exclaimed with sudden excitement, 'you don't say you know her!'

The pocket had stopped swaying: they heard some metallic sound and the sliding squeak of a latch.

'I know her all right,' whispered Spiller. 'She makes my winter clothes.'

'Quiet,' urged Pod; 'we've arrived.' He had heard the sound of an opening door and could smell an indoor smell.

'You know *Lupy?*' Homily persisted, unaware even that the pocket had become darker. 'But what are they doing? And where are they living – she and Hendreary? We thought they was eaten by foxes, children and all . . .'

'Quiet, Homily,' implored Pod. Strange movements seemed to be going on, doors were opening and shutting; so stealthily the boy was walking the pocket now hung still.

'Tell us, Spiller, quick,' went on Homily; but she dropped her voice to an obedient whisper. 'You must know! Where are they living now?'

Spiller hesitated – in the semi-darkness he seemed to smile.

'They're living here,' he said.

The boy now seemed to be kneeling.

As the fingers came down again, feeling amongst them, Homily let out a cry. 'It's all right,' whispered Pod, as she burrowed back among the crumbs. 'Keep your head – we got to come out sometime.'

Spiller went first; he sailed away from them – nonchalantly astride a finger, without even bothering to glance back. Then it was Arrietty's turn. 'Oh my goodness me . . .' muttered Homily, 'wherever will they put her?'

Pod's turn next; but Homily went with him. She scrambled aboard at the last moment by creeping under the thumb. There was hardly time to feel sick (it was the swoosh through the empty air which Homily always dreaded), so deftly and gently they found themselves set down.

A gleam of firelight struck the tiny group as they stood beside the hearth, against a high, wooden wall: it was, they discovered later, the side of the log-box. They stood together – close and scared, controlling their longing to run. Spiller, they noticed, had disappeared.

The boy, on one knee, towered above them – a terrifying mountain of flesh. The firelight flickered on his down-turned face: they could feel the draught of his breathing.

'It's all right,' he assured them, 'you'll be all right now.' He was staring with great interest, as a collector would stare at a new-found specimen. His hand hovered above them as though he longed to touch them, to pick one of them up, to examine each more closely.

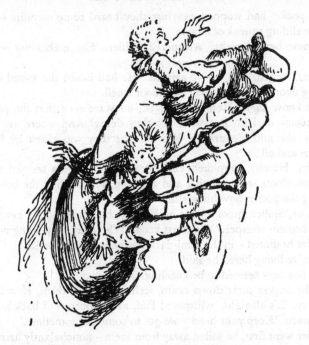

Nervously Pod cleared his throat. 'Where's Spiller?' he asked.

'He'll be back,' said the boy. After a moment he added: 'I got six altogether in there.'

'Six what?' asked Homily nervously.

'Six borrowers,' said the boy. 'I reckon I got the best collection of borrowers in two counties. And,' he added, 'me grandad ain't seen one. His eyes is sharp enough, yet he ain't ever seen a borrower.'

Pod cleared his throat again. 'He ain't supposed to,' he said.

'Some I got in there' – the boy jerked his head towards the log-box – 'I never sees neither. Scared. Some folks say you can't never tame 'em. You can give 'em the earth, 'tis said, but they'll never come out and be civil.'

'I would,' said Arrietty.

'Now you behave yourself,' snapped Homily, alarmed.

'Spiller would, too,' said Arrietty.

'Spiller's different,' replied Homily, with a nervous glance towards the boy – Spiller, she felt, was the boy's curator: the go-between of this rare collection. 'Gets so much a head, I wouldn't wonder?'

'Here he is,' said Arrietty, looking towards the corner of the log-box. Noiselessly he had come upon them.

'She won't come out,' said Spiller to the boy.

'Oh,' exclaimed Homily, 'does he mean Lupy?'

No one answered. Spiller stood silent, looking up at the boy. The boy frowned thoughtfully; he seemed disappointed. He looked them over once more, examining each of them from head to foot as though loath to see them go; he sighed a little. 'Then take 'em in,' he said.

CHAPTER TWENTY

'LONG LOOKED FOR COMES AT LAST'
Vasco da Gama rounded Cape of Good Hope, 1497
[*Extract from Arrietty's Diary and Proverb Book, 20th November*]

THEY filed in through the Gothic-shaped hole in the wainscot, a little nervous, a little shy. It was shadowy inside like a cave; disappointingly it felt uninhabited and smelled of dust and mice. 'Oh dear,' muttered Homily incredulously, 'is this how they live . . .?' She stopped suddenly and picked up some object from the floor. 'My goodness,' she whispered aside excitedly to Pod, 'do you know what this is?' and she brandished a whitish object under his nose.

'Yes,' said Pod, 'it's a bit of quill pipe-cleaner. Put it down, Homily, and come on, do. Spiller's waiting.'

'It's the spout of our old oak-apple teapot,' persisted Homily, 'that's what it is. I'd know it anywhere and it's no good telling me any different. So they *are* here . . .' she mused wonderingly as she followed Pod into the shadows to where Spiller with Arrietty stood waiting.

'We go up here,' said Spiller, and Homily saw that he stood with his hand on a ladder. Glancing up to where the rungs soared away above them into dimness, she gave a slight shudder: the ladder was made of matchsticks, neatly glued and spliced to two lengths of split cane, such as florists use to support potted plants.

'I'll go first,' said Pod. 'We better take it one at a time.'

Homily watched fearfully until she heard his voice from above.

'It's all right,' he whispered from some invisible eyrie; 'come on up.'

Homily followed, her knees trembling, and emerged at last on to the dim-lit platform beside Pod – an aerial landing stage, that was what it looked like – which creaked a little when she stepped on it and almost seemed to sway. Below lay hollow darkness; ahead an open door. 'Oh my goodness,' she muttered, 'I do hope it's safe . . . don't look down,' she advised Arrietty, who came up next.

But Arrietty had no temptation to look down: her eyes were on the lighted doorway and the moving shadows within; she heard the faint sound of voices and a sudden high-pitched laugh.

'Come on,' said Spiller, slipping past her, and making towards the door.

Arrietty never forgot her first sight of that upstairs room: the warmth, the sudden cleanliness, the winking candle-light, and the smell of home-cooked food.

And so many voices . . . so many people . . .

Gradually, in a dazed way, she began to sort them out: that must be Aunt Lupy embracing her mother – Aunt Lupy so round and glowing, her mother so smudged and lean. Why did they cling and weep, she wondered, and squeeze each other's hands? They had never liked each other – all the world knew that. Homily had thought Lupy stuck-up because, back in the big house, Lupy had lived in the drawing-room and (she had heard it rumoured) changed for dinner at night. And Lupy despised Homily for living under the kitchen and for pronouncing parquet 'parkett'.

And here was Uncle Hendreary, his beard grown thinner, telling her father that this could not be Arrietty, and her father, with pride, telling Uncle Hendreary it could. Those must be the three boy cousins – whose names she had not caught – graduated in size but as like as peas in a pod. And this thin, tall, fairylike creature, neither old nor young, who hovered shyly in the background with a faint uneasy smile, who was she?

Homily screamed when she saw her and clapped her hand to her mouth. 'It can't be Eggletina!'

It evidently could. Arrietty stared too, wondering if she had heard aright: Eggletina, that long-lost cousin who one fine day escaped from under the floor and was never seen again? A kind of legend she had been to Arrietty and a life-long cautionary tale. Well, here she was, safe and sound, unless they all were dreaming.

And well they might be.

There was something strangely unreal about this room – furnished with doll's-house furniture of every shape and size, none of it matching or in proportion. There were chairs upholstered in rep or velvet, some of them too small to sit in and some too steep and large; there were chiffoniers which were too tall and occasional tables far too low; and a toy fire-place with coloured plaster coals and its fire-irons stuck down all-of-a-piece with the fender; there were two make-believe windows with curved pelmets and red satin curtains, each hand-painted with an imitation view – one looked out on a Swiss mountain scene, the other a Highland glen ('Eggletina did them,' Aunt Lupy boasted in her rich society voice. 'We're going to have a third when we get the curtains – a view of Lake Como from Monte S. Primo'); there were table lamps and standard lamps, flounced, festooned, and tasselled, but the light in the room, Arrietty noticed, came from humble, familiar dips like those they had made at home.

Everybody looked extraordinarily clean and Arrietty became even shyer. She threw a quick glance at her father and mother and was not reassured: none of their clothes had been washed for weeks nor, for some days, had their hands and faces. Pod's trousers had a tear in one knee and Homily's hair hung down in snakes. And here was Aunt Lupy, plump and polite, begging Homily please to take off her things in the kind of voice, Arrietty imagined, usually reserved for feather boas, opera cloaks, and freshly cleaned white kid gloves.

But Homily, who back at home had so dreaded being 'caught out' in a soiled apron, knew one worth two of that. She had, Pod and Arrietty

noticed with pride, adopted her woman-tried-beyond-endurance role backed up by one called yes-I've-suffered-but-don't-let's-speak-of-it-now; she had invented a new smile, wan but brave, and had – in the same good cause – plucked the two last hair-pins out of her dust-filled hair. 'Poor dear Lupy,' she was saying, glancing wearily about, 'what a lot of furniture! Whoever helps you with the dusting?' And swaying a little, she sank on a chair.

They rushed to support her, as she hoped they might. Water was brought and they bathed her face and hands. Hendreary stood with the tears in his brotherly eyes. 'Poor valiant soul,' he muttered, shaking his head, 'your mind kind of reels when you think of what she's been through . . .'

Then, after a quick wash and brush up all round and a brisk bit of eye-wiping, they all sat down to supper. This they ate in the kitchen, which was rather a come-down except that, in here, the fire was real: a splendid cooking range made of a large, black door-lock; they poked the fire through the keyhole, which glowed handsomely, and the smoke, they were told, went out through a series of pipes to the cottage chimney behind.

The long, white table was richly spread: it was an eighteenth-century finger-plate off some old drawing-room door – white-enamelled and painted with forget-me-nots, supported firmly on four stout pencil stubs where once the screws had been; the points of the pencils emerged slightly through the top of the table; one was copying-ink and they were warned not to touch it in case it stained their hands.

There was every kind of dish and preserve – both real and false; pies, puddings, and bottled fruits out of season – all cooked by Lupy, and an imitation leg of mutton and a dish of plaster tarts borrowed from the doll's house. There were three real tumblers as well as acorn cups and a couple of green glass decanters.

Talk, talk, talk . . . Arrietty, listening, felt dazed: she saw now why they had been expected. Spiller, she gathered, having found the alcove bootless and its inmates flown, had salvaged their few possessions and had run and told young Tom. Lupy felt a little faint suddenly when they mentioned this person by name, and had to leave the table. She sat a while in the next room on a frail gilt chair placed just inside the doorway – 'between draughts' as she put it – fanning her round red face with a lark's feather.

'Mother's like this about humans,' explained the eldest cousin. 'It's no good telling her he's tame as anything and wouldn't hurt a fly!'

'You never know,' said Lupy darkly, from her seat in the doorway. 'He's nearly full grown! And that, they say, is when they start to be dangerous . . .'

'Lupy's right,' agreed Pod, 'I'd never trust 'em meself.'

'Oh, how can you say that?' cried Arrietty. 'Look at the way he snatched us up right out of the jaws of death!'

'Snatched you up?' screamed Lupy from the next room. 'You mean – *with his hands?*'

Homily gave her brave little laugh, listlessly chasing a globule of raspberry around her too slippery plate. 'Naturally . . .' She shrugged. 'It was nothing really.'

'Oh, dear . . .' stammered Lupy faintly, 'oh, you poor thing . . . imagine it! I think,' she went on, 'if you'll excuse me a moment, I'll just go and lie down . . .' and she heaved her weight off the tiny chair, which rocked as she left it.

'Where did you get all this furniture, Hendreary?' asked Homily, recovering suddenly now that Lupy had gone.

'It was delivered,' her brother told her, 'in a plain white pillow-case. Someone from the big house brought it down.'

'From our house?' asked Pod.

'Stands to reason,' said Hendreary. 'It's all stuff from that doll's house, remember, they had upstairs in the school-room. Top shelf of the toy cupboard, on the right-hand side of the door.'

'Naturally I remember,' said Homily, 'seeing that some of it's mine. Pity,' she remarked aside to Arrietty, 'that we didn't keep that inventory,' she lowered her voice, 'the one you made on blotting-paper, remember.'

Arrietty nodded: there were going to be fireworks later – she could see that. She felt very tired suddenly; there seemed too much talk and the crowded room felt hot.

'Who brought it down?' Pod was asking in a surprised voice. 'Some kind of human being?'

'We reckon so,' agreed Hendreary. 'It was lying there t'other side of the bank. Soon after we got turned out of the badgers' set and had to set up house in the stove –'

'What stove was that?' asked Pod. 'Not the one by the camping site?'

'That's right,' Hendreary told him; 'two years we lived there, off and on.'

'A bit too close to the gipsies for my liking,' said Pod. He cut himself a generous slice of hot boiled chestnut and spread it thickly with butter. He remembered suddenly that pile of fragile bones.

'You got to be close,' Hendreary explained, 'like it or not, when you got to borrow.'

Pod, about to bite, withdrew the chestnut: he seemed amazed. 'You borrowed from caravans?' he exclaimed. 'At your age!'

Hendreary shrugged slightly and was modestly silent.

'Well I never,' said Homily admiringly, 'there's a brother for you! You think what that means, Pod –'

'I am thinking,' said Pod. He raised his head. 'What did you do about smoke?'

'You don't have none,' Hendreary told him, 'not when you cook on gas.'

'On gas!' exclaimed Homily.

'That's right. We borrowed a bit o' gas from the gas company: they got a pipe laid all along that bank. The stove was resting on its back, like, you remember? We dug down behind through a flue, a good six weeks we spent in that tunnel. Worth it in the end, though: three pin-hole burners, we had down there.'

'How did you turn 'em on and off?' asked Pod.

'We didn't – once lit, we never let them out. Still burning they are to this day.'

'You mean that you still go back there?'

Hendreary, yawning slightly, shook his head (they had eaten well and the room felt very close). 'Spiller lives there,' he said.

'Oh,' exclaimed Homily, 'so that's how Spiller cooked! He might have told us,' she went on, looking about in a hurt way, 'or, at any rate, asked us in –'

'He wouldn't do that,' said Hendreary. 'Once bitten, twice shy, as you might say.'

'How do you mean?' asked Homily.

'After we left the badgers' set –' began Hendreary, and broke off: slightly shamefaced, he seemed, in spite of his smile. 'Well, that stove was one of his places: he asked us in for a bite and a sup and we stayed a couple o' years –'

'Once you'd struck gas, you mean,' said Pod.

'That's right,' said Hendreary. 'We cooked and Spiller borrowed.'

'Ah!' said Pod. 'Spiller borrowed? Now I understand . . . You and me, Hendreary; we got to face up to it – we're not as young as we was. Not by a long chalk.'

'Where is Spiller now?' asked Arrietty suddenly.

'Oh, he's gone off,' said Hendreary vaguely; he seemed a little embarrassed and sat there frowning and tapping the table with a pewter spoon (one of a set of six, Homily remembered angrily: she wondered how many were left).

'Gone off where?' asked Arrietty.

'Home, I reckon,' Hendreary told her.

'But we haven't thanked him,' cried Arrietty. 'Spiller saved our lives!'

Hendreary threw off his gloom. 'Have a drop of blackberry cordial,' he suggested suddenly to Pod. 'Lupy's own make? Cheer us all up . . .'

'Not for me,' said Homily firmly, before Pod could speak. 'No good never comes of it, as we've found out to our cost.'

'But what will Spiller think?' persisted Arrietty, and there were tears in her eyes. 'We haven't even thanked him.'

Hendreary looked at her, surprised. 'Spiller? He don't hold with thanks. He's all right . . .' and he patted Arrietty's arm.

'Why didn't he stay for supper?'

'He don't ever,' Hendreary told her; 'doesn't like company. He'll cook something on his own.'

'Where?'

'In his stove.'

'But that's miles away!'

'Not for Spiller – he's used to it. Goes part way by water.'

'And it must be getting dark,' Arrietty went on unhappily.

'Now don't you fret about Spiller,' her uncle told her. 'You eat up your pie . . .'

Arrietty looked down at her plate (pink celluloid, it was, part of a tea-service which she seemed to remember); somehow she had no appetite. She raised her eyes. 'And when will he be back?' she asked anxiously.

'He don't come back much. Once a year for his new clothes. Or if young Tom sends 'im special.'

Arrietty looked thoughtful. 'He must be lonely,' she ventured at last.

'Spiller? No, I wouldn't say he was lonely. Some borrowers is made like that. Solitary. You get 'em now and again.' He glanced across the room to where his daughter, having left the table, was sitting alone by the fire. 'Eggletina's a bit like that . . . pity, but you can't do nothing about it. Them's the ones as gets this craze for humans – kind of man-eaters, they turns out to be . . .'

When Lupy returned, refreshed from her rest, it all began again: talk, talk, talk . . . and Arrietty slipped unnoticed from the table. But, as she wandered away towards the other room, she heard it going on: talk about living arrangements; about the construction of a suite of rooms upstairs; about what pitfalls there were in this new way of life and the rules they had made to avoid such pitfalls – how you always drew the ladder up last thing at night but that it should never be moved while the men were out borrowing; that the young boys went out as learners, each in turn, but that, true to borrowing tradition, the women would stay at home; she heard her mother declining the use of the kitchen. 'Thank you, Lupy,' Homily was saying; 'it's very kind of you but we'd better begin as we mean to go on, don't you think? quite separate.'

'And so it starts again,' thought Arrietty, as entering the next room she seated herself in a stiff arm-chair. But no longer quite under the floor – up a little, they would be now, among the lath and plaster: there would be ladders instead of dusty passages, and that platform, she hoped, might do instead of her grating.

She glanced about her at the over-furnished room: the doll's-house left-overs suddenly looked silly – everything for show and nothing much for use; the false coals in the fire-place looked worn as though scrubbed too often by Lupy, and the painted view in the windows had finger-marks round the edge.

She wandered out to the dim-lit platform; this, with its dust and shadows, had she known of such things, was something like going back-stage. The ladder was in place, she noticed – a sign that someone was out – but in this case, not so much 'out' as 'gone'. Poor Spiller . . . solitary, they had called him. 'Perhaps,' thought Arrietty self-pityingly, 'that's what's the matter with me . . .'

There was a faint light, she saw now, in the chasm below her; what at first had seemed a lessening of darkness seemed now a welcoming glow. Arrietty, her heart beating, took hold of the ladder and set her foot on the first rung. 'If I don't do it now,' she thought desperately, 'this first evening – perhaps, in the future, I should never dare again.' There seemed too many rules in Aunt Lupy's house, too many people, and the rooms seemed too dark and too hot. 'There may be compensations,' she thought, her knees trembling a little as rung after rung she started to climb down, 'but I'll have to discover them myself.'

Soon she stood once again in the dusty entrance hall; she glanced about her and then nervously she looked up; she saw the top of the ladder outlined against the light and the jagged edge of the high platform. It made her feel suddenly dizzy and more than a little afraid: suppose someone, not realizing she was below, decided to pull it up?

The faint light, she realized, came from the hole in the wainscot: the log-box, for some reason, was not laid flush against it – there might well be room to squeeze through. She would like to have one more peep at the room in which, some hours before, young Tom had set them down – to have some little knowledge, however fleeting, of this human dwelling which from now on would compose her world.

All was quiet as she stole towards the Gothic-shaped opening. The log-box, she found, was a good inch and a half away. It was easy enough to slip out and ease her tiny body along the narrow passage left between the side of the box and the wall. Again a little frightening: suppose some human being decided suddenly to shove the log-box into place. She would be squashed, she thought, and found long afterwards, glued to the wainscot, like some strange, pressed flower. For this reason she moved fast, and reaching the box's corner, she stepped out on the hearth.

She glanced about the room. She could see the rafters of the ceiling, the legs of a Windsor chair, and the underside of its seat. She saw a lighted candle on a wooden table, and, by its leg, a pile of skins on the floor – ah this, she realized, was the secret of Spiller's wardrobe.

Another kind of fur lay on the table, just beyond the candle above a piece of cloth – tawny yellow and somehow rougher. As she stared it seemed to stir. A cat? A fox? Arrietty froze to stillness, but she bravely stood her ground. Now the movement became unmistakable: a roll over and a sudden lifting up.

Arrietty gasped – a tiny sound, but it was heard.

A face looked back at her, candle-lit and drowsed with sleep, below its thatch of hair. There was a long silence. At last the boy's lips curved softly into a smile – and very young he looked after sleeping, very harmless. The arm on which he had rested his head lay loosely on the table and Arrietty, from where she stood, had seen his fingers relax. A clock was ticking somewhere above her head; the candle flame rose, still and steady, lighting the peaceful room; the coals gave a gentle shudder as they settled in the grate.

'Hallo,' said Arrietty.

'Hallo,' replied young Tom.

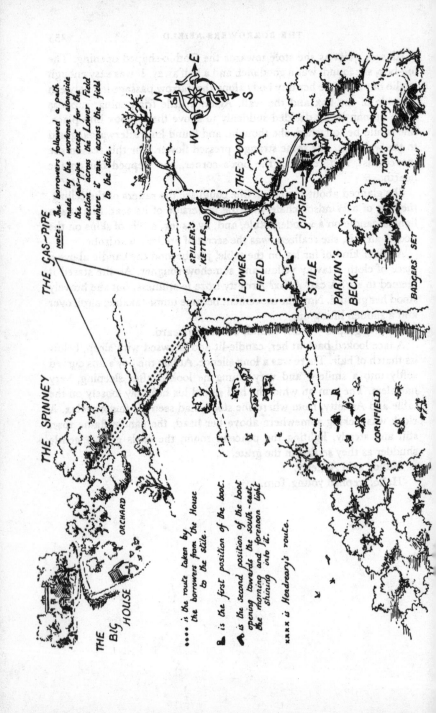

THE SPINNEY

THE BIG HOUSE

ORCHARD

THE GAS-PIPE

note: The borrowers followed a path made by the workmen alongside the gas-pipe except for the section across the Lower Field where it ran across the field to the stile.

N
E
W
S

THE POOL

SPILLER'S KETTLE

GIPSIES

LOWER FIELD

STILE

PARKIN'S BECK

TOM'S COTTAGE

BADGERS' SET

CORNFIELD

•••• is the route taken by the borrowers from the House to the stile.

B is the first position of the boot.

◣ is the second position of the boot opening towards the south-east the morning and forenoon light shining into it.

××××× is Hendreary's route.

THE
BORROWERS
AFLOAT

WITH ILLUSTRATIONS BY
Diana Stanley

CHAPTER ONE

'BUT what do they talk about?' asked Mr Beguid, the lawyer. He spoke almost irritably as of foolish goings-on.

'They talk about the borrowers,' said Mrs May.

They stood beneath the shelter of the hedge among wet, tree-like cabbages which tumbled in the wind. Below them on this dark, dank afternoon, a lamp glowed warmly through the cottage window. 'We could have an orchard here,' she added lightly as though to change the subject.

'At our time of life,' remarked Mr Beguid, gazing still at the lighted window below them in the hollow, 'yours and mine – it's wiser to plant flowers than fruit . . .'

'You think so?' said Mrs May. She drew her ulster cape more closely about her against the eddying wind. 'But I'll leave her the cottage, you see, in my will.'

'Leave whom the cottage?'

'Kate, my niece.'

'I see,' said Mr Beguid, and he glanced again towards the lighted window behind which he knew Kate was sitting: a strange child, he thought; disconcerting – the way she gazed through one with wide unseeing eyes and yet would chatter by the hour with old Tom Goodenough, a rascally one-time gamekeeper. What could they have in common, he asked himself, this sly old man and eager, listening child? There they had been now (he glanced at his watch) for a good hour and a quarter, hunched by the window, talking, talking . . .

'Borrowers . . .' he repeated, as though troubled by the word; 'what kind of borrowers?'

'Oh, it's just a story,' said Mrs May lightly, picking her way gingerly amongst the rain-soaked cabbages towards the raised brick path; 'something we used to tell each other, my brother and I, when we stayed down here as children.'

'At Firbank Hall, you mean?'

'Yes, with great-aunt Sophy. Kate loves this story.'

'But why,' asked Mr Beguid, 'should she want to tell it to him?'

'To old Tom? Why not? As a matter of fact I believe it's the other way round: I believe he tells it to her.'

As he followed Mrs May along the worn brick path Mr Beguid became silent. He had known this family most of his life and a strange lot (he had begun to think lately) they were.

'But a story made up by you?'

'Not by me, no' – Mrs May laughed as though embarrassed – 'it was my brother, I think, who made it up. If it was made up,' she added suddenly, just above her breath.

Mr Beguid pounced on the words: 'I don't quite follow you. This story you speak of, is it something that actually happened?'

Mrs May laughed. 'Oh no, it couldn't have actually happened. Not possibly.' She began to walk on again, adding over her shoulder: 'It's just that this old man, this old Tom Goodenough, seems to know about these people.'

'What people? These cadgers?'

'Not cadgers – borrowers . . .'

'I see,' said Mr Beguid, who didn't see at all.

'We called them that,' and turning on the path, she waited for him to catch up with her, 'or rather they called themselves that – because they had nothing of their own at all. Even their names were borrowed: the family we knew – father, mother, and child – were called Pod, Homily, and little Arrietty.' As he came beside her she smiled: 'I think their names are rather charming.'

'Very,' he said, a little too dryly. And then, in spite of himself, he smiled back at her: always, he remembered, there had been in her manner this air of gentle mockery; even as a young man, though attracted by her prettiness, he had found her disconcerting. 'You haven't changed,' he said.

She at once became more serious: 'But you can't deny that it was a strange old house?'

'Old, yes. But no more strange than' – he looked down the slope – 'than this cottage, say.'

Mrs May laughed. 'Ah, there Kate would agree with you! She finds this cottage quite as strange as we found Firbank, neither more nor less. You know, at Firbank, my brother and I – right from the very first – had this feeling that there were other people living in the house besides the human beings.'

'But!' exclaimed Mr Beguid, exasperated, 'there can be no such things as "people" other than human beings. The terms are synonymous.'

'Other personalities then. Something far smaller than a human being but like them in all essentials – a little larger in the head, perhaps, a little longer in the hands and feet. But very small and hidden. We imagined that they lived like mice – in the wainscots, or behind the skirtings, or under the floorboards . . . and were entirely dependent on what they could filch from the great house above. Yet you couldn't call it stealing: it was a kind of garnering. On the whole they only took things that could well be spared.'

'What sort of things?' asked Mr Beguid and, suddenly feeling foolish, he sprang ahead of her to clear a trail of bramble from her path.

'Oh, all sorts of things. Any kind of food, of course, and any other small movable objects which might be useful – matchboxes, pencil ends, needles, bits of stuff . . . anything they could turn into tools or clothes or furniture. It was rather sad for them, we thought, because they had a sort of longing for beauty; and to make their dark little holes as charming and comfortable as the homes of human beings. My brother used to help them.' Mrs May hesitated suddenly as though embarrassed. 'Or so he said,' she concluded lamely, and for the sake of appearances she gave a little laugh.

'I see,' said Mr Beguid again. He became silent as they skirted the side of the cottage to avoid the dripping thatch. 'And where does Tom Goodenough come in?' he asked at last as she paused beside the water-butt.

She turned to face him. 'Well, it's extraordinary, isn't it? At my age – nearly seventy – to inherit this cottage and find him still here in possession?'

'Not in possession, exactly – he's the outgoing tenant.'

'I mean,' said Mrs May, 'to find him here at all. In the old days, when they were boys, he and my brother used to go rabbiting – in a way they were great companions. But that all ended – after the rumpus.'

'Oh,' said Mr Beguid, 'so there was a rumpus?' They stood together by the weather-worn front door and, intrigued against his wish, he withdrew his hand from the latch.

'There most certainly was,' exclaimed Mrs May. 'I should have thought you might have heard about it. Even the policeman was implicated – you remember Ernie Runacre? – it must have gone all over the village: the cook and the gardener got wind of these creatures and determined to smoke them out. They got in the local rat-catcher and sent up here for Tom to bring his ferret. He was a boy then, the gamekeeper's grandson – a little older than we were, but still quite young. But' – Mrs May turned suddenly towards him – 'you *must* have heard something of this?'

Mr Beguid frowned. Past rumours stirred vaguely in his memory . . . some nonsense or other at Firbank Hall; a cook with a name like Diver or Driver; things missing from the cabinet in the drawing-room . . .

'Wasn't there,' he said at last, 'some trouble about an emerald watch?'

'Yes, that's why they sent for the police.'

'But' – Mr Beguid's frown deepened – 'this woman, Diver or –'

'Driver! Yes, that was the name.'

'And this gardener – you mean to say they believed in these creatures?'

'Obviously,' said Mrs May, 'or they would not have made all this fuss.'

'What happened?' asked Mr Beguid. 'Did they catch them? No, no – I don't mean that! What I meant to say is – what did they turn out to be? Mice, I suppose?'

'I wasn't there myself at the time – so I can't say "what they turned out to be". But according to my brother they escaped out of doors through a grating just in the nick of time: one of those ventilator things set low down in the brickwork outside. They ran away across the orchard and' – she looked around her in the half light – 'up into these fields.'

'Were they seen to go?'

'No,' said Mrs May.

Mr Beguid glanced swiftly down the mist-enshrouded slopes: against the pallid fields the woods beyond looked dark – already wrapped in twilight.

'Squirrels,' he said, 'that's what they were, most likely.'

'Possibly,' said Mrs May. She moved away from him to where, beside the wash-house, the workmen that morning had opened up a drain. 'Wouldn't this be wide enough to take sewage?'

'Wide enough, yes,' he agreed, staring down at the earthenware sections, 'but the sanitary inspector would never allow it: all these drains run straight down to the stream. No, you'll have to have a septic tank, I'm afraid.'

'Then what was this used for?'

He nodded towards the wash-house. 'Dish-water, I suppose, from the sink.' He glanced at his watch. 'Could I give you a lift anywhere? It's getting rather late . . .'

'That's very kind of you,' said Mrs May as they moved towards the front door.

'An odd story,' remarked Mr Beguid, putting his hand to the latch.

'Yes, very odd.'

'I mean – to go to the lengths of sending for the police. Extraordinary.'

'Yes,' agreed Mrs May, and paused to wipe her feet on a piece of torn sacking which lay beside the step.

Mr Beguid glanced at his own shoes and followed her example. 'Your brother must have been very convincing.'

'Yes, he was.'

'And very inventive.'

'Yes, according to my brother there was quite a colony of these people. He talked about another lot, cousins of the ones at Firbank, who were supposed to live in a badger's set – up here on the edge of these woods. Uncle Hendreary and Aunt Lupy . . .' She looked at him sideways. 'This lot had four children.'

'According to your brother,' remarked Mr Beguid sceptically, and he reached again for the latch.

'And according to old Tom,' she laughed and lowered her voice. 'Old Tom swears that the story is true. But *he* contends that they did not live in the badger's set at all; or that, if they did, it could not have been for long. He insists that for years and years they lived up here, in the lath and plaster beside the fireplace.'

'Which fireplace?' asked Mr Beguid uneasily.

'This fireplace,' said Mrs May. As the door swung open she dropped her voice to a whisper: 'Here in this very cottage.'

'Here in this very cottage . . .' repeated Mr Beguid in a startled voice, and, standing aside for Mrs May to pass, he craned his neck forward to peer within without advancing across the threshold.

The quiet room seemed empty: all they could see at first was yellow lamplight spilling across the flag-stones and dying embers in the grate. By the window stood a stack of hazel wands, split and trimmed for thatching, beside them a wooden arm-chair. Then Kate emerged rather suddenly from the shadows beside the fireplace. 'Hallo,' she said.

She seemed about to say more but her gaze slid past Mrs May to where Mr Beguid hovered in the doorway. 'I was looking up the chimney,' she explained.

'So I see – your face is black!'

'Is it?' said Kate, without interest. Her eyes looked very bright and she seemed to be waiting – either, thought Mrs May, for Mr Beguid to shut the door and come in or for Mr Beguid to shut the door and depart.

Mrs May glanced at the empty arm-chair and then past Kate towards the door of the wash-house: 'Where's Tom?'

'Gone out to feed the pig,' said Kate. Again she hesitated, then, in a burst, she added: 'Need we go yet? It's only a step across the fields, and there's something I terribly want to show you –'

Mr Beguid glanced at his watch. 'Well, in that case –' he began.

'Yes, please don't wait for us,' interrupted Mrs May impulsively. 'As Kate says, it's only a step . . .'

'I was only going to say,' continued Mr Beguid stolidly from his neutral position on the threshold, 'that as this lane's so narrow and the ditches so full of mud I propose to drive on ahead and turn the car at the cross-roads.' He began to button up his overcoat. 'Perhaps you would listen for the horn?'

'Yes, yes, indeed. Thank you . . . of course. We'll be listening . . .'

When the front door had closed and Mr Beguid had gone, Kate took Mrs May by the hand and drew her urgently towards the fireplace: 'And I've heaps to tell you. Heaps and heaps . . .'

'We weren't rude, were we?' asked Mrs May, 'I mean to Mr Beguid? We didn't shoo him off?'

'No, no, of course not. You thanked him beautifully. But look,' Kate went on, 'please look!' Loosing Mrs May's hand, she ran forward and – with much tugging and panting – dragged out the log-box from where it was jammed against the wall beside the hearth: a rat-hole was revealed in the skirting – slightly Gothic in shape. 'That's where they lived . . .' cried Kate.

Mrs May, in spite of herself, felt a curious sense of shock; staring down at it she said uneasily: 'We mustn't be too credulous, Kate. I mean, we can't believe *quite* everything we hear. And you know what they say about old Tom?'

'In the village? Yes, I know what they say – "the biggest liar in five counties". But all that started *because* of the borrowers: at first, you see, he used to talk about them. And that was his mistake. He thought people would be interested. But they weren't interested – not at all: they just didn't believe him.' Kate knelt down on the hearth and, breathing rather heavily, she peered into the darkness of the hole. 'There was only one other human being, I think, who really believed in the borrowers . . .'

'Mrs Driver, you mean, the cook at Firbank?'

Kate frowned, sitting back on her heels: 'No, I don't really think that Mrs Driver *did* believe in them. She saw them, I know, but I don't think she trusted her eyes. No, the one I was thinking of was Mild Eye, the gipsy. I mean, he actually shook them out of his boot on to the floor of his caravan. And there they were – right under his nose – and no two ways about it. He tried to grab them, Tom says, but they got away. He wanted to put them in a cage and show them for pennies at the fair. It was Tom who rescued them. With the help of Spiller, of course.'

'Who was Spiller?' asked Mrs May – she still stared, as though spellbound, at the rat-hole.

Kate seemed amazed: 'You haven't heard of Spiller?'

'No,' said Mrs May.

'Oh,' cried Kate, throwing her head back and half closing her eyes, 'Spiller was wonderful!'

'I am sure he was,' said Mrs May; she pulled forward a rush-seated chair and rather stiffly sat down on it, 'but you and Tom have been talking for days, remember . . . I'm a little out of touch; what was Spiller supposed to be – a borrower?'

'He *was* a borrower,' corrected Kate, 'but rather on the wild side – he lived in the hedgerows, and wore old mole-skins, and didn't really wash –'

'He doesn't sound so *tremendously* wonderful.'

'Oh, but he was: Spiller ran for Tom and Tom rushed down and rescued them; he snatched them up from under the gipsies' noses and pushed them into his pockets; he brought them up here – all four of them – Spiller, Pod, Homily, and Arrietty. And he set them down very carefully, one by one' – Kate patted the warm flagstones – 'here, on this very spot. And then, poor things, they ran away into the wall through that rat-hole in the skirting' – Kate lowered her head again, trying to peer in – 'and up a tiny ladder just inside to where the cousins were living . . .' Kate scrambled up suddenly and, stretching one arm as far as it would go, she tapped on the plaster beside the chimney. 'The cousins' house was somewhere up here. Quite high. Two floors they had – between the lath and plaster of the wash-house and the lath and plaster of this one. They used the chimney, Tom says, and they tapped the wash-house pipes for water. Arrietty didn't like it up there: she used to creep down in the evenings and talk to young Tom. But our lot did not stay there long. Something happened, you see . . .'

'Tell me,' said Mrs May.

'Well, there isn't really time now. Mr Beguid will start hooting . . . And old Tom's the one to tell it: he seems to know everything – even what they said and did when no one else was there . . .'

'He's a born story-teller, that's why,' said Mrs May, laughing. 'And he knows people. Given a struggle for life people react very much alike – according to type, of course – whatever their size or station.' Mrs May leaned forward as though to examine the skirting. 'Even I,' she said, 'can imagine what Homily felt, homeless and destitute, faced with that dusty hole . . . And strange relations living up above who didn't know she was coming, and whom she hadn't seen for years . . .'

CHAPTER TWO

⋯

BUT Mrs May was not quite right: she had under-estimated their sudden sense of security – the natural joy a borrower feels when safely under cover. It is true that, as they filed in through the Gothic-shaped hole in the skirting, they had felt a little nervous, a little forlorn: this was because, at first glance, the cave-like space about them seemed disappointingly uninhabited: empty, dark, and echoing, it smelled of dust and mice . . .

'Oh dear,' Homily had muttered incredulously, 'they can't live here!' But as her eyes became used to the dimness she had stooped suddenly to pick up some object from the floor. 'My goodness,' she whispered excitedly to Pod, 'do you know what this is?'

'Yes,' Pod had told her, 'it's a bit of quill pipe-cleaner. Put it down, Homily, and come on, do. Spiller's waiting.'

'It's the spout of our old oak-apple teapot,' Homily had persisted. 'I'd know it anywhere and it's no good telling me different. So they *are* here . . .' she mused wonderingly as she followed Pod into the shadows, 'and from somewhere, somehow, they've got hold of some of our things.'

'We go up here,' said Spiller, and Homily saw that he stood with his hand on a ladder. Glancing up to where the rungs soared away above them into dimness, she gave a slight shudder: the ladder was made of matchsticks, neatly glued and spliced to two lengths of split cane, such as florists use to support potted plants.

'I'll go first,' said Pod. 'We better take it one at a time.'

Homily watched fearfully until she heard his voice from above.

'It's all right,' he whispered from some invisible eyrie; 'come on up.'

Homily followed, her knees trembling, and emerged at last on to the dim-lit platform beside Pod – an aerial landing-stage, that was what it seemed like – which creaked a little when she stepped on it and almost seemed to sway. Below lay hollow darkness; ahead an open door. 'Oh, my goodness,' she muttered, 'I do hope it's safe . . . don't look down,' she advised Arrietty, who came up next.

But Arrietty had no temptation to look down: her eyes were on the

lighted doorway and the moving shadows within; she heard the faint
sound of voices and a sudden high-pitched laugh.

'Come on,' said Spiller, slipping past, and making towards the door.

Arrietty never forgot her first sight of that upstairs room: the warmth,
the sudden cleanliness, the winking candlelight, and the smell of home-
cooked food.

And so many voices . . . so many people . . .

Gradually, in a dazed way, she began to sort them out: that must be
Aunt Lupy embracing her mother – Aunt Lupy so round and glowing,
her mother so smudged and lean. Why did they cling and weep, she
wondered, and squeeze each other's hands? They had never liked each

other – all the world knew that. Homily had thought Lupy stuck-up because, back in the big house, Lupy had lived in the drawing-room and (she had heard it rumoured) changed for dinner at night. And Lupy despised Homily for living under the kitchen and for pronouncing parquet 'parkett'.

And here was Uncle Hendreary, his beard grown thinner, telling her father that this could not be Arrietty, and her father, with pride, telling Uncle Hendreary it could. Those must be the three boy cousins – whose names she had not caught – graduated in size but as like as peas in a pod. And this thin, tall, fairy-like creature, neither old nor young, who hovered shyly in the background with a faint uneasy smile, who was she? Could it be Eggletina? Yes, she supposed it could.

And there was something strangely unreal about the room – furnished with doll's-house furniture of every shape and size, none of it matching or in proportion. There were chairs upholstered in rep or velvet, some of them too small to sit in and some too steep and large; there were chiffoniers which were too tall and occasional tables far too low; and a toy fireplace with coloured plaster coals and its fire-irons stuck down all-of-a-piece with the fender; there were two make-believe windows with curved pelmets and red satin curtains, each hand-painted with an imitation view – one looked out on a Swiss mountain scene, the other a Highland glen ('Eggletina did them,' Aunt Lupy boasted in her rich society voice. 'We're going to have a third when we get the curtains – a view of Lake Como from Monte S. Primo'); there were table lamps and standard lamps, flounced, festooned, and tasselled, but the light in the room, Arrietty noticed, came from humble dips like those they had made at home.

Everybody looked extraordinarily clean and Arrietty became even shyer. She threw a quick glance at her father and mother and was not reassured: none of their clothes had been washed for weeks nor, for some days, had their hands and faces. Pod's trousers had a tear in one knee and Homily's hair hung down in snakes. And here was Aunt Lupy, plump and polite, begging Homily please to take off her things in the kind of voice, Arrietty imagined, usually reserved for feather boas, opera cloaks, and freshly cleaned kid gloves.

'Poor dear Lupy,' Homily was saying, glancing wearily about, 'what a lot of furniture! Whoever helps you with the dusting?' And swaying a little, she sank on a chair.

They rushed to support her, as she hoped they might. Water was brought and they bathed her face and hands. Hendreary stood with the tears in his brotherly eyes. 'Poor valiant soul,' he muttered, shaking his head, 'your mind kind of reels when you think of what she's been through . . .'

Then, after a quick wash and brush up all round and a brisk bit of eye-wiping, they all sat down to supper. This they ate in the kitchen, which was rather a come-down except that, in here, the fire was real: a splendid cooking-range made of a large, black door-lock; they poked the fire through the key-hole, which glowed handsomely, and the smoke, they were told, went out through a series of pipes to the cottage chimney behind.

The long, white table was richly spread: it was an eighteenth-century finger-plate off some old drawing-room door – white-enamelled and painted with forget-me-nots, supported firmly on four stout pencil stubs where once the screws had been; the points of the pencils emerged slightly through the top of the table; one was copying-ink and they were warned not to touch it in case it stained their hands.

There was every kind of dish and preserve – both real and false; pies, puddings, and bottled fruits out of season – all cooked by Lupy, and an imitation leg of mutton and a dish of plaster tarts borrowed from the doll's house. There were three real tumblers as well as acorn cups and a couple of green glass decanters.

Talk, talk, talk . . . Arrietty, listening, felt dazed. 'Where is Spiller?' she asked suddenly.

'Oh, he's gone off,' said Hendreary vaguely; he seemed a little embarrassed and sat there frowning and tapping the table with a pewter spoon (one of a set of six, Homily remembered angrily: she wondered how many were left).

'Gone off where?' asked Arrietty.

'Home, I reckon,' Hendreary told her.

'But we haven't thanked him,' cried Arrietty. 'Spiller saved our lives!'

Hendreary threw off his gloom. 'Have a drop of blackberry cordial,' he suggested suddenly to Pod. 'Lupy's own make. Cheer us all up . . .'

'Not for me,' said Homily firmly, before Pod could speak. 'No good never comes of it, as we've found out to our cost.'

'We haven't even thanked him,' persisted Arrietty, and there were tears in her eyes.

Hendreary looked at her, surprised. 'Spiller? He don't hold with thanks. He's all right . . .' and he patted Arrietty's arm.

'Why didn't he stay for supper?'

'He don't ever,' Hendreary told her; 'doesn't like company. He'll cook something on his own.'

'Where?'

'In his stove.'

'But that's miles away!'

'Not for Spiller – he's used to it. Goes part way by water.'

'And it must be getting dark,' Arrietty went on unhappily.

'Now don't you fret about Spiller,' her uncle told her. 'You eat up your pie . . .'

Arrietty looked down at her plate (pink celluloid, it was, part of a tea-service which she seemed to remember); somehow she had no appetite. She raised her eyes. 'And when will he be back?' she asked anxiously.

'He don't come back much. Once a year for his new clothes. Or if young Tom sends 'im special.'

Arrietty looked thoughtful. 'He must be lonely,' she ventured at last.

'Spiller? No, I wouldn't say he was lonely. Some borrowers is made like that. Solitary. You get 'em now and again.' He glanced across the room to where his daughter, having left the table, was sitting alone by the fire. 'Eggletina's a bit like that . . . pity, but you can't do nothing about it. Them's the ones as gets this craze for humans – kind of man-eaters, they turns out to be . . .'

Very dark it was, this strange new home, almost as dark as under the floorboards at Firbank, and lit by wax dips fixed to upturned drawing-pins (how many human dwellings must be burned down, Arrietty realized suddenly, through the carelessness of borrowers running about with lighted candles). In spite of Lupy's polishings the compartments smelled of soot and always in the background a pervading odour of cheese.

The cousins all slept in the kitchen – for warmth, Lupy explained: the ornate drawing-room was only rarely used. Outside the drawing-room was the shadowed platform with its perilous matchstick ladder leading down below.

Above this landing, high among the shadows, were the two small rooms allotted them by Lupy. There was no way up to them as yet, except by climbing hand over hand from lath to lath and scrabbling blindly for footholds, to emerge at length on a rough piece of flooring made by Hendreary from the lid of a cardboard shoe-box.

'Do those rooms good to be used,' Lupy had said (she knew Pod was a handyman), 'and we'll lend you furniture to start with.'

*

'To start with,' muttered Homily that first morning as, foot after hand, she followed Pod up the laths – unlike most borrowers, she was not very fond of climbing. 'What are we meant to do after?'

She dare not look down. Beneath her, she knew, was the rickety platform below which again were further depths and the matchstick ladder gleaming like a fishbone. 'Anyway,' she comforted herself, feeling clumsily for foot-holes, 'steep it may be, but at least it's a separate entrance . . . What's it like Pod?' she asked as her head emerged suddenly at floor level, through the circular trap-door – very startling it looked, as though decapitated.

'It's dry,' said Pod non-committally; he stamped about a bit on the floor as though to test it.

'Don't stamp so, Pod,' Homily complained, seeking a foothold on the quivering surface. 'It's only cardboard.'

'I know,' said Pod. 'Mustn't grumble,' he added as Homily came towards him.

'At least,' said Homily, looking about her, 'back home under the kitchen we was on solid ground . . .'

'You've lived in a boot since,' Pod reminded her, 'and you've lived in a hole in a bank. And nearly starved. And nearly frozen. And nearly been captured by the gipsies. Mustn't grumble,' he said again.

Homily looked about her. Two rooms? They were barely that: a sheet of cardboard between two sets of laths, divided by a cloth-covered book-cover, on which the words 'Pig Breeders' Annual, 1896' were stamped in tarnished gold. In this dark purple wall Hendreary had cut a door. Ceilings there were none and an eerie light came down from somewhere far above – a crack, Homily supposed, between the floorboards and the whitewashed walls of the gamekeeper's bedroom.

'Who sleeps up there,' she asked Pod, 'that boy's father?'

'Grandfather,' said Pod.

'He'll be after us, I shouldn't wonder,' said Homily, 'with traps and what-not.'

'Yes, you've got to be quiet,' said Pod, 'especially with gamekeepers. Out most of the day, though, and the young boy with him. Yes, it's dry,' he repeated, looking about him, 'and warm.'

'Not very,' said Homily. As she followed him through the doorway she saw that the door was hung by the canvas binding which Hendreary had not cut through. 'Soon fray, that will,' she remarked, swinging the panel to and fro, 'and then what?'

'I can stitch it,' said Pod, 'with me cobbler's thread. Easy.' He laid his hands on the great stones of the farther wall. ''Tis the chimney casing,' he explained; 'warm, eh?'

'Um,' said Homily, 'if you lean against it.'

'What about if we sleep here – right against the chimney?'

'What in?' asked Homily.

'They're going to lend us beds.'

'No, better keep the chimney for cooking.' Homily ran her hands across the stones and from a vertical crevice began to pick out the plaster. 'Soon get through here to the main flue . . .'

'But we're going to eat downstairs with them,' Pod explained. 'That's what's been arranged – so that it's all one cooking.'

'All one cooking and all one borrowing,' said Homily. 'There won't be no borrowing for you, Pod.'

'Rubbish,' said Pod. 'Whatever makes you say a thing like that?'

'Because,' explained Homily, 'in a cottage like this with only two human beings, a man and a boy, there aren't the pickings there were back at Firbank. You mark my words: I been talking to Lupy. Hendreary and the two elder boys can manage the lot. They won't be wanting competition.'

'Then what'll I do?' said Pod. A borrower deprived of borrowing – especially a borrower of Pod's standing? His eyes became round and blank.

'Get on with the furniture, I suppose.'

'But they're going to lend us that.'

'Lend us!' hissed Homily. 'Everything they've got was ours!'

'Now, Homily –' began Pod.

Homily dropped her voice, speaking in a breathless whisper: 'Every single blessed thing. That red velvet chair, the dresser with the painted plates, all that stuff the boy brought us from the doll's house –'

'Not the keyhole stove,' put in Pod, 'not that dining-table they've made from a door-plate. Not the –'

'The imitation leg of mutton – that was ours,' interrupted Homily, 'and the dish of plaster tarts. All the beds were ours, and the sofa. And the palm in a pot . . .'

'Now listen, Homily,' pleaded Pod, 'we've been into all that, remember. Findings keepings as they say. Far as they knew we was dead and gone – like as we might be lost at sea. The things all came to them in a plain white pillow-case delivered to the door. See what I mean? It's like as if they was left them in a will.'

'I would never have left anything to Lupy,' remarked Homily.

'Now, Homily, you've got to say they've been kind.'

'Yes,' agreed Homily, 'you've got to say it.'

Unhappily she gazed about her. The cardboard floor was scattered with lumps of fallen plaster. Absent-mindedly she began to push these towards the gaps where the floor, being straight-edged, did not fit against the rough cob. They clattered hollowly down the hidden shaft into Lupy's kitchen.

'Now you've done it,' said Pod. 'And that's the kind of noise we mustn't make, not if we value our lives. To human beings,' he went on, 'droppings and rollings means rats or squirrels. You know that as well as I do.'

'Sorry,' said Homily.

'Wait a minute,' said Pod. He had been gazing upwards towards the crack of light and now in a flash he was on the laths and climbing up towards it.

'Careful, Pod,' whispered Homily. He seemed to be pulling at some object which was hidden from Homily by the line of his body. She heard him grunting with the effort.

'It's all right,' said Pod in his normal voice, beginning to climb down again. 'There isn't no one up there. Here you are,' he went on as he landed on the floor and handed her an old bone toothbrush, slightly taller than herself. 'The first borrowing,' he announced modestly and she saw that he was pleased. 'Someone must have dropped it, up there in the bedroom, and it wedged itself in this crack between the floorboards and the wall. We can borrow from up there,' he went on, 'easy; the wall's fallen away like or the floorboards have shrunk. Farther along it gets even wider . . . And here you are again,' he said and handed her a fair-sized cockle-shell he had pulled out from the cob. 'You go on sweeping,'

he told her, 'and I'll pop up again, – might as well, while it's free of human beings . . .'

'Now, Pod, go careful . . .' Homily urged him, with a mixture of pride and anxiety. She watched him climb the laths and watched him disappear before, using the cockle-shell as a dustpan, she began to sweep the floor. When Arrietty arrived to tell them a meal was ready, a fair-sized haul was laid out on the floor: the bottom of a china soap-dish for baths, a crocheted table-mat in red and yellow which would do as a carpet, a worn sliver of pale green soap with grey veins in it, a large darning-needle (slightly rusted), three aspirin tablets, a packet of pipe-cleaners, and a fair length of tarred string.

'I'm kind of hungry now,' said Pod.

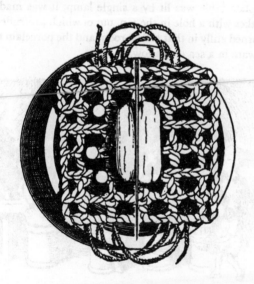

CHAPTER THREE

THEY climbed down the laths on to the platform – keeping well away from the edge, through Lupy's drawing-room, into the kitchen.

'Ah, here you are,' cried Lupy, in her loud, rich, aunt-like voice – very plump she looked in her dress of purple silk, and flushed from the heat of the stove. Homily, beside her, looked as thin and angular as a clothes-peg. 'We were just going to start without you.'

The door-plate table was lit by a single lamp; it was made from a silver salt shaker with a hole in the top, out of which protruded a wick. The flame burned stilly in that airless room and the porcelain table top, icily white, swam in a sea of shadow.

Eggletina, by the stove, was ladling out soup which Timmus, the young boy, unsteadily carried round in yellow snail-shells: very pretty they looked – scoured and polished. They were rather alike – Eggletina and Timmus – Arrietty thought, quiet and pale and watchful-seeming. Hendreary and the two elder boys were already seated, tucking into their food.

'Get up, get up,' cried Lupy archly, 'when your aunt comes in,' and her two elder sons rose reluctantly and quickly sat down again. 'Harpsichord manners . . .' their expressions seemed to say. They were too young to remember those gracious days in the drawing-room of the big house – the Madeira cake, little sips of China tea, and music of an evening. Churlish and shy, they hardly ever spoke. 'They don't much like us,' Arrietty decided as she took her place at the table. Little Timmus, his hands in a cloth, brought her a shell of soup. The thin shell was piping hot and she found it hard to hold.

It was a plain meal, but wholesome: soup and boiled butter-beans with a trace of dripping – one bean each. There was none of that first evening's lavishness when Lupy had raided her store cupboards. It was as though she and Hendreary had talked things over, setting more modest standards. 'We must begin,' she had imagined Lupy saying to Hendreary in a firm, self-righteous voice, 'as we mean to go on.'

There was, however, a sparrow's egg omelette, fried in a tin lid, for Hendreary and the two boys. Lupy saw to it herself. Seasoned with thyme and a trace of wild garlic it smelled very savoury and sizzled on the plate. 'They've been borrowing, you see,' Lupy explained, 'out of doors all morning. They can only get out when the front door's open and on some days they can't get back. Three nights Hendreary spent once in the woodshed before he got his chance.'

Homily glanced at Pod, who had finished his bean and whose eyes had become strangely round. 'Pod's done a bit, too, this morning,' she remarked carelessly, 'more high than far; but it does give you an appetite . . .'

'Borrowing?' asked Uncle Hendreary. He seemed amazed, and his thin beard had ceased the up and down movement which went with his eating.

'One or two things,' said Pod modestly.

'From where?' asked Hendreary, staring.

'The old man's bedroom. It's just above us . . .'

Hendreary was silent a moment and then he said: 'That's all right, Pod,' but as though it wasn't all right at all. 'But we've got to go steady. There isn't much in this house, not to spare like. We can't all go at it like bulls at gates.' He took another mouthful of omelette and consumed it slowly while Arrietty, fascinated, watched his beard and the shadow it threw on the wall. When he had swallowed, he said: 'I'd take it as a favour, Pod, if you'd just leave borrowing for a while. We know the territory, as you might say, and we work to our own methods. Better we lend you things, for the time being. And there's food for all, if you don't mind it plain.'

There was a long silence. The two elder boys, Arrietty noticed, shovelling up their food, kept their eyes on their plates. Lupy clattered about at the stove. Eggletina sat looking at her hands, and little Timmis stared wonderingly from one to another, eyes wide in his small pale face.

'As you wish,' said Pod slowly, as Lupy bustled back to the table.

'Homily,' said Lupy brightly, breaking the awkward silence, 'this afternoon, if you've got a moment to spare, I'd be much obliged if you'd give me a hand with Spiller's summer clothes . . .'

Homily thought of the comfortless rooms upstairs and of all she longed to do to them. 'But of course,' she told Lupy, trying to smile.

'I always get them finished,' Lupy explained, 'by early spring. Time's getting on now: tomorrow's the first of March.' And she began to clear the table. They all jumped up to help her.

'Where is Spiller?' asked Homily, trying to stack the snail-shells.

'Goodness knows,' said Lupy; 'off on some wild-goose chase. No one knows where Spiller is. Nor what he does for that matter. All I know is,' she went on, taking the plug out of the pipe (as they used to do at home, Arrietty remembered) to release a trickle of water, 'is that I make his moleskin suits each autumn and his white kid ones each spring and that he always comes to fetch them.'

'It's very kind of you to make his suits,' said Arrietty, watching Lupy rinse the snail-shells in a small crystal salt-cellar and standing by to dry them.

'It's only human,' said Lupy.

'Human!' exclaimed Homily, startled by the choice of words.

'Human – just short like that – means "kind",' explained Lupy, remembering that Homily, poor dear, had had no education, being dragged up as you might say under a kitchen floor. 'It's got nothing at all to do with human beings. How could it have?'

'That's what I was wondering . . .' said Homily.

'Besides,' Lupy went on, 'he brings us things in exchange.'

'Oh, I see,' said Homily.

'He goes hunting, you see, and I smoke his meat for him – there in the chimney. Some we keep and some he takes away. What's over I make into paste with butter on the top – keeps for months that way. Birds' eggs, he brings, and berries and nuts . . . fish from the stream. I smoke the fish too, or pickle it. Some things I put down in salt . . . And

if you want anything special, you tell Spiller – ahead of time, of course
– and he borrows it from the gipsies. That old stove he lives in is just by
their camping site. Give him time and he can get almost anything you
want from the gipsies. We have a whole arm of a waterproof raincoat,
got by Spiller, and very useful it was when the bees swarmed one
summer . . . we all crawled inside it.'

'What bees?' asked Homily.

'Haven't I told you about the bees in the thatch? They've gone now.
But that's how we got the honey, all we'd ever want, and a good, lasting
wax for the candles . . .'

Homily was silent a moment – enviously silent, dazzled by Lupy's
richness. Then she said, as she wiped up the last snail-shell: 'Where do
these go, Lupy?'

'Into that wickerwork hair-tidy in the corner. They won't break – just
take them on the tin lid and drop them in . . .'

'I must say, Lupy,' Homily remarked wonderingly as she dropped
the shells one by one into the hair-tidy (it was horn-shaped with a loop
to hang it on and a faded blue bow on the top), 'that you've become
what they call a good manager . . .'

'For one,' agreed Lupy laughing, 'who was brought up in a drawing-
room and never raised a hand.'

'You weren't *brought up* in a drawing-room,' Homily reminded her.

'Oh, I don't remember those Rain-Pipe days,' said Lupy blithely; 'I
married so young. Just a child . . .' And she turned suddenly to Arrietty:
'Now, what are you dreaming about, Miss-butter-wouldn't-melt-in-
her-mouth?'

'I was thinking of Spiller,' said Arrietty.

'A-ha!' cried Aunt Lupy, 'she was thinking of Spiller!' And she
laughed again. 'You don't want to waste precious thoughts on a
ragamuffin like Spiller. You'll meet lots of nice borrowers, all in good
time. Maybe, one day, you'll meet one brought up in a library: they're
the best, so they say, gentlemen all, and a good cultural background.'

'I was thinking,' continued Arrietty evenly, keeping her temper, 'that
I couldn't imagine Spiller dressed up in white kid.'

'It doesn't stay white long,' cried Lupy, 'of that I can assure you! It
has to be white to start with because it's made from an evening glove.
A ball glove, shoulder length – it's one of the few things I salvaged from
the drawing-room. But he will have kid – says it's hard wearing. It
stiffens up, of course, directly he gets it wet, but he soon wears it soft
again. And by that time,' she added, 'it's all colours of the rainbow.'

Arrietty could imagine the colours; they would not be 'all colours of the rainbow': they would be colours without real colour, the shades which made Spiller invisible – soft fawns, pale browns, dull greens, and a kind of shadowy gun-metal. Spiller took care about 'seasoning' his clothes: he brought them to a stage where he could melt into the landscape, where one could stand beside him, almost within touching distance, and yet not see him. Spiller deceived animals as well as gipsies. Spiller deceived hawks and stoats and foxes . . . and Spiller might not wash but he had no Spiller scent: he smelled of hedgerows, and bark and grasses and of wet sun-warmed earth; he smelled of buttercups, dried cow dung, and early morning dew . . .

'When will he come?' Arrietty asked. But she ran away upstairs before anyone could tell her. She wept a little in the upstairs room, crouched down beside the soap-dish.

To talk of Spiller reminded her of out of doors and of a wild, free life she might never know again. This new-found haven among the lath and plaster might all too soon become another prison . . .

CHAPTER FOUR

IT was Hendreary and the boys who carried the furniture up the laths, with Pod standing by to receive it. In this way Lupy lent them just what she wished to lend and nothing they would have chosen. Homily did not grumble, however; she had become very quiet lately as slowly she realized their predicament.

Sometimes they stayed downstairs after meals, helping generally or talking to Lupy. But they would gauge the length of these visits according to Lupy's mood: when she became flustered, blaming them for some small mishap brought on by herself, they would know it was time to go. 'We couldn't do right today,' they would say, sitting empty-handed upstairs on Homily's old champagne corks which Lupy had unearthed for stools. They would sit by the chimney casing in the inner room to get the heat from the stones. Here Pod and Homily had a double bed, one of those from the doll's house: Arrietty slept in the outer room, the one with the entrance hole. She slept on a thickish piece of wadding, borrowed in the old days from a box of artist's pastels, and they had given her most of the bed-clothes.

'We shouldn't have come, Pod,' Homily said one evening as they sat alone upstairs.

'We had no choice,' said Pod.

'And we got to go,' she added, and sat there watching him as he stitched the sole of a boot.

'To where?' asked Pod.

Things had become a little better for Pod lately: he had filed down the rusted needle and was back at his cobbling. Hendreary had brought him the skin of a weazel, one of those nailed up by the gamekeeper to dry on the outhouse door, and he was making them all new shoes. This pleased Lupy very much and she had become a little less bossy.

'Where's Arrietty?' asked Homily suddenly.

'Downstairs, I shouldn't wonder,' said Pod.

'What does she do downstairs?'

'Tells Timmus a story and puts him to bed.'

279

'I know that,' said Homily, 'but why does she stay so long? I'd nearly dropped off last night when we heard her come up the laths . . .'

'I suppose they get talking,' said Pod.

Homily was silent a moment and then she said: 'I don't feel easy. I've got my feeling . . .' This was the feeling borrowers get when human beings are near; with Homily it started at the knees.

Pod glanced up towards the floorboards above them from whence came a haze of candlelight: 'It's the old man going to bed.'

'No,' said Homily, getting up, 'I'm used to that. We hear that every night.' She began to walk about. 'I think,' she said at last, 'that I'll just pop downstairs . . .'

'What for?' asked Pod.

'To see if she's there.'

'It's late,' said Pod.

'All the more reason,' said Homily.

'Where else would she be?' asked Pod.

'I don't know, Pod. I've got my feeling and I've had it once or twice lately,' she said.

Homily had grown more used to the laths: she had become more agile, even in the dark. But tonight it was very dark indeed. When she reached the landing below she felt a sense of yawning space and a draught from the depths which eddied hollowly around her; feeling her way to the drawing-room door, she kept well back from the edge of the platform.

The drawing-room too was strangely dark and so was the kitchen beyond; there was a faint glow from the keyhole fire and a rhythmic sound of breathing.

'Arrietty?' she called softly from the doorway, just above a whisper.

Hendreary gave a snort and mumbled in his sleep; she heard him turning over.

'Arrietty . . .' whispered Homily again.

'What's that?' cried Lupy, suddenly and sharply.

'It's me . . . Homily.'

'What do you want? We were all asleep. Hendreary's had a hard day . . .'

'Nothing,' faltered Homily, 'it's all right. I was looking for Arrietty . . .'

'Arrietty went upstairs hours ago,' said Lupy.

'Oh,' said Homily, and was silent a moment. The air was full of breathing. 'All right,' she said at last, 'thank you. I'm sorry . . .'

'And shut the drawing-room door on to the landing as you go out. There's a howling draught,' said Lupy.

As she felt her way back across the cluttered room, Homily saw a faint light ahead, a dim reflection from the landing. Could it come from above, she wondered, where Pod, two rooms away, was stitching? Yet it had not been there before . . .

Fearfully she stepped out on the platform. The glow, she realized, did not come from above but from somewhere far below: the matchstick ladder was still in place and she saw the top rungs quiver. After a moment's pause she summoned up the courage to peer over. Her startled eyes met those of Arrietty, who was climbing up the ladder and had nearly reached the top. Far below Homily could see the Gothic shape of the hole in the skirting: it seemed a blaze of light.

'Arrietty!' she gasped.

Arrietty did not speak. She climbed off the last rung of the ladder, put her finger to her lips, and whispered: 'I've got to draw it up. Move back.' And Homily, as though in a trance, moved out of the way as Arrietty drew the ladder up rung over rung until it teetered above her into the darkness and then, trembling a little with the effort, she eased it along and laid it against the laths.

'Well . . .' began Homily in a sort of gasp. In the half light from below they could see each other's faces: Homily's aghast with her mouth hanging open; Arrietty's grave, her finger to her lips. 'One minute,' she whispered and went back to the edge. 'All right,' she called out softly into the space beneath; Homily heard a muffled thud, a scraping sound, the clap of wood on wood, and the light below went out.

'He's pushed back the log-box,' Arrietty whispered across the sudden darkness. 'Here, give me your hand . . . Don't worry,' she beseeched in a whisper, 'and don't take on! I was going to tell you anyway.' And supporting her shaking mother by the elbow she helped her up the laths.

Pod looked up startled. 'What's the matter?' he said as Homily sank down on the bed.

'Let me get her feet up first,' said Arrietty. She did so gently and covered her mother's legs with a folded silk handkerchief, yellowed with washing and stained with marking-ink, which Lupy had given them for a bed cover. Homily lay with her eyes closed and spoke through pale lips. 'She's been at it again,' she said.

'At what?' asked Pod. He had laid down his boot and had risen to his feet.

'Talking to humans,' said Homily.

Pod moved across and sat on the end of the bed. Homily opened her eyes. They both stared at Arrietty.

'Which ones?' asked Pod.

'Young Tom, of course,' said Homily. 'I caught her in the act. That's where she's been most evenings, I shouldn't wonder. Downstairs, they think she's up, and upstairs, we think she's down.'

'Well, you know where that gets us,' said Pod. He became very grave. 'That, my girl, back at Firbank was the start of all our troubles . . .'

'Talking to humans . . .' moaned Homily and a quiver passed over her face. Suddenly she sat up on one elbow and glared at Arrietty: 'You wicked thoughtless girl, how *could* you do it again!'

Arrietty stared back at them, not defiantly exactly, but as though she were unimpressed. 'But with this Tom downstairs,' she protested, 'I can't see why it matters: he knows we're here anyway. Because he put us here himself! He could get at us any minute if he really wanted to . . .'

'How could he get at us,' said Homily, 'right up here?'

'By breaking down the wall – it's only plaster.'

'Don't say such things, Arrietty,' shuddered Homily.

'But they're true,' said Arrietty. 'Anyway,' she added, 'he's going.'

'Going?' said Pod sharply.

'They're both going,' said Arrietty, 'he and his grandfather; the grandfather's going to a place called Hospital, and the boy is going to a place called Leighton Buzzard to stay with his uncle who is an ostler. What's an ostler?' she asked.

But neither of her parents replied: they were staring blankly at each other. Struck dumb, they seemed – it was rather frightening.

'We've got to tell Hendreary,' said Pod at last, 'and quickly.'

Homily nodded. Recovered from one fear to face another, she had swung her legs down from the bed.

'But it's no good waking them now,' said Pod. 'I'll go down first thing in the morning.'

'Oh, my goodness,' breathed Homily, 'all those poor children . . .'

'What's the matter?' asked Arrietty. 'What have I said?' She felt scared suddenly and gazed uncertainly from one parent to the other.

'Arrietty,' said Pod, turning towards her – his face had become very grave – 'all we've told you about human beings is true; but what we haven't told you, or haven't stressed enough maybe, is that we, the borrowers, cannot survive without them.' He drew a long deep breath. 'When they close up a house and go away it usually means the end . . .'

'No food, no fire, no clothes, no heat, no water . . .' chanted Homily, almost as though she were quoting.

'Famine . . .' said Pod.

CHAPTER FIVE

NEXT morning, when Hendreary heard the news, a conference was called around the door-plate. They all filed in, nervous and grave, and places were allotted them by Lupy. Arrietty was questioned again.

'Are you sure of your dates, Arrietty?'

Yes, Arrietty was sure.

'And of your facts?' Quite sure: young Tom and his grandfather would leave in three days' time in a gig drawn by a grey pony called Duchess and driven by Tom's uncle, the ostler, whose name was Fred Tarabody and who lived in Leighton Buzzard and worked at the Swan Hotel – what was an ostler? she wondered again – and young Tom was worried because he had lost his ferret, although it had a bell round its neck and a collar with his name on: he had lost it two days ago down a rabbit-hole and was afraid he might have to leave without it, and even if he found it he wasn't sure they would let him take it with him.

'That's neither there nor here,' said Hendreary, drumming his fingers on the table.

They all seemed very anxious and at the same time curiously calm.

Hendreary glanced round the table. 'One, two, three, four, five, six, seven, eight, nine,' he said gloomily and began to stroke his beard.

'Pod, here,' said Homily, 'can help borrow.'

'And I could too,' put in Arrietty.

'And I could,' echoed Timmus in a sudden squeaky voice. They all turned round to look at him, except Hendreary, and Lupy stroked his hair.

'Borrow *what?*' asked Hendreary. 'No, it isn't borrowers we want; on the contrary' – he glanced across the table and Homily, meeting his eye, suddenly turned pink – 'it's something left to borrow. They won't leave a crumb behind, that boy and his grandad, not if I know 'em. We'll have to live from now on on just what we've managed to save . . .'

'For as long as it lasts,' said Lupy grimly.

'For as long as it lasts,' repeated Hendreary, 'and such as it is.' All their eyes grew wider.

'Which it won't do for ever,' said Lupy. She glanced up at her store shelves and quickly turned away again. She too had become rather red.

'About borrowing . . .' stammered Homily. 'I was meaning out of doors . . . the vegetable patch . . . beans and peas . . . and suchlike.'

'The birds will have that lot,' said Hendreary, 'with this house closed and the human beings gone. The birds always know in a trice . . . And what's more,' he went on, 'there's more wild things and vermin in these woods than in all the rest of the county put together – weasels, stoats, foxes, badgers, shrikes, magpies, sparrow-hawks, crows . . .'

'That's enough, Hendreary,' Pod put in quickly. 'Homily's feeling faint . . .'

'It's all right . . .' murmured Homily. She took a sip of water out of the acorn cup, and staring down at the table she rested her head on her hand.

Hendreary, carried away by the length of his list, seemed not to notice: '. . . owls, and buzzards,' he concluded in a satisfied voice. 'You've seen the skins for yourselves nailed up on the outhouse door, and the birds strung up on a thorn bush – gamekeeper's gibbet they call it. He keeps them down all right, when he's well and about. And the

boy, too, takes a hand. But with them two gone . . .!' Hendreary raised
his gaunt arms and cast his eyes towards the ceiling.

No one spoke. Arrietty stole a look at Timmus, whose face had
become very pale.

'And when the house is closed and shuttered,' Hendreary went on
again suddenly, 'how do you propose to get *out?*' He looked round the
table triumphantly as one who had made a point. Homily, her head on
her hand, was silent. She had begun to regret having spoken.

'There's always ways,' murmured Pod.

Hendreary pounced on him: 'Such as?' When Pod did not reply at
once Hendreary thundered on: 'The last time they went away we had
a plague of field-mice . . . the whole house awash with them, upstairs
and down. Now when they lock up they lock up proper. Not so much
as a spider could get in!'

'Nor out,' said Lupy, nodding.

'Nor out,' agreed Hendreary and, as though exhausted by his own
eloquence, he took a sip from the cup.

For a moment or two no one spoke. Then Pod cleared his throat. 'They won't be gone for ever,' he said.

Hendreary shrugged his shoulders. 'Who knows?'

'Looks to me,' said Pod, 'that they'll always need a gamekeeper. Say this one goes, another moves in like. Won't be empty long – a good house like this on the edge of the coverts, with water laid on in the wash-house . . .'

'Who knows?' said Hendreary again.

'Your problem, as I see it,' went on Pod, 'is to hold out over a period.'

'That's it,' agreed Hendreary.

'But you don't know for how long – that's your problem.'

'That's it,' agreed Hendreary.

'The farther you can stretch your food,' Pod elaborated, 'the longer you'll be able to wait . . .'

'Stands to reason,' said Lupy.

'And,' Pod went on, 'the fewer mouths you have to feed, the farther the food will stretch.'

'That's right,' agreed Hendreary.

'Now,' went on Pod, 'say there are six of you . . .'

'Nine,' said Hendreary, looking round the table, 'to be exact.'

'You don't count us,' said Pod. 'Homily, Arrietty, and me – we're moving out.' There was a stunned silence round the table as Pod, very calm, turned to Homily. 'That's right, isn't it?' he asked her.

Homily stared back at him as though he were crazy and, in despair, he nudged her with his foot. At that she swallowed hastily and began to nod her head. 'That's right . . .' she managed to stammer, blinking her eyelids.

Then pandemonium broke out: questions, suggestions, protestations, and arguments. 'You don't know what you're saying, Pod,' Hendreary kept repeating and Lupy kept on asking: 'Moving out – where to?'

'No good being hasty, Pod,' Hendreary said at last. 'The choice of course is yours, but we're all in this together, and for as long as it lasts' – he glanced around the table as though putting the words on record – 'and such as it is, what is ours is yours.'

'That's very kind of you, Hendreary,' said Pod.

'Not at all,' said Hendreary, speaking rather too smoothly; 'it stands to reason.'

'It's only human,' put in Lupy: she was very fond of this word.

'But,' went on Hendreary, as Pod remained silent, 'I see you've made up your mind.'

'That's right,' said Pod.

'In which case,' said Hendreary, 'there's nothing we can do but adjourn the meeting and wish you all good luck!'

'That's right,' said Pod.

'Good luck, Pod,' said Hendreary.

'Thanks, Hendreary,' said Pod.

'And to all three valiant souls – Pod, Homily, and little Arrietty – good luck and good borrowing!'

Homily murmured something and then there was silence, an awkward silence while eyes avoided eyes. 'Come on, me old girl,' said Pod at last, and turning to Homily he helped her to her feet. 'If you'll excuse us,' he said to Lupy, who had become rather red in the face again, 'we got one or two plans to discuss.'

They all rose and Hendreary, looking worried, followed Pod to the door: 'When you think of leaving, Pod?'

'In a day or two's time,' said Pod, 'when the coast's clear down below.'

'No hurry, you know,' said Hendreary. 'And any tackle you want . . .'

'Thanks,' said Pod.

'. . . just say the word.'

'I will,' said Pod. He gave a half-smile, rather shy, and went on through the door.

CHAPTER SIX

HOMILY climbed the laths without speaking: she went straight to the inner room and sat down on the bed. She sat there shivering slightly and staring at her hands.

'I had to say it,' said Pod, 'and we have to do it, what's more.'

Homily nodded.

'You see how we're placed?' said Pod.

Homily nodded again.

'Any suggestions?' Pod said. 'Anything else we could do?'

'No,' said Homily, 'we've got to go. And what's more,' she added, 'we'd have had to anyway.'

'How do you make that out?' said Pod.

'I wouldn't stay here with Lupy,' declared Homily, 'not if she bribed me with molten gold, which she isn't likely to. I kept quiet, Pod, for the child's sake. A bit of young company, I thought, and a family background. I even kept quiet about the furniture . . .'

'Yes, you did,' said Pod.

'It's only,' said Homily, and again she began to shiver, 'that he went on so about the vermin . . .'

'Yes, he did go on,' said Pod.

'Better a place of our own,' said Homily.

'Yes,' agreed Pod, 'better a place of our own . . .' But he gazed round the room in a hunted kind of way, and his flat round face looked blank.

When Arrietty arrived upstairs with Timmus she looked both scared and elated.

'Oh,' said Homily, 'here you are.' And she stared rather blankly at Timmus.

'He would come,' Arrietty told her, holding him tight by the hand.

'Well, take him along to your room. And tell him a story or something . . .'

'All right. I will in a minute. But first I just wanted to ask you –'

'Later,' said Pod, 'there'll be plenty of time: we'll talk about everything later.'

'That's right,' said Homily; 'you tell Timmus a story.'

289

'Not about owls?' pleaded Timmus. He still looked rather wide-eyed.

'No,' agreed Homily, 'not about owls. You ask her to tell you about the doll's house' – she glanced at Arrietty – 'or that other place – what's it called now? – that place with the plaster borrowers?'

But Arrietty seemed not to be listening. 'You did mean it, didn't you?' she burst out suddenly.

Homily and Pod stared back at her, startled by her tone. 'Of course we meant it,' said Pod.

'Oh,' cried Arrietty, 'thank goodness . . . thank goodness,' and her eyes filled suddenly with tears. 'To be out of doors again . . . to see the

sun, to –' Running forward, she embraced them each in turn: 'It will be all right – I know it will!' Aglow with relief and joy, she turned back to Timmus: 'Come, Timmus, I know a lovely story – better than the doll's house – about a whole town of houses: a place called Little Fordham . . .'

This place, of recent years, had become a kind of legend to borrowers. How they got to know it no one could remember – perhaps a conversation overheard in some kitchen and corroborated later through dining-room or nursery – but know of it they did. Little Fordham, it appeared, was a complete model village. Solidly built, it stood out of doors in all weathers in the garden of the man who had designed it, and it covered half an acre. It had a church, with organ music laid on, a school, a row of shops, and – because it lay by a stream – its own port, shipping and custom houses. It was inhabited – or so they had heard – by a race of plaster figures, borrower size, who stood about in frozen positions; or who, wooden-faced and hopeless, rode interminably in trains. They also knew that from early morning until dusk troupes of human beings wound around and about it, removed on asphalt paths and safely enclosed by chains. They knew – as the birds knew – that these human beings would drop litter – the ends of ice-cream cones, sandwich crusts, nuts, buns, half-eaten apples. ('Not that you can live on those,' Homily would remark. 'I mean, you'd want a change . . .') But what fascinated them most about the place was the plethora of empty houses – houses to suit every taste and every size of family: detached, semi-detached, stuck together in a row, or standing comfortably each in its separate garden – houses which were solidly built and solidly roofed, set firmly in the ground and which no human being, however curious, could carelessly wrench open – as they could with dolls' houses – and poke about inside. In fact, as Arrietty had heard, doors and windows were one with the structure – there were no kind of openings at all. But this was a drawback easily remedied. 'Not that they'd open up the front doors,' she explained in whispers to Timmus as they lay curled up on Arrietty's bed; 'borrowers wouldn't be so silly: they'd burrow through the soft earth and get in underneath . . . and no human being would know they were there.'

'Go on about the trains,' whispered Timmus.

And Arrietty went on. And on. Explaining and inventing, creating another kind of life. Deep in this world she forgot the present crisis, her parents' worries, and her uncle's fears; she forgot the dusty drabness of the rooms between the laths, the hidden dangers of the woods outside, and that already she was feeling rather hungry.

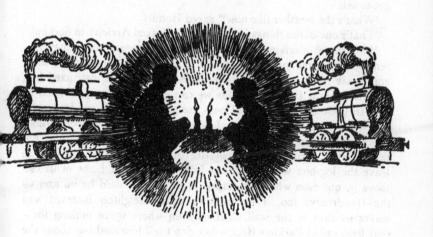

CHAPTER SEVEN

'BUT where are we going *to*?' asked Homily for about the twentieth time. It was two days later and they were up in Arrietty's room sorting things for the journey, discarding and selecting from oddments spread round on the floor. They could only take – Pod had been very firm about this – what Lupy described as hand luggage. She had given them for this purpose the rubberized sleeve of the waterproof raincoat, which they had cut up neatly into squares.

'I thought,' said Pod, 'we'd try first to make for that hole in the bank.'

'I don't think I'd relish that hole in the bank,' said Homily, 'not without the boot.'

'Now, Homily, we've got to go somewhere. And it's getting on for Spring.'

Homily turned and looked at him: 'Do you know the way?'

'No,' said Pod, and went on folding the length of tarred string; 'we've got to ask.'

'What's the weather like now?' asked Homily.

'That's one of the things,' said Pod, 'I've asked Arrietty to find out.'

With some misgivings, but in a spirit of 'needs must', they had sent her down the matchstick ladder to interview young Tom. 'You've got to ask him to leave us some loophole,' Pod had instructed her, 'no matter how small so long as we can get out of doors. If need be we can undo the luggage and pass the pieces through one by one. If the worst came to the worst, I wouldn't say no to a ground-floor window and something below to break the drop. But like as not they'll latch those tight and shutter them across. And tell him to leave the log-box well pulled out from the skirting. None of us can move it, not even when it's empty. A nice pickle we'd be in, and all the Hendrearys too, if he trundles off to Leighton Buzzard and leaves us shut in the wall. And tell him where we're making for – that field called Parkin's Beck – but don't tell him nothing about the hole in the bank – and get him to give you a few landmarks, something to put us on our way. It's been a bit chilly indoors lately, for March: ask him if there's snow. If there's snow we're done: we've got to wait . . .'

But could they wait? he wondered now as he hung the coil of tarred string on a nail in the lath and thoughtfully took up his hat-pin. Hendreary had said in a burst of generosity: 'We're all in this together.' But Lupy had remarked afterwards, discussing their departure with Homily: 'I don't want to seem hard, Homily, but in times like these it's each one for his own. And in our place you'd say the same.' She had been very kind about giving them things – the mackintosh sleeve was a case in point -- and the Christmas-pudding thimble with a ring on its tip for Homily to hang round her neck – but the store shelves, they noticed, were suddenly bare: all the food had been whisked away and hidden out of sight; and Lupy had doled out fifteen dried peas which she had hoped would 'last them'. These they kept upstairs, soaking in the soap-dish, and Homily would take them down three at a time to boil them on Lupy's stove.

To 'last them' for how long? Pod wondered now, as he rubbed a speck of rust off his hat-pin. Good as new, he thought, as he tested the point, pure steel and longer than he was. No, they would have to get off, he realized, the minute the coast was clear, snow or no snow . . .

'Here's someone now,' exclaimed Homily; 'it must be Arrietty.' They went to the hole and helped her on to the floor: the child looked pleased, they noticed, and flushed with the heat of the fire. In one hand she carried a long steel nail, in the other a sliver of cheese. 'We can eat this now,' she said excitedly; 'there's a lot more downstairs: he pushed it through the hole behind the log-box. There's a slice of dry bread, some more cheese, six roasted chestnuts, and an egg.'

'Not a hen's egg?' said Pod.

'Yes.'

'Oh my!' exclaimed Homily. 'Who's going to get it up the laths?'

'And how are we going to cook it?' asked Pod.

Homily tossed her head: 'I'll boil it with the peas on Lupy's stove. It's our egg: no one can say a word.'

'It's boiled already,' Arrietty told them, 'hard boiled.'

'Thank goodness for that,' exclaimed Pod. 'I'll take down the razor-blade – we can bring it up in slices. What's the news?' he asked Arrietty.

'Well, the weather's not bad at all,' she said; 'spring-like, he says, when the sun's out, and pretty warm.'

'Never mind that,' said Pod; 'what about the loophole?'

'That's all right too. There's a worn-out place at the bottom of the door – the front door, where feet have been kicking it open, like Tom does when his arms are full of sticks. It's shaped like an arch. But they've nailed a piece of wood across it now to keep the field-mice out. Two nails it's got, one on either side. This is one of them,' and she showed them the nail she had brought. 'Now all we've got to do, he says, is to swing the bit of wood up on the other nail and prop it up safely, and we can all go through – underneath. After we've gone Hendreary and the cousins can knock it in again – that is if they want to.'

'Good,' said Pod, 'good.' He seemed very pleased. 'They'll want to all right because of the field-mice. And when did he say they were leaving – him and his grandpa, I mean?'

'What he said before: the day after tomorrow. But he hasn't found his ferret.'

'Good,' said Pod again: he wasn't interested in ferrets. 'And now we'd better nip down quick and get that food up the laths, or someone might see it first.'

Homily and Arrietty climbed down with him to lend a hand. They brought up the bread and cheese and the roasted chestnuts, but the egg they decided to leave. 'There's a lot of good food in a hen's egg,' Pod pointed out, 'and it's all wrapped up already, as you might say, clean and neat in its shell. We'll take that egg along with us and we'll take it just as it is.' So they rolled the egg along inside the wainscot to a shadowy corner in which they had seen shavings.

'It can wait for us there,' said Pod.

CHAPTER EIGHT

On the day the human beings moved out the borrowers kept very quiet. Sitting round the door-plate table they listened to the bangings, the bumpings, the runnings up and down stairs with interest and anxiety. They heard voices they had not heard before and sounds which they could not put a name to. They went on keeping quiet . . . long after the final bang of the front door had echoed into silence.

'You never know,' Hendreary whispered to Pod; 'they might come back for something.' But after a while the emptiness of the house below seemed to steal in upon them, seeping mysteriously through the lath and plaster – and it seemed to Pod a final kind of emptiness. 'I think it's all right now,' he ventured at last; 'suppose one of us went down to reconnoitre?'

'I'll go,' said Hendreary, rising to his feet. 'None of you move until I give the word. I want the air clear for sound . . .'

They sat in silence while he was gone. Homily stared at their three modest bundles lying by the door, strapped by Pod to his hat-pin. Lupy had lent Homily a little moleskin jacket – for which Lupy had grown too stout. Arrietty wore a scarf of Eggletina's: the tall, willowy creature had placed it round her neck, wound it three times about, but had said not a word. 'Doesn't she ever speak?' Homily had asked once, on a day when she and Lupy had been more friendly. 'Hardly ever,' Lupy had admitted, 'and never smiles. She's been like that for years, ever since that time when as a child she ran away from home.'

After a while Hendreary returned and confirmed that the coast was clear. 'But better light your dips; it's later than I thought . . .'

One after another they scrambled down the matchstick ladder, careless now of noise. The log-box had been pulled well back from the hole and they flowed out into the room – cathedral high, it seemed to them, vast and still and echoing – but suddenly all on their own: they could do anything, go anywhere. The main window was shuttered as Pod had foreseen, but a smaller, cell-like window, sunk low and deep in the wall, let in a last pale reflection of the sunset. The younger cousins and Arrietty went quite wild, running in and out of the shadows

among the chair legs, exploring the cavern below the table top, the underside of which, cobweb-hung, danced in the light of their dips. Discoveries were made and treasures found – under rugs, down cracks in the floor, between loose hearthstones ... here a pin, there a matchstick; a button, an old collar-stud, a blackened farthing, a coral bead, a hook without its eye, and a broken piece of lead from a lead pencil. (Arrietty pounced on this last and pushed it into her pocket: she

had had to leave her diary behind, with other non-essentials, but one never knew ...) Then dips were set down and everybody started climbing – except for Lupy, who was too stout, and for Pod and Homily, who watched silently, standing beside the door. Hendreary tried an overcoat on a nail for the sake of what he might find in the pockets, but he had not Pod's gift for climbing fabric and had to be rescued by one of his sons from where he hung, perspiring and breathing hard, clinging to a sleeve button.

'He should have gone up by the front buttonholes,' Pod whispered to Homily; 'you can get your toes in and pull the pocket towards you, like, by folding in the stuff. You never want to make direct for a pocket . . .'

'I wish,' Homily whispered back, 'they'd stop this until we're gone.' It was the kind of occasion she would have enjoyed in an ordinary way – a glorious bargain hunt – findings keepings with no holds barred; but the shadow of their ordeal hung over her and made such antics seem foolish.

'Now,' exclaimed Hendreary suddenly, straightening his clothes and coming towards them as though he had guessed her thought, 'we'd better test out this loophole.'

He called up his two elder sons, and together the three of them, after spitting on their hands, laid hold of the piece of wood which covered the hole in the door.

'One, two, three – hup!' intoned Hendreary, ending on a grunt. They gave a mighty heave and the slab of wood pivoted slowly, squeaking on its one nail, revealing the arch below.

Pod took his dip and peered through: grass and stones he saw for a moment and some kind of shadowy movement before a draught caught the flame and nearly blew it out. He sheltered the flame with his hand and tried again.

'Quick, Pod,' gasped Hendreary, 'this wood's heavy . . .'

Pod peered through again: no grass now, no stones – a rippling blackness, the faintest snuffle of breath and two sudden pin-points of fire, unblinking and deadly still.

'Drop the wood,' breathed Pod. He spoke without moving his lips. 'Quick,' he added under his breath as Hendreary seemed to hesitate. 'Can't you hear the bell?' and he stood there as though frozen, holding his dip steadily before him.

Down came the wood with a clap and Homily screamed. 'You saw it?' said Pod, turning. He set down his dip and wiped his brow on his sleeve: he was breathing rather heavily.

'Saw it?' cried Homily. 'In another second it would have been in here amongst us.'

Timmus began to cry and Arrietty ran to him: 'It's all right, Timmus, it's gone now. It was only an old ferret, an old tame ferret. Come, I'll tell you a story.' She took him under a rough wooden desk where she had seen an old account book. Setting it up on its outer leaves she made it into a tent. They crept inside, just the two of them, and between the sheltering pages they soon felt very cosy.

'Whatever was it?' cried Lupy, who had missed the whole occurrence.

'Like she said – a ferret,' announced Pod; 'that boy's ferret, I shouldn't wonder. If so, it'll be all round the house from now on seeking a way to get in . . .' He turned to Homily. 'There'll be no leaving here tonight,' he said.

Lupy, standing in the hearth where the ashes were still warm, sat down suddenly on an empty matchbox which gave an ominous crack. 'Nearly in amongst us,' she repeated faintly, closing her eyes against the ghastly vision. A faint cloud of wood ash rose slowly around her which she fanned away with her hand.

'Well, Pod,' said Hendreary after a pause, 'that's that.'

'How do you mean?' said Pod.

'You can't go that way. That ferret'll be round the house for weeks.'

'Yes . . .' said Pod, and was silent a moment. 'We'll have to think again.' He gazed in a worried way at the shuttered window: the smaller one was a wall aperture, glazed to give light but with the glass built in – no possibility there.

'Let's have a look at the wash-house,' he said. This door luckily had been left ajar and, dip in hand, he slid through the crack. Hendreary and Homily slid through after him, and after a while Arrietty followed. Filled with curiosity she longed to see the wash-house, as she longed to see every corner of this vast human edifice now that they had it to themselves. The chimney, she saw, in the flickering light of the dip, stood back to back with the one in the living-room; in it there stood a dingy cooking-stove; flags covered the floor. An old mangle stood in one corner; in the other a copper for boiling clothes. Against the wall, below the window, towered a stone sink. The window above the sink was

heavily shuttered and rather high. The door, which led outside, was
bolted in two places and had a zinc panel across the bottom reinforcing
the wood.

'Nothing doing here,' said Hendreary.

'No,' agreed Pod.

They went back to the living-room. Lupy had recovered somewhat
and had risen from the matchbox, leaving it slightly askew. She had
brushed herself down and was packing up the borrowings preparatory
to going upstairs. 'Come along, chicks,' she called to her children; 'it's
nearly midnight and we'll have all day tomorrow . . .' When she saw
Hendreary she said: 'I thought we might go up now and have a bite of
supper.' She gave a little laugh. 'I'm a wee bit tired – what with ferrets
and so on and so forth.'

Hendreary looked at Pod. 'What about you?' he said, and as Pod
hesitated Hendreary turned to Lupy: 'They've had a hard day too –
what with ferrets and so on and so forth – and they can't leave here
tonight . . .'

'Oh?' said Lupy and stared. She seemed slightly taken aback.

'What have we got for supper?' Hendreary asked her.

'Six boiled chestnuts' – she hesitated – 'and a smoked minnow each
for you and the boys.'

'Well, perhaps we could open something,' suggested Hendreary after
a moment. Again Lupy hesitated and the pause became too long. 'Why,
of course –' she began in a flustered voice, but Homily interrupted.

'Thank you very much; it's very kind of you but we've got three roast
chestnuts ourselves. And an egg.'

'An egg,' echoed Lupy, amazed. 'What kind of an egg?'

'A hen's egg.'

'A *hen's* egg,' echoed Lupy again as though a hen were a pterodactyl
or a fabulous bird like the phoenix. 'Wherever did you get it?'

'Oh,' said Homily, 'it's just an egg we had.'

'And we'd like to stay down here a bit,' put in Pod, 'if that's all right
with you.'

'Quite all right,' said Lupy stiffly. She still looked amazed about the
egg. 'Come, Timmus.'

It took some minutes to round them all up. There was a lot of running
back for things; chatter at the foot of the ladder; callings, scoldings,
giggles, and 'take-cares'. 'One at a time,' Lupy kept saying, 'one at a
time, my lambs.' But at last they were all up and their voices became
more muffled as they left the echoing landing for the inner rooms

beyond. Light running sounds were heard, small rollings, and the faintest of distant squeakings.

'How like mice we must sound to humans,' Arrietty realized as she listened from below. But after a while even these small patterings ceased and all became quiet and still. Arrietty turned and looked at her parents: at last they were alone.

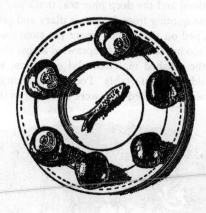

CHAPTER NINE

'BETWEEN the devil and the deep blue sea, that's us,' said Pod with a wan smile: he was quoting from Arrietty's diary and proverb book.

They sat grouped on the hearth where the stones were warm. The iron shovel, still too hot to sit on, lay sprawled across the ashes. Homily had pulled up the crushed matchbox lid on which, with her lighter weight, she could sit comfortably. Pod and Arrietty perched on a charred stick; the three lighted dips were set between them on the ash.

Shadows lay about them in the vast confines of the room and now the Hendrearys were out of earshot (sitting down to supper most likely), they felt drowned in the spreading silence.

After a while this was broken by the faint tinkle of a bell – quite close it seemed suddenly – there was a slight scratching sound and the lightest most delicate of snuffles. They all glanced wide-eyed at the door which, from where they sat, was deeply sunk in shadow.

'It can't get in, can it?' whispered Homily.

'Not a hope,' said Pod; 'let it scratch . . . we're all right here.'

All the same Arrietty threw a searching glance up the wide chimney: the stones, she thought, if the worst came to the worst, looked uneven enough to climb. Then suddenly, far, far above her, she saw a square of violet sky and in it a single star, and, for some reason, felt reassured.

'As I see it,' said Pod, 'we can't go and we can't stay.'

'And that's how I see it,' said Homily.

'Suppose,' suggested Arrietty, 'we climbed up the chimney on to the thatch?'

'And then what?' said Pod.

'I don't know,' said Arrietty.

'There we'd be,' said Pod.

'Yes, there we'd be,' agreed Homily unhappily, 'even supposing we could climb a chimney, which I doubt.'

There were a few moments' silence, then Pod said solemnly: 'Homily, there's nothing else for it . . .'

'But what?' asked Homily, raising a startled face: lit from below it looked curiously bony and was streaked here and there with ash. And Arrietty, who guessed what was coming, gripped her two hands beneath her knees and stared fixedly down at the shovel which lay sideways across the hearth.

'But to bury our pride, that's what,' said Pod.

'How do you mean?' asked Homily weakly, but she knew quite well what he meant.

'We got to go, quite open-like, to Lupy and Hendreary and ask them to let us stay . . .'

Homily put her thin hands on either side of her thin face and stared at him dumbly.

'For the child's sake . . .' Pod pointed out gently.

The tragic eyes swivelled round to Arrietty and back again.

'A few dried peas, that's all we'd ask for,' went on Pod, very gently, 'just water to drink and a few dried peas . . .'

Still Homily did not speak.

'And we'd say they could keep the furniture in trust, like,' suggested Pod.

Homily stirred at last. 'They'd keep the furniture anyway,' she said huskily.

'Well, what about it?' asked Pod after a moment, watching her face.

Homily looked round the room in a hunted kind of way, up at the chimney then down at the ashes at their feet. At last she nodded her head. 'Should we go up now,' she suggested after a moment in a dispirited kind of voice, 'while they're all at supper, and get it over with?'

'Might as well,' said Pod. He stood up and put out a hand to Homily. 'Come on, me old girl,' he coaxed her. Homily rose slowly and Pod turned to Arrietty, Homily's hand pulled under his arm. Standing beside his wife he drew himself up to his full five inches. 'There's two kinds of courage I know of,' he said, 'possibly there's more, but your mother's got 'em all. You make a note of that, my girl, when you're writing in your diary . . .'

But Arrietty was gazing past him into the room: she was staring white-faced into the shadows beyond the log-box towards the scullery door.

'Something moved,' she whispered.

Pod turned, following the direction of her eyes. 'What like?' he asked sharply.

'Something furry . . .'

They all froze. Then Homily, with a cry, ran out from between them. Amazed and aghast they watched her scramble off the hearth and run with outstretched arms towards the shadows beyond the log-box. She seemed to be laughing – or crying – her breath coming in little gasps: 'The dear boy, the good boy . . . the blessed creature!'

'It's Spiller!' cried Arrietty on a shout of joy.

She ran forward too, and they dragged him out of the shadows, pulled him on to the hearth and beside the dips where the light shone warmly on his suit of moleskins, worn now, slightly tattered, and shorter in the leg. His feet were bare and gleaming with black mud. He seemed to have grown heavier and taller. His hair was still as ragged and his pointed face as brown. They did not think to ask him where he had come from – it was enough that he was there. Spiller, it seemed to Arrietty, always materialized out of air and dissolved again as swiftly.

'Oh, Spiller!' gasped Homily, who was not supposed to like him, 'in the nick of time, the very nick of time!' And she sat down on the charred stick which flew up the farther end scattering a cloud of ash, and burst into happy tears.

'Nice to see you, Spiller,' said Pod, smiling and looking him up and down. 'Come for your summer clothes?' Spiller nodded: bright eyed, he gazed about the room, taking in the bundles strapped to the hat-pin, the pulled-out position of the log-box, the odd barenesses and rearrangements which signify human departure. But he made no comment: countrymen, such as Spiller and Pod were, do not rush into explana-tions; faced with whatever strange evidence they mind their manners and bide their time. 'Well, I happen to know they're not ready,' Pod went on. 'She's sewn the vest, mind, but she hasn't joined up the trousers . . .'

Spiller nodded again. His eyes sought out Arrietty who, ashamed of her first outburst, had become suddenly shy and had withdrawn behind the shovel.

'Well,' said Pod at last, looking about as though aware suddenly of strangeness in their surroundings, 'you find us in a nice sort of pickle . . .'

'Moving house?' asked Spiller casually.

'In a manner of speaking,' said Pod. And as Homily dried her eyes on her apron and began to pin up her hair he outlined the story to Spiller in a few rather fumbling words. Spiller listened with one eyebrow raised and his mocking V-shaped mouth twisted up at the corners. This was Spiller's famous expression Arrietty remembered, no matter what you were telling him.

'And so,' said Pod, shrugging his shoulders, 'you see how we're placed?'

Spiller nodded, looking thoughtful.

'Must be pretty hungry now, that ferret,' Pod went on, 'poor creature. Can't hunt with a bell: the rabbits hear him coming. Gone in a flash the rabbits are. But with our short legs he'd be on us in a trice – bell or no bell. But how did *you* manage?' Pod asked suddenly.

'The usual,' said Spiller.

'What usual?'

Spiller jerked his head towards the wash-house. 'The drain, of course,' he said.

CHAPTER TEN

'WHAT drain?' asked Homily, staring.

'The one in the floor,' said Spiller as though she ought to have known. 'The sink's no good – got an S-bend. And they keep the lid on the copper.'

'I didn't see any drain in the floor . . .' said Pod.

'It's under the mangle,' explained Spiller.

'But,' went on Homily, 'I mean, do you always come by the drain?'

'And go,' said Spiller.

'Under cover, like,' Pod pointed out to Homily, 'doesn't have to bother with the weather.'

'Or the woods,' said Homily.

'That's right,' agreed Spiller; 'you don't want to bother with the woods. Not the woods,' he repeated thoughtfully.

'Where does the drain come out?' asked Pod.

'Down by the kettle,' said Spiller.

'What kettle?'

'His kettle,' put in Arrietty excitedly. 'That kettle he's got by the stream . . .'

'That's right,' said Spiller.

Pod looked thoughtful. 'Do the Hendrearys know this?'

Spiller shook his head. 'Never thought to tell them,' he said.

Pod was silent a moment and then he said: 'Could anyone use this drain?'

'No reason why not,' said Spiller. 'Where you making for?'

'We don't know yet,' said Pod.

Spiller frowned and scratched his knee where the black mud, drying in the warmth of the ash, had turned to a powdery grey. 'Ever thought of the town?' he asked.

'Leighton Buzzard?'

'No,' exclaimed Spiller scornfully, 'Little Fordham.'

Had Spiller suggested a trip to the moon they could not have looked more astonished. Homily's face was a study in disbelief as though she thought Spiller was romancing. Arrietty became very still

306

– she seemed to be holding her breath. Pod looked ponderously startled.

'So there is such a place?' he said slowly.

'Of course there is such a place,' snapped Homily; 'everyone knows that: what they don't know exactly is – *where*? And I doubt if Spiller does either.'

'Two days down the river,' said Spiller, 'if the stream's running good.'

'Oh,' said Pod.

'You mean we have to swim for it?' snapped Homily.

'I got a boat,' said Spiller.

'Oh, my goodness . . .' murmured Homily, suddenly deflated.

'Big?' asked Pod.

'Fair,' said Spiller.

'Could she take passengers?' asked Pod.

'Could do,' said Spiller.

'Oh, my goodness . . .' murmured Homily again.

'What's the matter, Homily?' asked Pod.

'Can't see myself in a boat,' said Homily, 'not on the water, I can't.'

'Well, a boat's not much good on dry land,' said Pod. 'To get something you got to risk something – that's how it goes. We got to find somewhere to live.'

'There might be something, say, in walking distance,' faltered Homily.

'Such as?'

'Well,' said Homily unhappily, throwing a quick glance at Spiller, 'say, for instance . . . Spiller's kettle.'

'Not much accommodation in a kettle,' said Pod.

'More than there was in a boot,' retorted Homily.

'Now, Homily,' said Pod, suddenly firm, 'you wouldn't be happy, not for twenty-four hours, in a kettle; and inside a week you'd be on at me night and day to find some kind of craft to get you downstream to Little Fordham. Here you are with the chance of a good home, fresh start, and a free passage, and all you do is go on like a maniac about a drop of clean running water. Now, if it was the drain you objected to –'

Homily turned to Spiller. 'What sort of boat?' she asked nervously. 'I mean, if I could picture it like . . .'

Spiller thought a moment. 'Well,' he said, 'it's wooden.'

'Yes?' said Homily.

Spiller tried again. 'Well, it's like . . . you might say it was something like a knife-box.'

'How much like?' asked Pod.

'Very like,' said Spiller.

'In fact,' declared Homily triumphantly, 'it *is* a knife box?'

Spiller nodded. 'That's right,' he admitted.

'Flat-bottomed?' asked Pod.

'With divisions, like, for spoons, forks, and so on?' put in Homily.

'That's right,' agreed Spiller, replying to both.

'Tarred and waxed at the seams?'

'Waxed,' said Spiller.

'Sounds all right to me,' said Pod. 'What do you say, Homily?' It sounded better to her too, Pod realized, but he saw she was not quite ready to commit herself. He turned again to Spiller. 'What do you do for power?'

'Power?'

'Got some kind of sail?'

Spiller shook his head. 'Take her down-stream, loaded – with a paddle; pole her back up-stream in ballast . . .'

'I see,' said Pod. He sounded rather impressed. 'You go often to Little Fordham?'

'Pretty regular,' said Spiller.

'I see,' said Pod again. 'Sure you could give us a lift?'

'Call back for you,' said Spiller, 'at the kettle, say. Got to go up-stream to load.'

'Load what?' asked Homily bluntly.

'The boat,' said Spiller.

'I know that,' said Homily, 'but with what?'

'Now, Homily,' put in Pod, 'that's Spiller's business. No concern of ours. Does a bit of trading up and down the river, I shouldn't wonder. Mixed cargo, eh, Spiller? Nuts, birds' eggs, meat, minnows . . . that sort of tackle – more or less what he brings Lupy.'

'Depends what they're short of,' said Spiller.

'They?' exclaimed Homily.

'Now, Homily,' Pod admonished her. 'Spiller's got his customers. Stands to reason. We're not the only borrowers in the world, remember. Not by a long chalk . . .'

'But these ones at Little Fordham,' Homily pointed out. 'They say they're made of plaster?'

'That's right,' said Spiller, 'painted over. All of a piece . . . Except one,' he added.

'One live one?' asked Pod.

'That's right,' said Spiller.

'Oh, I wouldn't like that,' exclaimed Homily, 'I wouldn't like that at all: not to be the one live borrower among a lot of dummy waxworks or whatever they call themselves. Get on my nerves that would . . .'

'They don't bother him,' said Spiller, 'leastways not as much, he says, as a whole lot of live ones might.'

'Well, that's a nice friendly attitude, I must say,' snapped Homily. 'Nice kind of welcome we'll get, I can see, when we turn up there unexpected.'

'Plenty of houses,' said Spiller; 'no sort of need to live close . . .'

'And he doesn't own the place,' Pod reminded her.

'That's true,' said Homily.

'What about it, Homily?' said Pod.

'I don't mind,' said Homily, 'providing we live near the shops.'

'There's nothing in the shops,' explained Pod in a patient voice, 'or so I've heard tell, but bananas and suchlike made of plaster and all stuck down in a lump.'

'No, but it sounds nice,' said Homily, 'say you were talking to Lupy –'

'But you won't be talking to Lupy,' said Pod. 'Lupy won't even know we're gone until she wakes up tomorrow morning thinking that she's got to get us breakfast. No, Homily,' he went on earnestly, 'you don't want to make for shopping centres and all that sort of caper: better some quiet little place down by the water's edge. You won't want to be everlastingly carting water. And, say Spiller comes down pretty regular with a nice bit of cargo, you want somewhere he can tie up and unload . . . Plenty of time, once we get there, to have a look round and take our pick.'

'Take our pick . . .' Suddenly Homily felt the magic of these words: they began to work inside her – champagne bubbles of excitement welling up and up – until, at last, she flung her hands together in a sudden joyful clap. 'Oh, Pod,' she breathed, her eyes brimming as, startled by the noise, he turned sharply towards her, 'think of it – all those houses . . . we could try them *all* out if we wanted, one after another. What's to prevent us?'

'Common sense,' said Pod; he smiled at Arrietty: 'What do you say, lass? Shops or water?'

Arrietty cleared her throat. 'Down by water,' she whispered huskily, her eyes shining and her face tremulous in the dancing light of the dip. 'At least to start with . . .'

There was a short pause. Pod glanced down at his tackle strapped to the hat-pin and up at the clock on the wall. 'Getting on for half past one,' he said; 'time we had a look at this drain. What do you say, Spiller? Could you spare us a minute? And show us the ropes like?'

'Oh,' exclaimed Homily, dismayed, 'I thought Spiller was coming with us.'

'Now, Homily,' explained Pod, 'it's a long trek and he's only just arrived – he won't want to go back right away.'

'I don't see why not if his clothes aren't ready – that's what you came for, isn't it, Spiller?'

'That and other things,' said Pod; 'dare say he's brought a few oddments for Lupy.'

'That's all right,' said Spiller, 'I can tip 'em out on the floor.'

'And you will come?' cried Homily.

Spiller nodded. 'Might as well.'

Even Pod seemed slightly relieved. 'That's very civil of you, Spiller,' he said, 'very civil indeed.' He turned to Arrietty: 'Now, Arrietty, take a dip and go and fetch the egg.'

'Oh, don't let's bother with the egg,' said Homily.

Pod gave her a look. 'You go and get that egg, Arrietty. Just roll it along in front of you into the wash-house, but be careful with the light near those shavings. Homily, you bring the other two dips and I'll get the tackle . . .'

CHAPTER ELEVEN

As they filed through the crack of the door on to the stone flags of the wash-house they heard the ferret again. But Homily now felt brave. 'Scratch away,' she dared it happily, secure in their prospect of escape. But when they stood at last, grouped beneath the mangle and staring down at the drain, her new-found courage ebbed a little and she murmured: 'Oh, my goodness . . .'

Very deep and dark and well-like, it seemed, sunk below the level of the floor. The square grating which usually covered it lay beside it at an angle and in the yawning blackness she could see the reflections of their dips. A dank draught quivered round the candle flames and there was a sour smell of yellow soap, stale disinfectant, and tea leaves.

'What's that at the bottom?' she asked, peering down. 'Water?'

'Slime,' said Spiller.

'Jellied soap,' put in Pod quickly.

'And we've got to wade through that?'

'It isn't deep,' said Spiller.

'Not as though this drain was a sewer,' said Pod, trying to sound comforting and hearty. 'Beats me though,' he went on to Spiller, 'how you manage to move this grating.'

Spiller showed him. Lowering the dip, he pointed out a short length of what looked like brass curtain rod, strong but hollow, perched on a stone at the bottom of the well and leaning against the side. The top of this rod protruded slightly above the mouth of the drain. The grating, when in place, lay loosely on its worn rim of cement. Spiller explained how, by exerting all his strength on the rod from below, he could raise one corner of the grating – as a washerwoman with a prop can raise up a clothes-line. He would then slide the base of the prop on to the raised stone in the base of the shaft, thus holding the contraption in place. Spiller would then swing himself up to the mouth of the drain on a piece of twine tied to a rung of the grating: 'only about twice my height,' he explained. The twine, Pod gathered, was a fixture. The double twist round the light iron rung was hardly noticeable from above and the length of the twine, when not in use, hung downwards into the drain.

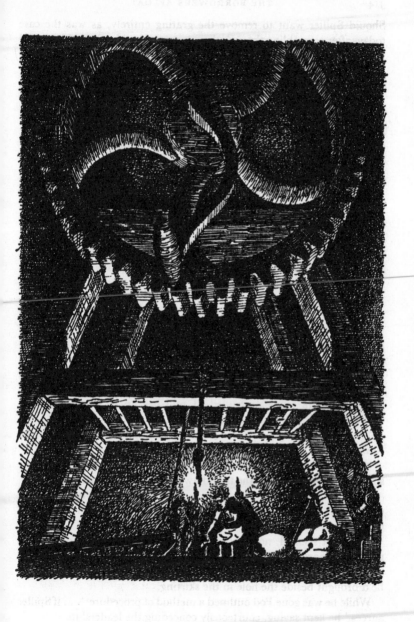

Should Spiller want to remove the grating entirely, as was the case today, after scrambling through the aperture raised by the rod he would pull the twine after him, fling it around one of the stays of the mangle above his head, and would drag and pull on the end. Sometimes, Spiller explained, the grating slid easily, at other times it stuck on an angle. In which event Spiller would produce a small but heavy bolt, kept specially for the purpose, which he would wind into the free end of his halyard and, climbing into the girder-like structure at the base of the mangle, would swing himself out on the bolt which, sinking under his weight, exerted a pull on the grating.

'Very ingenious,' said Pod. Dip in hand he went deeper under the mangle, examined the wet twine, pulled on the knots and finally, as though to test its weight, gave the grating a shove – it slid smoothly on the warn flagstones. 'Easier to shove than to lift,' he remarked. Arrietty, glancing upwards, saw vast shadows on the wash-house ceiling – moving and melting, advancing and receding – in the flickering light from their dips: wheels, handles, rollers, shifting spokes . . . as though, she thought, the great mangle under which they stood was silently and magically turning . . .

On the ground, beside the drain, she saw an object she recognized: the lid of an aluminium soapbox, the one in which the summer before last Spiller had spun her down the river, and from which he used to fish. It was packed now with some kind of cargo and covered with a piece of worn hide – possibly a rat skin – strapped over lid and all with lengths of knotted twine. From a hole bored in one end of the rim a second piece of twine protruded. 'I pull her up by that,' explained Spiller, following the direction of her eyes.

'I see how you get up,' said Homily unhappily, peering into the slime, 'but it's how you get down that worries me.'

'Oh, you just drop,' said Spiller. He took hold of the twine as he spoke and began to drag the tin lid away towards the door.

'It's all right, Homily,' Pod promised hurriedly, 'we'll let you down on the bolt,' and he turned quickly to Spiller. 'Where you going with that?' he asked.

Spiller, it seemed, not wishing to draw attention to the drain, was going to unpack next door. The house being free of humans and the log-box pulled out there was no need to go upstairs – he could dump what he'd brought beside the hole in the skirting.

While he was gone Pod outlined a method of procedure: '. . . if Spiller agrees,' he kept saying, courteously conceding the leadership.

Spiller did agree, or rather he raised no objections. The empty soap-box lid, lightly dangling, was lowered on to the mud: into this they dropped the egg – rolling it to the edge of the drain as though it were a giant rugby football, with a final kick from Pod to send it spinning and keep it clear of the sides. It plopped into the soap-box lid with an ominous crack. This did not matter, however, the egg being hard-boiled.

Homily, with not a few nervous exclamations, was lowered next seated astride the bolt; with one hand she clung to the twine, in the other she carried a lighted dip. When she climbed off the bolt into the lid of the soap box the latter slid swiftly away on the slime, and Homily, for an anxious moment, disappeared down the drain. Spiller drew her back, however, hand over hand. And there she sat behind the egg, grumbling a little, but with her candle still alight. 'Two can go in the lid,' Spiller had announced, and Arrietty (who secretly had longed to try the drop) was lowered considerably, dip in hand, in the same respectful way. She settled herself opposite her mother with the egg wobbling between them.

'You two are the light-bearers,' said Pod. 'All you've got to do is to sit quite still and – steady the egg – move the lights as we say . . .'

There was a little shuffling about in the lid and some slightly perilous balancing as Homily, who had never liked travelling – as human beings would say – back to the engine, stood up to change seats with Arrietty. 'Keep a good hold on that string,' she kept imploring Spiller as she completed this manoeuvre, but soon she and Arrietty were seated again face to face, each with their candle and the egg between their knees. Arrietty was laughing.

'Now I'm going to let you go a little ways,' warned Spiller and paid out a few inches of twine. Arrietty and Homily slid smoothly under the roof of their arched tunnel, which gleamed wetly in the candlelight. Arrietty put out a finger and touched the gleaming surface: it seemed to be made of baked clay.

'Don't touch *anything*,' hissed Homily shudderingly, 'and don't breathe either – not unless you have to.'

Arrietty, lowering her dip, peered over the side at the mud. 'There's a fishbone,' she remarked, 'and a tin bottle top. And a hairpin . . .' she added on a pleased note.

'Don't even *look*,' shuddered Homily.

'A hairpin would be useful,' Arrietty pointed out.

Homily closed her eyes. 'All right,' she said, her face drawn with the effort not to mind. 'Pick it out quickly and drop it, sharp, in the bottom of the boat. And wipe your hands on my apron.'

'We can wash it in the river,' Arrietty pointed out.

Homily nodded: she was trying not to breathe.

Over Homily's shoulder Arrietty could see into the well of the drain; a bulky object was coming down the shaft: it was Pod's tackle, waterproof wrapped and strapped securely to his hat-pin. It wobbled on the mud with a slight squelch. Pod, after a while, came after it. Then came Spiller. For a moment the surface seemed to bear their weight then, knee deep, they sank in slime.

Spiller removed the length of curtain rod from the stone and set it up inconspicuously in the corner of the shaft. Before their descent he and Pod must have placed the grating above more conveniently in position: a deft pull by Spiller on the twine and they heard it clamp down into place – a dull metallic sound which echoed hollowly along the length of their tunnel. Homily gazed into the blackness ahead as though following its flight. 'Oh, my goodness,' she breathed as the sound died: she felt suddenly shut in.

'Well,' announced Pod in a cheerful voice, coming up behind them, and he placed a hand on the rim of their lid, 'we're off!'

CHAPTER TWELVE

SPILLER, they saw, to control them on a shorter length, was rolling up the towline. Not that towline was quite the right expression under the circumstances. The drain ran ahead on a slight downwards incline and Spiller functioned more as a sea anchor and used the twine as a brake.

'Here we go,' said Pod, and gave the lid a slight push. They slid ahead on the slippery scum, to be lightly checked by Spiller. The candlelight danced and shivered on the arched roof and about the dripping walls. So thick and soapy was the scum on which they rode that Pod, behind them, seemed more to be leading his bundle than dragging it behind him. Sometimes, even, it seemed to be leading him.

'Whoa, there!' he would cry on such occasions. He was in very good spirits, and had been, Arrietty noticed, from the moment he set foot in the drain. She too felt strangely happy: here she was, with the two she held most dear, with Spiller added, making their way towards the dawn. The drain held no fears for Arrietty: leading as it did towards a

317

life to be lived away from dust and candlelight and confining shadows
– a life on which the sun would shine by day and the moon by night.

She twisted round in her seat in order to see ahead, and as she did so
a great aperture opened to her left and a dank draught flattened the
flame of the candle. She shielded it quickly with her hand and Homily
did the same.

'That's where the pipe from the sink comes in,' said Spiller, 'and the
overflow from the copper . . .'

There were other openings as they went along, drains which branched
into darkness and ran away uphill. Where these joined the main drain
a curious collection of flotsam and jetsam piled up over which they had
to drag the soap-box lid. Arrietty and Homily got out for this to make
less weight for the men. Spiller knew all these branch drains by name
and the exact position of each cottage or house concerned. Arrietty
began, at last, to understand the vast resources of Spiller's trading. 'Not
that you get up into all of 'em,' he explained. 'I don't mind an S-bend,
but where you get an S-bend you're apt to get a brass grille or suchlike
in the plug hole.'

Once he said, jerking his head towards the mouth of a circular
cavern: 'Holmcroft, that is . . . nothing but bath water from now on . . .'
And, indeed, this cavern as they slid past it had looked cleaner than
most – a shining cream-coloured porcelain, and the air from that point
onwards, Arrietty noticed, smelled far less strongly of tea leaves.

Every now and again they came across small branches – of ash or
holly – rammed so securely into place that they would have difficulty

manoeuvring round them. They were set, Arrietty noticed, at almost regular intervals. 'I can't think how these tree things get down drains, anyway,' Homily exclaimed irritably when, for about the fifth time, the soap-box lid was turned up sideways and eased past and she and Arrietty stood ankle deep in jetsam, shielding their dips with their hands.

'I put them there,' said Spiller, holding the boat for them to get in again. The drain at this point dropped more steeply. As Homily stepped in opposite Arrietty the soap-box lid suddenly slid away, dragging Spiller after: he slipped and skidded on the surface of the mud but miraculously he kept his balance. They fetched up in a tangle against the trunk of one of Spiller's tree-like erections and Arrietty's dip went overboard. 'So that's what they're for,' exclaimed Homily as she coaxed her own flattened wick back to brightness to give Arrietty a light.

But Spiller did not answer straight away. He pushed past the obstruction and, as they waited for Pod to catch up, he said suddenly: 'Could be . . .'

Pod looked weary when he came up to them. He was panting a little and had stripped off his jacket and slung it round his shoulders. 'The last lap's always the longest,' he pointed out.

'Would you care for a ride in the lid?' asked Homily. 'Do, Pod!'

'No, I'm better walking,' said Pod.

'Then give me your jacket,' said Homily. She folded it gently across her knees and patted it soberly as though (thought Arrietty watching) it too were tired, like Pod.

And then they were off again – an endless, monotonous vista of circular walls. Arrietty after a while began to doze: she slid forward against the egg, her head caught up on one knee. Just before she fell asleep she felt Homily slide the dip from her drooping fingers and wrap her round with Pod's coat.

When she awoke the scene was much the same: shadows sliding and flickering on the wet ceiling, Spiller's narrow face palely lit as he trudged along and the bulky shape beyond which was Pod; her mother, across the egg, smiling at her bewilderment. 'Forgotten where you were?' asked Homily.

Arrietty nodded. Her mother held a dip in either hand and the wax, Arrietty noticed, had burned very low. 'Must be nearly morning,' Arrietty remarked. She still felt very sleepy.

'Shouldn't wonder . . .' said Homily.

The walls slid by, unbroken except for arch-like thickenings at regular intervals where one length of pipe joined another. And when they spoke their voices echoed hollowly, back and forth along the tunnel.

'Aren't there any more branch drains?' Arrietty asked after a moment.

Spiller shook his head. 'No more now. Holmcroft was the last . . .'

'But that was ages ago . . . we must be nearly there.'

'Getting on,' said Spiller.

Arrietty shivered and drew Pod's coat more tightly around her shoulders: the air seemed fresher suddenly and curiously free from smell. 'Or perhaps,' she thought, 'we've grown more used to it . . .' There was no sound except for the whispering slide of the soap-box lid and the regular plop and suction of Pod's and Spiller's footsteps. But the silt seemed rather thinner: there was an occasional grating sound below the base of the tin-lid as though it rode on grit. Spiller stood still. 'Listen,' he said.

They were all quiet but could hear nothing except Pod's breathing and a faint musical drip somewhere just ahead of them. 'Better push on,' said Homily suddenly, breaking the tension; 'these dips aren't going to last for ever.'

'Quiet!' cried Spiller again. Then they heard a faint drumming sound, hardly more than a vibration.

'Whatever is it?' asked Homily.

'Can only be Holmcroft,' said Spiller. He stood rigid, with one hand raised, listening intently. 'But,' he said, turning to Pod, 'whoever'd be having a bath at this time o'night?'

Pod shook his head. 'It's morning by now,' he said; 'must be getting on for six.'

The drumming sound grew louder, less regular, more like a leaping and a banging . . .

'We've got to run for it!' cried Spiller. Towline in hand he swung the tin-lid round and, taking the lead, flew ahead into the tunnel. Arrietty and Homily banged and rattled behind him. Dragged on the short line they swung shatteringly, thrown from wall to wall. But, panic-stricken at the thought of total darkness, each shielded the flame of her candle. Homily stretched out a free hand to Pod who caught hold of it just as his bundle bore down on him, knocking him over. He fell across it, still gripping Homily's hand, and was carried swiftly along.

'Out and up!' cried Spiller from the shadows ahead, and they saw the glistening twigs wedged tautly against the roof. 'Let the traps go!' he was shouting. 'Come on – climb!'

They each seized a branch and swung themselves up and wedged themselves tight against the ceiling. The over-turned dips lay guttering in the tin-lid and the air was filled with the sound of galloping water. In the jerking light from the dips they saw the first pearly bubbles and the racing, dancing, silvery bulk behind. And then all was choking, swirling, scented darkness.

After the first few panic-stricken seconds Arrietty found she could breathe and that the sticks still held. A mill-race of hot, scented water swilled through her clothes, piling against her at one moment, falling away the next. Sometimes it bounced above her shoulders, drenching her face and hair, at others it swirled steadily about her waist and tugged at her legs and feet. 'Hold on!' shouted Pod above the turmoil.

'Die down soon!' shouted Spiller.

'You there, Arrietty?' gasped Homily. They were all there and all breathing and, even as they realized this, the water began to drop in level and run less swiftly. Without the brightness of the dips the darkness about them seemed less opaque, as though a silver haze rose from the water itself, which seemed now to be running well below them and, from the sound of it, as innocent and steady as a brook.

After a while they climbed down into it and felt a smoothly running warmth about their ankles. At this level they could see a faint translucence where the surface of the water met the blackness of the

walls. 'Seems lighter,' said Pod wonderingly. He seemed to perceive some shifting in the darkness where Spiller splashed and probed. 'Anything there?' he asked.

'Not a thing,' said Spiller.

Their baggage had disappeared – egg, soap-box lid, and all – swept away on the flood.

'And now what?' asked Pod dismally.

But Spiller seemed quite unworried. 'Pick it up later,' he said; 'nothing to hurt. And saves carting.'

Homily was sniffing the air. 'Sandalwood!' she exclaimed suddenly to Arrietty. 'Your father's favourite soap.'

But Arrietty, her hand on a twig to steady herself against the warm flow eddying past her ankles, did not reply: she was staring straight ahead down the incline of the drain. A bead of light hung in the darkness. For a moment she thought that, by some miraculous chance, it might be one of the dips – then she saw it was completely round and curiously steady. And mingled with the scent of sandalwood she smelled another smell – minty, grassy, mildly earthy . . .

'It's dawn,' she announced in a wondering voice; 'and what's more,' she went on, staring spellbound at the distant pearl of light, 'that's the end of the drain.'

CHAPTER THIRTEEN

THE warmth from the bath water soon wore off and the rest of the walk was chilly. The circle of light grew larger and brighter as they advanced towards it until, at last, its radiance dazzled their eyes.

'The sun's out,' Arrietty decided. It was a pleasant thought, soaked to the skin as they were, and they slightly quickened their steps. The bath-water flow had sunk to the merest trickle and the drain felt gloriously clean.

Arrietty too felt somehow purged as though all traces of the old dark, dusty life had been washed away – even from their clothes. Homily had a similar thought:

'Nothing like a good, strong stream of soapy water running clean through the fabric . . . no rubbing or squeezing: all we've got to do now is lay them out to dry.'

They emerged at last, Arrietty running ahead on to a small sandy beach which fanned out sideways and down to the water in front. The mouth of the drain was set well back under the bank of the stream, which overhung it, crowned with rushes and grasses: a sheltered, windless corner on which the sun beat down, rich with the golden promise of an early summer.

'But you can never tell,' said Homily, gazing around at the weather-worn flotsam and jetsam spewed out by the drain, 'not in March . . .'

They had found Pod's bundle just within the mouth of the drain where the hat-pin had stuck in the sand. The soap-box lid had fetched up, upside-down, against a protruding root, and the egg, Arrietty discovered, had rolled right into the water: it lay in the shallow below a fish-boning of silver ripples and seemed to have flattened out. But when they hooked it on to the dry sand they saw it was due to refraction of the water: the egg was still its old familiar shape but covered with tiny cracks. Arrietty and Spiller rolled it up the slope to where Pod was unpacking the waterlogged bundles, anxious to see if the mackintosh covering had worked. Triumphantly he laid out the contents one by one on the warm sand. 'Dry as a bone . . .' he kept saying.

Homily picked out a change of clothes for each. The jerseys, though

clean, were rather worn and stretched: they were the ones she had knitted – so long ago it seemed now – on blunted darning-needles when they had lived under the kitchen at Firbank. Arrietty and Homily undressed in the mouth of the drain, but Spiller – although offered a garment of Pod's – would not bother to change. He slid off round the corner of the beach to take a look at his kettle.

When they were dressed and the wet clothes spread out to dry, Homily shelled off the top of the egg. Pod wiped down his precious piece of razor-blade, oiled to preserve it against rust, and cut them each a slice. They sat in the sunshine, eating contentedly, watching the ripples of the stream. After a while Spiller joined them. He sat just below them, steaming in the warmth, and thoughtfully eating his egg.

'Where is the kettle exactly, Spiller?' asked Arrietty.

Spiller jerked his head. 'Just round the corner.'

Pod had packed the Christmas-pudding thimble and they each had a drink of fresh water. Then they packed up the bundles again and, leaving the clothes to dry, they followed Spiller round the bend.

It was a second beach, rather more open, and the kettle lay against the bank at the far end. It lay slightly inclined, as Spiller had found it, wedged in by the twigs and branches washed by the river downstream. It was a corner on which floating things caught up and anchored themselves against a projection of the bank. The river twisted inwards at this point, running quite swiftly just below the kettle where, Arrietty noticed, the water looked deep.

Beyond the kettle a cluster of brambles growing under the bank hung out over the water – with new leaves growing among the tawny dead ones; some of these older shoots were trailing in the water and, in the tunnel beneath them, Spiller kept his boat.

Arrietty wanted to see the boat first but Pod was examining the kettle, in the side of which where it met the base was a fair-sized circular rust-hole.

'That the way in?' asked Pod.

Spiller nodded.

Pod looked up at the top of the kettle. The lid, he noticed, was not quite in and Spiller had fixed a piece of twine to the knob in the middle of the lid and had slung it over the arched handle above.

'Come inside,' he said to Pod. 'I'll show you.'

They went inside while Arrietty and Homily waited in the sunshine. Spiller appeared again almost immediately at the rust-hole entrance, exclaiming irritably: 'Go on, get out.' And, aided by a shove from

Spiller's bare foot, a mottled yellow frog leapt through the air and slithered swiftly into the stream. It was followed by two wood-lice which, as they rolled themselves up in balls, Spiller stooped down and picked up from the floor and threw lightly on to the bank above. 'Nothing else,' he remarked to Homily, grinning, and disappeared again.

Homily was silent a moment and then she whispered to Arrietty: 'Don't fancy sleeping in there tonight . . .'

'We can clean it out,' Arrietty whispered back. 'Remember the boot,' she added.

Homily nodded, rather unhappily: 'When do you think he'll get us down to Little Fordham?'

'Soon as he's been up-stream to load. He likes the moon full . . .' Arrietty whispered.

'Why?' whispered Homily.

'He travels mostly at night.'

'Oh,' said Homily, her expression bewildered and slightly wild.

A metallic sound attracted their attention to the top of the kettle: the lid, they saw, was wobbling on and off, raised and lowered from inside. 'According to how you want it . . .' said a voice. 'Very ingenious,' they heard a second voice reply in curiously hollow tones.

'Doesn't sound like Pod,' whispered Homily, looking startled.

'It's because they're in a kettle,' explained Arrietty.

'Oh,' said Homily again. 'I wish they'd come out.'

They came out then, even as she spoke. As Pod stepped down on the flat stone which was used as a door-step he looked very pleased. 'See that?' he said to Homily.

Homily nodded.

'Ingenious, eh?'

Homily nodded again.

'Now,' Pod went on happily, 'we're going to take a look at Spiller's boat. What sort of shoes you got on?'

They were old ones Pod had made. 'Why?' asked Homily. 'Is it muddy?'

'Not that I know of. But if you're going aboard you don't want to slip. Better go barefoot like Arrietty . . .'

CHAPTER FOURTEEN

ALTHOUGH she seemed nearly aground, a runnel of ice-cold water ran between the boat and the shore; through this they waded and Spiller, at the prow, helped them to climb aboard. Roomy but clumsy (Arrietty thought as she scrambled in under the gaiter) but, with her flat bottom, practically impossible to capsize. She was in fact, as Homily had guessed, a knife-box: very long and narrow, with symmetrical compartments for varying sizes of cutlery.

'More what you'd call a barge,' remarked Pod, looking about him: a wooden handle rose up inside to which, he noticed, the gaiter had been nailed. 'Holds her firm,' explained Spiller, tapping the roof of the canopy, 'say you want to lift up the sides.'

The holds were empty at the moment, except for the narrowest. In this Pod saw an amber-coloured knitting-needle which ran the length of the vessel, a folded square of frayed red blanket, a wafer thin butter-knife of tarnished Georgian silver, and the handle and blade of his old nail-scissor.

'So you've still got that?' he said.

'Comes in useful,' said Spiller. 'Careful,' he said as Pod took it up. 'I've sharpened it up a bit.'

'Wouldn't mind this back,' said Pod a trifle enviously, 'say, one day, you got another like it.'

'Not so easy to come by,' said Spiller; and as though to change the subject he took up the butter-knife: 'Found this wedged down a crack in the side . . . does me all right for a paddle.'

'Just the thing,' said Pod – all the cracks and joins were filled in now he noticed as, regretfully, he put back the nail-scissor. 'Where did you pick up this knife-box in the first place?'

'Lying on the bottom up-stream. Full of mud when I spotted her. Bit of a job to salvage. Up by the caravans, that's where she was. Like as not someone pinched the silver and didn't want the box.'

'Like as not,' said Pod. 'So you sharpened her up?' he went on, staring again at the nail-scissor.

'That's right,' said Spiller and, stooping swiftly, he snatched up the piece of blanket. 'You take this,' he said; 'might be chilly in the kettle.'

'What about you?' said Pod.

'That's all right,' said Spiller; 'you take it!'

'Oh,' exclaimed Homily, 'it's the bit we had in the boot . . .' and then she coloured slightly. 'I think,' she added.

'That's right,' said Spiller; 'better you take it.'

'Well, thanks,' said Pod and threw it over his shoulder. He looked around again: the gaiter, he realized, was both camouflage and shelter. 'You done a good job, Spiller. I mean . . . you could live in a boat like this – come wind, say, and wet weather.'

'That's right,' agreed Spiller and he began to ease the knitting-needle out from under the gaiter, the knob emerging forward at an angle. 'Don't want to hurry you,' he said.

Homily seemed taken aback. 'You going already?' she faltered.

'Sooner he's gone, sooner he's back,' said Pod. 'Come on, Homily, all ashore now.'

'But how long does he reckon he'll be?'

'What would you put it at, Spiller?' asked Pod. 'A couple of days? Three? Four? A week?'

'May be less, may be more,' said Spiller; 'depends on the weather. Three nights from now, say, if it's moonlight . . .'

'But what if we're asleep in the kettle?' said Homily.

'That's all right, Homily, Spiller can knock.' Pod took her firmly by the elbow: 'Come on now, all ashore – you too, Arrietty.'

As Homily, with Pod's help, was lowered into the water, Arrietty jumped from the side; the wet mud, she noticed, was spangled all over with tiny footprints. They linked arms and stood well back to watch Spiller depart. He unloosed the painter and, paddle in hand, let the boat slide stern foremost from under the brambles. As it glided out into open water it became unnoticeable suddenly and somehow part of the landscape: it might have been a curl of bark or a piece of floating wood.

It was only when Spiller laid down the paddle and stood up to punt with the knitting-needle that he became at all conspicuous. They watched through the brambles as, slowly and painstakingly, leaning at each plunge on his pole, he began to come back up-stream. As he came abreast of them they ran out from the brambles to see better. Shoes in hand they crossed the beach of the kettle and, to keep up with him, climbed round the bluff at the corner and on to the beach of the drain. There, by a tree root which came sharply into deepish water, they waved him a last good-bye.

'Wish he hadn't had to go,' said Homily, as they made their way back across the sand towards the mouth of the drain.

There lay their clothes, drying in the sun, and as they approached an iridescent cloud like a flock of birds flew off the top of the egg. 'Bluebottles!' cried Homily, running forward, then, relieved, she slackened her steps: they were not bluebottles after all, but cleanly, burnished river flies, striped blue and gold. The egg appeared untouched but Homily blew on it hard and dusted it up with her apron because, she explained, 'You never know . . .'

Pod, poking about among the flotsam and jetsam, salvaged the circular cork which Homily had used as a seat. 'This'll just about do it,' he murmured reflectively.

'Do what?' asked Arrietty idly. A beetle had run out from where the cork had been resting and, stooping, she held it by its shell. She liked beetles: their shiny, clear-cut armour, their mechanical joints and joins. And she liked just a little to tease them: they were so easy to hold by the sharp edge of their wing casings, and so anxious to get away.

'One day you'll get bitten . . .' Homily warned her as she folded up the clothes which still, though dry, smelled faintly and pleasantly of sandalwood, 'or stung, or nipped, or whatever they do, and serve you right.'

Arrietty let the beetle go. 'They don't mind, really,' she remarked, watching the horned legs scuttle up the slope and the fine grains of dislodged sand tumbling down behind them.

'And here's a hairpin!' exclaimed Pod. It was the one Arrietty had found in the drain, clean-washed now – and gleaming. 'You know what we should do,' he went on; 'while we're here, that is?'

'What?' asked Homily.

'Come along here regular, like, every morning, and see what the drain's brought down.'

'There wouldn't be anything I'd fancy,' said Homily, folding the last garment.

'What about a gold ring? Many a gold ring, or so I've heard, gets lost down a drain . . . and you wouldn't say no to a safety-pin.'

'I'd sooner a safety-pin,' said Homily, 'living as we do now.'

They carried the bundles round the bluff on to the beach by the kettle. Homily climbed on the smooth stone which wedged the kettle at an angle and peered in through the rust-hole. A cold light shone down from above where the lid was raised by its string: the interior smelled of rust and looked very uninviting.

'What we want now, before sundown,' said Pod, 'is some good clean dried grass to sleep on. We've got the piece of blanket . . .'

He looked about for some way of climbing the bank. There was a perfect place, as though invented for borrowers, where a cluster of tangled roots hung down from the lip of the cliff which curved deeply in behind them. At some time the stream had risen and washed the roots clean of earth and they hung in festoons and clusters, elastic but safely anchored. Pod and Arrietty went up, hand over hand: there were hand-holes and footholds, seats, swings, ladders, ropes . . . It was a borrower's gymnasium and almost a disappointment to Arrietty when – so soon – they reached the top.

Here among the jade-like spears of new spring growth were pale clumps of hair-like grasses bleached to the colour of tow. Pod reaped these down with his razor-blade and Arrietty tied them into stooks. Homily, below, collected these bundles as they pushed them over the cliff edge and carried them up to the kettle.

When the floor of the kettle was well and truly lined Pod and Arrietty climbed down. Arrietty peered in through the rust-hole: the kettle now smelled of hay. The sun was sinking and the air felt slightly colder. 'What we all need now,' remarked Homily, 'is a good hot drink before bed . . .' But there was no means of making one so they got out the egg instead. There was plenty left: they each had a thickish slice, topped up by a leaf of sorrel.

Pod unpacked his length of tarred string, knotted one end securely and passed the other through the centre of the cork. He pulled it tight.

'What's that for?' asked Homily, coming beside him, wiping her hands on her apron (no washing up, thank goodness: she had carried the egg-shells down to the water's edge and had thrown them into the stream).

'Can't you guess?' asked Pod. He was trimming the cork now, breathing hard, and bevelling the edges.

'To block up the rust-hole?'

'That's right,' said Pod. 'We can pull it tight like some kind of stopper once we're all safely inside.'

Arrietty had climbed up the roots again. They could see her on top of the bank. It was breezier up there and her hair was stirring slightly in the wind. Around her the great grass blades, in gentle motion, crossed and recrossed against the darkening sky.

'She likes it out of doors . . .' said Homily fondly.

'What about you?' asked Pod.

'Well,' said Homily after a moment, 'I'm not one for insects, Pod, never was. Nor for the simple life – if there is such a thing. But tonight' – she gazed about her at the peaceful scene – 'tonight I feel kind of all right.'

'That's the way to talk,' said Pod, scraping away with his razor-blade.

'Or it might,' said Homily, watching him, 'be partly due to that cork.'

An owl hooted somewhere in the distance, on a hollow, wobbling note . . . a liquid note, it seemed, falling musically on the dusk. But Homily's eyes widened. 'Arrietty!' she called shrilly. 'Quickly! Come on down!'

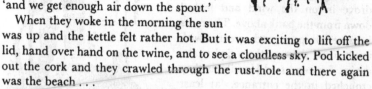

They felt snug enough in the kettle – snug and secure, with the cork pulled in and the lid let down. Homily had insisted on the latter precaution. 'We won't need to *see*,' she explained to Pod and Arrietty, 'and we get enough air down the spout.'

When they woke in the morning the sun was up and the kettle felt rather hot. But it was exciting to lift off the lid, hand over hand on the twine, and to see a cloudless sky. Pod kicked out the cork and they crawled through the rust-hole and there again was the beach . . .

They breakfasted out of doors. The egg was wearing down but there were two-thirds left to go. 'And sunshine feeds,' said Pod. After breakfast Pod went off with his hat-pin to see what had come down the drain; Homily busied herself about the kettle and laid out the blanket to air; Arrietty climbed the roots again to explore the top of the bank. 'Keep within earshot,' Pod had warned them, 'and call out now and again. We don't want accidents at this stage – not before Spiller arrives.'

'And we don't want them then,' retorted Homily. But she seemed curiously relaxed: there was nothing to do but wait – no housework, no cooking, no borrowing, no planning. 'Might as well enjoy ourselves,' she reflected and settled herself in the sun on the piece of red blanket. To Pod and Arrietty she seemed to be dozing but this was not the case at all: Homily was busy day-dreaming about a house with front door and windows – a home of their very own. Sometimes it was small and compact, sometimes four storeys high. And what about the castle? she wondered.

For some reason the thought of the castle reminded her of Lupy: what would they be thinking now – back there in that shuttered house? That we've vanished into thin air – that's what it will seem like to them.

Homily imagined Lupy's surprise, the excitement, the conjectures . . . And, smiling to herself, she half closed her eyes: never would they hit on the drain. And never, in the wildest dreams, would they think of Little Fordham . . .

Two halcyon days went by, but on the third day it rained. Clouds gathered in the morning and by afternoon there was a downpour. At first Arrietty, avid to stay outdoors, took shelter among the roots under the overhanging bank, but soon the rain drove in on the wind and leaked down from the bank above. The roots became slippery and greasy with mud, so all three of them fled to the drain. 'I mean,' said Homily as they crouched in the entrance, 'at least from here we can see out, which is more than you can say for the kettle.'

They moved from the drain, however, when Pod heard a drumming in the distance. 'Holmcroft!' he exclaimed after listening a moment. 'Come on, get moving . . .' Homily, staring at the grey veil of rain outside, protested that, if they were in for a soaking, they might just as well have it hot as cold.

CHAPTER FIFTEEN

It was a good thing they moved, however: the stream had risen almost to the base of the bluff round which they must pass to get to the kettle. Even as it was they had to paddle. The water looked thick and brownish. The delicate ripples had become muscular and fierce and, as they hurried across the second beach, they saw great branches borne on the flood, sinking and rising as the water galloped past.

'Spiller can't travel in this . . .' moaned Homily as they changed their clothes in the kettle. She had to raise her voice against the drumming of the rain-drops on the lid. Below them, almost as it might be in their cellar, they heard the thunder of the stream. But the kettle, perched on its stone and wedged against the bank, felt steady as a citadel. The spout was turned away from the wind and no drop got in through the lid. 'Double rim,' explained Pod; 'well made, these old-fashioned kettles . . .'

Banking on Spiller's arrival they had eaten the last of the egg. They felt very hungry and stared with tragic eyes through the rust-hole when, just below them, a half-loaf went by on the flood.

At last it grew dark and they pulled in the cork and prepared to go to sleep. 'Anyway,' said Pod, 'we're warm and dry. And it's bound to clear up soon . . .'

But it rained all next day. And the next. 'He'll never come in this,' moaned Homily.

'I wouldn't put it past him,' said Pod. 'That's a good solid craft that knife-box, and well covered in. The current flows in close here under those brambles. That's why he chose this corner. You mark my words, Homily, he might fetch up here any moment. Spiller's not one to be frightened by a drop of rain.'

That was the day of the banana. Pod had gone out to reconnoitre, climbing gingerly along the slippery shelf of mud beneath the brambles. The current, twisting in, was pouring steadily through Spiller's boat-house, pulling the trailing brambles in its wake: caught up in the branches where they touched the water Pod had found half a packet of sodden cigarettes, a strip of waterlogged sacking, and a whole, rather overripe banana.

Homily had screamed when he pushed it in inch by inch through the rust-hole. She did not recognize it at first and, later, as she saw what it was she began to laugh and cry at the same time.

'Steady, Homily,' said Pod, after the final push, as he peered in, grave-faced, through the rust-hole, 'get a hold on yourself.'

Homily did – almost at once. 'You should have warned us,' she protested, still gasping a little and wiping her eyes on her apron.

'I did call out,' said Pod, 'but what with the noise of the rain . . .'

They ate their fill of the banana – it was overripe already and would not last for long. Pod sliced it across, skin and all; he thus kept it decently covered. The sound of the rain made talking difficult. 'Coming down faster,' said Pod. Homily leaned forward, mouthing the words: 'Do you think he's met with an accident?'

Pod shook his head: 'He'll come when it stops. We got to have patience,' he added.

'Have what?' shouted Homily above the downpour.

'Patience,' repeated Pod.

'I can't hear you . . .'

'Patience!' roared Pod.

Rain began to come in down the spout. There was nothing for it but to sacrifice the blanket. Homily stuffed it in as tightly as she could and the kettle became very airless. 'Might go on for a month,' she grumbled.

'What?' shouted Pod.

'For a month,' repeated Homily.

'What about it?'

'The rain!' shouted Homily.

After that they gave up talking: the effort seemed hardly worth while. Instead they lay down in the layers of dried grasses and tried to go to sleep. Full-fed and in that airless warmth it did not take them long. Arrietty dreamed she was at sea in Spiller's boat: there was a gentle rocking motion which at first seemed rather pleasant and then in her dream the boat began to spin. The spinning increased and the boat became a wheel, turning . . . turning . . . She clung to the spokes, which became like straw and broke away in her grasp. She clung to the rim, which opened outwards and seemed to fling her off, and a voice was calling again and again: 'Wake up, Arrietty, wake up . . .'

Dizzily she opened her eyes and the kettle seemed full of a whirling half light. It was morning, she realized, and someone had pulled the

blanket from the spout. Close behind her she made out the outline of
Pod; he seemed in some strange way to be glued to the side of the kettle.
Opposite her she perceived the form of her mother, spread-eagled
likewise in the same fixed, curious manner. She herself, half sitting, half
lying, felt gripped by some dreamlike force.

'We're afloat,' cried Pod, 'and spinning.' And Arrietty, besides the
kettle's spin, was aware of a dipping and a swaying. 'We've come adrift.
We're in the current,' he went on, 'and going down-stream fast . . .'

'Oh, my . . .' moaned Homily, casting up her eyes: it was the only
gesture she could make, stuck as she was like a fly to a fly-paper. But
even as she spoke the speed slackened and the spinning turns slowed
down, and Arrietty watched her mother slide slowly down to a sitting
position on the squelching, waterlogged floor. 'Oh, my goodness . . .'
Homily muttered again.

Her voice, Arrietty noticed, sounded strangely audible: the rain had
stopped at last.

'I'm going to get the lid off,' said Pod. He, too, as the kettle ceased
turning, had fallen forward to his knees and now rose slowly, steadying

himself by a hand on the side, against the swaying half-turns. 'Give me a hand with the twine, Arrietty.'

They pulled together. Water had seeped in past the cork in the rust-hole and the floor was awash with sodden grass. As they pulled they slithered, but gradually the lid rose and above them they saw, at last, a circle of bright sky.

'Oh, my goodness,' Homily kept saying, and sometimes she changed it to, 'Oh, my goodness me . . .' But she helped them stack up Pod's bundles. 'We got to get out on deck, like,' Pod had insisted; 'we don't stand a chance down below.'

It was a scramble: they used the twine, they used the hat-pin, they used the banana, they used the bundles and somehow, the kettle listing steeply, they climbed out on the rim to hot sunshine and a cloudless sky. Homily sat crouched, her arms gripped tightly round the stem of the arched handle, her legs dangling below. Arrietty sat beside her holding on to the rim. To lighten the weight Pod cut the lid free and cast it overboard: they watched it float away.

'. . . seems a waste,' said Homily.

CHAPTER SIXTEEN

THE kettle turned slowly as it drifted – more gently now – down-stream. The sun stood high in a brilliant sky: it was later than they had thought. The water looked muddy and yellowish after the recent storm, and in some places had overflowed the banks. To the right of them lay open fields and to the left a scrub of stunted willows and taller hazels. Above their heads golden lamb's-tails trembled against the sky and armies of rushes marched down into the water.

'Fetch up against the bank any minute now,' said Pod hopefully, watching the flow of the stream. 'One side or another,' he added; 'a kettle like this don't drift on for ever . . .'

'I should sincerely hope not,' said Homily. She had slightly relaxed her grip on the handle and, interested in spite of herself, was gazing about her.

Once they heard a bicycle bell and, some seconds later, a policeman's helmet sailed past just above the level of the bushes. 'Oh, my goodness,' muttered Homily, 'that means a footpath . . .'

'Don't worry,' said Pod. But Arrietty, glancing quickly at her father's face, saw he seemed perturbed.

'He'd only have to glance sideways,' Homily pointed out.

'It's all right,' said Pod; 'he's gone now. And he didn't.'

'What about Spiller?' Homily went on.

'What about him?'

'He'll never find us now.'

'Why not?' said Pod. 'He'll see the kettle's gone. As far as Spiller's concerned, all we've got to do is bide our time, wait quietly – wherever we happen to fetch up.'

'Suppose we don't fetch up and go on past Little Fordham?'

'Spiller'll come on past looking for us.'

'Suppose we fetch up amongst all those people?'

'What people?' asked Pod a trifle wearily. 'The plaster ones?'

'No, those human beings who swarm about on the paths.'

'Now, Homily,' said Pod, 'no good meeting trouble half-way.'

'Trouble?' exclaimed Homily. 'What are we in now, I'd like to know?'

She glanced down past her knees at the sodden straw below. 'And I suppose this kettle'll fill up in no time.'

'Not with the cork swollen up like it is,' said Pod. 'The wetter it gets the tighter it holds. All you got to do, Homily, is to sit there and hold on tight, and, say we come near land, get yourself ready to jump.' As he spoke he was busy making a grappling hook out of his hat-pin, twisting and knotting a length of twine about the head of the pin.

Arrietty, meanwhile, lay flat on her stomach gazing into the water below. She was perfectly happy: the cracked enamel was warm from the sun, and with one elbow crooked round the base of the handle she felt curiously safe. Once in the turgid water she saw the ghostly outline of a large fish – fanning its shadowy fins and standing backwards against the current. Sometimes there were little forests of water-weeds where blackish minnows flicked and darted. Once a water-rat swam swiftly past the kettle, almost under her nose: she called out then

excitedly – as though she had seen a whale. Even Homily craned over to watch it pass, admiring the tiny air bubbles which clung like moonstones among the misted fur. They all stood up to watch it climb out on the bank and shake itself hurriedly into a cloud of spray before it scampered away into the grasses. 'Well I never,' remarked Homily. 'Natural history,' she added reflectively.

Then, raising her eyes, she saw the cow. It stood quite motionless above its own vast shadow, hock deep and silent in the fragrant mud. Homily stared aghast and even Arrietty felt grateful for a smoothly floating kettle and a stretch of water between. Almost impertinently safe she felt – so near and yet so far – until a sudden eddy in the current swung them in towards the bank.

'It's all right,' called Pod as Arrietty started back; 'it won't hurt you . . .'

'Oh, my goodness . . .' exclaimed Homily, making as though to climb down inside the rim. The kettle lurched.

'Steady!' cried Pod, alarmed. 'Keep her trimmed!' And, as the kettle slid swiftly shorewards, he flung his weight sideways, leaning out from the handle. 'Stand by . . .' he shouted as with a vicious twist they veered round sharply, gliding against the mud. 'Hold fast!' The great cow backed two paces as they careered up under her nose. She lowered her head and swayed slightly as though embarrassed and then, sniffing the air, she clumsily backed again.

The kettle teetered against the walls and craters of the cow-tracks, pressed by the current's flow: a faint vibration of drumming water quivered through the iron. Then Pod, leaning outwards, clinging with one hand to the rim, shoved his hat-pin in against a stone: the kettle bounced slightly turning into the current and, in a series of bumps and quivers, began to turn away.

'Thank goodness for that, Pod . . .' cried Homily, 'thank goodness . . . thank goodness . . . Oh my, oh my, oh my!' She sat clinging to the base of the handle, white-faced and shaking.

'It would never hurt you,' said Pod as they glided out to mid stream, 'not a cow wouldn't.'

'Might tread on us,' gasped Homily.

'Not once it's seen you it wouldn't.'

'And it did see us,' cried Arrietty, gazing backwards. 'It's looking at us still . . .'

Watching the cow, relaxed and relieved, they were none of them prepared for the bump. Homily, thrown off balance, slid forward with

a cry – down through the lid hole on to the straw below. Pod just in
time caught hold of the handle rail, Arrietty caught hold of Pod.
Steadying Arrietty, Pod turned his head: the kettle, he saw, had fetched
up against an island of sticks and branches, plumb in the middle of the
stream. Again the kettle thrummed, banging and trembling against the
obstructing sticks; little ripples rose up and broke like waves among
and around the weed-strewn, trembling mass.

'Now we are stuck,' remarked Pod, 'good and proper.'

'Get me up, Pod – do . . .' they heard Homily calling from below.

They got her up and showed her what had happened. Pod, peering down, saw part of a gate-post and coils of rusted wire: on this projection a mass of rubbish was entangled, brought down by the flood, a kind of floating island, knitted up by the current and hopelessly intertwined.

No good shoving with his pin: the current held them head on and, with each successive bump, wedged them more securely.

'It could be worse,' remarked Homily surprisingly, when she had got her breath. She took stock of the nest-like structure: some of the sticks, forced above water, had already dried in the sun. The whole contraption, to Homily, looked pleasantly like dry land. 'I mean,' she went on, 'we could walk about on this. I wouldn't say, really, but what I don't prefer it to the kettle . . . Better than floating on and on, and ending up, as well might be, in the Indian Ocean. Spiller could find us here easy enough . . . plumb in the middle of the view.'

'There's something in that,' agreed Pod. He glanced up at the banks: the stream here was wider, he noticed. On left bank, among the stunted willow which shrouded the towpath, a tall hazel leaned over the water; on the right bank the meadows came sloping down to the stream and, beside the muddy cow-tracks, stood a sturdy clump of ash. The tall boles, ash and hazel, stood like sentinels one each side of the river. Yes, it was the kind of spot Spiller would know well; the kind of place, Pod thought to himself, to which humans might give a name. The water on either side of the mid-stream obstruction flowed dark and deep, scooped out by the current into pools . . . yes, it was the kind of place, he decided – with a slight inward tremor of his 'feeling' – where in the summer human beings might come to bathe. Then, glancing down-stream, he saw the bridge.

CHAPTER SEVENTEEN

IT was not much of a bridge – wooden, moss-grown, with a single handrail – but, in their predicament, even a modest bridge was still a bridge too many: bridges were highways, built for humans, and command long views of the river.

Homily, when he pointed it out, seemed strangely unperturbed: shading her eyes against the sunlight she gazed intently down-river.

'No human being that distance away,' she decided at last, 'could make out what's on these sticks . . .'

'You'd be surprised,' said Pod. 'They spot the movement like –'

'Not before we've spotted them. Come on, Pod, let's unload the kettle and get some stuff dried out.'

They went below and, by shifting the ballast, they got the kettle well heeled over. When they had achieved sufficient list Pod took his twine and made the handle fast to the sunken wire netting. In this way, with the kettle held firm, they could crawl in and out through the lid hole.

346

Soon all the gear was spread out in the warmth and, sitting in a row on a baked branch of alder, they each fell to on a slice of banana.

'This could be a lot worse,' said Homily, munching and looking about her. She was thankful for the silence and the sudden lack of motion. Down between the tangled sticks were well-like glintings of dark water, but it was quiet water and, from her high perch, far enough away to be ignored.

Arrietty, on the contrary, had taken off her shoes and stockings and was trailing her feet in the delicate ripples which played about the outer edges.

The river seemed full of voices, endless, mysterious murmurs like half-heard conversations. But conversations without pauses – breathless, steady recountings. 'She said to me, I said to her. And then . . . and then . . . and then . . .' After a while Arrietty ceased to listen as, so often, she ceased to listen to her mother when Homily, in the vein, went on and on and on. But she was aware of the sound and the deadening effect it would have on sounds farther afield. Against this noise, she thought, something could creep up on you and, without hint or warning, suddenly be there. And then she realized that nothing can creep up on an island unless it were afloat or could swim. But, even as she thought this thought, a blue-tit flew down from above and perched beside her on a twig. It cocked its head sideways at the pale ring of banana skin which had enclosed her luncheon slice. She picked it up and threw it sideways towards him – like a quoit – and the blue-tit flew away.

Then she crept back into the nest of flotsam. Sometimes she climbed

under the dry twigs on to the wet ones below. In these curious hollows, cut with sunlight and shadow, there was a vast choice of handholds and notches on which to tread. Above her a network of branches criss-crossed against the sun. Once she went right down to the shadowed water and, hanging perilously above it, saw in its blackness her pale reflected face. She found a water-snail clinging to the underside of a leaf and once, with a foot, she touched some frog's spawn, disturbing a nest of tadpoles. She tried to pull up a water-weed by the roots but, slimily, it resisted her efforts – stretching part way like a piece of elasticized rubber, then suddenly springing free.

'Where are you, Arrietty?' Homily called from above. 'Come up here where it's dry . . .'

But Arrietty seemed not to hear: she had found a hen's feather, a tuft

of sheep's wool, and half a ping-pong ball which still smelled strongly of celluloid. Pleased with these borrowings she finally emerged. Her parents were suitably impressed, and Homily made a cushion of the sheep's wool, wedged it neatly in the half-ball and used it as a seat. 'And very comfortable too,' she assured them warmly, wobbling slightly on the curved base.

Once two small humans crossed the bridge, country boys of nine or ten. They dawdled and laughed and climbed about, and threw sticks into the water. The borrowers froze, staring intently as, with backs turned, the two boys hung on the railings watching their sticks drift down-stream.

'Good thing we're up-stream,' murmured Pod from between still lips.

The sun was sinking and the river had turned to molten gold. Arrietty screwed up her eyelids against the glitter. 'Even if they saw us,' she whispered, her eyes on the bridge, 'they couldn't get at us – out here in deep water.'

'Maybe not,' said Pod, 'but the word would get around . . .'

The boys at length disappeared. But the borrowers remained still, staring at the bushes and trying to hear above the bubble of the river any sound of human beings passing along the footpath.

'I think they must have gone across the fields,' said Pod at last. 'Come on, Arrietty, give me a hand with this waterproof . . .'

Pod had been preparing a hammock bed for the night where four sticks lay lengthwise in a hollow: a mackintosh groundsheet, their dry clothes laid out on top, the piece of sheep's wool for a pillow and, to cover them, another groundsheet above the piece of red blanket. Snug, they would be, in a deep cocoon – protected from rain and dew and invisible from the bank.

As the flood water began to subside their island seemed to rise higher. Slimy depths were revealed among the structure, and gazing down between the sticks at the rusted wire they discovered a water-logged shoe.

'Nothing to salvage there,' remarked Pod after a moment's thoughtful silence, 'except maybe the laces.'

Homily, who had followed them downwards, gazed wonderingly

about her. It had taken courage to climb down into the depths: she had tested every foothold – some of the branches were rotten and broke away at a touch, others less securely wedged were apt to become detached and quivers and slidings took place elsewhere – like a distant disturbance in a vast erection of spillikins. Their curious island was only held together, she realized, by the interrelation of every leaf, stick, and floating strand of weed. All the same, on the way up, she snapped off a living twig of hawthorn for the sake of the green leaf buds. 'A bit of salad, like, to eat with our supper,' she explained to Arrietty. 'You can't go on for ever just on egg and banana . . .'

CHAPTER EIGHTEEN

THEY ate their supper on the up-stream side of the island where the ripples broke at their feet and where the kettle, tied on its side, had risen clear of the water. The level of the stream was sinking fast and the water seemed far less muddy.

It was not much of a supper: the tail end of the banana which had become rather sticky. They still felt hungry, even after they had finished off the hawthorn shoots, washing them down with draughts of cold water. They spoke wistfully of Spiller and a boat chock full of borrowings.

'Suppose we miss him?' said Homily. 'Suppose he comes in the night?'

'I'll keep watch for Spiller,' said Pod.

'Oh, Pod,' exclaimed Homily, 'you've got to have your eight hours.'

'Not tonight,' said Pod, 'nor tomorrow night. Nor any night while there's a full moon.'

'We could take it in turns,' suggested Homily.

'I'll watch tonight,' said Pod, 'and we'll see how we go.'

Homily was silent, staring down at the water. It was a dream-like evening: as the moon rose the warmth of the day still lingered on the landscape in a glow of tranquil light. Colours seemed enriched from within, vivid but softly muted.

'What's that?' said Homily suddenly, gazing down at the ripples, 'something pink . . .'

They followed the direction of her eyes. Just below the surface something wriggled, held up against the current.

'It's a worm,' said Arrietty after a moment. Homily stared at it thoughtfully. 'You said right, Pod,' she admitted after a moment. 'I have changed . . .'

'In what way?' asked Pod.

'Looking at that worm,' said Homily, 'all scoured and scrubbed, like – clean as a whistle – I was thinking.' She hesitated. 'Well, I was thinking . . . I could eat a worm like that . . .'

'What, raw?' exclaimed Pod, amazed.

'No, stewed of course,' retorted Homily crossly, 'with a bit of wild garlic.' She stared again at the water. 'What's it caught up on?'

Pod craned forward. 'I can't quite see . . .' Suddenly his face became startled and his gaze, sharply intent, slid away on a rising curve towards the bushes.

'What's the matter, Pod?' asked Homily.

He looked at her aghast – a slow stare. 'Someone's fishing,' he breathed, scarcely above his breath.

'Where?' whispered Homily.

Pod jerked his head towards the stunted willows. 'There – behind those bushes . . .'

Then Homily, raising her eyes at last, made out the fishing line. Arrietty saw it too. Only in glimpses was it visible: not at all under water but against the surface here and there. They perceived the hair-thin shadow. As it rose it became invisible again, lost against the dimness of the willows, but they could follow its direction.

'Can't see nobody,' whispered Homily.

'Course you can't!' snapped Pod. 'A trout's got eyes, remember, just like you and me . . .'

'Not *just* like –' protested Homily.

'You don't want to show yourself,' Pod went on, 'not when you're fishing.'

'Especially if you're poaching,' put in Arrietty. Why are we whispering? she wondered. Our voices can't be heard above the voices of the river.

'That's right, lass,' said Pod, 'especially if you're poaching. And that's just what he is, I shouldn't wonder – a poacher.'

'What's a poacher?' whispered Homily.

Pod hushed her, raising his hand: 'Quiet, Homily,' and then he added aside: 'A kind of human borrower.'

'A human borrower . . .' repeated Homily in a bewildered whisper: it seemed a contradiction in terms.

'Quiet, Homily,' pleaded Pod.

'He can't hear us,' said Arrietty, 'not from the bank. Look!' she exclaimed. 'The worm's gone.'

So it had, and the line had gone too.

'Wait a minute,' said Pod; 'you'll see – he sends it down on the current.'

Straining their eyes they made out the curves of floating line and, just below the surface, the pinkness of the worm sailing before them. The worm fetched up in the same spot, just below their feet, where again it was held against the current.

Something flicked out from under the sticks below them: there was a flurry of shadow, a swift half-turn, and most of the worm had gone.

'A fish?' whispered Arrietty.

Pod nodded.

Homily craned forward: she was becoming quite excited. 'Look, Arrietty – now you can see the hook!'

Arrietty caught just a glimpse of it and then the hook was gone.

'He felt that,' said Pod, referring to the fisherman; 'thinks he got a bite.'

'But he did get a bite,' said Arrietty.

'He got a bite but he didn't get a fish. Here it comes again . . .'

It was a new worm this time, darker in colour.

Homily shuddered: 'I wouldn't fancy that one, whichever way you cooked it.'

'Quiet, Homily,' said Pod as the worm was whisked away.

'You know,' exclaimed Homily excitedly, 'what we could do – say we had some kind of fire? We could take the fish off the hook and cook and eat it ourselves . . .'

'Say there was a fish *on* the hook,' remarked Pod, gazing soberly towards the bushes. Suddenly he gave a cry and ducked sideways, his hands across his face. 'Look out!' he yelled in a frantic voice.

It was too late: there was the hook in Homily's skirt, worm and all. They ran to her, holding her against the pull of the line while her wild shrieks echoed down the river.

'Unbutton it, Homily! Take the skirt off! Quick . . .'

But Homily couldn't or wouldn't. It might have had something to do with the fact that underneath she was wearing a very short red flannel petticoat which once had belonged to Arrietty and did not think it would look seemly, or she might quite simply just have lost her head. She clung to Pod and, dragged out of his grasp, she clung to Arrietty. Then she clung to the twigs and sticks as she was dragged past them towards the ripples.

They got her out of the water as the line for a moment went slack, and Arrietty fumbled with the small jet bead which served Homily's skirt as a button. Then the line went taut again. As Pod grabbed hold of Homily he saw out of the corner of his eye that the fisherman was standing up.

From this position, on the very edge of the bank, he could play his rod more freely: a sudden upward jerk and Homily, caught by her skirt and shrieking loudly, flew upside-down into the air with Pod and Arrietty fiercely clinging each to an arm. Then the jet button burst off, the skirt sailed away with the worm, and the borrowers, in a huddle, fell back on the sticks. The sticks sank slightly beneath the impact and rose again as gently, breaking the force of their fall.

'That was a near one,' gasped Pod, pulling his leg out of a cleft between the branches. Arrietty, who had come down on her seat, remained sitting: she seemed shaken but unhurt. Homily, crossing her arms, tenderly massaged her shoulders: she had a long graze on one cheek and a jagged tear in the red flannel petticoat. 'You all right, Homily?'

Homily nodded, and her bun unrolled slowly. White-faced and shaking she felt mechanically for hairpins: she was staring fixedly at the bank.

'And the sticks held,' said Pod, examining his grazed shin. He swung the leg slightly. 'Nothing broken,' he said. Homily took no notice: she sat, as though mesmerized, staring at the fisherman.

'It's Mild Eye,' she announced grimly after a moment.

Pod swung round, narrowing his eyes. Arrietty stood up to see better: Mild Eye, the gipsy . . . there was no mistaking the ape-like build, the heavy eyebrows, the thatch of greying hair.

'Now we'll be for it,' said Homily.

Pod was silent a moment. 'He can't get at us here,' he decided at last, 'right out here in mid stream: the water's good and deep out here, on both sides of us, like.'

'He could stand in the shallows and reach,' said Homily.

'Doubt if he'd make it,' said Pod.

'He knows us and he's seen us,' said Homily in the same expressionless voice. She drew a long, quivering breath: 'And, you mark my words, he's not going to miss us again!'

There was silence except for the voices of the river. The babbling murmur, unperturbed and even, seemed suddenly alien and heartless.

'Why doesn't he move?' asked Arrietty.

'He's thinking,' said Homily.

After a moment Arrietty ventured timidly: 'Of what he's going to charge for us, and that, when he's got us in a cage?'

'Of what he's going to do next,' said Homily.

They were silent a moment, watching Mild Eye.

'Look,' said Arrietty.

'What's he up to now?' asked Pod.

'He's taking the skirt off the hook!'

'And the worm too,' said Pod. 'Look out!' he cried as the fisherman's arm flew up. There was a sudden jerk among the sticks, a shuddering series of elastic quivers. 'He's casting for us!' shouted Pod. 'Better we get under cover.'

'No,' said Homily as their island became still again; she watched the caught branch, hooked loose, bobbing away down-river. 'Say he drags this obstruction to bits, we're safer on top than below. Better we take to the kettle –'

But even as she spoke the next throw caught the cork in the rust-hole. The kettle, hooked by its stopper and tied to the sticks, resisted the drag of the rod: they clung together in silent panic as just below them branches began to slide. Then the cork bounced free and leapt away on

the end of the dancing line. Their island subsided again and, unclasping each other, they moved apart, listening wide-eyed to the rhythmic gurgle of water filling the kettle.

The next throw caught a key branch, one on which they stood. They could see the hook well and truly in, and the trembling strain on the

twine. Pod clambered alongside and, leaning back, tugged downwards against the pull. But strain as he might the line stayed taut and the hook as deeply embedded.

'Cut it,' cried someone above the creaking and groaning. 'Cut it . . .' the voice cried again tremulously faint, like the rippling voice of the river.

'Then give me the razor-blade,' gasped Pod. Arrietty brought it in a breathless scramble. There was a gentle twang and they all ducked down as the severed line flew free. 'Now why,' exclaimed Pod, 'didn't I think of that in the first place?'

He glanced towards the shore. Mild Eye was reeling in; the line, too light now, trailed softly on the breeze.

'He's not very pleased,' said Homily.

'No,' agreed Pod, sitting down beside her, 'he wouldn't be.'

'Don't think he's got another hook,' said Homily.

They watched Mild Eye examine the end of his line and they met his baleful glare as, angrily raising his head, he stared across the water.

'Round one to us,' said Pod.

CHAPTER NINETEEN

THEY settled themselves more comfortably on the sticks, preparing for a vigil. Homily reached behind her into the bedding and pulled out the piece of red blanket. 'Look, Pod,' she said in an interested voice as she tucked it about her knees, 'what's he up to now?' They watched intently as Mild Eye, taking up his rod again, turned towards the bushes. 'You don't think he's given it up?' she added as Mild Eye, making for the towpath, disappeared from view.

'Not a hope,' said Pod, 'not Mild Eye. Not once he's seen us and knows we're here for the taking.'

'He can't get us here,' said Homily again, 'right out in deep water. And it'll be dark soon.' She seemed strangely calm.

'Maybe,' said Pod, 'but look at that moon rising. And we'll still be here in the morning.' He took up his razor-blade: 'Might as well free that kettle: it's only a weight on the sticks . . .'

Homily watched him slice through the twine and, a little sadly, they watched the kettle sink.

'Poor Spiller,' said Arrietty. 'He was kind of fond of that kettle . . .'

'Well, it served its purpose,' said Pod.

'What if we make a raft?' suggested Homily suddenly. Pod looked about at the sticks and down at the twine in his hand. 'We could do,' he said, 'but it would take a bit of time. And with him about' – he jerked his head towards the bushes – 'I reckon we're as safe here as anywhere.'

'And it's better here,' said Arrietty, 'for being seen.'

Homily, startled, turned and looked at her. 'Whatever do you want to be seen for?'

'I was thinking of Spiller,' said Arrietty. 'With this kind of moon and this sort of weather he'll come tonight most likely.'

'Pretty well bound to,' agreed Pod.

'Oh dear,' said Homily, pulling the blanket around her, 'whatever will he think? I mean, finding me like this – in Arrietty's petticoat?'

'Nice and bright,' said Pod. 'Catch his eye nicely, that petticoat will.'

357

'Not short and shrunk up like it is,' complained Homily unhappily, 'and a great tear in the side, like.'

'It's still bright,' said Pod, 'a kind of landmark. And I'm sorry now we sunk the kettle. He'd have seen that too. Well, can't be helped –'

'Look!' whispered Arrietty, gazing at the bank.

There stood Mild Eye. Just beside them he seemed now. He had walked down the towpath behind the bushes and had emerged on the bank beside the leaning hazel. In the clear shadowless light he seemed extraordinarily close. They could even see the pallor of his one blue eye in contrast to the fiercely glaring black one; they could see the joints in his fishing rod and the clothes-pegs and coils of clothes-line in his basket, which he carried half slung on his forearm and tilted towards them. Had it been dry land between them four good strides would have brought him across.

'Oh dear,' muttered Homily, 'now what?'

Mild Eye, leaning his rod against the hazel, set down the basket from which he took two fair-sized fish strung together by the gills. These he wrapped carefully in several layers of dock leaves.

'Rainbow trout,' said Arrietty.

'How do you know?' asked Homily.

Arrietty blinked her eyelids. 'I just know,' she said.

'Young Tom,' said Pod; 'that's how she knows, I reckon – seeing his grandad's the gamekeeper. And that's how she knew about poachers, eh, Arrietty?'

Arrietty did not reply: she was watching Mild Eye as he returned the fish to the basket. Very carefully he seemed to be placing them, deep down among the clothes-pegs. He then took up two coils of clothes-line and laid these carelessly on top.

Arrietty laughed. 'As if,' she whispered scornfully, 'they wouldn't search his basket!'

'Quiet, Arrietty,' said Homily, watching intently as Mild Eye, staring across at them, advanced to the edge of the bank. 'It's early yet to laugh . . .'

On the edge of the bank Mild Eye sat down and, his eyes still fixed on the borrowers, began to unlace his boots.

'Oh, Pod,' moaned Homily suddenly, 'you see those boots? They are the same, aren't they? I mean – to think we lived in one of them! Which was it, Pod, left or right?'

'The one with the patch,' said Pod, alert and watching. 'He won't make it,' he added thoughtfully, 'not by paddling.'

'Think of him wearing a boot patched up by you, Pod.'

'Quiet, Homily,' pleaded Pod as Mild Eye, barefoot by now, began to roll up his trousers. 'Get ready to move back.'

'And me getting *fond* of that boot!' exclaimed Homily just above her breath. She seemed fascinated by the pair of them, set neatly together now, on the grassy verge of the stream.

They watched as Mild Eye, a hand on the leaning hazel, lowered himself into the water. It came to just above his ankles. 'Oh, my,' muttered Homily, 'it's shallow. Better we move back –'

'Wait a minute!' said Pod. 'You watch!'

The next step took Mild Eye in to well above the knee, wetting the turn-up of his trousers. He stood, a little nonplussed, holding tight to the leaning branch of the hazel.

'Bet it's cold,' whispered Arrietty.

Mild Eye stared as though measuring the distance between them, and then he glanced back at the bank. Sliding his hand farther out along the branch he took a second step. This brought him in almost to the thigh. They saw him start as the coldness of the water seeped through his trousers to the skin. He glanced at the branch above. It was already bending: he could not with safety move farther. Then, his free arm outstretched towards them, he began to lean . . .

'Oh my –' moaned Homily as the swarthy face came nearer. The outstretched fingers had a greedy steadiness about them. Reaching, reaching . . .

'It's quite all right,' said Pod.

It was as though Mild Eye heard him. The black eye widened slightly while the blue one smoothly stared. The stream moved gently past the soaking corduroys. They could hear the gipsy's breathing.

Pod cleared his throat. 'You can't do it,' he said. Again the black eye widened and Mild Eye opened his mouth. He did not speak but his breathing became even deeper and he glanced again at the shore. Then clumsily he began to retreat, clinging to his branch, and feeling backwards with his feet for rising ground on the slimy bottom. The branch creaked ominously under his weight and, once in shallower water, he quickly let it go and splashed back unaided to the bank. He stood there dripping and gasping and staring at them heavily. There was still no expression on his face. After a while he sat down, and rather unsteadily, still staring, he rolled himself a cigarette.

CHAPTER TWENTY

'I TOLD you he couldn't make it,' said Pod; 'needed a good half-yard or another couple of feet . . .' He patted Homily on the arm: 'All we've got to do now is to hold out till dark. And Spiller will come for sure.'

They sat in a row on the same stick, facing upstream. To watch Mild Eye they had to turn slightly sideways to the left.

'Look at him now,' whispered Homily. 'He's still thinking.'

'Let him think,' said Pod.

'Supposing Spiller came now?' suggested Arrietty, gazing hopefully along the water.

'He couldn't do anything,' said Pod, 'not under Mild Eye's nose. Say he did come now – he'd see we were all right, like, and he'd take cover near by until dark. Then he'd bring his boat alongside on the far side of the island and take us all aboard. That's what I reckon he'd do.'

'But it won't ever get dark,' Arrietty protested, 'not with a full moon.'

'Moon or no moon,' said Pod, 'Mild Eye won't sit there all night. He'll be getting peckish soon. And as far as he calculates, he's got us all tied up, like, and safe to leave for morning. He'll come along then, soon as it's light, with all the proper tackle.'

'What is the proper tackle?' asked Homily uneasily.

'I hope,' said Pod, 'that not being here we won't never need to know.'

'How does he know we can't swim?' asked Arrietty.

'For the same reason as we know he can't: if he could've swum he'd have swum. And the same applies to us.'

'Look,' said Arrietty; 'he's standing up again . . . he's getting something out of the basket!'

They watched intently as Mild Eye, cigarette dangling out of the corner of his mouth, fumbled among the clothes-pegs.

'Oh my,' said Homily, 'see what he's doing? He's got a coil of clothes-line. Oh, I don't like this, Pod. This looks to me' – she caught her breath – 'a bit like the proper tackle.'

'Stay quiet and watch,' said Pod.

Mild Eye, cigarette in mouth, was deliberately unfolding several lengths of line which, new and stiff, hung in curious angles. Then, an end of rope in his hand, he stared at the trunk of the hazel. 'I see what he's going to do,' breathed Homily.

'Quiet, Homily – we all see. But' – Pod narrowed his eyes, watching intently as Mild Eye attached the length of rope above a branch high on the trunk of the hazel – 'I can't quite figure where it gets him . . .'

Climbing down off a curve of root Mild Eye pulled on the rope, testing the strength of the knot. Then, turning towards them, he gazed across the river. They all turned round, following the direction of his eyes. Homily gasped: 'He's going to throw it across . . .' Instinctively she ducked as the coil of rope came sailing above their heads and landed on the opposite bank.

The slack of rope, missing their island by inches, trailed on the surface of the water. 'Wish we could get at it,' muttered Homily but, even as she spoke, the current widened the loop and carried it farther away. The main coil seemed caught in the brambles below the alder. Mild Eye had disappeared again. He emerged at last, a long way farther down the tow-path almost beside the bridge.

'Can't make out what he's up to,' said Homily as Mild Eye, barefoot still, hurried across the bridge, 'throwing that rope across. What's he going to do – walk the tightrope or something?'

'Not exactly,' said Pod; 'the other way round, like. It's a kind of overhead bridge, as you might say, and you get across by handholds. Done it myself once, from a chair back to lamp-table.'

'Well, you need both hands for that,' exclaimed Homily. 'I mean, he couldn't pick *us* up on the way. Unless he does it with his feet.'

'He doesn't need to get right across,' explained Pod – he sounded rather worried – 'he just needs something to hang on to that's a bit longer than that hazel branch, something he knows won't give way. He just wants a bit more reach, a bit more safe lean-over . . . he was pretty close to us that time he waded, remember?'

'Yes . . .' said Homily uneasily, watching as Mild Eye picked his way rather painfully along the left bank and made towards the ash-tree. 'That field's full of stubble,' she remarked unkindly, after a moment.

The rope flew up, scattering them with drops, as Mild Eye pulled it level and made it fast to the ash-tree. It quivered above them, still dripping slightly – taut, straight, and very strong-looking. 'Bear a couple of men his weight,' said Pod.

'Oh, my goodness . . .' whispered Homily.

They stared at the ash-tree: a cut end of clothes-line hung the length

of the bole, still swinging slightly from Mild Eye's efforts. 'Knows how
to tie a knot . . .' remarked Homily.

'Yes,' agreed Pod, looking even more glum. 'You wouldn't undo that
in a hurry.'

Mild Eye took his time walking back. He paused on the bridge and
stared awhile up the river as though to admire his handiwork.
Confident, he seemed suddenly, and in no particular hurry.

'Can he see us from there?' asked Homily, narrowing her eyes.

'I doubt it,' said Pod, 'not if we're still. Might get a glimpse of the
petticoat . . .'

'Not that it matters either way,' said Homily.

'No, it don't matter now,' said Pod. 'Come on now,' he added as
Mild Eye left the bridge, and behind the bushes was starting along
the towpath. 'What we better do, I reckon, is get over to the far side
of the island and each of us straddle a good thick twig: something to
hold on to. He may make it and he may not, but we got to keep
steady now, all three of us, and take our chance. There ain't nothing
else we can do.'

They each chose a thickish twig, picking the ones that seemed light enough to float and sufficiently furnished with handholds. Pod helped Homily, who was trembling so violently that she could hardly keep her balance. 'Oh, Pod,' she moaned, 'I don't know what I feel like — perched up here on my own. Wish we could all be together.'

'We'll be close enough,' said Pod. 'And maybe he won't even get within touching distance. Now you hold tight and, no matter what happens, don't you let go. Not even if you end up in the water.'

Arrietty sat on her twig as though it were a bicycle: there were two footholds and places for both hands. She felt curiously confident: if the twig broke loose, she felt, she could hold on with her hands and use her feet as paddles. 'You know,' she explained to her mother, 'like a water-beetle . . .' But Homily, who in shape was more like a water-beetle than any of them, did not seem comforted.

Pod took his seat on a knobbly branch of elder. 'And make for this far bank,' he said, jerking his head towards the ash-tree, 'if you find you can make for anywhere. See that piece of rope he's left dangling? Well, we might make a grab at that. Or some of those brambles where they trail down into the water . . . get a hold on one of them. Depends where you fetch up . . .'

They were high enough to see across the sticks of their island and Homily, from her perch, had been watching Mild Eye. 'He's coming now,' she said grimly. In her dead, expressionless voice there was a dreadful kind of calm.

They saw that this time he laid both hands on the rope and lowered himself more easily into the water. Two careful steps brought him thigh deep on his foremost leg: here he seemed to hesitate. 'Only wants that other couple of feet,' said Pod.

Mild Eye moved his foremost hand from the rope and, leaning carefully, stretched out his arm towards them. He waggled his fingers slightly, calculating distance. The rope, which had been so taut, sagged a little under his weight and the leaves of the hazel rustled. He glanced behind him, as he had done before, and seemed reassured by the lissom strength of the tree; but the light was fading and, from across where they waited, they could not see his expression. Somewhere in the dusk a cow lowed sadly and they heard a bicycle bell. If only Spiller would come . . .

Mild Eye, sliding his grasp forward, steadied himself a moment and took another step. He seemed to go in deep, but he was so close now that the height of their floating island hid him from the waistline down

They could no longer see the stretching fingers, but they heard the sticks creak and felt the movement: he was drawing their island towards him.

'Oh, Pod,' cried Homily as she felt the merciless pull of that unseen hand and the squeakings and scrapings below her, 'you've been so good to me. All your life you been so good. I never thought to tell you, Pod, never once – how good you've always been –'

She broke off sharply as the island lurched, caught on the barbed wire obstruction, and, terror-stricken, clutched at her twig. There was a dull crack and two outside branches dislodged themselves slowly and bobbed away downstream.

'You all right, Homily?' called Pod.

'So far,' she gasped.

Then everything seemed to happen at once. She saw Mild Eye's expression turn to utter surprise as, lurching forward to grab their island, he pitched face downwards into the water. They went down with him in one resounding splash – or rather, as it seemed to Homily, the water rushed up to them. She had opened her mouth to scream but closed it just in time. Bubbles streamed past her face and tendrils of clinging weed. The water was icily cold but alive with noise and movement. No sooner had she let go her twig, which seemed to be dragging her down, than the hold on the sticks was released and the island rushed up again. Gasping and coughing, Homily broke surface: she saw the trees again, the rising moon, and the dim, rich evening sky. Loudly she called out for Pod.

'I'm here,' cried a choked voice from somewhere behind her. There was a sound of coughing. 'And Arrietty too. Hold tight, like I said! The island's moving . . .'

The island swung as though on a pivot, caught by one end on the wire. They were circling round in a graceful curve towards the bank of the ash-tree. Homily realized, as she grabbed for a handhold, that Mild Eye in falling had pushed on their floating sticks.

They stopped a little short of the bank and Homily could see the trailing brambles and the trunk of the ash-tree with its piece of hanging cord. She saw Pod and Arrietty had clambered down to the sticks which were nearest the shore, at which, with their backs to Homily, they seemed to be staring intently. As she made her way towards them, slipping and sliding on the wet branches, she heard Arrietty talking excitedly, clutching her father by the arm. 'It is,' she kept saying, 'it is . . .'

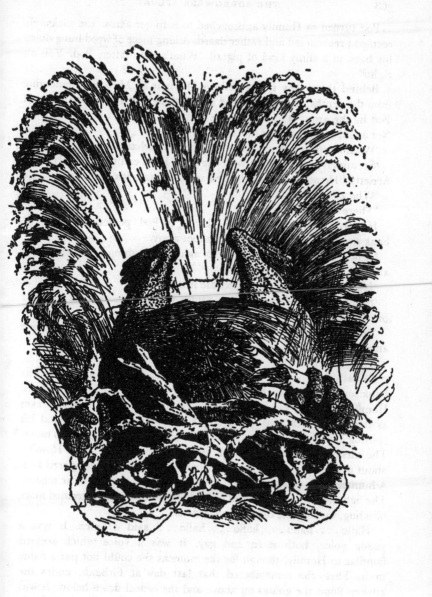

Pod turned as Homily approached to help her across the sticks. He seemed preoccupied and rather dazed. A long piece of weed hung down his back in a slimy kind of pigtail. 'What's the matter, Pod? You all right?'

Behind them they heard bellows of fright as Mild Eye, emerging from the depths, struggled to find a foothold; Homily, alarmed, gripped Pod by the arm. 'It's all right,' he told her, 'he won't bother with us. Not again tonight at any rate . . .'

'What happened, Pod? The rope broke – or what? Or was it the tree?'

'Seemingly,' said Pod, 'it were the rope. But I can't see how. Hark at Arrietty.' He nodded towards the bank. 'She says it's Spiller's boat –'

'Where?'

'There under the brambles.'

Homily, steadying herself by clinging to Pod, peered forward. The bank was very close now – barely a foot away.

'It is, I know it is,' cried Arrietty again, 'that thing under there like a log.'

'It's like a log,' said Pod, 'because it is a log.'

'Spiller!' called Homily on a gentle rising note, peering into the brambles.

'No good,' said Pod, 'we been calling. And, say it was his boat, he'd answer. Spiller,' he called again in a vehement whisper, 'you there?'

There was no reply.

'What's that?' cried Pod, turning. A light had flashed on the opposite bank somewhere near the towpath. 'Someone's coming,' he whispered. Homily heard the sudden jangle of a bicycle and the squeak of brakes as it skidded to a stop. Mild Eye had ceased his swearing and his spitting and, though still in the water, it seemed he had ceased to move. The silence was absolute, except for the running of the river. Homily, about to speak, felt a warning grip on her arm. 'Quiet,' whispered Pod. A human being on the opposite bank was crashing through the bushes. The light flashed on again and circled about. This time it seemed more blinding, turning the dusk into darkness.

'Hallo . . . hallo . . . hallo . . . hallo . . .' said a voice. It was a young voice, both stern and gay. It was a voice which seemed familiar to Homily, though for the moment she could not put a name to it. Then she remembered that last day at Firbank, under the kitchen floor: the goings on above and the ordeal down below. It was the voice, she realized, of Mrs Driver's old enemy – Ernie Runacre, the policeman.

She turned to Pod. 'Quiet!' he warned her again as the circle of light trembled across the water. On the sticks – if none of them moved – he knew they would not be seen. Homily, in spite of this, gave a sudden loud gasp. 'Oh, Pod!' she exclaimed.

'Hush,' urged Pod, tightening his grip on her arm.

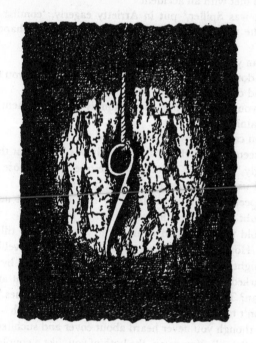

'It's our nail-scissor,' persisted Homily, dropping her voice to a breathy kind of whisper. 'You must look, Pod. Half-way down the ash-tree . . .'

Pod swivelled his eyes round: there it hung, glittering against the bark. It seemed attached in some way to the spare end of rope which Mild Eye had left dangling.

'Then it *was* Spiller's boat,' Arrietty whispered excitedly.

'Keep quiet, can't you,' begged Pod through barely opened lips, 'till he shifts the beam of the light!'

But Ernie Runacre, on the opposite bank, seemed taken up with Mild Eye. 'Now then,' they heard him say in the same brisk, policeman's voice, 'what's going on here?' And the light beam flicked away to concentrate on the gipsy.

Pod drew a sigh of relief. 'That's better,' he said, relaxing slightly and using his normal voice.

'But where is Spiller?' fussed Homily, her teeth chattering with cold. 'Maybe he's met with an accident.'

'But that was Spiller,' put in Arrietty eagerly, 'coming down the tree with the nail-scissor. He'd have it slung by the handle on his shoulder.'

'You mean you saw him?'

'No, you don't see Spiller. Not when he doesn't want you to.'

'He'd kind of match up with the bark,' explained Pod.

'Then if you didn't see him,' said Homily after a moment, 'how can you be certain?'

'Well, you can't be certain,' agreed Pod.

Homily seemed perturbed. 'You think it was Spiller cut the rope?'

'Seemingly,' said Pod; 'shinned up the tree by that loose bit of left-over. Like I used to with my name-tape, remember?'

Homily peered at the brambles. 'Say that is his boat under there, which I doubt – why didn't he just come and fetch us?'

'Like I told you,' said Pod wearily; 'he was laying up till dark. Use your head, Homily. Spiller needs this river – it's his livelihood, like. True, he might have got us off. But – say he was spotted by Mild Eye; he'd be marked down by the gipsies from then on – boat and all. See what I mean? They'd be on the watch for him. Sometimes,' Pod went on, 'you don't talk like a borrower. You and Arrietty both – you go on at times as though you never heard about cover and suchlike, let alone about being "seen". You go on, the both of you, like a couple of human beings . . .'

'Now, Pod,' protested Homily, 'no need to get insulting.'

'But I mean it,' said Pod. 'And as far as Spiller knew we was all right here till dark. Once the hook had gone.'

They were quiet a moment, listening to the splashes across the water. Homily, caught by the sound of that brisk, familiar voice, moved away from Pod in order to hear what was happening. 'Come on now,' Ernie Runacre was saying, 'get your foot on that root. That's right. Give us your hand. Bit early, I'd say, for a dip. Wouldn't choose it myself. Sooner try me hand at a bit of fishing . . . providing, of course, I weren't too particular about the by-laws. Come on now' – he caught his breath as though to heave – 'one, two, three – hup! Well, there you are! Now, let's take a look at this basket . . .'

Homily, to get a glimpse of them, had hauled herself up on a twig when she felt Pod's hand on her arm. 'Watch!' she exclaimed excitedly, gripping his fingers with hers. 'He'll find that borrowed fish! That rainbow trout or whatever it's called . . .'

'Come on now,' whispered Pod.

'Just a minute, Pod –'

'But he's waiting,' insisted Pod. 'Better we go now, he says, while they're taken up with that basket . . . And that light on the bank, he says, will make the river seem darker.'

Homily turned slowly. There was Spiller's boat, bobbing alongside, with Spiller and Arrietty in the stern. She saw their faces, pale against the shadows, lit by the rising moon. All was quiet, except for the running of the ripples.

Dazedly she began to climb down. 'Spiller . . .' she breathed. And, missing a foothold, she stumbled and clung to Pod.

He supported and gently guided her down to the water. As he helped her aboard he said: 'You and Arrietty better get under the canopy. Bit of a squeeze now because of the cargo, but it can't be helped . . .'

Homily hesitated, gazing dumbly at Spiller, as they met face to face in the stern. She could not, at that moment, find words to thank him, nor dare she take his hand. He seemed aloof, suddenly, and very much the captain: she just stood and looked at him until, embarrassed, he frowned and looked away. 'Come, Arrietty,' said Homily huskily and, feeling rather humbled, they crept in under the gaiter.

CHAPTER TWENTY-ONE

PERCHED on top of the cargo, which felt very knobbly, Homily and Arrietty clung together to share their last traces of warmth. As Pod let go the painter and Spiller pushed off with his butter-knife, Homily let out a cry.

'It's all right,' Arrietty soothed her; 'see, we're in the current. It was just that one last lurch.'

The knife-box now rode smoothly on the ripples, gracefully veering with the river's twists and turns. Beyond the canopy and framed in its arch they could see Pod and Spiller in the stern. What were they talking about? Arrietty wondered. And wished very much she could hear.

'Pod'll catch his death,' muttered Homily unhappily, 'and so will we all.'

As the moon gained in brilliance the figures in the stern became silvered over. Nothing moved except Spiller's hand on the paddle as deftly, almost carelessly, he held the boat in the current. Once Pod laughed, and once they heard him exclaim: 'Well, I'm danged!'

'We won't have any furniture or anything,' said Homily after a while, 'only the clothes we stand up in – say we were standing up, I mean. Four walls, that's all we'll have: just four walls!'

'And windows,' said Arrietty. 'And a roof,' she added gently.

Homily sneezed loudly. 'Say we survive,' she sniffed, fumbling about for a handkerchief.

'Take mine,' said Arrietty, producing a sodden ball; 'yours went away with the skirt.'

Homily blew her nose and pinned up her dripping hair; then, clinging together, they were silent awhile, watching the figures in the stern. Homily, very tense, seemed to be thinking. 'And your father's lost his hacksaw,' she said at last.

'Here's papa now,' Arrietty remarked as a figure darkened the archway. She squeezed her mother's arm: 'It will be all right. I know it will. Look, he's smiling . . .'

Pod, climbing on to the cargo, approached them on hands and knees. 'Just thought I'd tell you,' he said to Homily, slightly lowering his voice, 'that he's got enough stuff in the holds he says to start us off housekeeping.'

'What sort of stuff?' asked Homily.

'Food mostly. And one or two tools and such to make up for the nail-scissor.'

'It's clothes we're short of . . .'

'Plenty of stuff for clothes, Spiller says, down at Little Fordham. Any amount of it: dropped gloves, handkerchiefs, scarves, jerseys, pull-overs – the lot. Never a day passes, he says, without there isn't something.'

Homily was silent. 'Pod,' she said at last, 'I never even thanked him.'

'That's all right. He don't hold with thanks.'

'But, Pod, we got to do something.'

'I been into that,' said Pod; 'there's no end to the stuff we could collect up for him once we get settled, like, in a place of our own. Say every night we whipped round quick after closing time. See what I mean?'

'Yes,' said Homily uncertainly. She could never quite visualize Little Fordham.

'Now,' said Pod, squeezing past them, 'he's got a whole lot of sheep's wool, he says, up for'ard. Better you both undress and tuck down into it. Might get a bit of sleep. We won't be there, he says, not much before dawn . . .'

'But what about you, Pod?' asked Homily.

'That's all right,' said Pod, poking about for'ard; 'he's lending me a suit. Here's the sheep's wool,' he said and began to pass it back.

'A suit?' echoed Homily, amazed. 'What kind of a suit?' Mechanically she stacked up the sheep's wool. It smelled a little oily but there seemed to be plenty of it.

'Well,' said Pod, 'his summer clothes.' He sounded rather self-conscious.

'So Lupy finished them?'

'Yes, he went back for them.'

'Oh,' exclaimed Homily, 'did he tell them anything about us?'

'Not a word. You know Spiller. They did the telling. Very upset Lupy was, he says. Went on about you being the best friend she ever had. More like a sister to her, she says. Seems she's gone into mourning.'

'Mourning! Whatever for?'

'For us, I reckon,' said Pod. He smiled wanly and began to unbutton his waistcoat.

Homily was silent a moment. Then she too smiled – a little puffed up, it seemed, by the thought of Lupy in black. 'Fancy!' she said at last and, suddenly cheerful, she began to unbutton her blouse.

Arrietty, already undressed, had rolled herself into the sheep's wool. 'When did Spiller first spot us?' she asked sleepily.

'Saw us in the air,' said Pod, 'when we were on the hook.'

'Goodness . . .' murmured Arrietty. Drowsily she seemed trying to think back: 'And that's why we didn't see him.'

'And why Mild Eye didn't either. Too much going on. Spiller took his chance like a flash: slid on quick, close as he could get, and drove in under those brambles.'

'Wonder he didn't call out to us,' said Homily.

'He did,' exclaimed Pod, 'but he wasn't all that close. And what with the noise of the river –'

'Hush!' whispered Homily. 'She's dropping off . . .'

'Yes,' went on Pod, lowering his voice, 'he called all right – it was just that we didn't seem to hear him. Excepting, of course, that once.'

'When was that?' asked Homily. 'I never heard nothing.'

'That fourth throw,' whispered Pod, 'when the hook caught in our stick, remember? And I was down there pulling? Well, he yelled out then at the top of his lungs: remember a voice calling "Cut it"? Thought it was you at the time . . .'

'Me?' said Homily. In the wool-filled dimness there were faint clicking, mysterious unbuttonings . . .

'But it was Spiller,' said Pod.

'Well, I never . . .' said Homily. Her voice sounded muffled: in her modest way she was undressing under the sheep's wool and had disappeared from view. Her head emerged at last, and one thin arm with a sudden bundle of clothes. 'Anywhere we can hang these out, do you think?'

'Leave them there,' said Pod as, grunting a little, he struggled with Spiller's tunic, 'and Arrietty's too. I'll ask Spiller . . . dare say we'll manage. As I see it,' he went on, having got the tunic down past his waist and the trousers dragged up to meet it, 'in life as we live it – come this thing or that thing – there's always some way to manage. Always has been and, like as not, always will be. That's how I reckon. Maybe we could fly the clothes, like, strung out on the knitting-needle . . .'

Homily watched him in silence as he gathered the garments together. 'Maybe . . .' she said after a moment.

'Lash the point, say, and fly the knob.'

'I meant,' said Homily softly, 'what you said before: that maybe there is always some way to manage. The trouble comes, like, or so it seems to me, in whether you hit on it.'

'Yes, that's the trouble,' said Pod.

'See what I mean?'

'Yes,' said Pod. He was silent a moment, thinking this out. 'Oh, well . . .' he said at last, and turned as if to go.

'Just a minute, Pod,' pleaded Homily, raising herself on an elbow, 'let's have a look at you. No, come a bit closer. Turn round a bit . . . that's right. I wish the light was better . . .' Sitting up in her nest of fleece, she gave him a long look – it was a very gentle look for Homily. 'Yes,' she decided at last, 'white kind of suits you, Pod.'

EPILOGUE

In the large kitchen at Firbank Hall, Crampfurl, the gardener, pushed his chair back from the table. Picking his teeth with a whittled matchstick, he stared at the embers of the stove. 'Funny . . .' he said.

Mrs Driver, the cook, who was clearing the dishes, paused in her stacking of the plates; her suspicious eyes slid sideways: 'What is?'

'Something I saw . . .'

'At market?'

'No – tonight, on the way home . . .' Crampfurl was silent a moment, staring towards the grate. 'Remember that time – last March, wasn't it – when we had the floor up?'

Mrs Driver's swarthy face seemed to darken. Tightening her lips, she clattered the plates together and, almost angrily, she threw the spoons into a dish. 'Well, what about it?'

'Kind of nest, you said it was. Mice dressed up, you said . . .'

'Oh, I never –'

'Well, you ask Ernie Runacre: he was there – nearly split his sides laughing. Mice dressed up, you said. Those were the very words. Saw them running, you said . . .'

'I swear I never.'

Crampfurl looked thoughtful: 'You've a right to deny it. But couldn't help laughing meself. I mean, there you was, perched up on that chair and –'

'That'll do.' Mrs Driver drew up a stool and sat down heavily. Leaning forward, elbows on knees, she stared into Crampfurl's face. 'Suppose I did see them – what then? What's so funny? Squeaking and squawking and running every which way . . .' Her voice rose. 'And what's more . . . now I *will* tell you something, Crampfurl.' She paused to draw a deep breath. 'They were more like *people* than mice. Why, one of 'em even –'

Crampfurl stared back at her: 'Go on. Even what?'

'One of 'em even had its hair in curlers . . .'

She glared as she spoke, as though daring him to smile. But Crampfurl did not smile. He nodded slowly. He broke his matchstick in half and threw it into the fire. 'And yet,' he said, rising to his feet, 'if there'd been anything, we'd have found it at the time. Stands to reason – with the floor up and that hole blocked under the clock.' He yawned noisily, stretching his forearms. 'Well, I'll be getting on. Thanks for the pie . . .'

Mrs Driver did not stir. 'For all we know,' she persisted, 'they may be still about. Half the rooms being closed, like.'

'No, I wouldn't say that was likely: we been more on the watch-out and there'd be some kind of traces. No, I got an idea they escaped – say there *was* something here in the first place.'

'There was something here all right! But what's the good of talking . . . with that Ernie Runacre splitting his sides. And' – she glanced at him sharply – 'what's changed you all of a sudden?'

'I don't say I have changed. It's just that I got thinking. Remember that scarf you was knitting – that grey one? Remember the colour of the needles?'

'Needles . . . kind of coral, wasn't they? Pinkish like . . .'

'Coral?'

'Soon tell. I've got them here.' She crossed to the dresser, pulled out a drawer, and took out a bundle of knitting-needles tied about with wool. 'These are them, these two here. More pinkish than coral. Why do you ask?'

Crampfurl took up the bundle. Curiously he turned it about. 'Had an idea they was yellow . . .'

'That's right too – fancy you remembering! I did start with yellow but I lost one: that day my niece came, remember, and we brought up tea to the hayfield?'

Crampfurl, turning the bundle, selected and drew out a needle: it was amber-coloured and slightly translucent. He measured it thoughtfully between his fingers: 'One like this, weren't it?'

'That's right. Why? You found one?'

Crampfurl shook his head: 'Not exactly.' He stared at the needle, turning it about: the same thickness, that other one, and, allowing for the part that was hidden, about the same length . . . Fragile as glass it had looked in the moonlight, with the darkened water behind, as – staring, staring – he had leaned down over the bridge. The paddle, doubly silvered, had flashed like a fish in the stern. As the strange craft came nearer, he had caught a glimpse of the butter-knife, observed the shape of the canopy, and the barge-like depth of the hull. The set of signals flying from the mast-head seemed less like flags than miniature garments strung like washing in the breeze – a descending scale of trousers, pants, and drawers, topped gallantly (or so it had seemed) by a fluttering red-flannel petticoat – and tiny shreds of knitted stocking whipped eel-like about the mast. Some child's toy, he had thought . . . some discarded invention, abandoned and left to drift . . . Until, as the craft approached the shadow of the bridge, a face had looked up from the stern, bird's-egg pale and featureless in the moonlight, and with a mocking flick of the paddle – a fish-tail flash which broke the surface to spangles – the boat had vanished beneath him.

No, he decided, as he stood there twisting the needle, he would not tell Driver of this. Nor how, from the farther parapet, he had seen the boat emerge and had watched its course down-stream. How blackly visible it had looked against the glittering water, the mast-head garments now in fluttering silhouette . . . How it had dwindled in size until a tree shadow, flung like a shawl across the moonlit river, had absorbed it into darkness.

Crampfurl sighed and, putting the needle back with the others, he gently closed the drawer. No, he wouldn't tell Driver of this. Leastways, not tonight, he wouldn't . . .

THE
BORROWERS
ALOFT

WITH ILLUSTRATIONS BY
Diana Stanley

This story is dedicated with love to
TOM BRUNSDON AND FRANCES RUSH
*and to all the children in the world who
have promised their parents never to play with gas,
and who keep their promises*

SOME people thought it strange that there should be two model villages, one so close to the other (there was a third as a matter of fact belonging to a little girl called Agnes Mercy Foster, which nobody visited, and which we need not bother about because it was not built to last).

One model village was at Fordham, called Little Fordham: it belonged to Mr Pott. Another was at Went-le-Craye, called Ballyhoggin, and belonged to Mr Platter.

It was Mr Pott who started it all, quietly and happily for his own amusement; and it was the business-like Mr Platter, for quite another reason, who copied Mr Pott.

Mr Pott was a railway-man who had lost his leg on the railway: he lost it at dusk one evening on a lonely stretch of line – not through carelessness, but when saving the life of a badger. Mr Pott had always been anxious about these creatures: the single track ran through a wood, and in the half light the badgers would trundle out, sniffing their

383

way across the sleepers. Only at certain times of the year were they in any real danger, and that was when the early dusk (the time they liked to sally forth) coincided with the passing of the last train from Hatter's Cross. After the train passed, the night would be quiet again; and foxes, hares and rabbits could cross the line with safety; and nightingales would sing in the wood.

In those early days of the railway, Mr Pott's small, lonely signal-box was almost a home from home. He had there his kettle, his oil-lamps, his plush-covered table and his broken-springed railway armchair. To while away the long hours between trains, he had his fret-saw, his stamp collection and a well-thumbed copy of the Bible which sometimes he would read aloud. Mr Pott was a good man, very kind and gentle. He loved his fellow creatures almost as much as he loved his trains. With the fret-saw he would make collecting-boxes for the Railway Benevolent Fund; these were shaped like little houses and he made them from old cigar-boxes, and no two of his houses were alike. On the first Sunday of every month Mr Pott, on his bicycle, would make a tour of the village, armed with a screwdriver and a small black bag. At each home or hostelry he would unscrew the roof of a little house and count out the contents into his bag. Sometimes he was cheated (but not often) and would mutter sadly as he rode away: 'Fox been at the eggs again.'

Occasionally, in his signal-box, Mr Pott would paint a picture, very small and detailed. He had painted two of the church, three of the vicarage, two of the post office, three of the forge and one of his own signal-box. These pictures he would give away as prizes to those who collected most for his fund.

On the night of which we speak the badger bit Mr Pott – that was the trouble. It made him lose his balance, and in that moment's delay the train wheels caught his foot. Mr Pott never saw the marks of the badger's teeth because the leg it bit was the leg they cut off. The badger itself escaped unharmed.

The Railway Benevolent were very generous. They gave Mr Pott a small lump sum and found him a cottage just outside the village, where three tall poplar-trees stood beside a stream. It was here, on a mound in his garden, that he started to build his railway.

First he bought at second hand a set of model trains. He saw them advertised in a local paper with the electric battery on which to run them. Because there was no room large enough in his tiny cottage he set up the lines in his garden. With the help of the blacksmith he made the rails but he needed no help with the sleepers: these he cut to scale and

set them firmly, as of old he had set the big ones. Once these were set
he tarred them over, and when the sun was hot they smelled just right.
Mr Pott would sit on the hard ground, his wooden leg stretched out
before him, and close his eyes and sniff the railway smell. Lovely it was,
and magic – but something was missing. Smoke, that's what it was!
Yes, he badly needed some smoke – not only the tang of it, but the sight
of it as well. Later, with the help of Miss Menzies of High Beech, he
found a solution.

When he made his signal-box, he built it of solid brick. It was exactly

like his old one, wooden stairs and all. He glazed the windows with real
glass and made them to open and shut (it wasn't for nothing, he realized
then, that he had kept the hinges of all the cigar-boxes passed on to him
by his directors). The bricks he made from the red brick of his
tumbledown pigsty; he pounded these down to a fine dust and mixed
them loosely with cement. He set the mixture in a criss-cross mould
which he stood on a large tin tea-tray. The mould was made of old steel
corset-bones – a grill of tiny rectangles soldered by the blacksmith.
With his contraption, Mr Pott could make five hundred bricks at a
time. Sometimes to vary the colour he stirred in powdered ochre or a

drop of cochineal. He slated the roof of his signal-box with thin flakes of actual slate, neatly trimmed to scale – these too from his ruined pigsty.

Before he put the roof on he took a lump of builder's putty. Rolling and rubbing it between his stiff old hands, he made four small sausages for arms and legs and a thicker, shorter one for the body. Rolling and squeezing, he made an egg for the head and smoothed it squarely on to the shoulders. Then he pinched it here and there and carved bits out, scraping away with a horny thumb-nail.

But it wasn't very good, even as an effigy – let alone as a self-portrait. To make it more like himself he took off the leg at the knee and stuck in a matchstick. Then when the putty was hardened he painted the figure over with a decent suit of railway blue, pinked up the face, gummed on a thatch of greying hair made from that creeper called old-man's-beard, and set it up in his signal-box. There it looked much more human – and really rather frightening, standing so still and stiff and staring through the windows.

The signal-box seemed real enough though – with its outside stairway of seasoned wood, yellow lichen on the slates, weathered bricks with their softly blended colours, windows ajar and, every now and again, the living clack of its signals.

The children of the village became rather a nuisance. They would knock on his front door and ask to see the railway. Mr Pott, once settled comfortably on the hard ground, his wooden leg stuck out before him, found it hard to rise quickly. But, being very patient, he would heave himself up and stump along to let in his callers. He would greet them civilly and conduct them down the passage, through the scullery and out into the garden. There precious building time was lost in questions, answers and general exclamation. Sometimes while they talked his cement would dry, or his soldering-iron grow cold. After a time he made the rule that they could only come at week-ends, and on Saturdays and Sundays he would leave his door ajar. On the scullery table he set a small collecting-box and the grown-ups, who now came too, were asked to pay one penny: the proceeds he sent to his Fund. The children still came free.

After he made his station, more and more people were interested and the proceeds began to mount up. The station was an exact copy of Fordham's own station, and he called it Little Fordham. The letters were picked out in white stone on a bank of growing moss. He furnished the inside before he put the roof on. In the waiting-rooms, hard dark

benches, and in the station-master's office, pigeon-holes for tickets and a high wooden desk. The blacksmith (a young man called Henry who by now was deeply interested) welded him a fireplace of dark wrought iron. They burned dead moss and pine-needles to test the draught and they saw that the chimney drew.

But once the roof was on all these details were lost. There was no way to see inside except by lying down and peering through the windows, and when the platform was completed you couldn't do even this. The platform roof was edged by Mr Pott with a wooden fringe of delicate fretwork. There were cattle-pens, milk-churns; and old-fashioned station lamps in which Mr Pott could burn oil.

With Mr Pott's meticulous attention to detail and refusal to compromise with second best, the building of the station took two years and seven months. And then he started on his village.

CHAPTER TWO

MR POTT had never heard of Mr Platter, nor Mr Platter of Mr Pott.

Mr Platter was a builder and undertaker at Went-le-Craye, the other side of the river, of which Mr Pott's stream was a tributary. They lived quite close, as the crow flies, but far apart by road. Mr Platter had a fine, new red brick house on the main road to Bedford, with a gravel drive, and a garden which sloped to the water. He had built it himself and called it Ballyhoggin. Mr Platter had amassed a good deal of money. But people weren't dying as they used to; and when the brick factory closed down there were fewer new inhabitants. This was because Mr Platter, building gimcrack villas for the workers, had spoiled the look of the countryside.

Some of Mr Platter's villas were left on his hands, and he would advertise them in county papers as 'suitable for elderly retired couples'. He was annoyed if, in desperation, he had to let to a bride and bridegroom: because Mr Platter was very good at arranging expensive funerals and he liked to stock up on an older type of client. He had a tight kind of face and a pair of rimless glasses which caught the light so that you could not see his eyes. He had, however, a very polite and gentle manner; so you took the eyes on trust. Dear Mr Platter, the mourners said, was always 'so very kind', and they seldom questioned his bill.

Mr Platter was small and thin but Mrs Platter was large. Both had rather mauvish faces: Mr Platter's had a violet tinge while Mrs Platter's inclined more to pink. Mrs Platter was an excellent wife and both of them worked very hard.

As villas fell vacant and funerals became scarcer, Mr Platter had time on his hands. He had never liked spare time. In order to get rid of it he took up gardening. All Mr Platter's flowers were kept like captives – firmly tied to stakes: the slightest sway or wriggle was swiftly punished – a lop here or a cut there. Very soon the plants gave in – uncomplaining as guardsmen they would stand to attention in rows. His lawns too were a sight to behold as, weed-repelled and mown in stripes, they sloped down to the river. A glimpse of Mr Platter with his weeding-tools was enough to make the slyest dandelion seed smartly change

course in mid air, and it was said of a daisy plant that, realizing suddenly where it was, the pink-fringed petals turned white overnight.

Mrs Platter, for her part – and with an eye to the main road and its traffic – put up a notice which said TEAS, and she set up a stall on the grass verge for the sale of flowers and fruit. They did not do very well, however, until Mrs Platter had an inspiration and changed the wording of the notice to RIVERSIDE TEAS. Then people did stop. And once conducted to the tables behind the house they would have the 'set tea' because there was no other. This was expensive, although there was margarine instead of butter and falsely pink, oozy jam bought by Mrs Platter straight from the factory in large tin containers. She also sold soft drinks in glass bottles with marble stoppers, toy balloons and paper windmills. People kept coming and the Platters began to do well; the cyclists were glad to sit down for a while, and the motorists to take off their dust-coats and goggles and stretch their legs.

The falling-off was gradual. At first they hardly noticed it. 'Quiet Whitsun,' Mr Platter would say as they changed the position of the tables so as not to damage the lawn. He thought again about an ice-cream machine, but decided to wait: Mr Platter was a great believer in what he described as 'laying out money', but only where he saw a safe return.

Instead of this he mended up his old flat-bottomed boat and, with the aid of a shrimping-net, he cleared the stream of scum. 'Boating' he

wanted to add to the tea-notice; but Mrs Platter dissuaded him. There might be complaints, she thought, as with the best will in the world and a bit of pulling and pushing, you could get the boat round the nettle-infested island but that would be about all.

August Bank Holiday was a fiasco: only ten set teas sold on what Mrs Platter called 'The Saturday'; eleven on the Sunday and seven on the Monday. 'I can't make it out,' Mrs Platter kept saying, as she and Agnes Mercy threw the stale loaves into buckets for the chickens. 'Last year they were standing for tables . . .'

Agnes Mercy was fifteen now. She had grown into a large, slow, watchful girl, who seemed older than her age. This was her first job – called 'helping Mrs Platter with the teas'.

'Mrs Read's doing teas too now,' said Agnes Mercy one day, when they were cutting bread and butter.

'Mrs Read of Fordham? Mrs Read of the Crown and Anchor?' Mrs Platter seldom went to Fordham – it was what she called 'out of her way'.

'That's right,' said Agnes Mercy.

'Teas in the garden?'

Agnes Mercy nodded. 'And in the orchard. Next year they're converting the barn.'

'But what does she give them? I mean, she hasn't got a river. Does she give them strawberries?'

Agnes Mercy shook her head. 'No,' she said, 'it's because of the model railway . . .' and in her slow way, under a fire of questions, she told Mrs Platter about Mr Pott.

'A model railway . . .' remarked Mrs Platter thoughtfully, after a short reflective silence. 'Well, two can play at that game!'

Mr Platter whipped up a model railway in no time at all. There was not a moment to lose: and he laid out money in a big way. Mr Pott was a slow worker but he was several years ahead. All Mr Platter's builders were called in. A bridge was built to the island; the island was cleared of weeds; paths and turf were laid down; electric batteries installed. Mr Platter went up to London and bought two sets of the most expensive trains on the market, goods and passengers. He bought two railway stations, both exactly alike, but far more modern than the railway station at Little Fordham. Experts came down from London to install his signal-boxes and to adjust his lines and points. It was all done in less than three months.

And it worked. By the very next summer to RIVERSIDE TEAS they added the words MODEL RAILWAY.

And the people poured in.

Mr Platter had to clear a field and face it with rubble for parking the motor-cars. In addition to the set teas, it cost a shilling to cross the bridge and visit the railway. Half way through the summer the paths on the island became worn down and he refaced them with asphalt, and built a second bridge to keep people moving. And he put the price up to one and sixpence.

There was soon an asphalted car park and a special field for wagonettes, and a stone trough with running water for the horses. Parties would often picnic in this field, leaving it strewn with litter.

But none of this bothered Mr Pott. He was not particularly anxious for visitors: they took up his time and disturbed his work. If he encouraged sightseers at all it was just out of loyalty to his beloved Railway Benevolent.

He took no precautions for their comfort. It was Mrs Read of the Crown and Anchor saw to that side of things, and who benefited accordingly. The whole of Mr Pott's railway could be seen from the back-door step which led on to his garden and sightseers had to pass through his house – they were welcome, of course, as they went through the kitchen, to a glass of cool water from the tap.

When Mr Pott built his church it was an exact copy of the Norman church at Fordham, with added steeple, gravestones and all. He collected stone for over a year before he started to build. The stone-breakers helped him, as they chipped beside the highway. So did Mr Flood, the mason. By now Mr Pott had several helpers in the village: besides Henry, the blacksmith, he had Miss Menzies of High Beech. Miss Menzies was very useful to Mr Pott, she designed Christmas cards for a living, wrote children's books and her hobbies were wood-carving, hand-weaving and barbola waxwork. She also believed in fairies.

When Mr Platter heard of the church – it took some time, because until it was finished, during visiting hours, Mr Pott swathed it in sacking – Mr Platter put up a larger one with a much higher steeple, based on Salisbury Cathedral. At a touch the windows lit up, and with the aid of a phonograph he laid on music inside. Takings had once more fallen off slightly at Ballyhoggin, now they leapt up again.

All the same, Mr Pott was a great worry to Mr Platter – you never

quite knew what he might be up to, in his gentle plodding way. When Mr Pott built two cob cottages and thatched them, Mr Platter's takings fell off for weeks. Mr Platter was forced to screen off part of his island and build, at lightning speed, a row of semi-detached villas and a public house. The same thing happened when Mr Pott built his village shop and filled the window with miniature merchandise in painted barbola work – a gift from Miss Menzies of High Beech. Immediately, of course, Mr Platter built a row of shops and a hairdresser's establishment with a striped pole.

After a while, Mr Platter found a way of spying on Mr Pott.

CHAPTER THREE

He mended up the flat-bottomed boat, which, for lack of use, had again become waterlogged.

Between the two villages, the weed-clogged river and its twisting, deep-cleft tributaries formed an irritating network, only to be circumvented by roads to distant bridges or by clambering and wading on foot. But if, thought Mr Platter, you could force a boat through the rushes you had a short cut and could spy on Mr Pott's house through the willows by his stream.

And this he did – after business hours on summer evenings. He did not like these expeditions but felt them to be his duty. Plagued by gnats, stung by horse-flies, scratched by brambles, when he arrived back to report to Mrs Platter he was always in a very bad temper. Sometimes he got stuck in the mud and sometimes, when the river was low, he had to clamber out into slime and frog-spawn to lift the boat over hidden obstructions such as drowned logs or barbed wire. But he found a place, a little past the poplars, where, standing on the stump of a willow, he could see the whole layout of Mr Pott's model village, and be screened himself by the flicker of silvery leaves.

'You shouldn't do it, love,' Mrs Platter would say when, panting, puce and perspiring, he sank on a bench in the garden. 'Not at your age and with your blood pressure.' But she had to agree, as she dabbed his gnat bites with ammonia or his wasp stings with dolly-blue, that taking it by and large his information was priceless. It was only due to Mr Platter's courage and endurance that they found out about the model station-master and about Mr Pott's two porters and the vicar in his cassock who stood at Mr Pott's church door. Each of these tiny figures had been modelled by Miss Menzies and dressed by her in suitable clothes which she oiled to withstand the rain.

This discovery had shaken Mr Platter. It was just before the opening of the season. 'Lifelike . . .' he kept saying, 'that's how you'd describe 'em. Madame Tussaud's isn't in it. Why any one of 'em might *speak* to you, if you see what I mean. It's enough to ruin you,' he concluded, 'and would have if I hadn't seen 'em in time.'

However, he *had* seen them in time; and soon both the model villages were inhabited. But Mr Platter's figures seemed far less real than Mr Pott's. They were hurriedly modelled, ready dressed in plaster of Paris and brightly varnished over. To make up for this they were far more varied and there were many more of them – postmen, milkmen, soldiers, sailors and boy scouts. On the steps of his church he put a bishop, surrounded by choir-boys, each of the choir-boys looked like the others,

each had a hymn-book and a white plaster cassock; all had wide-open mouths.

'Now they are what I *would* call lifelike . . .' Mrs Platter used to say proudly. And the organ would boom in the church.

Then came the awful evening, long to be remembered, when Mr Platter, returning from a boat trip, almost stumbled as he climbed back on to the lawn. Mrs Platter, at one of the tables, her large white cat on her lap, was peacefully counting out the takings; the littered garden was bathed in evening sunlight, and the sleepy birds sang in the trees.

'Whatever's the matter?' exclaimed Mrs Platter when she saw Mr Platter's face.

He sank down heavily in the green chair opposite, shaking the table and dislodging a pile of half-crowns. The cat, alarmed and filled with foreboding, streaked off towards the shrubbery. Mr Platter stared dully at the half-crowns as they rolled away across the greensward but he did not stoop to pick them up. Neither did Mrs Platter; she was staring at Mr Platter's complexion: it looked most peculiar – a kind of greenish heliotrope, very delicate in shade.

'Whatever's the matter? Go on, tell me? What's he been and done now?'

Mr Platter looked back at her without any expression. 'We're done for,' he said.

'Nonsense. What he can do, we can do. And it's always been like that. Remember the smoke. Now come on, tell me!'

'Smoke,' exclaimed Mr Platter bitterly, 'that was nothing – a bit of charred string! We soon got the hang of the smoke. No, this is different; this is the end. We're finished,' he added wearily.

'Why do you say that?'

Mr Platter got up from his chair and mechanically, as if he did not know what he was doing, he picked up the fallen half-crowns. He piled them up neatly, and pushed the pile towards her. 'Got to look after the money now,' he said in the same dull expressionless voice, and he slumped again in his chair.

'Now, Sidney,' said Mrs Platter, 'this isn't like you – you've got to show fight.'

'No good fighting,' said Mr Platter, 'where the odds are impossible. What he's done now is plain straightforward impossible.'

His eyes strayed to the island where, touched with golden light among the long evening shadows, the static plaster figures glowed dully, frozen in their attitudes – some seeming to run, some seeming to walk, some about to knock on doors and others simply sitting. Several windows of the model village glowed with molten sunlight as if they were afire. The birds hopped about amongst the houses, seeking for crumbs dropped by the visitors. Except for the birds, nothing moved . . . stillness and deadness.

Mr Platter blinked. 'And I'd set my heart on a cricket pitch,' he said huskily, 'bowler and batsmen and all.'

'Well, we still *can* have,' said Mrs Platter.

He looked at her pityingly. 'Not if they don't *play* cricket – don't you understand? I'm *telling* you – what he's done now is plain, straightforward impossible.'

'What has he done then?' asked Mrs Platter in a frightened voice, infected at last by the cat's foreboding.

Mr Platter looked back at her with haggard eyes. 'He's got a lot of live ones,' he said slowly.

CHAPTER FOUR

BUT Miss Menzies – who believed in fairies, had seen them first. And in her girlish, excited, breathless way she had run to Mr Pott.

Mr Pott, busy with an inn-sign for his miniature Crown and Anchor, had said 'Yes' and 'No' and 'Really'. Sometimes hearing her voice rise to fever pitch, he would exclaim 'Get away' or 'You don't mean it'. The former expression had rather worried Miss Menzies at first. In a puzzled way her voice would falter and her blue eyes fill with tears. But soon she learned to value this request as the ultimate expression of Mr Pott's surprise: when Mr Pott said 'Get away' she took it as a compliment and would hug her knees and laugh.

'But it's *true!*' she would protest, shaking her head. 'They're alive! They're as much alive – as you and I are, and they've moved into Vine Cottage. . . . Why, you can see for yourself if you'd only look where they've even worn a path to the door!'

And Mr Pott, pincers in hand and inn-sign dangling, would glance down the slope towards his model of Vine Cottage. He would stare at the model for just long enough to please her and then, wondering what she was talking about, he would grunt a little and return to his work. 'Well, I never did,' he would say.

Mr Pott, once she 'got started', as he put it, never dreamed of listening to Miss Menzies. Through nodding and smiling, he would make his mind a blank. It was a trick which he had learned with his late wife, who was also known as a 'talker'. And Miss Menzies spoke in such a high, strange, fanciful voice – using the oddest words and most fly-away expressions; sometimes, to his dismay, she would even recite poetry. He did not dislike her, far from it; he liked to have her about, because in her strange, leggy, loping way she always seemed girlishly happy, and her prattle, like canary song, kept him cheerful. And many a debt he owed to those restless fingers – concocting this and fashioning that: not only could they draw, paint, sew, model and wood-carve, but they could slide into places where Mr Pott's own fingers, stiffer and stubbier, got stuck or could not reach. Quick as a flash, she was; gay as a lark and steady as a rock. '. . . none of us perfect,' he'd tell himself, 'you got to have something . . .' and with her it was 'talking'.

He knew she was not young, but when she sat beside him on the rough grass, clasping her thin wrists about her bent knees, swaying back and forth, her closed eyes raised to the sun and chattering nineteen

zen, she seemed to Mr Pott like some kind of overgrown
 And sweet eyes she had too, when they were open – that he
would say – for such a long, bony face: shy eyes, which slid away when
you looked too long at them – more like violets, he'd say her eyes were,
than forget-me-nots. They were shining now and so were the knuckles
of her long fingers clasped too tightly about her knees; even her mouse-
grey silky hair had a sudden lustre.

'The great secret, you see, is never to show that you've seen them.
Stillness, stillness, that's the thing – and looking obliquely and never
directly. Like with bird-watching . . .'

'. . . bird-watching,' agreed Mr Pott, as Miss Menzies seemed to
pause. Sometimes, to show his sympathy and disguise his lack of
attention, Mr Pott would repeat the last word of Miss Menzies's last
sentence; or sometimes anticipate Miss Menzies's last syllable. If Miss
Menzies said 'King and Coun—', Mr Pott would chip in, in an
understanding voice, with '. . . tree'. Sometimes, being far away in
mind, Mr Pott would make a mistake and Miss Menzies, referring to
'garden-produce', would find herself presented with '. . . roller' instead,
and there would be bewilderment all round.

'I can't quite really, you know, make out quite *what* they are. I mean,
from the size and that, you'd say they were fairies. Now, wouldn't you?'
she challenged him.

'That's right,' said Mr Pott, testing the swing of his inn-sign with a
stubby finger and wondering where he had left the oil.

'But you'd be wrong, you know. This little man I saw with this sack
thing on his back – he was panting. Quite out of breath, he was. Now,
fairies don't pant.' As Mr Pott was silent, Miss Menzies added sharply:
'Or do they?'

'Do they what?' asked Mr Pott, watching the swing of his inn-sign
and wishing it did not squeak.

'Pant!' said Miss Menzies, and waited.

Mr Pott looked troubled. What could she be talking about? 'Pant?'
he repeated. Mentally, he put the word into the plural, and with a
glance at her face, took it out again. 'I wouldn't like to say,' he conceded
cagily.

'Nor would I,' agreed Miss Menzies gaily, much to his relief. 'I mean
– by and large – we know so little about fairies . . .'

'That's right,' said Mr Pott. He felt safe again.

'. . . what their habits are. I mean, whether or not they get tired or
old like we do and go to bed, cook and do the housework. Or what they

do about food. There's so little data. We don't even know what they . . .'

'. . . eat,' said Mr Pott.

'. . . are,' corrected Miss Menzies. 'What they are made of . . . surely not flesh and blood?'

'Surely not,' agreed Mr Pott. Then suddenly looked startled – a strange word echoed in his mind: had she said 'blood'? He laid down the inn-sign and turned to look at her. '*What* was you saying?' he asked.

Miss Menzies was away again. 'I was saying this lot couldn't be fairies – not on second thoughts and sober reflection. Why, this little fellow had a tear in his trousers and there he was – panting and puffing and toiling up the hill. There's another one in skirts – or maybe two in skirts. I can't make out how many there are; whether it's just one that keeps changing, or what it is. There was a little hand cleaning a window – rubbing and rubbing from the inside. But you couldn't see what it belonged to. White as a bluebell stalk, it looked, when you pull it out of the earth. And about that thickness – waving and swaying. And then I found my glasses and I saw it had an elbow. I could hardly believe my eyes. There it was, a cloth in its hand and going into the corners. And yet, in a way, it seemed natural.'

'In a way,' agreed Mr Pott. But he was looking rather lost.

CHAPTER FIVE

THEN began for Miss Menzies what afterwards seemed almost the happiest time of her life. She had always been a great watcher: she would watch ants in the grass, mice in the corn, spinnings of webs and buildings of nests. And she could keep very quiet, because, watching a spider plummet from a leaf, she would almost become a spider herself, and having studied the making of web after web she could have spun one herself to almost any shape, however awkward. Miss Menzies, in fact, had become quite critical of web-making.

'Oh, you silly thing . . .' she would breathe to the spider as it swayed in the air, '. . . not that leaf – it's going to fall. Try the thorn . . .'

Now, sitting on the slope, her hands about her knees, she would watch the little people, screened – as she thought – by a tall clump of thistle. And everything she saw she described to Mr Pott.

'There are three of them,' she told him some days later. 'A mother, a father and a thin little girl. Difficult to tell their ages. Sometimes I think there's a fourth . . . something or someone who comes and goes. A shadowy sort of creature. But that, of course' – she sighed happily – 'might just be my . . .'

'. . . fancy,' said Mr Pott.

'. . . imagination,' corrected Miss Menzies. 'It's strange, you know, that *you* haven't seen them!'

Mr Pott, busy brick-building, did not answer. He had decided the subject was human; village gossip of some kind, referring not to his Vine Cottage, but to the original one in Fordham.

'They've done wonders to the house,' Miss Menzies went on. 'The front door was stuck, you know. Warped, I suppose, with the rain. But he was working on it yesterday with a thing like a razor-blade. And there's another thing they've done. They've taken those curtains I made for your Crown and Anchor and put them up in Vine Cottage, so now you can't see inside. Not that I'd dare to look – you couldn't go that close, you see. And the High Street's so narrow. But isn't it exciting?'

Mr Pott grunted. Stirring his brick-dust and size, he frowned to himself and breathed rather heavily. Gossip about neighbours – he had never held with it. Nor, until now, had Miss Menzies. A talker, yes, but a lady born and bred. This wasn't like her, he thought unhappily ... peeping in windows ... no, it wasn't like her at all. She was on now about the station-master's coat.

'... she took it, you see. That's where it went. She took it for *him*, gold buttons and all, and he wears it in the evening, after sundown when the air gets chilly. I would not be at all surprised if, one day, she snapped up the vicar's cassock. It's so like a dress, you see, and would fit her perfectly. Except, of course, that might seem too obvious. They're very clever, you know. One would be bound to notice a vicar bereft of his cassock – there on the church steps for all to see. But to see the station-master you have to look right into the station. And you can't do that now; he could be without his coat for weeks and none of us any the wiser.'

Mr Pott stopped stirring to glare at Miss Menzies. She looked back in alarm at his round, angry eyes. 'But what is the matter?' she asked him uneasily after a moment.

Mr Pott drew a deep breath. 'If you don't know,' he said, 'then I won't tell you!'

This did not seem very logical. Miss Menzies smiled forgivingly and laid a hand on his arm. 'But there's nothing to be frightened of,' she assured him; 'they're quite all right.'

He shook his arm free and went on stirring, breathing hard and clattering with his trowel. 'There's plenty to be frightened of,' he said sternly, 'when there's gossip on the tongue. Homes ruined, I've seen, and hearts broken.'

Miss Menzies was silent a moment. 'I didn't grudge her the coat,' she said at last. Mr Pott snorted and Miss Menzies went on: 'In fact, I intend to make them some clothes myself. I'd thought I'd just leave the clothes about for them to find, so they'll never know where they came from ...'

'That's better,' said Mr Pott, scraping at a brick. There was a long pause – so strangely long that Mr Pott became aware of it. Had he been a little too sharp, he wondered, and glanced sideways at Miss Menzies. With clasped knees, she sat smiling into space.

'I love them, you see,' she said softly.

After this Mr Pott let her talk again: if her interest stemmed from affection, that was another matter. Day after day he nodded and smiled, as Miss Menzies unfolded her story. The words spilled over him, soothing and gay, and slid away into the sunlight; very few caught his attention. Even on that momentous afternoon – one day in June – when, bursting with fresh news, she flung herself breathlessly beside him.

He was re-tarring a line of sleepers and, pot in one hand, brush in the other, he edged himself along the ground, his wooden leg stretched out before him. Miss Menzies, talking away, edged along to keep up with him.

'. . . and when she spoke to me,' gasped Miss Menzies, 'I was amazed, astounded! Wouldn't you have been?'

'Maybe,' said Mr Pott.

'This tiny creature – quite unafraid. Said she'd been watching me for weeks.'

'Get away,' said Mr Pott amiably. And he wiped a drop of tar off the rail. 'That's better,' he said, admiring the steely gleam . . . 'Not a trace of rust anywhere,' he thought happily.

'And now I know what they're called and everything. They're called Borrowers . . .'

'Burroughs?' said Mr Pott.

'No, Borrowers.'

'Ah, Burroughs,' said Mr Pott, stirring the tar, which stood in a can of hot water. 'Getting a bit thick,' he thought, as he raised the stick and critically watched the trickle.

'It's not their family name,' Miss Menzies went on; 'their family name is Clock. It's their racial name – the kind of creatures they are. They live like mice . . . or birds . . . on what they can find, poor things. They're an offshoot of humans, I think, and live from human left-overs. They don't own anything at all. And of course they haven't any money. . . . Oh, it's perfectly all right,' said Miss Menzies, as in absent-minded sympathy Mr Pott clicked his tongue and gently shook his head. 'They wouldn't care about money. They wouldn't know what to do with it. But they have to live . . .'

'. . . and let live,' said Mr Pott brightly. He felt mildly pleased with this phrase and hoped it would fit in somewhere.

'But they do let live,' said Miss Menzies. 'They never take anything that matters. Except of course . . . well, I'm not sure about the station-master's overcoat. But when you come to think of it, the station-master didn't need it for warmth, did he? Being made as he is of barbola? And it wasn't his, either – I made it; come to that, I made *him*, too. So it really belongs to me. And I don't need it for warmth.'

'Not warmth,' agreed Mr Pott absently.

'These Borrowers do need warmth. They need fuel and shelter and water and they terribly need human beings. Not that they trust them. They're right, I suppose: one has only to read the papers. But it's sad, isn't it? That they can't trust us, I mean. What could be more charming for someone – like me, say – to share one's home with these little creatures? Not that I'm lonely, of course. My days' – Miss Menzies's eyes became over-bright suddenly and the gay voice hurried a little – 'are *far* too full ever to be lonely. I've so many interests, you see. I keep up with things. And I have my old dog and the two little birds. All the same, it would be nice. I know their names now – Pod, Homily and little Arrietty. These creatures talk, you see. And just think I'd' – she laughed suddenly – 'I'd be sewing for them from morning until night. I'd make them things. I'd buy them things. I'd – oh, but you understand . . .'

'I understand,' said Mr Pott. 'I get you . . .' But he didn't understand. In a vague sort of way he felt it rather rude of Miss Menzies to refer to her new-found family of friends as 'creatures'. Down on their luck, they might be, but all the same . . . But then, of course, she did use the strangest expressions.

'And I think that's why she spoke to me,' Miss Menzies went on; 'she must have felt safe, you see. They always . . .'

'. . . know,' put in Mr Pott obligingly.

'Yes. Like animals and children and birds and . . . fairies.'

'I wouldn't commit meself about fairies,' said Mr Pott. And, come to think of it, he would not commit himself about animals, either: he thought of the badger whose life he had rescued – if *it* had 'known' he would still have had his leg.

'They've had an awful time, poor things, really ghastly . . .' Miss Menzies gazed down the slope at the peaceful scene, the groups of miniature cottages, the smoking chimneys, the Norman church, the forge, the gleaming railway lines. 'It was wonderful, she told me, when they found this village.'

Mr Pott grunted. He shifted himself along a couple of feet and drew the tar-pot after him. Miss Menzies, lost in her dreams, did not seem to notice. Knees clasped, eyes half closed, she went on as though reciting.

'It was moonlight, she told me, the night they arrived. You can imagine it, can't you? The sharp shadows. They had heaps to carry and had to push their way up through those rushy grasses down by the water's edge. Spiller – that was the untamed one – took Arrietty round the village. He took her right inside the station, and there were those figures I made – the woman with the basket, the old man and the little girl – in a row on the seat, so still, so still . . . and just beside them the soldier with his kit-bag. They were speckled by moonlight and the fretted shadow of the station roof. They looked very real, she said, but like people under a spell or listening to music which neither she nor Spiller could hear. Arrietty too stood silent – staring and wondering at the pale moonlit faces. Until suddenly there was a rustling sound and

a great black beetle ran right over them and she saw they were not alive. She doesn't mind beetles herself, she rather likes them, but this one made her scream. She said there were toadstools in the ticket office, and when they went out of the station, the field-mice were busy in the High Street, running in and out of the shadows. And there, on the steps of the church, stood the vicar in his cassock – so silent, so still. And moonlight everywhere . . .'

'Homily, of course, fell in love with Vine Cottage. And you can't blame her – it is rather charming. But the door was stuck, warped, I suppose, by the rain, and when they opened the window it seemed to be full of something and it smelled very damp. Spiller put his hand in and

– do you know? – it was filled with white grass stalks, right up to the roof. White as mushrooms, they were, through growing up in the dark. So that night they slept out of doors.

'Next day, though, she said, was lovely – bright sunshine, spring smells and the first bee. They can see things so closely, you see: every hair of the bee, the depth of the velvet, the veins on its wings and the colours vibrating. The men' – Miss Menzies laughed – 'I mean, you must call them men – soon cleared the cottage of weeds, reaping them down with a sliver of razor-blade and a kind of half nail-scissor. Then they dug out the roots. Spiller found a chrysalis, which he gave to Arrietty. She kept it until last week. It turned out to be a red admiral. She watched it being born. But when its wings appeared and they began to see the size of it, there was absolute panic. Just in the nick of time they got it out of the front door. Its wing span would almost have filled their parlour from wall to wall. Imagine your own parlour full of butterfly and no way to let it out! When you come to think of it, it's quite fantas . . .'

'. . . tick,' added Mr Pott.

'About a week later they found your sandpile; and when they had dug up the floor they sanded it over and trod it down. Dancing and stamping like maniacs. She said it was rather fun. This was all in the very early morning. And about three weeks ago they borrowed your size. It was already mixed – when you were making that last lot of bricks, remember? Anyway, now what with sizing it over and one thing

and another, she tells me, their floor has quite a good surface. They sweep it with thistle-heads. But it's early for these, she said, the blooms are too tightly packed. The ones which come later are far more practical . . .'

But Mr Pott had heard at last. 'My sandpile . . .' he said slowly, turning to stare at her.

'Yes.' Miss Menzies laughed. 'And your size.'

'My size?' repeated Mr Pott. He was silent a moment, as though thinking this out.

'Yes,' laughed Miss Menzies, 'but so little of it – so very, very little.'

'My size . . .' repeated Mr Pott. His face grew stern, almost belligerent he seemed suddenly as he turned to Miss Menzies.

'Where are these people?' he asked.

'But I've told you!' Miss Menzies exclaimed, and as he still looked angry, she took his horny hand in both of hers as though to help him up. 'Come,' she whispered, but she was still smiling, 'come very quietly, and I'll show you!'

CHAPTER SIX

'STILLNESS . . . that's the thing,' Pod whispered to Arrietty, the first time he saw Miss Menzies crouching down behind her thistle. 'They don't expect to see you, and if you're still they somehow don't. And never look at 'em direct – always look at 'em sideways like. Understand?'

'Yes, of course I understand – you've told me often enough. Stillness, stillness, quiet, quiet, creep, creep, crawl, crawl . . . What's the good of being alive?'

'Hush,' said Pod and laid a hand on her arm. Arrietty had not been herself lately. It was as though, thought Pod, she had something on her mind. But it wasn't often she was as rude as this. He decided to ignore it: getting to the awkward age – that's what it was, he wouldn't wonder.

They stood in a clump of coarse grass, shoulder high to them, with only their heads emerging. 'You see,' breathed Pod, speaking with still lips out of the corner of his mouth, 'some kind of plant or flowers, that's what we look like to her. Something in bud, maybe.'

'Supposing she decided to pick us,' suggested Arrietty irritably. Her ankles were aching and she longed to sit down; ten minutes had become quarter of an hour and still neither party had moved. An ant climbed up the grass stem beside her, waved its antennae in the air and swiftly climbed down again. A slug lay sleeping under the plantain leaf, every now and again there was a slight ripple where the frilled underside of its body appeared to caress the earth.

'It must be dreaming,' Arrietty decided, admiring the silver highlights in the lustrous gun-metal skin. 'If my father were less old-fashioned,' she thought guiltily, 'I would tell him about Miss Menzies, and then we could walk away.' But in his view and in that of her mother it was still a disgrace to be 'seen', not only a disgrace but almost a tragedy; to them it meant broken homes, wearisome treks across unexplored country and the labour of building anew. By her parents' code, to be known to exist at all put their whole way of life into jeopardy, and a borrower once 'seen' must immediately move away.

In spite of all this, in her short life of fifteen years, Arrietty herself had been 'seen' four times. What was this longing, she wondered, which drew her so strongly to human beings? And on this – her fourth occasion

of being 'seen' – actually to speak to Miss Menzies? It was reckless and stupid, no doubt, but also strangely thrilling to address and be answered by a creature of so vast a size, who yet could seem so gentle; to see the giant eyes light up and the great mouth softly smile. Once you had done it and no dreadful disaster had followed, you were tempted to try it again. Arrietty had even gone so far as to lay in wait for Miss Menzies. Perhaps because every incident she described seemed so to delight and amaze her and – when Spiller was not there – Arrietty was often lonely.

Those few first days had been such wonderful fun! Spiller taking her on the trains – nipping into some half-empty carriage and, when the train moved, sitting so stiff and so still – pretending they too, like the rest of the passengers, were made of barbola wax. Round and round they would go, passing Vine Cottage a dozen times, and back again over the bridge. Other faces besides Mr Pott's stared down at them, and by Mr Pott's back door they saw rows of boots and shoes, fat legs, thin legs, stockinged legs and bare legs. They heard human laughter and human squeals of delight. It was terrifying and wonderful, but somehow, with Spiller, she felt safe. A plume of smoke ran out behind them. The same kind of smoke which was used for the cottage chimneys, parcel string soaked in nitrate and secured in a bundle by a twist of invisible hairpin. ('Have you seen my invisible hairpins?' Miss Menzies had one day asked Mr Pott – a question which to the puzzled Mr Pott seemed an odd contradiction in terms.) In Vine Cottage, however, Pod had hooked down the smouldering bundle and had lit a real fire instead, which Homily fed with candle-grease, coal-slack and tarry lumps of cinder. On this she cooked their meals.

And it was Spiller, wild Spiller, who had helped Arrietty to make her garden and to search for plants of scarlet pimpernel, small blue-faced bird's eyes, fern-like mosses and tiny flowering sedum. With Spiller's help she had gravelled the path and laid a lawn of moss.

Miss Menzies, behind her thistle clump, had watched this work with delight. She saw Arrietty; but Spiller, that past master of invisibility, she could never quite discern. Both still and swift, with a wild creature's instinct for cover, he could melt into any background, and disappear at will.

With Spiller too Arrietty had explored the other houses, fished for minnows and bathed in the river, screened by the towering rushes. 'Getting too tomboyish by half,' Homily had grumbled. She was nervous of Spiller's influence. 'He's not our kind really,' she would complain to Pod, in a sudden burst of ingratitude, 'even if he did save our lives.'

Standing beside her father in the grass and thinking of these things, Arrietty began to feel the burden of her secret. Had her parents searched the world over, she realized uneasily, they could not have found a more perfect place in which to settle – a complete village tailored to their size and, with so much left behind by the visitors, unusually rich in borrowings. It had been a long time since she had heard her mother sing as she sang now at her housework, or her father take up again his breathy, tuneless whistle as he pottered about the village.

There was plenty of 'cover' but they hardly needed it. There was little difference in size between themselves and the borrowers made of wax and except during visiting hours Pod could walk about the streets quite freely, providing he was ready to freeze. And there was no end to the borrowing of clothes. Homily had a hat again at last and would never leave the house without it. 'Wait,' she would say, 'while I put on my hat,' and took a fussed kind of joy in pronouncing the magic word. No, they could not be moved out now: that would be too cruel. Pod had even put a lock on the front door, complete with key. It was the lock of a pocket jewel-case belonging to Miss Menzies. He little knew to whom he owed this find – that she had dropped the case on purpose beside the clump of thistle to make the borrowing easy. And Arrietty could not tell him. Once he knew the truth (she had been through it all before), there would be worry, despair, recriminations and a pulling up of stakes.

'Oh dear, oh dear,' she breathed aloud unhappily, 'whatever should I do . . .?'

Pod glanced at her sideways. 'Sink down,' he whispered, nudging her arm. 'She's turned her head away. Sink slowly into the grasses . . .'

Arrietty was only too grateful to obey. Slowly their heads and shoulders lowered out of sight and after a moment's pause to wait and listen they crawled away among the grass stems, and taking swift cover by the churchyard wall they slid to safety through their own back door.

CHAPTER SEVEN

ONE day Miss Menzies began to talk back to Arrietty. At first her amazement had kept her silent, and confined her share of their conversations to the few leading questions which might draw Arrietty out. This for Miss Menzies was a most unusual state of affairs and could not last for long. As the summer wore on, she had garnered every detail of Arrietty's short life and a good deal of data besides. She had heard about the borrowed library of Victorian miniature books, through which Arrietty had learned to read and to gain some knowledge of the world. Miss Menzies, in her hurried, laughing, breathless way, helped to add to this knowledge. She began to tell Arrietty about her own girlhood, her parents and her family home, which she always described as 'dear Gadstone'. She spoke of London dances and of how she had hated them; of someone called 'Aubrey', her closest and dearest friend – 'my cousin, you see. We were almost brought up together. He would come to dear Gadstone for his holidays.' He and Miss Menzies would ride and talk and read poetry together. Arrietty, listening and learning about horses, wondered if there was any kind of animal which she could learn to ride. You could tame a mouse (as her cousin Eggletina had done), but a mouse was too small and too 'scuttley': you couldn't go far on a mouse. A rat? Oh no, a rat was out of the question. She doubted even if Spiller would be brave enough to train a rat. Fight one, yes – armed with Pod's old climbing-pin – Spiller was capable of that but not, she thought, of breaking a rat into harness. But what fun it would have been to go riding with Spiller, as Miss Menzies had gone riding with Aubrey.

'He married a girl called Mary Chumley-Gore,' said Miss Menzies. 'She had very thick ankles.'

'Oh . . . !' exclaimed Arrietty.

'Why do you say "Oh" in that voice?'

'I thought he might have married you!'

Miss Menzies smiled and looked down at her hands. 'So did I,' she said quietly. She was silent a moment and then she sighed. 'I suppose he knew me too well. I was almost like a sister.' She was quiet again as though thinking this out, and then she added more cheerfully: 'They were happy though, I gather; they had five children and lived in a house outside Bath.'

And Miss Menzies, even before Arrietty explained to her, understood about being 'seen'. 'You need never worry about your parents,' she assured Arrietty. 'I would never – even if you had not spoken – have looked at them directly. As far as we are concerned – and I can speak for Mr Pott – they are safe here for the rest of their lives. I would never even have looked at you directly, Arrietty, if you had not crept up and spoken to me. But even before I saw any of you I had begun to wonder – because, you see, Arrietty, your chimney sometimes smoked at quite the wrong sort of times; I only light the string for the visitors, you see, and it very soon burns out.'

'And you would never pick us up, any of us? In your hands, I mean?'

Miss Menzies gave an almost scornful laugh. 'As though I would dream of such a thing!' She sounded rather hurt.

Miss Menzies also understood about Spiller: that when he came for his brief visits, with his offerings of nuts, corn grains, hard-boiled sparrows' eggs and other delicacies, she would not see so much of Arrietty. But after Spiller had gone again, she liked to hear of their adventures.

All in all, it was a happy, glorious summer for everyone concerned.

There were scares of course. Such as the footsteps before dawn, human footsteps, but not those of the one-legged Mr Pott, when something or someone had fumbled at their door. And the moonlight night when the fox came, stalking silently down their village street, casting his great shadow and leaving his scent behind. The owl in the oak-tree was of course a constant source of danger. But, like most owls, he did his hunting farther afield, and once the vast shape had wafted over the river and they had heard his call on the other side of the valley, it was safe to sally forth.

Much of the borrowing was done at night before the mice got at the scraps dropped by the visitors. Homily at first had sniffed fastidiously when presented with, say, the remains of a large ham sandwich. Pod had to persuade her to look at the thing more practically – fresh bread, pure farm butter and a clean paper bag; what had been good enough for human beings should be good enough for them. What was wrong, he asked her, with the last three grapes of a stripped bunch? You could wash them, couldn't you, in the stream? You could peel them? Or what

was wrong with a caramel, wrapped up in transparent paper? Half-eaten bath-buns, he agreed, were a bit more difficult . . . but you could extract the currants, couldn't you, and collect and boil down those crusted globules of sugar?

Soon they had evolved a routine of collecting, sorting, cleaning and conserving. They used Miss Menzies's shop as a storehouse, with – unknown to Pod and Homily – her full co-operation. She had cheated a little on the furnishings, having (some years ago now) gone into the local town and bought a toy grocer's shop, complete with scales, bottles, cans, barrels and glass containers. With these, she had skilfully furnished the counter and dressed up the windows. This little shop was a great attraction to visitors – it was a general shop and post office modelled on the one in the village – bow windows, thatched roof and all. A replica of old Mrs Purbody (slimmed down a little to flatter her) stood behind the counter inside. Miss Menzies had even reproduced the red knitted shawl which Mrs Purbody wore on her shoulders, both in summer and winter, and the crisp white apron below. Homily would borrow this apron when she worked on her sortings in the back of the shop, but would put it back punctually in time for visitors. Sometimes she washed it out, and every morning – regular as clockwork – she would dust and sweep the shop.

The trains made a good deal of noise. They very soon got used to this, however, and learned, in fact, to welcome it.

When the trains began to clatter and the smoke unfurled from the cottage chimneys, it warned them of Visiting Hours. Homily had time to take off the apron, let herself out of the shop and cross the road to her home, where she engaged herself in pleasant homely tasks until the trains stopped and all was quiet again and the garden lay dreaming and silent in the peaceful evening light.

Mr Pott, by this time, would have gone inside to his tea.

CHAPTER EIGHT

'THERE must be something we can do,' said Mrs Platter despairingly for about the fifth time within an hour. 'Look at the money we've sunk.'

'Sunk is the right word,' said Mr Platter.

'And it isn't as though we haven't tried.'

'Oh, we've tried hard enough,' said Mr Platter. 'And what annoys me about this Abel Pott is that he does it all without seeming to try at all. He doesn't seem to mind if people come or not. MODEL VILLAGE WITH LIVE INHABITANTS – that's what he'll put on the notice – and then we'll be finished. Finished for good and all! Better pack it in now, that's what I say, and sell out as a going concern.'

'There must be something . . .' repeated Mrs Platter stubbornly.

They sat as before at a green table on their singularly tidy lawn. On this Sunday evening it was even more singularly tidy than usual. Only five people had come that afternoon for RIVERSIDE TEAS. There had been three quite disastrous week-ends: on two of them it had rained, and on this particular Sunday there had been what local people spoke of as 'the aeronaut' – a balloon ascent from the fairground, with tea in tents, ice-cream, candy-floss and roundabouts. On Saturday people drove out to see the balloon itself (at sixpence a time to pass the rope barriers) and today in their hundreds to see the balloon go up. It had been a sad sight indeed for Mr and Mrs Platter to watch the carriages and motors stream past Ballyhoggin with never a glance nor a thought for RIVERSIDE TEAS. It had not comforted them either, when at about three o'clock in the afternoon the balloon itself sailed silently over them, barely clearing the ilex tree which grew beside the house. They could even see 'the aeronaut', who was looking down – mockingly, it seemed – straight into the glaring eyes of Mr Platter.

'No good saying "there must be something",' he told her irritably. 'Night and day I've thought and thought and you've thought too. What with this balloon mania and Abel Pott's latest, we can't compete. That's all: it's quite simple. There isn't anything – short of stealing them.'

'What about that?' said Mrs Platter.

'About what?'

'Stealing them,' said Mrs Platter.

Mr Platter stared back at her. He opened his mouth and shut it again. 'Oh, we couldn't do that,' he managed to say at last.

'Why not?' said Mrs Platter. 'He hasn't shown them yet. Nobody knows they're there.'

'Why, it would be – I mean, it's a felony.'

'Never mind,' said Mrs Platter, 'let's commit one.'

'Oh, Mabel,' gasped Mr Platter, 'what things you do say!' But he looked slightly awestruck and admiring.

'Other people commit them,' said Mrs Platter firmly, basking in the glow of his sudden approbation. 'Why shouldn't we?'

'Yes, I see your argument,' said Mr Platter. He still looked rather dazed.

'There's got to be a first time for everything,' Mrs Platter pointed out.

'But' – he swallowed nervously – 'you go to prison for a felony. I don't mind a few extra items on a bill, I'm game for that, dear. Always was, as you well know. But this – oh, Mabel, it takes *you* to think of a thing like this!'

'Well, I said there'd be something,' acknowledged Mrs Platter modestly. 'But it's only common sense, dear. We can't afford not to.'

'You're right,' said Mr Platter; 'we're driven to it. Not a soul could blame us.'

'Not a living soul!' agreed Mrs Platter solemnly in a bravely fervent voice.

Mr Platter leaned across the table and patted her hand. 'I take my hat off to you, Mabel, for courage and initiative. You're a wonderful woman,' he said.

'Thank you, dear,' said Mrs Platter.

'And now for ways and means . . .' said Mr Platter in a suddenly business-like voice. He took off his rimless glasses and thoughtfully began polishing them. 'Tools, transport, times of day . . .'

'It's simple,' said Mrs Platter. 'You take the boat.'

'I realize that,' said Mr Platter with a kind of aloof patience. He put his rimless glasses back on his nose, returned the handkerchief to his pocket, leaned back in his chair and with the fingers of his right hand drummed lightly on the table. 'Allow me to think a while . . .'

'Of course, Sidney,' said Mrs Platter obediently, and folded her hands in her lap.

After a few moments he cleared his throat and looked across at her. 'You'll have to come with me, dear,' he said.

Mrs Platter, startled, lost all her composure. 'Oh, I couldn't do that, Sidney. You know what I'm like on the water. Couldn't you take one of the men?'

He shook his head. 'Impossible, they'd talk.'

'What about Agnes Mercy?'

'Couldn't trust her, either; it would be all over the county before the week was out. No dear, it's got to be you.'

'I *would* come with you, Sidney,' faltered Mrs Platter, 'say we went round by road. That boat's kind of small for me.'

'You can't get into his garden from the road, except by going through the house. There's a thick holly hedge on either side with no sort of gate or opening. No, dear, I've got it all worked out in my mind: the only approach is by water. Just before dawn, I'd say, when they're all asleep, and that would include Abel Pott. We shall need a good strong cardboard box, the shrimping-net and a lantern. Have we any new wicks?'

'Yes, plenty up in the attic.'

'That's where we'll have to keep them – these ... er ... well, whatever they are.'

'In the attic?'

'Yes, I've thought it all out, Mabel. It's the only room we always keep locked – because of the stores and that. We've got to keep them warm and dry through the winter while we get their house built. They *are* part of the stores in a manner of speaking. I'll put a couple of bolts on the door, as well as the lock, and a steel plate across the bottom. That should settle 'em. I've got to have time, you see,'

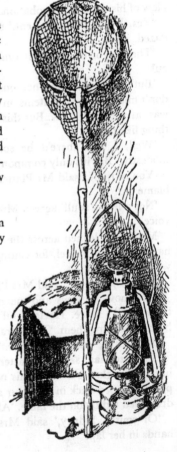

Mr Platter went on earnestly, 'to think out some kind of house for them. It's got to be more like a cage than a house and yet it's got to *look* like a house, if you see what I mean. You've got to be able to see them inside and yet make it so they can't get out. It's going to take a lot of working on, Mabel.'

'You'll manage, dear,' Mrs Platter encouraged him. 'But' – she thought a moment – 'what if *he* comes here and recognizes them? Anybody can buy a ticket.'

'He wouldn't. He's so taken up with his own things that I doubt if he's ever heard of us or of Ballyhoggin or even Went-le-Craye. But say he did? What proof has he? He's been keeping them dark, hasn't he? Nobody's seen them – or the news would be all over the county. In the papers most likely. People would be going there in hundreds. No, dear, it would be his word against ours – that's all. But we've got to act quickly, Mabel, and you've got to help me. There are two weeks left to the end of the season; he may be keeping them to show next year. Or he may decide to show them at once – and then we'd be finished. You see what I mean? There's no knowing . . .'

'Yes . . .' said Mrs Platter. 'Well, what do you want me to do?'

'It's easy: you've only got to keep your head. I take the cardboard box and the lantern and you carry the shrimping-net. You follow me ashore and you tread where I tread, which you'll see by the lantern. I'll show you their house, and all you've got to do is to cover the rear side with the shrimping-net, holding it close as you can against the wall and partly over the thatch. Then I make some sort of noise at the front – they keep the front door locked now, I've found out that much. As soon as they hear me at the front door – you can mark my words – they'll go scampering, out of the back. Straight into the net. You see what I mean? Now you'll have to keep the net held tight up against the cottage wall. I'll have the cardboard box in one hand by then, and the lid in the other. When I give the word, you scoop the net up into the air, with them inside it, and tumble them into the box. I clap the lid on and that will be that.'

'Yes,' said Mrs Platter uncertainly. She thought a while and then she said: 'Do they bite?'

'I don't know that. Only seen them from a distance. But it wouldn't be much of a bite.'

'Supposing one fell out of the net or something?'

'Well, you must see they don't, Mabel, that's all. I mean, there are only three or four of 'em, all told. We can't afford any losses . . .'

'Oh, Sidney, I wish you could take one of the men. I can't even row.'

'You don't have to row. I'll row. All you have to do, Mabel, is to carry the net and follow me ashore. I'll point out their cottage and it'll be over in a minute. Before you can say Jack Robinson, we'll be back in the boat and safely home.'

'Does he keep a dog?'

'Abel Pott? No, dear, he doesn't keep a dog. It will be quite all right. Just trust me and do what I say. Like to come across to the island now and have a bit of practice on one of our own houses? You run up to the attic now and get the net and I'll get the oars and the boat-hook. Now, you've got to face up to it, Mabel,' added Mr Platter irritably, as Mrs Platter still seemed to hesitate; 'we must each do our part. Fair's fair, you know.'

CHAPTER NINE

THE next day it began to rain and it rained on and off for ten days. Even Mr Pott had a falling-off of visitors. Not that he minded particularly; he and Miss Menzies employed themselves indoors at Mr Pott's long kitchen table – repairing, remodelling, repainting, restitching and oiling . . . The lamplight shed its gentle glow around them. While the rain poured down outside, the glue-pot bubbled on the stove and the kettle sang beside it. At last came October the first, the day when the season ended.

'Mr Pott,' said Miss Menzies, after a short but breathy silence (she was quilting an eiderdown for Homily's double bed and found the work exacting), 'I am rather worried.'

'Oh,' said Mr Pott. He was making a fence of matchsticks, glueing them delicately with the aid of pincers and a fine sable brush. 'In fact,' Miss Menzies went on, 'I'm very worried indeed. Could you listen a moment?'

This direct assault took Mr Pott by surprise. 'Something wrong?' he asked.

'Yes, I think something is wrong. I haven't seen Arrietty for three days. Have you?'

'Come to think of it, no,' said Mr Pott.

'Or any of them?'

Mr Pott was silent a moment, thinking back. 'Not now you mention it – no,' he said.

'I had an appointment with her on Monday, down by the stream, but she didn't turn up. But I wasn't worried, it was raining anyway and I thought perhaps Spiller had arrived. But he hadn't, you know. I know now where he keeps his boat and it wasn't there. And then, when I passed their cottage, I saw the back door was open. This isn't like them, but it reassured me as I assumed they wouldn't be so careless unless they were all inside. When I passed again on my way home for tea, the door was still open. All yesterday it was open, and it was open again this morning. It's a bit . . .'

'. . . rum,' agreed Mr Pott.

'. . . odd,' said Miss Menzies – they spoke on the same instant.

'Mr Pott, dear,' went on Miss Menzies, 'after I showed them to you, so very carefully, you remember – you didn't go and stare at them or anything? You didn't frighten them?'

'No,' said Mr Pott, 'I been too busy closing up for winter. I like to see 'em, mind, but I haven't had the time.'

'And their chimney isn't smoking,' Miss Menzies went on. 'It hasn't been smoking for three days. I mean, one can't help being . . .'

'. . . worried,' said Mr Pott.

'. . . uneasy,' said Miss Menzies. She laid down her work. 'Are you still listening?' she asked.

Mr Pott tipped a matchstick with glue, breathing heavily. 'Yes, I'm thinking . . .' he said.

'I don't like to look right inside,' Miss Menzies explained. 'For one thing, you can't look in from the front because there's not room to kneel in the High Street, and you can't kneel down at the back without spoiling their garden, and the other thing is that, say they *are* inside – Pod and Homily, I mean – I'd be giving the whole game away. I've explained to you what they're like about being "seen"? If they hadn't gone already, they'd go then because I'd "seen" them. And we would be out of the frying-pan into the fire . . .'

Mr Pott nodded; he was rather new to borrowers and depended on Miss Menzies for his data – she had, he felt, through months of study, somehow got the whole thing taped. 'Have you counted the people?' he suggested at last.

'Our people? Yes, I thought of that – and I've been through every one twice. A hundred and seven, and those two being mended. That's right, isn't it? And I've examined them all very carefully one by one and been through every railway carriage and everything. No, they're either in their house or they've gone right away. You're sure you didn't frighten them? Even by accident?'

'I've told you,' said Mr Pott. Very deliberately, he gave her a look, laid down his tools and went to the drawer in the table.

'What are you going to do?' asked Miss Menzies, aware that he had a plan.

'Find my screwdriver,' said Mr Pott. 'The roof of Vine Cottage comes off in a piece. It was so we could make the two floors – you remember?'

'But you can't do that – supposing they *are* inside. It would be fatal!'

'We've got to take the risk,' said Mr Pott. 'Just get your coat on now and find the umbrella.'

Miss Menzies did as she was told; relieved, she felt suddenly, to surrender the leadership. Her father, she thought, would have acted just like this. And so, of course, would have Aubrey.

Obediently she followed him into the rain and held the umbrella while he went to work. Mr Pott took up a careful position within the High Street and Miss Menzies (feet awkwardly placed to avoid damage) teetered slightly above Church Lane and the back garden. Stooping anxiously they towered above the house.

Several deft turns of the screwdriver and a good deal of grunting soon loosened the soaking thatch. Lid-like, it came off in a piece. 'Bone dry inside,' remarked Mr Pott as he laid it aside.

They saw Pod and Homily's bedroom – a little bare it looked, in spite of the three pieces of doll's-house furniture which once Miss Menzies had bought and left about to be borrowed. The bed, with its handkerchief sheets, looked tousled as though they had left it hurriedly. Pod's working-coat, carefully folded, lay on a chair and his best suit hung on a safety-pin coat-hanger suspended against the wall; while Homily's day clothes were neatly ranged on two rails at the foot of the bed.

There was a feeling of deadness and desertion – no sound but the thrum of the rain as it pattered on the soaked umbrella.

Miss Menzies looked aghast. 'But this is dreadful – they've gone in their night clothes! What could have happened? It's like the *Marie Celeste* –'

'Nothing's been inside,' said Mr Pott, staring down, screwdriver in hand, 'no animal marks, no signs of what you'd call a scuffle . . . Well, we better see what's below. As far as I remember this floor comes out all in a piece with the stairs. Better get a box for the furniture.'

'The furniture!' thought Miss Menzies as she squelched back to the house, picking her way with great Gulliver-like strides over walls and

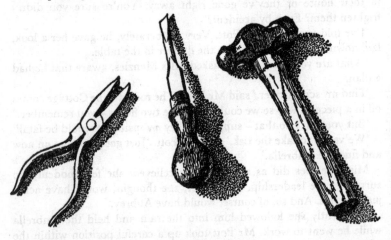

railway lines, streets and alleyways. Just beside the churchyard her foot slipped on the mud, and to save herself she caught hold of the steeple; beautifully built, it held firm, but a bell rang faintly inside: a small, sad, ghostly protest. No; 'the furniture', she realized, was too grand an expression for the contents of that little room. If she had known she would have bought them more things, or left more about for them to borrow. She knew how clever they were at contriving but it takes time, she realized, to furnish a whole house from left-overs. She found a box at last and picked her way back to Mr Pott.

He had lifted out the bedroom floor with the ladder stairway attached and was gazing into the parlour. Neat but bare, Miss Menzies saw again: the usual match-box chest of drawers, a wood-block for a table, bottle-lid cooking-pots beside the hearth and Arrietty's truckle-bed pushed away in a corner; it was the deeper half of a velvet-lined case which must once have contained a large cigar-holder. She wondered where they had found it – perhaps Spiller had brought it to them? Here too the bedclothes had been thrown back hurriedly and Arrietty's day clothes lay neatly folded on a pill-box at the foot.

'I can't bear it,' said Miss Menzies in a stifled voice, feeling for her handkerchief. 'It's all right,' she went on hurriedly, wiping her eyes, 'I'm not going to break down. But what can we do? It's no good going to the police – they would only laugh at us in a polite kind of way and secretly think we were crazy. I know because of what happened when I saw that fairy. People would be polite to one's face, but . . .'

'I wouldn't know about fairies,' said Mr Pott, staring disconsolately into the gutted house, 'but *these* I seen with my own two eyes.'

'I am so glad and thankful that you did see them!' exclaimed Miss Menzies warmly, 'or where should I be now?' For once, it was almost a conversation.

'Well, we'll pack up these things,' said Mr Pott, suiting the action to the word, 'and set the roof back. Got to keep the place dry.'

'Yes,' said Miss Menzies, 'at least we can do that. Just in case . . .' her voice faltered and her fingers trembled a little, as carefully she took up the wardrobe. It had no hooks inside, she noticed – toy-makers never quite completed things – so she laid it flat and packed it like a box with the little piles of clothes. The cheap piece of looking-glass flashed suddenly in a watery beam of sunlight and she saw the rain had stopped.

'Are we doing right?' she asked suddenly. 'I mean, shouldn't we leave it all as we found it? Supposing quite unexpectedly they did come back?'

Mr Pott looked thoughtful. 'Well,' he said, 'seeing as we got the place all opened up like, I thought maybe I'd make a few alterations.'

Miss Menzies, struggling with the rusty catch of Mr Pott's umbrella, paused to stare at him. 'You mean – make the whole place more comfortable?'

'That's what I do mean,' said Mr Pott. 'Do the whole thing over like – give them a proper cooking-stove, running water and all.'

'Running water! Could you do that?'

'Easy,' said Mr Pott.

The umbrella shut with a snap, showering them with drops, but Miss Menzies seemed not to notice. 'And I could furnish it,' she exclaimed; 'carpets, beds, chairs, everything . . .'

'You got to do something,' said Mr Pott, eyeing her tear-marked face, 'to keep your mind off.'

'Yes, yes, of course,' said Miss Menzies.

'But don't be too hopeful about their coming back, you got to keep ready to face the worst. Say they had a fright and ran off on their own accord: that's one thing. Like as not, once the fright's over, they'd come back. But, say, they were *took*. Well, that's another matter altogether – whoever it was that took them, took them to *keep* them, see what I mean?'

'*Whoever?*' repeated Miss Menzies wonderingly.

'See this,' said Mr Pott, moving aside his wooden leg and pointing with his screwdriver to a soggy patch in the High Street. 'That's a human footprint – and it's neither mine nor yours; the pavement's broken all along and the bridge is cracked as though someone has stood on it. Neither you nor me would do that, now would we?'

'No,' said Miss Menzies faintly. 'But,' she went on wonderingly, 'no one except you and I knew of their existence.'

'Or so we thought,' said Mr Pott.

'I see,' said Miss Menzies, and was silent a moment.

Then she said slowly: 'I am thinking now, whether they laugh at us or not, I must report this loss to the police. It would stake our claim. In case,' she went on, 'they should turn up somewhere else.'

Mr Pott looked thoughtful. 'Might be wise,' he said.

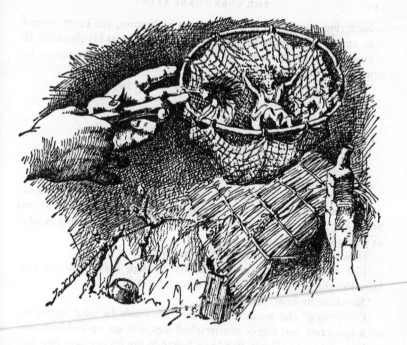

CHAPTER TEN

AT first they lay very still in the corner of the cardboard box, recovering from the shock. Since the lid had been removed they were aware of vastness and of great, white, sloping ceilings. Two dormer windows, high in the tent-like walls, let in a coldish light. The edges of the box obscured the floor.

Arrietty felt very bruised and shaken: she glanced at her mother, who lay back limply, in her long white nightgown, her eyes still doggedly closed, and knew that, for the present, Homily had given up. She glanced at her father, who was leaning forward lost in thought, his hands limply on his knees, sat and noticed that he alone had managed to snatch up a garment – a patched pair of working trousers which he had pulled on over his nightshirt.

Shivering a little in her thin cambric nightgown, she crept towards him, and crouching beside him laid her cheek against his shoulder. He did not speak but his arm came loosely about her, and he patted her gently in an absent-minded way.

'Who are they?' she whispered huskily. 'What happened, Papa?'

'I don't rightly know,' he said.

'It was all so quick – like an earthquake . . .'

'That's right,' he said.

'Mother won't speak,' whispered Arrietty.

'I don't blame her,' said Pod.

'But she's all right, I think,' Arrietty went on; 'it's just her nerves . . .'

'We'd better take a look at her,' said Pod. They crawled towards her on their knees across the washed-out blanket with which the box was lined. For some reason – perhaps their old instinct for cover – neither as yet had dared stand upright.

'How are you feeling, Homily?' asked Pod.

'Just off dead,' she muttered faintly through barely moving lips. Dreadful she looked – lying so straight and so still.

'Anything broken?' asked Pod.

'Everything,' she moaned. But when anxiously he tried to feel the stick-like arms and fragile outstretched legs, she sat up suddenly and exclaimed crossly: 'Don't, Pod,' and began to pin up her hair. She then sank back again, and in a faint voice murmured: 'Where am I?' and with a loose, almost tragic gesture, flung the back of her hand on her brow.

'Well, we could all ask ourselves *that*,' said Pod. 'We're in some kind of room in some kind of human house.' He glanced up at the distant windows. 'We're in an attic; that's where we are. Take a look . . .'

'I couldn't,' said Homily, and shivered.

'And we're alone,' said Pod.

'We won't be for long,' said Homily. 'I've got my "feeling", and I've got it pretty sharp.'

'She's right,' said Arrietty, and gripped her father's shoulder. 'Listen!'

With beating hearts and raised faces they crouched together tensely in the corner of the box – there were footsteps below them on the stairs.

Arrietty sprang up wildly but her father caught her by the arm. 'Steady, girl, what are you after?'

'Cover,' gasped Arrietty, as the footsteps became less muffled. 'There must be somewhere . . . Come on, quick, let's hide!'

'No good,' said Pod; 'they know we're here. There'd only be

searchings and pokings and sticks and pullings-out; your mother couldn't stand it. No, better we stay dead quiet.'

'But we don't know what they'll do to us,' Arrietty almost sobbed. 'We can't just be here and let them!'

Homily suddenly sat up and took Arrietty in her arms. 'Hush, girl, hush,' she whispered, strangely calm all at once. 'Your father's right. There's nothing we can do.'

The footsteps grew louder as though the stairs were now uncarpeted, and there was a creaking of wooden treads. The borrowers clung more tightly together. Pod, face raised, was listening intently.

'That's good,' he breathed in Arrietty's ear. 'I like to hear that – gives us plenty of warning – they can't burst in on us unexpected like.'

Arrietty, still sobbing below her breath, clung to her mother's waist – never had she been more terrified. 'Hush, girl, hush . . .' Homily kept saying.

The footsteps now had reached the landing. There was heavy breathing, outside the door, the clink of keys and the tinkle of china. There was the thud of a drawn bolt; and then another, and a key squeaked and turned in the lock.

'Careful,' said a voice; 'you're spilling it!'

Then the floorboards creaked and trembled as the two pairs of footsteps approached. A great plate loomed suddenly over them, and behind the plate, a face. Extraordinary it looked – pink and powdered, with piled-up golden hair, on each side of this face two jet earrings dangled towards them. Down it came, closer, closer – until they could see each purple vein in the powdered bloom of the cheeks and each pale eyelash of the staring light-blue eyes; and the plate was set down on the floor.

Another face appeared hanging beside the first – tighter and lighter, with rimless glasses, blank and pale with light. A saucer swung sharply towards them and was set down beside the plate.

The pinkish mouth of the first opened suddenly and some words came tumbling out. 'Think they're all right, dear?' it said – on a warm gust of breath which ruffled Homily's hair.

From the other face they saw the rimless glasses removed suddenly, polished and put back again. Scared as he was, Pod could not help thinking: 'I could use those for something, and that great silk handkerchief, too.' 'Bit out of shape,' the thinner mouth replied; 'you bumped them a bit in the box.'

'What about a drop of brandy in their milk, dear?' the pink mouth suggested. 'Have you got your hip flask?'

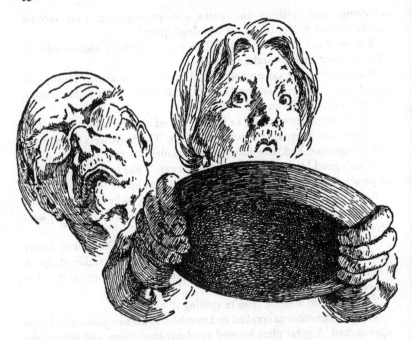

The rimless glasses receded, disappeared for a moment and there was the clink of metal on china. Pod, in some message to Homily, tightened his grip on her hand. Quite strongly, she squeezed his back as the first voice said: 'That's enough, Sidney, you don't want to overdo it.'

Again the two faces loomed over them, staring, staring . . .

'Look at their little faces – hands, hair, feet and everything. What *are* they, do you think, Sidney?'

'They're a find, that's what they are! They're a goldmine! Come, dear, they won't eat while we're here.'

'Suppose I picked one up?'

'No, Mabel, they shouldn't be handled.' (Again Pod squeezed Homily's hand.)

'How do you know?'

'It stands to reason – we haven't got them here as pets. Leave them be now, Mabel – and let's see how they settle. We can come back a bit later on.'

CHAPTER ELEVEN

'MABEL and Sidney,' said Arrietty, as the footsteps died away. She seemed quite calm suddenly.

'What do you mean?' asked Pod.

'Those are their names,' said Arrietty lightly. 'Didn't you listen when they were talking?'

'Yes, I heard them say that we mustn't be handled and they would put a drop of brandy in our milk . . .'

'As though we were cats or something!' muttered Homily.

But suddenly they all felt relieved; the moment of terror had passed – at least they had seen their captors.

'If you ask me,' said Pod, 'I'd say they were not too bright. Clever enough maybe, in their way – but not what you'd rightly call "bright".'

'Mabel and Sidney?' said Arrietty. She laughed suddenly and walked to the edge of the box.

Pod smiled at her tone. 'Yes, them,' he said.

'Food,' announced Arrietty, looking out over the box edge. 'I'm terribly hungry, aren't you?'

'I couldn't touch a thing!' said Homily. But after a moment she seemed to change her mind. 'What *is* there?' she asked faintly.

'I can't quite recognize it from here,' Arrietty told her, leaning over.

'Wait a moment,' said Pod, 'something's just come to me – something important, and it's come to me like a flash. Come back here, Arrietty, sit down beside your mother – the food won't run away.'

When both were seated, waiting expectantly, Pod coughed to clear his throat. 'We don't want to underrate our position,' he began. 'I been thinking it over and I don't want to frighten you like – but our position is bad, it's very bad indeed.' He paused, and Homily took Arrietty's hand in both of hers and patted it reassuringly, but her eyes were on Pod's face. 'No borrower,' Pod went on, 'at least none that I've ever heard tell of – has lived in the absolute power of a set of human beings. The absolute power!' he repeated, gravely, looking from one scared face to the other. 'Borrowers have been "seen" – we've been "seen" our-selves – borrowers have been starved out or chased away – but I never

433

heard tell of this sort of caper – not ever in the whole of my life. Have you, Homily?'

Homily moistened her lips. 'No,' she whispered. Arrietty looked very grave.

'Well, unless we can hit on some sensible way of escape that's what's going to happen to us. We're going to live out our lives in the absolute power of a set of human beings. The absolute power . . .' he repeated again slowly as though to brand the phrase on their minds. There was an awed silence, until Pod spoke again. 'Now, who is the captain of our little ship?'

'You are, Pod,' said Homily huskily.

'Yes, I am. And I'm going to ask a lot of you both – and I'm going to make rules as we go – depending on what's needed. The first rule, of course, is obedience . . .'

'That's right,' nodded Homily, squeezing Arrietty's hand.

'. . . And the second rule – this is the thing that came to me – is: we must none of us speak a word.'

'Now, Pod . . .' began Homily reasonably, aware of her own limitations.

Arrietty saw the point. 'He means to Mabel and Sidney.'

Pod smiled again at her tone, albeit rather wryly. 'Yes, them,' he said. 'Never let 'em know we can speak. Because' – he struck his left palm with two fingers of his right to emphasize his meaning – 'if they don't think we can speak, they'll think we don't understand. Just as they are with animals. And if they think we don't understand, they'll talk before us. *Now* do you get my meaning?'

Homily nodded several times in quick succession: she felt very proud of Pod.

'Well,' he went on in a more relaxed tone, 'let's take a look at this food, and after we've eaten we're going to begin a tour of this room – explore every crack and cranny of it from floor to ceiling. May take us several days . . .'

Arrietty helped her mother to her feet. Pod, at the box edge, swung a leg and lightly dropped to the floor. Then he turned to help Homily. Arrietty followed and made at once for the plate.

'Cold rice pudding,' she said, walking round it, 'a bit of mince, cold cabbage, bread' – she put out a finger to touch something black, she sucked the finger – 'and half a pickled walnut.'

'Careful, Arrietty,' warned Homily, 'it may be poisoned.'

'I wouldn't reckon so,' said Pod. 'Seems like they want us alive. Wish I knew for why.'

'But how are we supposed to drink this milk?' complained Homily.

'Well, take it up in your hands, like.'

Homily knelt down and cupped her hands. Her face became very milky but as she drank a reviving warmth seemed to flow through her veins, and her spirits lifted. 'Brandy,' she said. 'Back home at Firbank they kept it in the morning-room and those Overmantels used to –'

'Now, Homily,' said Pod, 'this is no time for gossip. And that was whisky.'

'Something anyway, and dead drunk they used to be – or so they say – every time the bailiff came in to do the accounts. What's the mince like, Arrietty?'

'It's good,' she replied, licking her fingers.

CHAPTER TWELVE

'Now,' said Pod some time later when they had finished eating, 'we better start on the room.'

He looked upwards. In each sharply sloping wall was set a dormer window, at what seemed a dizzy height; the windows were casement-latched and each had a vertical bolt. Above each was a naked curtain rail, hung with rusted rings. Through one window Pod could see the bough of an ilex tree tossing in the wind.

'It's odd,' Arrietty remarked, 'how from starting under the floor we seem to get higher and higher . . .'

'And it isn't natural,' put in Homily quickly, 'for borrowers to get high. Never leads to no good. Look at those Overmantels, for instance, back in the morning-room at Firbank. Stuck up they were, through living high. Never so much as give you good day, say you were on the floor. It was as though they couldn't see you. Those windows are no good,' she remarked, 'doubt if even a human being could reach up there. Wonder how they clean them?'

'They'd stand on a chair,' said Pod.

'What about the gas-fire?' Homily suggested.

'No hope there,' said Pod, 'it's soldered into the chimney surround.'

It was a small iron gas-fire, with a separate ring – on which, in a pan, stood a battered glue-pot.

'What about the door?' said Arrietty. 'Suppose we cut a piece out of the bottom?'

'What with?' asked Pod, who was still examining the fireplace.

'We might find something,' said Arrietty, looking about her.

There were plenty of objects in the room. Beside the fireplace stood a dressmaker's dummy, upholstered in a dark green rep: it was shaped like an hour-glass, had a knob for a head and below the swelling hips a kind of wire-frame petticoat – a support for the fitting of skirts. It stood on three curved legs with swivel wheels. Its dark green bosom was stuck with pins and on one shoulder, in a row, three threaded needles. Arrietty had a strange thought: did human beings look like this, she wondered, without their clothes? Were they, unlike the borrowers, perhaps not made of flesh and blood at all? Come to think of it, as 'Mabel' had put down the plate, there had been a kind of creaking; and it stood to reason that, to keep such bulk erect, there must surely be some hidden form of scaffolding.

Above the mantel-shelf, on either side, were swivel gas-brackets of tarnished brass. From one hung a length of measuring tape, marked in inches. On the shelf itself she saw the edge of a chipped saucer, the blades of what must be a pair of cutting-out scissors, and a large iron horseshoe propped upside down.

At right angles to the fireplace, pulled out from the sloping wall, she saw a treadle sewing-machine; it was like one she remembered at Firbank. Above the sewing-machine, hanging on a nail, were the inner tube of a bicycle tyre and a bunch of raffia. There were two trunks, several piles of magazines and some broken slatted chairs. Between the trunks, leaning at an angle, was the shrimping-net which had achieved their capture. Homily glanced at the bamboo handle and, shuddering, averted her eyes.

On the other side of the room, a fair-sized kitchen table was pushed against the wall, and beside it a ladder-back chair. The table was piled with various neat stacks of plates and saucers, and other things which from floor level were difficult to recognize.

On the floor, beyond the chair and immediately below the window, stood a solid box of walnut veneer, inlaid with tarnished brass. The veneer was cracked and peeling. 'It's a dressing-case,' said Pod, who had seen something like it at Firbank, 'or one of those folding writing-desks. No, it isn't though,' he went on as he walked round to the far side, 'it's got a handle . . .'

'It's a musical-box,' said Arrietty.

After a moment of seeming stuck, the handle wound quite easily. They could turn it as one turned an old-fashioned mangle, though the upward swing at its highest limit was difficult to control. Homily could manage, though, with her long wrists and arms; she was a little taller

than Pod. There was a grinding sound from within the box and suddenly the tune tinkled out. It was fairylike and charming, but somehow a little sad. It ended very abruptly.

'Oh, play it again!' cried Arrietty.

'No, that's enough,' said Pod, 'we've got to get on.' He was staring towards the table.

'Just once,' pleaded Arrietty.

'All right,' he said, 'but hurry up. We haven't got all day . . .'

And while they played their encore he stood in the middle of the room, gazing thoughtfully at the table top.

When at last they came beside him, he said: 'It's worth while getting up there!'

'Don't see quite how you could,' said Homily.

'Quiet,' said Pod, 'I'm getting it . . .'

Obediently they stood silent, watching the direction of his eyes as he gauged the height of the ladderback chair, and then, turning his back on it, glanced up at the raffia on the opposite wall, took in the position of the pins in the bosom of the dressmaker's dummy, and turned back again to the table. Homily and Arrietty held their breaths, aware some great issue was at stake.

'Easy,' said Pod at last, 'child's play,' and, smiling, he rubbed his hands: it always cheered him to solve a professional problem. 'Some good stuff up there, I shouldn't wonder.'

'But what good can it do us?' asked Homily, 'seeing there's no way out?'

'Well, you never know,' said Pod. 'Anyway,' he went on briskly, 'keeps your hand in and your mind off.'

CHAPTER THIRTEEN

THE next two or three days established their daily routine. At about nine o'clock each morning Mr or Mrs Platter – or both – would arrive with their food. They would air the attic, clear away the dirty plates and generally set the borrowers up for the day. Mrs Platter, to Homily's fury, persisted with the cat treatment: a saucer of milk, a bowl of water and a baking tin of ashes, set out daily beside their food on a clean sheet of newspaper.

Towards evening, at between six and seven o'clock, the process was repeated and was called 'putting them to bed'. It was dark by then and sometimes they would have dozed off – to be woken suddenly by the scrape of a match and the flare of a roaring gas-jet. It was one of Pod's rules that, however active they might be between whiles, the Platters' arrival should always find them once again in their box. The footsteps on the stairs gave them plenty of warning. 'And never let them know we can climb.'

The morning food seemed to consist of the remains of the Platters' breakfast; the evening food, the remains of the Platters' midday meal, was slightly more interesting. Anything they left on the plate was never served up again. 'After all,' they had heard Mr Platter say, 'there are no books about them, no way to find out what they live on except by trial and error. We must try them out with a bit of this and that, and we'll soon see what agrees.'

Except on the rare occasions when Mr or Mrs Platter decided to do a repairing job in the attic or to stagger upstairs with trays of china or cutlery to be put away for the winter, the hours between meals were their own.

They were very active hours. On that first afternoon Pod, with the aid of a bent pin and a knotted strand of raffia, achieved the ascent of the table, and once safely ensconced, showed Arrietty how to follow. Later, he said, they would make a raffia ladder.

Gradually they worked their way through various cardboard boxes; some contained teaspoons and cutlery; some contained paper windmills, others toy balloons. There were boxes of nails and assorted screws and

there was a small square biscuit-tin without a lid,
filled with a jumble of keys. There was a tottering
pile of pink-stained strawberry baskets and there
were sets of neatly packed ice-cream cones, hermetically sealed in transparent grease-proof
paper.

There were two drawers in the table, one of
which was not quite closed. They squeezed
through the crack, and in the half light saw it was
full of tools. Pod's leg went down between a
spanner and a screwdriver, in extricating which
he rolled the screwdriver over and struck Arrietty
on the ankle. Although neither injury was serious,
they decided the drawer was a dangerous place
and put it out of bounds.

By the fourth day the operation was complete:
they had learned the position and possible use of
every object in the room. They had even succeeded
in opening the lid of the musical-box, in a vain
hope of changing the tune. It slid up quite easily
on a brass arm which, clinking into a locked
position, held the lid in place. It closed, rather
faster but almost as easily, by pressure on a knob.
They could not change the tune, however; the
brass cylinders, spiked with an odd pattern of
steel prickles, were too heavy for them to lift, and
they could only look longingly at the five unknown
tunes on the equally heavy cylinders ranged at the
back of the box. But with each new
discovery – such as the steel backing
of the lower part of the door and the
dizzy height of the dormer windows
from which the sloping walls slid
steeply away – their hopes grew
fainter: there still seemed no way of
escape.

Pod spent more and more of his time just sitting and thinking.
Arrietty, tired of the musical-box, had discovered on the magazine pile
several tattered copies of the *Illustrated London News*. She would drag
them one at a time under the table, and turning over the vast sail-like

pages would walk about on them listlessly, looking at the pictures and sometimes reading aloud.

'You see nobody knows where we are,' Pod would exclaim, breaking a dreary silence, 'not even Spiller.'

'And not even Miss Menzies . . .' Arrietty would think to herself, staring unhappily at a half-page diagram of a dam to be built on the lower reaches of the Nile.

As the mornings became chillier Homily tore some strips off the worn blanket and she and Arrietty fashioned themselves sarong-like skirts and pointed shawls to draw round their shoulders.

Seeing this, the Platters decided to light the gas-fire and would leave it burning low. The borrowers were glad, because, although sometimes the air grew dry and stuffy, they were able to toast up scraps of the duller foods and make their meals more appetizing.

One day Mrs Platter bustled in and, looking very purposeful, went to the closed drawer of the table. Watching her from their box in the corner as she pulled out some of the contents they saw it contained rags and rolls of old stuff, neatly tied round with tape. She unrolled a piece of yellowed flannel and, taking up the cutting-out scissors, came and stared down on them with narrowed, thoughtful eyes.

They stared back nervously at the waving scissor blades. Was she going to snip and snap and tailor them to size? But no – with a little creaking and much heavy breathing, she kneeled down on the floor and, spreading the stuff doubled before her, cut out three combination garments, each one all of a piece, with magyar sleeves and legs. These she seamed up on the sewing-machine, 'tutting' to herself under her breath when the wheel stuck or the thread parted. When her thimble rolled away under the treadle of the sewing-machine they noted its position: a drinking-cup at last!

Breathing hard, and with the aid of a bone crochet-hook, Mrs Platter turned the garments inside out. 'There you are,' she said, and threw them into the box. They lay there stiffly like little headless effigies. None of the borrowers moved.

'You can put them on yourselves, can't you?' said Mrs Platter at last. The borrowers stared back at her, with wide, unblinking eyes, until, after waiting a moment, she turned and went away.

They were terrible garments, stiff and shapeless, fitting nowhere at all. But at least they were warm; and Homily could now rinse out their own clothes in the bowl of drinking water and hang them before the

gas-fire to dry. 'Thank heavens, I can't see myself,' she remarked grimly, as she gazed incredulously at Pod.

'Thank goodness you can't,' he replied, smiling, and he turned rather quickly away.

CHAPTER FOURTEEN

As the weeks went by they learned gradually of the reason for their capture and the use to which they would be put. As well as the construction of the cage-like house on the island, Mr and Mrs Platter – assured of vast takings at last – were installing a turnstile in place of the gate to the drive.

One side of their cage-house, they learned, was to be made of thick plate-glass, exposing their home life to view. 'Good and heavy' the glass would have to be – Mr Platter had insisted, describing the 'layout' to Mrs Platter – nothing the borrowers could break; and fixed in a slot so the Platters could raise it for cleaning. The furniture was to be fixed to the floor and set in such a way that there should be nothing behind which they might hide.

'You know those cages at the Zoo with sleeping-quarters at the back, where you wait and wait, and the animal never comes out? Well, we don't want anything like that. Can't have people asking for their money back . . .'

Mrs Platter had agreed. She saw the whole project in her mind's eye and thought Mr Platter very far-seeing and wonderful. 'And you've got to set the cage,' he went on earnestly, 'or house, or whatever we decide to call it, in a bed of cement. You can't have them burrowing.'

No, that wouldn't do, Mrs Platter had agreed again. And as Mr Platter went ahead with the construction of the house, Mrs Platter, they learned, had arranged with a seamstress to make them an entirely new wardrobe. She had taken away their own clothes to serve as patterns for size. Homily was very intrigued by Mrs Platter's description to Mr Platter of a green dress 'with a hint of a bustle – like my purple plaid, you remember?' 'Wish I could *see* her purple plaid,' Homily kept worrying, 'just so as to get the idea . . .'

But Pod's thoughts were set on graver matters. Every conversation overheard brought day by day an increasing awareness of their fate: to live out the rest of their lives under a barrage of human eyes – a constant, unremitting state of being 'seen'. Flesh and blood could not stand it, he thought; they would shrivel up under these stares – that's

what would happen – they would waste away and die. And people would watch them even on their deathbeds – they would watch, with necks craned and shoulders jostling – while Pod stroked the dying Homily's brow or Homily stroked the dying Pod's. No, he decided grimly, from now on there could be but one thought governing their lives – a burning resolve to escape: to escape while they were still in the attic; to escape before spring. Cost what it might, he realized, they must never be taken alive to that house with a wall of glass!

For these reasons, as the winter wore on, he became irritated by Homily's fussings over details such as the ash-pan and Arrietty's unheeding preoccupation with the *Illustrated London News*.

CHAPTER FIFTEEN

DURING this period (mid November to December) several projects were planned and attempted. Pod had succeeded in drawing out four nails which secured a patch of mended floorboard below the kitchen table. 'They don't walk here, you see,' he explained to his wife and child, 'and it's in shadow like.' These four stout nails he replaced with slimmer ones from the tin box on the table. The finer nails could be lifted out with ease and the three of them together could move the boards aside. Below they found the familiar joists and crossbeams, with a film of dust which lay – ankle-deep to them – on the ceiling plaster of the room below. ('Reminds me of the time when we first moved in under the floor at Firbank,' said Homily. 'I thought sometimes we would never get it straight, but we did.')

But Pod's project was nothing to do with homemaking – he was seeking a way which might lead them to the lath and plaster walls of the room immediately below. If they could achieve this, he thought, there was nothing to stop them climbing down through the whole depth of the house, with the help of the laths within the walls: mice did it, rats did it; and as he pointed out, risky and toilsome as it was, they had done it several times themselves. ('We were younger then, Pod,' Homily reminded him nervously, but she seemed quite willing to try.)

It was no good, however; the attic was in the roof and the roof was set fairly and squarely on the brickwork of the main house, bedded and held in some mixture like cement. There was no way down to the laths.

Pod's next idea was one of breaking a small hole in the plaster of the ceiling below, and with the aid of the swinging ladder made of raffia, descend without cover into whatever room it might turn out to be.

'At least,' he said, 'we'd be one floor down, the window will be lower and the door unlocked . . .' First, though, he decided to borrow a packing-needle from the tool drawer and make a peephole. This, too, was hazardous: not only might the ceiling crack but there was bound to be some small fall of plaster on to the floor below. They decided to risk it, however; borrowers' eyes are particularly sharp: they could manage with a very small hole.

447

When at last they had made the hole and to their startled gaze the room below sprang into view, it turned out to be Mr and Mrs Platter's bedroom. There was a large brass bed, a very pink, shiny eiderdown, a Turkey carpet, a wash-hand-stand with two sets of flowered china, a dressing-table and a cat-basket. And what was still more alarming, Mrs Platter was having her afternoon's rest. It was an extraordinary sight to see her vast bulk from this angle, propped against the pillows. Very peaceful and unconcerned she looked, reading a home journal – leisurely turning the pages and eating butterscotch from a round tin. The cat lay on the eiderdown at her feet. A powdery film of ceiling plaster had settled in a ring on the pinkness of the eiderdown just beside the cat. This, Pod realized thankfully, would be swiftly shaken off when Mrs Platter arose.

Trembling and silent the borrowers backed away from their peephole, and noiselessly felt their way through the blanketing dust to the exit in the floorboards. Silently they lifted the small plank into place and gingerly dropped back the nails.

'Phew! . . .' said Pod, sinking back, as they reached their box in the corner. He wiped his brow on his sleeve, 'didn't expect to see that!' He looked very shaken.

'Nor did I,' said Homily. She thought a while. 'But it might be useful.'

'Might,' agreed Pod uncertainly.

The next attempt concerned the window – the one through which they could see the waving branch of the ilex. This branch was their only link with out of doors. 'Wind's in the east today,' Mrs Platter would sometimes say as she opened the casements to air the attic – this she achieved by standing on a chair – and the borrowers took note of what she said, and by the streaming of the leaves in one direction or another could roughly foretell the weather: 'wind in the east' meant snow.

When the flakes piled up on the outer sill they liked to watch them dance and scurry, but were thankful for the gas-fire. This was early January and not the most auspicious weather for Pod's study of the window, but they had no time to lose.

Homily, on occasion, was apt to discourage him. 'Say we did get it open, where would we be? On the roof! And you can see how steep it is by the slope of these ceilings. I mean, we're better in here than on the roof, Pod. I'm game in most things, but if you think I'm going to make a jump for that branch, you'll have to think again.'

'You couldn't make a jump for that branch, Homily,' Pod would tell her patiently, 'it's yards and yards away. And what's more, it's never still. No, it's not the branch I'm thinking of . . .'

'What are you thinking of, then?'

'Of where we are,' said Pod, 'that's what I want to find out. You might *see* something from the roof. You've heard them talk – about Little Fordham and that. And about the river. I'd like just to know where we *are*.'

'What good does that do us,' retorted Homily, 'if we can't get out, anyway?'

Pod turned and looked at her. 'We've got to keep trying,' he explained.

'I know, Pod,' admitted Homily quickly. She glanced towards the table, under which, as usual, Arrietty was immersed in the *Illustrated London News*, 'and we both want to help you. I mean, we did make the raffia ladder. Just tell us what to do.'

'There isn't much you *can* do,' said Pod, 'at least not at the moment. What foxes me about this window is that, to free the latch you have to turn the handle of the catch upwards. See what I mean? The same with that vertical bolt – you've got to pull it out of its socket *upwards*. Now say to open the window you had to turn the handle of the catch downwards – that would be easy! We could fling a piece of twine or something over, swing our weight on the twine like and the catch would slide up free.'

'Yes,' said Homily thoughtfully, staring at the window. 'Yes, I see what you mean.' They were silent a moment – both thinking hard. 'What about that curtain rod?' asked Homily at last.

'The curtain rod? I don't quite get you . . .'

'Is it fast in the wall?'

Pod screwed up his eyes. 'Pretty fast, I'd say, it's brass. And with those brackets . . .'

'Could you get a bit of twine over the curtain rod?'

'Over the curtain rod?'

'Yes, and use it like a pulley.'

A change came over Pod's face. 'Homily,' he said, 'that's it! Here am I – been weeks on the problem . . . and you hit on the answer first time . . .'

'It's nothing,' said Homily, smiling.

Pod gave his orders; and swiftly they all went to work: the ball of twine and a small key to be carried to the table and up to the topmost

box (this to bring Pod, sideways on, to within easier throwing distance of the curtain rod); the horseshoe to be knocked from the mantel-shelf to the floor, and to be dragged to a spot beside the musical-box, and immediately below the window; several patient swinging throws by Pod from the box pile on the table of the key attached to the twine, aimed at the wall above the curtain rod, which stood out slightly on its twin brass brackets (and suddenly there had been the welcome clatter of the key against the glass and the key falling swiftly as Arrietty paid out the twine – down past the window, past the sill, to Homily on the floor, beside the horseshoe); the removal of the key by Homily and the knotting of the raffia ladder to the twine to be wound back again by Arrietty, to bring the head of the ladder even with the window catch; the tying, by Homily, of the base of the swinging ladder to the horseshoe on the floor; the twine to be pulled taut and made fast by Arrietty to a table leg; the descent of Pod to the floor.

It was wonderful. The ladder rose tautly from the horseshoe, straight up the centre join of the casement windows to the catch, held firmly by the twine around the curtain rod.

Up the raffia ladder went Pod, watched by Arrietty and Homily from the floor. When on a level with the window catch, he hooked the first rung over the curtain rail, making – for a few essential moments – the ladder independent of the twine. Arrietty, beside the table leg, paying out several inches from the ball, enabling Pod to knot the twine about the iron handle of the catch. Pod then descending to the floor from the table leg and bringing the ball directly below the window.

'So far, so good,' he said. 'Now we've all got to pull on the twine. You behind Arrietty, Homily, and I'll bring up the rear.'

Obediently they did as he said. With a twist of twine tug-of-war-like around each tiny fist, they leaned backwards into the room, panting and straining and digging in their heels. Slowly, steadily the handle of the latch moved upward and the hammer-shaped head dipped down in a sliding half-circle, until at last it left one casement free.

'We've done it,' said Pod. 'You can let go now. That's the first stage.' They all stood rubbing their hands and feeling very happy. 'Now for the bolt,' Pod went on. And the whole performance was repeated; more efficiently, this time – more swiftly. The small bolt, easy in its groove, lifted gently and hung above its socket. 'The window's open,' cried Pod. 'There's nothing holding it now except for the snow on the sill!'

'And we could brush that off – if, say, we went up the ladder,' said Homily. 'And I'd like to see the view.'

'You can see the view in a minute,' said Pod, 'but what we mustn't touch is that snow. You don't want Mabel and Sidney coming upstairs and finding we've been at the window. At least, not yet awhile . . . What we must do now, and do quickly, is shut it up again. How do you feel, Homily? Like to rest a moment?'

'No, I'm all right,' she said.

'Then we better get going,' said Pod.

CHAPTER SIXTEEN

UNDER Pod's direction, and with one or two small mistakes on the parts of Homily and Arrietty, the process was reversed and the latch and bolt made fast again. But not before – as Pod had promised – all three had climbed the ladder in solemn file, and rubbing the misted breath from the glass, had stared out over the landscape. They had seen, so far below them, the dazzling slope of Mr Platter's lawn, the snake-like river, black as a whiplash, curving away into the distance; they had seen the snow-covered roofs of Fordham – and beside a far loop of the stream the three tall poplars, which as they knew marked the site of Little Fordham. They looked very far away – even, thought Homily, as the crow flies . . .

They did not talk much after they had seen these things. They felt overawed by the distance, the height and the whiteness. On Pod's orders they set about storing the tackle below the floorboard, where, though safely hidden, it would always be ready to hand. 'We'll practise that window job again tomorrow,' said Pod, 'and every other day from now on.'

As they worked the wind rose again and the underside of the ilex leaves showed grey as the grey sky. Before dusk it began to snow again. When they had set back the board and replaced the nails, they crept up close to the gas-fire and sat there thinking, as the daylight drained from the room. There still seemed no way of escape. 'We're too high,' Homily kept saying. 'Never does and never has done borrowers any good to be high . . .'

At last the footsteps of Mrs Platter on the stairs drove them back to their box. When the match scraped and the gas-jet flared they saw the room again and the blackness of the window with the snow piled high on the outer sill. The line of white rose softly as they watched it with each descending snowflake.

'Terrible weather,' muttered Mrs Platter to herself, as she set down their plate and their saucer. She stared at them anxiously as they lay huddled in the box and turned up the gas-fire a little before she went away. And they were left as always to eat by themselves in the dark.

CHAPTER SEVENTEEN

THE snow and frost and leaden cold continued into early February. Until one morning they woke to soft rain and the pale clouds running in the sky. The leaves of the ilex branch, enamelled and shining, streamed black against the grey and showed no silvery glimpse of underside. 'Wind's in the south,' announced Pod that morning in the satisfied voice of an experienced weather prophet. 'We're likely to have a thaw.'

In the past weeks they had employed their time as best they could. Against the weight of snow on the sill they had practised the raising of the latch and had brought the process to a fine art. Mr and Mrs Platter, they gathered, had been held up on the building of the cage-house, but the borrowers' clothes had arrived, laid out between layers of tissue-paper in a cardboard dress-box. It took them no time at all to get the lid off and with infinite care and cunning to examine the contents and in secret to try them on. The seamstress had nimbler fingers than those of Mrs Platter and had worked in far finer materials. There was a grey suit for Pod with – instead of a shirt – a curious kind of dicky with the collar and tie painted on; there was a pleated and ruched dress for Arrietty with two pinafores to keep it clean. Homily, although ready to grumble, took to her green dress with its 'hint of a bustle', and would wear it sometimes to a moment of danger – the dread sound of footsteps on the stairs.

To Pod these goings-on seemed frivolous and childish. Had they forgotten, he wondered, their immediate danger and the fate which day by day became closer as the weather cleared and Mr Platter worked away on the house? He did not reproach them, however. Let them have their little bit of happiness, he decided, in face of misery to come.

But he became very 'down'. Better they all should be dead, he told them one day, than in lifelong public captivity; and he would sit and stare into space.

He became so 'down' that Homily and Arrietty grew frightened. They stopped dressing up and conferred together in corners. They tried

to liven him with little jokes and anecdotes; they saved him all the titbits from the food. But Pod seemed to have lost his appetite. Even when they reminded him that spring was in the air and soon it would be March – 'and something always happens to us in March' – he evinced no interest. 'Something *will* happen to us in March,' was all he said before retreating again into silence.

One day Arrietty came beside him as he sat there, dully thinking, in the corner of the box. She took his hand. 'I have an idea,' she said.

He made an effort to smile and gently squeezed her hand. 'There isn't anything,' he said; 'we've got to face it, lass.'

'But there is something,' Arrietty persisted. 'Do listen, Papa. I've thought of the very thing!'

'Have you, my girl?' he said gently, and, smiling a little, he stroked back the hair from her cheek.

'Yes,' said Arrietty, 'we could make a balloon.'

'A what?' he exclaimed. And Homily, who had been toasting up a sliver of bacon at the gas-fire, came across to them, drawn by the sharpness of his tone.

'We needn't even make it!' Arrietty hurried on. 'There are heaps of balloons in those boxes and we have all those strawberry baskets, and there are diagrams and everything . . .' She pulled his hand. 'Come and look at this copy of the *Illustrated London News*.'

There was a three-page spread in the *Illustrated London News* – with diagrams, photographs and an expert article, set out comprehensively in columns, on the lately revived sport of free ballooning.

Pod could count and add up, but he could not read, so Arrietty, walking about on the page, read the article aloud. He listened attentively, trying to take it in. 'Let's have that again, lass,' he would say, frowning with his effort to understand.

'Well, move, Mother – please,' Arrietty would say, because Homily,

weak from standing, had suddenly sat down on the page. 'You're on the piece about wind velocity . . .'

Homily kept muttering phrases like: 'Oh, my goodness – oh, my goodness gracious me . . .' as the full implications of their plan began to dawn on her. She looked strained and a little wild, but awake now to their desperate plight, was resigned to a lesser evil.

'I've got that,' Pod would say at last, after several repetitions of a paragraph concerning something described as 'the canopy or envelope'. 'Now let's have that bit about the valve line and the load ring. It's up near the top of the second column.' And he and Arrietty would walk up the page again and patiently, clearly, although stumbling now and again on the big words, Arrietty would read aloud.

In the tool drawer, no longer out of bounds, they had found the stub of a lead pencil. Pod extracted the lead and sharpened it to a fine point, for Arrietty to underline key headings and to make lists.

At last, on the third day of concentrated homework, Pod announced: 'I'm there!'

He was a changed man suddenly; what had once seemed a ridiculous flight of fancy on the part of Arrietty could now become sober fact, and he was practical enough to see it.

The first job was swiftly to dismantle the shrimping-net. On this, in more senses than one, would hang all their hopes of success. Homily, with a cut-down morsel of fret-saw blade, taken from a box in the tool drawer, was to cut the knots which secured the net to the frame. Pod would then saw up the frame into several portable lengths and take off the bamboo handle.

'That whole shrimping-net's got to disappear,' Pod explained, 'as though it had never existed. We can't have them seeing the frame with the netting part cut away. Once it's in pieces, like, we can hide it under the floor.'

It took less time than they had foreseen and as they laid back the floorboard and dropped the nails into place, Pod – who was not often given to philosophizing – said: 'Funny, when you come to think of it, that this old net we were caught in should turn out to be our salvation.'

That night, when they went to bed, they felt tired but a good deal happier. Pod for some time lay awake, thinking another great test lay before them on the morrow. Could the balloon be filled from the gas-jet? There was a real danger in meddling with gas, he realized uneasily; even adult human beings had met with accidents, let alone disobedient children. He had warned Arrietty about gas in the days when they lived at Firbank, and she, good girl, had respected his advice and had understood the peril. He would of course take every precaution: first the window must be opened wide and the cock of the gas-jet shut off, and the fire allowed to cool down until not a spot of red remained. There was plenty of pressure in the gas-jet; even this very evening, when Mrs Platter had first lit it, he remembered how fiercely it had roared; she had always – he had noticed – to turn it a fraction lower. The ascent to the mantel-shelf could be made via the dummy. It was no use worrying, he decided at last, they were bound to have this try-out and to abide by the result. All the same, it was a long time – several hours it seemed – before Pod fell asleep.

CHAPTER EIGHTEEN

The balloon filled perfectly. Lashed around the nozzle of the gas-jet and anchored to the horseshoe on the floor by a separate piece of twine, it first swelled slightly in a limp mass which hung loosely down against the burner and then – to their startled joy – suddenly shot upright and went on swelling. Bigger and bigger it grew – until it became a vast, tight globe of a rich translucent purple. Then Pod, firmly perched among the ornate scrollwork of the bracket, leaned sideways and turned off the gas.

As though making a tourniquet, he tied the neck of the balloon above the nozzle and undid the lashing just below. The balloon leapt free almost with a jump but was brought up short by the tethering string which Pod had anchored to the horseshoe.

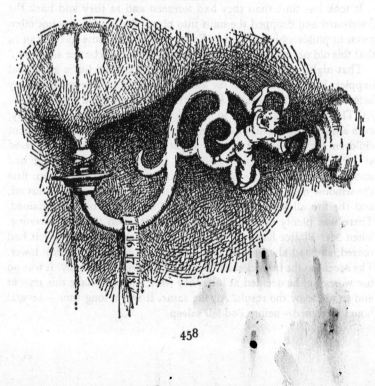

Homily and Arrietty on the floor beside the horseshoe let out their 'Aaahs' and 'Ohs' . . . and Arrietty ran forward and, seizing the string, tried her weight on it. She swung a little to and fro as the balloon bumped against the ceiling.

'Gently!' cried Pod from the bosom of the dummy. He was climbing down slowly on carefully set footholds of pins. When he reached the caged part below the dummy's hips he swung down more quickly from one wire rung to another.

'Now, we'll all three take hold,' he told them, running to grasp the string. 'Pull,' he cried, 'as hard as you can. Hand over hand!'

Hand over hand they pulled and swung and slowly the balloon came down. A swift double turn of the twine through a nail-hole in the horseshoe and there it was – tethered beside them, gently swaying and twisting.

Pod wiped his brow on his sleeve. 'It's too small,' he said.

'Too small!' exclaimed Homily. She felt dwarfed and awed by the great bobbing purple mass. But it gave her a feeling of delightful power to push it and make it sway; and a sideways stroke of her fingers would send it into a spin.

'Of course it's too small,' explained Pod in a worried voice. 'We shouldn't be able to pull it down like that. A balloon that size might take Arrietty alone, but it would not take the three of us – not with the net and the basket added. And we got to have ballast too.'

'Well,' said Homily, after a short, dismayed silence, 'what are we going to do?'

'I've got to think,' said Pod.

'Suppose we all stopped eating and thinned down a bit?' suggested Homily.

'That wouldn't be any good. And you're thin enough already.' Pod seemed very worried. 'No, I've got to think.'

'There is a bigger balloon,' said Arrietty. 'It's in a box by itself. At least, it looked bigger to me.'

'Well, let's take a look,' said Pod, but he did not sound very hopeful.

It did seem bigger and was covered with shrivelled white markings. 'I think it's some kind of lettering,' Arrietty remarked, turning over the box-lid. 'Yes, it says here: "Printed to your own specification" – I wonder what it means . . .'

'I don't care what it means,' exclaimed Pod, 'so long as there's room for a lot of it. Yes, it's bigger,' he went on, 'a good deal bigger, and it's heavier. Yes, this balloon may just do us nicely. Might as well try it at once, now we've got the fire off and the window open.'

'What shall we do with this one?' asked Homily from the floor. She tapped it sharply so that it trembled and spun.

'We better burst it,' said Pod on his way down from the table via the raffia ladder which swung on bent pins from the chair back, 'and hide the remains. Nothing much else that we *can* do.'

He burst it with a pin. The report seemed deafening and the balloon, deflating, jumped about like a mad thing; Homily screamed and ran for

safety into the wire cage below the dummy. There was a terrible smell of gas.

'Didn't think it would make such a noise,' said Pod, pin in hand and looking rather startled. 'Never mind, with the window open – the smell will soon wear off.'

The new balloon was more cumbersome to climb with and Pod had to rest awhile on the mantel-shelf before he tackled the gas-jet.

'Like me to come up and help you, Papa?' Arrietty called out from the floor.

'No,' he said, 'I'll be all right in a minute. Just let me get my breath . . .'

The heavier balloon remained limp for longer; until, almost as though groaning under the effort, it raised itself upright and began to fill. 'Oh,' breathed Arrietty, 'it's going to be a lovely colour . . .' It was a deep fuchsia pink, becoming each moment – as the rubber swelled – more delicately pale. As it swayed a little on the gas-jet white lettering began to appear. STOP! was the first word, with an exclamation mark after it. Arrietty, reading the word aloud, hoped it was not an omen. Below STOP came the word BALLYHOGGIN, and below that again in slightly smaller print: 'World Famous Model Village and Riverside Teas.'

The balloon was growing larger and larger. Homily looked alarmed. 'Careful, Pod,' she begged; 'whatever you do, don't burst it!'

'It can go a bit more yet,' said Pod. They watched anxiously until at last Pod, in a glow of pink shadow from the swaying monster above him, said: 'That's about it,' and leaning sideways to the wall, sharply turned off the gas. Climbing back, he took up the tape-measure which still hung from the gas-bracket and measured the height of the letter 'i' in 'Riverside Teas'. 'A good three inches,' he said, 'that gives us something to check by the next time we inflate.' He now spoke more often in current ballooning terms and had acquired quite a fair-sized vocabulary concerning such things as flying ballast, rip lines, trail ropes or grapnel hooks.

This time the balloon, soaring to the ceiling, half lifted the horseshoe and dragged it along the floor. With great presence of mind Homily sat down on the horseshoe while Arrietty leapt for the string.

'That looks more like it,' said Pod as he climbed once again down the bosom of the dummy. As he started down excitely his foot slipped on a pin, but leaning sideways he pushed the pin back in again almost to the head and made the foothold secure. But for the rest of the climb he controlled his eagerness and took the stages more slowly. By the time he reached the floor, in spite of the cold air from the window, he looked very hot and dishevelled.

'Any give on the line?' he asked Arrietty as he waited to recover his breath.

'No,' gasped Arrietty. Then they all three pulled together but the balloon merely twisted on the ceiling as though held there by a magnet.

'That's enough,' said Pod, after they had all three lifted their feet from the floor and had swung about awhile, still with no effect on the balloon. 'Let her go. I've got to think again.'

They were quiet while he did so, but watched anxiously as he paced about frowning with concentration. Once he untethered the balloon from the horseshoe and, tow-line in hand, walked it about on the ceiling. It bumped a little but followed him obediently as he sketched out its course from the floor.

'Time's getting on, Pod,' Homily said at last.

'I know,' he said.

'I mean,' Homily went on in a worried voice. 'How are we going to get it down? I'm thinking of Mabel and Sidney. We've got to get it down before supper, Pod.'

'I know that,' he said. He walked the balloon across the room until he stood below the lip of the table. 'What we need is some kind of winch – some kind of worm and worm-wheel.' He stared up at the knob of the tool drawer.

'Worm and worm-wheel . . .' said Homily in a mystified voice. '*Worm?*' she repeated incredulously.

Arrietty, up to date now with almost every aspect of free ballooning, including the use of winches, laughed and said: 'It's a thing that takes the weight – supposing, say, you were turning a handle. Like the –' she stopped abruptly, struck by a sudden thought. 'Papa!' she called out excitedly, 'what about the musical-box?'

'The musical-box?' he repeated blankly. Then, as Arrietty nodded, a light dawned and his whole expression changed. 'That's it!' he exclaimed. 'You've hit it. That's our winch-handle, weight, cylinder, worm and wheel and all!'

CHAPTER NINETEEN

IN no time at all they had the musical-box open and Pod, standing on an upturned match-box, was staring down at the works. 'We've got a problem,' he said, as they scrambled up beside him. 'I'll solve it, mind, but I've got to find the right tool. It's those teeth,' he pointed out.

Gazing into the works, they saw he meant a row of metal points suspended downwards from a bar, these were the strikers which, brushing the cylinder as it turned, rang from each prickle one tinkling note of the tune. 'You've got to have those teeth out, or they'd mess up the tow-line. If they're welded in it's going to be difficult, but looks to me as though they're all in a piece held in by those screws.'

'It looks to me like that too,' said Arrietty, leaning forward to see better.

'Well, we'll soon have those screws out,' said Pod.

While he climbed once again to the tool drawer, Homily and Arrietty played one last tune. 'Pity we never heard the others,' said Arrietty, 'and we never shall hear them now.'

'If we get out of here alive,' said Homily, 'I don't care if I never see or hear any kind of musical-box again in the whole of the rest of my life!'

'Well, you are going to get out of here alive,' remarked Pod in a grimly determined voice. He had come back amongst them with the smallest screwdriver he could find; even then it was as tall as himself. He walked out on the bar and, feet apart, holding the handle at chest level, took his position above the screw and set the edge into the slot. After a short resistance the screw turned easily as Pod revolved the handle. 'Light as watch screws,' he remarked as he loosened the others. 'It's well made, this musical-box.'

Soon they could lift out the row of spiked teeth and make fast the tow-line to the cylinder. It swayed loosely as the balloon above it surged against the ceiling. 'Now,' said Pod, 'I'll take the first turn and we'll see how it goes ...'

Arrietty and Homily held their breaths as he grasped the handle of the musical-box and slowly began to turn. The line tautened and

became dead straight. Slowly and steadily, as Pod put more effort into his turning, the balloon started down towards them. They watched it anxiously, with upturned faces and aching necks, until at last – swaying and pulling slightly at its moorings – it was brought within their reach.

'What about that?' said Pod in a satisfied voice. But he looked very white and tired.

'What do we do now?' asked Homily.

'We deflate it,' he said.

'Let the gas out,' explained Arrietty as Homily still looked blank.

'We've to find some kind of a platform,' announced Pod, 'to set across the top of this musical-box, something we can walk about on . . .' He looked about the room. Under the gas-ring, on which stood the empty glue-pot, was a small oblong of scorched tin, used to protect the boards of the floor. 'That'll do us,' said Pod.

All three were very tired by now, but they managed to slide the strip of tin from below the gas-ring and hoist it across the opened top of the musical-box. From this platform Pod could handle the neck of the balloon and begin to untie the knot. 'You and Arrietty keep your distance,' he advised Homily. 'Better go under the table. No knowing what this balloon might do.'

What it did, when released from the knotted twine, was to sail off sideways into the air and, descending slowly, to bump along the floor. With each bump the smell of gas became stronger. It seemed to Arrietty, as she watched it from under the table, that the balloon was dying in jerks. At last the envelope lay still and empty and Arrietty and Homily emerged from under the table and stood looking down at it with Pod.

'What a day!' said Homily. 'And we've still got to close the window . . .'

'It's been a worth-while day,' said Pod.

But by the time they had gone through the elaborate process of closing up the window and had hidden all traces of the recent experiment below the floorboard, they were utterly worn out. It was not yet dusk before they crept wearily into their blanket-lined box and stretched their aching limbs.

By the time Mr and Mrs Platter brought their supper all three were lost to the world in a deep, exhausted sleep. They did not hear Mrs Platter exclaim because the fire was out. Nor did they see Mr Platter sniffing delicately and peering about the room, and complaining that 'You ought to be more careful, Mabel – there's a wicked smell of gas.'

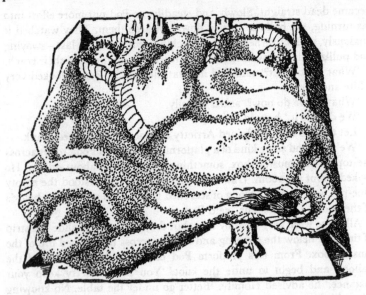

Mrs Platter, very indignant, protested her innocence. 'It was you who lit the gas-fire this morning, Sidney.'

'No, that was yesterday,' he said. And as each knew the other (when caught out in misdoing) to have little regard for truth, they disbelieved each other and came to no conclusion.

'Anyhow,' Mrs Platter summed up at last, 'the weather's too mild now for gas-fires . . .' And they never lit it again.

CHAPTER TWENTY

THE next ten days were confined to serious experiment, controlled and directed by Pod. 'We want to go at it steady now,' he explained. 'Keep to a programme, like, and not try too much at a time. It's a big undertaking, Homily – you don't want to rush it. "Step by step climbs the hill"!'

'But when do they open, Pod?'

'Riverside Teas? April the first, if the cage-house is finished.'

'I'll wager it's finished now. And we're getting well into March . . .'

'You're wrong, Homily. They've not delivered the plate-glass, nor the handle to lift it up with. And something went wrong with the drainage. They had a flood, remember? Didn't you listen when they were talking?'

'Not if they're talking about the cage-house I don't listen,' said Homily. 'It gives me the creeps to hear them. Once they start on about the cage-house, I go right under the blanket.'

During these busy ten days Pod and Arrietty walked about so much on the open pages of the *Illustrated London News* that the print became quite blurred. They had to discard the idea of a valve at the top of the canopy, to be controlled from below by a line which passed through the open neck into the basket because, as Pod explained to Arrietty, of the nature of the canopy. He touched the diagram with his foot. 'With this kind of fabric balloon you *can* have the valve line through the neck . . . but rubber's like elastic, squeezes the gas out . . . we'd all be gassed in less than ten minutes if we left the neck open like they do.'

He was disappointed about this because he had already invented a way to insert a control valve where it should be – in the top of the canopy, and had practised on the smaller balloons, of which they had an endless supply.

In the meantime, as Homily with a needle ground down by Pod worked on the shaping of the net, he and Arrietty studied 'equilibrium and weight disposal'. A series of loops was made in the tow-line on which, once the balloon was inflated, they would hang up various objects – a strawberry basket, the half-shaped net, a couple of keys, a

467

hollow curtain ring, a tear-off roll of one-and-sixpenny entrance tickets to Ballyhoggin, and lastly they would swing on the line themselves. There came a day when they achieved a perfect balance. Half a dozen one-and-sixpenny entrance tickets, torn off by Arrietty, would raise the balloon two feet; and one small luggage key, hooked on by Pod, would bring it down with a bump.

Still, they could find no way of controlling the gas through the neck. They could go up, but not down. Untying what he called 'the guard knot' at the neck – or even loosening the guard knot – would, Pod thought, be a little too risky. The gas might rush out in a burst (as they had seen it do so often by now) and the whole contraption – balloon, basket, ballast and aeronauts – would drop like a stone to the earth. 'We can't risk that, you know,' Pod said to Arrietty. 'What we need is some sort of valve or lever . . .' and for the tenth time that day he climbed back into the tool drawer.

Arrietty joined Homily in her corner by the box to help her with the load-ring. The net was shaping up nicely and Homily, instructed by Pod and Arrietty, had threaded in and made secure the piece of slightly heavier cord which, as it encircled the balloon round its fullest circumference, was suitably called 'the equator'. She was now attaching the load-ring which, when the balloon was netted, would encircle the neck and from which they would hang the basket. They had used the hollow curtain ring, whose weight was now known and tested. 'It's lovely, Mamma! You are clever . . .'

'It's easy,' said Homily, 'once you've got the hang of it. It's no harder than tatting.'

'You've shaped it so beautifully.'

'Well, your father did the calculations . . .'

'I've got it!' cried Pod from the tool drawer. He had been very quiet for a very long while and now emerged slowly with a long cylindrical object almost as tall as himself, which he carefully stowed on the table. 'Or so I believe,' he added, as he climbed up after it by means of the repair kit. In his hand was a small length of fret-saw blade.

Arrietty ran excitedly across the room and swiftly climbed up to join him. The long object turned out to be a topless fountain-pen, with an ink-encrusted nib, one prong of which was broken. Pod had already unscrewed the pen and taken it apart, and the nib end now lay on the table attached to its worm-like rubber tube, with the empty shaft beside it.

'I cut the shaft off here,' said Pod, 'about an inch and a half from the top, just above the filling lever; then I'll cut off the closed end of this inner tube – but right at the end, like – so it sticks out a good inch and a half beyond the cut-off end of the pen casing. May be more. Now' – he went on, speaking cheerfully but rather ponderously, as though giving a lesson (a 'do-it-yourself' lesson, thought Arrietty, remembering the Household Hints section in her Diary and Proverb Book) – 'we screw the whole thing together again and what do we get? We get a capless fountain-pen with the top of its shaft cut off and an extra bit of tube. Do you follow me?'

'So far,' said Arrietty.

'Then,' said Pod, 'we unscrew the nib . . .'

'Can you?' asked Arrietty.

'Of course,' said Pod; 'they're always changing nibs. I'll show you.' He took up the pen and, straddling the shaft, he gripped it firmly between his legs, and taking the nib in both hands, he quickly unscrewed it at chest level. 'Now,' he said as he laid the nib aside, 'we have a circular hole where the nib was – leading straight into the rubber tube. Take a look . . .'

Arrietty peered down the shaft. 'Yes,' she said.

'Well, there you are,' said Pod.

But where? Arrietty wanted to say; instead she said, more politely: 'I don't think I quite . . .'

'Well,' said Pod in a patient voice as though slightly dashed by her slowness, 'we insert the nib end into the neck of the balloon – after inflation of course, and just below the guard knot. We whip it around with a good firm lashing of twine. I take hold of the filling lever and pull it down sideways at right angles to the pen shaft. That's the working position, with the gas safely shut off. We then untie the guard knot. And there we are: with the cut-off pen shaft and rubber tube hanging down into the basket.' He paused. 'Are you with me? Never mind,' he went on confidently, 'you'll see it as I do it. Now' – he drew a long satisfied breath – 'standing in the basket, I reach up my hand to the filling lever and I close it down slowly towards the shaft and the gas flows out through the tube. Feel,' he went on happily, 'the lever's quite loose,' and with one foot on the pen to steady it, he worked the filling lever gently up and down. Arrietty tried it, too. Worn with use, it slid easily.

'Then,' said Pod, 'I raise the lever back up so it stands out again at right angles – and the gas is now shut off.'

'It's wonderful,' said Arrietty, but suddenly she thought of something. 'What about all that gas coming down straight into the basket?'

'We leave it behind!' cried Pod. 'Don't you see, girl – the gas is rising all the time and rising faster than the balloon's descending? I thought of that: that's why I wanted that bit of extra tube; we can turn that tube-end upwards, sideways – where we like; but whichever way we turn it the gas'll be rushing upwards and we'll be dropping away from it. See what I mean? Come to think of it, we could bend the tube upwards to start with and clip it to the shaft of the pen. No reason why not.'

He was silent a moment, think-
ing this over.

'And there won't be all that much gas – not once I've sorted out the lever. You only let it out by degrees . . .'

During the next few days, which were very exciting, Arrietty often thought of Spiller – how deft he would have been at adjusting the net as the envelope filled at the gas-jet. This was Homily's and Arrietty's job – tiresome pullings by hand or with bone crochet-hook, while Pod controlled the intake of gas; the netted canopy would slowly swell above them until the letter 'i' in Riverside Teas had achieved its right propor- tion. The 'equator' of the net, as Pod told them, must bisect the envelope exactly for the load-ring to hang straight and keep the basket level.

Arrietty wished Spiller could have seen the first attachment of the basket by raffia bridles to the load-ring. This took place on the platform of the musical-box, with the basket at this stage weighted down with keys.

And on that first free flight up to the ceiling when Pod, all his attention on the fountain-pen lever, had brought them down so gently, Spiller – Arrietty knew – would have prevented Homily from making the fatal mistake of jumping out of the basket as soon as it touched the floor. At terrifying speed, Pod and Arrietty had shot aloft again, hitting the ceiling with a force which nearly threw them out of the basket, while Homily – in tears – wrung her hands below them. It took a long time to descend, even with the valve wide open, and Pod was very shaken.

'You must remember, Homily,' he told her gravely when, anchored once more to the musical-box, the balloon was slowly deflating, 'you weigh as much as a couple of Gladstone-bag keys and a roll and a half of tickets. No passenger must ever attempt to leave the car or basket until the envelope is completely collapsed.' He looked very serious. 'We were lucky to have a ceiling. Suppose we'd been out of doors – do you know what would have happened?'

'No,' whispered Homily huskily, drying her cheeks with the back of her trembling hand and giving a final sniff.

'Arrietty and me would've shot up to twenty thousand feet and that would have been the end of us . . .'

'Oh dear . . .' muttered Homily.

'At that great height,' said Pod, 'the gas would expand so quickly that it would burst the canopy.' He stared at her accusingly. 'Unless, of course, we'd had the presence of mind to open the valve and keep it open on the whole rush up. Even then, when we did begin to descend, we'd descend too quickly. We'd have to throw everything overboard – ballast, equipment, clothes, food, perhaps even one of the passengers –'

'Oh no!' gasped Homily.

'And in spite of all this,' Pod concluded, 'we'd probably crash just the same!'

Homily remained silent, and after watching her face for a moment, Pod said more gently:

'This isn't a joy-ride, Homily.'

'I know that,' she retorted with feeling.

CHAPTER TWENTY-ONE

BUT it did seem a joy-ride to Arrietty when – on 28th March, having opened the window for the last time and left it open, they drifted slowly out into the pale spring sunshine.

The moment of actual departure had come with a shock of surprise, depending as it did on wind and weather. The night before they had gone to bed as usual, and this morning, before Mabel and Sidney had brought their breakfast, Pod, studying the ilex branch, had announced that this was The Day.

It had seemed quite unreal to Arrietty and it still seemed unreal to her now. Their passage was so dreamlike and silent . . . At one moment they were in the room, which seemed now almost to smell of their captivity, and the next moment – free as thistledown – they sailed softly into a vast ocean of landscape, undulating into distance and brushed with the green veil of spring.

There was a smell of sweet damp earth and for a moment the smell of something frying in Mrs Platter's kitchen. There were myriad tiny sounds – a bicycle bell, the sound of a horse's hoofs and a man's voice growling 'Giddup . . .' Then suddenly they heard Mrs Platter calling to Mr Platter from a window: 'Put on your coat, dear, if you're going to stay out long . . .' And, looking down at the gravel path below them, they saw Mr Platter, tool-bag in hand, on his way to the island. He looked a strange shape from above – head down between his shoulders and feet twinkling in and out as he hurried towards his objective.

'He's going to work on the cage-house,' said Homily.

They saw with a kind of distant curiosity the whole layout of Mr Platter's model village, and the river twisting away beyond it to the three distant poplars which marked what Pod now referred to as their L.Z.[1]

During the last few days he had taken to using abbreviations of ballooning terms, referring to the musical-box as the T.O.P.[2] They were now, with the gleaming slates of roof just below them, feeling their way towards a convenient C.A.[3]

1. Landing Zone.   2. Take-off Point.   3. Chosen Altitude.

Strangely enough, after their many trial trips up and down from the ceiling, the basket felt quite home-like and familiar. Arrietty, whose job was 'ballast', glanced at her father, who stood looking rapt and interested – but not too preoccupied – with his hand on the lever of the cut-off fountain-pen. Homily, although a little pale, was matter-of-factly adjusting the coiled line of the grapnel, one spike of which had slid below the level of the basket. 'Might just catch in something,' she murmured. The grapnel consisted of two large open safety-pins, securely wired back to back. Pod, who for days had been studying the trend of the ilex leaves, remarked: 'Wind's all right but not enough of it . . .' as very gently, as though waltzing, they twisted above the roof. Pod, looking ahead, had his eye on the ilex.

'A couple of tickets now, Arrietty,' he said; 'takes a few minutes to feel the effect . . .'

She tore them off and dropped them overboard. They fluttered gently and ran a little on the slates of the roof and then lay still.

'Let's give her two more,' said Pod. And within a few seconds, staring at the ilex tree as slowly it loomed nearer, he added: 'Better make it three . . .'

'We've had six shillings' worth already,' Arrietty protested.

'All right,' said Pod, as the balloon began to lift, 'let's leave it at that.'

'But I've done it now,' she said.

They sailed over the ilex tree with plenty of height to spare and the balloon still went on rising. Homily gazed down as the ground receded.

'Careful, Pod,' she said.

'It's all right,' he told them, 'I'm bringing her down.' And in spite of the upturned tube they smelled a slight smell of gas.

Even from this height the noises were quite distinct. They heard Mr Platter hammering at the cage-house and, although the railway looked so distant, the sound of a shunting train. As they swept down rather faster than Pod had bargained for, they found themselves carried beyond the confines of Mr Platter's garden and drifting – on a descending spiral – above the main road. A farm cart crawled slowly beneath them on the broad sunlit stretch which, curving ribbon-like into the distance, looked frayed along one side by the shadows thrown from the hedges and from the spindly wayside woods. There was a woman on the shafts of the farm cart and a man asleep in the back.

'We're heading away from our L.Z.' said Pod. 'Better give her three more tickets – there's less wind down here than above . . .'

As the balloon began to lift they passed over one of Mr Platter's

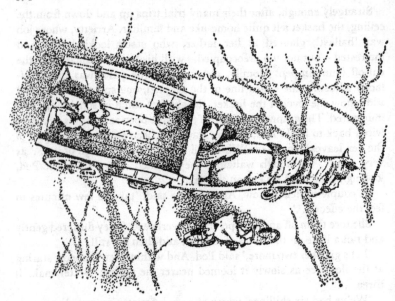

lately built villas in which someone was practising the piano – a stream
of metallic notes flowed up and about them. And a dog began to bark.

They began to rise quite swiftly – on the three legitimate tickets – and
an extra one-and-sixpenny-worth thrown down by Arrietty. She did it
on an impulse and knew at once that it was wrong. Their very lives
depended on obedience to the pilot, and how could the pilot navigate
if she cheated on commands? She felt very guilty as the balloon
continued to rise. They were passing over a field of cows which, second
by second, as she stared down at them, were becoming steadily smaller;
all the same, a tremulous 'Moo' surged up to them through the quiet
air and eddied about their ears. She could hear a lark singing – and
over a spreading cherry orchard she smelled the sticky scent of sun-
warmed buds and blossoms. 'It's more like mid April,' Arrietty thought,
'than the 28th of March.'

'Spiller would have liked this,' she said aloud.

'Maybe,' said Homily rather grimly.

'When I grow up I think I'll marry Spiller . . .'

'Spiller!' exclaimed Homily in an astounded voice.

'What's wrong with him?' asked Arrietty.

'There's nothing exactly wrong with him,' admitted Homily grudgingly. 'I mean if you tidied him up a bit . . . But where do you imagine you'd live? He's always on the move.'

'I'd be on the move too,' said Arrietty.

Homily stared at her. 'Whatever will you think of to say next? And what a place to choose to say it in. Marry Spiller! Did you hear that, Pod?'

'Yes, I heard,' he said.

The balloon was still rising.

'He likes the out-of-doors, you see,' said Arrietty, 'and I like it, too.'

'Marry *Spiller* . . .' Homily repeated to herself – she could not get over it.

'And if we were always on the move, we'd be freer to come and see you more often . . .'

'So it's got to "we"!' said Homily.

'. . . and I couldn't do that,' Arrietty went on, 'if I married into a family with a set house the other side of Bedfordshire –'

'But you're only sixteen!' exclaimed Homily.

'Seventeen – nearly,' said Arrietty. She was silent a moment and then she said, 'I think I ought to tell him –'

'Pod!' exclaimed Homily, 'do you hear? It must be the height or something, but this child's gone out of her senses!'

'I'm trying to find the wind,' said Pod, staring steadily upwards to where a slight film of mist appeared to drift towards the sun.

'You see,' Arrietty went on quietly (she had been thinking of her talks with Miss Menzies and of those blue eyes full of tears), 'he's so shy and he goes about so much, he might never think of asking me. And one day he might get tired of being lonely and marry some' – Arrietty hesitated – 'some *terribly nice* kind of borrower with very fat legs . . .'

'There isn't such a thing as a borrower with fat legs,' exclaimed Homily, 'except perhaps your Aunt Lupy. Not that I've actually ever seen her legs . . .' she added thoughtfully, gazing upwards as though following the direction of Pod's eyes. Then she snapped back again to the subject. 'What nonsense you do talk, Arrietty,' she said. 'I can't imagine what sort of rubbish you must have been reading in that *Illustrated London News*. Why, you and Spiller are more like brother and sister!'

Arrietty was just about going to say – but she couldn't quite find the words – that this seemed quite a good kind of trial run for what was after all a lifelong companionship, when something came between them and the sun and a sudden chill struck the basket. The top of the envelope had melted into mist and the earth below them disappeared from sight.

They stared at each other. Nothing else existed now except the familiar juice-stained basket, hung in a limbo of whiteness, and their three rather frightened selves.

'It's all right,' said Pod, 'we're in a cloud. I'll let out a little gas . . .'

They were silent while he did so, staring intently at his steady hand on the lever – it hardly seemed to move.

'Not too much,' he explained in a quiet conversational voice. 'The condensation on the net will help us: there's a lot of weight in water. And I think we've found the wind!'

CHAPTER TWENTY-TWO

THEY were in sunshine again quite suddenly and cruising smoothly and softly on a gentle breeze towards their still distant L.Z.

'Shouldn't wonder,' remarked Pod cheerfully, 'if we hadn't hit on our right C.A. at last.'

Homily shivered. 'I didn't like that at all.'

'Nor did I,' agreed Arrietty. There was no sense of wind in the basket and she turned up her face to the sun, basking gratefully in the suddenly restored warmth.

They passed over a group of cottages set about a small, squat church. Three people with baskets were grouped about a shop, and they heard a sudden peal of very hearty laughter. In a back garden they saw a

woman with her back to them, hanging washing on a line; it hung quite limply.

'Not much wind down there,' remarked Pod.

'Nor all that much up here,' retorted Homily.

They stared down in silence for a while.

'I wonder why no one ever looks up,' Arrietty exclaimed suddenly.

'Human beings don't look up much,' said Pod. 'Too full of their own concerns.' He thought a moment. 'Unless, maybe, they hear a sudden loud noise . . . or see a flash or something. They don't have to keep their eyes open like borrowers do.'

'Or birds,' said Arrietty, 'or mice . . .'

'Or anything that's hunted,' said Pod.

'Isn't there anything that hunts human beings?' Arrietty asked.

'Not that I know of,' said Pod. 'Might do 'em a bit of good if there was. Show 'em what it feels like, for once.' He was silent a moment and then said: 'Some say they hunt each other –'

'Oh no!' exclaimed Homily, shocked. (Strictly brought up in the borrowers' code of one-for-all and all-for-one, it was as though he had accused the human race of cannibalism.) 'You shouldn't say such things, Pod – no kind of creature could be as bad as that!'

'I've heard it said!' he persisted stolidly. 'Sometimes singly and sometimes one lot against another lot!'

'All of them human beings?' Homily exclaimed incredulously.

Pod nodded. 'Yes,' he said, 'all of them human beings.'

Horrified but fascinated, Homily stared down below at a man on a bicycle, as though unable to grasp such depravity. He looked quite ordinary – almost like a borrower from here – and wobbled slightly on the lower slopes of what appeared to be a hill. She stared incredulously until the rider turned into the lower gate of the churchyard.

There was a sudden smell of Irish stew, followed by a whiff of coffee.

'Must be getting on for midday,' said Pod, and as he spoke the church clock struck twelve.

'I don't like these eddies,' said Pod some time later, as the balloon once again on a downward spiral curved away from the river; 'something to do with the ground warming up and that bit of hill over there.'

'Would anybody like something to eat?' suggested Homily suddenly. There were slivers of ham, a crumbly knob of cheese, a few grains of cold rice pudding and a long segment of orange on which to quench their thirst.

'Better wait awhile,' said Pod, his hand on the valve. The balloon was moving downwards.

'I don't see why,' said Homily; 'it must be long past one.'

'I know,' said Pod, 'but it's better we hold off, if we can. We may have to jettison the rations, and you can't do that once you've eaten them.'

'I don't know what you mean,' complained Homily.

'Throw the food overboard,' explained Arrietty, who, on Pod's orders, had torn off several more tickets.

'You see,' said Pod, 'what with one thing and another, I've let out a good deal of gas.'

Homily was silent. After a while she said: 'I don't like the way we keep turning round; first the church is on our right, the next it's run round to the left. I mean, you don't know where you are, not for two minutes together.'

'It'll be all right,' said Pod, 'once we've hit the wind. Let go another two,' he added to Arrietty.

It was just enough; they rose gently and, held on a steady current, moved slowly towards the stream.

'Now,' said Pod, 'if we keep on this, we're all right.' He stared ahead to where, speckled by the sunshine, the poplar trees loomed nearer. 'We're going nicely now.'

'You mean we might hit Little Fordham?'

'Not unlikely,' said Pod.

'If you ask me,' exclaimed Homily, screwing her eyes against the afternoon sun, 'the whole thing's hit or miss!'

'Not altogether,' said Pod, and he let out a little more gas. 'We bring her down slowly, gradually losing altitude. Once we're in reach of the ground we steady her with the trail rope. Acts like a kind of brake. And directly I give her the word, Arrietty releases the grapnel.'

Homily was silent again. Impressed, but still rather anxious, she stared steadily ahead. The river swam gently towards them until and at last it came directly below. The light wind seemed to follow the river's course as it curved ahead into distance. The poplars now seemed to beckon as they swayed and stirred in the breeze, and their long shadows – even longer by now – were stretching directly towards them. They sailed as though drawn on a string.

Pod let out more gas. 'Better uncoil the trail rope,' he said to Arrietty.

'Already?'

'Yes,' said Pod, 'you got to be prepared . . .'

The ground swayed slowly up towards them. A clump of oak trees seemed to move aside and they saw just ahead and slightly tilted a bird's eye view of their long lost Little Fordham.

'You wouldn't credit it!' breathed Homily as, enraptured, they stared ahead.

They could see the railway lines glinting in the sunshine, the weathercock flashing on the church steeple, the uneven roofs along the narrow High Street and the crooked chimney of their own dear home. They saw the garden front of Mr Pott's thatched cottage, and beyond the dark green of the holly hedge a stretch of sunlit lane. A tweed-clad figure strode along it, in a loose-limbed, youthful way. They knew it was Miss Menzies – going home to tea. And Mr Pott, thought Arrietty, would have gone inside for his.

The balloon was sinking fast.

'Careful, Pod!' urged Homily, 'or you'll have us in the river!'

As swiftly the balloon sank down, a veil-like something suddenly appeared along the edge of the garden. As they swam down they saw it to be a line of strong wire fencing girding the bank of the river. Mr Pott had taken precautions and his treasures were now caged in.

'Time, too!' said Homily grimly. Then suddenly she shrieked and clung to the sides of the basket as the stream rushed up towards them.

'Get ready the grapnel!' shouted Pod. But even as he spoke the basket had hit the water and, tilted sideways in a flurry of spray, they were dragged along the surface. All three were thrown off balance and, knee-deep in rushing water, they clung to raffia bridles while the envelope surged on ahead. Pod just managed to close the valve as Arrietty, clinging on with one hand, tried with the other to free the grapnel. But Homily, in a panic and before anyone could stop her, threw out the knob of cheese. The balloon shot violently upwards, accompanied by Homily's screams, and then – just as violently – snapped back to a sickening halt. The roll of tickets shot up between them and sailed down into the water. Except for their grasp on the bridles the occupants would have followed; they were thrown up into the air, where they hung for a moment before tumbling back into the basket: a safety-pin of the grapnel had caught in the wire of the fence. The trembling, creakings, twistings and strainings seemed enough to uproot the fence, and Pod, looking downwards as he clung to the re-opened valve lever, saw the barb of the safety-pin slide.

'That won't hold for long,' he gasped.

The quivering basket was held at a terrifying tilt – almost pulled

apart, it seemed, between the force of the upward surge and the drag of the grapnel below. The gas was escaping too slowly – it was clearly a race against time.

There was a steady stream of water from the dripping basket. Their three backs were braced against the tilted floor and their feet against one side. As, white-faced, they all stared downwards they could hear each other's breathing. The angle of the opened pin was slowly growing wider.

Pod took a sudden resolve. 'Get hold of the trail rope,' he said to Arrietty, 'and pass it over to me. I'm going down the grapnel-line and taking the trail rope with me.'

'Oh, Pod!' cried Homily miserably, 'suppose we shot up without you!'

He took no notice. 'Quick!' he urged. And, as Arrietty pulled up the length of dripping twine, he took one end in his hand and swung over the edge of the basket on to the line of the grapnel. He slid away below them in one swift downward run, his elbow encircling the trail rope. They watched him steady himself on the top of the fence and climb down a couple of meshes. They watched his swift one-handed movements as he passed the trail rope through the mesh and made fast with a double turn.

Then his small square face turned up towards them.

'Get a hold on the bridles,' he called, 'there's going to be a bit of a jerk . . .' He shifted himself a few meshes sideways, from where he could watch the pin.

It slid free with a metallic ping, even sooner than they had expected, and was flung out in a quivering arch which, whiplike, thrashed the air. The balloon shot up in a frenzied leap but was held by the knotted twine. It seemed frustrated as it strained above them, as though striving to tear itself free. Arrietty and Homily clung together, half laughing and half crying, in a wild access of relief. He had moored them just in time.

'You'll be all right now,' Pod called up cheerfully; 'nothing to do but wait,' and after staring a moment reflectively, he began to climb down the fence.

'Where are you going, Pod?' Homily cried out shrilly.

He paused and looked up again. 'Thought I'd take a look at the house – our chimney's smoking, seems like there's someone inside.'

'But what about us?' cried Homily.

'You'll come down slowly, as the envelope deflates, and then you can climb down the fence. I'll be back,' he added.

'Of all the things,' exclaimed Homily, 'to go away and leave us!'

'What do you want me to do?' asked Pod. 'Just stand down below and watch? I won't be long and – say it's Spiller – he's likely to give us a hand. You're all right,' he went on. 'Take a pull on the trail rope as the balloon comes down, that'll bring you alongside.'

'Of all the things!' exclaimed Homily again incredulously, as Pod went on climbing down.

CHAPTER TWENTY-THREE

THE door of Vine Cottage was unlocked and Pod pushed it open. A fire was burning in an unfamiliar grate and Spiller lay asleep on the floor. As Pod entered he scrambled to his feet. They stared at each other. Spiller's pointed face looked tired and his eyes a little sunken.

Pod smiled slowly. 'Hallo,' he said.

'Hallo,' said Spiller, and without any change of expression he stooped and picked some nutshells from the floor and threw them on to the fire. It was a new floor, Pod noticed, of honey-coloured wood, with a woven mat beside the fireplace.

'Been away quite a while,' remarked Spiller casually, staring at the blaze. The changed fireplace, Pod noticed, now incorporated a small iron cooking-stove.

'Yes,' he said, looking about the room, 'we've been all winter in an attic.'

Spiller nodded.

'*You* know,' said Pod, 'a room at the top of a human house.'

Spiller nodded again and kicked a piece of fallen nutshell back into the grate. It flared up brightly with a cheerful crackle.

'We couldn't get out,' said Pod.

'Ah,' said Spiller non-committally.

'So we made a balloon,' went on Pod, 'and we sailed it out of the window.' Spiller looked up sharply, suddenly alert. 'Arrietty and Homily are in it now. It's caught on the wire fence.'

Spiller's puzzled glance darted towards the window and as swiftly darted away again: the fence was not visible from here.

'Some kind of boat?' he said at last.

'In a manner of speaking,' Pod smiled. 'Care to see it?' he added carelessly.

Something flashed in Spiller's face – a spark which was swiftly quenched. 'Might as well,' he conceded.

'May interest you,' said Pod, a note of pride in his voice. He glanced once more about the room.

'They've done the house up,' he remarked.

Spiller nodded. 'Running water and all . . .'

'Running water!' exclaimed Pod.

'That's right,' said Spiller, edging towards the door.

Pod stared at the piping above the sink but he made no move to inspect it. Tables and floor were strewn with Spiller's borrowings: sparrows' eggs and eggshells, nuts, grain and, laid out on a dandelion leaf, six rather shrivelled smoked minnows.

'Been staying here?' he said.

'On and off,' said Spiller, teetering on the threshold.

Again Pod's eyes travelled about the room: the general style of it emerged, in spite of Spiller's clutter – plain chairs, scrubbable tables, wooden dresser, painted plates, hand-woven rugs, all very Rossetti-ish and practical.

'Smells of humans,' he remarked.

'Does a bit,' agreed Spiller.

'We might just tidy round,' Pod suggested 'wouldn't take us a minute.' As though in apology, he added: 'It's first impressions with her, if you get my meaning. Always has been. And –' he broke off abruptly as a sharp sound split the silence.

'What's that?' said Spiller, as eye met startled eye.

'It's the balloon,' cried Pod, and, suddenly white-faced, he stared in a stunned way at the window. 'They've burst it,' he exclaimed and, pushing past Spiller, he dashed out through the door.

Homily and Arrietty, shaken but unharmed, were clinging to the wires. The basket dangled emptily and the envelope, in tatters, seemed threaded into the fence; the net now looked like a bird's nest.

'We got it down lovely,' Pod heard Homily gasping, as hand over hand, he and Spiller climbed up the mesh of the fence.

'Stay where you are,' Pod called out.

'Came down like a dream, Pod,' Homily kept on crying. 'Came down like a bird . . .'

'All right,' called Pod, 'just you stay quiet where you are.'

'Then the wind changed,' persisted Homily, half sobbing but still at the top of her voice, 'and swung us round sideways . . . against that jagged wire . . . But she came down lovely, Pod, light as thistledown. Didn't she, Arrietty?'

But Arrietty, too proud to be rescued, was well on her way to the ground. Spiller climbed swiftly towards her and they met in a circle of mesh. 'You're on the wrong side,' said Spiller.

'I know, I can soon climb through.' There were tears in her eyes, her cheeks were crimson and her hair blew about in wisps.

'Like a hand?' said Spiller.

'No, thank you. I'm quite all right,' and avoiding his curious gaze, she hurriedly went on down. 'How stupid, how stupid,' she exclaimed aloud when she felt herself out of earshot. She was almost in tears: it should never have been like this: he would never understand the balloon without having seen it inflated, and mere words could never make clear all they had gone through to make it and the extent of their dizzy success. There was nothing to show for this now but a stained old strawberry basket, some shreds of shrivelled rubber and a tangled bunch of string. A few moments earlier she and her mother had been bringing it down so beautifully. After the first flurry of panic Homily had had one of her sudden calms. Perhaps it was the realization of being home again; the sight of their unchanged village at peace in the afternoon light; and the filament of smoke which rose up unexpectedly from the chimney of Vine Cottage, a drifting pennant of welcome which showed the house was inhabited and that the fire had only just been lit. Not lit by Miss Menzies, who had long since passed out of sight; nor Pod, who had not yet reached the house, so they guessed it must be Spiller. They had suddenly felt among friends again and, proud of their great achievement, they had longed to show off their prowess. In a business-like manner they had coiled up the ropes, stacked the tackle and made the basket shipshape. They had wrung out their wet clothes and Homily had redone her hair. Then, methodically and calmly, they had set to work, following Pod's instructions.

'It's too bad,' Arrietty exclaimed, looking upwards, as she reached the last rung of the wire: there was her father helping Homily with footholds, and Spiller of course at the top of the fence busily engaged in examining the wreckage. Very dispirited, she stepped off the wire, drew down a plantain leaf by its tip, and flinging herself along its springy length she lay there glumly, staring upwards, her hands behind her head.

Homily too seemed very upset when, steered by Pod, she eventually reached the ground. 'It was nothing we did,' she kept saying, 'it was just a change of wind.'

'I know, I know,' he consoled her; 'forget it now – it served its purpose and there's a surprise for you up at the house. You and Arrietty go on ahead while Spiller and I do the salvage . . .'

When Homily saw the house she became a different creature: it was as though, thought Arrietty, watching her mother's expression, Homily had walked into paradise. There were a few stunned moments of quiet incredulous joy before excitement broke loose and she ran like a mad thing from room to room, exploring, touching, adjusting and endlessly exclaiming. 'They've divided the upstairs into two, there's a little room for you, Arrietty. Look at this sink, I ask you, Arrietty! Water in the tap and all! And what's that thing on the ceiling?'

'It's a bulb from a hand torch of some kind,' said Arrietty, after a moment's study. And beside the back door, in a kind of lean-to shed, they found the great square battery.

'So we've got electric light . . .' breathed Homily, slowly backing away, 'better not touch it,' she went on, in an awestruck and frightened voice, 'until your father comes. Now help me clear up Spiller's clobber,' she continued excitedly; 'I pity any unfortunate creature who ever keeps house for *him* . . .' But her eyes were alight and shining. She hung up her new dress beside the fire to dry and, delighted to find them again, she changed into old clothes. Arrietty, who for some reason still felt dispirited, found she had grown out of hers.

'I look ridiculous in this,' she said unhappily, trying to pull down her jersey.

'Well, who's to see you,' Homily retorted, 'except your father and Spiller?'

Panting and straining, she worked away, clearing and stacking and altering the positions of the furniture. Soon nothing was where it had been originally and the room looked rather odd.

'You can't do *much* with a kitchen–living room,' Homily remarked when, panting a little, she surveyed the general post, 'and I'm still not sure about that dresser.'

'What about it?' said Arrietty, who was longing to sit down.

'That it wouldn't be better where it was.'

'Can't we leave the men to do it?' said Arrietty. 'They'll be back soon – for supper.'

'That's just the point,' said Homily. 'If we move it at all we must do it now, before I start on the cooking. It looks dreadful there,' she went on crossly. 'Spoils the whole look of the room. Now come on, Arrietty – it won't take us a minute.'

With the dresser back in its old position the other things looked out of place. 'Now that table could go here,' Homily suggested, 'if we move this chest of drawers. You take one end, Arrietty . . .'

There were several more reshuffles before she seemed content. 'A lot of trouble,' she admitted happily, as she surveyed the final result, 'but worth it in the end. It looks a lot better now, doesn't it, Arrietty? It suddenly looks kind of *right*.'

'Yes,' said Arrietty dryly, 'because everything's back where it was.'

'What do you mean?' exclaimed Homily.

'Where it was before we started,' said Arrietty.

'Nonsense,' snapped Homily crossly, but she looked about her uncertainly. 'Why – that stool was under the window! But we can't waste time arguing now: those men will be back any moment and I haven't started the soup. Run down to the stream now, there's a good girl, and get me a few leaves of watercress . . .'

CHAPTER TWENTY-FOUR

LATER that night when – having eaten and cleared away – the four of them sat round the fire, Arrietty began to feel a little annoyed with Spiller. Balloon crazy – that's what he seemed to have become; and all within a few short hours. No eyes, no ears, nor thoughts for anyone or anything except for those boring shreds of shrivelled rubber, now safely stored with the other trappings in the back of the village shop. He had listened, of course, at supper when Arrietty, hoping to interest him, had tried to recount their adventures, but if she paused even for a moment the bright dark glance would fly again to Pod and again, in his tense, dry way he would ply Pod with questions: 'Oiled silk instead of rubber next time for the canopy? The silk would be easy to borrow – and Mr Pott would have the oil . . .' Questions on wind velocity, trail ropes, moorings, grapnels, inflation – there seemed no end to these nor to his curiosity which, for some masculine reason Arrietty could not fathom, could only be satisfied by Pod. Any timid contribution on the part of Arrietty seemed to slide across his mind unheard. 'And I know as much about it as anybody,' she told herself crossly, as she huddled in the shadows. 'More in fact. It was I who had to teach Papa.' She stared in a bored way about the firelit room: the drawn curtains, plates glinting on the dresser, the general air of peace and comfort. Even this, in a way, they owed entirely to her: it was she who had had the courage to speak to Miss Menzies – and, in the course of this friendship, describe their habits and needs. How cosy they all looked in their ignorance, sitting smugly around the fire. Leaning forward suddenly, right into the firelight, she said: 'Papa, would you listen, please?'

'Don't see why not,' replied Pod, smiling slightly at the eager, firelit face and the breathless tone of her voice.

'It's something I've got to tell you. I couldn't once. But I can now . . .' As she spoke her heart began to beat a little faster: even Spiller, she saw, was paying attention. 'It's about this house; it's about why they made these things for us; it's about how they knew what we wanted . . .'

'What *we* wanted . . .?' repeated Pod.

'Yes, or why do you think they did it?'

Pod took his time. 'I wouldn't know for *why* they did it,' he said at last, 'any more than I'd know for *why* they built that church or the railway. Reckon they're refurnishing all these houses . . . one by one, like.'

'No,' exclaimed Arrietty, and her voice trembled slightly, 'you're wrong, Papa. They've only furnished one house and that's our house – because they know all about us and they like us and they want us to stay here!'

There was a short, stunned silence. Then Homily muttered: 'Oh, my goodness . . .' under her breath.

Spiller, still as stone, stared unblinkingly, and Pod said slowly: 'Explain what you mean, Arrietty. How do they know about us?'

'I told her,' said Arrietty.

'Her-r?' repeated Pod slowly, rolling his r-rs in the country way, his custom when deeply moved.

'Miss Menzies,' said Arrietty; 'the tall one with the long hands, who hid behind the thistle.'

'Oh, my goodness . . .' muttered Homily again.

'It's all right, Mother,' Arrietty assured her earnestly. 'There's nothing to be frightened of. You'll be safe here, safer than you've ever been – in the whole of all your life. They'll look after us, and protect us and take care of us – for ever and ever and ever. She promised me.'

Homily, though trembling, looked slightly reassured.

'What does your father think?' she asked faintly, and stared across at Pod. Arrietty too wheeled round towards him. 'Don't say anything, Papa, not yet, please . . . please! Not until I've told you everything, then' – at the sight of his expression she lost her nerve, and finished lamely – 'then you're practically sure to see.'

'See what?' said Pod.

'That it's quite all right.'

'Go on, then,' he said.

Hurriedly, almost pleadingly, Arrietty gave them the facts. She described her friendship with Miss Menzies right from the very beginning. She described Miss Menzies's character, her loyalty, her charity, her gifts, her imagination and her courage. She even told them about dear Gadstone and about Aubrey, Miss Menzies's 'best friend' (Homily shook her head there, and clicked her tongue. 'Sad when that happens,' she said musingly. 'It was like that with my younger sister, Milligram; Milli never married neither. She took to collecting dead flies' wings, making them into fans and suchlike. And pretty they looked, in certain lights, all colours of the rainbow . . .'), and went on to describe all she had learned from Miss Menzies concerning Mr Pott: how kind he was, and how gentle, and so skilled in making-do and invention that he might be a borrower himself.

'That's right,' Spiller said suddenly at this juncture. He spoke so feelingly that Arrietty, looking across at him, felt something stir in her memory.

'Was *he* the borrower you once told us about – the one you said lived here alone?'

Spiller smiled slyly. 'That's right,' he admitted; 'learn a lot from him, *any* borrower could.'

'Not when everything's laid on,' said Pod, 'and there's nothing left to borrow. Go on, Arrietty,' he said, as she suddenly seemed lost in thought.

'Well, that's all. At least all I can think of now.

'It's enough,' said Pod. He stared across at her, his arms folded, his expression very grave. 'You shouldn't have done it,' he said quietly, 'no matter what it's given us.'

'Listen, Pod,' Homily put in quickly, 'she has done it and she can't undo it now, however much you scold her. I mean' – she glanced about the firelit room, at the winking plates on the dresser, the tap above the sink, the unlit globe in the ceiling – 'we've a lot to be thankful for.'

'It all smells of humans,' said Pod.

'That'll wear off, Pod.'

'Will it?' he said.

Arrietty, suddenly out of patience, jumped up from her stool by the fire. 'I just don't know what any of you do want,' she exclaimed unhappily. 'I thought you might be pleased or proud of me or something. Mother's always longed for a house like this!' and fumbling at the latch, she opened the door, and ran out into the moonlight.

There was silence in the room after she had gone. No one moved until a stool squeaked slightly, as Spiller rose to his feet.

'Where are you off to?' asked Pod casually.

'Just to take a look at my moorings.'

'But you'll come back here to sleep?' said Homily; very hospitable, she felt suddenly, surrounded by new-found amenities.

'Thanks,' said Spiller.

'I'll come with you,' said Pod.

'No need,' said Spiller.

'I'd like the air,' said Pod.

Arrietty, in the shadow of the house, saw them go by in the moonlight.
As they passed out of sight, into darkness, she heard her father say:
'. . . depends how you look at it.' Look at what, she wondered? Suddenly
Arrietty felt left out of things: her father and mother had their house,
Spiller had his boat, Miss Menzies had Mr Pott and his village, Mr
Pott had Miss Menzies and his railway, but what was left for her? She
reached out and took hold of a dandelion stalk the size of a lamp-post
which had grown beside the house to the height of her bedroom window.
On a sudden impulse she snapped the stalk in half: the silver seeds
scattered madly into the moonlight and the juice ran out on her hands.
For a moment she stood there watching until the silky spikes, righting
themselves, had floated into darkness, and then, suddenly feeling cold,
she turned and went inside.

Homily still sat where they had left her, dreaming by the fire. But
she had swept the hearth and lighted a dip, which shed its glow
from the table. Arrietty, with a sudden pang, saw her mother's deep
content.

'Would you like to live here always?' she asked as she drew up a stool
to the fire.

'Yes,' said Homily, 'now we've got it comfortable. Why? Wouldn't
you?'

'I don't know,' said Arrietty. 'All those people in the summer. All the dust and noise . . .'

'Yes,' said Homily, 'you've got to keep on sweeping. But there's always something,' she added, 'and at least we've got running water.'

'And being cooped up during visiting hours . . .'

'I don't mind that,' said Homily; 'there's plenty to do in the house and I've been cooped up all my life. That's your lot, like, say you're born a borrower.'

Arrietty was silent a moment. 'It would never be Spiller's lot,' she said at last.

'Oh, him!' exclaimed Homily impatiently. 'I've never known nothing about those out-of-door ones. A race apart, my father used to say. Or house-borrowers just gone wild . . .'

'Where have they gone?'

'They're all over the place, I shouldn't wonder, hidden away in the rabbit holes and hedges.'

'I mean my father and Spiller.'

'Oh, them. Down to the stream to see to his moorings. And if I was you, Arrietty,' Homily went on more earnestly, 'I'd get to bed before your father comes in – your bed's all ready, new sheets and everything, *and*' – her voice almost broke with pride – 'under the quilt, there's a little silken eiderdown!'

'They're coming now,' said Arrietty. 'I can hear them.'

'Well, just say good night and run off,' urged Homily anxiously. As the latch clicked she dropped her voice to a whisper: 'I think you've upset him a bit with that talk about Miss – Miss –'

'Menzies,' said Arrietty.

CHAPTER TWENTY-FIVE

THERE was a strange aura about Pod when he entered the room with
Spiller: it was more than a night-breath of leaves and grasses and a
moon-cold tang of water; it was a strength and a stillness, Arrietty
thought when she went to kiss him good night, but he seemed very far
away. He received her kiss without a word and mechanically pecked at
her ear but, as she went off towards the stairs, he suddenly called her
back.

'Just a minute, Arrietty. Sit down, Spiller,' he said. He drew up a
chair and once more they encircled the fire.

'What's the matter, Pod?' asked Homily. She put out a nervous arm
and drew Arrietty close beside her. 'Is it something you've seen?'

'I haven't seen nothing,' said Pod, 'only moon on the water, a couple
of bats and this telltale smoke from our chimney.'

'Then let the child go to bed, it's been a long day.'

'I been thinking,' said Pod.

'It seems more like two days,' Homily went on, 'I mean, now you
begin to look back on it.' And suddenly, incredibly, it seemed to her,
that on this very morning they had wakened still as prisoners and here
they were – home again and united about a hearth! Not the same
hearth, a better hearth and a home beyond their dreams. 'You take the

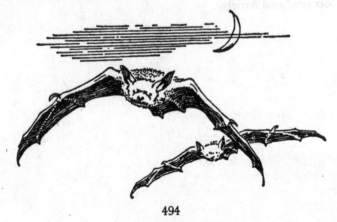

494

dip now,' she said to Arrietty, 'and get yourself into bed. Spiller can sleep down here. Take a drop of water up if you like to have a wash: there's plenty in the tap –'

'It won't do,' said Pod suddenly.

They all turned and looked at him. 'What won't do?' faltered Homily.

Pod waved an arm. 'All this. None of it will do. Not one bit of it. And Spiller agrees with me.'

Arrietty's glance flew across to Spiller: she noticed the closed look, the set gleam and the curt, unsmiling nod.

'What could you be meaning, Pod?' Homily moistened her lips. 'You couldn't be meaning this house?'

'That's just what I do mean,' said Pod.

'But you haven't really seen it, Pod,' Homily protested. 'You've never tried the switch, yet. Nor the tap either. You haven't even seen upstairs. You should see what they've done at the top of the landing, how Arrietty's room opens out of ours, like –'

'Wouldn't make no difference,' said Pod.

'But you liked it here, Pod,' Homily reminded him, 'before that attic lot took us away. You was whistling again and singing as you worked, like you did in the old days at Firbank. Wasn't he, Arrietty?'

'I didn't know then,' said Pod, 'the thing that we all know now – that these humans knew we was here.'

'I see,' said Homily unhappily, and stared into the fire. Arrietty, looking down at her, saw Homily's hunched shoulders and the sudden empty look of her loosely hanging hands.

She turned again to her father. 'These ones are different,' she assured him; 'they're not like Mabel and Sidney: they're tame, you see. I tamed Miss Menzies myself.'

'They're never tamed,' said Pod. 'One day they'll break out – one day, when you least expect it.'

'Not Miss Menzies,' protested Arrietty loyally.

Pod leaned forward. 'They don't mean it,' he explained, 'they just does it. It isn't their fault. In that they're pretty much like the rest of us: none of us means harm – we just does it.'

'You never did no harm, Pod,' protested Homily warmly.

'Not knowingly,' he conceded. He looked across at his daughter. 'Nor did Arrietty mean harm when she spoke to this Miss. But she did harm – she kept us deceived, like: she saw us planning away and not knowing – working away in our ignorance. And it didn't make her happy; now, did it, lass?'

'No,' Arrietty admitted, 'but all the same –'

'All right, all right,' Pod interrupted; he spoke quietly and still without reproach. 'I see how it was.' He sighed, and looked down at his hands.

'And she saw us, before we saw her,' Arrietty pointed out.

'I'd seen her,' said Pod.

'But you didn't know that she'd seen you.'

'You could have told me,' said Pod. He spoke so gently that the tears welled up in Arrietty's eyes. 'I'm sorry,' she gasped.

He did not speak for a moment and then he said: 'I'd have planned different, you see.'

'It wasn't Miss Menzies's fault that Mabel and Sidney took us.'

'I know that,' said Pod, 'but knowing different, I'd have planned different. We'd have been gone by then, and safely hidden away.'

'Gone? Where to?' exclaimed Homily.

'Plenty of places,' said Pod. 'Spiller knows of a mill – not far from here, is it, Spiller? – with one human. Never sees a soul except for flour carters. And short-sighted at that. That's more the place for us, Homily.'

Homily was silent: she seemed to be thinking hard. Although her hands were gripped in her lap, her shoulders had straightened again.

'She loves us,' said Arrietty. 'Miss Menzies really loves us, Papa.'

He sighed. 'I don't see for why. But maybe she does. Like they do their pets – their cats and dogs and birds and such. Like your cousin Eggletina had that baby mouse, bringing it up by hand, teaching it tricks and such, and rubbing its coat up with velvet. But it ran away in the end, back to the other mice. And your Uncle Hendreary's second boy once had a cockroach. Fat as butter, it grew, in a cage he made out of a tea-strainer. But your mother never thought it was happy. Never a hungry moment that cockroach had, but that strainer was still a cage.'

'I see what you mean,' said Arrietty uncertainly.

'Spiller sees,' said Pod.

Arrietty glanced across at Spiller: the pointed face was still but the eyes were wild and bright. So wildly bright, they seemed to Arrietty, that she quickly looked away.

'You wouldn't see Spiller in a house like this,' said Pod, 'with everything all done for him and a lady human being watching through the window.'

'She doesn't,' exclaimed Arrietty hotly, 'she wouldn't!'

'As good as,' said Pod. 'And sooner or later the word gets around once humans know where you are – or where you're to be found at certain times of day, like. And there's always one they wants to tell, and that one tells another. And that Mabel and Sidney, finding us gone, where do you think they'll look? Here, of course. And I'll tell you for why: they'll think this lot stole us back.'

'But now we've got the fence,' Arrietty reminded him.

'Yes,' said Pod, 'they've wired us in nice now, like chickens in a hen-run. But what's even worse,' he went on, 'it's only a question of time before one of us gets caught out by a visitor. Day after day, they come in their hundreds, and all eyes, as you might say. No, Homily, it isn't taps and switches that count. Nor dressers and eiderdowns neither. You can pay too high for a bit of soft living, as we found out that time with Lupy. It's making your own way that counts and being easy in your mind, and I wouldn't never be easy here.'

There was silence for a moment. Homily touched the fire with a rusty nail which Spiller had used as a poker, and the slack flared up with a sudden brightness, lighting the walls and ceiling and the ring of thoughtful faces. 'Well, what are we going to do?' Homily asked at last.

'We're going,' said Pod.

'When?' asked Homily.

Pod turned to Spiller. 'Your boat's in ballast, ain't it?' Spiller nodded. 'Well, as soon as we've got it loaded.'

'Where are we going to?' asked Homily, in a tone of blank bewilderment. How many times, she wondered now, had she heard herself ask this question?

'To where we belong,' said Pod.

'Where's that?' asked Homily.

'You know as well as I do,' said Pod, 'some place that's quiet-like and secret, which humans couldn't find.'

'You mean that mill?'

'That's what I reckon,' said Pod. 'And I'm going by Spiller – no human ain't never seen *him*. We got timber, water, sacks, grain, and what food the old man eats. We got outdoors as well as in. And, say Spiller here keeps the boat in trim, there's nothing to stop us punting up here of an evening for a quick borrow round, like. Am I right, Spiller?'

Spiller nodded, and again there was silence. 'But you don't mean tonight, Pod?' Homily said at last: she suddenly looked very tired.

He shook his head. 'Nor tomorrow neither. We'll be some days loading, and better we take our time. If we play it careful and put this fire out, they've no call to think we're back. Weather's fair now and getting warmer. No need to rush it. I'll take a look at the site first and plan out the stuff we need . . .' He rose stiffly and stretched his arms. 'What we need now,' he said, stifling a yawn, 'is bed. And a good twelve hours of it.' Crossing the room, he took a plate from the shelf and slowly, methodically, he scooped up the ashes to cover the glowing slack.

As the room became darker, Homily said suddenly: 'Couldn't we try out the light?'

'The electric?' said Pod.

'Just once,' she pleaded.

'Don't see why not,' he said, and went to the switch by the door. Homily blew out the dips and, as almost explosively the room sprang to brightness, she covered her eyes with her hands. Arrietty, blinking hard, gazed interestedly about her: white and shadowless, the room stared starkly back. 'Oh, I don't like it,' she said.

'No more do I,' said Homily.

'But you see what I mean, Papa,' Arrietty pointed out as though still seeking some acknowledgement, 'we could never have done this by ourselves!'

'And you'll see what *I* mean,' he said quietly, 'when you get to be a little older.'

'What has age got to do with it?' she replied.

Pod's glance flickered across to Spiller and back again to Arrietty. Very thoughtful he looked, as though carefully choosing his words. 'Well, it's like this,' he said, 'if you can try to get my meaning: say, one day, you had a little place of your own. A little family maybe – supposing, like, you'd picked a good borrower. D'you think you'd go making up to humans? Never,' he said, and shook his head. 'And I'll tell you for why: you wouldn't want to do nothing to put that family in danger. Nor that borrower either. See what I mean?'

'Yes,' said Arrietty. She felt confused; and glad suddenly that, facing Pod, she stood with her back to Spiller.

'You won't always have us to look after you,' Pod went on, 'and I tell you now there's nothing never been gained by borrowers talking to humans. No matter how they seem, or what they say, or which things they promise you. It's never been worth the risk.'

Arrietty was silent.

'And Spiller agrees with me,' said Pod.

Homily, watching from her corner by the fireside, saw the tears well up in Arrietty's eyes and saw Arrietty swallow. 'That's enough for tonight, Pod,' she said quickly. 'Let's put out the light now and get ourselves to bed.'

'Let her just promise us,' said Pod, 'here under the electric, that she'll never do it again.'

'No need to promise, Pod – she understands. Like she did about the gas. Let's get to bed now.'

'I promise,' said Arrietty suddenly. She spoke quite loudly and clearly, and then she burst into tears.

'Now there's no need for that, Arrietty,' said Pod, going quickly towards her as Homily rose to her feet. 'No need to cry, lass, we was speaking for your own good, like.'

'I know,' gasped Arrietty from between her fingers.

'What's the matter, then? Tell us, Arrietty. Is it about the mill?'

'No, no,' she sobbed, 'I was thinking about Miss Menzies . . .'

'What about her?' asked Homily.

'Now I've promised,' gasped Arrietty, 'there'll be no one to tell her. She'll never know we escaped. She'll never know about Mabel and Sidney. She'll never know about the balloon. She'll never know we came back. She'll never know anything. All her life she'll be wondering. And lying awake in the nights . . .'

Above Arrietty's bowed head, Pod and Homily exchanged looks: neither seemed to know what to say.

'I didn't promise,' said Spiller suddenly, in his harshest, most corncrakey voice. They all turned and looked at him, and Arrietty took her hands from her face.

'You,' she exclaimed, staring. Spiller looked back at her, rubbing his ear with his sleeve. 'You mean,' she went on, forgetting, in her amazement, her tear-stained cheeks and her usual shyness of Spiller, 'that *you*'d come back and tell her? You who've never been seen! You who're so crazy about cover! You who never even speak!'

He nodded curtly, looking straight back at her, his eyes alert and steady. Homily broke the silence. 'He'd do it for *you*, dear,' she said gently. And then, for some reason, she suddenly felt annoyed. 'But I've got to try and like him,' she excused herself irritably. 'I've really got to try.' As she saw the disbelief on Arrietty's face change slowly to joyous surprise, she turned aside to Pod, and said brusquely: 'Put the light out now, for goodness' sake. And let's all get to bed.'

THE
BORROWERS
AVENGED

WITH ILLUSTRATIONS BY
Pauline Baynes

To
all our dear ones
at the
Old Rectory, Monks Risborough

CHAPTER ONE

MR POMFRET, the village constable at Little Fordham, was a thin young man with very soft, brown eyes (Miss Menzies often said he looked 'wistful').

'Sometimes, I think –' she would say to Mr Pott, '– that Mr Pomfret does not really care for being a policeman.'

He was married to a small, bustling woman – as fair as he was dark – and they had one very large, quiet baby.

The windowsills of the flat above the police station were always strewn with furry toys. Miss Menzies usually found this disarming but as she walked down the path on this particular, drizzly autumn afternoon (October the third, to be exact) the glassy-eyed teddy bears and lop-eared rabbits staring down through the panes above somehow failed to comfort her. For some reason, her errand, which two days before had seemed the only right and sensible course, suddenly seemed less so. She felt a little shaky as she pressed the bell: dear Mr Pomfret had always been so kind, she dreaded now to forfeit his respect. Yet what she had to tell him was perfectly honest and straightforward: she pulled back her shoulders, regaining some of her courage, and pushed the bell.

It was Mrs Pomfret who opened the door, a little flushed, her hair awry. 'Oh, Miss Menzies, come in, do. You want to see my husband?'

A clothes-horse stood by the stove in the public side of the office; it was hung with towelling squares, steaming in the glow. Mrs Pomfret whisked this shut. 'Not much of a drying day,' she explained apologetically, as she made for an inner door.

'Do leave it,' said Miss Menzies but Mrs Pomfret had gone.

Miss Menzies carefully closed her umbrella and stood it beside the hearth. As she stretched out her hands to the fire, she noticed they trembled slightly. 'Oh, dear, oh dear . . .' she muttered; and thrusting them deep in her pockets she squared her shoulders again.

Mr Pomfret entered, quite cheerfully for him. Disturbed in the middle of his tea, he was wiping his mouth on his handkerchief. 'Good afternoon, Miss Menzies. Dreadful weather!'

'Yes, indeed,' said Miss Menzies faintly.

'Do sit down. Here, by the fire.'

Wordlessly, Miss Menzies sat down. Mr Pomfret drew a chair from the far side of the desk and joined her by the stove. There was a short silence, then Mr Pomfret went on: 'Thought it might clear up around dinner time . . . quite a bit of blue sky . . .' The silence continued, and Mr Pomfret repeated 'around dinner time'. Then hurriedly blew his nose. 'The farmers like it, though,' he went on, stuffing his handkerchief into his pocket. Very cheerful and casual, he seemed.

'Oh, yes,' agreed Miss Menzies nervously, 'the farmers like it.' She

moistened her lips with her tongue, staring across the hearth at his kind brown eyes as though beseeching them to be even kinder.

In the ensuing silence, Mrs Pomfret bustled in again with a cup of milky tea, which she set on a stool by Miss Menzies. 'Oh, how very kind,' gasped Miss Menzies as Mrs Pomfret bustled out again.

Miss Menzies stared thoughtfully at the tea, then, taking up the spoon, began very slowly to stir it. At last she raised her eyes. 'Mr Pomfret,' she said, in a clear and steady voice, 'I want to report a loss. Or it may be a theft,' she added as Mr Pomfret drew out his note-book. She laid down the spoon and clasped her hands together in her lap: the long, thin, curiously girlish face looked grave. 'Or missing persons – that might be more accurate.' Mr Pomfret unscrewed the top of his fountain-pen and waited politely for her to make up her mind. 'In fact,' she went on suddenly in a rush, 'you might even call it a case of kidnapping!'

Mr Pomfret became thoughtful, gently tapping his lower lip with his fountain-pen top. 'Suppose,' he suggested gently, after a moment, 'you just told me simply what happened?'

'I couldn't tell you simply,' said Miss Menzies. She thought awhile. 'You know Mr Pott and his model village?'

'Yes, indeed,' said Mr Pomfret. 'Quite a tourist attraction. They say that Mr Platter of Went-le-Craye is setting up some kind of model village, too.'

'Yes, I heard that.'

'A bit more modern, like, they say it's going to be, seeing as he's a builder.'

'Yes, I heard that, too.' Miss Menzies ran a nervous tongue across her lips again. 'Well –' she hesitated a moment and then went on boldly, '– to get back to *our* village, Mr Pott's and mine: you know we're sort of partners? That he makes all the houses and I make the model figures – the people, as you might say?'

'Yes, indeed, and very lifelike they are, too!'

'Yes.' Miss Menzies' hands tightened slightly, as she clasped them together in her lap. 'Well, it's like this – I didn't make all the figures. I didn't make the ones that are missing.'

Mr Pomfret managed to look both concerned and relieved at the same time. 'Ah, now I see it –' he gave a small laugh. 'It's some of them that's missing, is it? I thought for a moment – I mean, when you said kidnapping –'

'That I meant live ones?' She looked at him steadily. 'I do.'

Mr Pomfret looked alarmed. 'Now, that's different.' Very serious suddenly, he poised his pen above his book. 'Person or persons?'

'Persons.'

'How many?'

'Three. A father, mother and child.'

'Name?' said Mr Pomfret, writing busily.

'Clock.'

'Clock?'

'Yes, Clock.'

'How do you spell it?'

'C-l-o-c-k.'

'Oh, Clock,' said Mr Pomfret, writing it down. He stared at the word: he seemed puzzled. 'Father's occupation?'

'Shoemaker, originally.'

'And now?'

'Well, I suppose he's still a shoemaker. Only he doesn't do that for a living –'

'What does he do for a living?'

'Well, I – er – I mean, I don't suppose you've heard of it: he's a borrower.'

Mr Pomfret looked back at her without any recognizable expression, 'Yes, I've heard of it,' he said.

'No, no, it's not in the sense you mean. It is an occupation. A rare one. But I think you *could* call it an occupation –'

'Yes,' said Mr Pomfret, 'I agree with you. That's what I do mean. I think you could call it an occupation.'

Miss Menzies drew in a long breath. 'Mr Pomfret,' she said, in a rush, 'I must explain to you – I thought you'd realized it – that these people are very *small*.'

Mr Pomfret laid down his pen: he studied her face with his kind brown eyes. He seemed more than a little bewildered: what could their height have to do with it? 'Do I know them?' he asked. 'Do they live in the village?'

'Yes. I've just told you. They live in *our* village, the model village, Mr Pott's and mine.'

'The model village?'

'Yes. In one of the model houses. They're as small as that.'

Mr Pomfret's gaze became curiously fixed. 'How small?' he asked.

'Five or six inches, something like that. They're very unusual, Mr

Pomfret. Very rare. That is why I think they've been stolen. People could get a lot of money for a little family like that.'

'Five or six inches?'

'Yes.' Miss Menzies' eyes suddenly filled with tears; she opened her bag and felt around for her handkerchief.

Mr Pomfret was silent. After a moment, he said, 'Are you sure you didn't make them?'

'Of course I'm sure.' Miss Menzies blew her nose. 'How could I make them?' she went on in a strangled voice. 'These creatures are *alive*.'

Once again Mr Pomfret began to bang his pen against his lower lip: his gaze had become more distant.

Miss Menzies wiped her eyes and leaned towards him. 'Mr Pomfret,' she said in a steadier voice, 'I think perhaps we are talking at cross-purposes. Now, how can I put things more clearly . . .' She hesitated and Mr Pomfret waited patiently. 'With your experience of houses, have you ever had the feeling . . . the impression, that there are other people living in a house besides the human beings?'

Mr Pomfret looked even more thoughtful. Other 'people' – *besides* human beings: the terms were synonymous, surely?

'I can't say I have,' he admitted at last, almost apologetically.

'But you must have wondered about the mysterious way small objects seem to disappear. Nothing of great value – small things, like pencil stubs, safety-pins, stamps, corks, pill-boxes, needles, cotton-reels – all those sort of things?'

Mr Pomfret smiled. 'We usually put it down to our Alfred. Not that we'd ever let him get at a pill-box –' he added hastily.

'But you see, Mr Pomfret, factories go on making needles and pen-nibs and blotting paper, and people go on buying them, and yet there never is a safety-pin just when you want one, or the remains of a stick of sealing-wax. Where do they all go to? I'm sure your wife is often buying needles and yet all the needles she ever bought in her life can't be just lying about this house . . .'

'Not about this house, no,' he said: he was rather proud of his neat, new residence.

'No, perhaps, not this house,' agreed Miss Menzies. 'They usually like somewhere older and shabbier – with loose floorboards, and age-old panelling, and all that sort of thing; they make their homes in the oddest nooks and crannies. Most of them live behind wainscots, or even under the floor . . .'

'Who do?' asked Mr Pomfret.

'These little people. The ones I'm trying to tell you about –'

'Oh? I thought you said –'

'Yes, I said I had three of them. We made a little house for them. They call themselves "borrowers". And now they've gone –'

'Oh, I see,' said Mr Pomfret, tapping his lip with his pen. But, Miss Menzies realized, he did not see at all.

After a moment, in spite of himself, Mr Pomfret asked in a puzzled voice, 'But why would they *want* these kind of things?'

'They furnish their houses with them: they can adapt anything. They're very clever. I mean, for little people like that, a good piece of thick blotting paper makes an excellent carpet and can always be renewed.'

Blotting paper was quite obviously not Mr Pomfret's idea of 'an excellent carpet'. He became silent again and Miss Menzies realized unhappily that she was getting herself into even deeper water.

'It's not so extraordinary, Mr Pomfret, although it must sound so. Our ancestors spoke openly about "the little people". In fact, there are many places in these islands where they are spoken of even today . . .'

'And *seen*?' asked Mr Pomfret.

'No, Mr Pomfret, they must never be seen. Never to be *seen* – by any human being – is their first and most serious rule of life.'

'Why?' asked Mr Pomfret (he wondered afterwards what had induced him to go even this far).

'Because,' explained Miss Menzies, 'to be seen by a human being might be the death of their race!'

'Oh, dear,' said Mr Pomfret: he hardly knew what else to say. After a moment a thought occurred to him. 'But you say you've seen them?' he ventured.

'I have been very privileged,' said Miss Menzies.

Again there was silence. Mr Pomfret had begun to look worried and Miss Menzies, too, felt she had said too much: this conversation was becoming more than a little embarrassing. She had always liked and respected Mr Pomfret as he had always liked and respected her. How could she get things back on a less uneven keel? She decided to adopt a more normal and decisive tone, and somehow lighten the atmosphere. 'But please don't worry, Mr Pomfret, or go out of your way, or anything like that. All I'm asking you to do, if you *would* be so kind, is just to record the loss. That's all. In case,' she went on, 'they might turn up somewhere else . . .'

Still Mr Pomfret did not write. 'I'll make a mental note of it,' he said. He closed his book, and slid a black elastic round the covers. He stood up suddenly as though more easily to put it in his pocket.

Miss Menzies stood up too. 'Perhaps,' she said, 'you might like a word with Mr Pott?'

'I might,' said Mr Pomfret guardedly.

'He'd bear me out about the size and everything.'

'You mean,' said Mr Pomfret, eyeing her almost sternly, 'that Mr Pott has seen them, too?'

'Of course he's seen them. We talk of little else. At least –' suddenly, she faltered. Was it she, perhaps, who talked of little else? And had Mr Pott ever really seen them? Looking back, in a sudden kind of panic, she could think of no occasion when he had actually admitted to having done so: she had been so strict about not having them disturbed; about leaving them alone to live their lives. Even on that one day, when she had persuaded him to make a vigil near the little house, none of the family had appeared, she remembered, and Mr Pott, nodding drowsily in the sunshine, had fallen off to sleep. Perhaps, through all these months, Mr Pott – never really listening – had simply tried to humour her: he was a kind, good man with manias of his own.

Mr Pomfret, she realized, was still gazing at her, half expectantly, with his warm brown eyes. She gave a little laugh. 'I think I'd better go now,' she said rather hurriedly, looking at her watch, 'I'm due at the church at six to help Mrs Whitlace with the flowers.' As he opened the door for her, she lightly touched his arm. 'Just report the loss, Mr Pomfret, that's all. Or make a mental note as you said . . . Thank you so much. Look, it's stopped raining . . .'

Mr Pomfret stood in the doorway for a moment, staring after her as she loped away along the shining asphalt with those long-legged, girlish strides. How old would she be now, he wondered, forty-eight? fifty? Then he went inside.

'Dolly –' he called tentatively. Then, seeming to change his mind, he went beside the stove and gazed unseeingly into the fire. He appeared to be thinking deeply. After a while, he took out his note-book again, unloosed the elastic and stared down at the almost blank page. He thought again for a while, before licking his pencil. 'October 3rd, 1911'. After writing these words, he licked his pencil again and underlined them heavily. 'Miss Menzies,' he wrote next and hesitated. What to write now? He decided at last to put a question mark.

*

Miss Menzies walked down the path to the church holding her umbrella close to her head as if to cover her embarrassment. She was thinking hard about her little people (people . . .? Of course they were people. Pod, Homily, and her young Arrietty) for whom she had made a home (a safe home, she had thought) in Mr Pott's model village. Pod and Homily she had only observed from a distance, as it were, as she crouched down to watch them from behind a waving clump of thistles, but Arrietty – fearless, bright-eyed Arrietty – had almost become a friend. And then there was Spiller. But Miss Menzies had never seen Spiller. No one ever saw Spiller unless he willed it: he was a master of concealment; could melt into any background; lurk near, when thought to be far; arrive when least expected and disappear as fast. She knew he was a loner who lived wild in the hedgerows; she knew he could navigate streams; had built a boat out of an old wooden knife-box, caulked at the seams with beeswax and dried flax; and that for shorter trips he used the battered lid of an old tin soap-box . . . Yes, Arrietty had talked a lot about Spiller, now Miss Menzies came to think about it. Arrietty's mother thought him dirty but, to Arrietty, he had smelt of the whole wide out-of-doors.

Miss Menzies sighed. Perhaps Spiller would find them and help them if they were in trouble . . . wherever they were.

CHAPTER TWO

WHEN Miss Menzies reached the church, she found Mrs Whitlace and Lady Mullings in the vestry drinking tea.

'I'm so sorry to be late,' said Miss Menzies hurriedly, hanging up her mackintosh.

'Don't worry, my dear,' said Lady Mullings. 'There was little to do today except to change the water. Bring up a chair and sit down. Mrs Whitlace has brought us some drop scones.'

'How delicious,' exclaimed Miss Menzies, taking a seat between them. She looked a little flushed from her walk.

Lady Mullings was large and statuesque (and given to floating veils). She was a widow and lived alone, having lost two sons in the Boer War. She had a sweet, sad face, always heavily powdered (a habit which in those days was considered rather worldly). Miss Menzies, on occasion, had even suspected a touch of lip-salve, but one could never be sure. All the same, Miss Menzies was devoted to Lady Mullings, who was kindness itself and who, some years before, had cured Miss Menzies's arthritic hip.

For Lady Mullings was a faith-healer. She took no credit for it: 'Something or someone works through me,' she would say, 'I am only the channel.' She was also, Miss Menzies remembered suddenly, a 'finder': she could locate lost objects or, rather, visualize in her mind the surroundings in which such objects might be found. 'I see it in a dark place . . .' she had said of Mrs Crabtree's ring, '. . . sunk sideways, there's kind of mud . . . no, more like jelly . . . something is moving now . . . yes, it's a spider. Now, there's water . . . oh, the poor spider!' The ring had been found in the S-trap of the sink.

'I came a little early,' Lady Mullings was saying now, reaching for her gloves, 'and must leave a little early, I'm afraid, because someone is coming to see me at six-thirty . . . someone in trouble, I'm afraid – so I'd better hurry. Oh dear, oh dear, what about these tea things . . .?'

'Oh, I'll see to those,' said Miss Menzies, 'and Mrs Whitlace will help me – won't you, Mrs Whitlace?'

'I will, of course!' exclaimed Mrs Whitlace, jumping up from her seat. She began to collect up the plates and Miss Menzies, in spite of her present worries, found herself smiling. Why, she wondered, did Mrs Whitlace always seem so happy? Well, perhaps not always, but nearly always . . .

Miss Menzies had a very warm regard for Kitty Whitlace who, before her marriage, had been a Kitty O'Donovan who had come over from Ireland at the age of fifteen to be kitchen-maid at Firbank Hall – in the 'good old days' as they were called now. Lonely and homesick as she had been at first, her winning ways and eagerness to please had gradually won over the sour old cook, Mrs Driver. After several years, these same winning ways had also won the heart of Bertie Whitlace, an undergardener. Whitlace later left to become sole gardener at the rectory and, after their marriage, Kitty had followed him, and become cook-general in the same old house.

Alas, the old rectory was empty now, but the Whitlaces had stayed on as caretakers. The Tudor rectory was listed as 'an historic building' to be preserved by the parish, as was the church, with its famous rood-screen. Mr Whitlace was appointed verger and Mrs Whitlace cleaner of the church. They lived very happily in the deserted old house – in the kitchen annexe, which was almost a cottage in itself.

There was a sink for the flower-arrangers in the far corner of the vestry. As she filled the battered kettle which stood on the draining-board, lit the somewhat rusty gas ring which, for safety's sake, stood on the stone flags beneath it, Miss Menzies had a sudden thought: should she, *dare* she, confide in Lady Mullings, who after all was meant to be a 'finder'? Waiting for the kettle to boil, she washed out a few spare flower-vases in cold water, still thinking hard. But how, she wondered unhappily, could she explain the borrowers to Lady Mullings? She was still smarting from that embarrassing interview with Mr Pomfret. He had clearly thought her quite mad. Perhaps not *quite* mad, but he had obviously been very puzzled. What, she wondered, had he said afterwards to Mrs Pomfret? Up until now – and she knew it well – Miss Menzies had been a much respected member of the village community. And yet, and yet . . . should any stone be left unturned?

'Perhaps,' thought Miss Menzies, as she dried up the crockery, 'we are all a little "touched"?' Lady Mullings with her 'findings', Mr Pott with his model village, herself with her 'borrowers'. Even sensible Mrs Whitlace, brought up as she had been on the far coast of West Cork, was apt to go on about 'fairies'.

'I've never seen one myself,' she would explain. 'But they're all about,

mostly after dark. And, say you offend them, like, there's not a dirty trick they wouldn't stoop to.'

'I'll be coming down the village with ye,' she was saying now. 'Whitlace will be wanting his evening paper.' Mrs Whitlace always called her husband 'Whitlace': it was the name he had been known by at Firbank. She had tried 'Bertie' a few times after they had first married but somehow it wouldn't fit. He had always been called 'Whitlace' and 'Whitlace' he seemed to remain.

'Oh, good –' said Miss Menzies, putting a small piece of net edged with blue beads over the top of the milk jug, which she placed in a bowl of cold water. This was for Mrs Whitlace's elevenses next morning, after she had cleaned the church.

Mrs Whitlace gathered up the leaves and flower stalks and put them into the waste-paper basket, with a half-eaten drop scone. These she would transfer to the larger dustbin next morning. She tidied up the piles of hymn-books which stood on top of the disused harmonium. The sugar bowl she put in the cupboard among the chalices, candlesticks and offertory plate. She turned the key of the great oaken cupboard, and locked the vestry door.

As the two women walked down the aisle, to let themselves out through the main entrance, Miss Menzies was struck by the beauty of the little church and again by the cleverness with which Mr Pott had constructed its exact replica in his model village: the way the light fell through the intricate carving of the famous rood-screen, making patterns on the pale flagstones of the aisle. Their footsteps struck hollow sounds into the silence, the door groaned loudly as they opened it and clanged to when they shut it behind them with a sound which sent its echoes crashing down the nave. Even the turning of the key in the lock seemed to grate on the silence.

Before they reached the lychgate, they felt the first few drops of rain. Mrs Whitlace hesitated, her hand to her new straw hat trimmed with velvet violets. 'My umbrella,' she exclaimed, 'I've left it in the vestry.' Selecting the vestry key from the bunch she carried, she sped away around the church.

'I'll wait for you here by the lychgate,' Miss Menzies called after her.

The rain became heavier as Miss Menzies stood under the thatch of the lychgate, and she was glad of its shelter. Pensively she watched the puddles filling in the rutted lane beyond. She thought of Lady Mullings and of how she might approach her. Not again would she betray herself as she had with Mr Pomfret. But she knew that for this interview she must take some intimate belongings for Lady Mullings to get her 'feeling'. She could not take clothes, their size would arouse wonder: Lady Mullings would, of course, mistake them for dolls' clothes. She must take something which a human being might have used. She thought suddenly of bedclothes – their sheets: these could be taken for handkerchiefs (and one *was*, she remembered). Yes, that was what she should take. But should she go at all? Was it wise? Was it fair on Lady Mullings to seek her help and hold back so much vital information? Yet, if she told all, might she not (in some way unforeseen) betray her little people? Would Lady Mullings believe her even? Might she not see, in Lady Mullings' face, the same odd blank expression she had seen on Mr Pomfret's? No, she thought, that would be beyond bearing. And supposing Lady Mullings *did* believe her, might not she get too excited, too involved, too enthusiastic? Taking over the search herself, for instance? A search which, for the sake of the borrowers, should be quiet, methodical and secret?

Miss Menzies sighed and looked towards the church. From the lychgate, she could not see the door of the vestry, only the main door under the porch. Mrs Whitlace seemed to be taking her time. Had she slipped through the small wicket gate which led straight into the rectory? Perhaps she had left her umbrella there? Ah, here she was at last . . .

Mrs Whitlace hurried down the path. She seemed a little upset and the umbrella wobbled slightly in the speed of her advance. When she reached Miss Menzies she did not open the gate but closed her umbrella and stared into Miss Menzies' face. 'Miss Menzies,' she said, 'there's something after happening you might call odd.' Miss Menzies noticed the usually rosy face looked strangely pale.

'What was it, Mrs Whitlace?'

'Well,' Kitty Whitlace hesitated, 'I mean –' again she hesitated, then went on with a rush, '– you wouldn't call me fanciful?'

'No, indeed,' Miss Menzies assured her. 'Anything but that!' (Except, Miss Menzies reminded herself suddenly, about fairies.)

'I could have sworn on my sacred oath that we'd left the church empty –'

'Yes, of course we did,' said Miss Menzies.

'Well, when I turned the key in the lock and began to open the door, didn't I hear voices . . .?'

'Voices?' echoed Miss Menzies. She thought a moment. 'Those jackdaws in the belfry sometimes make an awful racket. Perhaps that was what you heard.'

'No. This was in the vestry itself. I stood there quite silent at the door. And somebody seemed to say something. Quite clear, it was. You know how sound carries in that church?'

'What did they seem to say?' asked Miss Menzies.

'They seemed to say "What?"'

'What?' repeated Miss Menzies.

'Yes – "what?", just like that.'

'How odd,' said Miss Menzies.

'And the curtain, you know the one, between the vestry and the Lady

Chapel, was moving slightly as though someone had touched it. And there was a rustle of paper. Or something.'

'Perhaps,' said Miss Menzies, 'it was the draught from the open door.'

'Perhaps,' agreed Mrs Whitlace uncertainly. 'Anyway, I gave the church a good going over. Except the belfry. Whatever I heard was quite close. I mean, it – whatever it was – couldn't have got up into the belfry. Not in the time.'

'You should have come back for me. I'd have helped you.'

'I thought of mice. I mean, the paper rustling and that. I went all through the waste-paper basket.'

'There are mice in that church, you know,' said Miss Menzies. 'Field mice. They come in from the long grass in the churchyard. You remember that time of the Harvest Festival?'

'Strong mice, then,' said Mrs Whitlace, 'I threw half a drop scone into that basket. Everything else was there, but devil a bit of scone.'

'You mean it had gone?'

'Clean gone.'

'You're sure you threw it in?'

'Sure as I stand here!'

'That is odd,' agreed Miss Menzies. 'Would you like me to go back with you? Perhaps we could get Mr Pomfret –' Mrs Menzies blushed as she said his name, at the thought of her recent embarrassment. No, she would not like, quite as soon as this, and under these circumstances, to enlist his help again.

'You know what I think, Mrs Whitlace?' she said after a moment. 'That since the robbery – those candlesticks on the altar were very valuable, Mrs Whitlace, more valuable than any of us really knew – that we have all become a little nervous. Not alarmed exactly, but a little nervous. And things do speak, you know – inanimate things. I had a fretsaw once which every time I used it seemed to say "Poor Freddie". You couldn't mistake it – "Poor Freddie, poor Freddie" . . . It was quite uncanny. And there was a tap that dripped which seemed to say "But *that* . . . But *that* . . ." With a terrific emphasis on the "that". I mean to say,' explained Miss Menzies, 'that a tap, that tap over the sink in the vestry, for instance, could easily say "What?" '

'Maybe,' said Mrs Whitlace opening her umbrella again (she still looked preoccupied). 'Well, if you'll excuse me, Miss, we'd better be getting on. Whitlace will be a-waiting for his tea.'

Later that evening, after tea, when Whitlace was ensconced by the stove with his evening paper, Kitty Whitlace told her story again. She told it more fully, as he barely listened when working out the racing odds, and she was free – as it were – to think aloud. 'I told her,' she said, in a worried, slightly hurt voice, 'that I heard something, or somebody, say "What?". The thing I didn't tell her – because nobody, least of all you, Whitlace, would deny I'm a good cook and, as you might say, you can't have too much of a good thing – what I didn't tell her was what the other voice said.'

'What other voice?' asked Mr Whitlace, absently.

'I told you, Whitlace, that I heard *voices*, not just one voice.'

'What did it say, then?' asked Mr Whitlace, laying down his paper.

'It said, "Not drop scones AGAIN!" '

In February, Miss Menzies went away to stay with her sister in Cheltenham, returning on the second of March. She found Mr Pott very busy with his model village, preparing for the summer season. The snows of winter had inflicted a certain amount of damage to the little houses, so that most of her spare time was spent in helping to put things right.

Almost her first action in the garden had been to lift the roof off the borrowers' house and sadly stare inside. A little bit of damp had got in and Miss Menzies prevented further damp by digging a small channel to carry off the rainwater which had collected in puddles on many of the miniature roads. If – oh, IF! – her little people ever returned, they must find their toylike house as neat and dry as when they had left it. This was the least she could do. The roof when she put it back seemed sound and firm. Yes, she had done her best: even to the extent (in an embarrassed and roundabout way) of reporting the loss to the police. That, perhaps, had been the greatest ordeal of all!

By mid March, in spite of several days of rain, the model village began to look more like itself. Once she had cleaned it out, it did not occur to Miss Menzies to examine the little house again: it had been deserted for so long and, if they were to open in time for Easter, there was so much else to do: new figures to make, old ones to refurbish, rolling stock to be oiled and painted, roofs to mend, gardens to be weeded . . . Mr Pott had been clever with his drainpipes and such water as there was now flowed smoothly into the stream. Miss Menzies was especially proud of her oak trees – stout stalks of curly parsley, dipped in glue and varnished over.

It was Miss Menzies, too, who persuaded Mr Pott to put up the pig-wire fence along the river bank. She felt sure that whoever had stolen the borrowers had approached the model village from the water. 'Don't seem much point to me,' Mr Pott had protested, 'seeing as they've gone now . . .' But he hammered in the stakes all the same and wired them up securely. He had never quite believed in the borrowers himself but realized, in his quiet way, that the idea of these creatures had meant a great deal to Miss Menzies.

And so the long winter passed. Until – at last, at last! – came the first intimations of spring. And (for all the characters concerned) a strange spring it turned out to be . . .

CHAPTER THREE

AT a house called Ballyhoggin, at Went-le-Craye, Mr and Mrs Platter sat staring at each other across their kitchen table. They appeared to be in a state of shock – they *were* in a state of shock. Words had now utterly deserted them.

Mr Platter was a builder and decorator, who sometimes acted (under certain conditions) as the village undertaker. He had a dry, shrivelled, somewhat rat-like face and rimless glasses through which, when the light caught them, one could not see his eyes. Mrs Platter was large and florid but, at this moment, florid no longer. Her heavy, rather lumpy face had turned to a curious shade of beige.

On the table three small saucers were set out in a row. They contained something gooey. It looked like over-cooked rice, but Mrs Platter called it 'kedgeree'.

At long last, Mr Platter spoke. He spoke very slowly and deliberately in his dry, cold, rasping voice. 'I shall take this whole house to pieces brick by brick,' he said. 'Even –' he went on, '– if I have to hire a couple of extra men!'

'Oh, Sidney –' gasped Mrs Platter. Two tears rolled down her pendulous cheeks. With a fumbling hand, she reached for a tea-towel and wiped them away.

'Brick by brick,' repeated Mr Platter. Mrs Platter could see his eyes now: they were round and hard, like blue pebbles.

'Oh, Sidney –' gasped Mrs Platter again.

'It's the only way,' said Mr Platter.

'Oh, Sidney –' Mrs Platter had covered her face with the tea-towel. She was really crying now. 'It's the nicest house you ever built . . .' Her sobs were barely muffled by the tea-towel. 'It's our *home*, Sidney.'

'Considering what's at stake,' went on Mr Platter stonily. He hardly seemed to notice his wife's distress. 'We had a fortune in our hands. A fortune!'

'Yes, Sidney, I know . . .'

'Houses!' exclaimed Mr Platter. 'We could have built all the houses we should ever want. Bigger and better houses. Houses such as you

519

have never even dreamed of! We could have shown these creatures all over the world. And for any money. And now' – his pupils became pinpoints – 'they've gone!'

'It's not my fault, Sidney,' Mrs Platter wiped her eyes.

'I know it's not your fault, Mabel. But the fact remains – they've gone!'

'It was I who gave you the idea of getting hold of them in the first place.'

'I know that, Mabel. Don't think I'm not grateful. We committed a felony. It was very brave of you. But now –' His face was still stony. 'Someone or something has stolen them back.'

'But nobody knew they were here. No one, Sidney, except us.' She gave her face a final clean-up with the tea-towel. 'And we always went up to the attic together, didn't we, Sidney? To check on the locking of the door. In case one of us forgot. And there was that piece of zinc at the bottom of the door, in case they bored through, like –'

'We found the window open,' said Mr Platter.

'But how could little things like that open a window?'

'I've explained to you how they opened it, Mabel. The cord and the pulley and all that . . .' He thought awhile. 'No, someone must have come up with a ladder. They must have had help –'

'But nobody knew they were here. *Nobody*, Sidney. And they were there at breakfast time, when we took up their porridge. You saw them yourself. Now, didn't you? And who'd bring a ladder in broad daylight? No, if you ask me, Sidney, they can't have got far. Not on those little legs of theirs . . .'

'They must have had help,' repeated Mr Platter.

'But no one's even seen them, only us –' She hesitated. 'Except –'

'Yes, that's what I do mean –'

'You mean that Miss Menzies, or whatever she's called? And that Abel Pott? I can't see Abel Pott climbing a ladder. Not with his wooden leg, I can't. And that Miss Menzies, she's not the type for a ladder. And how would they know to come here?'

'There's that Lady Mullings down at Fordham. Ever heard tell about her?'

'Can't say I have.' She thought for a moment. 'Oh, yes I have – I tell a lie – didn't you do her roof once?'

'That's right. They say she's a "finder".'

'A finder?'

'Finds things. Sort of sees where they are. They say she found Mrs Crabtree's ring. And she found those burglars that took the candle-sticks . . .'

'What candlesticks?'

'Those silver-gilt candlesticks out of the church. Said she saw them in a pawnshop, next to two china dogs. Gave the address and all. And that's where they were. You wouldn't credit it . . .'

'No, you wouldn't, would you?' said Mrs Platter slowly. She was looking thoughtful. 'Oh, well – we mustn't give up hope. Suppose we go up now and have just one more look . . .?'

'Mabel,' Mr Platter glanced at the clock on the wall, 'we've been looking for four hours and thirty-five minutes. And not a sign of them. If they're still in this house, they'd be inside the walls, under the floor . . . anywhere! Remember that bit of loose floorboard I hitched up?'

'Where they could see into our room? Yes.'

'Well,' said Mr Platter, as though that settled the matter. 'And talking of houses,' he went on, 'in my opinion, the best house I ever made in my life was that showcase I made for *them* for our model village. The trouble I took over that showcase. The trouble. Stairs, ventilation, drainage, furniture, real carpet, electric light . . . And that plate-glass front, slotted, so you could lift it up for cleaning. Real home-like it looked and yet – this was the trick – there wasn't a corner they could get themselves into where the public couldn't see them. Day or night –'

'There wouldn't be public at night, Sidney.'

'Evenings,' said Mr Platter, 'winter evenings. This wouldn't have been no tourist summer show, girl. Not like the Riverside Teas, or Pott's model village. And there it sits' – there was real grief in his voice now – 'a perfect miniature house out in the tool-shed, covered with a blanket.'

There was a gloomy silence. After a while, Mrs Platter said, 'I been thinking, Sidney, before you start taking our home to bits – brick by brick, as you say – that it might be a good idea to take a run down to Abel Pott's . . .'

'The model village?'

'Yes, that's where they'd aim for, wouldn't they?'

'Maybe. Yes. But it's a pretty good step. At their kind of pace, it might take them a week to get there.'

'All the better. Let them settle in and feel safe, like.'

'Yes, you've got a point there.' He thought for a moment. 'And yet, on the other hand . . .'

'What, Sidney?'

He began to smile. 'We got the boat, haven't we? Say we went down ahead and laid in wait for them?'

'What? *Now*?'

Mr Platter looked irritated. 'Not *now*, this minute. As I say, it'll take them a bit of time to get there. Tomorrow, say, or the day after . . .'

CHAPTER FOUR

'I DON'T know where your father's got to,' exclaimed Homily for about the fourth time that evening as she and Arrietty sat by the fireless grate in the far too tidy room, 'Spiller said he'd found a place . . .'

Although through the tiny glass panes they could see the neat roofs of Mr Pott's model village, here indoors a grey dimness had stolen all the colour from their bright and toylike home. Home? Was it really 'home'? This miniature village made by Mr Pott? More of a hide-away, perhaps – after that long, dark winter in the Platters' attic.

Arrietty glanced at the neatly strapped bundles ranged against the farther wall. 'We'll be ready when they do come,' she said. We were all right here, she thought, before those Platters stole us. All the same, it lacked something – it was, perhaps, too ordered, too perfect and in some way too confined. Improvisation is the breath of life to borrowers, and here was nothing they had striven for, planned or invented: all had been 'given', arranged by a kind but alien taste.

'When they *do* come? They've been gone two days!'

'Perhaps,' said Arrietty, 'it's a good sign really: it may mean they've found somewhere.'

'Pity that old mill wasn't any good. But, anyway, we couldn't have lived on corn.'

'Nor could the miller,' Arrietty pointed out, 'that's to say, when he was alive.'

'All tumbled down, they said it was. And the rats something fierce.'

'Spiller will find somewhere,' said Arrietty.

'But where? What sort of place? I mean, there's got to be human beans or we'll have nothing to live on! And this idea of everywhere by boat! Something could easily have happened to them! Or suppose those Platters got them again?'

'Mother –' began Arrietty, unhappily. She got up suddenly and went to the window and stared out at the fading sky. Then she turned, a dark outline against the dim light. Homily could not see her face. 'Mother –' she said again in a more controlled voice, '– don't you see that you and I, sitting here in this model village, the very place the Platters stole us from, are in far more danger than Papa or Spiller?'

'There's that pig-wire along the river bank.'

'They'd be through that in a trice. They'd get some things called wire-cutters. And if you want to take *all* our stuff, we've *got* to go by water.'

'That knife-box of Spiller's! Suppose it sank? You and your father can swim, but what about me?'

'We'd fish you out,' said Arrietty patiently. 'And it never has sunk yet.' She knew her mother in this mood. After all, Homily had been brave enough in their other escapes: in their home-made balloon, brave enough in the boot and, come to think of it, extremely courageous in the kettle. A worrier she might be but she would always rise to an emergency.

'Spiller will find somewhere,' she said again. 'I know he will. And it might be somewhere lovely . . .'

'I've liked it here,' said Homily. Glancing round the room, she shivered, crossing her arms. 'I wish we could light the fire . . .'

'But we can't!' exclaimed Arrietty. 'Someone might see the smoke – we promised Papa!'

'Or put the light on,' Homily went on.

'Oh, Mother!' cried Arrietty. 'That would be madness! You know it really . . .'

'Or have something to eat that wasn't Spiller's nuts . . .'

'We were lucky to have those nuts.'

'They take such an age to crack,' said Homily.

Arrietty was silent: she had heard these kind of grumbles so many times before. And yet, she thought (coming back to her stool as the room grew slowly dark) that perhaps in her heart Homily understood the need for this speedy removal better than she pretended. Three human beans, at least, perhaps four – perhaps even more – knew they had been here, knew they had departed but (unless they gave the game away) there was no one, as yet, who knew they had returned.

It was for this reason Pod had forbidden them the use of light or fire, had kept them away from the windows and, throughout the daylight hours, confined them to the miniature house. Such days, with Pod and Spiller away, could sometimes seem very long. It was late March and three days had passed since their dramatic escape by home-made balloon from the Platters' attic. Looking back on it now, Arrietty realized what a wonderful feat this had been. 'Why do things always happen to us in March?' she wondered. She came back to her stool and, curling her legs round slightly, laid her head on her knees. Both she and Homily were very tired: the packing had not been easy – beds taken down, mattresses rolled, arm-chairs clamped together; each bundle arranged in such a way that everything would fit into Spiller's boat. And still Pod and Spiller had not come.

She remembered her father's face on their first arrival back: the way he had glanced about the tidy little room, with its doll's-house furniture and polished wooden floor. How he had looked up with a rueful shrug at the pocket-torch bulb hanging from the ceiling. Battery controlled, this contraption meant more to him than any other of Miss Menzies's inventions ('Clever . . . she's bright, you know'). He wished he had thought of it himself. And Arrietty remembered he had sighed a little. No, it hadn't been easy for any of them.

'Hark!' said Homily suddenly. Noiselessly Arrietty sat up, holding her breath in the silence. A faint scrape on the door – a breath of nothing. Neither moved: it might be a passing vole, a beetle or even a grass-snake. Homily stole from her stool and melted into the shadows beside the threshold. Arrietty could just perceive her bent head and the stooped, listening outline.

'Who's there?' Homily whispered at last, just above her breath.

'Me,' said a familiar voice.

As Homily opened the door, a waft of air flew into the room, scented with spring and evening, and there against the pale sky was the solid outline.

Eagerly Homily pulled him by the arm. 'Well, what news? Where's Spiller? Did you find anything?' She pushed forward her own stool. 'Here you are. Sit down. You look all out.'

'I am all out,' said Pod. Sighing, he laid his borrowing bag on the floor. There was something in it, Arrietty noticed, but not much. 'Walking, walking, climbing, climbing . . . it takes it out of you.' He looked round wearily at the stacked furniture in its neat piles. 'Would there be a drop of something?' he asked.

'There's a few tea leaves,' suggested Homily, 'I could warm them up over the candle.' She bustled towards the luggage, 'If I can find them –' She pulled at a few bundles. 'What with everybody packing, you don't know what's in what . . .'

'I could do with something a bit stronger,' said Pod.

'There's that sloe gin,' said Homily. 'But you don't like it . . .'

'That'll do,' said Pod.

She brought it to him in part of a broken nut-shell. It was some of Miss Menzies's making. 'I was going to leave it behind,' Homily said: she had always been a little jealous of Miss Menzies as a provider.

Pod sipped the drink slowly. Then slowly he began to smile. 'You'll never guess,' he said. They could not – in that dusky half-light – see his expression but his voice sounded amused.

'You mean you've found somewhere?'

'Could be.' He took another sip of gin. 'But I've found *someone*. At least, Spiller has . . .'

'Who, Pod? Who?' Homily, leaning forward, tried to see his face.

'And what's more,' Pod went on stolidly, 'he's known about them all the time.'

'Them!' repeated Homily sharply.

'The Hendrearies,' said Pod.

'No!' exclaimed Homily. The little room became tense with shock. Thoughts raced shadow-like around it from floor to ceiling, as Homily sat with clasped hands, head and shoulders in rigid outline against the half-light of the window. 'Where?' she asked at last, in an oddly colourless voice.

'In the church,' said Pod.

'The church!' Homily's head swung sharply round towards the window.

'Not the model church,' said Pod, 'the real one –'

'The human church,' explained Arrietty.

'Oh, my goodness,' cried Homily, 'what a place to choose!'

'There wasn't all that choice,' said Pod.

'Oh, my goodness me,' muttered Homily again, 'what a thing! But how did they get there? I mean, the last we saw of them, they were locked up in that gamekeeper's cottage, with just enough food for six weeks. I never did quite take to Lupy, as you well know, but many a time I've thought of them, wondering how they made out. Famine! That's what they were facing. You said it yourself, remember? When the humans go and the place gets locked up (and locked up it was – every crevice, didn't we know it? – against the field mice!). And that ferret, sniffing about outside . . .'

'How did they get out?' asked Arrietty, listening intently. She had edged her way along the floor and was sitting by her father's feet. 'I'd love to see Timmus,' she added. She hugged her knees suddenly.

Pod patted her shoulder. 'Yes, he's there. But not the two bigger boys. Seems they went back to the badgers' set. And Eggletina went to

keep house for them. Well –' Pod moved uneasily, '– seems they got out
the same way as we did.'

'By *our* drain?' exclaimed Homily. 'In the scullery?'

'That's right. Spiller went for them.'

'And brought them down by our stream?' There was slight affront in
her voice.

'That's right. Just like he did us. And a nice dry run he said it was,
too. No bathwater and no floods. It was when we was shut up in the
attic. You see, Homily, as the weeks went by and turned into months,
Spiller never thought he'd see us no more. It was his escape route, not
ours: he'd a perfect right to use the drain.'

'Yes, but you know the way Lupy talks . . .'

'Now, Homily, who's she got to talk to? And you wouldn't have wanted them to starve – now, would you?'

'No,' said Homily grudgingly, 'not starve exactly. But Lupy could well lose a fair bit of weight.'

'Maybe she has,' said Pod.

'You mean, you didn't see them?'

Pod shook his head. 'We didn't go into the church.'

'Why ever not?'

'There wasn't time,' said Pod.

'Then where are we supposed to live? Not that I hold with a church. Not for borrowers. Arrietty's read all about churches: they're one of the places that get absolutely chock-a-block of human beans. Where they congregate, as you might say, like starlings or something . . .'

'Only at regular hours, like. A church can be a good sort of place to be. Say there's a stove that heats the water. For the radiators, like –'

'What are radiators?'

'Oh, you know, Homily! Those things they had at Firbank –'

'You forget, Pod,' said Homily, with some dignity, 'that at Firbank, I never went upstairs.'

'Radiators –' said Arrietty, '– I remember: those things that bubbled?'

'That's right. Full of hot water. Keeps the house warm in winter . . .'

'And they've got those in the church?'

'That's right. And the stove they have burns coke.'

Homily was silent, for almost a full minute. After that, she said slowly, 'Coke's as good as coal, wouldn't you say?'

'That's right,' said Pod. 'And they've got candles.'

'What sort of candles?'

'Great long things. There's a drawer that's full of them. And they throw away the candle ends.'

'Who do?' asked Homily.

'The human beans.'

Homily was silent again. After a while, she said slowly, 'Well, if we've *got* to live in a church . . .'

Pod laughed. 'Who said we'd got to live in a church?'

'Well, you did, Pod. In a manner of speaking . . .'

'I said no such thing. The place that Spiller and I had in mind is somewhere quite different.'

'Oh, my goodness,' said Homily, 'whatever next?' Her voice sounded frightened.

'There's an old empty house, not a stone's throw from the church. Spiller and I have been all over it . . .'

'Empty!' exclaimed Homily. 'What would we live on then?'

'Wait!' said Pod. He took another sip of sloe gin. 'When I say "empty", I mean no one lives in it, except –' he drained the nut-shell, '– the caretakers.' Homily was silent. 'Now, these caretakers, name of Witless, they live in the very far end of the house, which used to be the kitchen. There's the kitchen, the scullery and the larder . . .'

'A larder . . .' breathed Homily. Awe-struck, she sounded as though granted a heavenly vision.

'Yes, a larder,' repeated Pod, 'with slate shelves. And,' he added, 'a mite of lovely stuff laid out on them.'

'A larder . . .' breathed Homily again.

'And that reminds me,' went on Pod. He stooped down and opened his borrowing bag. He drew out a fairly large piece of rich plum cake and a rather hacked-off morsel of breast of chicken. 'I guess you and Arrietty have been on pretty short commons these last two days . . . Fall to,' he went on, 'Spiller and I had our fill. There was some stuff called "brawn" but wasn't sure if you would like it . . .'

'I remember it at Firbank,' said Homily. She tore off a morsel of chicken and handed it to Arrietty. 'Here, child, try this. Go on, Pod –'

'There's a small staircase that goes up from the scullery and some bedrooms above. Not the main staircase that goes curving up and up –'

'How do you know all this, Pod?' Daintily, she tore off a piece of chicken for herself.

'I told you: Spiller and I went all over.'

'How could you, Pod, without your climbing pin? I mean, how could you get up the stairs?'

'You don't have to,' he said. She could tell he was smiling. 'The house is covered with creeper – ivy, jasmine, clematis, honeysuckle – everything you can think of. You can get just about anywhere.'

'Were the windows open?'

'Some were. And some of the panes were broken. It's all that criss-cross stuff. Lattice, I think they call it.'

'And in the main house, you're sure there's no one?'

'No one,' said Pod. He thought for a moment. 'Except ghosts!'

'That's all right,' said Homily, breaking off another piece of chicken. With little finger crooked, she took a ladylike bite. She would have preferred to unpack a plate.

'She comes through now and again, this Mrs Witless, with a broom and a duster. But not often, she's frightened of the ghosts.'

'They always are, human beans,' remarked Homily. 'I can't think why.'

'She calls them "fairies",' said Pod.

'Fairies! What nonsense! As if there were such things!'

Arrietty cleared her throat: she felt her voice might tremble. 'I would be,' she said.

'Be what?'

'Frightened of ghosts.' (Her voice *did* tremble.)

'Oh, Arrietty,' exclaimed Homily irritably, 'it's nice you can read and that, but you read too much of all that human stuff. Ghosts is air. Ghosts can't hurt you. Besides, they keep human beans away. My mother lived in a house once where there was a headless maiden. Real good times they had with her, as children, running through her and out the other side – kind of fizzy it felt, she said, and a bit cold. It's human beans that can't abide them, for some reason. Never occurs to them that ghosts is too self-centred to take a blind bit of notice of human beans . . .'

'Let alone borrowers,' said Pod.

Homily was silent. She was thinking quietly of the larder – of cold smoked ham, or half-eaten apple tarts, of cheddar cheese, of celery in glass jars, of early cherries . . .

As if reading her thoughts, Pod said, 'He keeps up the kitchen garden, this Witless. Grows everything, Spiller says . . .'

'Where's Spiller now?' asked Homily.

'Down by the stream. Making the boat fast –'

'What to?'

'The pig-wire, of course:' Pod stretched out his legs wearily, 'Finish up that bit of cake. We got to start loading.'

'Tonight!' gasped Homily.

'Of course, tonight. While there's a bit of light left . . .' He rose to his feet. 'Then we just lie low awhile till the moon rises. Then we'll be off: Spiller's got to see to navigate . . .'

'You mean we're going to that place tonight!'

Pod, from where he stood, leaned forward, placing two tired hands on the shelf above the fireplace. He bowed his head. Then, after a moment, he slowly raised it. 'Homily,' he said, 'I don't want to scare you. Nor you neither, Arrietty. But you got to realize that every minute – any minute – that we're here, we're in grave danger.' He turned round and faced them. 'You don't want to be taken back to that attic. Now, do you? Nor to be put on show for the public to stare at? In a glass-fronted cage, like they were making – those Platters? For the rest of our lives . . .' He paused a moment. 'For the rest of our lives . . .' he repeated slowly.

There was a long silence. Then Arrietty whispered huskily, 'No.'

Pod straightened up. 'Then let's get busy,' he said.

CHAPTER FIVE

It was not easy to get all the bundles through the squares of the pig-wire; even with Spiller's help. The bedsteads were the worst. They had to dig away the earth on the bank of the stream with their bare hands and slide the bedsteads underneath. The squares of mesh were wide enough for most things but not wide enough for the beds. 'I wish we still had our old mustard spoon,' Homily grumbled, 'it would have come in useful here . . .'

'If you ask me –' panted Pod, as, stooping, he pushed the last bundle through to Spiller in the boat, '– if you ask me –' he repeated, standing upright to relieve his aching back, '– we shan't use half this junk.'

'Junk!' exclaimed Homily. 'All these lovely chairs and tables, made for us special! And all our very own, as you might say – to take or leave –'

'What have you *left*?' asked Pod wearily. Irritated as they were, they kept their voices down.

'Well, the kitchen sink, for one thing – being a fixture, like. And think of all those lovely clothes, washed and ironed, and fitting us a treat . . .'

'And who's to see us in them?' asked Pod.

'You never know,' said Homily. 'I've always kept a good home, Pod. And fitted you and Arrietty out proper. And it hasn't always been easy –'

'I know, I know,' Pod whispered more gently. He patted her on the shoulder. 'Well, we'd better be getting aboard –'

Arrietty took one last look round at the miniature village. The slate roofs glinted palely under the rising moon, the thatched ones seemed to disappear. There was no light in the window of Mr Pott's house, he must have gone to bed. A tinge of sadness mingled with the feeling of tired excitement. Why, she wondered? And then she thought of Miss Menzies. Miss Menzies would miss them. How she would miss them! And, in Miss Menzies, Arrietty knew she was losing a friend. Why, she thought, did she, a borrower born and bred, succumb to this fatal longing to talk to human beans?

It always brought trouble: she had to admit that now. Perhaps, as she grew wiser and older, she would grow out of it? Or, perhaps (and this was a strange thought) this hidden race to which she belonged once *had* been human beans themselves? Getting smaller and smaller in size as their ways of life became more secret? Or, perhaps even (as she remembered The Boy at Firbank had hinted), their race *was* dying out . . .

She shivered slightly and turned towards the pig-wire and, with Spiller's help, climbed down into the boat.

Homily was arranging down quilts and pillows in what had been the teaspoon compartment of Spiller's old knife-box. 'We'll have to get some sleep,' she was saying.

'You'll get that right enough,' said Pod. 'We'll have to lay up till morning.'

'Where?' Homily's voice sounded startled.

'Where the stream turns into the rectory garden. It comes from the pond, like: there's a spring. We aren't none of us going up across that lawn in the moonlight. Owls galore, they say there are. No, we'll hole-in against the bank under the alders. Nothing'll see us there . . .'

'But what about crossing that lawn in the daylight? Carrying all this stuff?'

'The stuff stays in the boat – until we've got our bearings. Some corner of the house that's safe. Safe to settle down in, as you might say.'

Spiller was fixing the shabby leather gaiter over the cargo. Once this was done, except to very sharp eyes, the knife-box would look like some old floating log. 'And we'd not be needing – not even a quarter of this stuff – say I'd got my tools.'

'Yes,' agreed Homily, in a sad whisper, 'that's a real shame, that is. To lose your tools . . .'

'They weren't lost, not in the meaning of the word. What did we take away from that gamekeeper's cottage, except one hard-boiled egg?'

'That's right,' said Homily. She sighed. 'But needs must.'

'I could make anything, *anything* we really needed, like, say I had my tools.'

'I know that,' said Homily. There was real understanding in her voice as she thought of the partitions, the gates, and the passages under the floor at Firbank. 'And that cigar-box bedroom you made for Arrietty! There's not a soul alive who wouldn't call that a triumph . . .'

'It wasn't bad,' said Pod.

Arrietty, who had been helping Spiller with the last lashings-down of the gaiter (a leather legging such as in those days most of the gamekeepers wore), heard her own name and became suddenly curious. Edging her way along the side of the knife-box, she heard her father saying, 'Wouldn't be surprised if the Hendrearies had got them . . .'

'Got what?' she asked, leaning towards them.

'Keep your voice down, girl.'

'We was talking about your father's tools,' explained Homily, 'he thinks the Hendrearies may have taken them. Not that they hadn't a right to, I suppose, seeing as we left them behind . . .'

'Left them behind – where?' Arrietty's voice sounded puzzled.

'In that gamekeeper's cottage. When we escaped down the drain. Where,' she added rather acidly, 'you used to talk to that boy. What was his name now?'

'Tom Goodenough,' said Arrietty. She still sounded puzzled. After a moment, she said, 'But the tools are here in this boat!'

'Oh, don't be silly, girl! How could they be?' Homily sounded really impatient. 'All we took away from that cottage was one hard-boiled egg!'

Arrietty was silent for a moment. Then she said slowly, 'Spiller must have rescued them.'

'*Now* what are you on about, girl? You'll only worry your father . . .' Pod, she noticed, had kept strangely silent.

Arrietty slid down from her perch and came between them. 'When we were loading, Spiller and I,' she had dropped her voice to a whisper, 'there was a blue bag, like one of Uncle Hendreary's – I sort of knocked against it, and it nearly fell into the water. Spiller jumped forward and saved it. Just in time.'

'Well, what about it?'

'When we stowed it, I heard something rattle inside.'

'That could be anything,' said Homily, thinking of her pots and pans.

'And it seemed fairly heavy. Spiller seemed quite angry. As he grabbed hold of it, I mean. And he said –' Arrietty swallowed. She seemed to hesitate, as though to recall the words.

'What did Spiller say?' asked Pod, in a strained voice. He had been standing very still.

'He said "Look out what you're doing! Them's your father's tools!" '

There was a stunned silence. Then Homily spoke: 'Arrietty, are you *sure* he said that?' She glanced across at her husband. His head and shoulders were outlined faintly in the moonlight. Still he had not moved.

'That's what it sounded like. I didn't give it two thoughts. Not with the bag nearly falling into the water . . .' As neither parent spoke, she went on, 'Yes, that's what he said all right. He nearly shouted it: "Them's your father's tools!" '

'You're sure he said "tools"?'

'Yes, *that* was the word he shouted. Never seen Spiller cross like that. That's what I was thinking of most . . .' She looked from one dim shape to the other. 'Why? What's the matter?'

'Nothing's the matter!' Arrietty thought she heard a short sob. 'Everything's wonderful! Wonderful . . .' Homily was really crying now. 'Oh, Pod –' she rushed forward, flinging her arms around the still figure. 'Oh, Pod,' she sobbed, 'I think it's true!'

He held her closely, patting her back. 'Seems like it,' he said gruffly.

'I don't understand,' faltered Arrietty. 'Spiller must have told you . . .'

'No, lass,' said Pod quietly, 'he didn't tell us nothing.' He felt around for something with which to wipe Homily's face. But she broke away from him and rubbed it on the small pillow she had been holding in her hand. 'You see, Arrietty,' she said, still gasping a little, 'church or rectory, or whatever it is, we can begin to live now. Really live. Now we've got his tools . . .' She threw down the pillow, and seemed to be straightening her hair. 'But why, Pod, *why* didn't he tell us?'

CHAPTER SIX

It was pleasant to be on the water again. Spiller's boat, fastened securely at the prow, swayed softly – drawn and released by the current of the stream. Fragile wisps of cloud drifted across the moon, and sometimes obscured the stars. But not for long: a gentle radiance seemed to quiver upon the water, and a faint hint of wind stirred the rushes on the farther bank. All was silent – except for Homily's humming. Brisk and light-hearted once more, she was making up the beds. A difficult business this was, as the teaspoon compartment in which she and Arrietty were to sleep was only partly under the gaiter. It meant a lot of crawling back and forth for careful tuckings-in of Miss Menzies's flannel blankets and handmade, quilted eiderdowns. If it rained, their heads and shoulders would be dry: but what about their feet, Arrietty wondered?

She stood in the one free place in the stern, breathing in great draughts of the welcome night air, and idly watching Pod and Spiller moving about in the prow. Spiller, stooping, was drawing out his punt pole, the long yellow knitting needle which once – so long ago – had belonged to Mrs Driver. Out it came from under the gaiter, inch by inch, and he laid it down across the thwarts. He stood up cheerfully and rubbed his hands; then turned towards Pod who, stooping towards the fence, was fumbling with the twine. Then, suddenly – swift as whiplash – Spiller swung round, staring upstream. Pod too, rather more slowly, straightened himself and followed the direction of Spiller's eyes.

Arrietty leant quickly forward and laid a warning hand on her mother's arm, as Homily, a little dishevelled, emerged once again from under the gaiter. 'Hush!' she whispered. Homily stopped her humming. They both listened. It was unmistakable – not very near, as yet – the sound of oars!

'Oh, my goodness . . .' breathed Homily. She stood up, peering bleakly ahead. Arrietty's hand on her arm tightened to a painful grip. 'Quiet, Mother! We mustn't panic . . .'

Homily, hurt (in more senses than one), turned reproachfully towards her daughter and Arrietty knew that she was about to protest that she never panicked, that all her life 'calm' had been her watchword, that she had never been one to fuss, that – But Arrietty pinched her arm more tightly and, grumpily, she remained silent, staring blankly ahead.

Spiller had moved quickly beside Pod. Somehow, the twine had got wet or someone had tied the knots too tightly. There was something desperate about the two bent backs. Arrietty, suddenly contrite, released her grip and laid a comforting arm about her mother's shoulders and drew her closer. Homily took Arrietty's free hand and squeezed it gently. This was no time for quarrels.

At last, the twine slid free. They saw Spiller snatch up his punt pole and, driving it hard into the bank below the fence, he spun the boat into mid-stream. Homily and Arrietty clung more closely together as, with strong rhythmic strokes, Spiller propelled them against the current. Upstream? Towards the sound of oars? Towards danger? Why?

'Oh, my goodness gracious . . .' breathed Homily again.

But on they went, stroke after stroke, the knife-box shuddering slightly on the shallow ripples of the current. The sound of oars became clearer and, with it, another sound – a kind of scrape and a splash. Homily, wild-eyed but silent, clung more closely to Arrietty and Arrietty, twisting in her mother's grasp, cast a desperate glance backwards. Yes, they had left the wire fence behind – the fence, the model village and all that their 'home' there had stood for. But where, oh where, could Spiller be making for now?

They soon saw: the knitting needle swung up in a moonlit flash across the boat and down on the other side. Two swift, deep strokes from Spiller and they were plunged among the rushes of the farther bank. Not plunged exactly, more crashing into them, the head of Spiller's boat being square.

There was no longer any sound of approaching oars. Whoever was rowing had heard the noise. A frightened frog plopped out of the rushes. Then all was silent again.

The sudden, sharp, unexpected swerve had bowled Homily and Arrietty over. They lay where they had fallen, listening hard. There was no sound except for the murmur of the gently flowing stream. Then an owl hooted, answered faintly by its mate across the valley. Silence again.

Arrietty rose stealthily to her knees and edged her way towards the stern of the boat. She could just see over.

Moonlight fell fully on her face and (she realized unhappily) on the exposed stern of the boat. She turned and glanced forward: Pod and

Spiller, lost among the deeper shadows, were scarcely visible now but she could see they were moving, moving and leaning. And then the boat began to stir: steadily, silently, inexorably, Pod and Spiller were pulling them more deeply into the rushes. A strong scent of bruised spearmint drifted back to her, and a faint smell of cow dung. Then the knife-box became still. Once more there was silence.

Arrietty, in shadow now, looked back over the stern. Between the bent and flattened rushes, she could still see the open stream and still she felt exposed.

'Could have been an otter . . .?' said a voice. Startlingly close it sounded, and it was a voice she recognized.

All the borrowers froze. Again there came the sound of a scrape and a splash.

'More likely a water-rat,' said another voice drily – nearer still now.

'Oh, my goodness . . .' breathed Homily again in Arrietty's ear, 'it's them! Those Platters . . .'

'I know,' whispered Arrietty, barely above her breath. 'Keep still . . .' as Homily made an instinctive move towards the gaiter.

Then the boat came into view, drifting down on the current. It was a small dinghy – the one the Platters had used at Riverside Teas for children's trips round the island – and the two figures in it, outlined against the moonlit bank, looked top-heavy and enormous. The oars, pulled in from the rowlocks, stuck up against the sky. The larger figure leaned forward. Again there was the scrape and a splash.

'I never thought we'd spring leaks like this, Sidney,' said the first voice.

'Stands to reason. Boat's been laid up all winter – she'll soon settle down once the timbers begin to swell.'

Another scrape, another splash. 'Oh, drat, something's gone into the bilges. I think it's the mutton sandwiches . . .'

'I told you, Mabel, this wasn't going to be easy.'

'I made them so nice, Sidney, with chutney and all.' There was a short silence and Arrietty held her breath, watching intently as the other boat drifted by. 'It's all right, Sidney,' she heard the first voice say. 'It was only the hard-boiled eggs . . .'

Again there was silence, except for the scrape and the splash. Arrietty turned her head, and there was Pod climbing towards them along the curve of the gaiter. He put his finger to his lips and she kept obediently still.

As he let himself down beside her, they heard the sound of oars again. Pod cocked his head, listening quietly. After a moment, under cover of the splashings, he said, 'They've gone past?' Arrietty nodded. Her heart was still beating wildly.

'Then *that's* all right, then.' He spoke in almost his normal voice.

Arrietty groped for his hand. 'Oh, Papa –'

'I know, I know,' he said, 'but it's all right now. Listen! They'll be tying up soon . . .'

Even as he spoke, they heard the clatter of the oars withdrawn from the rowlocks, and Mabel's voice, more distant now but carrying tremulously across the water. 'Oh, please, Sid, gently! You'll wake old Pott!'

'Him?' they heard Mr Platter say. 'He's deaf as a post. And his light's out. Been asleep this good couple of hours, I shouldn't wonder . . .' And again they heard the sound of baling.

'Could they sink?' whispered Arrietty hopefully.

''Fraid not,' said Pod.

Once more Mabel's voice came to them across the water: 'Have I got to keep this up all night?'

'Depends,' said Mr Platter. Then there were some murmurings and slight creaks and scufflings. They made out a few words like 'Can't seem to get my hand on the painter . . . mixed up with the umbrellas . . .' Then Mrs Platter complaining about 'too much stuff . . .'

'Too much stuff!' they heard Mr Platter repeat indignantly. 'You'll thank your stars for some of it before the night's out. I warned you what we were in for, didn't I, Mabel?' There was no reply, and they heard the hard voice rasp on. 'A vigil! That's what we're in for – a vigil! Tonight, tomorrow night and, if need be, many a night to come . . .'

'Oh, Sid –' (The borrowers, listening intently, caught the note of dismay.)

'We'll get them back, Mabel, if we die for it. *Or* –' here Mr Platter's tone became less certain, '– somebody else does . . .'

'Somebody else . . .? Oh no, Sidney. I mean, vigils and felonies – those I can get used to. But what you're suggesting now . . . well, that wouldn't be very nice, not murder, dear. Might involve the police –' As he did not reply at once, she added lamely, 'If you see what I mean . . .'

'It may not be necessary,' said Mr Platter loftily.

There were more creakings, faint scrapes of wood on wood, an occasional watery plop . . . 'Careful, Sidney, you nearly had me out!' and other small, half-frightened exclamations.

'They're tying up,' whispered Pod. 'Now's our moment!' He was

speaking to Spiller who, silent as a shadow, had joined them in the stern, punt pole in hand. 'Get hold of the rushes – you, too, Homily. Come on, Arrietty . . . that's right, that's right. Pull – gently now, gently . . .'

Slowly, slowly, they slid out – stern foremost – into more open water but, suddenly, it became dark, as dark as it had been among the rushes. 'I can't see,' whimpered Homily, 'I can't see nothing, Pod.' She stood up, cold hands dripping water. She sounded very frightened.

'No more can they,' Pod whispered back – very confident, he sounded. 'Stay where you are, Homily. Now, Spiller –'

As the boat shot forward, Arrietty looked up. The stars were bright but a cloud had come over the moon. Turning, she looked back but could see very little: all was dimness down by the fence. She felt the boat turn, sharply, against the stream. Oh, blessed cloud! Oh, blessed Spiller! Oh, blessed, silent knitting needle, driving them swiftly forward in Spiller's nimble hands! Upstream, stern foremost – it didn't matter: they were getting away!

Gauzily, magically, the last traces of cloud drifted away across the moon and the gentle radiance shone down again. She could see her parents' faces and looking back she could see the wire fence, silver in the moonlight, and the moving shadows beside it. If I can see them, she thought, they could see us. Her father, too, she noticed, was staring at the fence. 'Oh, Papa,' she faltered, 'suppose they see us?'

Pod did not reply for a moment, his eyes on the moving figures. 'They won't look,' he said at last. Smiling, he laid a hand on her shoulder and all fear suddenly left her. After a moment, he went on – in the same low, confident voice, 'The stream curves about here, and then we'll be out of sight . . .'

And so it was. In a few minutes Arrietty, looking back, saw only the peaceful water: the fence had disappeared from view. They all relaxed, except for Spiller steadily poling ahead.

'There's a butter-knife somewhere,' said Pod. 'I left it handy . . .' He turned, as though to climb back over the gaiter and then he hesitated: 'You and your mother better go to bed. You'll need all the sleep you can get. It'll be a busy day tomorrow . . .'

'Oh, Papa, not yet –' pleaded Arrietty.

'Do as I say, girl. And you, too, Homily. You look all out –'

'What on earth do you want with the butter-knife, Pod?' Her voice did sound very tired.

'What it was meant for,' said Pod, 'a rudder. Now, creep along under, the two of you, and get tucked in.' He turned away. They watched him as he made his careful way over the gaiter. 'A born climber,' breathed Homily proudly. 'Come along, Arrietty, we'd better do as he says. It's getting chilly and there's nothing we can do to help . . .'

Still Arrietty hesitated. To her, it seemed the fun was just beginning. There would be things to see on the banks – new things – and the joy of the great out-of-doors. Ah, there was a bat! And another one. There must be midges about. No, not midges so early in the year. And it was chilly. But spring was just round the corner. Lovely spring! And a new life . . . But it *was* chilly. Homily had disappeared from view.

Reluctantly, Arrietty felt her way under the gaiter. Very stealthily, she extracted the small pillow and drew it to the end of their bed. At least, she would sleep with her head out of doors!

Creeping between Miss Menzies's home-made bedclothes, she soon began to feel warmer. Lying flat on her back, she could only see the sky. And there was the moon again, sometimes obscured by a sudden tangle of overhanging branches, sometimes by filmy cloud. Now and again, there were strange night noises. Once, she heard a fox bark.

To what kind of new life were they going, she wondered? How long would it take them to reach this unknown house? A large human house, this much she knew. Larger than Firbank – this she had gathered from Pod – and Firbank had been large enough. There was a lawn, it seemed, which sloped down towards a pond – a pond with its own spring which fed this very stream up which they were so silently travelling. Oh, how she loved ponds! She remembered the one at the bottom of the field, that time they had been living in the boot. What fun she had had with that pond. Fishing for minnows, paddling about in Spiller's old tin soap-dish, learning to swim . . . How long ago it all seemed now! She thought of Mild Eye and his caravan; the succulent smell of his pheasant stew as she and her parents, terrified and hungry, crouched under the dubious shelter of Mild Eye's tousled bunk; and of that fierce-faced woman, who was Mild Eye's wife. Where were they now? Not too near, she hoped.

She thought again of Firbank, and of her childhood under the floor; the darkness, the dusty passages between the joists. And, yet, how clean and bright Homily had kept the tiny rooms in which they actually lived! What work it must have been! She should have helped more, she realized uncomfortably . . .

And then that glorious day when Pod had taken her 'upstairs' and her first delirious glimpse of the Great Outdoors and her meeting with

The Boy (her first real sight of a living human bean!) and what trouble it had caused . . .

But – how much she had gleaned from reading aloud to him; how strange were some of the books he had brought down into the garden from the great house above. How much she had learned about the mysterious world in which they all existed – herself, The Boy, the old woman upstairs – strange animals, strange customs, peculiar ways of thought. Perhaps the strangest of all creatures were the human beings themselves ('beings' not 'beans', as her father and mother still called them). Was she a 'being'? She must be. But not a human one, thank goodness! No, she would not like to be one of those: no borrower ever robbed another borrower; possessions did slide about between them – that was true – small things left behind or discarded by previous owners (or things just 'found'): what one borrower did not make use of, another one could. That made sense: nothing should be wasted. But no borrower would deliberately 'take' from another borrower: that, in their small precarious world, would be unthinkable!

This was what she had tried to explain to The Boy. She would always remember his scornful voice when he had cried out in sudden irritation: ' "Borrowing" you call it! I call it "stealing"!'

At the time, this had made her laugh. She had laughed and laughed at his ignorance. How silly he was (this great clumsy creature) not to know that human beans were made for borrowers, as bread for butter, cows for milking, hens for eggs: you might say (thinking of cows) that borrowers *grazed* on human beans. What else (she had asked him) were human beans *for*? And he had not quite known, now she came to think of it . . .

'For us, of course,' Arrietty told him firmly. And he had begun to see her point.

All the same, as she lay there – gazing up at the moon – she found all this very puzzling. Looking back, she saw how long it had taken her to realize how many millions of human beings there were in the world, and how few borrowers. Until those long days of reading aloud to The Boy, she had thought it the other way round. How could she think otherwise, brought up, as she had been, under the floor at Firbank – seeing so little and hearing less? Until she met The Boy, she had never laid eyes on a human bean. Of course, she had known they existed, or how else could borrowers exist? And she had known they were dangerous – the most dangerous animals on earth – but she thought they must be rare . . .

Now she began to know better.

Somewhere, far in the distance, she seemed to hear the sound of a church clock. Drowsily, she counted the notes: they seemed to add up to seven.

CHAPTER SEVEN

Looking back to that morning of their first arrival, the thing that Arrietty remembered most clearly was the long, long walk: an impossible walk it had seemed at times.

They had all slept well, even Pod and Spiller had slipped in an hour or two of rest: the journey, it seemed, had taken less time than any of them had expected. She had not woken, nor had Homily, when Spiller eventually ran them aground on what turned out to be a small pebbly beach under a cliff-like overhang of roots and mud. This was where the vast rectory lawn joined the curve of the out-flowing stream. She had not seen the lawn at first, only the dim tangled branches of a juniper bush which cut out all view of the sky and shed its darkness over this hidden anchorage. Could this be *it?* Had they really arrived? Or was this cavernous place just a resting place on what might turn out to be a much longer journey?

No, this *was* it! They had arrived: she heard the church clock, much nearer now, striking the hour of nine. She could see Pod and Spiller splashing about in the shallows among the pebbles and, between them, was Spiller's soap-box lid, bobbing emptily as Pod made it fast to a root. He turned and saw her as she stood, shivering slightly, wrapped in her eiderdown quilt. Homily, looking dazed and dishevelled, was emerging from under the gaiter. 'So you've stirred yourselves, at last!' said Pod cheerfully. 'Well, here we are! What do you think of it?'

Arrietty did not quite know what she thought of it: except, perhaps, that it was secret, dark, and felt, somehow safe. Homily, now standing uncertainly beside her, also wrapped in a quilt, nodded her head towards the soap-dish. 'Where are we supposed to be going in that?' she asked suspiciously. Spiller, Arrietty noticed, had begun climbing up the bluff: the tangled roots gave a wide choice of handholds.

'We're not going anywhere in that,' Pod told her. 'We're going to pack it up with a few things for the night. Where we're going, we're going on our own two feet . . .'

'Where *are* we going?' asked Homily.

'Up to the house,' said Pod. 'You'll see in a minute . . . And we'd

better get going – while there's no one about: Spiller says they're out for the day . . .'

'Who are?'

'Witless and Mrs Witless, of course: he does jobbing gardening, and she's gone to town on the bus. Now then, Homily,' he went on, coming up just below them, 'pass me down them eiderdowns and any other bedclothes. And, Arrietty, you'll find a bit of twine up for'ard . . .'

Reluctantly, they divested themselves of their warm coverings and Arrietty went for'ard to find the twine.

'What about some cooking-pots?' asked Homily as, half-heartedly, she began to fold up the quilts.

'There won't be no cooking tonight,' said Pod briskly.

'We got to eat –'

'Spiller's seen to all that. Now come on –'

Arrietty came back with the twine and they began to work more quickly, passing the folded bedclothes down to Pod who splashed back and forth loading up the soap-dish. 'Stream's risen a bit,' he remarked, 'it rained in the night . . .'

'Not here,' said Homily, laying a hand on the gaiter. 'This Thing's as dry as a bone . . .'

'Stands to reason,' he glanced up at the thick leafage above them, 'we're good and sheltered here. Better take your boots and stockings off, and I'll help you over the side –'

As Arrietty, still shivering a little, sat down to undo her boots, she thought of the Platters and almost pitied them, crouched by the fence all night in their leaky small boat under their dripping umbrellas. Spiller, she noticed, had disappeared over the bluff.

'Did you get any sleep, Pod?' asked Homily, one leg over the edge of the boat. 'You and Spiller?'

'Enough,' said Pod, reaching up as she leaned forward and catching her under the arms, 'we got in well before midnight – didn't you hear the clock? That's the way . . . let yourself go. That's right!'

'Oh,' squealed Homily, as she splashed down on to the pebbles, 'this water's cold!'

'Well, what do you expect at this time of year?'

Arrietty had slid down by herself, boots and socks in her hand; she was longing for a climb up the roots. Homily seemed less enthusiastic.

'Now up you go, you two!' said Pod (he was untying the soap-dish). 'There's nothing to it, Homily: you can do it easy . . . No need to fuss –'

'I haven't said a word,' remarked Homily coldly. She eyed the small cliff with distaste. 'Will you take my boots, Pod?' she asked after a moment.

'Yes, give them here,' said Pod. He took them rather roughly, and pushed them under the lashing which secured the bedclothes in the soap-box. 'Now, up you go!'

Arrietty, already climbing, held out a welcoming hand. 'It's lovely! It's easy! Come on . . . I'll help you –'

Stolidly, Homily began to climb. If it is possible to climb up a mass of overhanging, tangled roots with dignity, Homily managed it that morning – steadily, calmly, and with no hesitation. Pod, following her up – one end of the mooring string in his hand – smiled to himself with an amused, grim kind of pride. There was no one like her – not once she had set her mind to a thing!

Reaching the top, Arrietty looked round for Spiller but she could not see him. This was nothing new: he could melt into any background provided (this she remembered) that background was out of doors. Instead, she gazed at a vast expanse of lawn, not mown to a velvet smoothness (as once it must have been) but roughly cut with a scythe. She knew about scythes: her father's was made from a razor-blade; and she knew about mowing-machines: there had been one at Firbank. But what caught her sharp attention and made her heart beat faster was the sight she saw in the distance – a long, low, gabled house, whose roofs caught the morning sunshine but whose front seemed vague and windowless. It must (as her father had told them) be covered with creeper – creeper gone wild. The Old Rectory – oh, what climbings there would be, what hidings, what freedom! And then she noticed that between the place on which she stood and the distant-seeming house, there was a pond – a rush-bound pond with an island in the middle. She could see the flat, round leaves of still unopened water lilies . . .

Then she was aware of some sort of commotion behind her: Spiller, Pod and Homily on the edge of the bank seemed locked in some sort of struggle. Panting and heaving, they were pulling on the mooring string of the soap-dish. She ran to help them, and Spiller slipped over the edge to disentangle some part which had been caught up among the roots. He managed to get it free and, guiding it with one hand, followed its progress upwards as the others pulled and steered it from above. At last it was beside them and they could all sit down. Pod rubbed his face on his sleeve and Homily flapped at hers with her apron; Spiller lay flat on his back. Anybody who had felt chilly down below, now felt chilly no longer.

Arrietty sat up on her elbow and looked at Spiller as he lay spread-eagled on the ground. Odd that she had never thought of Spiller as one who could be tired. Or even as one who slept. And yet somehow, during the night, he and Pod (on that packed, uncomfortable boat) had found a place in which to close their eyes – while she and her mother had lain so cosily tucked up in Miss Menzies's bedclothes. How kind Spiller had always been to them! And yet, in a way, so distant: one could never talk to Spiller except about the barest essentials. Oh well, she supposed one could not have everything . . .

She rose to her feet to have another look at the distant house. After a moment, the others got up too. They all stared, each with a different thought.

'The tower of that church,' said Homily wonderingly, 'is the spitting image of the one down in the model village –'

'Or vice versa,' said Pod, laughing. Arrietty was pleased to hear her father laugh: it seemed like a good omen. Homily tossed her head: Pod sometimes used words she failed to understand, and this always seemed to annoy her. 'Well, I'm going to put my boots on,' she announced, and sat down among the dry leaves under the juniper bush. 'And you'd better do the same, Arrietty. That grass will be wet after the rain . . .' But Arrietty, always admiring of Spiller's horny feet, preferred to go barefoot.

And then began the long, long walk.

CHAPTER EIGHT

THEY had to keep close to the pond (more like a lake it seemed to them) where the sedges and water plants provided cover. On the end of its towing-line, the soap-dish slid easily over the wet grass. Spiller went first, then Pod, Arrietty next, and Homily bringing up the rear; the cord passing from shoulder to shoulder. At first they barely felt the pull of it.

A more direct route would have been straight across the lawn but, in spite of Pod's assurances that the great house would be empty, they could never quite lose the inborn fear of prying, human eyes.

The tiredness came on slowly at first. Some of the grasses were coarse and tiresome, and sometimes they came across some of last year's thistles, beaten down by weather, but prickly just the same. The little new ones, pushing up among the grass stems, were soft and silvery, and furry to the touch. All the same, Arrietty began to miss her boots. But as Spiller showed no sign of stopping, pride kept her silent.

On and on they plodded. Sometimes a shrew mouse would dart away at their approach, woken at last from its long winter sleep. Frogs were there in plenty, plopping here and there, and there were aconites among the grasses. Yes, spring was here . . .

At last (after hours it seemed), Pod called, 'We'll take a break, Spiller.'

And they all sat down, back to back, on the tightly packed soap-box.

'That's better,' Homily breathed, stretching out her aching feet. Arrietty put on her shoes and the rough warm stockings Homily had knitted so skilfully on a pair of blunted darning needles.

'How did Spiller know, Pod,' Homily asked after a while, 'that there'd be no one in the house?'

'I told you, didn't I? That black thing in the hall –'

'What black thing?' Homily did not like the sound of this.

'It's a black thing they have in the hall. They turn a handle and tell it things. They grind the handle round and round, like, and tell it where they're going and this and that . . .'

'And who hears them?'

'Well, Spiller does, for one – say he's about. Spiller knows that house backwards. You'll see . . .'

Homily was silent for some moments. She could not visualize 'that black thing in the hall'. How black? How big? Which hall?

'That black thing – do they tell it the truth?' she asked at last.

Spiller gave his small grunt of a laugh. 'Sometimes,' he said.

Homily was silent again: she was not reassured.

Pod rose to his feet. 'Well, if you're rested, we'd better get going again.'

'Just a minute, Pod,' pleaded Homily. 'My legs ache something dreadful.'

'So do mine, if it comes to that,' said Pod. 'And Arrietty's, too, I shouldn't wonder. And you know for why? We're out of condition – that's for why. Nigh on six months cooped up in an attic – it stands to reason. Exercise, that's what we need . . .'

'Well, we're getting it now,' said Homily wearily as she rose to her feet.

And on they plodded.

There was one place where they had to leave the pond and cross the open grass. Here, they broke the procession, leaving Spiller to tow the soap-dish, as they made for the shelter of a small shrubbery. This was a group of overgrown azalea bushes, whose tender twigs were glinting into bud. It seemed like a forest to them. Here they rested again. The crumbly ground was covered with last year's dead leaves, and the branches above them hung with tattered spiders' webs.

'I wish we could spend the night here,' said Homily, 'camping, like . . .'

'No, girl,' said Pod. 'Once we get the soap-dish through this lot, we'll be right up by the house. You'll see . . .'

It was a struggle to get the soap-dish through the low-hanging, rootlike branches; but at last it was done and they found themselves in the open again, at the foot of a grassy bank. To their left, they could see a flight of mossy steps. Only the lower treads were visible, spreading fanlike into what had once been lawn.

'We're not going up *them*, Pod,' complained Homily, 'are we?' They were shallow steps, but not that shallow; and Pod was walking towards them.

'No, you and Arrietty stay where you are,' he called back quietly. 'Spiller and I'll go up by the coping and pull the soap-dish up from above.' He turned round again. 'Or you *could* start climbing the bank . . .'

'Could we!' exclaimed Homily, and sat down firmly, wet grass or no wet grass. After a moment, Arrietty sat down beside her: she too could do with the rest. 'They won't take long,' she told her mother.

Homily laid her weary head on her clasped knees. 'I don't care if they take forever,' she said.

They did not take forever. It seemed quite a short time before they heard the soft call from above. Arrietty rose slowly to her feet. 'Are you there, Arrietty?'

Arrietty said, 'Yes . . .'

'Pick up the string and start climbing.'

'Is it long enough?'

'What do you say?'

'I said, "Is it long enough?" '

'Plenty. We'll come down to meet you –'

Homily raised her head from her knees and watched as Arrietty, the tow-line in one hand, picked her way up the bank, occasionally pulling on the grasses. Then the grasses hid her from view. But Homily could hear the sound of subdued voices: 'Give it here, girl . . . that's right . . . that's splendid . . . where's your mother?'

Slowly and stiffly, Homily rose to her feet. She stared at the bank: the climb had not looked too bad and, unlike Arrietty, she would have both hands free. But she did not intend to hurry . . . did them no harm to rest. She could still hear the mumble of their voices.

At last, she pushed through the last of the grasses and found herself standing on weedy gravel; and there was the great house towering above her.

'Good girl!' said Pod, taking her hand. He turned and looked up at the house. 'Well, here it is – we're home!'

'Home?' echoed Homily wanly, looking across the uneven gravel to the iron-studded front door. Ivy everywhere and other kinds of creepers. Some of the latticed windows were almost hidden.

'You'll see,' said Pod. 'Wait till I take you inside.'

'How do we get in?' asked Homily.

'Come on. I'll show you –' He turned to the right, away from the direction of the front door. The soap-dish, dragged by Spiller, made a scraping noise on the stones. Homily glanced fearfully at the dark latticed windows: might there be other eyes looking out from within? But all seemed peaceful: the house had an empty feeling.

Perhaps that 'black thing' in the hall had been told the truth for once . . .

The sunlight fell slantingly on the front of the house but when they turned the corner they suddenly felt its rich warmth: this side of the house must face full south. And the windows here were different, as though added at a later date – tall, great windows with low sills and squared panes, dimmed a little by time and weather. Homily's home-making instincts rose to the surface: if somebody cleaned them, she told herself, those panes would look 'lovely'.

They passed by three of these long windows, the soap-dish scraping behind them, until the wall of the house ended in a built-out erection

of glass. Homily peered in through the dingy panes, some of which were cracked. 'It's the conservatory,' Pod told her, 'where they used to grow the flowers in winter. Come on –' Spiller led them on to the corner, where they turned again at right angles: glass panes again, peeling white paint, and a shabby glass door, cracked and rotten at the base where the wood met the weedy gravel. Here they halted.

'This is where we get in,' Pod told them, 'and you don't want to disturb them weeds: they hide the entrance, like . . .'

Very carefully, he parted a clump of ragwort and dead-looking grass stems. 'Careful of the nettles,' he said. 'Spiller keeps them down – much as he can – but they spring up again fast as he cuts them . . .'

'I thought you said this Witless was a gardener,' remarked Homily as, gingerly, she followed Pod through the gap.

'He only keeps up the kitchen garden. The main garden's gone too far. And he keeps up the churchyard as well.'

Arrietty, preparing to follow, glanced about her. What she had taken to be trees, she saw were box hedges run up to a great tangled height. Cover! Cover everywhere. What a place, she thought, what a wonderful place!

Stooping a little, she followed Pod and Homily through a jagged hole under the door. When she touched the wet wood to steady herself, a piece came away in her hand. 'Careful,' said Pod, 'we don't want this hole any bigger.'

Inside, the place felt gloriously warm, with the sun pouring down through the sloping glass roof. It smelt of dead geranium leaves and a cindery smell like coal dust. Old cracked plant-pots stood about, some in piles. There were several bits of sacking. There were one or two rusty stands which must have held plants. The floor was tiled in a pattern of dull reds and browns but many of the tiles were broken.

Pod had gone back through the hole to help Spiller with the soap-dish and Homily, standing still just inside the door, gazed about her in a kind of dazed bewilderment. Every few seconds, they heard a soft plop. It came from a tap in the corner. Below the tap, set in the tiles, Arrietty saw there was a grating. By the sound of the plop, Arrietty guessed that there was water below the grating. In the opposite corner stood a curious brick stove whose pipe went up through the roof. It had a door like an oven door, which stood half open, stuck fast on its rusty hinges.

'What a place!' said Homily.

'I think it's lovely,' said Arrietty. 'Water and everything. You could cook on that stove . . .'

'No, you couldn't,' said Homily, looking at it with distaste, 'someone 'ud see the smoke.' And she sat down suddenly on a piece of prised-up tile. 'Oh, my legs . . .' she said.

On the farther wall, opposite the shabby door under which they had entered, there were double glass doors built in the style of french windows. These, Arrietty realized, must once (perhaps before the conservatory had been added) have led straight into the garden, like those drawing-room doors she remembered at Firbank. They stood slightly ajar. One door, Arrietty noticed, was handleless. She tiptoed towards it and pushed it gently. With a faint creak of rusted hinges, it slid open a few more inches. Arrietty peered inside.

She saw a long room (vast, it seemed to her) panelled with bookshelves in faded oak and there, too, on her left, she saw the three long windows, through which the great squares of sunlight streamed across the floor. Opposite the middle window, in the right-hand wall, she made out a fireplace, rather a small one: to Arrietty's eyes it looked more modern than the rest of the room. Each of the three windows had deep window seats of oak, faded now by years of glass-warmed sunlight.

So entranced she was, that she did not hear Pod come up beside her, and started slightly when she felt his hand on her shoulder. 'Yes,' said Pod, 'this was the library.' Arrietty looked up at the bookshelves: there indeed were a few old dilapidated books, some untidy piles of tattered magazines, and one or two other objects of the kind no longer needed or cared for by a previous owner: old tin boxes, a broken riding whip, a cracked flower-vase or two, a noseless bust of some Roman emperor, a dusty pile of dried-up pampas grass.

'Doesn't look to me as though anybody ever comes in here,' said Homily, who had crept up behind them.

'That's just the idea,' said Pod. 'It's perfect. Perfect!' he repeated happily.

Arrietty thought so too, but turned back reluctantly to help Spiller with the unlashing of the soap-box. Pod and Homily turned back as well and Homily, still looking exhausted, sank down limply on her piece of prised-up tiling. 'Perfect, it may be,' she said, 'but where are we going to sleep tonight?'

'In the stove,' said Pod.

'What – among all that ash!'

'There's not much ash on the bars,' said Pod, 'it's all underneath.'

'Well,' said Homily, 'I never thought I'd be asked to sleep in a stove . . .'

'You slept *under* one at Firbank.'

'Oh, Firbank –' moaned Homily, '– why did we ever have to leave . . .'

'You know quite well why we had to leave,' said Pod. 'No, Arrietty,' he went on, 'get a bit of something – a strip of old sacking will do – and clean a bit of dust off them bars.' He moved towards the door. 'And I'll get a few green leaves –'

'Where's Spiller?' asked Homily, looking about her. He had been there a moment before.

'Slipped round to the larder to get a bite to eat, I shouldn't wonder.'

There was a sudden whirring sound and they all looked up as (very close it seemed now) the church clock began to strike. Pod raised his hand: he seemed to be counting. Homily and Arrietty watched Pod's trance-like expression: they seemed to be counting, too. 'Eleven,' said Homily as the last chime died away.

'Twelve,' said Pod. 'What did you get, Arrietty?'

'I got twelve, too.'

'That's right. Your mother missed a stroke. Well,' he went on, with an odd little smile, 'now we know: takes a good three hours to cross that lawn on foot . . .'

'Seemed more like three years to me,' said Homily. 'Hope we don't have to do it often.'

'There are ways and means,' said Pod darkly, as he made his way towards the entrance hole.

'Ways and means!' repeated Homily, as he disappeared from view. 'What can he mean? Ways and means . . . he'll be teaching us to fly next!'

Arrietty wondered, too, as she tore off a piece of loose sacking. Soon Pod was back with a bundle of leaves – box, they were, dark green and springy – soon the soap-dish was empty and the beds made up.

'Could be worse,' said Homily, dusting her hands together. It had really looked quite cosy: the blankets and quilts spread out on the springy leaves. 'Wish we could close the door . . .'

'Well, you couldn't call it open,' said Pod. 'Just room to get in and out –'

'I think I'll get in,' said Homily, moving back to the stove.

'No,' said Pod.

'What do you mean "no"?'

'Well, don't you want to see round the house?'

Homily hesitated. 'Well, after I've had a bit of a lie-down. We've been going all morning, Pod.'

'I know that. We're all a bit weary, like. But –' he went on, '– we may never get another chance like this. I mean, they're all out, aren't they? The human beans? And won't be back for hours . . .'

Still Homily hesitated. A bell shrilled. They all turned, like figures moved by clockwork, and stared at the double doors. The bell became silent.

'Whatever was it?' breathed Homily, moving backwards towards the stove, nervous hands feeling for the door.

'Wait!' said Pod sharply.

They waited, still as statues, and the bell shrilled out again. Three times it rang, and still they did not move.

'Well, that's all right,' said Pod, after a moment. 'Proves what I say.' He was smiling.

'How do you mean?'

'That black thing in the hall: when the bell goes, the human beans always come running –'

And then Arrietty remembered. Something The Boy had told her . . . What was it called now? A telegraph? No that was something else. What had be called it? The word seemed on the tip of her tongue. Ah, yes . . .

'I think it's a telephone –' she said uncertainly. She spoke rather shyly: sometimes it embarrassed her to know more about the great human world than either of her parents. 'Miss Menzies had one,' she added as though to excuse her startling knowledge.

It took a lot of explaining – wires, poles, speaking from house to house . . .

'Whatever will they think of next!' exclaimed Homily at last.

Pod remained silent for a moment, and then he said, 'Difficult to get the hang of it. At least, the way you explain it, Arrietty. But there's one thing I'm certain of –'

'What's that?' asked Homily sharply.

'That thing out in the hall – we're going to thank our stars for it!'

'How do you mean, Pod?'

'For what it tells us,' said Pod.

Homily looked bewildered. 'I never heard it say a word –'

'That the house is empty. That's what it told us, plain as plain. You mark my words, Homily, that black thing in the hall is going to be a . . .' (in his happy excitement, he seemed at a loss for the word) . . . 'a . . .'

'Godsend?' ventured Arrietty.

'Safeguard,' said Pod.

But, in the end, they did not explore the house that day. Homily seemed uneasy at the thought of being left on her own, and Spiller arrived with a tempting feast of titbits garnered from the larder. So they all sat down on bits of broken tile and ate a delicious luncheon. There were goodies they had not seen or tasted for what seemed like years: smoked ham, pink and tender; anchovy butter; small scraps of flaky pastry; grapes – to be carefully peeled; something wrapped in a lettuce leaf which Homily hailed as pigeon pie; a whole slice of home-made bread and a small, uneven chunk of rich plum cake.

After this meal, as sometimes happens, they all began to feel sleepy. Even Pod seemed aware of a sudden tiredness. Homily gathered up the leftovers and wondered where to put them (leftovers – they had forgotten there could be such things!). 'I'll get you a dock leaf,' said Pod, moving towards the door. But he moved rather slowly and Spiller forestalled him and was soon back with a selection of rather rusty-looking leaves. But Spiller, Arrietty noticed, had not eaten anything: he had never been one for eating in company.

But where to put the food where no stray eye might discover it? Even the broken tiles, Pod had explained, must be put back exactly as they had found them: there must be nothing to arouse attention or suspicion.

'We could put it outside among these weeds,' suggested Homily.

'No,' said Pod, 'it 'ud only attract the rats. And that we don't want . . .'

At length, Homily decided to take the leftovers to bed with her. 'They'll make a nice breakfast,' she told them, as she climbed up into the nest of eiderdown quilts.

Arrietty helped her father replace the bits of tiling (Spiller, in his sudden way, had silently disappeared). After this, there seemed nothing more to do so, feeling tired, she decided to join her mother in their comfortable, make-shift bed. Before she fell asleep, she heard the church clock strike four. Only four o'clock! But all the same, it had seemed a long, long day . . .

CHAPTER NINE

ARRIETTY was the first to wake in the morning. It was almost too warm under such a mound of quilts as all three had gone to bed fully dressed. She had awakened once in the night, disturbed by a strange noise – a banging, a tapping, a shuddering sort of noise followed by a silence and then by a series of gurgles. Pod and Homily awakened too. No one had spoken. 'What is it?' asked Arrietty after a moment. Pod had given a short grunt and had turned back on his side. 'It's the pipes,' he had muttered, 'the hot water pipes. Keep quiet, now, there's a good girl: we were up a bit late, me and Spiller . . .' and he pulled the bedclothes over his ears.

'Oh yes,' Arrietty remembered those radiators . . . 'A bit old-fashioned,' Pod had told them, but she supposed any caretaker must keep the house aired: that was what caretakers were for.

Carefully, she crept out through the narrow gap by the barely opened stove door, the hinges of which had become so rusted that it was quite immovable. It had been a clever place, she realized, in which to take shelter. She let herself down on to the shallow cluttered tiles, still strewn with the ashes she had brushed from the bars above, and took cover between the bricks on which the old stove had been built. She stared out cautiously, much as she and Pod had stared out from under the clock at Firbank.

All looked just as it had done the day before: the piled plant-pots, the cracked panes of glass, the garden beyond. The tap dripped rhythmically at its long intervals. No, this was different: a slightly thinner sound, more a plink than a plonk. Arrietty leaned forward, still careful to keep under cover. There seemed to be something blue on the grating under the tap. She narrowed her eyes, straining to see better. Something very blue. Some kind of utensil, something in which when the drop fell it went plink instead of plonk.

Filled with curiosity, she took a careful step forward. And then she saw what it was – they had had one in their storeroom at Firbank – it was a glass eye-bath. Homily had never used the one they had at Firbank because of its weight and its awkward shape: she hadn't patience with it. Well, here must be somebody who did have patience with it and somebody (Arrietty realized with beating heart) must be another borrower.

For one moment, she was tempted to turn back and waken her parents. Then she decided against it. No, she would stay here and watch and wait. After a while the eye-bath would be filled to the brim and, sooner or later, whoever had put it there would come back and fetch it. Arrietty sat down and, leaning against the brick support, she drew up her legs and clasped them in her arms. Chin on knees, she could watch in comfort.

Her thoughts began to stray a little. She thought of Spiller. Of his kindness and his wildness, of his reserve and independence. Of his deadly bow and arrow. He only shot for the pot. She herself would like to learn to use a bow but never, never, she realized, could she bring herself to kill anything living: in her case, it would be just for 'self-defence' as, when in danger, Pod might use his hat-pin. And yet, and yet – she remembered uncomfortably – how often, hungrily and gratefully, they had devoured the game which Spiller had procured for them. No questions asked – at least, none that she had been aware of – just a savoury dish on their table. Would Spiller come and live in this house with them, she wondered? Helping them to borrow and taking Pod's place perhaps when Pod got older? Would she herself ever learn to borrow? Not a cautious bit here or there, but fearlessly and well, learning the rules, knowing the tools . . . The answer, she felt, to the first question was 'no': Spiller, that outdoor creature, would never live in a house, never throw his lot in with theirs. But he would help them – always help them, of that she was sure. The answer to that second question was 'yes': she knew in her bones that she would learn to borrow, and learn to borrow well. Times had changed: there would be new methods, new techniques. And, as part of the rising generation, some of these she might even invent!

Suddenly there was a sound. It was quite a small sound and seemed to come from the library next door. Arrietty stood up and, keeping her body covered by the brick support, peeked her head forward.

All was quiet. She watched and waited. From where she stood, she could see the tap and, to the left of this, the place where the tiles ended and the library floorboards began. She could see a little way into the library, part of the fireplace and the light from the long windows but not the windows themselves. As she stood there under the stove, still as the crumbled bricks which supported it, she could feel the quickening pulse of her own heartbeats.

The next sound was very slight. She had to strain her ears to hear it. It was a faint continuous squeak. As though, she thought, someone was working a machine, or turning some miniature handle. It grew – not louder exactly, but nearer. And then, with a catch of the breath, she saw the tiny figure.

It was a borrower – no doubt of that – a borrower with a limp, dragging some contraption behind him. Whatever the contraption was, it moved easily – almost magically – not like Spiller's soap-box which was rather apt to bump. In this case, it was the borrower who bumped. One of his shoulders went right down with each step taken: he was very lame. And fairly young, Arrietty noticed, as he came on towards the tap. He had a soft mop of tow-coloured hair and a pale, pale face. The thing he dragged was on wheels. What a wonderful idea, Arrietty thought: why had not her own family ever owned such a thing? There had been plenty of old toys, she had been told, pushed away in the playroom cupboard at Firbank and some of them must have had wheels. It was these four wheels, she realized, which produced the fairylike squeaking.

When the young borrower reached the drain, he turned his truck so the rear end faced the eye-bath. Then, stooping down, he took a drink of water. Arrietty drew back a little when, wiping his mouth on his sleeve, he moved towards the glass door which led to the garden. He stood there for some moments, his back to Arrietty, gazing out through the panes. 'He's watching the birds,' she thought, 'or seeing what sort of day it is . . .' And it was a lovely day. Arrietty could see that for herself. No wind, pale sunlight, and the birds were starting to build. After a while he turned and limped his way back to the eye-bath. Stooping, he tried to lift it. But it seemed very heavy and was slippery with water. No wonder Homily had had no patience with such an object: there was nothing you could get a grip on.

He tried again. Suddenly, she longed to help him; but how to announce herself without giving him a fright? She coughed, and he turned quickly, then remained frozen.

Their eyes met. Arrietty kept quite still. His heart, she realized, must be beating just as hard as hers was. After a moment, she smiled. She tried to think of something to say. 'Hallo!' might sound too sudden. Perhaps she should say 'Good morning'? Yes, that was it. 'Good morning,' she said. Her voice, to her ears, sounded tremulous, even a little husky, so she added quickly on a brighter, clearer note. 'It's a lovely day!'

He was still staring at her, as though unable to believe his eyes. Arrietty returned his stare and kept quite still. She tried to hold on to her smile. 'Isn't it?' she added.

Suddenly, he gave a half laugh, and sat down on the edge of the drain. He ran his hand rather ruefully through the mop of his hair, and laughed again. 'You gave me a fright,' he said.

'I know,' said Arrietty, 'I'm sorry . . .'

'Who are you?'

'Arrietty Clock.'

'I haven't seen you before.'

'I – we only came last night.'

'We?'

'My mother and father. And me . . .'

'Are you going to stay here?'

'I don't know. It depends –'

'On what?'

'On whether it's safe. And nice. And – you know . . .'

'Oh, it's nice,' he said. 'Considering –'

'Considering what?'

'Considering other places. And it used to be safe . . .'

'Isn't it now?'

He gave her a small, half-rueful smile and shrugged his shoulders. 'How can one tell?'

'That's true,' said Arrietty. 'You never know –' She liked his voice, she realized: he spoke each word so clearly, in a clipped kind of way, but the general tone was gentle.

'What is your name?' she asked.

He laughed, and tossed his hair back out of his eyes. 'They call me Peagreen,' he said, still smiling – as though she might find it ridiculous.

'Oh,' said Arrietty.

'It's spelt P-E-R-E-G-R-I-N-E.'

Arrietty thought for a moment. 'Peregrine,' she said.

'That's it.' He stood up then, as though suddenly aware that all this time he had been sitting. 'I'm sorry . . .' he said.

'What for?'

'For flopping down like that.'

'You had a bit of a shock,' said Arrietty.

'A bit,' he admitted, and added, 'who taught you to spell?'

'I –' Arrietty hesitated: suddenly it seemed too long a story. 'I just learned,' she said. 'My father knew a little. Enough to start me off . . .'

'Can you write?'

'Yes, very nicely. Can you?'

'Yes.' He smiled. 'Very nicely.'

'Who taught you?'

'Oh, I don't know. All the Overmantels can read and write. The human children used to have lessons in that library,' he jerked his head towards the double doors. 'It goes back generations. You only had to listen, and the books were always left on the table . . .'

Arrietty moved forward suddenly from between the bricks, her face alight and interested. 'Are you one of the Overmantels?'

'I was until I fell off the chimneypiece.'

'How wonderful! I don't mean falling off the chimneypiece. I mean – that you're an Overmantel! I never thought I'd meet a real Overmantel. I thought they were something in the past –'

'Well, they are now, I suppose.'

'Peregrine Overmantel,' breathed Arrietty, 'what a lovely name . . . Peregrine Overmantel! We're just Clocks – Pod, Homily and Arrietty Clock. It doesn't sound very grand, does it?'

'It depends on the clock,' said Peagreen.

'It was a grandfather clock.'

'Old?'

'Yes, I suppose so.' She thought a moment. 'Yes, it was very old.'

'Well, then!' said Peagreen laughing.

'But we mostly lived under the kitchen.'

Peagreen laughed again. 'Ah-ha,' he said, and there was mischief in his face. Arrietty looked puzzled: had she made some sort of joke? Peagreen seemed to think so.

'Where do you –' she began and then put her hand to her mouth. She remembered suddenly that it was not done to ask strange borrowers where they lived: their homes, of necessity, must be hidden and secret – unless, of course, they happened to be one's relations.

But Peagreen did not seem to mind. 'I don't live anywhere just at present,' he said lightly, answering her half-asked question.

'But you must sleep somewhere –'

'I'm moving house. As a matter of fact, you could say I've moved. But I haven't slept there yet.'

'I see,' said Arrietty. Somehow suddenly the day seemed less bright and the future more uncertain. 'Are you going far?'

He looked at her speculatively. 'It depends what you call "far" . . .'
He turned back to the eye-bath and laid his hands on the rim. 'It's a bit
too full,' he said.

Arrietty was silent for a moment, then she said, 'Why don't you tip
a bit out?'

'That's just what I was going to do.'

'I'll help you,' she said.

Together they tilted the eye-bath. It had a lip on either side. As the
water gurgled down the drain, they set it back on its base. Then

Peagreen moved to his cart to push it nearer. Arrietty came beside him.
'My father would like this truck,' she said, running a finger along the
curved front: the rear was open like a lorry without a tailboard. 'What's
it made of?'

'It's the bottom half of a date box. I have the top, too. But that hasn't
got wheels. It was useful though, when they had carpets.'

'When who had carpets?'

'The human beings who lived here. The ones who took down the
overmantel. That's when I fell off the chimneypiece.' He went back to
the eye-bath. 'If you could take one lip, I'll take the other . . .'

Arrietty could and did, but her mind was reeling with what she had just heard: the overmantel gone, a whole lifestyle destroyed! When did it happen, and why? Where were Peagreen's parents now? And their friends and, perhaps, other children . . . She kept silent until they had set the eye-bath down on the lorry. Then she said casually, 'How old were you when you fell off the chimneypiece?'

'I was quite small, five or six. I broke my leg.'

'Did somebody come down and rescue you?'

'No,' he said, 'I don't think they noticed.'

'Didn't notice that a little child had fallen off the chimneypiece!'

'They were packing up, you see. There was a kind of panic. It was night, and they knew they had to get out before daylight. Perhaps they missed me afterwards . . .'

'You mean they went without you!'

'Well, I couldn't walk, you see.'

'But what did you do?'

'Some other borrowers took me in. Ground-floor borrowers. They were going too, but they kept me until my leg got better. And when they went, they left me the house, though, and some food and that. They left me quite a few things. I could manage.'

'But your poor leg!'

'Oh, I can climb all right. But I'm not too good at running, so I don't go out of doors much: things can happen out of doors, when you have to run. It was all right, and I had the books . . .'

'You mean the books in the library? But how did you get up to the shelves?'

'Oh, it's easy: all those shelves are adjustable. There are notches cut out in the uprights, it's like climbing a rather steep staircase. You just prise out the book you want, and let it drop. But you can't put it back. My house got full of books.'

Arrietty was silent, thinking all this over. After a while she said, 'What were they like, those human beings – those ones who pulled down the overmantel?'

'Dreadful. Always pulling things down and putting things up. You never knew where you were from one day to another. It was a nightmare. They blocked up the old open fireplace and put a small grate there instead . . .'

'Yes, I saw it,' said Arrietty. Even she had thought it spoiled the look of the room, with its glazed tile surround painted with writhing tulips – very snake-like, those tulips.

'Art-nouveau,' Peagreen told her, but she did not know what that meant. 'They said the old one was draughty, and it was rather: if you stood inside you could look up and see the sky. And sometimes the rain came down. But not often. In the old days, they burned great logs in it – logs as big as trees, the grown-ups used to tell us . . .'

'What sort of other things did they do? I mean, those human beings –'

'Before they went, they put in the telephone. And the central heating. And the electric light. Very newfangled they were: everything had to be "modern".' He laughed, 'They even put a generator into the church.'

'What's a generator?'

'A thing that makes electric light. All the lights in the church can go on at one go. Not like lighting the gas jets one by one. But all the same . . .'

'All the same what?'

'They went, too. Said the place was creepy. In this house, you never know what you're going to get in the way of human beings. But there's just one thing you can be sure of –'

'What's that?' asked Arrietty.

'They may *come* – but they always *go*!'

'Why's that, I wonder?'

'It's because of the ghosts. For some silly reason, human beings can't abide them.'

Arrietty swallowed. She put out a hand as though to steady herself on the rim of the date box. 'Are there – are there many ghosts?' she faltered.

'Only three that I know of,' said Peagreen carelessly. 'And one of those you can't see: it's only footsteps. Footsteps never hurt anybody.'

'And the others?'

'Oh, you'll see for yourself in time.' He smiled at her and picked up the cord attached to his truck. 'Well, I'd better be getting along: those Whitlaces will be up by seven.'

Arrietty increased her grip on the edge of the truck, as though to detain him. 'Can you speak to ghosts?' she asked him hurriedly.

'Well, you could. But I doubt if they'd answer you.'

'I wish you weren't going,' said Arrietty, as she removed her hand from the truck. 'I'd like you to meet my father and mother: there's so much you could tell them!'

'Where are they now?'

'They're asleep in that stove. We were all very tired.'

'In the stove?' He sounded surprised.

'They've got bedclothes and everything.'

'Better let them sleep,' he said. 'I'll come back later.'

'When?'

'When the Whitlaces have gone out.' He thought for a moment. 'About two o'clock, say? She goes down to the church and He'll be up in the kitchen garden, by then . . .'

'That would be wonderful,' and she stood there watching as he pulled his truck towards the double doors and into the library beyond. The fairylike squeaking became fainter and fainter until she could hear it no longer.

CHAPTER TEN

'ARRIETTY!'

It was a hoarse whisper. Arrietty broke out of her dream and turned quickly towards the stove. Yes, of course, it was her mother: Homily stood peering out of the stove, her hair tousled and her face drawn and worried. Arrietty ran towards her. 'Oh, Mother, what is it?'

Homily leaned a little further forward, still speaking in the same tense whisper: 'You were talking to somebody!' Her frightened eyes flicked round the sunlit conservatory as though, thought Arrietty, some monster might appear.

'Yes, Mother, I know.'

'But, Arrietty, you promised –' Homily seemed to be trembling.

'Oh, Mother, it wasn't a human bean! I was talking to a *borrower*!'

'A borrower!' Homily was still trembling. 'What sort of a borrower?'

'An Overmantel, to be exact.'

'An Overmantel!' Homily's voice now became shrill with incredulity. 'But how – I don't see . . . An Overmantel!' Her eyes flicked about again. 'Besides,' she went on, her voice becoming firmer, 'I never heard, not in my whole life, of an Overmantel bothering to talk to the likes of us.'

Arrietty remembered only too well her mother's dislike of Overmantels. 'A stupid stuck-up lot!' she had called them, who only lived for pleasure and were careless of their children. Pod had pointed out that somehow they always managed to get their children educated. 'Only to show off!' Homily had retorted.

'This one was quite young. Only a boy, Mother –'

'Don't tell me any more,' said Homily, 'I'm going to get your father –' As she disappeared through the crack, Arrietty heard her mutter, 'What with Hendrearies down at the church . . . and now, of all things, an Overmantel!'

Arrietty, once again, leaned against the brickwork thoughtfully biting a thumbnail. What was going to happen now, she wondered? She could hear their voices: a good many exclamations from Homily, a few quiet words from Pod. He came out first, combing his tousled hair with the little silver eyebrow comb they had borrowed from the showcase at Firbank. 'What's this,' he said mildly, 'you've met another borrower?' He climbed down (a little awkwardly for him) on to the tiles.

'Yes,' said Arrietty.

'What's he like?'

'Quite young. Well, at first, I thought he was not much older than me. His name is Peagreen.'

Pod was silent. Thoughtfully, he pushed the comb back into his pocket as Homily appeared. She, too, Arrietty noticed, had tidied her hair. She came beside her husband and both stood quietly, looking at Arrietty.

'Your mother tells me he's an Overmantel,' Pod said, at last.

'Well, he *was*,' said Arrietty.

'Once an Overmantel, always an Overmantel. Well,' he went on, 'there's nothing wrong in that: they come in all kinds!'

'Not really –' began Homily excitedly. 'You remember those ones in the morning-room at Firbank? They –'

Pod raised a quiet hand to silence her. 'Does he live alone?' he asked Arrietty.

'Yes, I think so. Yes, I'm sure he does. You see, it's like this . . .' And she told him, perhaps a little too eagerly, of Peagreen's accident, his early life, all the troubles and dangers and hungers and lonelinesses she had imagined for him (not that he had ever mentioned these himself) '. . . it must have been too awful!' she finished breathlessly.

Homily had listened silently: she had not known quite what to think. To feel pity for an Overmantel: that would be a development for which she would need time.

'You don't know where he lives?' asked Pod.

'No,' said Arrietty, 'he's just moved house.'

'Oh, well,' said Pod, 'he's a grown man now: it's none of our business. We've more important things of our own to go into now – Spiller and me, we was talking late last night: we got decisions to make and we've got to make them quickly.' He pulled out a piece of tile and sat down on it. 'What about that bit of breakfast, Homily? We can talk as we eat . . .'

'It's like this,' said Pod, when they were all seated and had opened up the dock leaf, 'with this weather and a full moon, we could unload the boat tonight.'

'Oh, Pod,' groaned Homily, 'not across that lawn again! Not so soon!' She was holding up a piece of limp ham which, during the long night, had become a good deal paler.

'Who said anything about walking across lawns?' Pod retorted. 'Just you listen quietly, Homily, and I'll tell you Spiller's idea.' He broke off a corner of dry bread and laid a sliver of ham across it. 'You know that pond? – well, you might call it a lake –' They waited anxiously until he had finished his first mouthful. At last, he swallowed. 'That lake, as you might have noticed, comes right up to the steps. If you didn't notice, it was because we cut away from it, through those bushes, to the bank, remember?'

Homily nodded. Arrietty, her eyes fixed on her father, stretched out her hand for a grape. She had begun to feel excited and was more thirsty than hungry.

'Now,' Pod went on, 'Spiller, with his punt pole and with the help of the paddle –'

'What paddle?' asked Homily.

'The butter-knife,' whispered Arrietty.

'– Can turn his boat into the stream and take it into the main lake, across the lake, and right up to the steps. Once on the lake, the going is smooth as silk, no currents there once he's out of the stream . . .'

'Then why didn't he do it yesterday?' complained Homily, 'instead of all that walking?'

'Because,' said Pod patiently, 'it was broad daylight. What sort of cover, I ask you, could you expect to find in the middle of a lake? No, Homily, moving our stuff by boat is a night-time job. Though I wouldn't say no to a bit of a moon . . .'

'That lake doesn't come right up to the bank, Pod,' said Homily after a moment.

'Near enough for us to unload and bring the stuff up the bank.'

'That'll take us all night,' said Homily, 'if all we've got to help us is Spiller's soap-box.'

'The first things I'll need out of that boat is me tools and the ball of twine.'

'What about my cooking-pots? Say we wanted a drink? Now, with our breakfast? There's that tap in the corner, dripping away, but we've nothing to put under it.'

'You must use your cupped hands,' said Pod, in the same patient voice, 'for the time being.'

They were not quarrelling, Arrietty realized, this was a 'discussion': later on, even she might venture to join in.

'There's an awful lot of stuff, Pod,' Homily pointed out, 'tables, chairs, beds . . .'

Was Pod going to remind her, Arrietty wondered, of his repeated warnings not to bring too much? No, she realized, he wasn't: he was too kind (and what good would it do now?).

'This move,' he said, 'must be done in two operations: everything up the bank and on to the gravel. And then, piece by piece, we bring it along here.'

There was a short silence. Then Arrietty swallowed nervously. 'Papa –' she began.

'Yes, Arrietty?'

'Where are we going to put all this stuff when we get it along here?'

Homily looked about her at the vast, empty conservatory. Then she looked back at Pod. 'The child's got a point, Pod. Where *are* we going to put it? Seeing as we have to put every tile back just where it was, so nothing should look out of place . . .'

Pod was silent a moment. Then he said gravely, 'You're right: that is a bit of a problem.'

They were all silent. After a while, Homily said, 'Seems like we have to find some sort of place first.' She looked towards the library.

'There's nowhere in there,' said Pod, turning his head to follow her gaze, 'barring the shelves and they're all open to view, as you might say.' He turned back and linked his hands together across his bent knees. He stared down at them thoughtfully. 'Yes, now I come to think of it, this is more than a bit of a problem.'

'You've been in the hall, Pod. What about those other rooms, as you go along the passage?'

'They keep them locked,' said Pod.

'What do you come to when you get to the end of the passage?'

'The old kitchen,' said Pod.

'What's that like?'

'Empty,' said Pod. 'They don't use it. Except for the cooking-stove in the corner. They keep that alight for hot water. And She simmers on it, Spiller says. They've got their own little kitchen beyond. Well, not a kitchen, exactly. It's a little place with a small sink and gas stove. The gas stove is very small – only takes one dish, Spiller says, and boils a kettle. And they get the hot water for the sink from the stove in the old kitchen. As I say, She simmers things on it and it keeps the place warm.'

'Might be useful for us,' said Homily thoughtfully.

'Might be,' said Pod.

'That old kitchen – there wouldn't be a place for us? To live in, like?'

'There could be,' said Pod, 'but say you've got a choice, better not choose a room where human beans are always coming in and out, bringing coal, carrying dishes . . . She cooks a lot for other people,' he added, 'takes it on as a job.'

Again there was silence: all were thinking hard.

'Are there any cupboards in the old kitchen?' Homily asked after a while.

'Plenty,' said Pod, 'and down at floor level underneath the dressers.'

'Suppose,' suggested Homily, 'we just stored the stuff in one of those? For the time being, say, till we found somewhere permanent?'

Pod thought this over. 'No,' he said, after a moment, 'it wouldn't do. Who's to say someone might not open that cupboard door? And that stuff – though it's safe enough now down in Spiller's boat – is all we've got in the world, Homily. Furthermore,' he went on (rather pleased with the word), 'there's so much of it. More than we need,' he sighed. 'But we'll let that pass now. As I see it, it's against the law of –' he paused.

'Averages,' suggested Arrietty.

'That's the word: it's against the law of averages that we could cart all that stuff all the way down that long passage, across the old kitchen, and stack it in an empty cupboard – and mind you, Homily, that kitchen is just below the place where they sleep, those Witlesses – without making a sound!'

'I suppose you're right,' said Homily, after a moment.

'I know I'm right,' said Pod. 'You can picture it: this house is dead quiet at night. One of them, Him or Her, would wake up, think it was rats or something, and there we'd be – caught red-handed!'

Homily was quiet for a moment, and then she said, 'Yes, I – I see what you mean.' Her voice sounded rather faint.

'And not only us,' Pod went on, 'all our possessions!'

A kind of burglary in reverse, Arrietty thought to herself, but she felt sorry to have had to be the one to point out all these difficulties. But difficulties they certainly were, and very grave ones.

'Then what are we going to do?' Homily said at last, after a long unhappy silence.

Pod stood up. 'It's obvious,' he said. He took a few restless steps across the tiles and then came back and sat down again. 'Go on as we are for the time being,' he announced firmly.

'What, live in that stove!' exclaimed Homily. But Arrietty felt a wave of relief: she had thought he might say that they must go away again. Suddenly she realized that she loved this house, the garden, the sense of freedom, and she felt that somehow, by some means yet to be discovered, they would find happiness here.

'Our stuff is safe enough where it is,' Pod went on, 'in Spiller's boat under that bank. And there it can stay, until we find some corner for ourselves . . .'

'But there doesn't seem to be one,' said Homily, 'not here on the ground floor. And I can't go climbing creepers at my age.' She was thinking of the rooms upstairs.

'Give me a few days,' said Pod.

Once Homily had made up their bed, there seemed nothing much else to do. Pod went off to make another exploration of the library but came back just as frustrated. They were waiting for Spiller who, at some point, was bound to appear, but time dragged very heavily. Once, the telephone rang. It rang three times, and they all rushed under the stove at the sound of scurrying footsteps in the passage. They heard Mrs Whitlace say, 'Hallo!' Then there was a pause, and she said, 'Yes – Yes.' There was another pause, and they heard her say, 'I will, of course!' in her cheerful, ringing voice. There was a click, and the footsteps scurried away again.

'I wonder what that was about,' said Homily, as they came out from under the stove. She was brushing herself down. 'Pod,' she went on, 'we've got to do something about these ashes . . .'

'I'll get you a wisp of box. You can sweep them to the side, like.'

'And how are we going to wash, I'd like to know? Drip by drip under that tap . . .'

'It may only be for a few days,' said Pod.

'How do we know?'

'Now, Homily, you be your old self: we've been through a lot worse than this, remember?'

'I was only asking,' said Homily as Pod turned towards the garden door. Arrietty jumped up and forestalled him. She held him back by clinging to his arm. 'Oh, Papa, could I go? It needn't be box: I saw a thistle head – a thistle head makes a lovely broom. Please, Papa!'

He let her go, rather unwillingly, but remembering his promise that, very soon now, he would teach her to borrow. All the same, he watched her anxiously through the dim glass panes as she darted about among the weeds and grasses. Soon she was back with two dried-up thistle heads, both a little damp with dew but, as she told Homily, they would sweep all the better for that. 'Are there any crumbs?' she asked her mother. 'There's a robin in that bush . . .'

'Plenty,' said Homily, and handed her the crumpled dock leaf.

'Now, Homily –' warned Pod. But Homily said, 'Oh, let her go, Pod. It's a lovely day and we can watch her from here . . .'

But, alas, as she crossed the path, the robin flew away. But she scattered the crumbs all the same and threw away the dock leaf. She went on to the untidy box hedge on the far side of the path and looked up into the branches. Very dark it looked up there, hemmed in by the thick clumps of leaves at the outer edges. It was a hollow kind of darkness but criss-crossed with a myriad sinewy twigs and branches. It was an easy climb and a hidden one. Arrietty barely hesitated: such a climb was beyond resistance . . . It was wonderful – no thorns, no scratchy pieces, only, here and there, soft curls of paper-thin bark. Up and up, she went: this climb was child's play, she thought, and, what was more, completely secure and hidden. Perhaps the leaves on the outside might rustle a little but what did that matter? Bushes were apt to rustle a little – birds could cause it, or even a puff of wind. But there was no wind today and as she got higher the surroundings became lighter until, at last, on a topmost branch she found herself in sunshine.

Oh, the view! There was the stable yard, with its mellowed roofs and beyond that the walled garden – the kitchen garden, Pod had called it. The walls were too high to see very far inside, but she could see the iron gate, with its upright bars: just wide enough, that gate, to take a wheelbarrow. It appeared to be padlocked.

On the other side, so close that it surprised her, was the squat tower of the church, with its small, low parapet and, just below this, the clock face. Around the church, obscured here and there by trees and bushes, the churchyard lay dreaming in the sunshine. Very peaceful it looked with its medley of gravestones. Some graves looked carefully tended, others old and forgotten, but they did not lie in rows. If anyone had asked her about the layout of the churchyard, she would have described it as 'higgledy-piggledy', but somehow, she thought, this made it seem beautiful. It made her long to explore it, to read the names on the headstones, and learn something of those who, when their time had come, had been so gently laid to rest. She had not quite realized how near the church was to the rectory, barely a step for a human being and not many more for a borrower.

Gazing at the church, she found herself comparing it with Mr Pott's

miniature counterpart in his model village. Looking at it now (as she swayed rather dreamily on a little seat she had found for herself between two upcurving boughs) she realized with what loving care Mr Pott had copied the original, almost – it seemed to her now – stone by stone. Was it true that her cousins, the Hendrearies, were living there? Spiller had said so, but her father had not seen them. Perhaps because he had not yet been inside the church? She had never liked Aunt Lupy, with her stout, important figure and her heavy, plummy voice. Nor, for that matter, had she particularly cared for her Uncle Hendreary, with his wispy beard and rather shifty eyes. She had never got to know the elder boys very well during those uncomfortable months she and her parents had stayed in their home: they were always out borrowing and seldom spoke at meals. And Eggletina had always seemed strange and withdrawn ('Never been the same, poor child,' Aunt Lupy would say, 'since that adventure with the cat . . .'). But she had liked Timmus, their youngest child.

Little Timmus, with his rosy cheeks and great, round, wondering eyes. Liked? No, that was not the word: she had loved Timmus! During those dull, long winter evenings in Aunt Lupy's house, she had kept him happy telling him stories (many of them the same stories she had read aloud to The Boy at Firbank). 'Quite the little mother, aren't you?' Aunt Lupy used to say, with her patronizing laugh. But Aunt Lupy, after all, had been kind enough to take them in – when they were homeless and what Homily called 'dessitute'. But, after the first rapturous reunion between Aunt Lupy and her mother the kindness had soon worn off. When danger threatened all of them, they had been made to feel unwelcome. Perhaps, Arrietty thought now, that was understandable. Too many mouths to feed, that had been the trouble . . .

Oh, well . . .

Yes, perhaps she had been 'a little mother' to Timmus; perhaps she had made his dull young life a little less dull? Curled up together on the foot of her uncomfortable bed, she had carried him into other worlds, and strange made-up adventures. But she had taken herself off, too. The chilly, twilit room had no longer contained them: they had flown away into fairy places and mysterious realms unknown. Yes, this was what she was realizing now: if perhaps she had helped Timmus, Timmus – with his loving, grateful ways – had certainly helped her.

And how seldom she had thought of him since. Imprisoned in the Platters' attic, they had been too busy planning their escape. And now they had this journey, the business of packing up for it, this exciting arrival at the rectory, the meeting this morning with Peagreen. In all this time, it never once occurred to her how Timmus must have missed her in his shut-up lonely life. How old would he be now? She tried to think, but all she could think of was that she must see Timmus again.

She looked back again towards the kitchen garden. It would (Pod had told them) be filled with good things in summer: they would never want for fruit or vegetables. And herbs for Homily's cooking. Not just the wild ones from the hedgerows (as had been the case so often before) but of rarer kinds and greater variety. But where would poor Homily do her cooking? Where, in the end, would they make their permanent home?

A sudden whirring from the church tower announced the clock was about to strike. She turned quickly, swaying slightly on her slender branch. The clock struck two. Two o'clock! It couldn't be! Where had the morning gone? Her parents must be out of their minds with worry. And Spiller must have arrived by now to bring them their luncheon. *And*, what was worse, she had forgotten to tell her parents that Peagreen might appear.

Down she went in careless haste, sliding, dropping, missing footholds. Why had she thought there was nothing 'scratchy' in this bush? There seemed plenty of scratchy things now.

Once on the ground, she dashed across the path, too hurriedly to notice that not one robin but two were feasting on her crumbs. They flew away at her approach into the bushes. She hardly bothered to avoid the nettles and nearly got stung several times (and a nettle sting was a big sting to a borrower) before she reached the hole under the door; dashing through it in her dew-wet boots she came to a sliding stop and looked around wonderingly at the silent, seated group.

CHAPTER ELEVEN

HER entrance did not cause the stir she had expected. Only Homily said, 'No need to come in like a thunderbolt,' but her voice sounded dispirited as though she had other matters on her mind. Arrietty had a feeling that, when she entered, they had all been sitting in silence. No. Spiller was not sitting exactly, he was lounging against the wall, idly running a lump of beeswax along the string of his bow.

She prised out a bit of tile and sat down facing them, her back towards the garden. A little tray of food lay, untouched, on the ground between them: why had nobody eaten? The tray, she realized, was a rather battered tin ashtray. No one spoke and no one seemed to notice her dishevelled appearance. What had been happening, she wondered? To what decision had they come?

At last Pod said, 'Well, that's how I see it,' and gave a great sigh.

'I suppose you're right,' said Homily glumly.

'I don't see what else there is to do. We can't keep on holding up Spiller's boat for ever . . . he'll be needing it soon. It's his livelihood, as you might say, borrowing for others.' Homily did not reply and Spiller, having raised his eyes for a moment, looked down again at his bow. 'And there should be a good bright moon tonight . . .' Pod added, as though to introduce a more cheerful note, '. . . and we've practically nothing to pack.'

So that was it: they were going! This lovely house, this dear house, had been found wanting. Although at first it had seemed so promising, for some reason now it would not 'do'. Arrietty felt the tears pricking into her eyes, and bowed her head so that they would not show.

'We might try the church of course,' said Pod. 'The Hendrearies seem to have managed to get along there . . .'

Homily threw up her head, her eyes flashing. 'Nothing,' she exclaimed, 'absolutely *nothing*, Pod, would persuade me to stay with Lupy again! Not wild horses, with wings of fire, down on their bended knees! Remember the last time we stayed with them!'

'Well, I didn't rightly mean stay with them,' said Pod, 'that church is a big place, Homily.'

Homily's eyes were still angry. 'Not even under the same roof!' she said firmly. 'However big . . .'

Pod knew when he was beaten. Once more, there was silence. Homily now sat again with her head bowed; very depressed she looked, and very tired. Why, Arrietty wondered, did all these decisions have to be made so quickly? Her mother's next listless words seemed to echo her thought.

'Why don't we just sleep on it tonight, Pod?' she suggested wearily.

'Because the weather might change,' said Pod.

Arrietty brushed a hand across her eyes and raised her head again and then, suddenly, she began to smile. She was looking at the double doors which led into the library: it was Peagreen! He stood there, hesitating a little shyly. He seemed ready to slip away again.

'Peagreen!' she exclaimed, and jumped to her feet.

Pod and Homily turned sharply: even Spiller straightened himself against the wall.

'Papa, this is Peagreen! We met this morning. Peagreen, this is my father and mother. And our friend Spiller . . . Peagreen, come in. Do . . .'

'Yes,' said Pod, slowly rising, 'come in and sit down. Arrietty, get him a piece of tile . . .'

Peagreen bowed and as he limped shyly forward his usually pale face looked faintly flushed. 'How do you do?' he said, as Arrietty placed a tile for him. He sat down on it a little uncertainly and rather towards the edge. There was a short surprised silence, and then Pod said, 'It's a lovely day, isn't it?' Homily just stared.

'Yes,' said Peagreen.

'Not that I've been out of doors yet,' Pod went on.

'I have,' Arrietty put in conversationally. 'I climbed that bush outside. It was lovely. You can see for miles . . .'

Peagreen smiled, 'So you've found my look-out?' he said.

'Your look-out?' repeated Pod. He sounded interested.

'Yes,' said Peagreen, turning courteously towards him. 'You'll find it very useful. Almost indispensable, in fact. I'm not much of a walker, but luckily I can climb.'

Homily was still looking amazed. So this was an Overmantel! Nothing like those she had ever heard about, except perhaps the voice, which she thought rather affected.

'Have you lived here long?' asked Pod politely.

'All my life,' said Peagreen.

'So you know all the ins and outs?'

'You could put it like that,' said Peagreen, smiling, 'but in my case, it's more "ins" than "outs". I'm not an open-air type – except by necessity.'

'And it's a nice old house,' Pod said. 'We're sorry to be leaving it.'

Peagreen looked surprised. 'But this young lady here . . . your daughter . . . well, I gathered from her you had only just come?'

'That's true,' said Pod, 'but there are difficulties . . .' He sighed.

'I'm sorry,' said Peagreen, still looking puzzled. He was too polite to ask what these difficulties might be.

'Well, it's like this –' began Pod, and hesitated, but looking back into that simple, boyish face he felt encouraged to go on. 'It's just this: there seems no place on this ground floor, no place at all, where it would seem safe for a family of borrowers to live. Not settle down in, like. Not to start a new life in. I like the house, no doubt about that, but you've got to face facts. Hard as it may be. And it *will* be hard for us . . .'

Peagreen leaned forward on his seat. 'I – I could make a suggestion,' he said, after a moment.

'I'd be glad if you would,' said Pod, but there was not much hope in his voice.

'I don't know what you'd think of it. It isn't much. And it's rather inconvenient, I'm afraid, but my old house is free now. And you'd be very welcome to it. For the time being, at least . . . I mean, until you can find somewhere better.' His flush had deepened and he seemed rather embarrassed. Nevertheless, his face looked eager and smiling.

'That's very kind of you,' said Pod, wary of committing himself, 'very kind indeed. But you see, my missus and I, we'll soon be getting on a bit and any house we settled in would have to be on the ground floor, like.'

'But my house *is* on the ground floor,' said Peagreen.

'I can't think where,' said Pod.

Peagreen jerked his head towards the double doors. 'In there . . .'

'In the library? Impossible!' exclaimed Pod.

Peagreen smiled. 'I can show you, if you like. It isn't far . . .' He rose to his feet.

'If it isn't too much trouble,' said Pod. He still looked very mystified, having searched – several times over – every crack and cranny in the library.

'No trouble at all,' said Peagreen. 'I'd better lead the way . . .' he added, and began to limp ahead.

Spiller, Arrietty noticed, had slung his bow over his shoulder and was making for the garden door. She took a few steps towards him. 'Aren't you coming, too, Spiller?'

He turned as he reached the door and shook his head. Then he slipped away through the hole.

Feeling slightly disappointed, Arrietty followed the others into the library; they were grouped, she noticed, in front of that strangely modern fireplace. Why had not Spiller come, she wondered? Was he shy? Was he a little suspicious of Peagreen? Or, being an outdoor borrower, was he just not interested in any kind of indoor home?

As Arrietty came up to them she noticed, where Peagreen was standing, a wide dark stain on the lighter wood of the floorboards. Peagreen glanced down. 'Yes,' he said, 'they used to put a rug over that. I'll explain later . . .' He turned again to Pod. 'The thing to remember,' he said, 'is that it's the third tile from the end.' Crossing the hearth, he gave the tile in question a slight kick. Nothing happened, so he kicked it again, slightly harder.

This time, the top of the tile slid forward a little from the base of the tile just above it. Peagreen, stretching his arms, got his fingers on the protruding edge and, with an effort, managed to pull it forward. Pod hurried up, anxious to save the tile from falling, but Peagreen said, 'It's all right: it won't fall; these tiles were made to fit exactly.' He tugged once more and with a grating sound the tile came free, Pod supporting it in front and Peagreen at the side. They paused a moment for breath. Then Peagreen said, 'Now, we just have to push it along a little . . .' This they did, and leaned it gently against the tile beside it. A gaping hole was revealed, very dark and somewhat forbidding.

'I see,' said Pod, 'very clever.' He ran his hand along the edge of the tile. 'You scraped off the cement?'

'Yes. At least the Wainscots did. There wasn't much cement –'

'No, there wouldn't be,' said Pod, 'not with tiles that fitted like these.'

'Who were the Wainscots?' asked Arrietty.

'The borrowers who took me in. Shall I go in first?' he said to Pod, who was peering into the hole. 'It's a bit dark at the entrance . . .'

'Thanks,' said Pod. 'Come along, Homily –' and he put out a hand to guide her. Arrietty brought up the rear.

They all trooped in through the cavern-like hole. Arrietty noticed it had been hacked out by hand and was almost a short tunnel. They found themselves in a vast dimly lit space, draughty and cold after the warmth of the sunlit conservatory. Looking up, to find out the source of light, she saw a patch of blue sky. They were somewhere inside the old chimneypiece.

'There should be a bit of old candle-end about,' Peagreen was saying. 'I usually left one here, and a few safety matches. To tell you the truth,' he went on, as he fumbled about in the semi-darkness, 'I don't use this entrance much myself.'

'Is there another?' asked Pod.

'Yes. But that's not too easy either. Ah!' he exclaimed in a satisfied voice: he had found the candle and was striking a light.

What a strange place it was! A cathedral sort of place, the soot-blackened walls going up and up, with the sky as a far distant canopy. The cracked floor was littered with twigs and sticks and, in one corner, a neat but high pile of ash beside which, to Arrietty's surprise, she recognized the eye-bath. But Peagreen now was moving the light towards the farther wall, so dutifully she followed its gleam. 'This is really what I wanted to show you,' Peagreen was saying, holding the candle high: and Arrietty saw, propped up at either end by two piles of slatey-looking stones, the prongs of a narrow hand-fork minus its handle: it was the kind of weeding fork, Arrietty realized, which a lady-gardener might use – someone like Miss Menzies, for instance; and now, when she came to think of it, Miss Menzies *had* owned such a fork but hers had a handle; and she kept it very clean. This one, in the flickering candlelight, looked very worn and blackened.

'You can cook on these prongs,' Peagreen told them. 'They found it in the conservatory –' he added, '– makes a kind of grill.'

Homily, hearing this, ventured a little closer; the expression on her face was one of extreme distaste: this was not her idea of a cooking-stove, nor was this vast, dusty cavern her idea of a kitchen.

'What about the smoke?' she whispered to Pod.

'There wouldn't be any smoke,' Pod told her, 'at least not that anyone would notice, with this great hearth and the chimney so high. What little there was the walls about'd absorb it, like. Think of the size of our fire compared with the ones this was built for!'

'*Our* fire?' echoed Homily. Her whisper was bitter: was Pod really thinking she would consent to live in this awful place?

'What on earth did they use to cook in?' It was only the second time Homily had addressed Peagreen directly.

'Tin lids mostly.' He nodded his head towards a deeply shadowed wall, 'There are some shelves over there.' He turned away from the grid, holding the candle high. 'Well, then, I'll show you the rest – such as it is. Careful of the wood,' he warned them as he kicked some branches aside. 'The jackdaws drop it down: every spring they try to nest on the corner of the chimney and every spring they fail,' he was leading them towards the entrance hole. 'As long as those jackdaws keep on building, you'll never be short of fuel. And keep on building they will . . .'

Pod paused for a moment to look at the tottering pile. 'Could do with a bit of stacking,' he said.

Peagreen paused too, and glanced at the untidy mess. 'I didn't bother,' he said. 'You see, I can't cook – at least, not much. I just used that grid to heat up water. For my bath,' he added, 'or an occasional cup of tea.'

Yes, thought Arrietty, looking at Peagreen in the candlelight, that was what had struck her at their first meeting: that he looked so very clean. How she longed for a bath herself: perhaps later it could be managed?

Peagreen had paused by the hole which led to the library. He turned to Arrietty. 'Would you take the candle for a moment?'

She took it from him and tried to hold it high as she watched him kneel down on the cracked stone of the floor. Some flat thing lay there: something that when they had entered in nearly pitch darkness she had taken for a kind of door-mat. Now she saw it was the back cover of a leather-bound book. He pushed it aside and there was another hole, one that led downwards. Arrietty drew back from it with a little gasp of dismay. Was the rest of Peagreen's house somewhere under the floor? If so, it would be beyond bearing. She thought of those early years at Firbank, the dusty passages, the dimly lit rooms, the long monotonous days, the sense of imprisonment, intermingled with fear. She had grown used to it, that she realized now, but only because she had known no other life. But now she had tasted freedom, the joy of running, the fun of climbing; the sight of birds, butterflies, flowers – of sunshine, rain and dew . . . No, not that again, not under floor!

Peagreen took the candle from her gently and held it over the hole. She felt he had sensed her dismay and had mistaken it for fear. 'It's all right,' he assured her, 'only a few steps down . . .' and slowly he disappeared from view. Pod went next and, after him, Homily – with almost as much unwillingness as Arrietty herself was feeling. There were about six steps made of stone and neatly set together.

It was just as she had feared: a long dark passage between the joists which supported the floor above, the library floor it must be;

it was quite straight and it seemed to go on and on. It was as dusty as the passages had been at Firbank, and smelt of mice droppings. Bringing up the rear of the procession, she felt there were tears on her cheeks. No good feeling in her pocket for a handkerchief: she had left it in the stove. Her only ally, she felt, was going to be her mother, and that not because of darkness but because of the awful kitchen. Pod seemed unconcerned.

At last, Peagreen paused at a second set of steps – these seemed to go upwards. He held the light steady until they had all caught up with him, and then he went on ahead.

'These steps are well made,' remarked Pod, 'can't think how the stones bind together.'

'Wainscot made them,' Peagreen called down from above. 'He was a better stone-mason than carpenter. Some kind of sticky stuff he used,' he went on, as Pod's head emerged to his level, 'something he mixed with resin from the fir trees.'

'Resin . . .' echoed Pod, as though to himself. In all the alterations he had made at Firbank, he had never thought of resin! And fir trees there had been there in plenty . . .

Peagreen had passed the candle to Pod and seemed to be busy with his hands. Suddenly the small staircase was lit up by a stream of light from above. And, to Arrietty's surprise and joy, the light was daylight! Pod blew out the candle.

One by one, they emerged into what seemed, to them, a very long room. It was (Arrietty suddenly realized) the enclosed space below one of the window seats. It must be the one (judging by their long walk under the floorboards) below the window which faced the fireplace. The space was even longer than it had seemed at first because one end of it was filled with a stack of books which rose almost to the ceiling. Otherwise, it was empty. And spotlessly clean. Chequered sunlight fell across the floor from what appeared to be a grating let in to the outside wall. It was a grating very like the one she remembered at Firbank: the one which she used to call *her* grating, and through which she would gaze for hours at the forbidden world outside. Her spirits lifted: perhaps, oh perhaps, everything was going to be all right . . .

Pod was staring up at the wooden ceiling. 'You could get another storey in here,' he said, 'plenty of height . . .'

'Yes, Wainscot thought of that,' Peagreen told him, 'but decided in the end it would take too much material. He couldn't think of a way to get the stuff in.'

'We'd hit on something,' said Pod.

Arrietty's spirits began to rise even higher. She could tell from her father's voice and the way he was looking about him that he was already making plans. He had now walked into the alcove which enclosed the grating. Heavy curtains, now drawn back, fell down on either side. In winter, Arrietty realized, these would cut off the draught.

'I'm leaving the curtains,' said Peagreen as he came beside Pod. 'I've no need for them where I'm going.' Where *was* he going, Arrietty wondered?

'I'm not looking at the curtains,' said Pod. He was staring upwards at the low ceiling of the alcove. Some sort of pulley hung there, from the inner ridge of which there hung down a piece of twine.

'Oh, that!' said Peagreen. He did not sound very enthusiastic. Arrietty moved close to see better. At Pod's feet she saw an old-fashioned iron weight, with a handle on top for lifting. To this the twine was fastened. The other end of the string, she saw, ran across the ridge of the pulley and was attached to the top of the grating. Whatever could this contraption be for?

'It works,' said Peagreen rather gloomily, 'I don't know where he found the pulley.'

'I do,' said Pod, smiling. 'He found that pulley in an old grandfather clock.'

'How do you know that?' asked Peagreen.

'Because,' said Pod, still smiling broadly, 'at Firbank, our house was under a clock. There's not a bit of mechanism in a grandfather clock that we don't know inside out: the times I've studied it all from below. Our name is Clock, by the way . . .'

'Ah, yes,' said Peagreen, suddenly remembering.

'The string from that pulley – in our clock, it was wire not string – was attached to one of two weights. Pulled the weight up and down, like.' He was silent a moment. 'Where's the rest of the clock now?'

'Stashed away somewhere,' said Peagreen. 'Most likely in the old game larder. There's a pile of old junk in there. But the clock never worked.'

'It wouldn't,' said Pod. 'Not without that pulley.' He seemed to be deep in thought. After a while he said, 'I gather that grating isn't fixed?'

'It used to be fixed,' said Peagreen, 'but Wainscot got it free. Now it just stands by its own weight.'

'So you can open and shut it? I mean with the help of that pulley?'

'Yes,' said Peagreen. 'You push on the top to free it, then you take hold of the string and gradually let it go. It opens out flat on to an old brick outside.'

'Very clever,' said Pod, 'quite a one, your friend, for scraping out cement. Although,' Pod went on, peering downwards through the grating, 'I'm not sure about that great brick outside . . .'

'You need the brick,' explained Peagreen, 'for the ventilator to rest on. Otherwise you might not get it up again. It's quite heavy: cast iron, you see.'

'Yes, I see that,' said Pod. 'It's just that we were brought up to think that a borrower should never use – when he's constructing his house, say – anything that a human bean might move.'

'No one ever has moved it,' said Peagreen, 'at least, not in my lifetime. It's a mossy kind of old brick: you'd hardly notice it, among all the weeds and things . . .'

'All the same –' said Pod.

'And I never did open it right down,' Peagreen went on, 'I'd just open it a little way so I could slip out sideways. Except, of course, during these last few days, when I had to get my things out.'

'Yes, that must have been quite a business,' said Pod.

'Oh, Papa –' Arrietty broke in, 'he has a little truck! Quite a big truck, really, it's half a date box. With wheels,' she added eagerly. 'Four wheels!'

'A truck, eh?' said Pod, looking at Peagreen with increased respect. 'With wheels?'

'I didn't make it,' Peagreen hastened to assure him, 'it belonged to the Wainscots. I'm not very good with my hands.' He glanced at the weight and pulley. 'I loathe that contraption. That's why I'm moving, partly.'

Pod turned back to the grating. 'Well, let's try it,' he said. 'What do you say, Homily?'

'No harm in trying,' she said timidly. Although she had kept so quiet, she had been watching closely. Arrietty could not quite make out her expression: it was an odd mixture of anxiety, hope and fear. Her hands were so closely clasped together against her chest that the knuckles looked white.

Pod went close up to the grating and, raising his arm above his head, he struck the top of it with the side of his closed fist. It began to slide forward and as the weight on the floor began to rise, Pod stepped aside quickly to avoid its sudden ascent. A bit too sudden, Arrietty thought, as the floor weight clashed up against the pulley. The ventilator lay fully open, resting, it seemed, on the brick. You could walk out on it, Arrietty realized, into the sunlit world outside.

'Well, that's that,' said Pod, rubbing the side of his hand: the blow he had given on cast iron had been a bit severe. 'Is there any way of working this thing more slowly?'

'Well,' said Peagreen, 'you can keep a guiding hand on the twine and pull it aside, if you see what I mean. Depending on how far you want to let the whole thing go. If you want to stop it at a certain place, you can give it a couple of twists round this –' He put up a hand and touched a piece of metal in the wall. 'Sort of cleat, don't they call it?'

'I see what you mean,' said Pod. 'I never noticed that.'

'It comes in useful,' Peagreen told him. 'Especially for someone like me. I hardly ever open that grating fully . . .'

'How do you shut it?' asked Pod.

'You pull on the weight,' said Peagreen.

'I see,' said Pod. He seemed very impressed. 'What do you think of it, Homily?'

'Very nice,' said Homily uncertainly. 'But –'

'But what?' Pod asked her.

'Say you pull that weight right down till it reaches the ground, what's to prevent it going up again?'

'Because,' said Pod, 'by the time that weight's on the ground, the grating will be back in position: there'll be no more strain on the twine, like.'

He turned his back to the sill of the now empty gap and, with a hand on either side, swiftly hitched himself up into a sitting position. He did this, Arrietty noticed, with something of his old athletic manner. Proudly she watched him as, swinging both legs around on to the grating, he swiftly rose to his feet. To her loving eyes, he seemed, quite suddenly, to have found his youth again. Swiftly she turned as though to speak to her mother but was silenced by what she saw. Homily, too, had been gazing at Pod. She seemed to be smiling but her lips were trembling and her eyes looked suspiciously bright. Catching Arrietty's glance, she opened her arms and Arrietty flew into them. They clung together. Were they laughing or crying? It was difficult to tell.

CHAPTER TWELVE

In the end, they all climbed out on to the grating. The sun, by now, had moved slightly round towards the west but its rays still poured down on this south side of the house. Through a thin fringe of weeds, Arrietty could see the path along which they had traipsed (was it really only yesterday?) dragging Spiller's soap-box. Where was Spiller now, she wondered? Why had he disappeared? He would have liked this place. Or perhaps he already knew about it?

Pod, his legs apart, was staring down at the grating. 'You know, Peagreen,' he was saying, 'this thing isn't resting on the brick at all: it's held in this straight-out position by that weight coming up against the pulley . . .'

'All the same,' went on Pod, 'that brick's a bit of a safeguard: supposing, say, the twine broke, or something . . .'

'Heaven forbid . . .' muttered Homily.

'It's all right, Homily, I've got plenty of twine among our stuff. Fishing line,' he explained to Peagreen, 'good and strong. Stronger than this, I shouldn't wonder.' Another idea seemed to strike him. 'What sort of fish do you have in that pond?'

Peagreen hesitated: he was not a fishing man. 'Roach, they say, and chub. Wainscot once caught a trout. Minnows . . .'

'Minnows will do for us,' said Pod, 'there's nothing tastier than a fresh-caught minnow, the way Homily cooks it.'

Homily, thinking of that dark, draughty cavern behind the fireplace, said, 'But we've got the larder now, Pod. Seems to be everything that we might ever need in that larder. And most of it ready-cooked . . .'

'Now, Homily,' said Pod, 'let's get this straight once and for all: I don't want you depending too much on that larder. A bit here, a bit there – well that's all right. That's how we managed at Firbank. But remember when we lived in the boot? We had to use our . . .' he hesitated, '. . . our . . .'

'Imagination?' suggested Arrietty.

'That's it. We got to use our imagination, and get back to our old ways, as far as we can. Suppose those Witlesses moved out sudden, like? Suppose Mrs Witless took ill? Suppose I got caught, stranded on one of those shelves? or Arrietty here – once she's learned to borrow? It's hard work, my girl, and dangerous work. Borrowers only borrow the things they can't live without. Not for the fun of it. Not out of greediness. And not out of laziness, neither. Borrowing for borrowers – and well you know it, Homily – is their only means of . . .' Again he hesitated, seeking the word.

'Subsistence?' murmured Arrietty tentatively.

'Survival,' said Pod firmly. He looked round at them all as though happy to have found the word for himself.

For a short while, there was a silence: it was a long time since they had heard Pod make such a long speech. And it seemed he had more to say:

'Now, don't get me wrong,' he went on, 'that walled garden, the kitchen garden, we can borrow from that to our hearts' content. Compare us, say, with the pigeons, the field mice, the slugs, the snails, the caterpillars . . . I mean one pod of peas would give us a meal, like, and who's there to grudge us that? Not Witless, that's for sure. Nor Mrs Witless neither. And there'd be Spiller with his bow, keeping down the field mice. There's a mite of things to keep down in a kitchen garden . . .'

'Who's to grudge us a sliver of cheese, a pinch or two of tea, a drop of milk?' said Homily, 'or a bit of ham off the bone before they throw the bone away? Or . . .'

'I don't say we won't never borrow from the larder, Homily, all I'm saying is we got to watch it.'

'I *have* to depend on the larder for everything,' said Peagreen glumly, 'that's why I'm moving house.'

They all turned to look at him, and he smiled rather wanly. 'You see,' he explained, 'for me to get to the larder, I have to open this grating a crack, slide out sideways, and walk round the corner of the conservatory, and on along that same path as far as the larder window and then back again by the same route. It's the safest way for someone who can't run fast. There's always that box hedge for cover but it's very inconvenient sometimes, especially in winter: one can get snowed up.'

'I see your point,' said Pod. 'You want to be nearer the larder?'

'Yes,' said Peagreen. 'Not that I eat so much, but it's all that walking. I find it a waste of time. Of course,' he went on, 'it might be a bit shorter down that passage and across the old kitchen. But I have to take it slowly and there's not much cover. Once there used to be a great old table in the middle of that kitchen, but it's gone now . . .'

'Yes,' said Pod, 'there's a good bit of open floor to cover. I see your point,' he repeated. There was a short silence, then Pod said, 'Your new house –' and he hesitated. Arrietty guessed that her father longed to know where Peagreen's new house might be, just as she herself had longed to know, but manners forbade his actually asking. 'I mean,' said Pod, 'this new house of yours? You'll find it easier?'

'Very much easier,' said Peagreen. Suddenly his face lit up. 'Would you like to see it?'

'Oh, I would!' cried Arrietty, running towards him across the opened grating.

'It's a bit of a walk,' said Peagreen to Pod.

Pod still seemed to hesitate out of some kind of politeness: perhaps he did not want to appear to pry. 'Another day,' he said, 'I'd like to poke about here a bit longer.' He looked at the gap in the wall and down again at the grating. 'I want to get the hang of this thing . . .'

'Can *I* go, Papa?' cried Arrietty eagerly. Her legs already were over the side of the grating. Pod looked down at her.

'I don't see why not,' he said, after a moment, 'providing you're quick,' he added.

'We'll be as quick as we can,' she promised, and slid off the grating into the grasses, 'come, Peagreen!' For the moment, she had forgotten Peagreen's lameness.

'Oh, Peagreen –' called Pod, as the latter was preparing to slide off the edge of the grating, 'there's just one thing –'

'What's that?' asked Peagreen, pausing.

Pod jerked his head towards the long, window-like gap in the brickwork. 'All those books in there, have you read them?'

'Yes,' said Peagreen.

'Do you want to read them again?'

'Not particularly. Are they in your way?' he went on. 'I just left them there because they were too big to fit into my new place.'

'No,' said Pod, 'they're not in my way. Not at all,' he added in a satisfied voice.

'If so, now the grating's open, we can chuck them out into the grasses and move them away after dark. I've got a lot of smaller ones . . .'

'And where would we hide these?' asked Pod. 'No, no, leave them be. I might have a use for them . . .'

'Right,' said Peagreen, and slid off the grating into the grasses.

CHAPTER THIRTEEN

ARRIETTY did not speak as, matching her step to Peagreen's, they passed along the western side of the conservatory. Her feeling of relief and happiness seemed almost too much to bear: so they were going to stay – that much had become obvious! A new life and a freedom such as she had never dared to dream of; and it was just about to begin: it *had* begun!

Once round the corner, Peagreen said 'Excuse me', and stooped rather gingerly to feel among the dried dock and nettles. He drew out a grimy piece of broken glass. 'I'm collecting these,' he said. He then took her arm and guided her across the path into the shelter of the box hedge. 'Safer to walk on this far side,' he said.

Arrietty stared with interest across the path at the ivy-clad wall of a part of the rectory she had not yet seen. The ivy was small-leaved and variegated, and clung stoutly to the dark red brick; its woody stems ran snake-like in all directions across the ancient surface. How easy, she realized, these root-like tentacles would be to climb. Could Peagreen's new house be on an upper floor? No, he had said that it was near to the larder. Then, a few steps ahead of them, she noticed a long cage-like erection firmly fixed, it seemed, to the old red bricks. As they came abreast of it, Peagreen halted. It consisted of several metal posts and cross bars, netted with torn and rusted chicken-wire. Inside it were what looked like several small dead trees, some of whose many branches had rotted away. In one corner stood a mossy-looking water barrel, full to the brim and with water flowing over. This was fed by a pipe running down from the roof. What could this place be? Some kind of fruit cage?

'It's the old aviary,' said Peagreen.

'Oh,' said Arrietty uncertainly: she was not quite sure what an 'aviary' might be.

'They kept birds in it,' Peagreen explained. 'All kinds of birds. Rare birds. I wish I had seen it in the old days . . .'

They stood looking at it for a little while longer. The ivy, Arrietty noticed, had spread itself like a tattered carpet over the whole floor of the aviary except in the very centre where a round stone trough stood up among the variegated leaves.

'The bird-bath,' Peagreen told her. 'Not as deep as it looks; it's raised up on a base. Come on, and I'll show you the larder window.'

A few paces further on, Arrietty saw a barred window set deep in the ivied wall. It was a latticed window and, from where she stood, peering hard at the bars, it seemed to her that one side of the window stood slightly ajar.

'It's open,' she said to Peagreen.

'Yes, they always leave it like that – to keep the larder aired. You can't quite see it from here, but they've got a bit of chicken-wire, from the aviary I suppose, tacked across the frame. Against the cats, when they used to have cats. I've untacked the bottom corner: you can sort of lift it. No one's ever noticed – not ever bothered, for that matter – seeing there are no cats here now.'

'I'm glad to hear that,' said Arrietty, 'my cousin Eggletina was supposed to have been eaten by a cat. But it came out that she escaped in the end. But she was never quite the same afterwards . . .'

'It's understandable . . .' said Peagreen.

'Cats and owls,' Arrietty went on, 'I suppose those are the two things borrowers really are frightened of. As frightened as human beans are supposed to be of ghosts.'

'Don't say "human beans",' said Peagreen.

'Why not?' retorted Arrietty, 'we always called them that under the floor at Firbank.'

'It sounds silly,' Peagreen remarked. 'And it isn't correct.' He looked at her thoughtfully. 'I don't mean to be rude but you must have picked up a lot of odd expressions, living – as you say you did – under the kitchen.'

'I suppose we did,' said Arrietty almost humbly. It occurred to her that there might be quite a lot to be learned from Peagreen, steeped as he was in book-learning. And an Overmantel to boot. 'All the same,' she went on firmly, 'I believe that any\ expression which was good enough for my father and mother should be good enough for me.' She was eyeing him rather coldly. 'Don't you agree?'

Peagreen flushed. And then he smiled his gentle, sideways smile. 'Yes,' he said, 'I do agree. And I agree with something else . . .'

'Oh?'

'Something you didn't say: that I'm a rotten snob!'

Arrietty laughed. 'Oh, you're just an Overmantel . . .' she said airily.

Then she laid a hand on his arm. 'Aren't you going to show me the larder?'

'I'll show you my house first.' He led her back beside the path until they stood once again in front of the aviary. 'That's where I'm going to live,' he said.

Arrietty stared in a puzzled way at the metal posts and the torn strips of rusted netting. 'Look up a bit,' said Peagreen. Arrietty raised her eyes and then she saw. A row of sun-bleached nesting-boxes were fixed to the ivied wall. Some were half concealed by tendrils of trailing leaves, others were fully exposed. In the front of each was a small round hole, a borrower-sized hole. 'The lids lift up,' Peagreen told her. 'You can put in all kinds of stuff from the top . . .'

Arrietty was breathless with admiration. 'How marvellous,' she breathed at last. 'What a wonderful idea!'

'It is rather,' Peagreen admitted modestly. 'And what's more, they're made of teak – a wood that lasts for ever . . .'

'For ever?' echoed Arrietty.

'Well, in a manner of speaking. Come rain or shine, it doesn't rot like other woods. The humans who built this aviary were not short of a few pennies.'

'Are rectors rich then?' asked Arrietty, still gazing admiringly at the nesting-boxes.

'Not nowadays,' said Peagreen. 'But from what I've heard and read, some of them used to be – horses, carriages, servants. The lot. And, of course, in the olden days, money went further . . .'

Arrietty knew about servants: Mrs Driver had been one. But she did not know much about money. 'What *is* money?' she decided to ask. 'I can never quite figure it out . . .'

'And you'll never need to,' Peagreen told her, laughing.

After a while, still staring bemused at the nesting-boxes, Arrietty said, 'Which one are you going to live in?'

'Well, the first will be my sitting-room, the next will be my bedroom in summer, the one after that I'll keep my books in and all my bits of paper. In the next one I'll keep my painting things, and the last one – the one nearest the larder window – I'll turn into my dining-room.'

This was a scale of living undreamed of by Arrietty: grandeur beyond grandeur – and all for one young borrower who lived alone!

'I suppose you must have a lot of furniture,' she said after a minute.

'Very little,' Peagreen told her. 'Nice rooms don't need much furniture.'

'What do you paint with your painting things?' asked Arrietty then.

'Pictures,' said Peagreen.

'On what you call your bits of paper?'

'Sometimes. But there's a roll of fine canvas on the top shelf of the library. Paper is very hard to come by. I try to keep it for writing.'

'Letters?' asked Arrietty.

'Poems,' said Peagreen, and he blushed. 'Most of the books I read are poetry,' he went on, as though to excuse himself, 'the smaller ones, up there,' he nodded towards the aviary, 'the ones I brought away.'

'Could you ever let me read a little of the poetry you write?' Arrietty spoke rather shyly.

Peagreen's blush deepened. 'It's not very good,' he said shortly and he turned away somewhat hurriedly. 'Come along, now I'll show you the larder.'

He looked swiftly from right to left to make sure the coast was clear then, taking her by the sleeve, he pulled her across the path, moving as fast as he was able. He dragged her rather roughly through one of the many gaps in the wire netting into (what seemed to them) a forest of ivy leaves which met above their heads. 'Excuse me a minute,' he said then; and, pushing aside a frond or two of green and white ivy, he laid down his piece of glass on an almost hidden pile of other grimy pieces.

'What are you going to use those for?' Arrietty asked as he rejoined her.

'I'm going to wash them in the bird-bath, and put them over the holes in the nesting-boxes.'

'To keep out the draughts?'

'No, to keep out the wrens and blue tits and goodness knows what else. Field mice for instance . . .'

'Why did you hurry me so, across the path? You said all the human beans were out –'

'You can't take chances. At least, not out of doors: there might be a visitor, or an errand boy; or possibly a postman . . . Come on, we've got to climb the ivy. Just follow me –'

Arrietty found that climbing the ivy was almost as much fun as climbing the look-out bush. Peagreen was making for the last of the nesting-boxes, the one that was to be his dining-room. They went up beside it and, both a little breathless, rested on the slightly sloping lid. Arrietty looked down. 'You've got a good view from here of anyone coming along the path.'

'I know,' said Peagreen. He slid off the nesting-box on to a thick branch of ivy. 'Come along. We've got to go sideways now. It's quite easy . . .'

It took no time at all to reach the sill of the larder window. How clever of Peagreen, thought Arrietty, to have planned all this out! And how proud he looked as he lifted the loose corner of rusty wire, holding it back for her to pass through! He came in beside her and they stood together on the narrow indoor sill. 'Well, this is it!' he said.

It was a long, narrow room. On one side were wide slate shelves; along the other a row of wooden bins, with sloping lids, rather like the lids of the nesting-boxes outside. In fact, Arrietty thought, they *were* rather like giant nesting-boxes except they were all joined together.

Peagreen followed the direction of her eyes. 'Yes, that's where in the olden days they used to keep the cereals – rice, dried beans, maize for poultry, flour – all those sort of things. And rock salt in lumps. All the stores that had to be kept dry. You see, that wall backs on to the old kitchen stove in the next room. It's quite warm in those bins. They used to be kept locked, but all the locks are broken now – except this end one just below us. That one, they can't *unlock* . . . Not that it matters, those bins are never used now. It's not like the old days: humans no longer store things in bulk. They just buy what they want when they want it.'

'With money, I suppose?' said Arrietty wonderingly.

Peagreen laughed. 'Yes, with money.'

'I still don't quite understand money,' Arrietty said in a puzzled voice. Then she turned her eyes to the wide slate shelves.

The upper ones seemed mainly to be stocked with bottled fruits, jams, pickles, ketchups and pudding basins of all sizes, tied round with cloths; these shelves above were narrower than the main shelf below them, on which many unrecognizable objects were laid out. Unrecognizable from where she stood because several of them were shrouded by clean white napkins, others by wire-mesh meat covers. Strings of onions hung down from hooks in the ceiling, also large bunches of bay and thyme. Between the main shelf and the stone-flagged floor, the space was filled by a honeycomb affair which Peagreen explained later was a wine rack. Not for the best wines (those had been kept in the cellars), but the home-made wines, which the cooks used to make in season: elderflower, dandelion, parsnip, gooseberry and so on. There were none left now. The door at the far end of the room was held ajar by a weight exactly like the one attached to Peagreen's pulley, except that this one was even larger. What giant scales they must have used in those 'old days'!

Peagreen, edging past her, made his way along the sill and stepped down on to the slate shelf which lay almost flush with it. 'You see,' he said, putting out a hand to encourage her to follow him, 'how easy it is!' It was indeed easy, Arrietty agreed, and what fun it all was!

'Now,' Peagreen went on, 'let's see what Mrs W. has got under these covers . . .'

They lifted up the first wire-mesh cover (to Arrietty's surprise it was quite light) and peered beneath it: two partridges, plucked and dressed for the table. They dropped the cover rather quickly: neither of them liked the smell. Next, they lifted the corner of a white napkin: a crusty pie, gleaming and golden. 'No good to us,' said Peagreen, 'unless they've cut into it first.' All the same, Arrietty broke off the tiniest edge of pastry; light as a feather it was, and tasted delicious. She was aware suddenly of feeling very hungry: neither she nor her parents had touched the food which Spiller had brought them in the ashtray, and that now seemed a long time ago.

Under another cover, were the appetizing remains of a roast sirloin of beef. Arrietty ate up several small crispy bits which had fallen on to the dish. They then found a large piece of cheddar cheese on a cheese board behind the sirloin. It looked deliciously moist and crumbly. Arrietty and Peagreen ate up the crumbs, carefully putting back the piece of butter muslin with which it had been covered. There was a glass jar of celery, crisp and scraped clean of its fibres. They broke off a little piece of this. Arrietty began to feel appeased. They by-passed the ham bone, although quite a lot of ham still adhered to it, but were tempted by a wire tray of freshly baked rock cakes, gleaming here and there with currants. 'We can't interfere much with cakes,' Peagreen advised her, 'there are exactly a dozen. She would be sure to wonder . . .' So they each dug out a currant and passed on to a row of small glass jars. They contained something pinkish and were topped with melted butter. 'Her potted meat,' said Peagreen, 'she sells it round the village and very good it is. But we can't touch these either, now the butter's hardened. Have you seen enough now?'

'What's in that brown bowl?' asked Arrietty, standing on tiptoe, but even then the sides were too high for her to see into it.

'Eggs,' said Peagreen, 'but they're no good to us either: you can't climb about carrying raw eggs.' He was making his way back among the various dishes towards the latticed window. 'Come on – I'll show you the way to climb down.'

Arrietty, following him, asked rather fearfully, 'Down to the floor?'

'Yes, we can go back by the old kitchen. And there's something else I want to show you . . .'

It was easy work climbing down the wine rack: a swift slide down on the wooden uprights, a short rest on the edge of the curved hole made to house each bottle; another slide or two and then they were on the floor. Climbing up might be harder, Arrietty thought to herself, but Peagreen showed her a dusty length of knotted rope attached to a nail below the lip of the shelf. Under the shadow of the windowsill, it had been hardly visible against the dark wood. 'You keep your feet to the uprights where they're built against the wall and sort of walk, and you're up in a minute. Rather like rock climbing but a lot easier . . .'

Arrietty remembered Pod's injunctions: 'A human bean could move that,' she pointed out (she was still determined to call them 'beans').

'They could, but they don't,' said Peagreen. 'They hardly ever look lower than the food shelves, except when they sweep the floor. And that's not often . . .' He was crossing the stone flagstones towards the locked bin which stood nearest the window. 'This is the thing I wanted to show you.' He went up to the corner where the front of the bin joined the whitewashed wall. Arrietty came beside him. It was a dark corner, still in the shadow of the windowsill above. 'It's this,' said Peagreen, putting out a hand; and Arrietty saw that there was a crack in the plaster at floor level where the wood was joined on to the wall. 'It's always been there,' said Peagreen, 'but I widened it a bit: you can just slide through —' He proceeded to do so. 'Come on,' he called from inside the bin, his voice sounding curiously hollow. It was a bit of a squash, but she managed to creep in after him. If, by scraping away some of the wall plaster, he had widened the crack, he had not widened it very much.

Inside, it was very dark. She was aware of an empty, imprisoning vastness and a clean, half-familiar smell. But it was warm. 'Come and feel this back wall,' said Peagreen. She followed him and laid her hands on the smooth, unseen surface. 'It *is* warm, isn't it?' said Peagreen, in a whisper. 'She keeps a good fire up.'

'What did they store in here?' asked Arrietty. She also spoke in a whisper – something to do with the enclosure and vastness of the unseen space about them.

'Soap,' said Peagreen, 'kitchen soap. In the old days, they used to make their own. Long soft blocks of it. They stored it in here to dry out. There's still a block of it there in a corner. Hard as nails, it is now. I'll show you later, when I get a bit of candle . . .'

'What are you going to use this place for?' asked Arrietty, after a moment.

'To keep warm in winter. I've got all summer to fix it up a bit. I'll get in a stock of candle ends and food will be no problem. If I can get hold of more paper, I'll most likely get on with my book.'

Arrietty was becoming more and more impressed. So he wrote poems, he painted pictures, and now he was writing a book! 'What's it about, your book?' she asked, after a moment.

'Well,' he said carelessly, 'I suppose it's a sort of history of the Overmantels. After all they've been in this house longer than any set of human beings have. Generation after generation. They've seen all the changes . . .'

Arrietty was silent again, her hands on the warm wall. She was thinking hard. 'Who's going to read your book?' she asked at last. 'I mean, so few borrowers can read or write.'

'That's true,' admitted Peagreen glumly. 'I suppose it depended on where you were brought up. In the old days, in a house like this, the human children had tutors and governesses and lesson books: the borrowers soon picked things up. My grandfather knew Greek and Latin. Up to a point . . .' he added, as though determined to be truthful. Then he seemed to cheer up a little. 'But you never know – there might be someone.'

Arrietty seemed less sure. 'A human bean I once knew,' she said slowly, 'said we were dying out. That the whole race of borrowers was dying out.' She was thinking of The Boy at Firbank.

Peagreen was silent for a moment, and then he said quietly, 'That may be so.' Then suddenly he seemed to throw such thoughts aside. 'But anyway we're here now! Come on, I'll take you back through the old kitchen . . .'

CHAPTER FOURTEEN

ONCE through the larder door, Arrietty stood still and looked about her. Peagreen came beside her and in a protective kind of way slid a hand under her elbow. Before them stretched a stone-flagged passage ending in what looked like an outside door. Beside this, a wooden staircase rose up, with bare, scrubbed treads, under which there seemed to be some kind of built-in cupboard. 'Those stairs lead up to their bedroom,' Peagreen whispered, 'and other rooms beyond.' Why were they still whispering? Because, thought Arrietty, they both felt themselves to be in some alien part of the house, a part in which the dreaded human beings lived out their mysterious existence.

Along the left-hand side of the passage hung a row of bells on coiled steel springs with, beyond them, some kind of cabinet. She knew what these were. Many a time at Firbank she had heard such bells, rung to summon Mrs Driver.

On the opposite side, facing the bells, were several doors, all closed. Immediately beside them, on their right, another door stood ajar and opposite it, on their left, a matching door which had no latch and was secured, Arrietty noticed, by a loop of wire fixed to a nail in the upright.

'What's in there?' she asked.

'It's the old game larder,' Peagreen told her, 'they don't use it now.'

'Can I look in?' She had seen that, in spite of the loop of wire, the door was not quite closed.

'If you like,' said Peagreen.

She tiptoed up and peered through the crack, and then she slipped inside. Peagreen followed.

It was a vast shadowy jumble of a place, lit by a grimy window just below a ceiling from which, she saw, hung row upon row of hooks. And something else – it looked like a longish log – hung, slightly on a slope, on two chains suspended on very stout hooks.

'What's that?' she asked.

'For hanging venison. You could hang a whole deer on that – with the legs hanging down each side . . .'

'A whole deer! Whatever for?'

'To eat – as soon as it got a bit smelly.' He thought a moment. 'Or perhaps they hung it the other way up with the four legs tied together. I don't really know: it was all before my time, you see. I only know they had a zinc bath underneath to catch the blood . . .'

'How horrible!'

Peagreen shrugged. 'They were horrible,' he said.

Arrietty shuddered and, turning her eyes away from the deer sling, glanced at several rows of musty antlers which hung against the wall. More dead deer, she supposed – used as hooks for hanging other game. She turned then to examine the jumble of objects on the floor: broken garden chairs, stained dressers, half-used pots of paint or distemper, an ancient kitchen stove which had lost a leg, slanting drunkenly to one side, old stone hot-water bottles, two paint-splashed step-ladders – one tall, one short – the top part of a grandfather clock, various bags which seemed to contain tools, battered tins, cardboard boxes . . .

'What a mess,' she said to Peagreen.

'A useful mess,' he replied.

She could see that. Her father would find it a gold mine. 'Are these the paints you use for your pictures?'

'No,' Peagreen laughed but he sounded rather scornful, 'there was an artist chappie staying here, left a lot of half-used tubes behind. And,' he added, 'quite a decent roll of canvas. We'd better get on now, we said we wouldn't be long . . .'

They slid out sideways. As they stood once again in the passage, Peagreen pointed out the various doors: 'That one, right at the end, used to be called "the tradesmen's entrance". It's the one the Whitlaces use now – the front door is hardly ever opened. That door beside the foot of the stairs was the servants' hall but the Whitlaces use it now as their sitting-room. The next one along was the butler's pantry, next to that is the one that leads to the cellar steps, and this one here –' he crossed the passage to the door opposite the old game larder, '– is the old kitchen.'

As Arrietty had noticed when she had first seen it, this door stood slightly ajar. 'What would happen if they closed it?' she asked, as she followed in Peagreen's wake. 'I mean if you wanted to get to the larder by way of the old kitchen?'

He paused. 'It wouldn't make any difference,' he said, 'you can see how cracked and worn these stones are – after years and years of cooks and kitchen-maids trotting backwards and forwards to the larders. Wainscot just took out a cracked piece of paving from below the door.

Say the door's shut, you can crawl underneath it. A bit inconvenient at times. It depends what you're carrying . . .'

And Arrietty, looking down, could see the missing piece of stone had left a small pit.

They were in the kitchen now, almost as dark and gloomy as the game larder, lit only by a long narrow window set high in a farther wall. The floor seemed to go on and on, the stone flags patched up here and there with dingy-looking concrete. Immediately on her right, as she stood just within the doorway, she saw the great black stove. It seemed to be a slightly newer model of the one discarded in the game larder except, in this case, the surface gleamed and shone and gave out a heartening warmth. Beside it stood a roughly made table covered with oil-cloth, on which stood an earthen jar filled with wooden spoons. On one end of the stove stood a large copper stockpot. It, too, was polished and gleaming. A faint wisp of steam escaped from under the lid, and with it a savoury smell.

'It's better really –' Peagreen was saying, '– to go round this kitchen keeping close in to the walls. But as the human beings are out and, perhaps, your family waiting, do you think you could face the open floor?'

Arrietty looked across the vast expanse where, she realized, there was no hope of cover. Almost opposite, in the far distance it seemed, she saw the outline of a door. 'If you think it's all right,' she said uncertainly. Peagreen, she remembered, could not walk very quickly.

'Then come on,' he said, 'let's chance it, for once. It's a longish walk if you have to stick to the walls . . .'

It seemed a longish walk anyway, and Arrietty had to fight an almost overwhelming instinct to run, in order to match her steps to Peagreen's. Never in her whole life had she felt so exposed as she did on this journey across the vast, disused kitchen, where only the stove and the wooden table created a kind of warm oasis.

As at last they approached the far door, she could make out some patches of cloth hanging loosely on its surface. Green baize? Yes, that was it: it was (or might have been) a padded, baize door like the one she remembered at Firbank. Yes, now she could see the rusty brass studs which once had secured the padding. Did all old houses have them, she wondered, to keep out the noise and smells from the kitchen? But, on this particular door, the baize was stained and motheaten, and some of it hung in tatters. She also noticed, as they drew closer, that the door swung slightly in the draught.

Arrietty stopped sharply in her tracks. She gripped Peagreen's arm. From somewhere far behind them, she had heard a sound, the fiddling of a key in a lock. Peagreen had heard it too. Both stood rigid as they caught the mutter of voices. A far door slammed to, and footsteps echoed loudly in the stone-flagged passage. Another door opened and the footsteps died away.

'It's all right,' breathed Peagreen, 'they've gone into the annexe. Come on! We'd better hurry –'

They had barely taken three paces when, once again, they froze. This time they heard the voice more clearly as the footsteps clattered out again. It was a woman's voice, calling back to someone: '. . . must just take a look at my stew.' And the footsteps came hurrying nearer.

Like a shot thing, Peagreen dropped to the floor, pulling Arrietty with him. 'Don't move,' he breathed in her ear, as they lay there prostrate. 'Not a muscle!'

Arrietty's heart was beating wildly. She heard the scrape of wood across the flagstones. The kitchen door through which they had sidled had been flung open more widely. Then the footsteps paused. It was a sudden, startled pause. They had been seen.

There were a few moments of complete silence, before the footsteps began cautiously to approach them. A thought flew through Arrietty's mind as she lay there, rigid with terror: Mrs Whitlace had seen something but, in this dim light and at that distance, she could not quite make out what it was . . .

At that moment there was a sudden hiss from the stove. Then a spitting sound, the clumsy bumping of a lid, and the acrid smell of burning fat. Lying there, unable to see or even turn her head, she heard the sudden rush of feet towards the stove, the sound of some heavy object pushed, with short gasps, across some uneven surface, followed by a sharp cry of pain. The hissing ceased immediately and Arrietty heard a faint whimper as the footsteps hurried away into the passage.

Peagreen sprang to his feet, more deftly than Arrietty would have believed possible. He seized her wrist, pulling her up beside him. 'Come,' he said, 'quickly, quickly!'

They reached the broken baize door which swung, rather drunkenly, to Peagreen's light touch and suddenly, almost magically it seemed, they were in the sunlight of the long main hall.

Arrietty, white and trembling, leaned against the outer jamb of the door.

'I'm sorry,' Peagreen was saying, 'I'm tremendously sorry. We should have gone around by the walls –'

'What happened?' asked Arrietty in a faint voice.

'She burned herself. Or scalded herself. Or something. It's all right. We're safe now. Whitlace will be seeing to her hand. It's all right, Arrietty. Neither of them would come along here . . . at least, not for the moment anyway.' He put a hand under her elbow and began to lead her down the hall. He still looked very distressed but, all the same, he tried to distract her, pausing at the foot of the great stairway. 'The drawing-room's up there,' he told her, 'they used to call it the saloon. And all kinds of other rooms. You can get to some of them from outside by climbing the ivy . . .'

But Arrietty did not seem to look at anything, her troubled eyes were gazing straight ahead. She was still aware of the acrid smell of burned stew. Yes, that was what these baize doors were for: to keep out such smells.

'And here's the front door,' Peagreen went on. 'I think you've seen it from outside. And there's the telephone, on the windowsill. With its paper and pad. I borrow my paper from there and the pencil when it gets down to a stub.'

Arrietty turned then, her eyes suddenly wide. 'Supposing it rang?'

'They'd let it ring,' Peagreen said. 'Come along.' He named several rooms on the left as they passed by the doors: dining-room, gun-room, smoking-room . . . 'All locked,' he told her.

'And what's that open door at the end?'

'Surely you know?' said Peagreen.

'How could I?'

'It's the library.'

Arrietty's face lost its sleep-walking expression. 'So we've come right round?' she said in a relieved voice.

'Yes, we've come right round. And now you've seen how your father can get to the larder without having to go out of doors.'

'That's what I can't bear,' said Arrietty, as they approached the open door. 'I can't bear the thought of my father crossing that great, empty terrible floor – with no cover anywhere!'

'He'll go at night – when they're safely upstairs and asleep. That's what I always did. They never stir once they've gone upstairs. Dog-tired, they are, by then.'

Once inside the library, Arrietty relaxed. It was strange to look down the long room from this unfamiliar end. Through the glass doors, she could see a strip of the conservatory, and into the garden beyond. Arrietty made a mental note of this danger zone. In future they would have to be careful to keep on either side of it.

She paused for a moment to examine the middle window seat: their future home! Were her parents still inside, she wondered, or had Pod by this time learned all the tricks of the grating? Peagreen, by the fireplace, guessed her thoughts. 'They won't be in there,' he said, examining the fire surround, 'the loose tile's back in its place. And your father's a wise man,' he went on, 'he wouldn't have left the grating open. They must be in the conservatory . . .'

As they came through the glass doors, Arrietty noticed that all the floor tiles were neatly back in place. Her mother was by the stove, holding the tin ashtray as though it were a very large tray. 'Oh, there you are!' she said, with evident relief. 'What an age you've been! We've kept a little food back for you. I was just going to put it away. Your father's very strict now about leaving things about . . .'

'Where *is* Papa?' asked Arrietty.

Homily nodded towards the garden. 'Out there: he's a bit worried about Spiller –'

'Hasn't Spiller turned up?'

'Not a sign of him.'

'Oh dear . . .' exclaimed Arrietty unhappily. She turned towards Peagreen, but found he was no longer beside her. He was limping across the library towards the door which led to the hall. 'Oh, Peagreen,' she cried, 'where are you going? Do come back!' Then she clapped her hand to her mouth, aware she had called out too loudly.

He turned and glanced at her, almost shamefacedly, and then his gaze flew to her mother. 'I'll be back later,' he mumbled and turned away again.

So that was it, Arrietty realized suddenly: he did not, at that moment, wish to face either of her parents. He had taken a risk with their precious child's safety and was keenly aware of it now. She watched him go without another word: she would reassure him later.

Homily was still talking away. 'If anything has happened to Spiller or his boat . . .'

'I know, I know!' cut in Arrietty, 'I'll go and speak to Papa.'

'Don't *you* disappear, too –' Homily called after her, as Arrietty made for the hole under the door.

Arrietty wove her way quickly through the weeds and grasses, and there was Pod on the path. He was standing quite still. 'Papa –' she called softly, as she emerged from the weeds. He did not turn.

'I'm looking at the moon,' he said. And, as Arrietty came beside him, puzzled because it was still daylight, Pod went on, 'Have you ever seen such a moon? And not a cloud in the sky! What a waste . . . what a waste!'

Arrietty never *had* seen such a moon. It hung pallidly in the sky, from which the colour was slowly draining, like a ghostly tennis ball.

'We couldn't have had a better moon,' said Pod. 'Not if we'd ordered it. Crossing the lawn to that river . . . all that unpacking. We'll need every bit of light we can get. And no rain. By tomorrow, the weather might change . . .'

Arrietty was silent. Then, after a while, she said, 'Peagreen has a truck.'

'Maybe,' said Pod, 'but a truck doesn't give light. And it's light we want. But where is Spiller?'

Arrietty pulled sharply on her father's arm. 'Look! I think . . . that's him, isn't it? He's coming now . . .'

Indeed, it was Spiller, coming round the corner of the house, dragging his soap-dish behind him! And, as if turned to stone, Pod awaited his approach. His relief, Arrietty sensed, was too great for words.

'Oh, there you are,' he said in a carefully composed voice as Spiller came beside them. 'What have you got in that?'

'Your tools,' said Spiller, 'and I made a new quiver.' Spiller's quivers were always made of short pieces of hollow bamboo, plenty of which grew on some marshy ground near the lake.

'You've been down to the boat?' exclaimed Pod.

'I brought the boat up here.'

'Up here! You mean this end of the lake?'

'It's there among the rushes. Thought it would be quicker unpacking. To have it nearer, like.'

'So that's what you've been doing all day!' Pod stared at him. 'But how did you know we had decided to stay?'

'He offered you a house,' said Spiller simply.

There was an amazed silence: he had known they would accept. Spiller, she realized, with his sharp wild instincts, understood them better than they understood themselves. And now, with the heavily laden boat so near, how much easier he had made their move!

'Well I never!' said Pod and a slow smile spread over his face.

'Nothing to do now but wait for the night . . .' He sighed a deep, happy sigh. 'Have you had anything to eat?'

'I sucked a robin's egg,' said Spiller.

'That's not enough. Better come inside and see what Homily can find.' He nodded towards the soap-box. 'You can push that thing into the weeds . . .'

When they had made their way in through the hole, Arrietty ran eagerly to her mother, seizing her by both hands. 'Oh Mother, wonderful news! Spiller's back! And Papa says we can move tonight – everything's quite near! And –'

But, just then, the telephone shrilled. Homily, about to speak, turned round in a startled way. She had been standing near the stove. All four

of them froze into stillness, their eyes on the library door. The telephone rang out four times and then came the slow advance of heavy footsteps. None of the borrowers moved.

A man's voice said, 'Hello –' There was a short silence, before the deep voice went on: 'Not tomorrow, she can't.' Again there was silence while, in Arrietty's imagination, some unknown female voice must still be twittering on. Then Whitlace said, 'She's hurt her hand, see . . .' Another silence. Then Whitlace said (it *must* be Whitlace), 'Maybe the day after tomorrow.' Another small silence. An embarrassed grunt from Whitlace (he was not one for the telephone) and they heard him replace the receiver. The footsteps moved away.

'They're back,' said Pod, as soon as there was silence again. 'At least, *He* is.'

Homily turned a glowing face towards Spiller, 'Oh, Spiller!' she almost gushed. 'It's good to see you, that I must say!' She ran towards him but stopped in sudden confusion. Had she been going to kiss him, Arrietty wondered? Not very likely, she decided, remembering how often in the past her mother had disapproved of Spiller. All the same, with Homily, one never knew . . .

Pod was looking thoughtful. 'It might be safer,' he said at last, 'if we waited out of doors.'

'Waited for what?' asked Homily.

'For the night,' said Pod.

'Oh, that lawn!' exclaimed Homily. 'Crossing it once by daylight – that was bad enough, but crossing *twice* by night! Not sure if I can face it, Pod . . .'

'You won't have to,' said Pod, and he told her about the boat. She listened wide-eyed, then turned again towards Spiller. Was it going to happen now, Arrietty wondered, that kiss? But no – something impassive in Spiller's expression seemed to put her off. 'Thank you, Spiller,' was all she said. 'Thank you very much.'

Pod looked up through the glass panes. 'The light's fading already, as you might say. We won't have so long to wait. Now, Homily, you and Arrietty go outside. Take something to wrap round you. And sit quietly in the grass at the edge of the path. Spiller and I will join you later. Spiller, will you come with me and give me a hand? I've got to open the grating while we've still got a bit of light in-doors.'

They all did as they had been asked. Quietly and with no fuss. Although it was a bit of a struggle to bundle one of Miss Menzies's feather quilts through the narrow hole under the door. But it was a mild and beautiful evening for so early in April and it was a joy to breathe in the soft air. As they settled themselves among the grasses, the coverlet round their shoulders, Arrietty looked up at the moon. It was becoming golden, and the sky around it turning a gentle grey. There were sleepy murmurs with a few sharp, quarrelsome high-notes as the birds, in the bushes opposite, began to settle in for the night. Arrietty slipped an arm below her mother's and gave it a comforting squeeze. Homily squeezed hers back. After that, they sat in silence, each busy with their very different thoughts.

*

By the time that Pod and Spiller joined them, the moon had become quite bright. 'But the shadows will be black,' he told them, as he squatted down. 'We must treat the shadows as cover.' Spiller squatted beside him, bow in hand and a quiver full of arrows at his back.

Pod, his hands linked upon his knees, was whistling softly, through his teeth. It was an irritating sound but Arrietty knew it of old: it meant that he was happy. All the same, after a while, she said, 'Hush, Papa . . .' and laid a hand upon his knee. She had heard another sound, a good deal farther away. 'Listen!' she said.

It was a faint squeaking; very faint, but gradually growing clearer. After a moment or two, she recognized the sound. 'It's Peagreen with his truck,' she whispered. They watched and waited until, at last, the tiny figure appeared in the middle of the path, indistinct in the strange half light of dusk and brightening moon. He stood for a moment, undecided, by the door of the conservatory. He could not see them, half hidden as they were by the shadows of the grasses.

'Peagreen –' Arrietty called softly. He started and looked about, and then he came towards them. He seemed surprised to see them, sitting there in a row.

'We're moving in tonight,' Arrietty told him in a whisper.

'I guessed you might be,' he said, sitting down beside her. 'I saw Spiller passing the corner of the house, and I saw the size of the moon.' He kicked out a foot towards his truck, 'So I brought this thing along.'

'And very useful, too,' said Pod, leaning forward to see it better.

'It's yours, if you want it,' Peagreen said. 'Where I'm living now, I don't really need it.'

'Well, we could share it, like,' said Pod, and, still leaning forward to get a better view of Peagreen, he explained to him about the position of the boat and Spiller's selfless journey. 'With the grating open and the five of us to help, we can move that stuff within the hour.' He stood up and looked about him: in that strangely blended half light, nothing looked very distinct. 'I don't see,' he said, turning round to them, 'why we shouldn't get going now. You see –' He broke off suddenly and dropped to the ground. An owl had hooted uncomfortably near.

'Oh, my goodness . . .' muttered Homily, clinging more tightly to Arrietty's arm. Peagreen remained calm. 'It's all right,' he said, 'but it's better not to move just yet.'

'Why did he say it's all right?' Homily whispered to Arrietty, in a trembling voice.

Peagreen heard her. 'You'll see in a minute,' he said. 'Keep your eyes on the top of that cedar tree.'

They all stared at the cedar tree, which was now lit up by the moon. Pod eased himself into a more comfortable position. After a while, he asked in a whisper, 'Are there many of them?'

'No,' whispered Peagreen, 'only that one, for the moment. But there's another one across the valley. This one will call again. In a minute or two, you'll hear the female answer . . .'

It was just as he said: the owl near them hooted again and, after a few tense listening seconds, they heard the distant reply: a faint echo. 'This can go on for quite a while,' said Peagreen. It did, a weaving shuttle of sound above the sleeping fields. Or were they sleeping? Had the night things begun to come out? Arrietty thought uncomfortably of foxes. 'It's a blessing,' whispered Homily, 'that we don't have to cross all that grassland.'

'There he goes . . .' said Peagreen. Had Arrietty seen that noiseless shadow, or had she imagined it? Pod had seen it: that was for sure. 'A tawny owl,' he said, 'but a big one.' He stood up. 'Now we can get going.'

Peagreen stood up, too. 'Yes,' he said, '*he* won't be back before dawn.'

'If that's his lady-love across the valley,' said Homily letting go of Arrietty's arm, 'I wish he'd move in with her.'

'He may,' said Peagreen, laughing, as he helped her to her feet.

CHAPTER FIFTEEN

MR and Mrs Platter had also seen the moon. They were busy in the kitchen, preparing for their second night's 'vigil'. Mrs Platter had finished making the sandwiches and was sitting down waiting for the eggs, which were boiling noisily on the stove. Mr Platter, sitting opposite, was oiling a pair of wire-cutters. 'We can put the picnic in the cat-basket,' he said.

Mrs Platter blew her nose. 'Oh, Sidney,' she said, 'I've got a dreadful cold. I'm not sure that I'm fit to go.'

'There won't be any rain tonight, Mabel. You've seen the sky. And you've seen the moon.'

'I know, Sidney, but all the same . . .' She was going to add that she was not exactly built for sitting in a small boat, hour after hour, on a narrow wooden seat, but thought better of it; she knew it would not move him. Instead she said, 'Say you went on your own, I could have a nice hot breakfast ready for you in the morning?' Mr Platter did not reply: he was busily shutting and opening the wire-cutters. So Mrs Platter, greatly daring, went on, 'And I have a feeling that they won't be there tonight.'

Mr Platter carefully wiped the wire-cutters with an oily rag, and laid them down on the table beside the cat-basket. Then he sat back and looked across at her. His eyes were steely. 'Why should you think that?' he asked coldly.

'Because,' said Mrs Platter, 'they may have come and gone. Or –'

Mr Platter took up a blunt-nosed chisel, and ran a finger along its edge. 'We'll soon find that out,' he said.

'Oh, Sidney! What are you planning to do?'

'Take the roof off their house,' he said.

It was Mrs Platter's turn to stare. 'You mean go right up into the model village?'

'That's what I mean,' said Mr Platter, and he laid down the chisel.

'But you can't walk about in that village,' objected Mrs Platter, 'those silly little streets are too narrow: you couldn't get one foot before another!'

'We can try,' said Mr Platter.

'We'd be sure to break something. The public only view it from that concrete catwalk . . .'

'We aren't the public,' said Mr Platter. He laid both hands firmly on the table and leaned towards her, staring with a cold kind of anger into her dismayed face.

'I don't think, Mabel,' he said, 'that, *even now*, you begin to understand the real seriousness of all this: our whole future depends on our catching these creatures! And I shall need you beside me, with the cat-basket, open.'

'We managed all right before we had them . . .' faltered Mrs Platter.

'Did we?' said Mr Platter. 'Did we, Mabel? You know the Riverside Teas were falling off. And that most of the tourists were going to Abel Pott. Said his model village was more picturesque, or some such nonsense. Ours was far more modern. And, as you noticed yourself, there haven't been many funerals lately. And no new houses built since we finished the council estate. The only job on our list at the moment is clearing Lady Mullings' roof gutters . . .' There was something about Mr Platter's expression which really alarmed Mrs Platter: she had never seen him quite so disturbed. It could not be only because he had taken so much time and trouble in constructing the beautiful glass-fronted case in which he had hoped to exhibit such rare specimens: there was something coldly desperate about his whole attitude.

'We're not exactly in want, Sidney,' she reminded him, 'we've got our savings.'

'Our savings!' he exclaimed scornfully. 'Our savings! What are our puny little savings compared to the kind of fortune we had here in our hands?' He opened his hands widely, and then dropped them again. Mrs Platter looked more and more alarmed: their savings, to her certain knowledge, amounted to several thousand pounds. 'You get this into your head, Mabel,' he went on, 'no one in the whole world believes such creatures exist – not until they see them, with their own eyes, walking and talking and eating . . .'

'Not going to the lavatory, Sidney: you made them a little bathroom. But –' she repeated the word: '*but* you must remember that they may huddle in that back place all day. And never come out, like some of those animals in the zoo . . .'

'Oh, I'd think of something to make them come out – at least in front of the public. Something electric, perhaps. After midnight, I don't care much what they do so long as they're on show in the morning.'

'But how can we hope to find them, Sidney dear?' She still found his mood rather frightening. 'Say, they're not in the model village? Five or six inches high, they could slip into any corner.'

'We shall find them in the end,' he said slowly, stressing every word, 'however long it takes, because we are the only living people who know of their existence!'

'Miss Menzies knows of their existence . . .'

'And who is Miss Menzies? A foolish spinster lady who couldn't say boo to a goose!' He laughed. 'And even if she did, the goose wouldn't take any notice. No, I'm not frightened of Miss Menzies, Mabel, nor any of her ilk.' He rose from the table, and she was glad to see him calmer. 'Well, we'd better get going. It's a mild night . . .'

He put the wire-cutters and chisel into the cat-basket. Mrs Platter added the sandwiches and a bottle of cold tea. 'Would you like a piece of cake?' she asked him. But he did not seem to hear her, so, picking up her coat, she followed him quietly out through the front door.

In spite of the mild weather, the tranquil moonlight and the uneventful run downstream, the Platters' evening did not turn out to be a particularly pleasant one. First, they had to wait for Abel Pott to put his lamp out. 'Staying up late tonight,' muttered Mr Platter. 'Hope he hasn't got visitors . . .' Then, on the upper road behind Mr Pott's thatched cottage, they saw a figure on a bicycle. As it passed by, too slowly for Mr Platter's comfort, he recognized the tall headgear of a policeman. What was Mr Pomfret doing out so late, Mr Platter wondered?

'Perhaps,' said Mrs Platter, perched uncomfortably on her narrow seat, 'he takes a look round like this every evening . . .'

'Well, anyway,' said Mr Platter, as the bicycle passed out of sight, 'we can get on quietly with the wire cutting.'

Their boat was moored to an iron upright, against which the wire fencing had been stretched and nailed to a formidable tightness. At the first cut, the wire flew back with a loud ping. In the utter quietness of that peaceful night, and to the ears of the Platters, it sounded as loud as a pistol shot. 'Better we wait until his light's out . . .' whispered Mrs Platter.

Mr Platter sat down again, nervously tapping the wire-cutters against his knee, his eyes on that unwelcome light in Mr Pott's window. 'Say we had our little bit of supper now?' suggested Mrs Platter in a whisper. 'And it would leave us a bit more room in the cat-basket.'

Mr Platter nodded impatiently. But even the unwrapping of the sandwiches (cold fried bacon tonight) created a rustle and a stir in the uncanny moonlit silence. Mrs Platter had forgotten to bring a cup, so they drank their cold tea from the bottle. They would have preferred something hot, but Thermos flasks, only just invented, were expensive items in those days – bound in leather, with silver-plated tops. Mr and Mrs Platter had not yet heard of them.

And still the light glowed on. 'What can he be doing at this time of night?' Mr Platter muttered. 'He's usually in bed by eight-thirty at the latest. He *must* have visitors . . .'

But Mr Pott did not have visitors. Had they but known it, he was seated quietly at his work table, his wooden leg stretched out before him, peering down in his short-sighted way at the delicate work in hand. This was the repainting of the tiny wicket gates, all of different shapes and sizes, which led into the miniature front gardens of his beloved model village. At Easter, he would reopen the village to the public and by that time every detail needed to be perfect.

At last, after what seemed hours to the Platters, the gentle lamplight was extinguished and, after another cautious wait, they both felt free to move. Mr Platter, fast and expert, soon freed the wire from the post. As it loosened, it did not ping so loudly, and he was able very soon to fold a section back.

'Now!' he said to Mrs Platter. And, taking the cat-basket from her, he helped her up the bank. It was slightly slippery from last night's rain but, at last, she was through the wire, and they could survey the miniature village by the light of the brilliant moon.

Mr Pott had set it on a slight slope, and the whole layout spread on the rise before them. The lines of the model railway glistened in the moonlight and so did the slated roofs. The thatched roofs were a little dimmer but the tiny winding roads and lanes were snake-like chasms of blackest darkness. However, from where they stood, they could plainly see Vine Cottage, the house Miss Menzies had once fitted out for the borrowers. The question was: how best to get to it? 'Follow me,' said Mr Platter.

He chose roads wide enough to take the width of one foot, if each foot was placed carefully before the other. It was a finicky business but, at last, they stood beside the tiny house from where, six months ago, they had so heartlessly stolen the 'little people'. History was repeating itself, thought Mr Platter complacently, as he carefully inserted his chisel under the eaves of the roof. It came off surprisingly easily. Somebody must have 'been at it', Mr Platter decided as he stared down inside. He produced a torch from his pocket to see better.

The house was empty, abandoned. On the night they had captured the borrowers, it had been fully furnished: chairs, dressers, tables, cooking utensils, clothes in tiny doll's-house wardrobes. Now there was nothing, except the fixtures – a cooking-stove and a tiny porcelain sink. Mrs Platter, peering down beside him, saw a scrap of white, beside the closed front door. She picked it out gingerly. It was a tiny apron, one which Homily had discarded in their rush to get away. She put it in her pocket.

Mr Platter swore. He swore quite loudly and rather rudely, which was quite unusual for him. He straightened up and stepped back angrily. There was a tinkle of breaking glass: he had put a careless heel through one of Mr Pott's miniature shop fronts.

'Hush, Sidney,' pleaded Mrs Platter in a hoarse whisper. She looked about her in a frightened way, and then she gave a gasp. 'Look! Abel Pott's put his light on again! Let's get out of here . . . Come, Sidney! Come quickly!'

Mr Platter turned sharply. Yes, there was the light – growing brighter every minute as Mr Pott turned up the wick. Mr Platter swore again and turned towards the river. In his disappointment and anger, all the houses between him and his boat seemed just a jumble to him now. He no longer bothered to seek out the roads. And Mrs Platter, feeling about for the cat-basket (it might, one day, be evidence against them), heard tinkles of breaking glass and sudden falls of masonry as Mr Platter made his clumsy way down the hill. She followed him, panting and crying and sometimes stumbling.

At last they reached the opened wire. 'Oh, Sidney –' sobbed Mrs Platter, '– he'll be out in a minute. I heard him unbolting the front door!'

Mr Platter, already in the boat, put out a hand; less to help her than to drag her in. She slipped on the mud and fell into the water. It was very shallow by the bank, and she soon climbed out again. But she had not been able to repress a slight scream. Mr Platter was fumbling for oars and took no more notice of her as she sat dripping in the stern. 'Oh, Sidney, he's coming after us! I know he is . . .'

'Let him come!' exclaimed Mr Platter fiercely. 'What do I care for old Abel Pott with his wooden leg. People have been found floating in the river before now . . .'

And with that, he began to row upstream.

*

Once safely back in their own house, Mrs Platter went straight through to the kitchen and pushed the large tea-kettle on to the hotter part of the stove. She raked up the embers beneath it until they began to glow red. Her cold felt much worse and she wondered if she had a temperature. She drove a hand into her coat pocket to find her handkerchief but pulled out Homily's rather grubby little apron instead. She tossed it on the table and felt in her other pocket. She found her handkerchief but it, too, was soaking wet.

'Would you like tea or cocoa?' she asked Mr Platter, who had followed her in. 'I'm going upstairs now to get into something dry . . .'

'Cocoa,' he said and picked up the little apron. He eyed it curiously. 'Oh, Mabel –' he called out just as she was reaching the door.

She turned back unwillingly. 'Yes?'

'What did you do with that other stuff they left behind upstairs?' He had the apron in his hand.

'Threw it away, of course, when I cleaned out the attic: there was nothing worth keeping . . .' and, before he could speak again, she had made her way towards the front hall.

Mr Platter sat down slowly. He was looking very thoughtful. He spread the small apron before him on the table, and stared at it musingly.

'Lady Mullings . . .?' he murmured to himself, and slowly, almost triumphantly, he began to smile.

CHAPTER SIXTEEN

ARRIETTY was to look back to that spring as one of the happiest periods of her life. Every day seemed full of excitement and interest, from that first night in their new home under the window seat when, worn out with carrying, they had slept at last in their own little beds among the cluttered piles of stacked furniture, to the week by week improvements instigated by Pod.

His inventiveness knew no bounds. He had his old tools and he constructed others and, as Arrietty had foreseen, the jumble in the old game larder provided him with an almost endless supply of useful objects, more than even he could make use of or need.

The first priority was the construction of a kitchen within a kitchen for Homily. She hated cooking in that shadowy vastness where she said she felt as though she never knew what might be coming up behind her. First, he and Spiller and Arrietty moved the distant shelves nearer to the grill, replaced the pronged fork with a brass wheel (from the discarded grandfather clock in the game larder) set on a pivot so that Homily could turn it, varying the degrees of heat from the embers below. On the outer rim she could simmer; towards the spokes near the middle she could grill. A battered old tobacco tin, scoured out and hammered straight, once Pod had loosened the hinges and supplied it with a handle, provided a Dutch oven. He found two white tiles and constructed a small tube to fit them. Homily was delighted with this: it was so easy to wipe down.

But how to wall it, this kitchen? How to enclose it in? This was Pod's great puzzle. There were plenty of strong old cardboard boxes in the game larder, tea chests, plywood and many odds and ends. But there seemed no way of introducing any large flat object through the very small openings which led into the chimney. The passage under the floorboards (now scrubbed and fresh-smelling) was far too narrow for any object large enough to serve as sides of a wall. The hard backs of two large atlases, such as Pod had seen on one of the library shelves, would have been ideal. But how to get them in? Except, perhaps, by climbing on the roof and dropping them down the chimney. But the getting of them up the side of the house on to the roof seemed too much labour to contemplate at this juncture. Besides, the chimneys themselves, where they emerged on the roof, might turn out to be too narrow.

It was Peagreen who solved the problem in the end. 'Supposing,' he said to Pod, 'you constructed a little cardboard shelter in some dark corner of the game larder? Then took it to pieces again, and I soaked the pieces in the birdbath and, when they had softened, we could roll them up, tie them with twine into . . . well . . . cylinders, you might say. We could then take those cylinders in through the grating and push them along the passage under the floor. Then build your little kitchen again round the fire in the old hearth. Keep a good cooking fire up for a day or two, and your walls would soon be stiff again . . .'

Pod was delighted, and very impressed. 'We'd have to flatten them out first, though,' he said.

'That'll be easy,' Peagreen told him, 'they'll be soaking wet. They'll almost flatten themselves out under their own weight of water. We can lay that book-cover down – the one that covers the hole to the steps – and walk about on it, say any of the cardboard started to curl up . . .'

Arrietty and Homily had been given the job of cleaning up the ancient hearthstones of the old chimneypiece, chopping and stacking the untidy piles of wood, sorting the tin lids and screw bottle-tops, on which it seemed the Wainscots had done their cooking. It was just a happy chance that Peagreen happened to be beside her when she was about to throw away a large charred tin lid containing something that looked like stiffened treacle. 'Don't throw that away!' he almost shouted. 'Let me see it first . . .' Distastefully, Arrietty handed it over and was surprised to see a slow smile spread over Peagreen's face as he stooped to smell the horrid-looking contents.

'It's some of Wainscot's resin mixture,' he told her. 'It can be melted down again . . .' Triumphantly he carried the precious burden to a safe corner. 'Your father will be pleased with this!'

The second brainwave came after the kitchen partitions had been erected. The sides were glued firmly together with the help of strong strips of material cut by Pod from a dry – but grubby – floorcloth, discarded by the caretakers. The little room had no ceiling, so that any smoke from Homily's fire would escape into the vast chimney above. But Pod had made her a little door from a small book called *Essays of Emerson*. He had removed all the inside pages, glued the back of the book to the cardboard wall, and had left the front cover to swing to and fro against a small opening cut to the right size.

All the same, for all Pod's cleverness and Peagreen's bright ideas, it did not look a particularly cheerful kitchen. The cardboard walls, now they stood erected, did not appear any too clean. There were foot-marks on them here and there and, in spite of Homily's efforts, they had collected grimy smears when laid out to dry on the floor. One could not wash so large an expanse of hearthstone with drops of water collected, drip by drip, into an eye-bath. One could only brush it, as thoroughly as one could, with the heads of dried-up teazles.

It was then that Peagreen had his second brilliant idea. He remembered the roll of canvas on the top shelf of the library. It, too, formed a kind of cylinder. Tied and rolled, he could knock it to the floor. Pod would remove the loose tile in the fire surround and between them they could push the canvas through the gap.

No sooner thought of than achieved: Homily's kitchen became lined and shining white, and its enclosing walls even stronger. They pasted the canvas over the bookend, hiding it altogether, and now the little leather door looked what it was – a little leather door. 'And if ever the canvas should get a bit dingy with smoke,' Peagreen told them, 'there's plenty of whitewash in the game larder . . .'

'Maybe . . .' mused Pod, his eyes narrowing thoughtfully, 'later on, I'll fix some sort of a hood over the fire. But she'll be pleased enough with it as it is – for the time being . . .'

He smiled at Peagreen. Poets and painters might not be so 'good with their hands' (whatever that meant) but they certainly were good with ideas. 'Sure you won't need some of this canvas for yourself?' he asked.

'There's plenty over,' Peagreen told him, looking down in a satisfied way at the odds and ends on the floor.

Homily was unwilling to visit the Hendrearies until her kitchen was finished. 'The kitchen is the Heart of the Home,' she told Pod. 'I don't mind, for the moment, leaving all that stacked-up stuff in our living quarters. We can see to all that later at our leisure . . .'

And then, of course, there were the ghosts but, as Peagreen had prophesied, Arrietty soon got used to these. All the same, her attitude towards them differed a little from that of her parents and Peagreen: she never quite lost a sense of curiosity and wonder. Why should they suddenly appear and then, for no apparent reason, disappear and not be seen again for weeks? There seemed no logic in it.

She soon got used to The Footsteps. The first time she heard them was after the telephone had shrilled three times. Ready for flight into the conservatory, in case she heard the warning scamper of feet along the tiles of the front hall, after a short silence she heard instead a slow and ponderous tread which seemed, as she stood beside Peagreen in the library, to be coming down the main staircase. Who could it be? Not Mrs Whitlace's light, running steps, nor Mr Whitlace's slightly slower ones, unless, of course, he might be carrying something inordinately heavy? The footsteps grew louder as they seemed to cross the hall. She waited tensely for the lifting of the receiver and for some kind of human voice. But nothing happened beyond the sound of a dull kind of stumble, followed by a sudden silence.

She turned an alarmed face to Peagreen, and saw that he was laughing. 'Nobody's answered the telephone . . .' she whispered uneasily.

'Ghosts don't,' said Peagreen.

Oh,' exclaimed Arrietty, 'was that . . .? Do you mean . . .?' She looked very scared.

'Those were The Footsteps. I told you about them.' He still seemed amused.

'But I don't understand. I mean, could they hear the telephone?'

'No, of course not,' said Peagreen. He was really laughing now. 'The telephone has nothing to do with it: it was just a coincidence.' He laid a hand on her arm. 'It's all right, Arrietty, there's nothing to be frightened about: the Whitlaces are out.'

Yes, Peagreen was quite right: the real danger lay with human beings – not with harmless noises, however unearthly they might seem. Feeling rather a fool, she walked off into the conservatory, which was filled with sunlight. But she never showed (or even felt) fear of The Footsteps again.

The second ghost was The Little Girl On The Stairs. Actually, during those first weeks, Arrietty did not see her. For one reason because she only appeared, slightly luminous, at night. And, for another, because Arrietty very seldom went into the front hall. On her rare visits to the larder, she preferred Peagreen's route along the ivy to the partly opened window. She really disliked that open, coverless trek across the vast kitchen floor and avoided it whenever she could. Pod had seen the vision regularly, on his nightly visits to collect old junk from the game larder. It was a little girl, dressed in her night clothes, crouched halfway up the curve of the main staircase. She seemed to be crying bitterly, although there was no sound. Pod had described her little nightcap, shaped like a baby's bonnet, tied neatly below her chin.

She was there most nights, he thought, weeping for a favourite brother, 'who had somehow got himself shot . . .' Peagreen had told them. The faint, pale light she gave out helped him to find his bearings as he made his way through the darkness of the hall. He found her very useful.

Last, but not least, was The Poor Young Man.

On that first morning after their arrival at the rectory, having risen early, Arrietty had glanced into the library through the half-open glass doors which led into the conservatory. Although she had not taken it in at the time, she remembered now seeing something she had taken for a rolled-up rug, lying on the floor just in front of the fireplace. Then the squeaking wheels of Peagreen's trolley, and the sudden appearance of Peagreen himself had made her forget all about it. She had never seen it since.

She remembered it again quite suddenly on the day when, the human beings being out, Peagreen – on the topmost of the library bookshelves – had manoeuvred the roll of white canvas so that it fell at the feet of Pod who had been waiting down below. She had turned away to the tap in the conservatory to get herself a drink of water and when she returned again to the doors of the library to see what was going on,

Peagreen and Pod, one at each end of it, were carrying the roll towards the hole in the fire surround left by the missing tile.

But there was something between them and it. Again she took it for a rug, or a piece of rolled-up carpet, and went forward to see better. It was not a rug, or a piece of old rolled carpet; to her terror she saw it was a human being, stretched full length in front of the hearth. Asleep? Dead? She jumped back and screamed.

Pod, panting a little as he supported the back end of the roll, turned his head irritably. 'Oh, do be quiet, Arrietty! We've got to concentrate . . .'

Arrietty clapped her hand to her mouth, her eyes staring. 'Gently does it . . .' Pod was saying to Peagreen, who had not turned his head.

'Oh, Papa!' gasped Arrietty, 'whatever is it?'

'It's nothing,' said Pod. 'It's often there. You must have seen it. Lift your end up a bit, Peagreen. You've got the steps, remember. We've got to take it in a slant . . .' Then as if suddenly aware of Arrietty's distress, he turned his head towards her. 'It's all right, girl, no need to fuss – it's not a human being: a poor lad, they say, who shot himself. A kind of ghost, like. It won't hurt you. A bit higher, Peagreen, once you're inside the hole . . .'

Arrietty watched, dumbfounded, as Peagreen walked straight through the object on the floor. He and her father grew a little dim as they passed through the apparition, but her eyes could plainly follow the white gleam of the canvas.

At last, Peagreen emerged at the far side, and went on in through the hole. Pod, clearly visible again, followed. There was a lot of panting and grunting and a few muffled orders, and Arrietty was left alone with the ghost.

To her surprise, her first feeling was one of pity. They should not have walked through him like that. It showed – what did it show? – some kind of lack of respect: thinking of nothing but the 'job in hand'? But Peagreen –? Well, she supposed that Peagreen, having lived at the rectory all his life, was so used to ghosts that he hardly noticed them.

Poor young man . . . She moved closer to look at his face. It was turned sideways, against the floor, and was very pale. Dark curls fell back against the boards. It was a beautiful face, the lips were gently parted and the long-lashed eyes seemed not quite closed. He wore a frilled shirt, knee-breeches and, looking back along the length of him, she could make out his buckled shoes. One arm was flung out sideways, the fingers curved as though they had held some object no longer to be seen. He looked very young. Why had he shot himself? What had made him so sad? But, even as she looked at him, her pity flowing over him, he began to disappear; to melt away into nothingness. It was, she felt, as though he had never been there. Perhaps he never had? She was left staring at the floorboards and the familiar dark stain.

'Well, that's that . . .' said a cheerful voice. She looked up. It was Peagreen, appearing in the entrance to the hole and rubbing his hands in a satisfied way. 'I thought we might never get that great roll up the steps. But it was easy. One good thing about these old hearths is they do give one plenty of room.' He turned. 'Oh, here's your father. We'd better get the tile back now . . .'

Arrietty stared at Peagreen, her look was accusing. 'You shouldn't have walked through him like that –'

'But I didn't. Who? What do you mean?'

'That poor young man!'

Peagreen laughed. 'Oh, that! I thought you were referring to your father . . .'

'Of course I wasn't: you couldn't walk through my father.'

'No, I suppose one couldn't,' he moved towards her. 'But, Arrietty, that "poor young man" as you call him, wasn't really there at all: it was just a –' he hesitated, 'a photograph on air.' He thought a moment, 'Or on Time, if you prefer. We had to get that canvas through the hole . . .'

'Yes, I know. But you could have waited.'

'Oh, Arrietty, if we had to wait for ghosts to disappear or appear all the time, we'd never get in or out of anywhere in this house.' He half turned. 'Look, your father's struggling with that tile. I'd better go and help him –'

After that Arrietty was never frightened of 'the poor young man' again, but she was always careful to walk round him.

CHAPTER SEVENTEEN

THE next excitement (as soon as Homily's kitchen was finished) was their long-delayed visit to the church.

'We can't put it off any longer,' Pod said to Homily, 'or Lupy will be offended. Spiller must have told them that we're here . . .'

'I don't intend to put it off any longer,' retorted Homily. 'Now my kitchen's finished, I'm ready to go anywhere.' She was very happy with her kitchen. 'And I'd like to see what sort of house they've got together. A church! Seems a funny kind of place to choose to live in . . . I mean, what is there to eat in a church?'

'Well, we'll see,' said Pod.

They chose a bright, clear morning without a threat of rain. The party consisted of Pod, Homily and Arrietty. Peagreen had excused himself, and Spiller was elsewhere. Homily had packed a few 'goodies' in a borrowing bag, so as not to arrive empty-handed and all three felt very cheerful. After all the days of gruelling work, this was an expedition – a welcome 'day off'.

It felt strange to be walking *away* from the rectory and down an unfamiliar path. Birds were building in the box hedge, and there was moss underfoot at edges of the gravel. Spiller had given them directions: 'When you see the vestry drain, that's your place.'

As they slipped through the palings of the wicket gate which led into the churchyard, Arrietty saw a little figure moving towards them on the edge of the path. 'Timmus!' she exclaimed and, leaving her more cautious parents standing, hurriedly dashed towards him. Yes, it was him – much thinner, a little taller, with a very brown sunburnt face. 'Oh, Timmus!' she exclaimed again, and was about to hug him but then she hesitated: he had become so still and so staring, as if he could not believe his eyes. 'Oh, Timmus, my Timmus . . .' she whispered again and laid an arm around his shoulders. Upon which, he stooped suddenly as though to pick up something on the ground. She stooped down beside him, her arm still about his shoulders.

'I thought I saw a grasshopper . . .' he mumbled, and she could hear a catch in his voice.

'Oh, Timmus . . .' she whispered, '. . . you're crying. Why are you crying?'

'I'm not crying,' he gulped. 'Of course I'm not crying . . .' Suddenly he turned his face towards her: it was aglow with happiness, but the tears were running down his cheeks. 'I thought I was never going to see you no more.'

'Any more . . .' said Arrietty from habit: she had always corrected Timmus's grammar.

'I was coming to find you,' he went on. 'I keep looking for you.'

'Right up to the rectory? Oh, Timmus, you'd never have found us, not in that great place: we're very hidden up there.' She had nothing to wipe his cheeks with, so she wiped them very gently with her fingers. 'And you might have got caught yourself!'

'What on earth are you two doing, crouched down there on the path?' Pod and Homily had come up beside them: 'How are you, Timmus?' Homily went on, as Arrietty and Timmus stood up. 'My, how you've grown! Come and give me a kiss.' Timmus did so: he was all smiles now. 'How did you know we were coming?'

'He didn't,' said Arrietty. 'He was on his way to the rectory to find us.'

Homily looked grave. 'Oh, you must never do that, Timmus, not on your own. You never know what you might find up at the rectory. A couple of human beans for a start! Is your mother in?'

'Yes, she's in,' he said. 'And my father, too.'

He led them to the drain beside the vestry wall. A lead pipe came out above it through a hole cut in the stones: there was plenty of room on one side of it for a borrower to squeeze past. Timmus went through first, agile as an eel. For the others it was stiffer going, but they soon found out the trick of it.

Inside, they found themselves beneath the stone sink, beside the rusty gas-ring. Here they paused and looked about them.

It was a largish room, and smelled faintly of stale cassocks. In the centre was a square table covered with a red plush cloth, against which several chairs were set. They were of the type usually found in kitchens. Exactly opposite to them, from where they stood, was a large oaken press set into the wall of the church. The original wall of the church, Pod realized; the vestry must have been added on at a much later date. The press was iron-studded and had a very large keyhole. On one side of the press stood a large, box-like piece of furniture which Pod learned later was a disused harmonium. This was piled, almost to the ceiling, with shabby hymn-books. On the other side of the press, was a tall old desk, on which stood an open ledger, an ink-well, and what he took to be a selection of old pens. To their right, a whole wall was taken up by cassocks and surplices hanging on hooks. To their left were floor-length curtains of faded mulberry plush. These hung on wooden rings, separating the vestry from the main church. In the far corner stood an ugly iron stove, usually described as a 'tortoise', whose pipe ran up through the ceiling.

They did not take all this in at first glance, because Timmus had run away from them across the flagstones. 'I'll just tell them you're here,' he called back, and disappeared into a dark, rectangular hole at the base of the harmonium.

'So that's where they live,' muttered Homily, 'I wonder what it's like inside.'

'Roomy,' said Pod.

After a few moments, Lupy appeared, wiping her hands on her apron – a thing, Homily noted, she would never have done in what might be called her grander days, when she had always been one to dress up smartly for visitors. She kissed Homily rather soberly, and then did the same to Pod. 'Welcome,' she said, with a gentle un-Lupyish smile, 'welcome to the house of the Lord . . .'

It was a strange greeting, Homily thought, as, equally soberly, she kissed Lupy back. At the same time, she noticed that Lupy had grown much thinner and lost something of her bounce. 'Come in, come in . . .' she was saying, 'Hendreary and Timmus are lighting the candles. We've been expecting you this many a long day.'

Hendreary then appeared at the entrance hole, shaking out the flame of a match. Timmus came out beside his father; his brown little face was still aglow. There were further greetings and polite compliments as the visitors were ushered inside. Arrietty, Lupy declared, had become 'quite the young lady' and Homily herself was 'looking very well'.

The vast interior was ablaze with light, there were candle stubs in every type of container. These warmed the great room as well as lighting it and Homily, looking about her at the familiar pieces of furniture, thought these had gained elegance because of the ample space surrounding them: she hardly recognized the little snuff-box settee which once had been their own. What an age it had taken, she remembered, to pad and line it; but she felt very proud of it now.

She laid her small offering on one of the tables, and stiffly took a seat. Lupy bustled about and produced some sawn-off nutshells, which she carefully filled with wine. 'You can drink this,' she said, 'with a clear conscience, because it has not yet been blessed . . .' Homily again was puzzled by the oddness of this remark, but she took a sip of the wine.

'Or perhaps,' went on Lupy, 'you'd prefer gooseberry: my own make?'

'This is fine,' Pod assured her, taking a sip. 'Never *was* one for gooseberry wine – strong, gouty stuff . . .'

'Hendreary's very partial to it . . .'

'Hope it's partial to him,' said Pod. 'A bit too acid for me, like.'

Hendreary, Homily saw, was showing Pod round the premises. 'This,' he was saying, pointing out the entrance hole, 'is where the pedals used to be. Up there,' he raised his head to the heights above them, 'was where they had the bellows, but they took those out when they moved the broken harmonium to make room in the church for the organ. But we've still got the pipes: Lupy finds them useful for hanging the clothes to dry . . .'

'Hendreary looks very well,' said Homily, taking another delicate sip of wine. And Arrietty wondered why, when people had not met for some time, they must always tell each other they looked 'well'. To her, Uncle Hendreary looked more scrawny than ever, and his funny little

tuft of a beard had become slightly grizzled. Did she herself look 'well', she wondered?

'He is, and he isn't,' Aunt Lupy was saying. 'With the boys away, he's finding the borrowing here rather heavy. But we manage,' she added brightly. 'Spiller brings us things, and the ladies are here twice a week . . .'

'What ladies?' asked Homily. She wondered if they were anything to do with 'the lord'.

'The ladies who do the flowers, and they always bring a little refreshment. And we have our ways with that. You see, they set their baskets down on the floor until Miss Menzies has laid the table. In fact, once they've finished the flowers they sit down to a very hearty tea.'

Arrietty jumped up from her chair. 'Miss Menzies?' she exclaimed. Only Timmus noticed her excitement.

'Yes, she's one of them. I know most of their names. There's Lady Mullings and Mrs Crabtree. And Mrs Witless, of course: she does most of the cooking; cakes, sausage-rolls – all those sort of things. And I must confess to you, Homily, that it's quite an entertainment to listen to their talk. I just sit here quietly and listen. Since we last met, Homily, I've learnt quite a lot about human beans. They come in all shapes and sizes. You wouldn't credit some of the things I've heard . . .'

Arrietty sat down again slowly and Timmus, on the arm of her chair, leaned against her. Something his mother had just said had obviously interested her: he wondered what it was. Her face was still a little pink.

'Does the lord live in the vestry?' asked Homily.

'Oh, dear me, no!' exclaimed Aunt Lupy – she sounded slightly shocked, 'the Lord only lives in the church.' Something about the way she pronounced the word 'Lord' warned Homily that it should be spoken as though it began with a capital letter. Lupy's normally loud voice had fallen respectfully to a note of awe. 'The vestry,' she said gently, as though explaining to a child, 'isn't really part of the church.'

'Oh, I see,' said Homily, although she didn't see at all. But she was determined not to reveal her ignorance.

'This church,' went on Lupy, 'by human standards, is a very small church. And the rector is inclined to be high. Because of this, we don't have a very large congregation . . .'

'Oh,' said Homily, but she could not quite see what the rector's height had to do with it.

'He does not use incense, or anything like that,' went on Lupy, 'but he does like lighted candles on the altar. And thank goodness for it, because we can always get hold of the leftovers.'

'So I see,' said Homily, looking round the brightly lighted room.

'Because of this, a great many of the locals go to the church at Went-le-Craye.'

'Because of the candles here on the altar?' asked Homily, astonished.

'Yes,' said Lupy, 'because the vicar at Went-le-Craye is very low.'

'Oh, I see,' said Homily again: a whole new world was opening before her. No wonder Lupy had said that human beans came in all 'shapes and sizes'.

'Of course, this "little" church – as they call it – is the more famous. It's far older, for one thing. And tourists come from all over the world to see the rood-screen . . .'

'Do they?' said Homily, wonderingly. She was feeling more and more puzzled.

'Of course, when we first came here, we went through a few hard times. Yes, indeed. There was one week when we lived entirely on bull's-eyes –'

'*Bull's* eyes?' exclaimed Homily. Whatever was she going to hear next?

'They're those stripey sweets, shaped like pin-cushions – the choirboys always bring a few bags of them to suck during the sermons. The trouble with them is that when they get warm, they're apt to stick together . . .'

The choirboys or the bull's-eyes? Homily decided to keep silent.

'Little rascals, those choirboys. The gigglings, the goings-on in the vestry. And Timmus is beginning to pick up some of their expressions. And yet,' she went on, 'when they go into church, they sing like little angels; and look like them, too.'

Timmus rose from his seat and came beside his mother: he looked as though he wished to ask her a question. Lupy put an arm round him, affectionately but absentmindedly; she still had plenty more to tell Homily.

'Do you know, Homily, what were the first words we ever heard spoken in this church?' Homily shook her head. How could she know?

'A voice was saying "Come unto me all ye that travel and are heavy-laden and I will give you rest." We *had* travelled and we *were* heavy-laden –' Yes, thought Homily, glancing again about the room, heavy-laden with a whole lot of household objects which once belonged to us. 'Wasn't that wonderful? And we did find rest. And have done ever since. And the hymns they sing! You can't imagine!'

With one arm round Timmus and the other held up as though to beat time, she broke out into a little air: ' "All things bright and beautiful, all creatures great and small . . ." Great and *small*, Homily. Although no one knew we were here, you will understand that we could not help but feel welcome, if you see what I mean.' She followed the direction of Homily's eyes. 'Yes, dear, I think there are one or two things here which once belonged to you and Pod. We never thought you'd need them again, going off in the night, like you did. But if there's anything you'd like to take away – just to help you start up life in the Old Rectory – just say the word: we'd only be too delighted. Anything we can do to help –'

Homily's astonished eyes swerved back to Lupy's face. She could hardly believe her ears. Lupy *offering* things! And, seemingly, with real sincerity. Although she did notice a little quiver about the lips, and a slightly nervous flutter of the eyelids. Homily looked round for Pod, but Hendreary had taken him out into the vestry. Some great change had taken place in Lupy, and Homily needed Pod to witness it. She turned back again to those eager, questioning eyes. 'Oh, Lupy,' she said, 'you're welcome to all that old stuff that came in the pillowcase. Up at the Old Rectory, we've got all we need now. And more.'

'Are you sure, dear? You're not just saying that?' Homily could hear the relief in her voice.

'Quite sure. It's a long story. I mean, there are some things that have happened to us since then that you'll hardly credit –'

'And the same with us, dear . . . What's the matter, Timmus?' She turned to him impatiently: he had been whispering in her ear. 'What are you saying? It's rude to whisper . . .'

'Could I take Arrietty into the church?'

'I don't see why not. If Arrietty wants to go.' And it might be a relief to get rid of two extra pairs of listening ears: there were still so many things she longed to recount to Homily.

As Arrietty and Timmus slipped away, Homily said, 'Timmus is very brown. I suppose he spends a lot of time out of doors?'

'No, very little, as a matter of fact. We never let him go out alone.'

'Then how –?' began Homily.

'All that brown? That's just a fad of his. I'll tell you about that later . . .' It was almost a relief to Homily to recognize a trace of Lupy's old impatience. Lupy leaned forward towards her. 'Now where had we got to? You were just going to tell me . . .'

'Ours is a long story,' said Homily, 'you tell me yours first.' Lupy did not need asking twice.

As Arrietty and Timmus crossed the vestry, Pod and Uncle Hendreary emerged from between the curtains which led into the church, each with his nutshell in hand. They were deep in conversation. 'Very fine,' Pod was saying, 'never seen carving like that, not anywhere. No wonder the – the – what-you-call-'ems come . . .'

'Tourists –' said Hendreary, '– from right across the world!'

'I can well believe it,' went on Pod as he and Hendreary, still talking, made their way into the harmonium.

Timmus and Arrietty slipped through the curtains and then, for a moment, Arrietty stood still. So this was the church!

The building was simple, with its pillars and arches, and its rows of orderly pews. If the human beans called this 'a little church' what, thought Arrietty, could a 'big church' be like? She almost trembled at the height and vastness. It had a strange smell and a strange feeling: it was a feeling she had never felt before. At the far end, behind the last row of pews, there was a pair of curtains very like the ones beside which she was standing. Beams of coloured light streamed in through the stained-glass windows. She felt more than a little afraid. Where did the Lord live, she wondered? She moved slightly closer to Timmus. 'What's behind those curtains at the end?' she whispered.

Timmus answered in his ordinary voice. 'Oh, that leads to the belfry chamber and the stairs to the belfry,' he said, cheerfully. 'I'll show you in a minute. And there are stone stairs to the belfry. But I don't use them myself.' His face suddenly filled with mischief. 'You can get out on to the roof,' he told her gleefully.

Arrietty did not answer his smile. Stone stairs! How could creatures their size get up stone stairs built for humans? Carpeted stairs had been another matter – in the days when Pod had still had his tape and hat-pin.

Timmus was pulling her sideways. 'Come on. I'll show you the rood-screen . . .'

She followed him across to the centre aisle. Here the stone flags had pictures engraved on them. Odd-looking pictures of stiff-looking people – right down the church, they went, in all shapes and sizes, as far as the curtains at the end. But Timmus was looking in the opposite direction. 'There it is,' he announced.

It was indeed a wonderful feat of carving, this rood-screen which divided the chancel from the nave. It rose from the floor at either side, with a wide arch in the middle. Through this arch, she could see the choir stalls which, unlike the pews, were set out lengthwise and, beyond these, facing her, she could make out the altar. Above the altar was a stained-glass window. Yes, there were the two branched candlesticks, which had once been stolen and since retrieved, and tall silver vases generously filled with flowers. The air was heavy with the scent of lilies of the valley.

Timmus was nudging her: evidently she was not paying enough attention to the rood-screen. She smiled at him and took a few paces backwards down the aisle to study it from a wider angle.

The background (if anything so frail-looking could be called a background) was a delicate lattice of leaves and flowers, from among which peered a myriad little forms and faces: some human, some

angelic, others devilish. Some were laughing, others looked very solemn. These last ones, Arrietty was told later, were most likely actual portraits of dignitaries of the time. At the very top of the arch was a larger face, very gentle and calm, with flowing hair. On each side of this a hand had been carved, the palms exposed, in a gesture which seemed to be saying, 'Look . . .' Or was it, 'Come . . .'?

Arrietty turned to Timmus. 'That bigger face up there, is that a portrait of the man who carved all this?'

'I don't know,' said Timmus.

'Or is it –' Arrietty hesitated, '– a portrait of the Lord?'

'I don't know,' said Timmus, 'my mother calls it the Creator.' He pulled on her sleeve. 'Now do you want to see the bell chamber?'

'In a minute,' said Arrietty: there was still so much to see in the rood-screen. A little gallery, she noted, ran along the top of it, with a quaintly designed balustrade. Halfway along the balustrade was the carved figure of a dove, with wings outstretched. It looked, thought Arrietty, as though it had just alighted there. Or, perhaps, was just about to take off. It was lifelike. The outstretched wings balanced and enhanced the outstretched hands just below them.

'It's beautiful . . .' she said to Timmus.

'Yes, and it's fun, too,' he told her and, as they turned aside to make their way down the aisle, he added suddenly, 'Would you like to see me run as fast as a mouse?'

'If you like,' said Arrietty. She realized suddenly that Timmus, who was not yet allowed out of doors alone, had only this church for a playground. She hoped the Lord liked little children. She rather thought he must do if Aunt Lupy had been right about 'all creatures great and small'.

She watched, smiling, as Timmus darted away from her towards the curtains of the alcove at the end. Yes, he could run: the little legs almost flew; and he fetched up panting before a low bench set just in front of the curtains. This bench, Arrietty noticed when at last she came up with him and had climbed up on a hassock, held neat piles of pamphlets about the church, a few picture postcards, and a brass-bound wooden collecting-box. There was an ample slit in the lid, almost long enough to take a letter. A notice, propped behind it, said 'THANK YOU'.

'Do you think –' Timmus was saying, still panting a little, '– that if I practised I could run as fast as a ferret?'

'Faster,' said Arrietty. 'Even rabbits can run faster than ferrets: ferrets can only catch rabbits by chasing them down their holes.'

Timmus looked pleased. 'Come on,' he said, and darting under the bench, he slipped through the gap in between the curtains.

The room inside was bare stone, but with a white, plastered ceiling. Three kitchen chairs were set along one wall and the staircase rose up along another. But what fascinated Arrietty most were the six round holes in the ceiling, through each of which protruded a long length of rope. A few feet up, along each rope, was a sausage-like piece of padding. So this was how they rang the bells! Since her family had been living in the Old Rectory, they had only heard a single bell and this was only for the services on Sunday. Each piece of rope ended in a 'tail' which lay in curves on the floor. It was thinner than the main rope.

Timmus leapt upon the first rope, clung there for a moment, then slid downwards so that he sat astride the 'tail'. 'Watch me,' he said, and eased off his shoes. As they tumbled off, Arrietty recognized them as a pair her father had made – some years ago now – for Timmus's elder brother. She looked down at her own shoes which were getting very shabby and had once belonged to Homily. She hoped that, when they were really settled in their new home, Pod would take up this trade again: he had been a wonderful shoemaker. All he would need was an old leather glove; and there must be plenty of those left in churches.

'Please look –' Timmus was begging. He was standing up now on the knot, his hands grasped the rope above his head. What was he going to do? She soon saw: if he could run like a mouse, he could climb like one, too. Up he went. Up and up, hands and feet moving like clockwork. Faster even than a mouse, more like a spider on a filament of web. Except the bell-rope was no filament: the coarse weave was heavy and thick, providing invisible footholds.

Arrietty watched, amazed, until at last he reached the ceiling. Without looking down, he disappeared through the hole. In just those few moments, Timmus had vanished from sight. Rooted to the spot, Arrietty stood there dumbfounded, craning her neck at the ceiling. Her neck began to ache but she dare not look away. What hours of practice this must have cost him! And she had thought that *she* could climb . . .

At last, the little face appeared, peering down at her through the hole. 'You see,' he called out, 'to get to the belfry, borrowers don't need stairs!'

He came down more slowly, perhaps a little tired by the effort, and sat himself comfortably astride the rope. 'You can get right up to the bells,' he told her, 'and there's a place where you can get right out on

to the roof. There used to be six bellringers but now there's only one –
except at Easter and a day they call Christmas.'

'Oh,' cried Arrietty, 'I know all about Christmas. My mother's
always talking about it. And the feasts they always had. When she was
a girl, there were a lot more borrowers in the house and that was the
time – Christmas time – when she first began to notice my father. The
feasts! There were things called raisins and crystal fruit and plum
puddings and turkey and game pie . . . and the *wine* they left in glasses!
My father used to get it out with a fountain-pen filler. He'd be up a fold
in the table-cloth almost before the last human being had left the room.
And my mother began to see what a wonderful borrower he might turn
out to be. He brought her a little ring out of something called a cracker
and she wore it as a crown . . .' She fell silent a moment, remembering
that ring. Where was it now, she wondered? She had worn it often
herself . . .

'Go on,' said Timmus: he hoped this might turn out to be one of her
stories.

'That's all,' said Arrietty.

'Oh –' Timmus sounded disappointed. After a while he said, 'What's
it like up at the rectory?'

'Nice. You could come and visit us . . .'

'They don't let me go out alone.'

'I could come and fetch you –'

'Could you? Could you really? Can you still tell stories?'

'I think so,' said Arrietty.

Timmus stood up, clasping the rope with his hands. 'Now, if you
like, we could go and climb the rood-screen,' he suggested.

Arrietty hesitated. 'I can't climb as well as you,' she said at last. And
then she added quickly, 'Yet.'

'It's easy. You can get about all over that rood-screen. I go up there
to watch the human beans . . .'

'What human beans?'

'The human beans who come to church. They can't see you. Not if
you stay quite still. They think you're part of the carving. That's why
I brown my face . . .'

'What with?' asked Arrietty.

'Walnut juice, of course.' He swung the rope a little. 'Could you give
me a bit of a push?'

Arrietty was bewildered. How quickly he went from one subject to
another! 'What sort of a push?' she said.

'On me. Just give a push on me . . .'

Hand over hand, he was climbing up the tail rope and once he had gripped it firmly between his feet and knees, Arrietty pushed him gently. This first bell-rope, she saw, hung lower than the others. Perhaps through constant use? The sausage-shaped pad looked frayed and shabby and had been cleverly reinforced by a piece of old carpet, neatly bound round with string. This, she supposed, was the bell they heard on Sundays.

'Harder!' cried Timmus. '*Much* harder!' So she gave him a massive shove. He leaned outwards from the rope and, by pushing his feet and pulling with his hands, he began to gain momentum. Backwards and forwards swung the bell-rope, farther and farther, higher and higher. Once he brushed the curtains which opened slightly. She became afraid he might hit the walls!

'Careful . . .!' she called in rising panic: the bell-rope was too long to be checked by its radius – it could go any distance within sight. 'Careful, Timmus!' she implored. '*Please* be careful . . .!'

He only laughed, lithe and confident. With a twist of his body, he made a circular swerve, brushing the other bell-ropes, so they too swung and trembled. The whole bell chamber became alive with movement. Supposing somebody came! Supposing the bells began to ring! Arrietty felt a sudden sense of guilt: this wild display was all for her benefit. 'Stop it, Timmus,' she begged him, almost in tears. She threw out her arms, as though to check him – a fruitless gesture at the speed he was going – and she had to dodge back swiftly as the bell-rope flew wildly past her through the gap in the curtains. She heard the sliding crash and the scrape of wood on stone. He had hit the bench. 'Oh, please don't let him be dead,' she cried out to herself as she rushed out through the curtains.

He wasn't dead at all: he was standing on the bench, surrounded by scattered pamphlets – the rope still held in his hand. He looked down on it in a bewildered way, then gently let it go. In her distress, Arrietty hardly noticed it as it sailed softly past her through the gaping curtains, and back to its usual place, curving and trembling as though it was alive.

There were pamphlets on the floor, the collecting-box was pushed sideways, and the bench was out of place. Not very much out of place, she noticed with relief. 'Oh, Timmus . . .!' she exclaimed and there was a world of reproach in her voice.

'I'm sorry,' he said and moved towards the edge of the bench, as if about to descend. It would have been a big drop.

'Stay where you are,' Arrietty ordered him. 'I'll get you down later. We've got to tidy this up . . . Have you hurt yourself?'

He still looked bewildered. 'Not much,' he said.

'Then collect all those papers together and put them back into piles. I'll pass you these ones on the floor . . .'

He did as he was told. He *was* moving rather stiffly but Arrietty, stooping to collect the scattered pamphlets on the flagstones, had no time to notice or look up. At least he could walk and bend.

On tiptoe, she passed her small collection of postcards and pamphlets up to him while he, perilously leaning over the edge of the polished bench stretched down to receive them. At last, all the papers were in place. The bench itself, alas, would have to remain crooked.

'Now, you'd better try to straighten up the collecting-box – if it's not too heavy . . .'

It was heavy, but he managed it after a struggle. Then Arrietty passed him up the card which said 'THANK YOU'. And that, at last, was that.

They walked back up the aisle very soberly. Neither of them felt very much like talking but, as they reached the rood-screen, Arrietty said, 'I don't think we'll climb that today.' Although he did not answer, Timmus appeared to agree with her.

CHAPTER EIGHTEEN

AFTER that, Arrietty went down to the church quite often: it was because of the 'new arrangements' – arrangements which made Arrietty very happy and became a turning point in her life: she was to be allowed to 'borrow' and not only that, but joy of joys, to borrow out of doors!

It came about like this: her Uncle Hendreary had been finding the long walk to the kitchen garden increasingly tiring and Timmus was too young to be sent out alone. He would go with his father sometimes to help to carry, but he would dash about and 'run like a mouse' and this exercise, too, Hendreary found tiresome, being prone to odd twinges of gout. It had been different when the two elder boys had been at home: they had always undertaken to do what Aunt Lupy called 'the donkey work' but now that they had returned to their old home in the badgers' set with Eggletina to keep house for them, seeking what they called their independence, the daily chores fell heavily on their father. 'I am not as young as I was,' he would say, and he would say it very often.

Pod could not help much: he had worked out a wonderful scheme for their living quarters under the window seat and the work this entailed took up all of his time. He was determined to divide up the fairly large space into three separate rooms: a little one for Arrietty, another for himself and Homily, and a bright, sun-filled sitting-room which would look out on to the grating. He would construct the partitions from the backs of the many odd books Peagreen had left behind. Montaigne's *Essays* in two volumes were the largest and these he had set up first, the smaller books he would use for doors. He kept back a good supply of the inside pages, with these he planned to paper the walls in vertical lines of news type. Homily thought the even lettering a little dull and uninteresting for the sitting-room: she would have preferred a touch of colour. 'You don't want a big room like this all *grey*. And that's what it'll look like if you don't look closely. Just *grey*: the print's so small-like . . .' But Arrietty and Pod persuaded her that this neutral shade would increase the feeling of space, and make a splendid background for the pictures Peagreen had promised to paint for them.

'You see, Mother,' Arrietty tried to explain, 'this room won't be furnished with bits and bobs – like the room under the floor at Firbank. I mean, now we've got all Miss Menzies's beautiful dolls'-house furniture . . .'

'Bits and bobs!' Homily had muttered crossly: she had been fond of their cosy room at Firbank. Especially fond of that beautiful knight from a chess set. She wondered where it was now.

But she would cook them splendid meals in her snow-white kitchen, well supplied with borrowings from the vegetable garden, and Spiller brought them an occasional minnow or freshwater crayfish from the stream, and – every now and again – a haunch of this or that, rich and gamey, but he would never say of *what*.

Pod hammered and sawed (and whistled under his breath), among the stacked furniture and general chaos under the window seat in the library. Peagreen would occasionally look in to inspect their work, and bring them some rare dainty or other from the larder, but he found it hard to tear himself away from his painting (which he was doing in secret so that each picture would be a surprise).

Everybody seemed happy, each with his own particular job, but perhaps the happiest of all were Arrietty and Timmus.

He would never 'run like a mouse' with Arrietty (except when danger threatened: they once had a very nasty encounter with a weasel). And, on their way to the kitchen garden, she would often tell him a story which would keep him enthralled. In those first early days of spring, there was little to borrow except brussels sprouts, parsley and winter kale, but as the weather grew warmer there were crowded rows of seedling lettuces which badly needed thinning: the borrowers thinned them. They also 'thinned' the tiny seedling onions and gathered sprigs of thyme. Then came the glorious day when Whitlace dug the first of the new potatoes and left in the soft earth a myriad of tiny tubors, some no larger than a hazel nut: with which he 'would not bother'. But Homily 'bothered' and so did Lupy. What a treat it was to serve up a whole dish of miniature new potatoes, flavoured with tender sprigs of early mint. And if Peagreen could produce a knob of butter from the larder! What a change from cutting off slices from tired old potatoes – potatoes so large that they had to be rolled along dusty floorboards into Homily's kitchen, as had been the case at Firbank.

Then came the promise of the first broad beans, the scarlet runners, the strawberry-beds and raspberry canes breaking into leaf. And those mysterious fruit trees trained along the southern wall. Peaches?

Nectarines? Victoria plums? They would have to wait and see. Oh, the bottlings and the dryings and the storings! Pod was hard put to it to find enough utensils. And yet the old disused game larder never seemed to fail him. With patient and persistent searchings, he could usually supply most needs.

Spiller would sometimes join them in the vegetable garden: with the aid of his bow and arrow, he kept down the largest pests. Pigeons were the greatest menace: they could strip a planting of early cabbage in less than a couple of hours. But they grew to detest the sting of his tiny arrows.

Borrowing for two families could sometimes be heavyish work. One brussels sprout was as big as a cabbage to Arrietty and Timmus and, besides all the other borrowings, they must always return with four, two for each household. All the same, in that warm and sheltered garden, there were quite long hours of fun and leisure: hide-and-seek among the parsley and, if it rained, they could shelter under the spreading leaves of rhubarb and play guessing games and such. They had, of course, to keep a sharp look-out for Whitlace. And there were rats among the compost. But Spiller saw to those. They, too, grew to know the 'ping' of that tiny bow.

On the way home, they would leave Arrietty's borrowings below the grating (where Pod would take them in), and then go on to the church. Sometimes Aunt Lupy would ask Arrietty to stay to tea, and Arrietty nearly always accepted: she was longing to catch a glimpse of Miss Menzies. Although she had solemnly promised her father never again to speak to a human bean, there might be some way of letting Miss Menzies know that they were safe. But though the other ladies appeared on Wednesdays and Saturdays to do the flowers, Miss Menzies was never among them.

Aunt Lupy, Arrietty noticed, was getting quite fond of her ladies. She was very used to genteel human conversation, having become a Harpsichord by marriage and lived so long with her first husband inside that instrument in the drawing-room at Firbank. It was here (as Homily maintained) she had picked up grander manners than those rougher ways current below the kitchen. ('Although,' Homily would always add, 'Lupy was only a Rainpipe from the stables before she married Harpsichord.') The harpsichord was never opened because so many of the strings were missing. All the same, superior though it might seem, it had not been an easy life: they had to subsist entirely on what was left over from afternoon tea. And their borrowing had to be done at lightning speed, between the time the ladies left to change for dinner and the butler appeared to clear away the tea things. And there was many a day (as she once confessed to Homily) when there had been nothing to drink except water from the flower-vases, and nothing to eat at all. Aunt Lupy seemed doomed, Arrietty thought, (with a few exceptional interludes) to make a home inside some kind of musical instrument.

Arrietty liked to hear Aunt Lupy's stories about the human beans and picked up many kinds of interesting information with which she would regale her mother and father on her return to supper. For instance, *why* the old rector no longer lived in the rectory, but in a neat, compact villa across the lane. She learned that Mrs Whitlace came down to the church every evening to lock away the offertory box in the press in the vestry, and how the solid old press (set deeply into the stones of the original church) housed 'priceless treasures' (Lady Mullings's description): gold and silver altar plates, a jewelled chalice, exquisite candlesticks far more ancient than those which had been stolen from the altar and many other historic objects, described in an awed voice by Lupy but of which Arrietty had forgotten the names.

'Fancy!' Homily exclaimed as Arrietty reeled off as many as she could remember. 'Whoever would have guessed it!'

And Pod remarked, 'Sounds like the display cabinet at Firbank . . .'

'Should all be under lock and key,' Homily said sternly.

'They *are* under lock and key,' Pod explained patiently. 'I've examined those doors: the oak is that hard with age that no one could drive so much as a nail into it. Not even a human bean could –'

'Lady Mullings,' Arrietty told them, 'thinks all those things should be put in a bank.'

'In a *bank!*' exclaimed Homily, thinking of a grassy slope.

'Yes, it sounded funny to me, too,' admitted Arrietty.

'Is that the Lady Mullings who's a "finder"?' asked Homily, after a moment.

'Yes. Well, she is for other people. But Aunt Lupy says she can never find anything she mislays herself. Aunt Lupy says she heard her telling Mrs Crabtree that she's lost the key of her attic and now she can't get at the things she laid aside for the jumble sale. And she's always leaving things in the church – umbrellas and handkerchiefs, gloves, and things like that . . .'

'I could do with a nice leather glove,' said Pod.

*

One afternoon, a little time later, Arrietty picked up courage to ask quite openly about Miss Menzies: why did she no longer come?

'Oh, poor thing!' exclaimed Aunt Lupy. 'She did come once to make her excuses. But she's been in dreadful trouble . . .'

Arrietty's heart sank. 'What . . . what kind of trouble?'

'Some vandals broke into the model village and knocked down all the houses!'

'*All* the houses?' gasped Arrietty, although she knew that Aunt Lupy was apt to exaggerate.

'Well, that's what it sounded like to me. Upset! I never heard a poor thing more upset. And it was nearly the end of Mr Pott. The brutes must have got in across the stream. They'd cut the wire and all. And there they both are – Miss Menzies and Mr Pott – working night and day to try to repair the damage. Poor things! They had wanted so much to get the place open for Easter. That's when the season starts . . .'

'When –' stammered Arrietty, '– I mean – how long ago did this happen?'

'Let me see . . .' Aunt Lupy looked thoughtful. 'About a week ago? No, it was more than that – more like two . . .' She wrinkled her brow, trying to remember. 'How long ago is it since you all first arrived here?'

'About two weeks . . .' said Arrietty.

'Well, it must have been about then. I seem to recall it was the night of a very full moon –'

'Yes,' Arrietty was leaning forward, her hands clasped so tightly in her lap that the nails dug into her palms, 'that was the night after we first arrived.' Her voice had trembled.

'What's the matter, child?'

'Oh, Aunt Lupy! Can't you see? If we'd delayed one night, just *one* night – and my mother wanted to – they'd have got us!'

'Who'd have got you?' Aunt Lupy looked alarmed.

'The Platters! They'd have taken the roof off, like they did before. And we'd have been in the house. Like rats in a trap, Aunt Lupy!'

'Goodness gracious me . . .' exclaimed Lupy.

'It wasn't vandals, Aunt Lupy, it was the Platters!'

'You mean those people who shut you up in the attic, and were going to show you in a showcase?'

'Yes, yes.' Arrietty was standing up now.

'But how do you know it was them?'

'I just know. My father was expecting them. I must go home now,

Aunt Lupy.' She was searching round frantically for her empty borrowing bag. 'I must tell all this to my parents . . .'

'But you're safe now, dear. Those people don't know that you're here.'

'I hope not,' said Arrietty. She found her bag and stooped hurriedly to kiss her aunt.

'The Lord takes care of his own,' said Lupy. 'Thank you for the lettuce. Go carefully, child.'

But Arrietty did not go very carefully. She was in such a hurry that she nearly ran into Kitty Whitlace, who was approaching the wicket gate from the far side. Luckily Arrietty heard her singing and recognized the singer by the song and had time to slip under the edge of a flat gravestone.

'In a dear little town in the old County Down,' sang Kitty, as she approached the gate, 'You must linger way down in my heart. Though it never was grand, it is my fairyland –' she paused to unlatch the gate, and carefully relatch it, before she went on, '– in a wonderful world apart.' Arrietty, peering out from under the lip of the gravestone, saw that Kitty, as she strolled along, was swinging a very large key on the forefinger of her right hand. Ah, yes! She suddenly remembered that this was the hour that Kitty Whitlace always went down to the church for a last look round and to lock up the collecting-box in the solid old press for the night. Swiftly, she slid out from under the gravestone and between the palings of the gate.

Her mother and father looked grave when they had heard her story. They seemed shaken and appalled at the narrowness of their escape. There was no crowing by Pod about his unheeded warnings to Homily. Nor did she concede, as she half longed to, how right those warnings had proved. This was no time for cheap triumphs nor recriminations. They were safe now, and that was all that mattered. But what a near thing it had been!

'How desperate they must have been, those Platters!' Pod said, at last.

'And still are, I shouldn't wonder,' said Homily.

'Well, they won't find us here,' said Pod. He looked round in a pleased way at their sitting-room, which was now taking shape: the chairs and sofa were now unstacked and they were sitting on them.

Homily rose to her feet. 'I've got a bit of supper all ready in the kitchen,' she told them, and led the way down the steps to the passage under the floor.

Pod took one last look round. 'I'll cut a nice piece of glass to fit that grating,' he said. 'Peagreen's got plenty. And then come winter, when they turn the central heating on, we'll be snug as houses . . .'

Homily was very silent during supper, and a little absent-minded. When they had finished eating, she sat with one elbow on the table and, leaning a cheek upon her hand, stared downwards at her plate. Pod, looking at her across the table, seemed puzzled.

'Is anything on your mind, Homily?' he asked, after a longish silence. He knew how easily she could become worried.

She shook her head. 'Not really . . .'

'But there *is* something?' persisted Pod.

'Nothing really,' said Homily and began to gather up the plates. 'It's only . . .'

'Only what, Homily?'

She sat down again. 'It's only . . . well, I wish sometimes they'd never told us about that Lady Mullings.'

'Why, Homily?'

'I don't sort of like the idea of a "finder",' she said.

THERE was no doubt that Homily very much enjoyed the snippets of human gossip with which Arrietty regaled her after visits to the church. Although the news of the Platters' invasion of poor Miss Menzies's model village had shocked and frightened her at the time, by next day, it had slid to the back of her mind, merging into a feeling of relief at their escape and the prospect of a safer and happier future.

Peagreen's pictures were a great success. They were the size of postage stamps and, as Homily said, 'went very well together'. Each painting was of a single object: a bumble bee with every glinting hair lovingly observed, its iridescent wings delicately transparent; blossoms of vetch, of speedwell and their familiar pimpernel; a striped fly; a snail emerging from its shell – all silver and gunmetal and whorling curves of golden brown, the head turned inquiringly towards them. 'Why,' she exclaimed, 'you could almost pick it up! Not that I would want to. And look at its eyes on stalks!'

Peagreen had stuck the fine canvas on to pieces of cardboard and, on the edge of each, he had painted a frame. It looked like a real frame: only by touching it did you find it was flat. (Some sixty years later, when repairs were being done to the house, these pictures were discovered by a human being; they aroused great wonder, and were put into a collection.)

'He says they're your Easter present,' Arrietty told her mother.

'What's Easter?' asked Homily wonderingly.

'Oh, I told you, Mother. Easter is next Sunday. And all the ladies will come and do the flowers for the church. Even Miss Menzies! I heard Lady Mullings say that, however busy she is, Miss Menzies would never miss helping with the flowers for Easter. Oh, Mother –' she sounded tearful, '– I wish Papa would let me speak to her – just *once!* After all, when you come to think of it, everything we have we owe to Miss Menzies – this lovely room, the chiffonier, the cooking-pots, our clothes . . . She loved us, Mother, she really did!'

'It wouldn't do,' said Homily. 'All our troubles started by you speaking to That Boy. And you might say he loved us, too . . .' She sounded sarcastic.

'He did,' said Arrietty.

'And much good it did us,' retorted Homily.

'Oh, Mother, he saved our lives!'

'Which wouldn't have been in danger, but for him. No, Arrietty, your father's right. Go down and *listen* to them as much as you like. But no speaking. No being *seen*. We've got to trust you, Arrietty. Especially now, when you've got all this newfangled liberty . . .' Seeing the expression on Arrietty's face, she added more gently, 'Not that you and Timmus aren't doing a very good job. And your Aunt Lupy thinks so, too . . .'

Some days before, Aunt Lupy and Uncle Hendreary had come to tea. It had taken a good deal of persuasion. The rectory was foreign ground to them and they did not know quite what to expect. Nowadays neither of them went much out of doors: the church was their territory and there they felt at home. And, although Aunt Lupy was thinner than she used to be, she did not much care for that scramble through the stone wall and the rough passage alongside the drainpipe: there was always the fear of getting stuck. However, Pod and Arrietty went to fetch them. Pod helped Lupy through the hole, and guided her courteously along the path, through the paling of the wicket gate and up to the opened grating. Arrietty stayed down in the church with Timmus – both of them delighted to miss the boredom of a grown-up tea party.

Once she was safely inside, Lupy was astonished at the grandeur of their doll's-house furniture. Homily, as polite as Pod on this occasion, took no credit for it. 'All *given*,' she trilled gaily, 'there's nothing here we chose ourselves. Nor made, for that matter – except the walls and doors.'

Aunt Lupy had looked round wonderingly. 'Very tasteful,' she said at last. 'I like your wallpaper.'

'*Do* you?' exclaimed Homily with feigned surprise, 'I thought it a bit dull.' Though, in reality, she had grown to admire it herself.

'I'd call it refined,' said Lupy.

'Oh, would you? I'm so glad. Of course there's a lot of good reading on it, if you bend yourself sideways . . .' The fact that neither Lupy nor Homily could read was gently ignored.

If there was a gleam of envy in Aunt Lupy's eye when Homily brought out the doll's tea-service, she suppressed it quickly. That it was a little out of proportion did not seem to matter: Miss Menzies had searched high and low for cups small enough to suit such tiny fingers and a teapot that would not be too heavy for a tiny hand to hold. But, large as the cups were, they were very pretty with their pattern of wild forget-me-nots, and Homily remembered always only to half-fill the teapot.

After tea, Lupy was taken to see the kitchen. She expressed some surprise at the long walk under the floor. 'I wouldn't like to have to carry *our* meals all this distance,' she said. 'At home, I have only to slip back from the gas-ring.'

'Yes. Very convenient,' agreed Homily politely. For some reason, she did not explain to Lupy that they never carried meals 'all this distance' but ate them comfortably at the tiled table in front of the kitchen fire.

'And in winter,' went on Lupy, 'they light up that big coke stove in the corner of the vestry. And what's more they keep it on all night.'

'Very cosy,' said Homily.

'And useful, for soups and stews and things like that.'

'Well, you were always a good manager, Lupy.'

By this time, they had reached the steps and Homily paused for a moment. Pod had gone ahead to light the candles and she wanted to give him time. Lupy was staring up the steps, mystified and very curious. 'It looks very dark up there . . .'

'Not really,' said Homily: she had seen the gleam of candlelight. 'Come along, I'll show you . . .' and she led the way up into the chimney.

Lupy looked round with something like horror at the great draughty space, the soot-darkened walls. She could not think of anything to say. Was this really their kitchen? Ah, there was a glint of light in the far corner . . .

'Better take my hand,' Homily was saying. 'Careful of the sticks. The jackdaws drop them down . . .' Stooping, she picked up two recent ones and threw them on to the neat pile.

When at last they reached the little door marked *Essays of Emerson*, Homily held it aside for Lupy to enter first. There was no mistaking the pride on her face, lit up as it was by the glow from two bright candles: the fire burning merrily (remade up by Pod), the shelves, Miss Menzies's cooking utensils, the spotless cleanliness . . .

'It's very nice,' Lupy said at last. She sounded rather breathless.

'It is rather,' Homily agreed modestly. 'No draughts in here . . . just a bit of fresh air from above.'

Lupy looked up and glimpsed the distant sky. 'Oh, I see, we're in some kind of chimney . . .'

'Yes, a very large one. Sometimes the rain comes in. But not in this corner. But sometimes below that far wall, there's quite a little pool.'

'You should keep a toad,' said Lupy firmly.

'A toad! Why?'

'To eat up the black beetles.'

'We have no black beetles,' retorted Homily coldly. How like Lupy to mention such a hazard! She felt deeply affronted. All the same, as they made their way back towards the entrance, she glanced at the pile of wood on the shadowy floor a little fearfully.

CHAPTER TWENTY

'WHERE are you going, Sidney?' asked Mrs Platter, as Mr Platter got up from the breakfast table, making his way rather, lackadaisically towards the back door.

'To catch the pony,' he said in a bored voice (once they had employed a boy to do these chores). 'I'll need the cart this morning. I'm not going to bicycle all the way to Fordham: that hill coming back just about kills you . . .'

'What are you on to at Fordham?' There was a note of hope in Mrs Platter's question. They had not been doing so well lately: people were not dying as often as they used to and, now the council estate was finished, nor did they seem to be building many houses. She hoped he was on to a good job?

'It's that Lady Mullings,' he told her, 'and hardly worth the journey. Some of her windows got stuck with the rain last winter – wood swelled up, like. And she's locked herself out of the attic, and lost the key . . . We had a box of old keys somewhere. Where did you put it?'

'I didn't put it anywhere. It's where you always keep it: on one of the bottom shelves of your workshop.' She stood up suddenly. 'Oh, Sidney –!' she exclaimed.

He looked surprised at the sudden emotion in her voice. 'What is it now?' he asked.

'Oh, Sidney!' she exclaimed again. 'Don't you see? This may be our last chance . . . Lady Mullings might get her "feeling". Take the little apron!'

'Oh, that,' he said uncomfortably.

'You ought to have taken it weeks ago. But there you were – going on about not knowing quite what to say to her. Feeling foolish, and all that. You should have taken it when you did her gutters.'

'It's not my line, Mabel – psychic or physic, or whatever they call it. It's such a silly little bit of a shred of a thing – who was I going to say it belonged to? It takes a bit of thinking about. I mean, how to bring the subject up, like, when all we was talking about was gutters. And I've got to bring up gutters again: she hasn't paid my bill yet . . .'

Mrs Platter went to a drawer in the dresser, and drew out a small beige envelope. She laid it firmly on the table. 'All you have to say to her, Sidney, is: "Lady Mullings, if it isn't too much trouble, could you find out who the owner of this is and where they are living now?" That's all you have to say, Sidney, quite casual, like. They are only *words*, Sidney, and what are words with our whole future at stake! Just hand it to her, as though it was your bill, or something. That's all you have to do.'

'I'll hand her my bill, too,' said Mr Platter grimly. He picked up the envelope, looked at it distastefully, and put it in his pocket. 'All right, I'll take it.'

'It's our last chance, Sidney, as I said before. It was you yourself who told me she was a "finder" and all about the church candlesticks and Mrs Crabtree's ring. If this fails, Sidney, we might just as well go to Australia.'

'Don't talk nonsense, Mabel!'

'It isn't nonsense. And I don't see much future for us here, unless – I say, *unless* – we can get back those tiresome creatures and show them in a showcase just as we had planned. As you have always said, there was money in them all right! But your brother's getting on now, and in the same line of business. And you remember what he said in his last letter? That he wouldn't have minded taking on a partner? That was a broad hint if ever there was one. And –'

'All right, all *right*, Mabel,' Mr Platter interrupted, 'I said I'd take the envelope,' and he made, more hurriedly this time, for the outside door.

'It's all washed and ironed and folded –' Mrs Platter called after him. But he did not seem to hear.

The door was opened for Mr Platter by Lady Mullings's stiff and starched old house-parlourmaid and he was ushered into the hall. 'Her Ladyship will be down in a minute,' he was told. 'Pray take a seat.' Mr Platter sat down on one of the straight-backed chairs beside the oak chest, took off his hat and placed it on his knees and his tool-bag beside him on the floor. Mr Platter had always been a 'front door caller', by reason of his status as undertaker, and comforter of the bereaved (no common handyman he!) but he was always willing to oblige his more favoured clients with small repairs in the hope of another funeral or a building contract to come. When at last Lady Mullings appeared, she seemed to be in a hurry. She flew down the stairs, hatted and veiled, and pulling on her gloves. At the same moment, her gardener appeared from the back premises carrying two large buckets filled to overflowing with a variety of spring flowers.

'Oh, Mr Platter, I am so relieved to see you, we are in a dreadful pickle here –' Mr Platter had risen and she was shaking him warmly by the hand. 'How are you? And how is Mrs Platter? Well, I hope. We can't get into the attic and it's so tiresome. All the stuff for the jumble stall is locked up in there and the church garden-party's on Easter Monday. And those new windows you put in last spring seemed to have hermetically sealed themselves during the winter. And there are one or two other things –' she was opening the front door. 'But Parkinson will explain to you . . .' She had turned to the gardener. 'Those look wonderful, Henry! Are you sure you can manage them as far as the church? We don't want any more bad backs, do we?' As the buckets were being carried through on to the pavement, she turned back to Mr Platter. 'I am so sorry, dear Mr Platter, to be in such a rush. But yesterday being Good Friday and tomorrow Easter Sunday, we have only this one day in which to decorate the whole church. It's always like this I'm afraid. It's the fault of the calendar . . .'

Mr Platter almost leapt forward to catch her before she closed the door. 'One moment, my lady –'

She hesitated. 'Only one, I'm afraid, Mr Platter. I'm late already –'

Mr Platter almost gabbled as he brought two beige envelopes out of his pocket. 'Should I take the liberty of adding the account of today's little jobs on to the account for the guttering?'

'Didn't I pay you for guttering, Mr Platter?'

'No, my lady, it must have slipped your memory.'

'Oh, dear, I *am* so sorry. What a juggins I am getting in my old age! Yes, yes. Add today's account on to the other one. Of course, of course. Now, I really must be . . .'

'It just occurs to me, my lady, that I might not be here when you get back from the church.' He only just stopped himself from holding on to the door.

'Then send it through the post, Mr Platter. Oh, no, I have my cheque-book. When you've finished here, why not come along to the church? I shall be there most of the day. It's only a step –'

'Very well, I'll do that, my lady.' He was pushing one beige envelope back into his pocket but the other one he was holding out towards her. This was the difficult moment but he was determined to get it over with: you never knew with these people. By the time he had got to the church, she might have gone off somewhere else – to tea with Miss Menzies or something. He couldn't go chasing her around the village. 'There's just one thing, if you'll forgive me detaining you just a bare second longer –'

Lady Mullings looked down at the envelope. 'Not another account, Mr Platter?'

Mr Platter tried to smile – and almost managed it, but the hand which held the envelope was trembling slightly. 'No, this is something quite different, something I promised my wife to do.' He had rehearsed this approach all the way down to Little Fordham: it was a manoeuvre he had once heard described as 'passing the buck' and he had decided to use it.

Lady Mullings seemed to hesitate. She liked men who tried to please their wives and, in all the long years she had known Mr Platter, he had always been so kind, so tactful, so obliging. She glanced up the road and was reassured to see her gardener plodding along towards the church with the buckets. She turned back to Mr Platter and took up the envelope. It felt soft. What could it be? Perhaps Mrs Platter had sent her a little present? A handkerchief, or something? She began to feel touched already.

'It is something my wife cares very much about,' Mr Platter was saying. 'She knows your great gift, my lady, of being a "finder" and she begs you that, when you have time and it isn't too much trouble, you might be able to tell her who is the owner of this little thing in the envelope and where that owner is living at present. Please don't bother to open it now,' as he saw Lady Mullings was about to do so, 'any time will do.'

'I'll do my best, Mr Platter. I never promise anything. Sometimes things happen, and sometimes they don't. I don't really have "a great gift", as you so kindly put it. Something just seems to work through me. I am just an empty vessel.' She felt in the little basket containing her picnic luncheon; took out her handbag and placed the envelope, almost reverently, inside. 'Please give my warmest regards to Mrs Platter, and tell her I'll do my very best,' and, smiling very kindly at Mr Platter, she closed the door gently behind her.

As Mr Platter picked up his tool-bag, he felt extremely pleased with himself. He felt he had 'handled' Lady Mullings very successfully, all due to his own foresight and hard thinking as he had driven along in his cart. What he did not take into account (and it would never have occurred to him to do so) was Beatrice Mullings's own character: that it was one which was incapable of thinking ill of others. And that, since the death of her husband and her two sons, she had devoted her life to her friends. Any call for help, however trivial, took first priority over all the other, more mundane, duties of her daily life. She would have no curiosity about the contents of the beige envelope, only that the object it contained was somehow dear to Mrs Platter, and that news of its owner's whereabouts must mean a great deal to her.

Mr Platter was really smiling now, as he went off to the nether regions in search of Parkinson (Miss Parkinson to him). It was as he feared. She had found a hundred extra jobs for him besides the windows and the door of the attic. Well, perhaps not a hundred but that's what it seemed like. Would he ever get home to his luncheon? He knew Mrs Platter was preparing Lancashire hot-pot: one of his favourites.

CHAPTER TWENTY-ONE

ARRIETTY had risen very early on that same Saturday morning. Aunt Lupy had impressed upon her that she must take Timmus off with plenty of time to spare before all the flower-arranging ladies invaded the church. 'The whole place gets awash with them,' Aunt Lupy had explained the night before, 'not just the ones we know: all sorts come – and they run about every which way, gabbling and arguing, strewing the place with petals and leaves, coats and picnic baskets all over the pews. Calling out to each other as if they were in their own houses. What the good Lord thinks about it, I just can't imagine. And it's a dreadful day for us: not a step dare we venture outside the harmonium. Food, water . . . everything has to be got in. And there we're stuck, hour after hour, in almost pitch darkness – you dare not light a candle – until at last they decide to go. And even then you don't feel safe. Someone or other is bound to come back with an extra bunch of flowers or to collect some belonging or other they've carelessly left behind. So you must take Timmus off early, dear, and don't bring him back until late . . .'

The vestry was indeed a wonderful sight when Arrietty entered through the hole that morning. Flowers in buckets, in tin baths, in great vases, in jam-jars – all over the floor, on the table, on the desk . . . everywhere. The curtains which led into the church proper were drawn back and even beyond these she could see pots of flowering shrubs, and tall budding branches of greenery. The scent was overpowering.

Timmus was waiting for her at the entrance to his home, his round little face alight with happiness: he had a treasure! Spiller had made him a miniature bow and a tiny quiver of miniature arrows. 'And he's going to teach me to shoot,' he told her ecstatically, 'and how to make my own arrows . . .'

'What are you going to shoot at?' Arrietty asked him. Her arm was round his shoulders, and she couldn't resist giving him a hug.

'Sunflowers. That's how you start,' he said, 'the nearest you can get to the heart of a sunflower!'

Aunt Lupy came out then and drove them off. 'Get along, you two. I've just heard a carriage drive up to the lychgate –'

And, indeed, the evening before, Arrietty having supper with her parents had heard the clip-clop of horses' hooves as pony-carts and carriages, one after another, had driven up to the church: delivering these flowers, she thought, as she and Timmus picked their way through the jungle of scented blooms – flowers from every garden in the parish. Suddenly the day began to feel like a holiday.

'Do you know what?' Arrietty said, when once they were out and hurrying along the path – at the same time keeping an eye out for whoever might have arrived in the carriage.

'No. What?' asked Timmus.

'After we've been to the vegetable garden, we're going to have lunch with Peagreen!'

'Oh, goody,' said Timmus. Peagreen had been giving him reading lessons and teaching him to write. Twice a week, Peagreen would come to Homily's parlour with sharpened pencil stubs and odd bits of paper and, being a poet and an artist, he could make these lessons a delight. He would always stay to tea and, sometimes, would read aloud to them afterwards. But Timmus had never been invited into any of Peagreen's nesting-boxes: these Peagreen kept strictly for working in solitude at his painting or writing.

'Oh, goody!' said Timmus again, and gave a little skip: he had always longed to climb the ivy. And this sunny Easter Saturday, minute by minute, began to seem more and *more* like a holiday. He had not even brought a borrowing bag because his mother (as she had explained to Arrietty) had 'got everything'.

So there was not very much to do in the kitchen garden but to play games and explore and tease the ants and earwigs and see who could get closest to a resting butterfly. The sunflowers were not out yet, so Timmus shot at a bumble-bee, which made Arrietty very cross. Not only because she loved bumble-bees but because (as she told him), 'You have only got six arrows and now you've lost one!' She made him promise not to start shooting again until Spiller had given him a lesson.

When the church clock struck twelve, Arrietty pulled up three tiny radishes and a lettuce seedling, and they began to make their way towards the house. They had to hide once when they saw Whitlace trundling a wheelbarrow along the path, filled with rhododendrons: he was heading for the church. Arrietty felt a sad little pang because she realized that her beloved Miss Menzies might be at the church by now but that she, Arrietty, would not be there – even to watch her from a distance.

Peagreen soon managed to cheer her up, however: he was delighted with the radishes which Arrietty had washed in the bird-bath, and the tiny lettuce went beautifully with the delicious cold food he had borrowed from the larder. The spring sunshine was so warm that they were tempted to eat out of doors but decided, in the end, that they would feel more at ease eating in Peagreen's dining-room, with the open lid of the nesting-box propped up by a stick. Peagreen's dining-table was made from the round lid of a pill-box, like the one Arrietty remembered at Firbank, but Peagreen had painted it carmine. For plates he had set out small-leaved nasturtiums, the roundest he could find, with a larger one in the centre of the table on which he had arranged the food. 'You can eat the plates, too,' he told Timmus, 'nasturtium goes well with salad.' Timmus thought this a great joke.

After luncheon, Timmus was allowed to go climbing among the ivy, with orders to freeze should anyone come along the path, and strictly forbidden to put even one foot inside the opened larder window. Peagreen and Arrietty just talked.

Arrietty described to Peagreen how sometimes she and Timmus would watch church services from the rood-screen. Timmus, being small, had his own comfortable little perch on the carved vine leaf, with the solemn face of a mitred bishop to lean back against, and from below he looked exactly like part of the carving. She herself, not wanting to brown her face, usually climbed up into the gallery which ran across the top. Here she could squat down behind the dove and peer out from below the spread wings. Weddings she liked best: weddings were beautiful. Funerals they liked next best: sad, but beautiful too. Except for that dreadful one at which Mr Platter had officiated as undertaker, and her heart had gone cold at the sight of that hated face. On that occasion, having raised her face once, she had never dared raise it again. In fact, it cured her of funerals.

At one point, she asked Peagreen why he never went down to the church. 'Well, it's a bit of a step for me,' he told her, smiling. 'I used to go more often before –' he hesitated.

'Before the Hendrearies came?'

'Perhaps you could say that,' he admitted rather sheepishly. 'And there are times when one prefers to be alone.'

'Yes,' said Arrietty. After a moment she added, 'Don't you like the Hendrearies?'

'I hardly know them,' he said.

'But you like Timmus?'

His face lit up. 'How could anybody not like Timmus?' He laughed amusedly. 'Oh, Timmus could go far . . .'

Arrietty jumped up. 'I hope he hasn't gone too far already!' She thrust her head out through the round hole in the nesting-box, and looked along the ivy. At last she saw him: he was hanging upside-down just above the larder window, trying to peer inside. She did not call out to him: his position looked too perilous. And, after all, she realized, he was obeying her to the letter: he had not 'set a foot inside'. She watched him anxiously until, with a snake-like twist, he reversed his position and made his way upwards among the trembling leaves. She drew in her head again. There was no need to worry. For one who could climb a bell-rope with such speed and confidence, ivy would be child's play.

When, at last, Timmus rejoined them, the clock was striking five. He looked very hot and dirty. Arrietty thought she had better take him home. 'But the church is full of "ladies",' protested Peagreen.

'I mean to *my* home. I'll have to clean him up a bit before his mother sees him.' She sighed happily. 'It's been a lovely afternoon . . .'

'How long will those women stay in the church?' asked Peagreen.

'I've no idea. Until they've finished the flowers, I suppose. I thought that, at about six o'clock, I'd climb that high box tree. You can see everything from there. All the comings and goings . . .'

'Do you want me to come with you?'

'Do you want to?'

'Yes. I'll feel like a climb by then.'

When Arrietty and Timmus reached home, they found Homily bustling towards the kitchen. As they walked across it, Arrietty noticed that the long dark hearth looked curiously neat. 'Somebody's restacked the wood pile,' she said to her mother, as they entered the bright kitchen.

'Yes, I did,' said Homily.

'All by yourself?'

'No, your father helped me. I got an idea in my head about black beetles . . .'

'Were there any?'

'No, only a couple of wood-lice. They're all right – clean as whistles, wood-lice are. But your father's thrown them out of doors, we don't want a whole family. Timmus, just look at your face!'

This was something Timmus could not do. So Homily washed it gently, and his little hands as well. She had always had a soft spot for

Timmus. She brushed down his clothes and smoothed back his hair. There was nothing she could do about the walnut juice.

At six o'clock, when Arrietty climbed up the tall bush, she found Peagreen already there. 'I think they've all gone now,' he told her, 'they've been coming out in twos and threes. I've been watching for ages . . .'

Arrietty put herself in a side-saddle position on a slender branch, and they both stared down at the empty path in silence. Nothing stirred in the churchyard. After about twenty minutes, both became a little bored. 'I think I'd better get Timmus now,' Arrietty said at last, 'he's waiting just beside the grating. I don't want him running out . . .' She was disentangling her skirt which had caught on a twig. 'Thank you for watching, Peagreen.'

'I've rather enjoyed it,' he said. 'I like to get a good look at a human being now and again. You never know what they're going to do next. Can you manage?' he asked as she started to climb down.

'Of course I can manage.' She sounded a little nettled. 'Aren't you coming?'

'I think I'll stay here and see you both safely in.'

CHAPTER TWENTY-TWO

When Arrietty and Timmus reached the vestry, they found it tidy and clean. The tablecloth was back on the table and the ledger on the desk, and the curtains leading into the church were demurely drawn to. But instead of the smell of stale cassocks there was a lingering fragrance of flowers. It drew Arrietty to part the curtains slightly and peer into the church. She caught her breath.

'Come and look, Timmus,' she whispered urgently. 'It's lovely!'

Every windowsill was a bower. But the sills being high and she so far below, she could only see the tops of the flowers – all the same, they were a riot of scent and colour. Timmus pushed past her, dashed straight through the curtains, and ran sharply to the right. 'You can't see from where you are –' he called back at her. He was making for his perch on the rood-screen. Of course! Arrietty stepped forward about to follow him when something or someone touched her on the arm. She swung round swiftly. It was Aunt Lupy, a finger to her lips, and looking very alarmed. 'Don't let him shout,' she whispered hurriedly, 'there are people still here!'

Arrietty looked down the seemingly empty church. 'Where?' she gasped.

'In the porch at the moment. Another whole hand-cart of flowers has arrived. They'll be bringing them in, in a moment. You'd better come inside with me . . .' She was pulling rather urgently at Arrietty's arm.

'What about Timmus? He's on the rood-screen . . .'

'He'll be all right. So long as he keeps still. And he will, because he'll see them from there.'

Arrietty turned unwillingly and followed her aunt under the table, whose hanging cloth gave them good cover. It was the Hendrearies' usual route when any kind of danger threatened and only meant one quick dash at the far end.

'Did Miss Menzies come?' Arrietty whispered, as they passed under the table.

'She's here now. And so's Lady Mullings. Come on, Arrietty, we'd better hurry. They may be coming in here for water . . .'

But Arrietty stood firm in her tracks. 'I *must* see Miss Menzies!' She tore her arm away from her aunt's urgent grasp, and disappeared under the hanging folds of the tablecloth, but not without having noticed her aunt's expression of dismay and astonishment. But there was no time to lose. As she sped along beside the foot of the rood-screen, she was aware of the great bank of flowers edging the chancel. Plenty of cover there! She glanced up at Timmus's perch. *That* was all right: to all intents and purposes, he had become invisible. But even as, breathlessly, she climbed up the side of the rood-screen towards the little gallery, she could hear Lady Mullings's voice (really annoyed for once) saying, 'Twelve huge pots of pelargonium, what on earth does she think we can do with them at this hour?'

Arrietty sped along the gallery and took cover under the spreading wings of the dove. She stared down. The great west door was wide open and the sun was streaming in from the porch. She saw Lady Mullings come in and move a little aside to let two men pass her, each carrying a large pot filled with a bush-like plant which, to Arrietty's eyes, resembled a striped geranium.

'Twelve, you say!' cried Lady Mullings despairingly. (How human voices echoed when the church was empty!)

'Yes, ma'am. We grew them special for the church. Where would you like them putting?'

Lady Mullings looked round desperately. 'Where do you suggest, Miss Menzies?' Arrietty craned forward over the edge of the gallery. Yes, there at last was her dear Miss Menzies, standing rather listlessly in the doorway to the porch. She looked somewhat pale and tired and, though very slim at the best of times, she seemed to have got a good deal thinner. 'Somewhere right at the back, don't you think?' she said faintly.

Then Kitty Whitlace entered in a rush, looking equally aghast. 'Whoever sent all these?' she exclaimed. She must have seen the cartload outside.

'Mrs Crabtree, wasn't it kind of her?' said Lady Mullings weakly. Then, pulling herself together, she added in a more normal voice, 'I think you know Mr Bullivant, Mrs Crabtree's head gardener?'

'Yes, indeed,' said Kitty. She made as though to put out her hand but, looking down at it, saw it was far from clean. 'I won't shake hands,' she added, 'I've just been carting all the leftover leaves and dirt and things away in the wheelbarrow . . .'

As the men went out for more pots, Kitty wheeled round to Lady

Mullings. 'Now, you two ladies sit down. You've done quite enough for one day. I've got the wheelbarrow outside and can give the men a hand with the pots. We'll have them all in in no time.'

'We thought we'd put them all at the back by the bell-chamber,' said Miss Menzies, as she and Lady Mullings slipped gratefully into the nearest pew, 'and sort of mass them all up against the curtains.'

'*Mass* them!' exclaimed Lady Mullings enthusiastically. 'What a wonderful idea! Build them up into a kind of pyramid of glorious pink against those dark curtains . . .' She jumped to her feet, very agile for a lady of her somewhat generous proportions. 'Now that is what I call a real inspiration!'

Miss Menzies rose, too, but a little more reluctantly, but Lady Mullings, now in the aisle, turned eagerly towards her. 'No, my dear, stay where you are. You've been overdoing things – anyone can see that – what with the model village and now the decorations: we ought not to have let you come. And yet we all know that you are the only one, the only truly artistic one, who can make such a show of the windowsills. Now, my dear,' she leant over the edge of the pew, her face alight with the prospect of her own turn at creation, 'take my bag, if you wouldn't mind, and sit back there quietly in your corner. I know exactly what to do!'

Miss Menzies was not reluctant to obey. As she sank back into her corner of the pew, her head against the wall, she heard Lady Mullings, hurrying towards the back of the church, say to Kitty Whitlace, 'Now, Kitty dear, the next thing is to find something to prop them up on . . .' Miss Menzies closed her eyes.

Arrietty, from her perch on the top of the rood-screen, stared down at her pityingly. How wicked it had been of those Platters to destroy those little houses and give her so much work! Perhaps she and Mr Pott had been up all night in their desperate attempt to be ready for Easter Monday? Then she turned her gaze towards Miss Menzies's windowsills and saw (as she had not been able to see from below) what Lady Mullings had meant. Each windowsill had been lined with moss (perhaps with earth below?) out of which the spring flowers seemed to be growing naturally. All in their right groups and colours: grape hyacinths, narcissi, late primroses, some bluebells, clumps of primulas . . . Each windowsill was a little garden in itself. And what was even better, Arrietty realized, was that, sprayed occasionally with water, Miss Menzies's little borders would last all week. How glad she was to have torn herself away from Aunt Lupy and reached the rood-screen just in time!

There was so much to watch. There was Lady Mullings removing all the pamphlets and the collecting-box from the bench in front of the far curtains, sweeping them aside, as it were, as though they were so much rubbish, and setting up plant pots along its length. Heavy as they were, she seemed to be given strength by the joy of her newly discovered talent. 'Just four along here, Kitty, and a space in the middle, and two standing higher up in the space. Now, what can we find to stand them up on?' Her eyes alighted on the collecting-box and she grabbed it up from the floor. 'Ah, this will do –'

'No, Lady Mullings, we can't use that. It's the tourists' collecting-box and people will be coming all next week – in their hundreds, I shouldn't wonder. What about a hassock?' She took the collecting-box from Lady Mullings and set it once again on the floor. When she brought out a rather dusty, sawdust-filled hassock from the back pew, Lady Mullings looked at it rather distastefully.

'It's a bit clumsy,' she said, 'and how are we going to hide the front of it? I know –' she exclaimed (it was her day for inspiration), '– we can drape it with a bit of pink aubretia, hanging down. There's some round the bottom of the pulpit.'

As she hurried down the aisle to fetch it, Kitty Whitlace tried to protest again. 'It's the two Miss Forbes's aubretia . . .' she pointed out.

'It doesn't matter,' Lady Mullings called back to her, 'I'll only take a little bit.' Nothing could stop her now.

At that moment something else caught Arrietty's eye. In the long patch of afternoon sunshine which streamed in from the west door, there lay a dark shadow. It was the shadow of a man. Why, oh why, did she have this sudden sense of foreboding? Was it perhaps because this shadow kept so still, thrown by a figure that was neither coming in nor intending to move away? A kind of 'watching' shadow? Her heart began to beat more heavily.

Lady Mullings came bustling back down the aisle, a clump of aubretia in her hand. Perhaps it had left rather a bald-looking patch at the foot of the pulpit, but she could see to that later by spreading the rest of it along. As she passed the open door, she glanced carelessly sideways to see who was standing on the threshold. 'Oh, Mr Platter,' she exclaimed, scarcely pausing in her step, 'I had forgotten all about you! Do come in. I shan't keep you a minute. Take a look round the

church. It's really worth it. The flowers are quite wonderful this year. *And –*' she called back to him gaily, as she hurried on, '– you're our first visitor . . .'

Mr Platter took off his hat and entered rather dubiously. He and Mrs Platter were very 'low church' (in fact, he had been brought up 'chapel') and he was not at all sure he approved of all these light-hearted goings-on on the eve of such a solemn feast as Easter. However, he was not a bad gardener himself, and, hat in hand, he made a slow but professional inspection. He quite liked the aubretia at the foot of the pulpit, but did not care much for those ashen-coloured roses below the lectern. The things that took his fancy most were the two long rows of variegated plants arranged along the foot of the rood-screen. Quite a herbaceous border, you might say! He sat down quietly on the front pew in order to study them better and while away the time until Lady Mullings should be ready to attend to him.

Arrietty peered down at him, her heart still beating heavily. From where she was stationed, she could not see Timmus and she hoped he was keeping still. She need not have worried. Mr Platter did not raise his eyes. He was not interested in rood-screens. After a while, he brought out an envelope, drew out a piece of paper, uncapped his fountain-pen and made a few jottings. He was adding to the list of extra jobs which Miss Parkinson had thrust upon him and wondering, in view of all the hours he had put in, whether or not he dare add a few inventions of his own.

Lady Mullings, down at the end of the church, was saying, 'Now we need something to top up the pinnacle. A few hymn-books would do . . .'

'A good idea,' Kitty Whitlace replied, 'I'll run and get them.' And hurried up the church towards the vestry. Aunt Lupy who, at that moment, had been peering out of her 'front door', heard her footsteps and darted back inside.

Lady Mullings, standing back to admire her handiwork, did not notice when another person entered the church; someone who looked around vaguely for a moment, then tiptoed up the side aisle. But Arrietty noticed, and also noticed that Mr Platter started slightly when he felt the figure take her place quietly beside him on the front pew. 'Mabel!' he gasped, in a sort of whisper.

'I thought something must have happened to you,' she whispered back, 'so I hopped on my bicycle.'

'They gave me a whole lot of extra jobs,' he told her, still in a whisper. But Arrietty could hear every word.

'They would,' hissed Mrs Platter. 'That Parkinson! Did they give you anything to eat?'

'They brought me something on a tray. Not much. Not what she and Cook were having in the kitchen.'

'I had a lovely hot-pot,' said Mrs Platter. She sounded almost wistful.

'I know.' He was silent a minute. 'What have you done with the bicycle?'

'Put it in the back of the pony-cart. I'm not going to bicycle back all the way up that hill . . .' Leaning more closely towards him, she put a hand on his arm. 'What I really wanted to know, Sidney, what really brought me down was – did you give that package to Lady Mullings?'

'Of course I did.'

'Oh, thank heavens for that! What did she say?'

'She said she'd do her best.'

'It's our only chance, Sidney. It's our last chance!'

'I know that,' he said uncomfortably.

CHAPTER TWENTY-THREE

LADY Mullings almost flung herself down beside Miss Menzies in the pew beside the west door. 'Well, that's done!' she exclaimed in a voice both exhausted and satisfied.

Miss Menzies, startled, opened her eyes. 'Have you finished? How splendid!' She blushed, 'I'm afraid I must have nodded off . . .'

'And I don't blame you, my dear, after having been up all night! Would you care to take a look at it? I always value your opinion . . .'

'I'd love to,' said Miss Menzies, although it was the last thing that she felt inclined to do at that moment.

She followed Lady Mullings out of the pew and down to the back of the church. It was indeed a startling erection, a beautiful burst of colour against the darker curtains and, facing straight down the aisle, adding a focal point to all the lesser decorations.

'It really is quite lovely,' exclaimed Miss Menzies with genuine admiration. 'I can't think how on earth you've managed to prop it all up –'

'With this and that,' said Lady Mullings modestly, but she was looking very pleased.

Kitty Whitlace was on her knees, tidying up the pamphlets which somehow seemed to have scattered themselves about the floor. She made a neat pile of these and another one of the postcards, and set them in an orderly fashion beside her rescued collecting-box. Then she sat back on her heels and looked up at Lady Mullings. 'What are we going to do with this lot?' she asked.

'Oh, dear! Yes . . . well, I see. Oh, I know! Just leave them where they are for the moment. I've a small card-table at home, which I can bring down later. With a pretty piece of brocade on top, we could set it by the west door.' She turned to Miss Menzies. 'Well, my dear, I really think we've all done enough for today. Where did you leave your bicycle?'

'Up at the rectory.'

'I'll ride it down for you,' said Kitty, 'or better still, I'll walk up with you and make you a nice pot of tea. You look as though you need one.

675

And I've got my cakes to see to . . .' These were cakes she was baking for the garden-party on Monday.

'Actually,' said Lady Mullings, 'I don't think there *is* any more to do. Except perhaps tidy up the pulpit.' She looked round the church. 'It all looks quite lovely, better even than last year –' She broke off abruptly, staring up towards the chancel. 'Oh, dear, there's Mr Platter! And Mrs Platter too. I'd forgotten all about him again. He's such a *quiet* man. Miss Menzies, dear, where did I leave my handbag?'

'In the pew. I'll get it. I've left mine there, too.'

In the end, they went together. Lady Mullings sat down. 'I'll just make sure I did bring my cheque-book.' She felt about in her handbag. 'Yes, here it is. And Mr Platter's bill –' She drew out a beige envelope. 'No, it isn't: it's the other thing he brought me. Do sit down for a minute, Miss Menzies, I really am a little curious to see what's inside . . .'

She slid a thumb under the flap of the envelope and drew out a very small, neatly folded piece of cambric. 'Oh, dear!' she exclaimed in an exasperated voice, crumpling the envelope and content together in her lap, 'I do wish people wouldn't send me things like this!'

'Why – whatever is it?' asked Miss Menzies.

'Washed and ironed! I can never do anything with things that have been washed and ironed. It leaves no trace whatever of the original owner. You see, dear,' she went on, turning to Miss Menzies, 'to get my "feeling", or whatever you might like to call it, it has to be from something that has recently been handled or worn, or close in some way to another human being. I couldn't get any "feeling" from this, except perhaps of soap-suds and Mrs Platter's ironing-board.'

'May I see?' asked Miss Menzies.

'Yes, of course,' Lady Mullings passed it to her, 'it's some kind of doll's apron . . .'

Miss Menzies, unfolding the scrap of material, gave a sharp gasp. 'Mr *Platter* brought you this?' Her voice sounded almost fearful with astonishment.

'Yes. He, or rather Mrs Platter, wanted to locate the owner.'

Miss Menzies was silent for a moment, staring down at the little object on the palm of her hand. 'Mr Platter?' she said again, in a tone of tremulous wonder.

'I must admit I was a little surprised myself. When you think of Mr Platter, it does seem a little out of character.' She laughed. 'I suppose I should feel flattered . . .'

'You *have* found the owner,' said Miss Menzies quietly.

'I don't quite understand –'

'I am the owner. I made it.'

'Good gracious me!' exclaimed Lady Mullings.

'I remember every stitch of it. You see these little stroked gathers? I thought I'd never get a needle fine enough . . . Mr Platter! I mean, how did he . . . ? It's quite extraordinary!'

'I suppose you made it for one of your little model figures?'

Miss Menzies did not reply: she was staring into space; never had a face looked more bewildered. Mr Platter? For some reason, she thought of the cut wire, the trampled streets, the broken shop-fronts, the general devastation in her model village. What thoughts were these? Why had they come to her? Mr Platter had a model village of his own (one might almost say a *rival* model village, if, as she was not, one was of a jealous disposition) and, as Lady Mullings had remarked, he was 'such a quiet man' – always courteous, so good at his job, so scrupulous in his building, such a comfort to those who found themselves bereaved. Miss Me..zies tried to resist these bad, unworthy thoughts which, somehow of their own accord, had crept into her mind.

'Well, my dear,' Lady Mullings was saying, 'I think we've solved Mr Platter's little problem.' She picked up her bag and gloves. 'Now, if you'll excuse me, I'll go and settle up with him.'

Arrietty, in her eyrie, had not quite heard the confidential exchanges going on halfway down the church: she had been too much taken up by trying to overhear the Platters. She *had* heard Miss Menzies's first, sharp repetition of Mr Platter's name, and thought perhaps the Platters had heard it too, because both had turned their heads warily to glance behind them. Even then Arrietty did not pay too much attention. All her anxiety now was concentrated on Timmus: would he be wise enough to keep absolutely still?

Then she noticed that Lady Mullings had eased herself out of her pew and, handbag in hand, was coming up the church towards the Platters. She held her breath: something was going to happen!

Mr Platter rose when she approached and so did Mrs Platter, with whom Lady Mullings shook hands. 'Ah, Mrs Platter, how very nice to see you! Come to see the decorations, have you? We're rather proud of them this year . . .' Mrs Platter mumbled some reply, but her face looked oddly anxious as the three of them sat down again.

Mr Platter produced his accounts, which took a little explaining. Lady Mullings listened amiably, nodding her head from time to time.

She completely trusted him. When she had written out his cheque and received his receipt, she rose to her feet. Mr Platter rose too.

'And that other little matter,' he said. 'I don't suppose you've had time –'

'Oh, the little thing you brought me – what a scatterbrain I am! I didn't *need* any time, Mr Platter: I find it belongs to Miss Menzies. She made it.' She turned to Mrs Platter. 'Here it is. Perhaps you'd like to give it back to her yourself? She's sitting down there by the west door . . .'

Mrs Platter did not seem to hear her. She was staring at the rood-screen. There was the strangest expression on her face and her mouth had fallen open. Lady Mullings, envelope in hand, looked puzzled. What was the matter with the woman? 'Well, here it is,' she said at last, and put the envelope down on the seat. Mrs Platter turned towards her then, her face still looking curiously dazed. But Lady Mullings saw that she was trying to pull herself together. 'No. Please –' she stammered, '– *you* give it to her. And thank you. Thank you very much. It was –' and her eyes flew back to the rood-screen.

Well, thought Lady Mullings as she made her way back towards Miss Menzies, I suppose there is rather a lot to look at in that rood-screen. Perhaps Mrs Platter had never seen it before? Perhaps it had rather shocked her, brought up (as Mr Platter had been) to a more austere form of worship. And, now she came to think of it, some of those medieval faces (although beautifully carved) did appear rather devilish . . .

Belongings were collected, and goodbyes said. Lady Mullings left by the west door, and Kitty and Miss Menzies came up the church to leave by the vestry, which gave them a short cut to the wicket gate. Mr Platter, too, was standing up as though preparing to leave, but Mrs Platter was still sitting down. It looked, as Kitty and Miss Menzies passed them – bidding them goodnight – as though Mrs Platter was gripping Mr Platter by the sleeve.

The church became very silent. Mrs Platter looked round cautiously. 'Don't go, Sidney . . .' she whispered urgently.

He pulled his arm away from her grip. 'Oh, come on, Mabel. We've played our trump card – and we've lost. I'm tired and I'm hungry. Is there any of that hot-pot left?'

'Oh, forget about the hot-pot, Sidney! This is serious –' Her voice seemed to be trembling with some kind of excitement.

'What is?'

She pulled on his sleeve again. 'Sit down and I'll tell you –' He sat down unwillingly. 'One of them *yawned*!'

'Well, what of it?' He thought she was referring to one of the ladies. But Arrietty, up above, understood immediately and went cold with fear.

Mrs Platter was pointing with a shaking finger at the rood-screen. 'One of those creatures up there – it *yawned*!'

'Oh, don't be silly, Mabel,' he attempted to stand up again. 'You're just imagining things . . .'

'Sidney, it *yawned* I'm telling you! You don't imagine a yawn. I saw the flash of its teeth –'

'Which one?'

Mrs Platter began to gabble. 'Well, you see that long kind of face, that one with a hat on – some kind of bishop something – there just by the edge of the arch. And you see there's a smaller face, just below its ear, sort of leaning against it – ? Well, that's the one that yawned!'

Mr Platter leaned forward peering hard in the direction of her pointing finger. 'Oh, Mabel, it couldn't have, it's carved out of wood!'

'It could be carved out of rock for all I care, but it yawned!'

From where Arrietty crouched, she could not see Timmus, except for one little leg which overhung the vine leaf. This was because the eaves of the gallery stood out a little on either side of the rood-screen. To see the whole of Timmus, she would have to lean right over. This, at the moment, for fear of being 'seen', she did not dare to do. Oh, why had she left him so long climbing about in the ivy? Of course he had yawned: he had tired himself out . . .

'It's one of *them*, Sidney, I know it is!' Mrs Platter was saying. 'And *one* would be better than none. Could you reach it, do you think?'

'I could try,' said Mr Platter. He rose to his feet and, rather gingerly, approached the massed blooms at the foot of the rood-screen. He leaned over, stretched up an arm, and rose up on tiptoe. 'It's no good, Mabel, I can't reach it.' He had very nearly overbalanced into the flowers. 'I'd need something to stand on.'

Mrs Platter looked around but could see nothing movable. Then her eye lighted on the two shallow steps leading into the chancel. 'Why don't you try from the other side?' she suggested, 'that's higher: you could put your hand round the edge of the arch, like . . .'

Arrietty was filled with a sudden anger: these two awful human beings were talking as though poor little Timmus had neither eyes nor ears.

Mr Platter went up the two steps and disappeared on the far side of the rood-screen. Arrietty, watching from above, saw the bony hand come out and feel its way along the smooth edge of the arch. '*Inwards* a bit more, Sidney, you're nearly there –' said Mrs Platter, watching excitedly. 'That's the bishop's face. Can you stretch a bit more? And then go lower –'

Arrietty decided to stand up and lean farther over: those dreadful feeling fingers were approaching the little leg. At last, they touched it. She heard Mr Platter give a strangled gasp as though he had been stung by a wasp, and the fingers flew away again. 'It's *warm*!' he cried out in a frightened voice. Arrietty realized then that Mr Platter had only been trying to humour Mrs Platter and had never believed that Timmus was alive.

'Of course it's warm!' Mrs Platter's voice had risen almost to a scream. 'Grab it, Sidney! Grab it! Quickly . . . quickly!' But the little leg had been withdrawn. The groping fingers, now in a panic of hurry, spun frenziedly about the vine leaf. It was empty. The prey had gone.

Mrs Platter burst into tears. As Mr Platter emerged in a crestfallen way from behind the rood-screen, Mrs Platter gasped out, 'You nearly had it! You actually touched it! How could you be so silly . . . !'

'It gave me a shock,' said Mr Platter and Arrietty, crouched back in her old position, could see he was looking pale. His eyes roved despondently over the rood-screen, but with little hope that among the myriad strange figures and faces he might see the one he sought.

'It's no good looking there,' gasped Mrs Platter, feeling for her handkerchief. 'It's down among those flowers. Or *was*. These creatures can move, I tell you!'

'Did it fall?'

'Fall! Of course it didn't fall. It nipped along to the edge of the screen, and slid down it into the flowers. Like greased lightning, it went!'

Mr Platter looked down at the flowers. 'Then it must be in there still,' he said.

'There's no "*must*" about it, Sidney. It could be anywhere by now –'

Mr Platter still stared down at the flowers, as if hoping to detect some kind of faint stir among the leaves and blossoms. He seemed to have got over his sudden attack of nervousness. Stooping, he put down a careful hand into the mass of colour. He felt about for a moment, and then withdrew it. He had discovered that, although the display had looked like a growing border, the cut stalks of each clump were set in some sort of container filled with water – jam-jars, tins, vases of all shapes and sizes – among which any creature small enough could move with ease. Well, that was that.

Sighing, he sat down beside his wife. 'We'll just have to watch and wait,' he said.

'What's the point of that, Sidney? It may have run out already.' She turned her head towards the open west door, where the sunlight seemed to be fading, 'and the light will be going soon . . .'

'If you didn't see anything run out – and you didn't did you?'

'No, of course I didn't.' But she wondered about those moments when she had been wiping her eyes.

'Then it stands to reason that it must still be in there somewhere.'

'But we can't sit here all night!' Was he really thinking of another 'vigil'?

He did not reply immediately: he seemed to be thinking hard. 'There's only one other thing we can do,' he said at last, 'that is to remove all these pots and vases one by one. You starting at one end and me at the other.'

'Oh, we can't do that, Sidney – supposing somebody came in . . .?'

Even as she spoke, they heard voices in the porch. Mrs Platter sprang to her feet. 'Sit down, Mabel, do!' hissed Mr Platter, 'we're not doing anything wrong.' Mrs Platter sat down again obediently but, all the same, both of them turned round to see who had come in.

It was Lady Mullings, followed by Parkinson who was carrying a small folding card-table. 'Just prop it up beside the door,' Lady Mullings was saying. 'And do ask Mrs Crabtree to come in –'

'She'd like to, but she's got the dog, my lady.'

'Oh, that doesn't matter on this sort of day, as long as she's got it on the lead. We won't be staying more than a minute or two, and I do want her to see her pelargoniums . . .' and she made off swiftly in the direction of her cherished flower arrangement. She did not even glance at the Platters sitting so quietly at the other end of the church. All her attention was centred elsewhere.

Mrs Crabtree was an extremely tall, elderly lady, dressed in shabby but very well-cut tweeds. The little dog was a young wire-haired terrier, and was pulling at the lead. 'Oh, come on, Pouncer,' she was saying irritably, as they made their way into church, 'don't be a fool! Walkies, after . . .'

'I'm here, dear,' called Lady Mullings, in her pleasant, rather musical voice, 'down by the bell-chamber.'

The Platters had half turned in their seats again to take note of the newcomer. Arrietty was watching, too. Mrs Platter seemed especially interested in Mrs Crabtree's frail right hand, as she hauled her unwilling little dog down the aisle. 'Just take a look at those diamonds,' she whispered to Mr Platter. Mr Platter said, 'Hush . . .' and turned away abruptly: the less attention they drew to themselves the better. But Mrs Platter went on staring.

The two ladies stood in silence for a moment before Lady Mullings's masterpiece. 'It's magnificent,' said Mrs Crabtree at last, 'quite magnificent!'

'I'm so glad you think so,' replied Lady Mullings, 'I did so want you to see it before the light failed . . .'

'I do congratulate you, my dear.'

'Well, you must take some of the credit, my dear Stephanie: it was you and Bullivant who grew the flowers.'

What persuaded Timmus to bolt then always remained a slight puzzle to Arrietty. Was it because he had overheard the conversation between Mr and Mrs Platter about moving the rood-screen flowers pot by pot? Or was he taking advantage of the unexpected distraction caused by the sudden entrance of two ladies and a dog? Or was he banking on the dimness of the aisle in this fading, pew-shadowed half light? But there he was, barely more than a shadow himself, streaking down towards the bell-chamber, as fast as his little, flailing legs would carry him!

She guessed his destination: under the curtain, on to the bell-rope, up through the hole in the ceiling, and then – *safety!*

But Mr Platter, facing forward, had seen him run out from among the flowers; Mrs Platter, looking backwards, had seen him chasing down the aisle, and Arrietty, watching so intently from her perch above the rood-screen, of course had seen every stage of his panic-stricken dash. And now (oh, horror of horrors!), the dog had seen him! Just as Timmus was about to chase round the far end of the collecting-box, which still was standing on the floor, the dog gave a joyous yelp and pounced, his lead freed in a second from Mrs Crabtree's frail and inattentive hand. He had not been named 'Pouncer' for nothing.

The collecting-box slithered along the floor, pushing Timmus with it. Arrietty saw two little hands come up and grip the top and, with an agile twist, the slim little body followed. Mrs Crabtree groped down for the lead and jerked the dog aside but not before Timmus, lithe as an eel, had slipped down through the slot. Was it only Arrietty, in the short sharp silence which followed the dog's first yelp, who heard a shifting and clinking of coins in the bottom of the collecting-box?

Lady Mullings came out of her dream. 'What was all that about?' she asked.

Mrs Crabtree shrugged. 'I don't know: he must have seen a mouse or something. I'd better take him home . . .' She patted Lady Mullings on the shoulder. 'Thank you, my dear, for showing me: you've worked wonders. I can have a good look at all the rest of the flowers after the service tomorrow – the light will be better then.'

As Mrs Crabtree went out, Kitty Whitlace came in, humming 'County Down' and swinging the key on her first finger as usual. Her cakes had turned out beautifully, she had put Miss Menzies to rest on the sofa, where she had fallen asleep again, and tomorrow was Easter Day. Kitty Whitlace was feeling very happy.

Not so Mr and Mrs Platter. A certain amount of anxiety still gnawed at their vitals. Neither could withdraw their gaze from the collecting-box. Both were standing up now. What must be their next move?

'At least, we know where it is,' whispered Mr Platter.

Mrs Platter nodded. After a minute, she said, her voice a little uncertain, 'It's a very young one.'

Mr Platter gave a grim little laugh. 'All the better: it'll last us longer!'

Kitty Whitlace and Lady Mullings had set up the card-table, spread with the piece of brocade, and Kitty had arranged the pamphlets, the picture postcards, and the visitors' book in a neat row towards the front. The collecting-box she tucked under her arm.

Arrietty shuddered as she heard the rush of coins to one end of it, hoping Timmus would not be hurt. Perhaps it contained a few of those rare pound notes which might act as buffers. American tourists could be very generous at times . . .

'I expect you'll be wanting to lock up now,' Lady Mullings was saying, glancing once more around the church. 'Oh, Mr and Mrs Platter, I didn't see you! I *am* sorry. It's all so beautiful that I suppose you're like the rest of us – almost impossible to tear oneself away.' Mr Platter nodded and smiled weakly. He didn't know quite what to say. Out of the corner of his eye, he could see Kitty Whitlace hurrying towards the vestry, the collecting-box under her arm. She returned almost immediately, swinging an even larger key, and went towards the door.

They all filed out. They had to: they could not keep her waiting. Mr and Mrs Platter came last. They walked like two people in a dream (or was it a nightmare?). Cheerful goodnights were said and see-you-tomorrows, and each went their separate ways. Mr and Mrs Platter walked reluctantly towards where they had tethered their pony-cart. Kitty Whitlace locked the church door.

CHAPTER TWENTY-FOUR

NEITHER spoke as Mr Platter untethered the pony and Mrs Platter – in her awkward way – climbed up on to the seat. Her bicycle lay safely in the back on top of Mr Platter's tool-bags. 'Where now?' she said in a dispirited voice as Mr Platter, reins in hand, took his place beside her.

He did not reply at once: just sat there staring down at his hands. 'We've got to do it,' he said at last.

'Do what?'

'Break into the church . . .'

'Oh, Sidney, but that's a felony!'

'It's not the first felony we've had to commit,' he reminded her glumly. 'We know exactly where that creature is –'

'Yes. Locked up, in a locked box, in a locked cupboard, in a locked church!'

'Exactly,' said Mr Platter, 'it's now or never, Mabel.'

'I don't like it, Sidney,' she looked round in the gathering dusk, 'it'll be dark soon and we won't be able to put a light on.'

'We can borrow a torch from Jim Sykes at the Bull. He's got a good one, for going round the cellars . . .'

'The Bull!' exclaimed Mrs Platter; the face she turned towards him looked almost stupid with surprise. Mr Platter had never been one for visiting village pubs.

'Yes, the Bull, Mabel. And what's more, we're going to stay there up to near on closing time. We'll have a nice glass of stout, a couple of roast-beef sandwiches, and some oats and water for the pony, and leave the cart there till we're ready for it. We're not going to leave that cart and pony parked outside the church – Oh no! It'd be evidence against us.'

'Oh, Sidney,' faltered Mrs Platter, 'you think of everything . . .' But she was feeling very nervous.

'No, Mabel, there was one thing I didn't think of.' He picked up the reins. 'When I took all my locksmith's tools down to Lady Mullings's to open up her attic, I never thought I'd need 'em again for a tricky job of this size. Giddup, Tiger!' And the pony trotted off.

*

When next they reached the church porch, night had completely fallen but, low above the yew trees, a pale moon was rising. Mr Platter threw it a glance, as though measuring it for size. They had come down on foot, Mrs Platter carrying the box of keys and Mr Platter his toolbag and the torch.

'Now, you hold the torch, Mabel, and pass me the box of keys. I took a good look this afternoon at the key that woman was using and I'll be blowed if I hadn't got one almost exactly like it. Most of these old church locks were made the same –' he was feeling about among the keys. 'I took it when they modernized the church at Went-le-Craye. Got antique value some of those old keys have . . .'

He was right – on all counts. After a bit of initial fumbling, they heard the lock grind back, and the heavy door squeaked open. 'What about that?' said Mr Platter in a satisfied voice.

They went inside, Mrs Platter on tiptoe. 'No need for that,' Mr Platter told her irritably, 'there's no one to hear us now.' But there was somebody to hear them.

As soon as Kitty Whitlace had locked the west door and silence reigned again in the church, Arrietty had climbed down from the rood-screen and had run to the harmonium, to break the dreadful news. Her Uncle Hendreary had his foot up on the sofa (as Pod had prophesied, he was becoming a martyr to gout) and her Aunt Lupy was busy preparing a little supper. The candles were all lighted again and the room looked very cosy. 'Oh, there you are!' Aunt Lupy had exclaimed, 'I couldn't get on till you came: I'm making a sparrow's-egg omelette. Where's Timmus?'

And then Arrietty had had to tell them. It had been a dreadful evening. There was nothing anyone could do. For almost the first time, Arrietty had realized the utter helplessness of their tiny race, when pitted against human odds. She had stayed on and on, trying to comfort them, although she knew her own parents must be getting worried. At last she said (thinking of Timmus's terror and loneliness), 'It will only be for one night. When Mrs Witless opens the press in the morning, he'll be out and away in a moment!'

'I hope you're right,' Aunt Lupy had said, but she did wipe away her tears and Arrietty, although she did not fancy the idea of the long walk back in the dark, now felt she might leave for home. It was then that they heard the squeak and scrape of the main door into the church.

'What's that?' whispered Aunt Lupy, and they all froze.

'Someone's come into the church,' said Hendreary, very low. He rose from his couch and, limping badly, blew out the candles one by one. They sat in the darkness, waiting.

A voice had spoken sharply, but they had not heard what it said. Footsteps were approaching the vestry. They heard the sudden rattle of the curtain-rings, and a strange light was flashing about. The borrowers drew together on the sofa, clasping each other's hands.

'Did you bring the key-box, Mabel?' Oh, that voice! Arrietty would have recognized it anywhere; it even haunted her dreams. She began to tremble.

'Shine the torch into my tool-bag, Mabel.' The voice was very close now. They could hear the sound of heavy breathing, the clank of metal, the shuffling of boots on the flagstones. 'And take the cloth off that table . . .'

'What are you going to do now, Sidney?' It was Mrs Platter. She sounded nervous.

'Nail that tablecloth up over the window. Then we can switch on the light. We might as well work in comfort, seeing as we've got all night, and the place to ourselves, like . . .'

'Oh, that will be better. I mean, a bit of light. I don't like it in here, Sidney. I don't like it in here at all!'

'Oh, don't be silly, Mabel. Take that other end –' The borrowers heard the sound of hammering. Then Mr Platter said, 'Draw those other curtains tight together, the ones leading to the church.' Again there was a rattle of curtain-rings, and the electric light flashed on. 'Ah, that's better. Now we can see what we're doing . . .'

The borrowers could now make out each other's faces, and very frightened faces they were. However, the sofa was well back from the glow which seeped in from their entrance.

There was silence. Mr Platter must be studying the lock. After about five minutes, he said in a pleased voice, 'Ah . . . now I think I see!'

The oddest sounds were heard as the operation got under way: squeaks, tappings, scrapings and, 'Pass me that, Mabel; no, not the thick one, the fine one; now that thing with a blunt end; put your finger here, Mabel; press hard; hold it steady; now that thing with a sharp point, Mabel,' and so on. Mabel did not say a word. At last, there was a long, loud, satisfied 'Ah . . .!' and the faint squeak of hinges: the door of the press was open!

There was an awed silence: the Platters had never seen such treasure.

Mr Platter's amazement was such that he did not make an immediate grab for the collecting-box which stood humbly on the middle shelf.

'Jewels, gold . . . all those stones are *real*, Mabel. The rector must be mad. Or is it the parish?' He sounded very disapproving. 'Stuff like this ought to be in a museum or a bank or something . . .' Arrietty listening was again surprised by the word 'bank' – a bank, to her, was something with grass growing on it. 'Oh, well,' Mr Platter went on sternly (he sounded genuinely shocked), 'I suppose it's their look-out. Glad I'm not a churchwarden!'

There was a pause, and the borrowers guessed that Mr Platter had picked up the collecting-box because they heard the faint clink of loose money.

'Careful, Sidney,' warned Mrs Platter. 'We don't want to damage it. I mean that creature inside. Set the box down here on the table.'

The borrowers heard a chair being pulled out, and then a second chair. Again there was silence (except for a little heavy breathing) while Mr Platter picked his second lock. This one did not take so long. Arrietty heard the rustle of paper money and the clink of coins as fingers felt about inside the box.

Mrs Platter broke the sudden shocked silence, 'It's gone! Look, Sidney, how he's piled up the half-crowns, and the florins, made a kind of staircase to get out, to reach the slot in the lid –'

'It's all right, Mabel, don't panic. He may have got out of the box but he couldn't have got out of the cupboard. He's in there all right, hiding among all that stuff.'

Again Arrietty heard the scrape of chairs, and the shuffle of footsteps on stone. 'Oh, goodness,' exclaimed Mrs Platter, 'here's a five-pound note – dropped on the floor!'

'Put it back, Mabel. I'll have to lock that box up again and place it back just where it was. But, first, we've got to take everything out of this middle shelf. You stand by the table and I'll pass things out to you. We'll get to him in the end. You'll see . . .'

Aunt Lupy began to cry again, and Arrietty put her arms round her – not so much, this time, to comfort her as to prevent her from breaking down into a storm of audible sobs.

The only sound they heard from the vestry was the faint clank of metal on wood. There were a few 'Ohs' and 'Ahs' of awestruck admiration when it seemed that Mr Platter had handed his wife some particularly beautiful object. Otherwise, they worked in methodical silence.

'He doesn't seem to be here . . .' said Mr Platter in a puzzled voice, 'unless he's behind that ivory thing at the back. Did you look inside all the chalices?'

'Of course I did,' said Mrs Platter.

There was a short silence. Then Mr Platter said, 'He's not on *this* shelf, Mabel . . .' He sounded more puzzled than desperate.

Then everything happened at once. A sudden shriek from Mrs Platter of 'There he is! There he is! There he goes . . .' and from Mr Platter, 'Where? Where? . . . Where?'

'Through the curtains into the church –'

'After him, Mabel. I'll put on the lights –'

Arrietty heard the sharp clicks, one after another: all lights in the church were controlled from the vestry and it was as though Mr Platter had run his hand down the whole set. There was a clashing of curtain-rings and Mr Platter, too, was gone.

She heard the panting voice of Mrs Platter echoing down the church. 'He was on the *bottom* shelf . . . !'

Arrietty ran out into the vestry. Yes. There was the cupboard wide open and the middle shelf bare. It was on the bottom shelf, the one at floor level, where Timmus must have been hiding: the shelf where the candlesticks were kept. Some of these were so tall and ornate that they nearly touched the shelf above. Timmus must have slid over the outer edge of the middle shelf on to a candlestick on the shelf below. Perhaps, thought Arrietty, in a strange old cupboard like this the edges of the shelves did not quite meet the backs of the doors when closed. There must have been a little space. Timmus had used it.

Now, if he could reach a bell-rope in time, he would be safe. She ran up to the curtains where Mr Platter had dragged them aside and peered round the edge of one into the church, but started back at the sound of a crash and a cry of pain. She knew what it was: someone, trying to get to the curtains leading to the belfry, had knocked over one of Mrs Crabtree's heavy flowerpots, on to somebody else's foot. Cautiously, she went back to the curtain and stared into the church. All the lights were on and there at the far end was Mr Platter hopping about and gripping his foot in both hands. Mrs Platter was nowhere to be seen. Arrietty guessed what had happened. Timmus had dashed under the curtains into the bell-chamber. And Mrs Platter had dashed after him and in her clumsy haste had knocked over one of the precious pelargoniums. Plant, plant-pot, shards and earth must now lie strewn on the ground below

Lady Mullings's cherished arrangement, completed with so much pride only a few hours before.

Then came a sound, so deep and resonant, that it seemed to fill the church, pass through its walls and throb into the still night air. A lingering sound. A sound which could be heard (by those who were still awake) in every house in the village. The sound of a church bell.

It was then that Mrs Platter began to shriek. Shriek after shriek. Even Aunt Lupy came out, followed by a limping Hendreary, to see what had happened. All they could see from the vestry steps was an empty church, ablaze with light. But the shrieks went on and on.

And the bell shuddered out again.

CHAPTER TWENTY-FIVE

KITTY WHITLACE was upstairs making up a bed for Miss Menzies when she heard the bell (she had managed to dissuade Miss Menzies from cycling 'down those lonely lanes at this hour of the night' and Miss Menzies had, at last, agreed). Kitty, trembling, and white as the sheets she had been smoothing, dropped the pillow and the case into which she had been inserting it, and stumbled down the stairs into the little sitting-room.

'Did you hear that?' she gasped.

'Yes,' said Miss Menzies. She had risen from the sofa on which Kitty had left her reclining. Whitlace had gone to bed.

'There's someone in the church!'

'Yes,' said Miss Menzies again.

'I left everything locked – everything. I must go down!'

'Not by yourself,' said Miss Menzies quickly. 'You must go and wake up your husband and we had better telephone Mr Pomfret. I'll do that, if you like?'

'You know where the lights are in the hall?' said Kitty.

'Yes, I think so.' Miss Menzies did not sound too certain. She knew the reputation of this house and did not much fancy feeling her way in the dark.

'All right then,' Kitty was saying, 'I'll go and wake up Whitlace. It takes a bit of doing once he's gone right off . . .' and she rushed upstairs again.

Mr Pomfret (who, by the sound of his voice, had also been asleep) said he would come at once and that no one was to go into the church until he arrived on his bicycle. 'You never know. I've got my truncheon but tell Whitlace to bring a stick . . .'

As Miss Menzies walked back through the empty old kitchen, firmly leaving the light on in the hall, she rather hoped there *would* be someone in the church even if they *were* a bit violent. She felt she would die of shame if, after her last interview with Mr Pomfret, this late-night call on a possibly weary policeman should turn out to be a false alarm. The bell rang out again. For some reason, this seemed to reassure her.

691

They waited for Mr Pomfret by the lychgate. Whitlace had pulled on a few clothes and was armed with a broom handle. There was someone in the church all right if the light from the windows was anything to go by. But even this was slightly dimmed by the brilliance of the moon.

'You're sure you didn't leave the lights on by mistake?' Miss Menzies asked Kitty anxiously.

'There weren't any lights. It was still daylight when I locked up. And what about the bell? There it goes again . . .'

'But not so loud.' As the sound died away, Miss Menzies went on to explain, 'A bell can go on quite a long time on its own momentum.'

'That's right,' said Whitlace. 'Once it's on the swing, like . . .'

Mr Pomfret arrived quietly and propped his bicycle against the wall. 'Well, here we are,' he said. 'Got your stick, Whitlace? We men better go first . . .' and led the way towards the church. Kitty Whitlace felt in her pocket to make sure she had brought the key. A great beam of moonlight lay across half the porch and Kitty could see that there seemed to be another key in the door. She pointed this out to Mr Pomfret and showed him her own. He nodded sagely, before trying out the one in the door. But the door had been left unlocked and opened easily (with its usual grinding squeak) and they all followed Mr Pomfret in. The bell tolled out again, even more quietly this time, as though on a dying fall.

The church looked empty, but somebody had been there all right. They saw the overturned flowerpot and, after the sound of the bell had died away, they heard a strange noise, a kind of regular gasping; or was it more like a grunting? Mr Pomfret went straight towards the back of the church, slid behind Lady Mullings's flowers, and (rather dramatically) flung back the curtains leading into the bell-chamber. Then he stood still.

The three others coming up behind saw the tableau framed, as on a stage, by the drawn-back curtains.

A largish lady seemed to have fallen to the floor, her hat askew, her hair awry. One leg stuck out before her, the other one seemed doubled somewhere underneath. It was Mrs Platter. It took him quite a minute to recognize her. She was sobbing and gasping, and seemed to be in pain. The bell-rope he saw was moving with a kind of steady indifference but the 'tail', like a frenzied snake, was threshing about the floor. Mr Platter, trying to keep clear of it, was rushing back and forth, hopping at times from one foot to the other. Mr Pomfret did not know very much about bells, but he had heard grim stories about the tail ends of

bell-ropes: they could whip your head off as likely as not. Mrs Platter seemed relatively safe: she was the centre of the storm.

The great bell sounded again, quite gently this time. The main rope was moving more slowly and the threshing 'tail' began to lose its impetus, until at last it settled down, like an exhausted serpent, in curls and whorls upon the floor.

They did not rush forward to assist Mrs Platter. They walked rather gingerly as if they feared the tangled serpent might revive and come alive again. It was Whitlace who ran a steady hand down the main rope, making sure that it was still; and then, quietly and matter-of-factly, he tidied up the 'tail'. 'You got to know about bells,' he told them, in a voice which sounded rather irritated, 'these were all set up for the ringers on Easter Day . . .'

But none of them listened. They were busy hoisting Mrs Platter up on to a kitchen chair. She was still sniffing and gasping. Miss Menzies produced a handkerchief and then, very gently, raised what seemed to be the injured foot on to a similar chair.

'It's broken,' sobbed Mrs Platter, 'I may be lame for life . . .'

'No, my dear,' Miss Menzies assured her (she had felt the ankle carefully: it was not for nothing Miss Menzies had been a Girl Guide). 'I think it's only a sprain. Just sit there quietly and Mrs Whitlace will get you a drink of water.'

'Of course I will,' said Kitty Whitlace in her cheerful way, and made off down the aisle towards the vestry.

'I'm bumps and bruises all over,' complained Mrs Platter. 'And my head! Cracked it on the ceiling . . . feel as though it's coming in half . . .'

'Good thing you were wearing that thick felt hat,' said Whitlace. 'Might have broken your neck.' There was little sympathy in his voice, and he still looked offended: his bells, his precious bells . . . set up so carefully! And what on earth did these people think they were doing, trying to ring them in the late hours of the night? And how had the Platters got into the church in the first place? And why?

Perhaps, by now, they were all thinking the same thoughts (Mr Pomfret certainly was) but they were too polite to voice them. Well, no doubt all would be explained later . . .

A sudden sound from the other end of the church caused Mr Pomfret to turn his head. It had been more an exclamation than a scream, and it seemed to come from the vestry. Mrs Whitlace? Yes, it must be she! As the whole group turned and stared up the aisle, Kitty Whitlace appeared between the curtains, holding them apart. 'Mr Pomfret,' she called, in a voice which it seemed she was trying to control, 'could you please step up here a minute?'

Light-footed Mr Pomfret was up the aisle in an instant: he had sensed the urgency in her tone. The others, though equally curious, followed more slowly. What were they going to witness now?

Mr Platter, bringing up the rear, was talking excitedly. But they did not quite hear all he said: it was too much of a gabble. Something about hearing intruders in the church . . . sense of duty . . . valuable stuff here . . . bit of a risk . . . but he and his missus had never lacked for courage . . . door locked . . . they had had to break in . . . intruders gone. But –'

At this point he seemed to run out of steam: they were in the vestry now. And all Mr Platter had been saying somehow did not quite *do*: not with the cupboard doors standing wide; the rare and lovely pieces laid out haphazardly on the table; and, on the floor, open for all to see, Mr Platter's familiar tool-bag. They all knew it well: there was hardly a house in the village where, sometime or another, Mr Platter had not done 'a little job'.

'Do you recognize these tools?' asked Mr Pomfret.

'I do,' replied Mr Platter with icy dignity, 'they happen to be mine.'

'Happen?' murmured Mr Pomfret and took out his note-book. Then another thought seemed to strike him. He looked sharply at Mr Platter. 'Your good lady – she must have thrown all her weight on that rope. Now, why would she do that, do you think?'

Mr Platter thought quickly. 'To raise the alarm. In the Middle Ages, you see . . .' But this did not quite *do* either – somehow. Mr Pomfret was writing in his note-book. 'We're not living in the Middle Ages now,' he remarked drily. 'I'm afraid, sir, I'll have to ask you to come down to the station.'

Mr Platter drew himself up. 'Not a thing has gone out of this church. Not a thing. So what are you going to charge me with?'

'Breaking and entering?' murmured Mr Pomfret, almost under his breath, as though he were speaking to himself. He was writing in the note-book. He looked up. 'And your good lady, will she be fit to come?'

'We're neither of us fit to come. Can't you leave it till the morning?'

Mr Pomfret was a kind man. 'I suppose I could,' he said. 'Say eleven-thirty?'

'Eleven-thirty,' agreed Mr Platter. He did look very tired. He glanced down at his tools, and around at the table. 'I think I'll leave this stuff here for tonight. No point in taking tools and bringing 'em down again: I've got to put these locks right, anyway.'

'A rum go,' said Mr Pomfret, shutting his note-book. He turned to Mr Platter, suddenly changing his tone. 'What were you doing, *really*?'

'Looking for something,' said Mr Platter.

'Something of yours?'

'Could be,' said Mr Platter.

'Oh, well,' Mr Pomfret put his note-book in his pocket. 'It's as I said, there'll be quite a bit of explaining to do. Goodnight all.'

After Mr Pomfret and Whitlace had departed and Miss Menzies and Kitty were tidying up the vestry, Arrietty heard Miss Menzies say in a thoughtful voice, 'I think, Kitty, the less we say about this evening in the village, the better. Don't you?'

'Yes, I do. The talk would be dreadful and most of it lies. Well, there's all the stuff back but I can't lock the cupboard . . .'

'It doesn't matter, just for one night.'

Dear Miss Menzies, thought Arrietty, protector of everyone, but all the same she wished they would go. She was longing to see Timmus, who she knew would not appear until the church was empty and the west door safely locked, although she guessed what must have happened down, almost, to the last detail. Mrs Platter had seen Timmus making his way up the rope, had nearly grabbed him with one hand, while twisting the other round the rope. Her weight had turned the bell right over and they both had sailed up to the ceiling. Timmus had been carried smoothly through the hole while Mrs Platter, after a painful crack on the head, had slithered to the floor.

At last Arrietty heard Miss Menzies say, 'Kitty dear, I think we'll leave the rest for the morning. I shall be here to help you. Oh dear, I don't know quite what we can do about Mrs Crabtree's plant . . .'

'Whitlace will re-pot it,' said Kitty.

'Oh, splendid! Let's go, then. I must admit I'm rather longing for bed – it's been quite an evening . . .'

Arrietty, back on the sofa, smiled and hugged her knees. She knew, once the door had closed behind them, Timmus would arrive back, safe and, she hoped, sound.

CHAPTER TWENTY-SIX

MUCH later that night, when Arrietty had climbed in through the partly opened grating and tumbled into their arms, Pod and Homily forgot the anxious hours of waiting and the dark unspoken dreads. There were tears but they were tears of joy. The church clock had struck two without being heeded before she had answered all their questions.

'Well, that's finished Platter,' said Pod at last.

'Do you think so, Pod?' quavered Homily.

'Stands to reason. The church broken into – at that hour of the night! Locks of the cupboard picked, cupboard bare, and all those vallyables out on the table . . .'

'But he tried to say there were intruders – or whatever they call them.'

Pod laughed grimly. 'Intruders wouldn't be using Sidney Platter's tools!'

Then next morning there was Peagreen to tell – and Spiller, too, if she could find him. By a happy chance, Arrietty found them together. Peagreen, among the ground-ivy near the path, had risen early to sort out his pieces of glass and Spiller, though bound on some other errand, had paused to watch him. Spiller, as Arrietty remembered, was always curious but would never ask a direct question. Both were suitably impressed by her story. As it went on, Arrietty and Peagreen sat down more comfortably on the dry ground below the ivy leaves. Even Spiller condescended to squat on his haunches, bow in hand, to hear it to the end. His eyes looked very bright but he did not speak a word.

'There's just one thing . . .' said Arrietty at last.

'What's that?' said Peagreen.

Arrietty did not reply at once and, to their surprise, they saw her eyes had filled with tears. 'It may seem silly to you, but . . .'

'But what?' asked Peagreen gently.

'It's Miss Menzies. I'd like to tell her we're all right.' The tears rolled out of her eyes.

'You mean –' said Peagreen in a tone of amazement, '– that *she* saw all this!'

'No, she didn't see anything. But I saw her. Sometimes, I was close enough to speak to her . . .'

'But you didn't, I hope!' said Peagreen sharply. He looked very shocked.

'No, I didn't. Because . . . because . . .' Arrietty seemed to swallow a sob, '. . . I promised my father, very gravely and sacredly, never to speak to any human being again. Not in my whole life.' She turned to Spiller. 'You were there that night. You heard me promise . . .' Spiller nodded.

'And your father was absolutely right,' said Peagreen. He had become very stern suddenly. 'It's madness. Utter madness. Every borrower worth his salt knows that!'

Arrietty put her head down on her knees and burst into tears. Perhaps her early rising after the strain of the past night had begun to take its toll. Or perhaps it was the angry tone of Peagreen's voice. Would anyone, ever, begin to understand . . . ?

They watched her helplessly: the little shoulders shaking with the sobs she tried to quench against her already damp pinafore. If he had been alone, Peagreen would have put out a hand to comfort her but, under Spiller's bright and curious eye, something made him hesitate.

Suddenly Arrietty raised an angry tear-stained face towards Spiller. 'You once said *you'd* tell her,' she accused him, 'that we were safe and that. But I knew you wouldn't. You're much too scared of human beans – even lovely ones like Miss Menzies. Let alone *speak* to one!'

Spiller sprang to his feet. His thin face had become curiously set. It seemed to Arrietty that the fierce glance he threw at her was almost one of loathing. Then he turned on his heel and was gone. Gone so swiftly and so silently that it was as though he had never been there. Not a leaf quivered among the ivy.

Between Arrietty and Peagreen there was a shocked silence. Then Arrietty said in a surprised voice, 'He's angry.'

'No wonder,' said Peagreen.

'I only said what was true.'

'How do you know it's true?'

'Oh, I don't know. It stands to reason. I mean . . . well surely *you* don't think he'd do it?'

'If he promised,' said Peagreen, 'and given the right time and place.'

He gave a grim little laugh. 'And be gone again before she could say a word. Oh, he'll do it all right. But he's a law unto himself, that one. He'll choose his own moment . . .'

Arrietty looked troubled. 'You mean I should have trusted him?'

'Something like that. Or not been in too much of a hurry.' He frowned. 'Not that I hold with any of this – this mad idea of talking to human beings. Foolhardy and stupid – that's what it is! And hardly fair on your father . . .'

'You didn't know Miss Menzies,' said Arrietty and, once again, her eyes filled with tears. She stood up. 'All the same, I wish I hadn't said all that . . .'

'Oh, he'll get over it,' said Peagreen cheerfully, and stood up beside her.

'You see, *really* I do rather like him . . .'

'We all do,' said Peagreen.

'Oh, well,' sighed Arrietty in a mournful little voice. 'I think I'd better be getting home now. I came out so early, and my parents may be wondering. And –' she dashed a quick hand across her eyes and tried an uncertain smile, '– to tell the truth, I'm getting rather hungry.'

'Oh,' said Peagreen, 'that reminds me.' He was feeling in his pocket. 'I hope I haven't broken it. No, here it is.'

He was holding out a very tiny egg – creamy pale with russet freckles. Arrietty took it gingerly, and turned it over between her hands. 'It's lovely,' she said.

'It's a blue tit's egg. I found it this morning in one of my nesting-boxes. Odd, because there wasn't a sign of a nest. I thought you might like it for breakfast . . .'

'It's so lovely. Just as it is. It seems a pity to eat it.'

'Oh, I don't know,' said Peagreen, 'today is a sort of egg day . . .'

'How do you mean?'

'Well, today's the day the humans call Easter Sunday . . .' He watched her thoughtfully as, very carefully, she wrapped the egg up into her pinafore. 'You know, Arrietty,' he went on after a moment, 'as a matter of fact, the less Spiller says the better; this human being . . . this Miss . . . Miss?'

'Menzies.'

'There's one thing that she must *never* find out – and I really mean NEVER – and that is where we are all living now.'

'I only wanted her to know we were *safe* . . .'

Peagreen looked back at her. He was smiling his quizzical, one-sided smile.

'Are we?' he said gently. 'Are we? Ever?'

It was not until a few years later, at the time of the First World War, that it occurred to Arrietty that those words of Peagreen's, spoken so quietly on that sunlit morning, might have a wider meaning: that they referred to others as well as themselves. What was that hymn so beloved of Aunt Lupy? The one that the family had heard at their first ('heavy-laden'), weary arrival at the church? Something about 'all creatures great and small'? And there was another one, wasn't there, which spoke of 'all creatures which on earth do dwell'? All creatures! That was the point, ALL creatures . . .

Dependent as they were on snippets of conversation overheard by Aunt Lupy, the borrowers never discovered *exactly* what happened to Mr Platter. Some said he had gone to prison; others that he had only been fined and cautioned; and then (many months later) that he and Mrs Platter had sold their house and departed for Australia where Mr Platter had a brother in the same line of business. Anyhow, the borrowers never saw the Platters again. Nor were they much spoken of by the ladies who came on Wednesdays and Fridays to do the flowers in the church.

POOR
STAINLESS

A 'Borrowers' Story

To
LIONEL

CHAPTER ONE

'AND now,' said Arrietty to Homily, 'tell me what-you-used-to-do . . .'

The phrase run together in one eager breath had lost its meaning as words – it described an activity, a way of passing the time while engaged in monotonous tasks. They were unpicking sequins from a square of yellowed chiffon: Homily unpicked while Arrietty threaded the glimmering circles on a string of pale blue silk. It was a fine spring day and they sat beside the grating let into the outside wall. The sunlight fell across them in criss-cross squares, and the soft air moved their hair.

'Well,' said Homily, after a moment, 'did I ever tell you about the time when I lit the big candle?'

'And burned a hole in the floorboards – and in the carpet upstairs? And human beings shrieked – and your father beat you with a wax matchstick? Yes, you've told me.'

'It was a candle my father borrowed to melt down for dips. It shined lovely,' said Homily.

'Tell me about the time when the cook upstairs upset the boiling marmalade and it all leaked down between the cracks –'

'Oh, that was dreadful,' said Homily, 'but we bottled it, or most of it, in acorn cups and an empty tube called morphia. But the mess, oh dear, the mess – my mother was beside herself. There was a corner of our carpet,' added Homily reflectively, 'which tasted sweet for months.' With a work-worn hand she smoothed down the gleaming chiffon which billowed smoke-like on the moving air.

'I know what,' cried Arrietty suddenly, 'tell me about the rat!'

'Oh, not again,' said Homily.

She glanced at herself in a sequin which – to her – was about the size of a hand-mirror. 'I'm going very grey,' she said. She polished up the sequin with a corner of her apron and stared again, patting her hair at the temples. 'Did I ever tell you about Poor Stainless?'

'Who was he?' asked Arrietty.

'One of the Knife Machine boys.'

'No . . .' said Arrietty uncertainly.

'That was the first time I went upstairs. To look for Stainless.'
Homily, staring into the sequin, lifted her hair a little at the temples.
'Oh dear,' she said, in a slightly dispirited voice.

'I like it grey,' said Arrietty warmly, gently retrieving the sequin;
'it suits you. What about Poor Stainless –'

'He was lost, you see. And we were all to go up and look for him.
It was an order,' said Homily. 'Some people thought it wrong that
the women should go, too, but there it was: it was an order.'

'Who gave it?' asked Arrietty.

'The grandfathers, of course. It was the first time I ever saw the
scullery. After that, once I knew the way, I used to sneak up there
now and again but no one ever knew. Oh dear, I shouldn't say this
to you!'

'Never mind,' said Arrietty.

'Poor Stainless. He was the youngest of that family. They used to
live down a hole in the plaster on a level with the table where the
knife machine used to stand. They did all their borrowing in the
scullery. Practically vegetarians they were – carrots, turnips, watercress, celery, peas, beans – the lot. All the stuff Crampfurl, the
gardener, used to bring in in baskets. Lovely complexions they had,
every one of them. Especially Stainless. Stainless had cheeks like
apple blossom. "Merry little angel" my mother used to call him.
All the grown-ups were mad about Stainless – he had a kind of
way with them. But not with us. We didn't like him.'

'Why not?' asked Arrietty, suddenly interested.

'I don't know,' said Homily; 'he had mean ways – well, more like
teasing kind of ways; and he never got found out. He'd coax black
beetles down our chute – great things with horns they were – and
we'd know it was him but we couldn't prove it. And many a time
he'd creep along above our floorboards, with a bent pin on a string
and hook at me through a crack in our ceiling: if we had a party,
he'd do it, because he was too young to be asked. But it wasn't any
fun, getting hooked by Stainless – caught me by the hair once, he
did. And in those days –' said Homily complacently, taking up
another sequin, 'my hair was my crowning glory.' She stared into
the sequin reflectively, then put it down with a sigh.

'Well, anyway,' she went on briskly, 'Stainless disappeared. What
a to-do! His mother, it seemed, had sent him out to borrow parsley.

Eleven-fifteen in the morning it was and, by evening, he hadn't returned. And he didn't return that night.

'Now you must understand about parsley – it's a perfectly simple borrow and a quick one. Five minutes, it should have taken him: all you had to do was to walk along the knife machine table onto a ledge at the top of the wainscot, drop down (quite a small drop) onto the draining board and the parsley always stood in an old jam jar at the back of the sink – on a zinc shelf, like, with worn holes in it.

'Some said, afterwards, Stainless was too young to be sent for parsley. They blamed the parents. But there was his mother, single-handed behind the knife machine getting a meal for all that family and the elder ones off borrowing with their father and, as I told you, Stainless was always out anyway directly his mother's back was turned – plaguing us and what not and whispering down the cracks: "I see you," he'd say – there was no privacy with Stainless until my father wall-papered our ceiling. Well, anyway,' went on Homily, pausing to get her breath, 'Stainless had disappeared and the next day, a lovely sunny afternoon, at three o'clock sharp – we were all to go up and look for him. It was Mrs Driver's afternoon out, and the maids would be having their rest.

'We all had our orders: some were to look among the garden boots and the blacking brushes; others in the vegetable bins; my father and your Uncle Hendreary's father and several of the stronger men had to carry a spanner with a wooden spoon lashed across it to unscrew the trap in the drain below the sink.

'I stopped to watch this, I remember. Several of us did. Round and round they went – like Crampfurl does with the cider-press – on the bottom of an upturned bucket under the sink. Suddenly there was a great clatter and the screw came tumbling off and there was a rush of greasy water all over the bucket top. Oh dear, oh dear,' exclaimed Homily, laughing a little but half ashamed of doing so, 'those poor men! None of their wives would have them home again until they had climbed up into the sink proper and had the tap turned on them. *Then* it was the hot tap, which was meant to be luke-warm. Oh dear, oh dear, what a to-do! But still no Stainless.

'We young ones were taken home then, but it was a good four hours before the men abandoned the search. We ate our tea in silence, I remember, while our mothers sniffed and wiped their eyes. After tea, my younger brother started playing marbles with three old dried peas he had, and my mother rebuked him and said, "Quiet now – have you no respect? Think of your father and of all those brave men Upstairs!" The way she said "Upstairs" made your hair stand on end.

'And, yet, you know, Arrietty, I liked the scullery, what I'd seen of it – with the sunshine coming through the yard door and falling warm on that old brick floor. And the bunches of bayleaf and dried thyme. But I did remember there had been a mouse trap under the sink and another under the boot cupboard. Not that these were dangerous – except for those who did not know – our father would roll a potato at them and then they would go click. But they'd jump a bit when they did it and that's what startled you. No, the real danger was Crampfurl, the gardener, coming in suddenly through the yard with the vegetables for dinner; or Mrs Driver, the cook, back from her afternoon out, to fill a kettle. And there were other maids then in the house who might take a fancy to a radish or an apple from the barrel behind the scullery door.

'Anyway, when darkness came the rescue party was called off. Our mothers made a great fuss of the men, thankful to see them back, and brought them their suppers and fetched their slippers. And no one spoke above a whisper. And we were sent to bed.

'By that time, we too felt grave. As we lay cosily under the warm covers, we could not help but think of Stainless. Poor Stainless. Perhaps he'd gone *past* the trap and down the drain of the sink into the sewers. We knew there were borrowers who lived in sewers and that they were dreadful people, wild and fierce like rats. Once, my little brother played with one and got bitten in the arm and his shirt stolen. And he got a dreadful rash.

'Next day, the two grandfathers called another meeting: they were the elders, like, and always made the decisions. One grandfather was my father's great uncle. I forget now who the other was . . .'

'Never mind,' said Arrietty.

'Well,' said Homily, 'the long and short of it was – we were all to go Upstairs, and go throughout every room. Firbank was full of borrowers, in those days – or so it seemed – and some we never knew. But we was to seek them out, any we could find, and ask about Poor Stainless. A house-to-house search they called it.'

'Goodness!' gasped Arrietty.

'We was all to go,' said Homily.

'Women and children, too?'

'*All*,' said Homily, 'except the little 'uns.'

She sat still, frowning into space, her face seemed graven by the memory. 'Some said the old men were mad,' she went on, after a moment. 'But it was wonderfully organized: we were to go in twos – two to each room. The elder ones and the young girls for the ground floor, the younger men and some quite young boys for the creepers.'

'What creepers?'

'The creepers up the house front, of course: they had to search the bedrooms!'

'Yes, I see,' said Arrietty.

'That was the only way you could get up to the first floor in those days. It was long before your father invented his hat-pin. There was no one could tackle the stairs – the height of the treads, you see, and nothing to grip on . . .'

'Yes. Go on about the creepers.'

'Early dawn it was, barely light, when the young lads were lined up on the gravel, marking from below which of the windows was open. One, two, three, GO – and they was off – all the ivy and wistaria leaves shaking like a palsy! Oh, the stories they had to tell about what they found in those bedrooms but never a sign of Stainless! One poor little lad slipped on a window-sill and gripped on a cord to save himself: it was the cord of a roller blind and the roller blind went clattering up to the ceiling and there he was – hanging on a thing like a wooden acorn. He got down in the end – swung himself back and forth until he got a grip on the pelmet, then down the curtain by the bobbles. Not much fun, though, with two great human beings in night caps, snoring away on the bed.

'We women and girls took the downstairs rooms, each with a man who knew the ropes, like. We had orders to be back by tea time, because of the little 'uns, but the men were to search on until dusk. I had my Uncle Bolty and they'd given us the morning-room. And it was on that spring day, just after it became light –' Homily paused significantly, 'that I first saw the Overmantels!'

'Oh,' exclaimed Arrietty, 'I remember – those proud kind of borrowers who lived above the chimney-piece?'

'Yes,' said Homily, 'them.' She thought for a moment. 'You never could tell how many of them there were because you always saw them doubled in the looking-glass. The overmantel went right up to the ceiling, filled with shelves and twisty pillars and plush-framed photographs. You saw them always gliding about behind the cape-gooseberries, or the jars of pipe cleaners, or the Japanese fans. They

smelled of cigars and brandy and – something else. But perhaps that
was the smell of the room. Russian leather – yes, that was it . . .'

'Go on,' said Arrietty, 'did they speak to you?'

'Speak to us! Did the Overmantels speak to us!' Homily gave a
short laugh, then shook her head grimly as though dismissing a
memory. Her cheeks had become very pink.

'But,' said Arrietty, breaking the odd silence, 'at least, you saw
them!'

'Oh, we saw them right enough. And heard them. There were
plenty of them about that morning. It was early, you see, and they
knew the human beings were asleep. There they all were, gliding
about, talking and laughing among themselves – and dressed up to
kill for a mouse hunt. And they saw us all right, as we stood beside
the door, but would they look at us? No, not they. Not straight, that
is: their eyes slid about all the time, as they laughed and talked
among themselves. They looked past us and over us and under us
but never quite at us. Long, long eyes they had, and funny light
tinkling voices. You couldn't make out what they said.

'After a while, my Uncle Bolty stepped forward: he cleared his
throat and put on his very best voice (he could do this voice, you see,
that's why they chose him for the morning-room). "Excuse and
pardon me," he said (it was lovely the way he said it), "for
troubling and disturbing you, but have you by any chance seen –"
And he went on to describe Poor Stainless lovely complexion and
all.

'Not a sign of notice did he get. Those Overmantels just went on
laughing and talking and putting on airs like as if they were acting
on a stage. And beautiful they looked, too (you couldn't deny it),
some of the women, in their long-necked Overmantel way. The early
morning sunlight shining on all that looking-glass lit them all up,
like, to a kind of pinky gold. Lovely it was. You couldn't help but
notice . . .

'My Uncle Bolty began to look angry and his face grew very red.
"High or low, we're borrowers all," he said in a loud voice, "and this
little lad –" he almost shouted it, "was the apple of his mother's
eye!" But the Overmantels went on talking in a silly, flustered way,
laughing a little still, and sliding their long eyes sideways.

'My Uncle Bolty suddenly lost his temper. "All right," he thundered, forgetting his special voice and going back to his country one,
"you silly feckless lot. High you may be but remember this – them as

dwells below the kitchen floor has solid earth to build on and we'll outlast you yet!"

'With that he turns away, and I go after him, crying a little – I wouldn't know for why. Knee high we were in the pile of the morning-room carpet. As we passed through the doorway a silence fell behind us. We waited in the hall and listened for a while. It was a long, long silence.'

Arrietty did not speak. She sat there lost in thought and gazing at her mother. After a moment, Homily sighed and said, 'Somehow, I don't seem to forget that morning, though nothing much happened really – when you come to think of it. Some of the others had terrible adventures, especially them who was sent to search the bedrooms. But your Great Uncle Bolty was right. When they closed up most of the house, after her Ladyship's accident, the morning-room wasn't used any more. Starved out, they must have been, those Overmantels. Or frozen out.' She sighed again and shook her head. 'You can't help but feel sorry for them . . .

'We all stayed up that night, even us young ones, waiting and hoping for news. The search parties kept arriving back in ones and twos. There was hot soup for all and some were given brandy. Some of the mothers looked quite grey with worry but they kept up a good front, caring for all and sundry as they came tumbling in down the chute. By morning, all the searchers were home. The last to arrive were three young lads who had got trapped in the bedrooms when the housemaids came up at dusk to close the windows and draw the curtains. It had come on to rain, you see. They had to crouch inside the fender for over an hour while two great human beings changed for dinner. It was a lady and gentleman and, as they dressed, they quarrelled – and it was all to do with someone called "Algy". Algy this and Algy that . . . on and on. Scorched and perspiring as these poor boys were, they peered out through the brass curlicues of the fender, and took careful note of everything. At one point, the lady took off most of her hair and hung it on a chair back. The borrowers were astonished. At another point, the gentleman, taking off his socks, flung them across the room and one landed in the fireplace. The borrowers were terrified and pulled it out of sight; it was a woollen sock and might begin to singe; they couldn't risk the smell.'

'How did they get away?'

'Oh, that was easy enough once the room was empty, and the

guests were safely at dinner. They unravelled the sock, which had a hole in the toe, and let themselves down through the banisters on the landing. The first two got down all right. But the last, the littlest one, was hanging in air when the butler came by with a soufflé. All was well, though, the butler didn't look up, and the little one didn't let go.

'Well, that was that. The search was called off and, for us younger ones at least, life seemed to return to normal. Then one afternoon – it must have been a week later because it was a Saturday, I remember, and that was the day our mother always took a walk down the drain-pipe to have tea with the Rain-Barrells and on this particular Saturday she took our little brother with her. Yes, that was it – anyway, we two girls, my sister and I, found ourselves alone in the house. Our mother always left us jobs to do and that afternoon it was to cut up a length of black shoe-lace to make armbands in memory of Stainless. Everybody was making them – it was an order "to show respect" – and we were all to put them on together in three days' time. After a while, we forgot to be sad and chattered and laughed as we sewed. It was so peaceful, you see, sitting there together and with no fear any more of black beetles.

'Suddenly my sister looked up, as though she had heard a noise. "What's that?" she said, and she looked kind of frightened.

'We both of us looked round the room, then I heard her let out a cry: she was staring at a knot-hole in the ceiling. Then I saw it, too – something moving in the knot-hole: it seemed to be black but it wasn't a beetle. We could neither of us speak or move: we just sat there riveted – watching this thing come winding down towards us out of the ceiling. It was a shiny snaky sort of thing, and it had a twist or curl in it which, as it got lower, swung round in a blind kind of way and drove us shrieking into a corner. We clung together, crying and staring, until suddenly my sister said, "Hush!" We waited, listening. "Someone spoke," she whispered, staring towards the ceiling. Then we heard it – a hoarse voice, rather breathy and horribly familiar. "I can see you!" it said.

'We were furious. We called him all sorts of names. We threatened him with every kind of punishment. We implored him to take the Thing away. But all he did was to giggle a little, and keep on saying, in that silly sing-song voice: "Taste it ... taste it ... it's lovely!"'

'Oh,' breathed Arrietty, 'did you dare?'

Homily frowned. 'Yes. In the end. And it was lovely,' she admitted grudgingly, 'it was a liquorice boot-lace.'

'But where had he been all that time?'

'In the village shop.'

'But –' Arrietty looked incredulous, 'how did he get there?'

'It was all quite simple really. Mrs Driver had left her shopping basket on the scullery table, with a pair of shoes to be heeled. Stainless, on his way to the parsley, heard her coming, and nipped inside a shoe. Mrs Driver put the shoes in the basket and carried them off to the village. She put down the basket on the shop counter while she gossiped awhile with the postmistress and, seizing the right opportunity, Stainless scrambled out.'

'But how did he get back home again?'

'The next time Mrs Driver went in for the groceries, of course. He was in a box of haircombs at the time but he recognized the basket.'

Arrietty looked thoughtful. 'Poor Stainless,' she said, after a moment, 'what an experience! He must have been terrified.'

'Terrified! Stainless! Not he! He'd enjoyed every minute of it!' Homily's voice rose. 'He'd had one wild, wicked, wonderful, never-to-be-forgotten week of absolute, glorious freedom – living on jujubes, walnut-whips, chocolate bars, bulls-eyes, hundreds-and-thousands and still lemonade. And what had he done to deserve it?' The chiffon between Homily's fingers seemed to dance with indignation. 'That's what we asked ourselves! We didn't like it. Not after all we'd been through: we never did think it was fair!' Crossly she shook out the chiffon and, with lips set, began to fold it. But gradually, as she smoothed her hands across the frail silk, her movements became more gentle: she looked thoughtful suddenly and, as Arrietty watched, a little smile began to form at the corners of her mouth. 'There was one thing, though, that we all took note of –' she said slowly, after a minute.

'What was that?' asked Arrietty.

'His cheeks had gone all pasty-like, and his eyes looked –' she hesitated, seeking the word, 'sort of *piggy*. There was a big red spot on his nose and a pink one on his chin. Yes,' she went on, thinking this over, 'all that sugar, you see! Poor Stainless! Pity, really, when you come to think of it . . .' she smiled again and slightly shook her head, '. . . good times or no good times, to have lost that wonderful complexion.'

PHILIPPA PEARCE

Author of *Tom's Midnight Garden*

Winner of the Whitbread Children's Book Award

'Did you expect a *real* dog?'

Can you *really* make a picture
of a dog come to life?

Ben's imagination can make
anything happen . . .

a dog so small

'No writer captures the dreamy intensity
of childhood better' – *Guardian*

puffin.co.uk